THE
Thackery T. Lambshead
CABINET of CURIOSITIES

Exhibits, Oddities, Images, and Stories from Top Authors and Artists

Other Books by Ann & Jeff VanderMeer

Best American Fantasy 1
(with Matthew Cheney)

Best American Fantasy 2
(with Matthew Cheney)

The New Weird

Steampunk

Fast Ships, Black Sails

Last Drink Bird Head: Flash Fiction for Literacy

The Kosher Guide to Imaginary Animals

Steampunk Reloaded

The Weird

Books by Jeff VanderMeer

FICTION

Dradin, in Love

The Book of Lost Places

Veniss Underground

City of Saints & Madmen

Secret Life

Shriek: An Afterword

The Situation

Secret Lives

Predator: South China Sea

Finch

The Third Bear

The Three Quests of the Wizard Sarnod

NONFICTION AND ANTHOLOGIES

Leviathan 1 (with Luke O'Grady)

Leviathan 2 (with Rose Secrest)

Leviathan 3 (with Forrest Aguirre)

Album Zutique

The Thackery T. Lambshead Pocket Guide to Eccentric & Discredited Diseases
(with Mark Roberts)

Why Should I Cut Your Throat?

Booklife: Strategies & Survival Tips for the 21st Century Writer

Monstrous Creatures: Explorations of Fantasy

The Steampunk Bible
(with S. J. Chambers)

THE Thackery T. Lambshead CABINET of CURIOSITIES

Edited by
Ann & Jeff VanderMeer

HARPER Voyager
An Imprint of HarperCollins*Publishers*

Page 317 serves as a continuation of the copyright page.

HarperCollins books may be purchased for educational, business, or sales promotional use. For information please write: Special Markets Department, HarperCollins Publishers, 10 East 53rd Street, New York, NY 10022.

FIRST EDITION

Harper Voyager and design is a trademark of HCP LLC.

Book designed by Paula Russell Szafranski

Library of Congress Cataloging-in-Publication Data has been applied for.

ISBN 978-0-06-200475-8

11 12 13 14 15 OV/RRD 10 9 8 7 6 5 4 3 2 1

Dedicated to the memory of Kage Baker,

a wonderful writer and a good friend of Dr. Lambshead.

You are not forgotten.

Contents

Microbial Alchemy and Demented Machinery: The Mignola Exhibits

The Miéville Anomalies

Further Oddities

Visits and Departures

THE
Thackery T. Lambshead
CABINET of CURIOSITIES

Exhibits, Oddities, Images, and Stories from Top Authors and Artists

A photograph of just one shelf in Lambshead's study displaying the "overflow" from his underground collection (1992). Some items were marked "return to sender" on the doctor's master list.

INTRODUCTION

The Contradictions of a Collection: Dr. Lambshead's Cabinet

By the Editors

To his dying day, Dr. Thackery T. Lambshead (1900–2003) insisted to friends that he "wasn't much of a collector." "Things tend to manifest around me," he told BBC Radio once, "but it's not by choice. I spend a large part of my life *getting rid of things.*"

Indeed, one of Lambshead's biggest tasks after the holiday season each year was, as he put it, "repatriating well-intentioned gifts" with those "who might more appropriately deserve them." Often, this meant reuniting "exotic" items with their countrymen and -women, using his wide network of colleagues, friends, and acquaintances hailing from around the world. A controversial reliquary box from a grateful survivor of ballistic organ syndrome? Off to a "friend in the Slovak Republic who knows a Russian who knows a nun." A centuries-old "assassin's twist" kris (see the Catalog entries) absentmindedly sent by a lord in Parliament? Off to Dr. Mawar Haqq at the National Museum in Kuala Lumpur, Malaysia. And so on and so forth.

He kept very little of this kind of material, not out of some loyalty to the Things of Britain, but more out of a sense that "the West still has a lot to answer for," as he wrote in his journals. Perhaps this is why Lambshead spent so much time in the East. Indeed, the east wing of his ever-more-extensive home in Whimpering-on-the-Brink was his favorite place to escape the press during the more public moments of his long career.

Regardless, over time, his cabinet of curiosities grew to the point that his semipermanent loans to various universities and museums became not so much philanthropic in nature as "acts of self-defense" (*LIFE* Magazine, "Hoarders: Curiosity or a New Disease?," May 19, 1975). One of the most frenzied of these "acts" occurred in "divesting myself of the most asinine acquisition I ever made, the so-called Clockroach"—documented in this very volume—"which had this ridiculous habit of starting all on its own and making a massacre of my garden and sometimes a stone fence or two. Drove my housekeeper and the groundskeeper mad."

Breaking Ground

This question of the cabinet's growth coincides with questions about its location. As early as the 1950s, there are rather unsubtle hints in Dr. Lambshead's journal of "creating hidden reservoirs for this river of junk" and "darkness and subterranean calm may be best for the bulk of it," especially since the collection "threatens to outgrow the house."

In the spring of 1962, as is well-documented, builders converged on Lambshead's abode and for several months were observed to leave through the back entrance carrying all manner of supplies while removing a large quantity of earth, wood, and roots.

Speculation began to develop as to Lambshead's intentions. "If even Dr. Lambshead despairs of compromise, what should the rest of us, who do not have

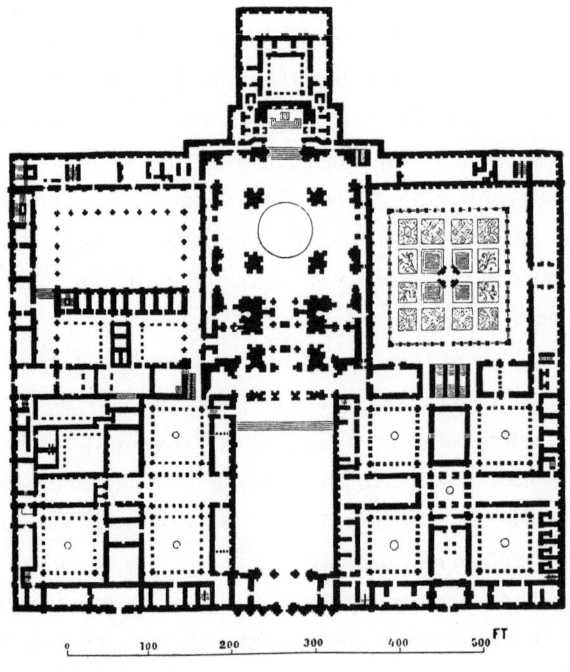

Floor plan found in Lambshead's private files, detailing, according to a scrawled note, "the full extent of a museum-quality cabinet of curiosities that will serve as a cathedral to the world, and be worthy of her."

the same privilege, do?" asked the editor of the *Socialist Union Guild Newsletter* that year, assuming that Lambshead, at the time a member, was building a "personalized bomb shelter with access to amenities many of us could not dream to afford in our everyday lives, nor wish to own for fear of capitalist corruption." In the absence of a statement from Lambshead, the Fleet Street press even started rumors that he had discovered gold beneath his property, or ancient Celtic artifacts of incredible value. Whatever Lambshead's motivations, he must have paid the builders handsomely, since the only recorded comment from the foreman is: "Something's wrong with the pipes. Full stop." (*Guardian,* "Avowed Socialist Builds 'Anti-Democracy' Bunker Basement," April 28, 1962)

Throughout the year, Lambshead ignored the questions, catcalls, and bullhorn-issued directives from the press besieging his gates. He continued to entertain guests at his by-now palatial home—including such luminaries as Maurice Richardson, Francis Bacon, Molly Parkin, Jerry Cornelius, George Melly, Quentin Crisp, Nancy Cunard, Angus Wilson, Philippe Jullian, and Violet Trefusis—and, in general, acted as if nothing out of the ordinary was occurring, even as the workmen labored until long after midnight and more than one guest reported "strange metallic smells and infernal yelping burps coming up from beneath the floorboards." Meanwhile, Lambshead's seemingly preternatural physical fitness fueled rumors involving "life-enhancing chambers" and "ancient rites." Despite being in his sixties, he looked not a day over forty, no doubt due to his early and groundbreaking experiments with human growth hormone.

Why the secrecy? Why the need to ignore the press? Nothing in Lambshead's journals can explain it. Indeed, given the damage eventually suffered by this subterranean space, there's not even enough left to map the full extent of the original excavation. We are left with two floor plans from Lambshead's private filing cabinet, one of which shows his estate house in relation to the basement area—and thus two contradictory possibilities. One of them, oddly enough, corresponds in shape to a three-dimensional model of an experimental flying craft. This coincidence has led to one of the stranger accusations ever leveled against Lambshead (not including those attributed to contamination scholar Reza Negarestani and obliteration expert Michael Cisco). Art critic Amal El-Mohtar, who for a time attempted to research part of Lambshead's cabinet, claimed that "It became obvious from Thackery's notes that he was creating a kind of specialized Ark to survive the extermination of humankind, each item chosen to tell a specific story, and his particular genius was to have all of these objects—this detritus of eccentric quality—housed within a container that would eventually double as a

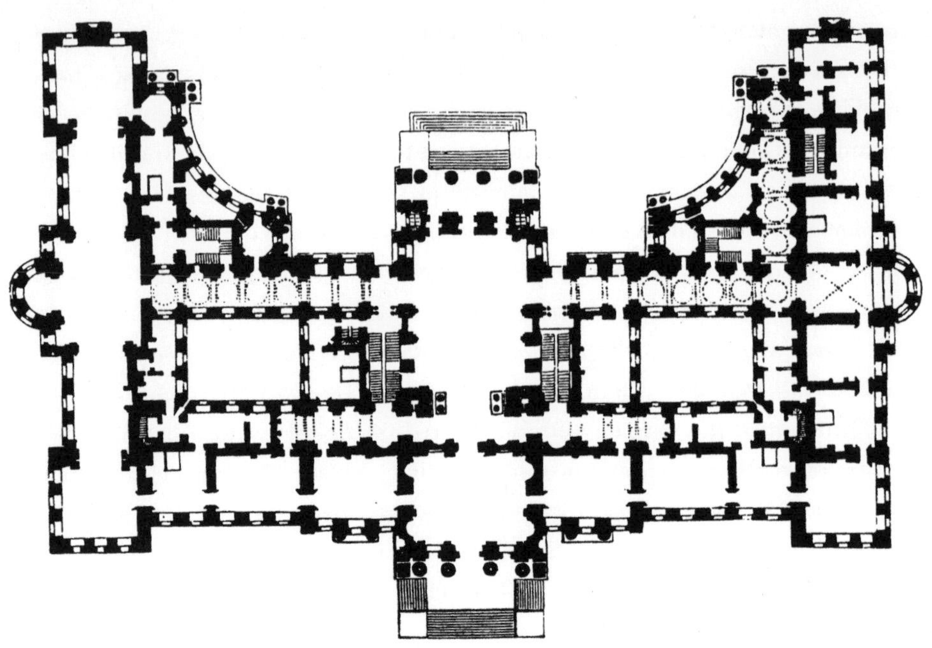

Floor plan of what Amal El-Mohtar called "a nascent spaceshop nee Ark," with a front view of Lambshead's house beneath it.

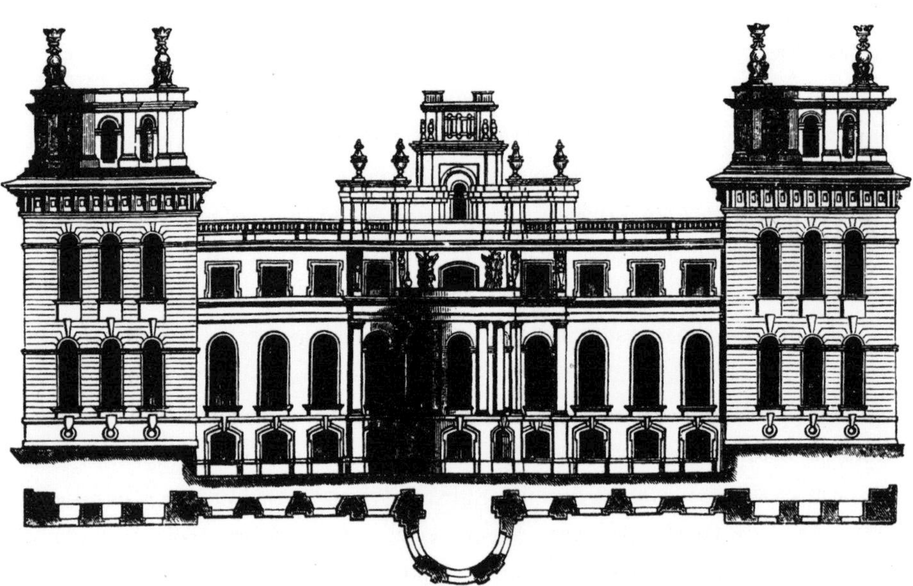

spaceship." However, it must be noted that this theory, leaked to various tabloids, came to El-Mohtar during a period of recovery in Cornwall from her encounter with the infamous singing fish from Lambshead's collection. Not only had her writings become erratic, but she was, for a period of time, fond of talking to wildflowers.

The most popular of other apocryphal theories originated with the performance artist Sam Van Olffen, who, since 1989, has seemed fixated on Lambshead and staged several related productions. The most grandiose, the musical *The Mad Cabinet of Curiosities of the Mad Dr. Lambshead,* debuted in 2008 in Paris and London, well after Lambshead's death. Perhaps the most controversial of Van Olffen's speculations is that Lambshead's excavations in 1962 were meant not to create a space for a cabinet of curiosities but to remodel an existing underground space that had previously served as a secret laboratory in which he was conducting illegal medical tests. A refrain of "Doctor doctor doctor doctor! / Whatcher got in there there? A lamb's head?" is particularly grating.

Certainly, nothing about the flashback scenes to the 1930s, or the hints of Lambshead's affiliation with underground fascist parties, did anything to endear Van Olffen's productions to fans of the doctor, or the popular press. *The Mad Cabinet of Curiosities* closed on both Les Boulevards and the West End after less than a month. The combined effect of media attention for this "sustained attack on the truth," as Lambshead's heirs put it in a deposition for an unsuccessful lawsuit in 2009, has been to distort the true nature of the doctor's work and career.

A Deep Emotional Attachment?

Despite irregularities and bizarre claims, one fact seems clear: Lambshead, especially in his later years, formed a deep emotional attachment to many of the objects in his collection, whether repatriated, loaned out, or retained in his house or underground cabinet.

A close friend of Lambshead, post–World War II literary icon Michael Moorcock, who first met the doctor in the mid-1950s at a party thrown by Mervyn Peake's family, remembered several such attachments to objects. "It became especially acute in the 1960s," Moorcock recalled in an interview, "when we spent a decent amount of time together because of affairs related to *New Worlds,*" the seminal science fiction magazine Moorcock edited at the time. "For a man of science, who resolutely believed in fact, he could be very sentimental. I remember how distraught he became during an early visit when he couldn't find an American Night Quilt he had promised to show both me and [J. G.] Ballard. He became so ridiculously agitated that I had to say, 'Pard, you might want to sit down

One of Sam Van Olffen's stage sets for the supposed laboratory of Dr. Lambshead, taken from the Parisian production of the musical *The Mad Cabinet of Curiosities of the Mad Dr. Lambshead* and supposedly inspired by Van Olffen's own encounter with the cabinet several years before. (*Le Monde*, March 2, 2008)

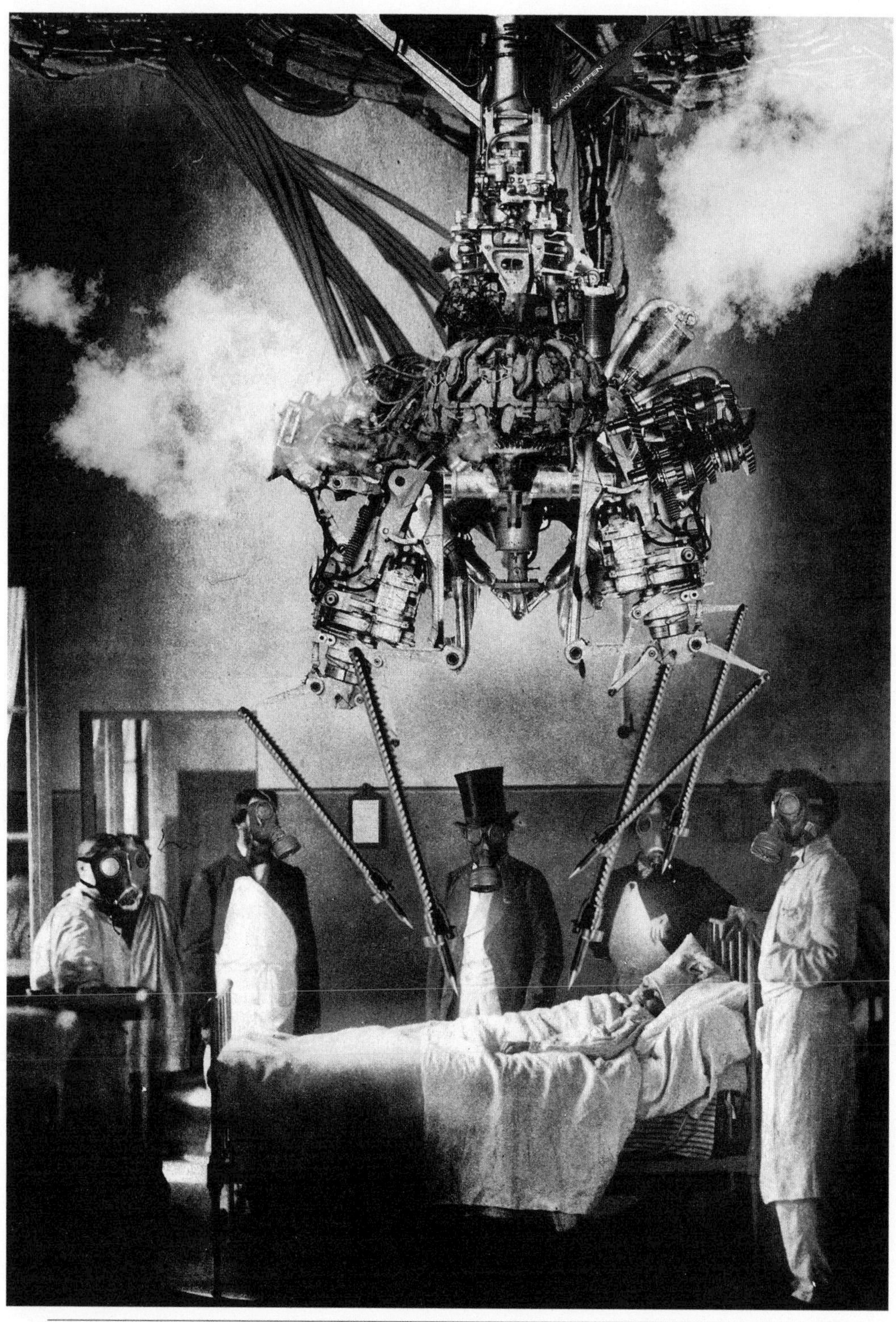

The "secret medical laboratory" stage set for *The Mad Cabinet of Curiosities of the Mad Dr. Lambshead*. A much less grandiose version of the musical was eventually turned into a SyFy channel film titled *Mansquito 5: Revenge of Dr. Lambshead*, but never aired. (*Le Monde*, March 2, 2008)

One of Lambshead's few attempts at art, admittedly created "under the influence of several psychotropic drugs I was testing at the time." Lambshead claims he was "just trying to reproduce the visions in my head." S. B. Potter (see: "1972" in Visits and Departures) claimed the painting provided "early evidence of brain colonization."

awhile.' Then he felt compelled to tell me that he and his first—his only—wife, Helen, who had passed on two or three years before, had watched the stars from the roof one night early in their relationship, and had snuggled under that quilt. One of his fondest memories of her." (*Independent*, "An Unlikely Friendship?: The Disease Doc and the Literary Lion," September 12, 1995)

A fair number of the artifacts in the cabinet dating from before 1961 would have reminded Lambshead of Helen Aquilus, a brilliant neurosurgeon whom he appears to have first met in 1939, courted until 1945, and finally married in 1950 (despite rumors of a chance encounter in 1919). She had accompanied him on several expeditions and emergency trips, as a colleague and fellow scientist. She had been present when Lambshead acquired many of his most famous artifacts, such as "The Thing in the Jar," a puzzler that haunted Lambshead until his death (see: Further Oddities). She also helped him acquire a number of books, including a rare printing of Gascoyne's *Man's Life Is This Meat.* Some have, in fact, suggested that Lambshead turned toward the preservation of his collection and building of a space for it as a distraction from his grief following Helen's death in an auto accident on a lonely country road in 1960.

Other items had significance to Lambshead because he had had a hand in their discovery, like St. Brendan's Shank, or in their creation, like the mask for Sir Ranulph Wykeham-Rackham, a.k.a. Roboticus. Perhaps most famous among these is the original of his psychedelic painting *The Family* from 1965, which for a time hung in the Tate Modern's exhibit "Doctors as Painters, Blood in Paint." In the painting, Death stares off into the distance while, behind it, a man who looks like Lambshead in his twenties stands next to a phantasmagorical rendering of Helen and her cousins.

In many cases, too, these objects, as he said, "remind me of lost friends"—for example, St. Brendan's Shank, which he came to possess during World War II, and which, as he wrote in his journal, "I spent many delightful days researching along with my comrades-in-arms, most of them, unfortunately, now lost to us from war, time, disease, accident, and heartbreak."

One of the few museum exhibit loans ever to have been photographed (Zurich, 1970s)—presented as evidence to support Caitlin R. Kiernan's accusations of Lambshead using artifacts to convey secret messages. She claims that Russian artist Vladimir Gvozdev, the creator of the mecha-rhino above, does not exist, and is a front for the "Sino-Siberian cells of a secret society."

Dr. Lambshead's Personal Life

In searching for a theme or approach to the cabinet, it may be relevant to return to the subject of Lambshead's wife. Throughout his life, and even after her death, Lambshead kept his attachment to Helen almost as secret as his cabinet, and *The Thackery T. Lambshead Pocket Guide to Eccentric & Discredited Diseases* never mentioned her, or referenced the marriage. Aquilus, a Cypriote Greek, came from a long line of dissenters and activists, and had originally left Athens to go to school at Oxford. She was and, at first, often seen as a beard for the doctor, since he was known to be bisexual and somewhat hedonistic in his appetites.

Aquilus, though, was a force and a character in her own right: a groundbreaking neuroscientist and surgeon in an era when females in those fields were unheard of; a researcher who worked for the British government during World War II to perfect triage for traumatic head wounds on the battlefield; and a champion at dressage who combined such a knack for negotiation with forcefulness of will that for a time she entered the political sphere as a spokesperson for the Socialist Party. Possessed of prodigious strength, she could also "shoot like a sniper" and "pilot or commandeer any damn boat, frigate, sampan, freighter, destroyer, or aircraft carrier you care to name," Lambshead wrote admiringly in a late 1950s letter to Moorcock.

All that ended in the one-car accident that left Lambshead in shock and Aquilus dead, her remains cremated and buried in a small, private ceremony almost immediately thereafter. Lambshead would never remarry, and often spoke of Helen as if she were still alive, a tendency that friends at first found understandable, then obsessional, and, finally, just "a quirk of Thackery's syntax," as Moorcock put it.

From 1963 on, however, despite his journals containing any number of elaborate descriptions of medical exploration and of artifacts acquired or sent off, there is only one mention of Helen. "Helen chose a different life," he writes in 1965, on the anniversary of her accident. The words are crossed out, then reinstated and emphasized overtop of the cross-out, with a violence that has torn the page, and several pages after, so that many entries thereafter are marked by and linked to that one sentence.

What to make of the statement "Helen has chosen another life"? Since 2005, when the journals first became available to the public through the British Library, many a researcher has attempted to make their reputation on an interpretation—everything from psychological profiling to outright conspiracy theories. Riffing off of the ideas, if not the political inclination, of the second endnote in Reza

Negarestani's "The Gallows-horse" (see: The Miéville Anomalies), unexplained-phenomena enthusiast and self-described "heretic Lambsheadean" Caitlín R. Kiernan has speculated that "Helen Aquilus did not die in a car crash in 1960. She staged her own death to join a secret society devoted to radical progressive change in the world, and spent the next half-century of her life in that struggle until a car bomb in Athens took her life in 2005, the body unclaimed for forty-eight hours and then mysteriously disappearing."

Evidence for this claim is flimsy at best, although Kiernan cites the speedy cremation of the body, the lack of any follow-up report, "due to the actions of a sleeper cell" within the police department, and "a damning history of collusion between the timing of Lambshead's museum loans/artifact purchases and the movements of known spies and double agents in the area. It must be assumed that encoded into such transactions were secret messages, some of them from Helen and some of them from Lambshead to Helen." Kiernan also notes the rapid reversal of some museum loans; in one case, involving "The Armor of Saint Locust," Lambshead rescinded his approval for the loan five days after the exhibit had opened to the public. She also references "the timing of Lambshead's visits to the Pulvadmonitor" (see: "Pulvadmonitor: The Dust's Warning," The Mignola Exhibits).

Kiernan saves her most pointed commentary for specific evidence: the rolled-up piece of parchment found inside a mechanical rhino in Zurich in 1976. "The text and image on this paper is ostensibly a *maskh* spell for constructing a pod for a journey toward the afterlife of the Elysian Fields. The spell is comprised of four main elements: a body wrapped in a shroud, one square and one rectangular chart, and lastly a scorpion, which in Middle Eastern folklore and talismans plays the role of a delivery system or a catalyst (here the scorpion is the engine for the pod to the afterlife). The dimensions of the pod (the shrouded body) have been given in the spell. The word 'scorpion' in Farsi has been hidden in this spell in the form of a cipher that looks like an abstract scorpion (the mark just above the word 'Elysian' at the bottom of the drawing). But what's also been hidden here, encrypted, is a series of messages from a husband to his wife that, if ever properly deciphered, would no doubt prove to be a hybrid of a love letter and a complex series of orders or *recognition of receipt of commands* that might have agency over several years, if not decades. *That* is the true scorpion in this image."

All of this "information" has been gleaned from what Kiernan calls "further encrypted evidence in Lambshead's journals from 1965 on—the year he learned that Helen wasn't dead—and supported by such circumstantial evidence as their heated public argument in 1959," also documented in the journals, in which

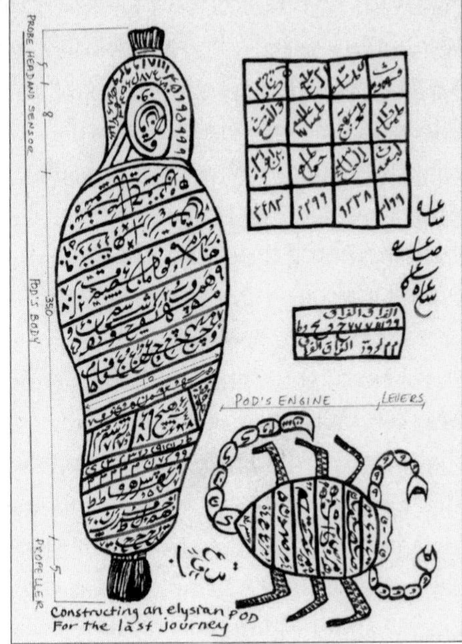

Spell or secret communication? The page found inside of the mecha-rhino, as photographed by Zurich investigator Kristen Alvanson.

Lambshead confesses, with no small amount of anguish, that "Helen is much more radical than I could ever be. How am I supposed to follow her in that?" Kiernan points to Lambshead's writings on "the second life of artifacts" in his "The Violent Philosophy of the Archive," which she claims "isn't about the objects at all, but about their repurposing by him."

Kiernan further claims that Helen attended Lambshead's funeral, "the mysterious woman in white standing at the back, next to Keith Richards and Deepak Chopra." However, photographs from the funeral clearly show many older women "standing at the back," several of them mysterious in the sense that they cannot be identified and are not on the guest list.

A theory put forward by Alan Moore, who knew Lambshead late in life better than anyone, is more reasonable and doesn't presume conspiracy and collusion. Moore suggests merely that the hectic pace Lambshead set from 1963 until his death in 2003 came from a sudden resolve: "It was merely one of the oldest stories, you see. A man attempting to outrun the knowledge of the continuing absence of the love of his life." (In the subtext of his pornographic masterpiece *The Lost Girls,* Moore would reference both Lambshead and Helen, through the device of a mirror separating them forever.)

Loans with Strings Attached: The Museum Exhibits

Of all of Kiernan's "evidence," the most fact-based concerned Lambshead's eccentric attitude toward the visual documentation of the contents of his cabinet, whether parts of it were at home or roaming abroad. Although it's hardly evidence of secret messages being included with his loans, Lambshead usually forbid even the usual photographs a museum will commission for catalogs or postcards. His sole recorded explanation? "It creates greater anticipation if the public has no preconceived idea of what they may be about to encounter. A photograph is a sad and lonely idea of an echo of something real." (*Guardian*, "Sir Ranulph Wykeham-Rackham. a.k.a. Robotikus, Still on Loan to Imperial War Museum, But Nowhere to Be Seen," June 4, 1998)

However, as even the barely suppressed emotion evidenced by the quote may suggest, it seems more likely that Lambshead's intense personal commitment to the core collection made the loaning of items, while necessary and part of what the doctor considered his "civic duty," also painful, and that forbidding photographs gave him a measure of control, a way he could allow the public to experience his cabinet and yet keep it from the Public Eye. As might be expected, the compilation of a book chronicling highlights from Lambshead's cabinet has been made much more difficult due to this eccentricity.

The Doctor Versus the Collector

For the majority of his career, due to his insistence on remaining true to his main passions, Lambshead existed on the fringes of medical science. He was well-respected by some of the world's best doctors, but it was only by becoming a kind of cult figure in the 1960s and 1970s, when he forged friendships with many of pop culture's elite, along with "sheer bloody persistence and endurance," that his medical exploits began to receive the media attention he believed they deserved. Later on, there would even be factions of Lambsheadologists who clashed in their interpretations of the doctor's theories, with Lambshead rarely if ever willing to put an end to such conflict with a definitive conclusion. "Definitive conclusions are for politicians, proctologists, and those who wear mascot costumes," he liked to say.

Despite the time spent on his cabinet, Lambshead's interests always manifested most concretely in *The Thackery T. Lambshead Pocket Guide to Eccentric & Discredited Diseases*. First published in 1921, the *Guide* gave agency and credence to real but obscure and often only anecdotally documented instances of diseases, parasites, and tumors. Not only did many young doctors from all over the world, who would later publish influential findings, receive a sympathetic welcome from the doctor, but marginalized peoples often found the *Guide* took up their cause, sometimes creating publicity for situations that local governments and foreign-relief agencies wished would just go away.

Published almost continuously until the doctor's death, the *Guide* received a controversial send-off with Bantam Books' commemorative eighty-third edition in 2003. That reviewers and readers were often confused as to whether the

Legendary Czech artist and animator Jan Svankmajer's tongue-in-cheek tribute to Dr. Lambshead's so-called "Skull Cucumber" hoax, perpetrated on London's Museum of Natural History in 1992, during as Lambshead put it, "a period of extreme boredom."

book constituted fact or fiction was the result of a colossal blunder by Bantam's marketing and PR departments, which were, as would be well documented later, largely dominated by pot-smokers. However, the doctor's legacy was vindicated by the fact that a large number of medical libraries now carry that edition in their medical-guides section.

However, as should be clear, the doctor's career was only half the story. Just as his exploration of eccentric diseases forms a secret history of the twentieth century, so, too, his cabinet of curiosities, in all of its contradictions, provides an eclectic record of a century—through folly and triumph, organized, if you will, by the imaginations of the eccentric and the visionary.

Resurrecting the Cabinet

Not until well after Lambshead's death of banal pulmonary failure did anyone except for his housekeeper seem to have had even an inkling of the full extent of the underground collection. This situation had been exacerbated by the old man's knowledge of his impending extinction. He had, for three years, been issuing a "recall" of sorts on many of his permanent loans. (This fact did not go unnoticed by Kiernan, who claimed these particular exhibits "had expired in their usefulness for communication with Helen.")

A long process of discovery awaited those assigned by the estate to take care of the house, which still begs the question: Why did it take so long to unearth the collection? Estate representatives have been vague on this point, perhaps hinting at some private foreknowledge and personal plundering prior to the British government, in 2008, declaring the property a national treasure—nothing was to be touched, except with extreme care, and certainly nothing removed.

But it is also true that Lambshead had left enough aboveground to keep archaeologists and appraisers busy for several lifetimes. In later years, Lambshead's housekeeper had gotten lackadaisical, and Lambshead made eccentric purchases of furniture—which, the week before his death, he'd hired movers to stack against the front door, as if to barricade the house against what he must have known by then was coming.

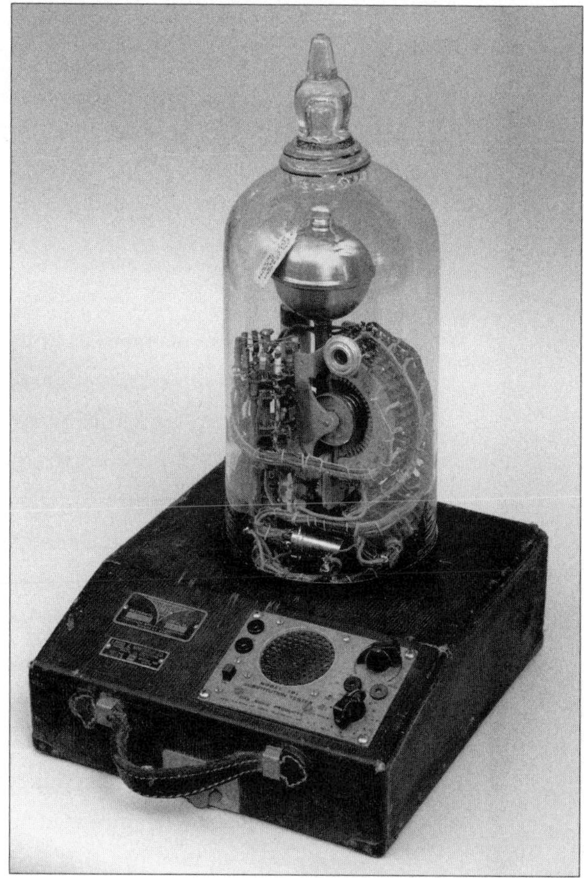

An invention commissioned from Jake von Slatt demonstrating the doctor's commitment to the future as well as the past. Some have speculated this device supports Amal El-Mohtar's "space Ark" theory. As described by Annalee Newitz, this image "illustrates an ideal system, where the knobs on the lower right demodulate cultural transmissions, and the amplifier beneath the bell transmits a psionic signal that can reach any analog neurological entity within 7,000 kilometers." (See Newitz's extended description in the Catalog section.)

More evidence of the disarray of the cabinet space, in a photograph taken during a 2009 appraisal. (Found in the display case at the back, a half-finished letter penned by Lambshead: "As Lichtenberg said of angels, so I say of dust. If they, or it, ever could speak to us, why in God's name should we understand? And even if so, how then should we reply?")

Therefore, the man's house was in a catastrophic state of disarray, with letters from heads of state mixed in with grocery lists, major medical awards propping up tables or sticking enigmatically out of the many cat litter boxes, and several hundred volumes of his personal journals shoved into random spaces in a library as shambolic as it was complete. The only clean, uncluttered space was Helen's study, which remained as it had been upon her death.

No doubt because of this disarray, and the introduction of an administrative red herring—Moorcock has suggested that Lambshead left instructions for someone to "plant the herring, no matter how badly it might begin to smell"—indicating that the collection had long ago been sent into storage in Berlin, it took caretakers until last year to unearth perhaps "the most stirring find," as *Le Monde* put it. In the basement space, lost under a collapsed floor, were found the remains of a "remarkable and extensive cabinet of curiosities" that "appeared to have been damaged by a fire that occurred sometime during the past decade."

(*Le Monde*, "Une merveille médicale: Le curieux cabinet d'un médecin renommé enflamme l'imagination," April 14, 2010) Strangely, there is no report of *any* fire from the many years Lambshead owned the house, and we have only a brief anecdotal (and probably false) statement from the doctor's estranged housekeeper to guide us to any sort of conclusion.

The cabinet of curiosities took more than eighteen months to unearth, reconstruct, document, and catalog. Many of the pieces related to anecdotes and stories in the doctor's personal diaries. Others, when shown to his friends, elicited further stories. In many cases, we had only descriptions of the items. Still, we were determined to build a book that would honor at least the spirit and lingering ghost of Lambshead's collection. Thus, in keeping with the bold spirit exemplified by Lambshead and his accomplishments, we are now proud to present highlights from the doctor's cabinet. These have been reconstructed not just through visual representations but also through text associated with their history and (sometimes) their acquisition by Lambshead. (As with any cabinet, real or housed within pages, it is, as Oscar Wilde once said about an exhaustive collection of poetry, a "browsing experience, to dip into and to savor, rather than take a wild carriage ride through.")

We also have Lambshead's own wistful words from his diary, written on a long-ago day in 1964: "It is never possible to completely reconstruct a person's life from what they leave behind—the absurdity of it all, the pain, the triumphs. What's lost is lost forever, and the silences are telling. But why mourn what we'll lose anyway? Laughter truly is the best medicine, and I find whisky tends to numb and burn what's left behind."

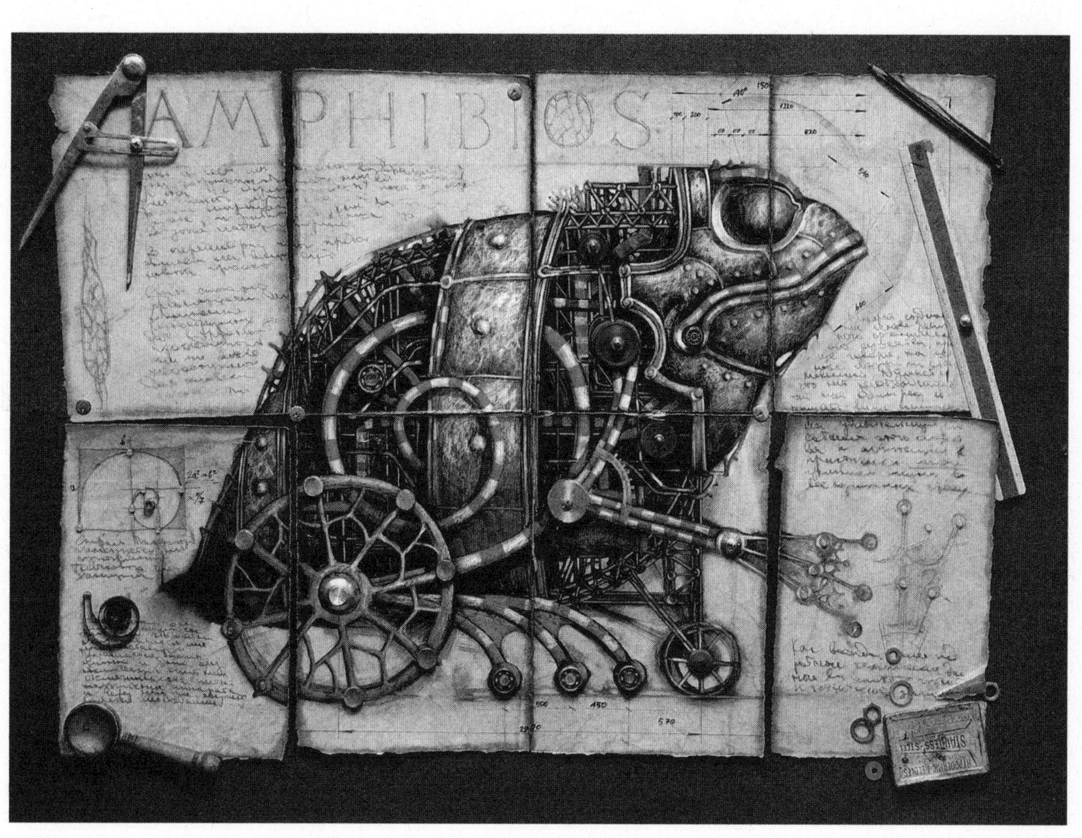
AMPHIBIOS

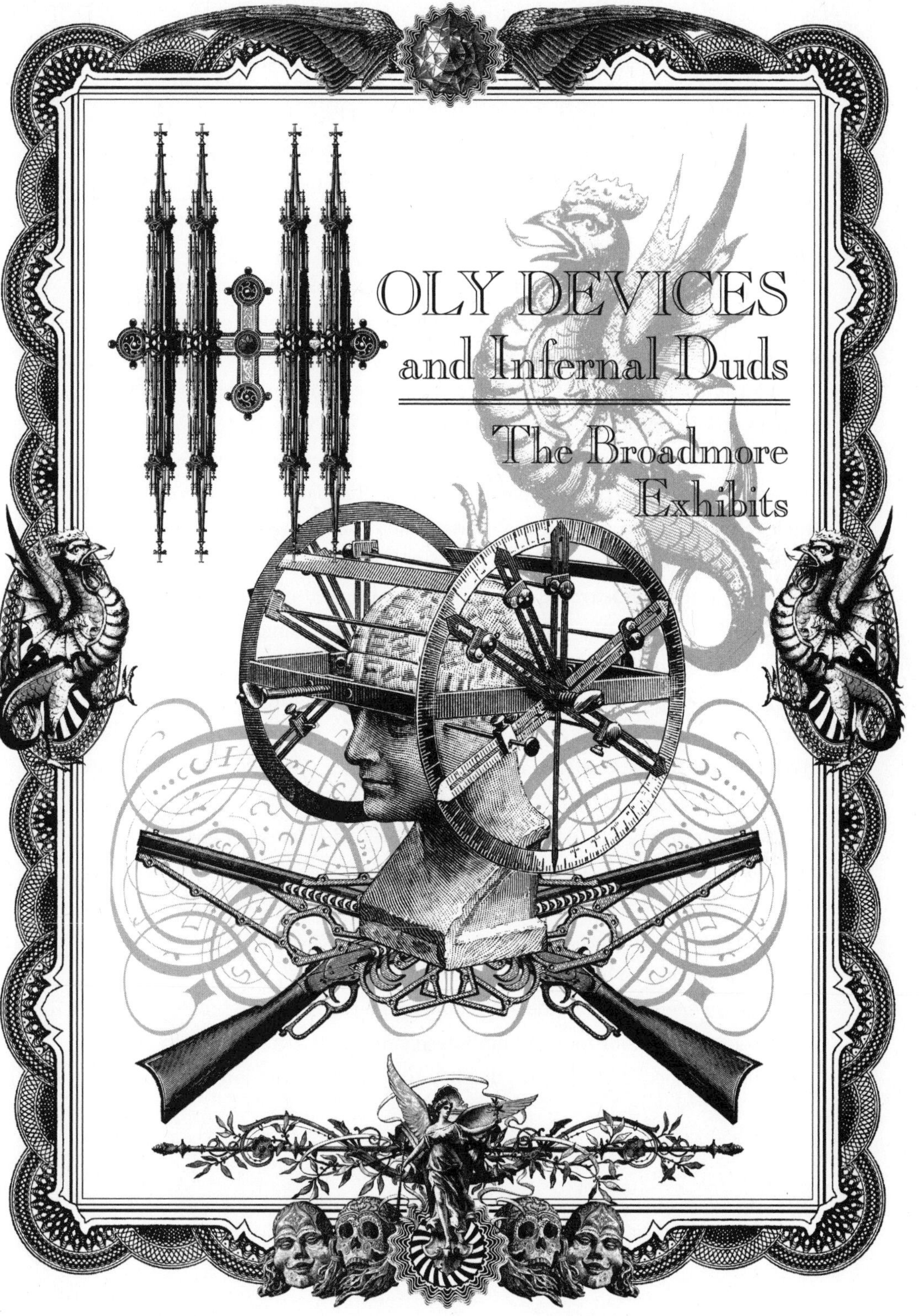
HOLY DEVICES
and Infernal Duds
The Broadmore
Exhibits

The Broadmore Exhibits

Greg Broadmore came by his interest in Lambshead's cabinet of curiosities honestly: through a familial connection. "Lambshead's family and mine were connected by an uncle, so even after my grandparents moved to New Zealand, they kept in touch."

On a trip to England at the age of twelve, Broadmore and his parents visited Lambshead. The artist remembers "a man in his eighties who looked more like fifty, but was as big a curmudgeon as you could possibly imagine. But he seemed to have a soft spot for me. At the very point where I was getting bored listening to them talk in the study, Lambshead suggested he step out to take me to the kitchen for some dessert . . . and instead he brought me down some steep steps into an underground space filled with wonders. The place was hewn out of solid stone and had that nice damp cool mossy smell you find in caves sometimes."

Broadmore remembers Lambshead giving him a wink and saying, "Don't break anything," and leaving him there with a glass of milk and some banana bread. "For me, it was like being given a free pass to an amazing fairyland—the outward expression of all of the visions in my head of anything miraculous. It had a deep and lasting effect on my art." For two hours, Broadmore roamed through Lambshead's collection, finding "countless old toys and ridiculously complex machines and scandalous artwork and comics and . . . well, I began to wonder what *wasn't* to be found there."

Broadmore never visited the cabinet again, and since then has, of course, gone on to forge a near-legendary career as an artist and creator aligned with Weta Workshop. "I was particularly saddened to hear of Lambshead's death a few years ago," Broadmore remembers. "It brought back all of those memories of those perfect hours in his cabinet of curiosities."

For this reason, among others, Broadmore kindly agreed to provide illustrative reconstructions for four of Lambshead's museum loans, which have never been photographed, even after his death, pursuant to instructions in his will.

The Electrical Neurheographiton

Documented by Minister Y. Faust, D.Phil

Constructed: March 14, 1914 (patent still pending)
Invented by: Nikola Tesla (Serbian subject of the Austrian Empire, later an American citizen, born July 10, 1856; "died" January 7, 1943)
History: Stolen from the "robotorium" (barn) of farmer-tinkerer Rhett Greene in St. John's, Dominion of Newfoundland, 1947, by Yugoslavian agents. Held in the Sub-Basement 6 of the Marshal Josip Broz Tito Museum of Yugoslavian Civilisation, until sold to Thackery T. Lambshead in 1997 and subsequently lent by his estate to the Slovenian National Museum of Electrical Engineering; L2010.01

Biographical Sketch

Few intellects in the history of Man achieved such Daedalian heights as those conquered by Serbian inventor, mechanical engineer, psychemetrician, and electrodynamist Nikola Tesla. Men as grand of conjecture and achievement as Tesla attract, along with their many accolades, such a volume of obloquy as to produce an aneurysm among all but the most robustly confident of souls. And while Mr. Tesla was confident indeed, even "galactically arrogant," as one detractor called him, he was also terrified of the charge that many of his foes in the scientific and journalistic establishments had hurled at him, *viz.*, that he was insane.

Indeed, as the twentieth century of our Lord unfolded, Tesla served for many cinematistes as the very archetype of the deranged natural physicist or "mad scientist." So it was that, in 1913, Tesla returned from his adopted America to the land of his birth to devote himself to constructing a mechanism that would ensure he never be chained in Bedlam's urine-spattered halls: the electrical neurheographiton (nyu-REY-o-GRAPH-i-ton, *lit.*, brain-wave writer).

Function of the Electrical Neurheographiton

Mr. Tesla's electrical neurheographiton (1914) was the forerunner of the electro-encephalogram and the electro-convulsive malady-eraser, and the estranged nephew of the intravenous mercury phrenological brain engine (known popularly as the "liquid silver guillotine").

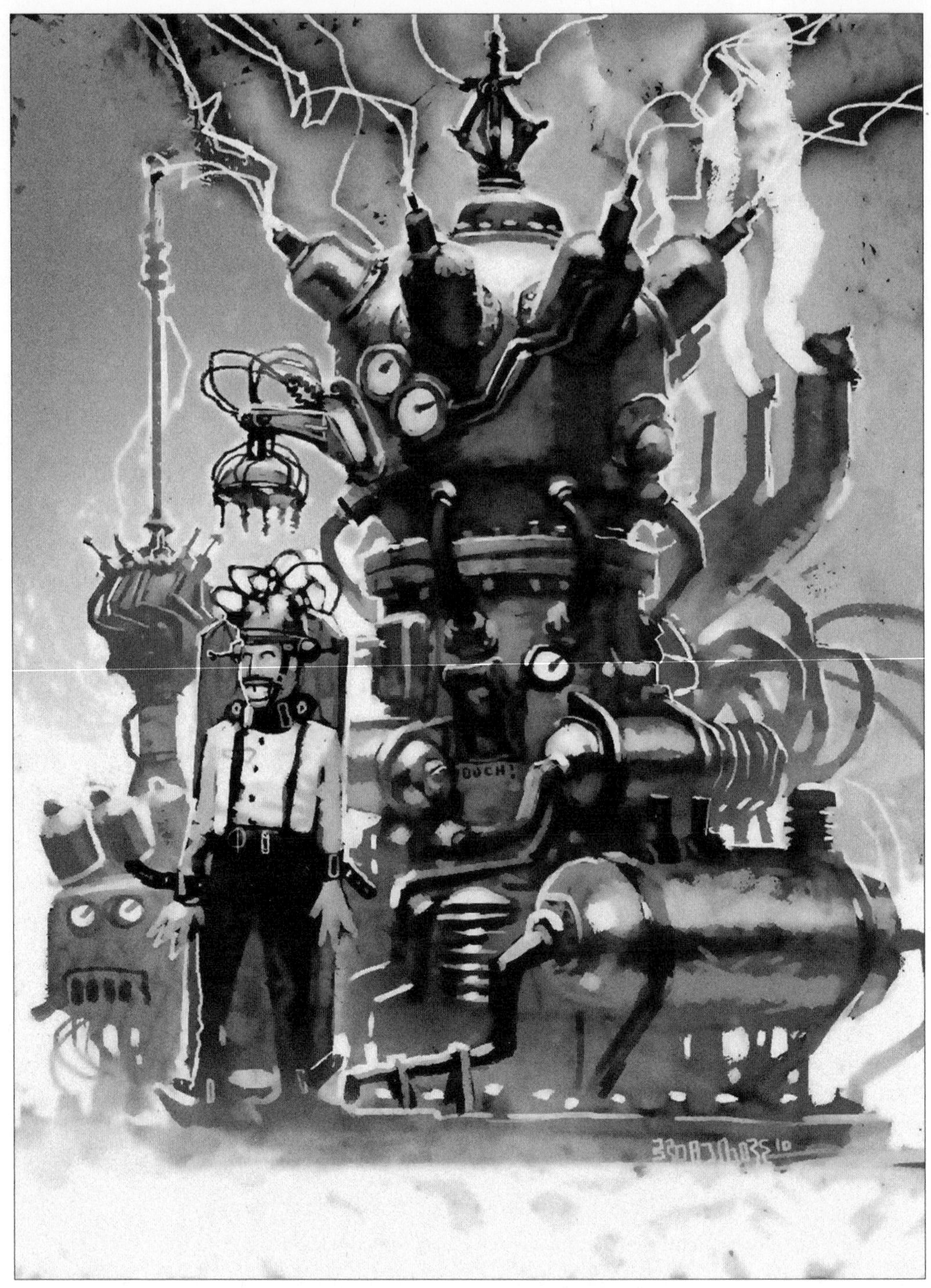

Tesla "ionically enthralled" by his electrical neurheographiton.

A massive mechanical device consisting of a generator and the most sophisticated magnetic-electrical scanner in the world at that time, the neurheographiton beamed electrical energy into a patient's cranium via a "healing helmet." The "electrical balm" demonstrably and immediately undercut the mania, enthusiasm, apostasy, anarchism, and other emotional morbidities of Tesla's numerous test subjects, apparently via relieving them of the burden of painful and traumatic memories (such as the recollection of childhood, adolescence, adulthood, and dotage), priming the patient's brain for emotional "rewriting" with whatever "biographical" data the therapist deemed appropriate. Following a single usage on himself, Tesla declared to his assistant, Mr. Igor Hynchbeck, that, "I'm cured, cured, cured, cured, cured, cured, cured, cured, cured, cured of all my obsessive impulsions! Absolutely, absolutely free of all of them!"

Electrophantasmic Discharges

A type of energetic pollution arising from the neurheographiton's manifold and highly charged internal mechanisms were what Mr. Tesla described in his *Apologia Electronika* as "electrophantasmic discharges"—plasmic fields that "disgorged horizontal ejaculations of lightning of a most disturbing and slaughterous composition." These discharges also warped light into phantasms that mimicked recognisable objects and people with resolute credibility. Such apparitions chiefly consisted of:

- **a.** A Bosnian Coarse-Haired Hound eating a clown composed entirely of human kidneys.
- **b.** A massive bust of influential English occultist Aleister Crowley that transmogrified into "a field of bunnies dancing with all the glee of becandied children."
- **c.** A politely dressed Central European man offering a 1907–24 issue Hotchkiss No. 4 Paper Fastener (i.e., a stapler) to an unseen coworker.

Controversy and a Continent Torn Asunder

That final apparition proved most unfortunate for Gavrilo Princip, a nineteen-year-old Bosnian Serb and subject of the Austro-Hungarian Empire. On June

14, 1914, a hungry fifty-eight-year-old Tesla, desperate for a wealthy sponsor after so many investors had deserted him in favour of archrival American electro-tycoon Thomas Edison, sought to attract the royal patronage of Austrian archduke Franz Ferdinand.

Nikola Tesla ca. 1890, well before the majority of this troubles.

An overly enthusiastic Mr. Tesla bade his assistants wheel his neurheographiton into the streets of Sarajevo near Tesla's laboratory in search of the archduke's motorcade. Mr. Tesla planned to project its "plasmic balm" directly through the air and into the crania of the manifold madmen and wild women who prowled the city at all hours of the day and night, so as to prove his device's capacity to unleash a torrent of industrialism among the newly sane, for the betterment of the Austro-Hungarian Empire.

Tesla, a fine statistician in his own right, predicted the likelihood of the neurheographiton unleashing an electrophantasmic discharge as less than 1 per cent. Alas for Tesla, and even more for the archduke and the archduchess, that 1 per cent manifested as a crackle of electrons that bored directly through their bodies like any American accent through any English gathering. And, unfortunately for Gavrilo Princip, the electrophantasm happened to resemble him down to the last detail, with the apparitional stapler appearing to be, to all mortified onlookers, a Browning FN model 1910 pistol.

Princip's absolute innocence—Princip's whereabouts were verified by more than a dozen eyewitnesses at a local Bohemian "cheese shop" (opium den)—was of no defense, largely because, since age eleven, he'd told any Sarajevan who would listen to him that he longed for nothing more than the chance to execute "any Austrian royalist bastard I can get my grimies on." Indeed, Princip had only a fortnight previously completed a tattoo across his back (employing, ironically, another of Mr. Tesla's inventions, the electrographic somatic autodecorator), depicting himself decapitating Austrian emperor Franz Josef I with a cricket bat.

A Second Try in America

Fearing that it was only a matter of time before the authorities connected the archduke's accidental death (and the subsequent Great War that engulfed all of Europe) to the neurheographiton and to him (or assumed that Princip had been

Tesla's human weapon aimed at the archduke), Mr. Tesla returned to the United States to resume developing his mentation engine.

Aleister Crowley, in mushroom cap, during the majority of his troubles.

But Tesla quickly found that his funding troubles were as dire as ever. While his protracted conflict with Edison yielded him nothing but grief, his failed lawsuit against Guglielmo Marconi over the patent for radio left him even further in debt.

The following decades were unkind to Mr. Tesla, consisting of quixotic struggles that included a rapid opposition to the League of Nations and increasingly violent claims that "secretive operatives ensconced inside black submarinal vessels patrolled the very oceans, seas, lakes, and rivers in order to spy upon us all with their telescoping looking-glasses!" Tesla developed impulsions, including the unquenchable urge to orbit buildings three times before he entered them, to have a stack of three folded napkins at every meal, and to produce neither less nor more than three bowel emissions at every 3 A.M. and 3 P.M. precisely. Finally, on March 3, 1933, Mr. Tesla's maddened certainty that he would win himself a sponsor granted him dividends. Word of his achievements and theories won him patronage of a Mr. Allen Dulles and a Mr. J. E. Hoover. For them, he constructed the Electrical Neurheographiton, Mark 2, which Tesla promised could not only rewrite mental histories but read them, making his device a deception-detector and espionage-recognition motor.

But, alas, patronage for Tesla was not to be. Mr. Tesla, in a bid to impress his sponsors that his device was no mere quackery or hocus-pocusion, arranged a private demonstration for Mr. Dulles and Mr. Hoover. While posterity does not record the contents of what Tesla revealed, Mr. Dulles was said to have quipped to a young Senator John Kennedy that Mr. Hoover found enormous distaste for Tesla's "sartorial speculations" about Mr. Hoover's leisure hours.

Triumph and Death of Tesla, and the Disappearance of the Neurheographiton

Effectively indexed by the elites who could fund his research, Mr. Tesla embarked on a new odyssey: touring the United States with the smaller, more portable Electrical Neurheographiton, Mark 3, as part of "Genius Nikola Tesla's Electric Circus," announcing "electrical exorcism of various mental afflictions and neurological maladies." Mr. Tesla eventually made enough money (and trade in chickens and illicit spirits) from his circus to fund his various researches for the remainder of his life, including into "electro-transdimensional portals."

Finally tendering "exclusive" sales of the technical specifications of the Mark 4 to Warner Bros. Studios, Metro-Goldwyn-Mayer, and United Artists in 1939, Tesla departed from public life, offering occasional anti-Relativity screeds while devoting most of his time to developing a "teleforce projector," or death ray.

On January 12, 1943, Mr. Tesla was claimed to have died, although reports were conflicting. Many in Hollywood conjectured immediately that assassins in the pay of Big Cinema had done in the Serbian genius for selling them "exclusive" rights to a device whose blueprints contained, in tiny print, the phrase "I have omitted an explanation only for the motive unit which makes the entire machine work, in fear that the alchemists of celluloid might enthrall their nation and the world with ludicrous tales of vacuous lives." Others believed that Mr. Tesla's madness finally claimed him, inflicting him with a Jovian "brain burst" that produced not Minerva but rather a puddle of bloodied grey matter upon Tesla's hotel room floor. Among the modern-day Fraternal Society of Teslic Scientific Investigators, there remains the belief that Tesla's "corpse" was an electrophantasmic discharge that had merged with organic materials in the hotel room to produce a permanent simulacrum of Tesla, while the "real" man departed from this world to explore the Universe, unhindered by the constraints of mortals.

Documentation released following the dissolution of Yugoslavia at least identifies the path that Mr. Tesla's inventions took following their master's putative death. Farmer and amateur inventor Mr. Rhett Greene tracked down every working or dysfunctional electrical neurheographiton and, by means of wagon train, transported their many parts back to his "robotorium" (barn) in the then Dominion of Newfoundland, where he, without success, laboured for several years to make them work. Then, on Christmas Day 1947, Yugoslavian agents forcibly entered Mr. Greene's barn under cover of darkness and extracted all of Mr. Tesla's creations they found there.

The Lambshead Imperative

Dr. Thackery T. Lambshead, who had long enjoyed Mr. Tesla's invectives against Dr. Einstein's theories of special and general relativity, in 1997 tracked the remains of Tesla's most bizarre device (that had actually worked) to the Sub-Basement 6 of the Marshal Josip Broz Tito Museum of Yugoslavian Civilisation.

Apparently long-forgotten, the neurheographiton had been used to produce an indiscernible, global, mental domination, *viz.*, to effect the export and sale of the Yugo. Because the Bosnian-Herzegovinian state held no interest in the ravings of a Serbian "madman," Lambshead was able to acquire the entirety of the Tesla collection for the sum of 100 marka (about US $66). By the conditions of Dr. Lambshead's will, Lambshead's estate lent Tesla's materials to the Slovenian National Museum of Electrical Engineering (L2010.01), where they were nearly destroyed in a terrorist attack by members of the Church of Electrology.

St. Brendan's Shank

Documented by Kelly Barnhill

Museum: The Museum of Medical Anomalies, Royal College of Surgeons, London

Exhibit: St. Brendan's Shank

Medium: Copper, silver

Date: 1270s (?) (disputed)

Origin: The monks of the Isle of St. Brendan, also known as the Isle of the Blessed (disputed); the Faroe Islands (undisputed point of collection)

St. Brendan's Shank is a small device—eight inches long from tip to tip—made from thirty-seven interlocking copper globes, circular hinges, a narrow headpiece (with burrowing snout), and a winding key connected to a clockwork interior (silver alloy and iron). The device itself has an uncannily efficient winding system—a single turn of the pin sets its lifelike wriggle in motion for days, even months, at a time. More than one biologist has noted the device's astonishing mimicry of the movements, behaviors, and habits of a tiny subspecies of the Turrilepad, or armored worm, called the Turrilepus Gigantis, found in the North Sea and other cold-water locations. Like its prehistoric cousins, the segmented body of the Turrilepus Gigantis was covered in a tough, calcitic armor, had a sharp, burrowing snout, and exhibited a distinct lack of fastidiousness when it came to its diet.

The name of the Shank originates with the brethren of the Order of Brendan, although not from the saint himself. St. Brendan (called the Navigator, the Voyager, and the Bold) was no inventor, being far more interested in the navigational utility of the heavenly stars, the strange insistence of the sea, and, in one famously preserved quotation, the curious hum of his small boat's leather hull against the foamy breasts of the ocean's waves: "So like the suckling child, I return, openmouthed, to the rocking bosom of the endless sea." He was not a man of science, nor of medicine, nor of healing. He was known for his ability to inspire blind devotion and ardent love in his followers, who willingly went to the farthest edges of the known world to found fortresses of prayer, only to have their beloved abbott leave them behind.

One such monastery existed for many centuries on the cliffs of the Isle of

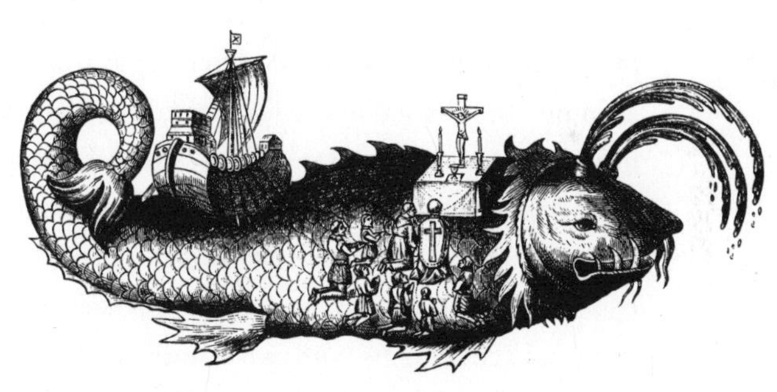

coast of Newfoundland, and once apparently passed so close to Iceland that the bards sang of "waving at the holy men," interpreted by some scholars as a reference to extreme drunkenness instead.

If the monks' own records can be believed—and these accounts are vague on many points—by the late 1200s, the monks had succeeded, perhaps in partnership with Arab scientists traveling to Africa, in fashioning a mechanical equivalent to what presumably must have been a kind of symbiotic relationship with a form of Turrilepus Gigantis.

Over time—due in part to the creation of copies and the reduction in the number of monks from fatalities from drowning, slipping on wet stone floors, and the like—each monk came to be in possession of a replica of his own, although from the few descriptions, most of these may have been crude, nonfunctional copies.

The Shank—*our Shank,* the monks said fondly—soon became sanctified as a holy object. It became friend, confidant, and spiritual guide to every monk on the island, from the lowliest of the novitiate to the interim abbott. The monks carried the replicas around in their pockets, held them delicately (desperately) to their mouths, whispering secrets in the dark. Given the extraordinarily long lives of the monks, they had more secrets than most to confess to their small, metal friends.

After the silence of the Dark Ages, the Shank came once again to the notice of the burgeoning medical community in the West in the form of a smattering of accounts that hailed it as a kind of miraculous relic, but noting that even though healed, the recipients of the Shank suffered from a strange melancholy bordering on mania, following their treatment. Such patients drew pictures of the Shank—both the clockwork Turrilepad and the Turrilepad in the flesh. They painted portraits and composed sonnets and sang odes. They whispered the name of the lost saint in their dreams, and, as though suddenly losing sight of their senses, they would call out to him during the day, responding to the ensuing silence with fits of weeping. They left their families, left their businesses and affairs, and took to the sea, their eyes scanning the horizon for . . . well, they would not say. It was generally believed that they *could* not say.

Indeed, by the year 1522, Pope Adrian VI—having had enough of talk of floating islands, healing that resulted in death by melancholia, bleeding, or worse, and other rumors that, in his opinion, were, at best, due to the infernal influence of the followers of that fallen priest, Martin Luther, or, at worst (and Heaven forbid!), an insidious Ottoman plot—banned the use of the Shank, banned mention of the

Shank, and excommunicated the ent
or absence of suffering is due wholly
an insult to thwart the divine Plan," h
his writings, he demonstrates an acute
died a year later. It is doubtful that the n
their excommunication, or, indeed, that

Throughout the historical record, the
gone assiduously *unmentioned* in its bri
Shank merely attested that it *worked,* rema
tant matters for quite some time.

Perhaps because of this very mystery, D
ested in locating one. Through his deep and m
tory of the medical arts, Lambshead had encou
to the Shank—particularly in his extensive re
Omnibus of Insidious Arctic Maladies, edited b
nard, long after his bitter and public feud with
kind of attempt through scholarship to reconcile.
object until many years later.

According to Dr. Lambshead's journals, volume
tered the Shank during World War II, while perform
the Island of Mykines, the Faroe Islands still under
soon return to his wartime efforts at London's Combu

On October 5, 1941, the doctor wrote: "Patient arri
rapid heartbeat, high fever, terrible bleeding from the
Lansing informed me that the ancient man was found cli
skiff that had wedged between two large rocks at the lee of
dressed in the manner of those bent toward monasticism
sandals, a rope binding the waist—and was impossibly old. H
leaves gone to mulch. His body was as light as paper and twic
fluttered and flapped as the breeze blew in cold gusts over the

Lambshead further notes, and the duty log from the day
claimed to be an abbot in the Order of St. Brendan, and ask
several times, but for what we had no clue, except for frequen
'weakness.' Where he had come from, we had no idea—due t
that place and a partial blockade by the Germans, it was all but
he had sailed his boat from another part of the island—he had to l
the sea." However, as Dr. Lambshead noted, there wasn't anothe

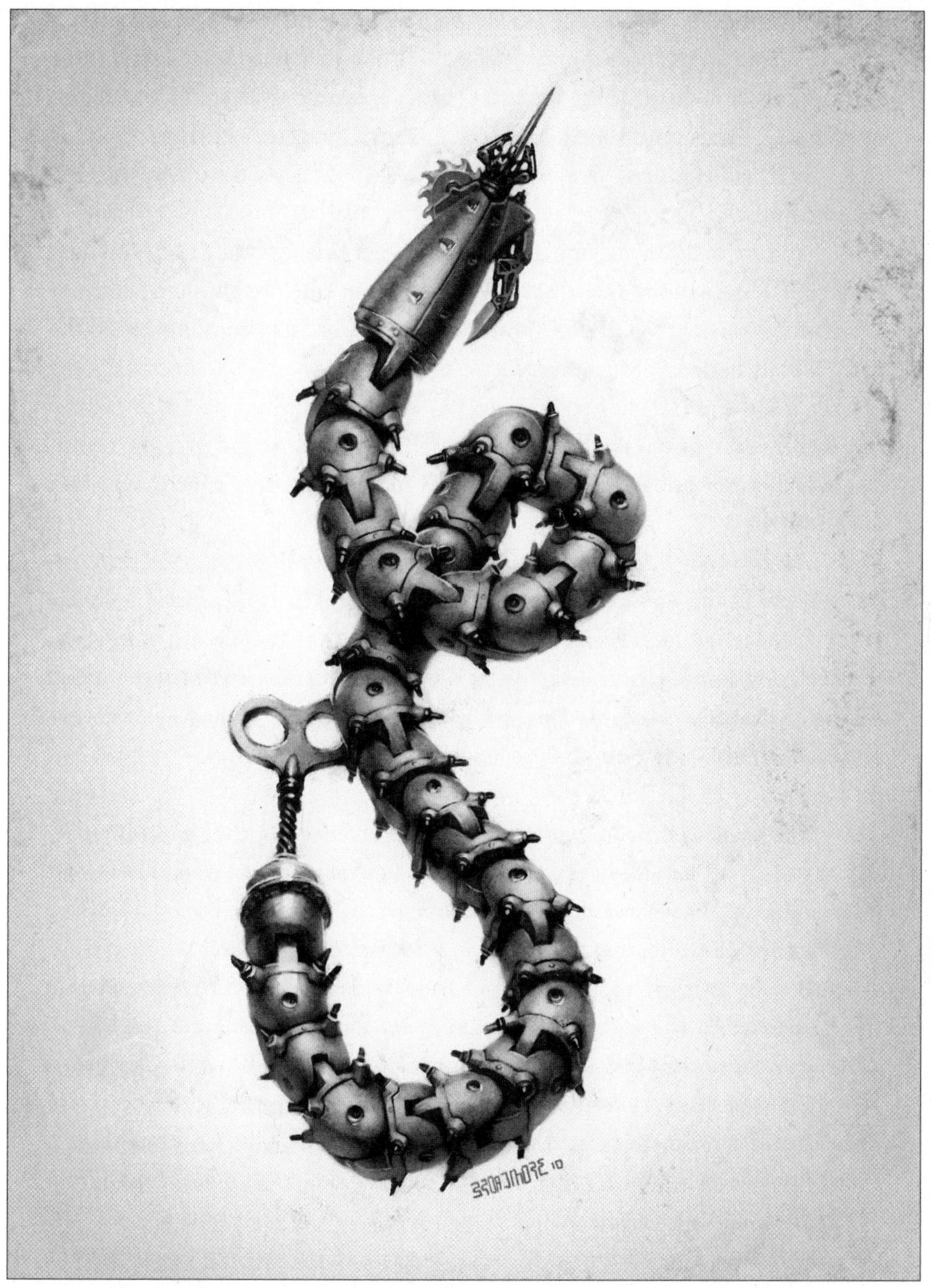

St. Brendan's Shank, made of interlocking copper pieces, with over thirty springs to keep the pieces in tension with one another.

St. Brendan—also known as the Isle of the Blessed—a lush, verdant island once inhabited by a strange pre-Coptic civilization that had since vanished, leaving only a series of man-made saltwater lakes that appeared to have some religious significance. The monks soon added to the many strange tales surrounding the place, for it was said that the monks themselves would never die unless they left the island.

It was here that the idea for the Shank appears to have originated, although the sophistication of the device has led to theories of outside collusion. Some, for example, believe that the device shows evidence of workmanship common to the Early Middle Period of Muslim scientific flowering in the 1200s, specifically the influence of the (nonmonastic) brothers known as Banu Musa, and their *Book of Ingenius Devices.* Given the amount of traveling the monks did over the centuries, it is not impossible that they came into contact with either the Banu Musa or equivalent.

Whether or not this legend is true, it seems incontestable that the development of the Shank followed eventually from an event in 1078, when the lonely order on the island found itself an unwilling host to the unstable and murderous son of Viking despot Olaf the Bloodless, King of Jutland. The arrival of the young Viking on the isle was recorded in the sagas of a bard known only as Sigi, who was present with the Viking entourage accompanying the prince.

> "The son of Olaf, upon hearing tell of an Isle populated by the Monks-Who-Cheated-Death, became inflamed by desire to find the place and conquer its secrets. The Isle, like a coward, made itself difficult to find, but the Prince did give chase through storm, through mist, and through ice until at last, the Isle was in our sights. We arrived with swords in hand, slicing open the first two monks who greeted us, as a demonstration of force and might. It was in this way that we learned that the Monks-Who-Cheated-Death had only cheated the death of cowards and slaves—a death in a bed, a death of age, a death of sickness. The death of Men cannot be cheated, nor can their Magics wish it away. And nothing, not even their craven God, is mightier than a Jutland sword. The monks knelt and trembled and wailed before us."

This account is contradicted in part by the journal of Brother Eidan, abbott of the order since the departure of their founder-saint: "The children of the children of the men who once laid waste to our homeland arrived upon our shores unexpectedly. They were tired and hungry and sick at heart. Our souls were moved to pity and we welcomed them with open arms. Their demands seemed beyond our abilities or strength to fulfill, but we had no choice but to try, as otherwise they would have put us all to the sword."

The prince suffered from a wasting disease that Sigi and other chroniclers had either covered up or had judiciously neglected to mention—this was the real reason the prince had come to the monks' island. What followed appeared to consist of a series of ablutions in the icy waters of the island's western bay. The monks told the prince they staved off death by stripping naked, bearing their skin to the morning light, and plunging into the water. Of course, if their other accounts are to be believed, any longevity, possible or impossible, came simply from prayer and from other essential properties of the island.

Nevertheless, after the young man stripped, winced, and shivered, submerging his body every morning for a full week, a miracle occurred. The son of King Olaf emerged from the water a new man, naked and shining, blessed with strength and health. "My disease is devoured and vanquished," he cried, and the Viking horde gave a halfhearted cheer. They left the island in a relatively unpillaged condition. No account tells of exactly *how* the prince was cured, however, despite the first reference in the literature to a "creature of healing." Nor is there any explanation for the prince's eventual death two years later, except for an obscure fragment from Sigi referring to "bleeding." Perhaps coincidentally or perhaps not, Brother Eidan died prior to the prince's recovery, and his successor, Brother Jonathan, notes only that "he made his sacrifice for our sake, and would that such a sacrifice not need be made again."[1]

A medieval representation of St. Brendan and his followers worshipping atop a floating sea monster.

The subsequent bleeding caught no one's attention, but news of the incredible healing spread slowly throughout Europe, with the result that many an expedition put forth into the northern seas. However, the island proved ridiculously difficult to find again. Many tried and failed, some sailing to their deaths. From these attempts grew the legend that the isle moved across the seas, from charted waters to the uncharted danger of "Here be dragons." Over the centuries, it would reportedly be sighted in view of the Canaries, in the midst of the Hebrides, off the coast of Newfoundland, and once apparently passed so close to Iceland that the bards sang of "waving at the holy men," interpreted by some scholars as a reference to extreme drunkenness instead.

If the monks' own records can be believed—and these accounts are vague on many points—by the late 1200s, the monks had succeeded, perhaps in partnership with Arab scientists traveling to Africa, in fashioning a mechanical equivalent to what presumably must have been a kind of symbiotic relationship with a form of Turrilepus Gigantis.

Over time—due in part to the creation of copies and the reduction in the number of monks from fatalities from drowning, slipping on wet stone floors, and the like—each monk came to be in possession of a replica of his own, although from the few descriptions, most of these may have been crude, nonfunctional copies.

The Shank—*our Shank,* the monks said fondly—soon became sanctified as a holy object. It became friend, confidant, and spiritual guide to every monk on the island, from the lowliest of the novitiate to the interim abbott. The monks carried the replicas around in their pockets, held them delicately (desperately) to their mouths, whispering secrets in the dark. Given the extraordinarily long lives of the monks, they had more secrets than most to confess to their small, metal friends.

After the silence of the Dark Ages, the Shank came once again to the notice of the burgeoning medical community in the West in the form of a smattering of accounts that hailed it as a kind of miraculous relic, but noting that even though healed, the recipients of the Shank suffered from a strange melancholy bordering on mania, following their treatment. Such patients drew pictures of the Shank—both the clockwork Turrilepad and the Turrilepad in the flesh. They painted portraits and composed sonnets and sang odes. They whispered the name of the lost saint in their dreams, and, as though suddenly losing sight of their senses, they would call out to him during the day, responding to the ensuing silence with fits of weeping. They left their families, left their businesses and affairs, and took to the sea, their eyes scanning the horizon for . . . well, they would not say. It was generally believed that they *could* not say.

Indeed, by the year 1522, Pope Adrian VI—having had enough of talk of floating islands, healing that resulted in death by melancholia, bleeding, or worse, and other rumors that, in his opinion, were, at best, due to the infernal influence of the followers of that fallen priest, Martin Luther, or, at worst (and Heaven forbid!), an insidious Ottoman plot—banned the use of the Shank, banned mention of the

Shank, and excommunicated the entire Order of St. Brendan. "Since the presence or absence of suffering is due wholly to the whims of God, it is a blasphemy and an insult to thwart the divine Plan," he wrote in October of that year, though, in his writings, he demonstrates an acute ignorance of *how* the Shank worked. He died a year later. It is doubtful that the monks on the wandering isle ever knew of their excommunication, or, indeed, that they would have cared.

Throughout the historical record, then, the actual *function* of the Shank had gone assiduously *unmentioned* in its brief appearances. The witnesses to the Shank merely attested that it *worked,* remaining curiously mum on other important matters for quite some time.

Perhaps because of this very mystery, Dr. Lambshead became keenly interested in locating one. Through his deep and multilayered explorations of the history of the medical arts, Lambshead had encountered several modern references to the Shank—particularly in his extensive rereading of *The Trimble-Manard Omnibus of Insidious Arctic Maladies,* edited by John Trimble and Rebecca Manard, long after his bitter and public feud with both Trimble and Manard—a kind of attempt through scholarship to reconcile. Still, he did not lay eyes on the object until many years later.

According to Dr. Lambshead's journals, volume 27, book 4, he finally encountered the Shank during World War II, while performing his duty as a surgeon on the Island of Mykines, the Faroe Islands still under the British flag. (He would soon return to his wartime efforts at London's Combustipol General Hospital.)

On October 5, 1941, the doctor wrote: "Patient arrived: an elderly gentleman, rapid heartbeat, high fever, terrible bleeding from the mouth and anus. Private Lansing informed me that the ancient man was found clinging to a leather-hulled skiff that had wedged between two large rocks at the lee of the island. The man was dressed in the manner of those bent toward monasticism—rough cloth, broken sandals, a rope binding the waist—and was impossibly old. His face had the look of leaves gone to mulch. His body was as light as paper and twice as fragile; his limbs fluttered and flapped as the breeze blew in cold gusts over the North Atlantic."

Lambshead further notes, and the duty log from the day confirms, that "He claimed to be an abbot in the Order of St. Brendan, and asked for forgiveness several times, but for what we had no clue, except for frequent references to his 'weakness.' Where he had come from, we had no idea—due to the currents in that place and a partial blockade by the Germans, it was all but impossible that he had sailed his boat from another part of the island—he had to have come from the sea." However, as Dr. Lambshead noted, there wasn't another island within one hundred miles, and the monk's boat could at best be classified "as a pathetic cockleshell."

The man carried with him "an intricate mechanical device that he clutched tightly in his hands." Although the artifact intrigued Lambshead, he had no time to examine it closely. The man was in need of immediate medical assistance. The bleeding was so profuse that it seemed to the doctor to have been caused by shrapnel, though that was "terribly unlikely." There had been no attacks in the last week against any of the islands—just a long, tense stalemate—and the wound "was fresh, and flowing."

The old monk explained that he had come from a place called Brendan's Isle after his craft became tempest-tossed in a sudden gale, and the island disappeared, and the monk was left alone on the undulating waves. Somehow, the doctor did not quite believe this explanation, although "to this day I couldn't say why I should doubt a dying monk."[2]

"Come back," the monk moaned, his eyes sliding past the rim of his sockets. "Oh, please come back with me."

"Does it hurt here?" the doctor asked, ignoring the monk as he palpated the belly.

"Was this the fate of our beloved Brendan?" the old man wheezed. "To realize too late that he was wrong to leave, that he wanted to come home." Tears leaked from the old man's rheumy eyes. "Always we wander, and it is so lonely. No matter where our island travels."

The doctor, assuming the man was raving, called the nurse to bring in the ether.

"Don't operate," the old monk raved, clutching his belly. "Oh, dear God, don't take it away."

"Don't take what away?" Lambshead said reasonably. "Your odd artifact is safe with us. You can have it back once we've operated." He wondered with growing irritation what on earth could be taking that nurse so long.

The monk's thin arm shot from the gurney, grabbed the doctor's crisp, white coat. "We were so alone," the monk whispered. "The Isle of the Blessed is a cold and lonely and desperate place without our beloved saint. And I am alone, and not alone. My brother! My brother! Don't take him!"

Lambshead reports that the monk shuddered so violently as the nurse came in, donning her surgical smock and mask, that he thought the monk might die right then, right there.

Five drops of ether, the doctor remembers thinking calmly. "Or, perhaps seven. Indeed, make it an even ten."

Soon, Lambshead opened up the anesthetized man's belly, and deep in the old monk's gut he found a very large tumor—nearly the size of a rugby ball, though three times as heavy—and inside the tumor, happily burrowing and eating away, "was a specimen of some form of Turrilepus Gigantis! The mirror image of the complex clockwork artifact we had found in the monk's pocket!"

After convincing the nurse to neither pass out nor leave the room, the doctor realized at once that the tumor, not the Turrilepus Gigantis—whether symbiotic or parasitic or belonging to some third classification—required immediate attention: "It was malignant and fast-growing, apparently too fast-growing to be mastered by the monk's little brother."

However, even Lambshead's best efforts were not enough.

"Exhausted and saddened by the outcome," Lambshead writes, "I nonetheless, in the interests of science, immediately performed an autopsy and attempted to preserve the Turrilepus Gigantis in an empty marmalade jar." What he found startled him: "This very old, tired man had had the organs and circulatory system of a twenty-five-year-old. If not for the aggressive growth of the tumor, a million-to-one anomaly that his symbiotic brother could not devour quickly enough, the monk might've lived another sixty or seventy years at least."

He also found that the mindless movements of the pre-wound replica had an oddly "hypnotic and vaguely dulling effect on me, its copper snout curling and uncurling rhythmically.

"What happened on the Isle of St. Brendan, I have no idea," Lambshead would write after the war, in a letter to the then-curator of the Museum of Medical Anomalies as part of the grant that included turning over the mechanical Shank and a half-dissolved, sad-looking Turrilepus Gigantis, "but I remain convinced that the last surviving member of Order of St. Brendan died on my operating table on 3 November 1941, and that this order had hitherto survived for centuries in part because of a symbiotic relationship with a creature that provided a high level of preventative medicine and thus conferred on these monks extremely long life. That extremely long life in such isolation may, in fact, be its own kind of illness I cannot speculate upon."

A month after the death and burial of the castaway monk, one Private Lansing wrote this in his journal: "Doctor Lambshead, always an odd duck, becomes odder by the day, afflicted as he is by a strange, growing sadness. He stands at all hours at the edge of the sea, his hand cupped over his eyes, scanning the horizon. He mutters to himself, and raves. And what's worse, he's given himself over to a bizarre religious fanaticism, calling out the name of a saint, waking, dreaming, again and again and again."

Whether this temporary melancholy was caused by the events of the war or by possession of the Shank is unknown, but in later years, Lambshead was known to remark, "I must say I was very happy to give the thing away."

Due to issues of medical ethics, the Shank displayed in this exhibit has yet to be tested on human patients. Nor have other specimens of this particular type of Turrilepus Gigantis ever been found.

ENDNOTES

1. There is unsubstantiated conjecture by Menard and Trimble that somehow the abbott conveyed his own seeming good health upon the Viking, as a way of saving the island, and that the monks then sought some way to avoid a similar catastrophe in future by creating an artifact that could, without a similar later sacrifice, perform the same function.
2. Later investigation would uncover nine reports from fishermen claiming to have found a castaway floating in the remains of a broken boat. Each report described a man dressed in the habit of a monk and impossibly old—a face like leaves gone to mulch, a body light as paper. Each man raved and raved about the Shank and a saint lost forever. In each instance, they died before reaching land, and their bodies were given over to the sea. If any of these men hid anything among their possessions, no record of it exists. What catastrophe they might have been fleeing is unknown, although German U-boat records do contain references to the sinking of at least two "ships" that do not correspond to any losses in the records of the Allies.

The Auble Gun

Documented by Will Hindmarch

Drs. Franz S. Auble and Lauritz E. Auble, Inventor/Designer
Auble Gun, 1884–1922
Purchased by Dr. Lambshead, January 1922
1922.11.1a&b

My goal is to create a new battlefield milieu in which a select few do battle for the sake of their ideals and their nations with science and engineering on their backs; a new generation of gallant combatants and miniaturized engines of war—knights not with horses and lances but with boilers and bullets.

—Dr. Franz Auble

The Development and Reputation of a Singular Weapon

According to Aidan Birch's book, *Cranks and Steam: The Story of the Auble Gun* (1921), Franz Auble came to America from Prague in 1855, at the age of eleven, with his mother. Though the Aubles were wealthy enough to buy Franz out of military service, due to a near-tragic misunderstanding he fought in the American Civil War as part of a Northern artillery battery and went deaf in his right ear as a result. Young Franz Auble's time among the deafening muskets and cannons may have inspired his idea for a shoulder-mounted weapon. "Franz Auble must very much enjoy being deaf," wrote Martin Speagel in the *St. Louis Gazette,* "for it means he hears only half of his bad ideas."

Although not widely known by the public, the Auble gun ranks among firearms and artillery enthusiasts as one of history's great curios. Not quite a personal firearm and not quite miniaturized artillery, the Auble is a man-portable, multibarreled *mitrailleuse* designed to be carried and fired on an operator's shoulder for "ease and haste of transport and displacement in tenuous battlefield circumstances," according to a lecture given by Franz Auble in 1882.

American humorist and essayist Edgar Douglas, while on a monologue tour in 1891, famously deemed it "the Awful gun." American shootists, in periodicals of the era, joked that it was the "Unstauble gun or Wobble gun."

The weapon's infamous instability was a result of the Aubles' innovative "human bipod" design. Franz Auble's vision cast able-bodied soldiers in the role of "specially trained mobile gunnery platforms," which would operate in three-man fire teams, triangulating on enemy positions. "Ideally," Franz Auble wrote, "the gun's very presence is enough to stymie or deter enemy soldiers, ending battles through superior military posture and displays of ingenious invention rather than outright bloodshed."

Word of Franz Auble's interest in "military posturing" over battlefield effectiveness led to his being labeled "a showman, not a shootist" by *Gentleman Rifleman* editor Errol MacCaskill in the periodical's winter 1882 issue. The Auble gun was still only in active development at the time. Billed as "a more personal approach to gentlemanly annihilation," perhaps tongue-in-cheek, an early hand-cranked prototype of the Auble gun debuted in 1883, just a year before the first demonstration of a proper machine gun: the Maxim gun, invented by Sir Hiram Maxim. Whereas the Maxim gun's reloading mechanism was powered by the weapon's own recoil action, the first Auble gun prototype was still powered by a hand crank. It looked somewhat like an oversized, shoulder-mounted film camera—and, indeed, some early design prototypes might have allowed shooters to shoot what they were shooting, so to speak.

When the Maxim gun first gained real attention, in the mid-1880s, Auble went back to the drawing board and the firing range. The era of the machine gun was coming, and in his journals, Franz would later bemoan his "fatally late understanding that the revolution would be in the field of ever-swifter reloading mechanisms, not the perfection of techniques to balance machinery on the human shoulder! Who knew?"

In the middle of 1884, however, Franz Auble was diagnosed with Brandywine syndrome, a rare and misunderstood disease in that day and age. Knowing he had limited time left to continue his work, he retreated to a cottage outside Boston, intent on designing a mechanism that would put the Auble gun into serious competition with the Maxim.

Journal entries from the time are chaotic—Franz combined his engineering notes with a dream journal analyzing months of fevered and torrid dreams of war and his dead wife—but on November 12, 1884, Franz wrote, "If I cannot escape my dreams, I must learn from them. I see smokestacks and gun barrels. I hear gurgling boilers and empty shells raining on cobblestones. It seems clear what the gun is asking me for!"

What he had arrived at was bold and, some said, insane: the creation of a steam engine to load rounds into the weapon automatically at the same time

The Auble Gun, probably being modeled by Dr. Lauritz E. Auble (from a badly damaged photograph, ca. 1912).

that it discarded spent cartridges. He produced detailed drawings. He had patent forms drawn up. He ordered smiths to forge new boilers and frames. He gave his famous interview to *Cranks and Steam* author Aidan Birch. Then he died.

A Son Continues His Father's Uncertain Legacy

It was edging toward the spring of 1885. Snow was melting into the mud on the day of Dr. Franz Auble's funeral in Massachusetts, and it seemed at first that his work might never be completed. Lauritz was a dutiful son and devoted business partner, but as he would later tell Aidan Birch, "I lacked my father's creative impulse. What came easily to him came to me with great difficulty. I did not have his head for numbers or his vision." Birch is reputed to have replied that this might be more boon than curse, and when Lauritz asked him to elaborate, said that "vision is not the same as sight." Thus bolstered, Lauritz set out to forge a future for the Auble gun.

Lauritz's first goal was to improve the weapon's stability, especially after early tests with the portable boiler revealed the weapon to be dangerously inaccurate. Between the bubbling boiler and the rattling barrels, the gun proved good at providing a harrowing base of fire . . . but little else. The boiler chugged. The gun trembled. The shooter shook. In one well-photographed demonstration in 1885, the gun walked itself upward in such a flash that it hurled the test-shooter onto his back, cracking the boiler and belching steam onto the shooter and his handlers.

In response to the accident, Lauritz Auble experimented with orangutan shooters with Auble guns upon their backs, but no orangutan would come near the steaming device. "Only humans," Lauritz wrote in his journal, "are bold enough to master the Auble gun and its formidable report."

Abandoning his flirtation with trained animals, Lauritz devised new "human quadrapod" braces for would-be shooters. Each brace was bound to the shooter's shoulder and upper arm, affixed to a long, crutch-like leg extending down to a rubber foot. This gave the shooter two additional points of contact with the ground—one spar from each elbow—thereby stabilizing the shooter and the gun. This refined design is what Lauritz Auble took to the U.S. Army and Navy for demonstrations in the winter of 1885.

It did not fare well.

According to one military observer, the demonstration shooter "moved about like a newborn calf with a Gatling gun on its back; unsteady and uncertain. . . ." The Navy passed on the gun altogether. The Army ordered one revised Auble gun, but canceled their order within the week. Demonstrations for the British Army, the Canadian Army, and a small band of fanatical freemasons fared no better.

Seemingly, Lauritz was out of options. The unwanted gun had become a mechanical albatross, one that could counterintuitively kill with the slightest misshrug, yet could scarcely hit a target.

"My father wouldn't quit if he were here," Lauritz wrote in his diary. "In all the hours I spent watching him in his workshops, no lessons were more clear than these: That my father loved me and that he would not abandon his work for anything short of death.

"Neither shall I."

The Repurposing of the Gun for Entertainment

However, unnoticed by Lauritz, something positive was happening at his demonstrations—something that caught the attention of entrepreneur Luther Fafnerd: crowds of civilians were coming out to see the Auble gun in action.

By 1885, Luther Fafnerd was known for two things: his famed, contest-winning mustache, and the traveling circus shows he produced with his cousin, Thaddeus. Luther Fafnerd visited Lauritz Auble in January of 1886 at the Auble townhouse in Boston, and, over brandy and cigars, devised a new function for the Auble gun (and for Lauritz Auble).

As reported by the local paper, Fafnerd famously said after the meeting, "I know spectacle, and what Lauritz Auble has there is spectacular. Bring your eyeballs, ladies and gentlemen, and your earplugs—we have a new attraction!"

Lauritz tapped into his experiences pitching the Auble gun to military men to transform himself from businessman to showman. He traveled Europe and America with the next-generation Auble gun on his shoulder, demonstrating the weapon's incredible power and phenomenal noise for audiences from San Francisco to Prague. He wore a top hat and tuxedo and touted the Auble as a gentleman's engine of war.

Lauritz eroded dummy armies with a withering barrage of lead. Children marveled. Lauritz blasted plaster bunkers to bits. Crowds applauded.

While visitors were cheering, Lauritz was going deaf, like his father. So he incorporated that into the act. Cries of "Wot wot wot Lauritz?!" greeted him every time he ascended the stage.

Encouraged beyond his wildest dreams, and desperate to keep his audience—which he saw as "vindication of my father's work"—Lauritz devised increasingly theatrical shows, casting himself as a dramatic star and his Auble gun as a variety of famous weapons. He drew the gun from a papier-mâché stone and became King Arthur. Then he shot the stone to pieces and slew a dozen mannequin Mordreds. He strode across a rocky field, perched atop an elephant with an Auble on his shoulder, and became Hannibal blasting cardboard centurions apart with a steam hiss and a rattling thrum.

"People demand not just a performance," Luther Fafnerd once said, "but *heroics!*" Lauritz imagined that he was delivering just that.

His plans grew out of control. He devised a fifty-man stunt show called *The Battle of the Nile* that would pit Auble-armed stuntmen in boats maneuvering and firing blanks at each other off the Chicago lakeshore, but the Fafnerds refused to pay for it. They had something else in mind.

American "automotive inventor" James Tasker had come to the Fafnerds with a new contraption—the Tasker Battle Carriage—and a simple sketch for a show: pit the rumbling Battle Carriage against lifelike animals preserved with rudimentary taxidermy.

Best of all, for outlandish sums, private citizens brought in by one of the Fafnerds' circus trains could ride the Battle Carriage and hunt animals loosed from pens into Tasker's private ranch for the occasion. Tasker had effectively found a way to monetize the testing process for his new weapon-wagon. As Tasker wrote the Fafnerds in 1908: "Auble provides a weapon you want to see—I provide a weapon that spectators actually wish they could fire first-hand. For a few, we make that wish come true!"

Thaddeus Fafnerd signed the deal with Tasker in the summer of 1908 without telling Lauritz. Soon after, Lauritz was out of a job.

The Auble gun had failed as a weapon of war and had gone out in a hail of glory as a novelty. What could the future possibly hold? "Perhaps a joke, perhaps a curious footnote," Lauritz is said to have muttered on more than one occasion.

The Aftermath and Dying Fall of the Auble Gun

In the years that followed, Lauritz gradually faded from the spotlight, even for weapons enthusiasts. Young weapons designers tended to associate the Auble gun with sideshows, and thus any of his attempts to serve as a consultant failed.

Immediately following his circus departure, Lauritz started to woo Daisy Fafnerd, the forty-year-old widowed daughter of Thaddeus the ringmaster. Thaddeus, an ordained minister and never one to let business come before love, married them the same summer that the Auble shows were finally canceled: 1908. The new couple traveled with the Fafnerd Cousins Circus for years afterward, managing performances and arranging venues.

Just shy of fifty specimens of the Auble gun, in various makes and models, were put into storage in a Fafnerd Cousins warehouse in Nebraska—only to be destroyed in a tornado in 1912. One local headline read, "Circus Warehouse Destroyed, Nothing Valuable Lost, Show Must Go On." The field around the warehouse was littered with top hats, clown shoes, and bent Auble barrels. Clown makeup smeared the grass for years. Only one working Auble gun, a model used during the early circus days and kept in Lauritz Auble's Boston townhouse, now remained intact.

As the Fafnerd cousins grew older, they sold off their circus piece by piece and retired. Lauritz and Daisy lived for a few years off their savings, but the Auble

The Tasker Battle Carriage in action, re-created by Sam Van Olffen from period newspaper descriptions for use in one of his interminable performance art productions.

family fortune was gone—spent on Auble guns—and their circus money was rapidly dwindling. They sold the Boston townhouse and moved into an apartment, with, according to Birch, "a third of the space given over to half-finished inventions."

After the Great War exploded in Europe, Lauritz donated his time to the stateside war effort, assembling and testing weapons for the U.S. Army until peace came in 1918. That same year, Laurtiz was diagnosed with Brandywine syndrome, inherited from his father. Daisy passed away from a bout of pneumonia the following year.

In 1921, *Cranks and Steam* was published to widespread acclaim, much to Lauritz's dismay. Inside, the Auble was touted as a turn-of-the-century marvel of steam engineering and a bizarre breakthrough in firearms design. Yet the work was not quite a celebration of Auble ingenuity. The Auble gun was the steam, but the Auble men were the cranks. And there, on page 201, was an interview with James Tasker about his "profound vision" for the next-generation Battle Carriage, along with a smug quote about the Auble gun.

Humiliated by the book, Lauritz withdrew from society.

It was in the earliest weeks of 1922, when Lauritz Auble was dwelling alone in his tiny flat, quietly withering away, that a young Thackery T. Lambshead came calling. He wanted to buy the last remaining Auble gun—the gun he had marveled at so many years before from the stands of the Fafnerd Cousins Circus—and install it in his burgeoning collection of antiquities and curios. Lambshead was offering the Aubles some measure of recognition for the marvelous thing they'd created, ridiculous and grand.

"It's a grand and curious thing, that gun," Lambshead supposedly told Lauritz. "It's the gun that war didn't want." Lambshead reportedly spent the day with Lauritz, hearing tales of Franz Auble and Daisy and of Lauritz's time with the circus. They drank port and smoked cigars. "Your gun might not have shot anyone, but its report echoed in imaginations from the California coast to the uttermost edge of Europe," Lambshead recalls telling Lauritz. "That's quite a difficult shot to make."

Of Lauritz's reply, there is no record.

Dacey's Patent Automatic Nanny

Documented by Ted Chiang

From the catalog accompanying the exhibition "Little Defective Adults—Attitudes Toward Children from 1700 to 1950"; National Museum of Psychology, Akron, Ohio

The Automatic Nanny was the creation of Reginald Dacey, a mathematician born in London in 1861. Dacey's original interest was in building a teaching engine; inspired by the recent advances in gramophone technology, he sought to convert the arithmetic mill of Charles Babbage's proposed Analytical Engine into a machine capable of teaching grammar and arithmetic by rote. Dacey envisioned it not as a replacement for human instruction, but as a labor-saving device to be used by schoolteachers and governesses.

For years, Dacey worked diligently on his teaching engine, and even the death of his wife, Emily, in childbirth in 1894 did little to slow his efforts.

What changed the direction of his research was his discovery, several years later, of how his son, Lionel, was being treated by the nanny, a woman known as Nanny Gibson. Dacey himself had been raised by an affectionate nanny, and for years assumed that the woman he'd hired was treating his son in the same way, occasionally reminding her not to be too lenient. He was shocked to learn that Nanny Gibson routinely beat the boy and administered Gregory's Powder (a potent and vile-tasting laxative) as punishment. Realizing that his son actually lived in terror of the woman, Dacey immediately fired her. He carefully interviewed several prospective nannies afterwards, and was surprised to learn of the vast range in their approaches to child-rearing. Some nannies showered their charges with affection, while others applied disciplinary measures worse than Nanny Gibson's.

Dacey eventually hired a replacement nanny, but regularly had her bring Lionel to his workshop so he could keep her under close supervision. This must have seemed like paradise to the child, who demonstrated nothing but obedience in Dacey's presence; the discrepancy between Nanny Gibson's accounts of his son's behavior and his own observations prompted Dacey to begin an investigation into optimal child-rearing practices. Given his mathematical inclination, he

Dacey's Patent Automatic Nanny in stand-by mode. In active mode, the arms meet so that the Automatic Nanny can rock the baby to sleep without the need for a cradle or even a blanket.

viewed a child's emotional state as an example of a system in unstable equilibrium. His notebooks from the period include the following: "Indulgence leads to misbehavior, which angers the nanny and prompts her to deliver punishment more severe than is warranted. The nanny then feels regret, and subsequently overcompensates with further indulgence. It is an inverted pendulum, prone to oscillations of ever-increasing magnitude. If we can only keep the pendulum vertical, there is no need for subsequent correction."

Dacey tried imparting his philosophy of child-rearing to a series of nannies for Lionel, only to have each report that the child was not obeying her. It appears not to have occurred to him that Lionel might behave differently with the nannies than with Dacey himself; instead, he concluded that the nannies were too temperamental to follow his guidelines. In one respect, he concurred with the conventional wisdom of the time, which held that women's emotional nature made them unsuitable parents; where he differed was in thinking that too much punishment could be just as detrimental as too much affection. Eventually, he decided that the only nanny that could adhere to the procedures he outlined would be one he built himself.

In letters to colleagues, Dacey offered multiple reasons for turning his attention to a mechanical nursemaid. First, such a machine would be radically easier to construct than a teaching engine, and selling them offered a way to raise the funds needed to perfect the latter. Second, he saw it as an opportunity for early intervention: by putting children in the care of machines while they were still infants, he could ensure they didn't acquire bad habits that would have to be broken later. "Children are not born sinful, but become so because of the influence of those whose care we have placed them in," he wrote. "Rational child-rearing will lead to rational children."

It is indicative of the Victorian attitude toward children that at no point does Dacey suggest that children should be raised by their parents. Of his own participation in Lionel's upbringing, he wrote, "I realize that my presence entails risk of the very dangers I wish to avoid, for while I am more rational than any woman, I am not immune to the boy's expressions of delight or dejection. But progress can only occur one step at a time, and even if it is too late for Lionel to fully reap the benefits of my work, he understands its importance. Perfecting this machine means other parents will be able to raise their children in a more rational environment than I was able to provide for my own."

For the manufacture of the Automatic Nanny, Dacey contracted with Thomas Bradford & Co., maker of sewing and laundry machines. The majority of the Nanny's torso was occupied by a spring-driven clockwork mechanism that controlled the feeding and rocking schedule. Most of the time, the arms formed a cradle for rocking the baby. At specified intervals, the machine would raise the baby into feeding position and expose an India-rubber nipple connected to a reservoir of infant formula. In addition to the crank handle for winding the mainspring, the Nanny had a smaller crank for powering the gramophone player used to play lullabies; the gramophone had to be unusually small to fit within the Nanny's head, and only custom-stamped discs could be played on it. There was also a foot pedal near the Nanny's base used for pressurizing the waste pump, which provided suction for the pair of hoses leading from the baby's rubber diaper to a chamber pot.

The Automatic Nanny went on sale in March 1901, with an advertisement appearing in the *Illustrated London News* (shown on the next page).

It is worth noting that, rather than promoting the raising of rational children, the advertising preys on parents' fears of untrustworthy nursemaids. This may have just been shrewd marketing on the part of Dacey's partners at Thomas Bradford & Co., but some historians think it reveals Dacey's actual motives for developing the Automatic Nanny. While Dacey always described his proposed teaching engine as an assistive tool for governesses, he positioned the Automatic Nanny as a complete replacement for a human nanny. Given that nannies came from the working class, while governesses typically came from the upper class, this suggests an unconscious class prejudice on Dacey's part.

Whatever the reasons for its appeal, the Automatic Nanny enjoyed a brief period of popularity, with over 150 being sold within six months. Dacey maintained that the families that used the Automatic Nanny were entirely satisfied with the quality of care provided by the machine, although there is no way to verify this; the testimonials used in the advertisements were likely invented, as was customary at the time.

What is known for certain is that in September 1901, an infant named Nigel Hawthorne was fatally thrown from an Automatic Nanny when its mainspring snapped. Word of the child's death spread quickly, and Dacey was faced with a deluge of families returning their Automatic Nannies. He examined the Hawthornes' Nanny, and discovered that the mechanism had been tampered with in an attempt to enable the machine to operate longer before needing to be rewound. He published a full-page ad, in which—while trying not to blame the Hawthorne parents—he insisted that the Automatic Nanny was entirely safe if operated properly, but his efforts were in vain. No one would entrust their child to the care of Dacey's machine.

Do not leave your child in the care of a woman whose character you know nothing about. Embrace the modern practice of scientific child-rearing by purchasing

DACEY'S PATENT AUTOMATIC NANNY

The ADVANTAGES of this UNIQUE SUBSTITUTE for a nanny are:

- **IT TEACHES YOUR BABY TO ADHERE TO A PRECISE SCHEDULE OF FEEDING AND SLEEPING.**
- **IT SOOTHES YOUR BABY WITHOUT ADMINISTERING STUPEFYING NARCOTICS.**
- **IT WORKS NIGHT AND DAY, REQUIRES NO SEPARATE QUARTERS, AND CANNOT STEAL.**
- **IT WILL NOT EXPOSE YOUR CHILD TO DISREPUTABLE INFLUENCES.**

CONSIDER THESE TESTIMONIALS FROM CUSTOMERS:

"Our child is now perfectly behaved and a delight to be near."
—Mrs. Menhenick, Colwyn Bay.
"An immeasurable improvement over the Irish girl we previously employed. It is a blessing for our household."
—Mrs. Hastings, Eastbourne.
"I wish I had been raised by one myself." —Mrs. Godwin, Andoversford.

THOMAS BRADFORD & CO.
68, FLEET STREET, LONDON; and MANCHESTER

To demonstrate that the Automatic Nanny was safe, Dacey boldly announced that he would entrust his next child to the machine's care. If he had successfully followed through with this, he might have restored public confidence in the machine, but Dacey never got the chance, because of his habit of telling prospective wives of his plans for their offspring. The inventor framed his proposal as an invitation to partake in a grand scientific undertaking, and was baffled that none of the women he courted found this an appealing prospect.

After several years of rejection, Dacey gave up on trying to sell the Automatic Nanny to a hostile public. Concluding that society was not sufficiently enlightened to appreciate the benefits of machine-based child care, he likewise abandoned his plans to build a teaching engine, and resumed his work on pure mathematics. He published papers on number theory and lectured at Cambridge until his death in 1918, during the global influenza pandemic.

The Automatic Nanny might have been completely forgotten were it not for the publication of an article in the *London Times* in 1925, titled "Mishaps of Science." It described in derisive terms a number of failed inventions and experiments, including the Automatic Nanny, which it labeled "a monstrous contraption whose inventor surely despised children." Reginald's son, Lionel Dacey, who by then had become a mathematician himself and was continuing his father's work in number theory, was outraged. He wrote a strongly worded letter to the newspaper, demanding a retraction, and when they refused, he filed a libel suit against the publisher, which he eventually lost. Undeterred, Lionel Dacey began a campaign to prove that the Automatic Nanny was based on sound and humane child-rearing principles, self-publishing a book about his father's theories on raising rational children.

Lionel Dacey refurbished the Automatic Nannies that had been in storage on the family estate, and in 1927 offered them for commercial sale again, but was unable to find a single buyer. He blamed this on the British upper class's obsession with status; because household appliances were now being marketed to the middle class as "electric servants," he claimed upper-class families insisted on hiring human nannies for appearance's sake, whether they provided better care or not. Those who worked with Lionel Dacey blamed it on his refusal to update the Automatic Nanny in any way; he ignored one business advisor's recommendation to replace the machine's spring-driven mechanism with an electric motor, and fired another who suggested marketing it without the Dacey name.

Like his father, Lionel Dacey eventually decided to raise his own child with the Automatic Nanny, but rather than look for a willing bride, he announced in 1932 that he would adopt an infant. He did not offer any updates in the following years, prompting a gossip columnist to suggest that the child had died at the machine's hands, but by then there was so little interest in the Automatic Nanny that no one ever bothered to investigate.

The truth regarding the infant would never have come to light if not for the work of Dr. Thackery Lambshead. In 1938, Dr. Lambshead was consulting at the Brighton Institute of Mental Subnormality (now known as Bayliss House) when he encountered a child named Edmund Dacey. According to admission records, Edmund had been successfully raised using an Automatic Nanny until the child was two years old, the age at which Lionel Dacey felt it appropriate to switch him to human care. He found that Edmund was unresponsive to his commands, and shortly afterwards, a physician diagnosed the child as "feebleminded." Judging such a child an unsuitable subject for demonstration of the Nanny's efficacy, Lionel Dacey committed Edmund to the Brighton Institute.

What prompted the institute's staff to seek Dr. Lambshead's opinion was Edmund's diminutive stature: although he was five, his height and weight were that of the average three-year-old. The children at the Brighton Institute were generally taller and healthier than those at similar asylums, a reflection of the fact that the institute's staff did not follow the still-common practice of minimal interaction with the children. In providing affection and physical contact to their charges, the nurses were preventing the condition now known as psychosocial dwarfism, where emotional stress reduces a child's levels of growth hormones, and which was prevalent in orphanages at the time.

The nurses quite reasonably assumed that Edmund Dacey's delayed growth was the result of substituting the Automatic Nanny's mechanical custody for actual human touch, and expected him to gain weight under their care. But after two years as a resident at the institute, during which the nurses had showered attention on him, Edmund had scarcely grown at all, prompting the staff to look for an underlying physiological cause.

Dr. Lambshead hypothesized that the child was indeed suffering from psychosocial dwarfism, but of a uniquely inverted variety: what Edmund needed was not more contact with a person but more contact with a machine. His small size was not the result of the years he spent under the care of the Automatic Nanny; it was the result of being deprived of the Automatic Nanny after his father felt he was ready for human care. If this theory were correct, restoring the machine would cause the boy to resume normal growth.

Dr. Lambshead sought out Lionel Dacey to acquire an Automatic Nanny. He gave an account of the visit in a monograph written many years later:

> [Lionel Dacey] spoke of his plans to repeat the experiment with another child as soon as he could ensure that the child's mother was of suitable stock. His feel-

ing was that the experiment with Edmund had failed only because of the boy's "native imbecility," which he blamed on the child's mother. I asked him what he knew of the child's parents, and he answered, rather too forcefully, that he knew nothing. Later on, I visited the orphanage from which Lionel Dacey had adopted Edmund, and learned from their records that the child's mother was a woman named Eleanor Hardy, who previously worked as a maid for Lionel Dacey. It was obvious to me that Edmund is, in fact, Lionel Dacey's own illegitimate son.

Lionel Dacey was unwilling to donate an Automatic Nanny to what he considered a failed experiment, but he agreed to sell one to Dr. Lambshead, who then arranged to have it installed in Edmund's room at the Brighton Institute. The child embraced the machine as soon as he saw it, and in the days that followed he would play happily with toys as long as the Nanny was nearby. Over the next few months, the nurses recorded a steady increase in his height and weight, confirming Dr. Lambshead's diagnosis.

The staff assumed that Edmund's cognitive delays were congenital in nature, and were content as long as he was thriving physically and emotionally. Dr. Lambshead, however, wondered if the consequences of the child's bond with a machine might be more far-ranging than anyone suspected. He speculated that Edmund had been misdiagnosed as feebleminded simply because he paid no attention to human instructors, and that he might respond better to a mechanical instructor. Unfortunately, he had no way to test this hypothesis; even if Reginald Dacey had successfully completed his teaching engine, it would not have provided the type of instruction that Edmund required.

It was not until 1946 that technology advanced to the necessary level. As a result of his lectures on radiation sickness, Dr. Lambshead had a good relationship with scientists working at Chicago's Argonne National Laboratory, and was present at a demonstration of the first remote manipulators, mechanical arms designed for the handling of radioactive materials. He immediately recognized their potential for Edmund's education, and was able to acquire a pair for the Brighton Institute.

Edmund was thirteen years old at this point. He had always been indifferent to attempts by the staff to teach him, but the mechanical arms immediately captured his attention. Using an intercom system that emulated the low-fidelity audio of the original Automatic Nanny's gramophone, nurses were able to get Edmund to respond to their voices in a way they hadn't when speaking to him directly. Within a few weeks, it was apparent that Edmund was not cognitively delayed in the manner previously believed; the staff had merely lacked the appropriate means of communicating with him.

With news of this development, Dr. Lambshead was able to persuade Lionel Dacey to visit the institute. Seeing Edmund demonstrate a lively curiosity and inquisitive nature, Lionel Dacey realized how he had stunted the boy's intellectual growth. From Dr. Lambshead's account:

> He struggled visibly to contain his emotion at seeing what he had wrought in pursuit of his father's vision: a child so wedded to machines that he could not acknowledge another human being. I heard him whisper, "I'm sorry, Father."
>
> "I'm sure your father would understand that your intentions were good," I said.
>
> "You misunderstand me, Dr. Lambshead. Were I any other scientist, my efforts to confirm his thesis would have been a testament to his influence, no matter what my results. But because I am Reginald Dacey's son, I have disproved his thesis twice over, because my entire life has been a demonstration of the impact a father's attention can have on his son."

Immediately after this visit, Lionel Dacey had remote manipulators and an intercom installed in his house and brought Edmund home. He devoted himself to machine-mediated interaction with his son until Edmund succumbed to pneumonia in 1966. Lionel Dacey passed away the following year.

The Automatic Nanny seen here is the one purchased by Dr. Lambshead to improve Edmund's care at the Brighton Institute. All the Nannies in Lionel Dacey's possession were destroyed upon his son's death. The National Museum of Psychology thanks Dr. Lambshead for his donation of this unique artifact.

HONORING LAMBSHEAD:
STORIES Inspired
by the Cabinet

Stories Inspired by the Cabinet

In early 2002, Ray Russell of prestigious specialty press Tartarus approached Lambshead about publishing a charity chapbook. It would celebrate Lambshead's life from an unusual angle: by focusing on the objects in the doctor's cabinet. Russell and Lambshead shared a fascination with supernatural literature that included a love for Arthur Machen, Elizabeth Jane Howard, and Thomas Ligotti. Several years earlier, Russell had even visited the cabinet for the express purpose of viewing some letters from Machen to Lambshead.

After some deliberation, Lambshead gave his blessing—"as long as all proceeds benefit the Museum of Intangible Arts and Objects and the Institute for Further Study," both of which he thought were underfunded and "staffed by wraiths in ragged clothes; it might be good for morale if they could afford sandwiches at least." Russell agreed and immediately embarked on the project, hoping to ride the coattails of the forthcoming Bantam/Pan Macmillan editions of *The Thackery T. Lambshead Pocket Guide to Eccentric & Discredited Diseases.*

Choosing from a list of items drawn up by Russell, several writers contributed, including the then-unknown Naomi Novik (who at the time wrote period ghost stories under the name N. N. Vasek). By January 2003, the chapbook was ready to be sent to the printer. It also included a somewhat overenthusiastic introduction titled "Virile Lambshead: Catch the Disease!," written by an editor at the medical journal the *Lancet.*

The inspiration for the stories varies greatly. For example, the actual foot that sparked Jeffrey Ford's "Relic" probably dates to the Crimean War's legendary Charge of the Light Brigade. As Lambshead put it, "unless the family mythology is wrong, this foot of my saintly grandfather was mummified due to the chance confluence of devastating military technologies and a freak dismount caused by a faulty stirrup." Similarly, Holly Black's story is mostly conjured up from the imagination, the item in question being "an odd Paddington knockoff that I felt sorry for."

However, Novik's teapot did, according to a Sotheby's auction catalog, belong to Edward John Moreton Drax Plunkett, a.k.a. Lord Dunsany. "Threads" by Carrie Vaughn gently mocks Lambshead's all-too-real predilection for scheduling interviews and then either not showing up or "observing my interview from afar." As for other allusions in the stories, Lambshead's involvement with various British secret service organizations is still murky, and the Meistergarten was probably never used by Lambshead to curb the rambunctious children of visiting relatives.

Unfortunately for readers, Lambshead died before publication, and the chapbook became a casualty of the free-for-all of lawsuits surrounding his estate. This decision was made easier for the estate because of an unfinished letter from Lambshead that began: "Dear Ray: Cease, desist, herewith take it upon yourself to remove me from . . ." (Russell claims the letter would have continued along the lines of either "from your overblown introduction" or "your annoying mailing list.")

Here, then, for the first time, in defiance of potential lawsuits, we are honored to publish those stories, along with all of the original art, sans Robert Mapplethorpe's piece for Novik's story. These tales do indeed form a bizarre tribute to Dr. Lambshead's cabinet, if not the man himself.

Threads

By Carrie Vaughn

Unicorn

For the twentieth time, Jerome reviewed the invitation that had brought him, more than prompt, to the parlor in the doctor's obscure manor house. *Mr. Kenelworth, Brief interview granted, ten minutes only, be prompt. Signed, Lambshead.* It appeared to be his actual signature, and not a note by some assistant.

The stooped housekeeper, who no doubt had been with Lambshead for decades, had guided him here to sit on a velvet-covered wingback chair and wait. The loudly ticking clock sitting at the center of the marble mantelpiece over the fireplace now showed that Lambshead was three minutes late. Would his ten-minute interview be reduced to seven minutes?

Not that sitting in the parlor wouldn't have been fascinating in itself, if he weren't so anxious. He'd arrived at the village the day before, to prevent any mishaps with the train, and spent the night in one of those little country inns with a decrepit public house in front and sparse rooms to let upstairs. The included breakfast had been greasy and now sat in his belly like lead. The village had exactly one taxi, whose driver was also the proprietor at the inn. Jerome had had to practically bribe him to drive him out here. He needed that interview, if for no other reason than to make sure the newspaper reimbursed him for his expenses.

But all he could do was wait. Breakfast gurgled at him. Perhaps he ought to review the questions he hoped to ask the doctor. *Doctor Lambshead, what of your sudden interest in occult experimentation? Is it true the Royal Academy has censured you over the debate about the veracity of certain claims made regarding your recent expedition to Ecuador?*

He ought to be making notes, so that his readers would understand what he was seeing. The parlor was filled with curios of the doctor's travels, glass-fronted cabinets displayed a bewildering variety of artifacts: elongated clay vases as thin as a goose's neck; squat, mud-colored jars, stopped with wax, containing who knew what horrors, wide baskets woven with grass in a pattern so complicated his eyes blurred. Weapons hung on the walls: spears, pikes, three-bladed daggers, swords as long as a man. Taxidermied creatures of the unlikeliest forms: a beaver that seemed to have merged with a lizard, a turkey colored scarlet.

The tapestry of a unicorn hanging in the center of one wall amid a swarm of serious-visaged portraits seemed almost ordinary—every country manor had at least one wall containing a mass of darkened pictures and a faded, moth-bitten Flemish unicorn tapestry. The beast in this one seemed a bit thin and constipated, gazing over a pasture of frayed flowers.

Jerome was sure that if he got up to pace, the eyes in the portraits would follow him, back and forth.

When he heard footsteps outside the parlor, he stood eagerly to greet the approaching doctor, and frowned when the doors opened and a young woman appeared from the vestibule. She stopped and stared at him, her eyes narrowed and predatory.

"Who are you?" they both said.

She wore smart shoes, a purplish skirt and suit jacket, and a short fur stole—fake, no doubt. A pillbox hat sat on dark hair that curled fashionably above her shoulders. She had a string of pearls, brown gloves, and carried a little leather-bound notebook and a pencil. He pegged her—a lady reporter. A rival.

In the same moment, she seemed to make the same judgment about him. Her jaw set, and her mouth pressed in a thin line.

"All right. Who are you with?" she said. Her accent was brash, American. An *American* lady reporter—even worse.

"Who are you with?" Jerome answered.

"I asked you first."

"It doesn't matter, I got here first, and I have an exclusive interview with the doctor."

"*I* have the exclusive interview. *You've* made a mistake."

He blinked, taken aback, then held out the note, which he'd crushed in his hands. Chagrined, he tried to smooth it out, but she took it from him before he could succeed. Her brow creased as she read it, then she shoved it back to him and reached into her handbag for a very similar slip of paper, and Jerome's heart sank. She offered it to him, and he read: brief interview granted, ten minutes only, for the exact same time. The exact same signature decorated the bottom of the page.

His spectacular opportunity was seeming less so by the moment.

"So the professor made a mistake and booked us both for exclusive interviews at the same time," she said.

"Evidently."

James A. Owen's depiction of the medieval tapestry from Lambshead's collection, the original so badly burned in the cabinet fire that only the fringe remains (now on display in the International Fabric Museum, Helsinki, Finland).

"Figures," she said. She crossed her arms, scanned the room, then nodded as if she had made a decision. Her curls bobbed. "Right, here's what we'll do. You get five minutes, I get five minutes. We coordinate our questions so we don't ask the same thing. Then we share notes. All right?"

"Hold on a minute—"

"It's the only fair way."

"I didn't agree to a press conference—"

"Two of us are hardly a press conference."

"But—"

"And don't try to blame me, it's the doctor who double-booked us."

I wasn't going to, Jerome thought, aggrieved. The afternoon was crumbling, and Jerome felt the portraits staring at him, a burning on the back of his neck. "I think that since I was here first it's only fair that I should have the interview. Perhaps you could reschedule—"

"Now how is that fair? I came all the way from New York to get this interview! You're from where, Oxford? You can show up on his doorstep anytime!"

He blinked again, put off-balance by her identifying his accent so precisely. He was the son of a professor there, and had scandalized the family by not going into academics himself. Roving reporting had seemed so much more productive. Romantic, even. So much for that. "I can see we've gotten off to a bad start—"

"Whose fault is that? I've been nothing but polite."

"On the contrary—"

Just then the double doors to the library opened once more, freezing Jerome and the woman reporter in place, her with one hand on her hip, waving her notebook; him pointing as if scolding a small child. The housekeeper, a hunched, wizened woman in a pressed brown cotton dress, scowled at them. Jerome tucked his hands behind his back.

"The doctor is very sorry, but he'll have to reschedule with both of you. He'll send letters to confirm a time." She stood next to the open door, clearly indicating that they should depart.

The woman reporter said, "Did he say why? What's he doing that he can't take ten minutes off to talk?"

"The doctor is very sorry," the housekeeper said again, her scowl growing deeper. She reminded Jerome of a headmistress at a particularly dank primary school. He knew a solid wall when he saw one.

Jerome gestured forward, letting the lady reporter exit first. She puckered her lips as if about to argue, before stalking out of the room. Jerome followed.

Once they were standing on the front steps of the manor, the housekeeper shut the door behind them with a slam of finality.

"Well. So much for that," he said. "I don't suppose you'd like to share a cab back to the village?"

"I'd rather walk," she said, and did just that, following the lane away from the building.

He watched her, astonished at the many unkind adjectives his mind was conjuring to describe her.

His cab arrived, and gratefully he rode it away, ignoring the hassled mutterings of the driver. They passed the woman reporter on the road, still marching, still with that look of witchy fury on her face, which was flushed now and streaked with sweat. A better man might have stopped and offered a ride yet again.

Further on the road, they passed an impressive black Bentley, filled with children. They seemed to be playing some game resembling badminton, in the backseat. And what were they doing, going to the doctor's manor? Lambshead didn't have children, did he? Grandchildren? Nieces and nephews? Jerome hadn't thought so, and he'd certainly never find out now.

He left it all—the doctor, the manor, the housekeeper, the car full of children, and the harridan of a reporter—behind, determined not to think on the day anymore. The pub and a pint awaited.

Mille-fleur

Their screaming certainly did carry in the close confines of the automobile.

The chauffeur scowled at Sylvia in the rearview mirror, and she turned away, her headache doubling.

"Children, please sit. All of you, sit now. Sit *down.*" She had been instructed by Lady Smythe-Helsing not to raise her voice at the children, as that would damage their fragile psyches. She had also been instructed not to ever lay a hand on any of them in an effort to control them—such efforts led to violence, which could not be tolerated. If she ever did any such thing out of Lady Smythe-Helsing's view, the children would report it. Never mind them, the chauffeur would report it. And he had the gall to glare at her for their misbehavior.

So here they were, the four little darlings scrambling all over the seats and each other, throwing their dolls and stuffed bears and India-rubber balls, kicking at the windows and ceilings, punching and screaming. Alice, Andrew, Anna, Arthur.

"That famous doctor is opening his house for tours, just for the afternoon, take the children to visit, it will be so educational," Lady Smythe-Helsing had announced this morning. Commanded. "Simpson will drive you. Hurry along, won't you?" The children had been lined up, tallest to shortest, oldest to youngest, ages ten to five, looking smart and crisp, the boys in their pressed suit jackets and ties—real, not clip-on—the girls in their pleated skirts and snow-white blouses with lace-trimmed Peter Pan collars. So lovely, weren't they? Their mother had kissed their rosy cheeks as they beamed up at her. Then Lady Smythe-Helsing had left Sylvia alone with them while she went to lead the latest meeting of the Oakwaddling Village Improvement Society.

The children had looked at Sylvia with such a piercing sense of anticipation.

Now that they had turned the interior of the car into a rugby pitch, the chauffeur looked at Sylvia, clearly thinking, *How could you let them carry on so?* He'd report to the mistress how the incompetent governess couldn't control a few innocent children.

"Miss Sylvia, are we there yet?" said the youngest boy, Arthur.

"Not yet, dear."

"I want to be there *now*!"

"Unless you've found a way to alter space and time, you'll have to wait."

He bit his lip and furrowed his brow, as if considering. If anyone could find a way to disrupt the workings of the universe, it would be one of the Smythe-Helsing children.

Meanwhile, Sylvia stared out the window, wishing *she* could speed up time. They had reached the drive leading to Dr. Lambshead's manor when they passed a woman in a dress suit walking away. She seemed angry. They'd also passed a car earlier—so the doctor's tours of his manor were popular. That many more people to notice the unruly children and tsk-tsk the poor governess who couldn't control them. Sylvia sighed.

Finally, the car stopped before the manor's carved front doors. Sylvia struggled to pop the door open, succeeded, and the children exploded out of the car. They ran laps around it, pulled each other's hair and sleeves and skirts and ties. Sylvia couldn't tell if they were screaming or laughing. Well, if they ran it out now, maybe they'd actually sleep tonight.

She glanced at the chauffeur, intending to discuss procedures for getting them all home. "I'll wait," he said, glaring.

Sighing again—she probably sighed more than she spoke—Sylvia moved to the bumper to head off the latest lap around the car. Andrew pulled up short in front of her, and the others crashed into him. Sylvia pointed to the house. "That way."

Screaming, they rocketed toward the ancient-looking and no-doubt fragile front doors, which obediently opened inward. The housekeeper, a stern-looking woman who seemed even more ancient and weathered than the doors, stood by them. Even the children fell silent at her appearance.

The old woman glared at Sylvia and said, "Here for a tour, miss?"

Sylvia swallowed and nodded. "Yes, if you please. The children really aren't so bad—"

"This way." The housekeeper disappeared into a darkened vestibule.

Alice, the oldest, glanced at Sylvia, sizing her up.

"Go on," Sylvia said, but the children had already raced inside. Sylvia hurried to follow them.

Housekeeper and children waited by another set of doors at the end of the entryway.

"If you would kindly keep the children in the parlor." The housekeeper glared with her beady, crab-like eyes, and opened the door. Sylvia and the children inched inside.

When Sylvia saw the parlor, she nearly cried. So many *things,* all of them smashable. Pottery, glassware, trinkets with gears and levers, arcane instruments made of spindly wire, fabric to be soiled, paper to be torn, entire cabinets to be toppled, and a wall full of art to be destroyed. Almost lost among portraits whose gazes followed her hung a floral tapestry in faded colors, which looked like it would disintegrate if one merely breathed on it. It was an odd, blurred thing that almost seemed to change shape if she turned her head just so.

The children trembled—vibrating, anticipating, potential energy waiting to burst forth—hoping for the chance to get their dirty little claws on everything. The housekeeper closed the double doors, her gaze still boring into Sylvia, as if expecting the worst and knowing it would be the governess's fault if even the smallest sliver broke free from the leg of a chair. The children would destroy it all, and the doctor would report the horror to Lady Smythe-Helsing, and Sylvia would be fired.

And would that really be such a bad thing? Perhaps she could leave right now, climb out a window and run . . .

She put a hand against her forehead, trying to stave off the headache building behind her eyes. "Children, do *behave,*" she said, by rote, out of habit, tired and unconvincing, even though the children hadn't moved since the closing of the door. It was only a matter of time before the human whirlwind.

Still, the children didn't move. Sylvia allowed herself to exhale. She attempted an actual instruction.

"Why don't you sit here on the sofa while we wait?" she said. Quietly, the children obeyed. They lined up on the sofa and sat, one after the other, no one pinching anyone.

Extraordinary. Truly extraordinary. Something was terribly, terribly wrong here.

Sylvia sat in a wingback chair across from them, watching. They sat, hands folded in laps, and waited, not making a sound, not even flinching. Somewhere, a clock ticked, and it sounded like the tolling of a funeral bell. Sylvia's heart was racing for no reason at all.

When the double doors opened again, she nearly shrieked, hand to her breast to still her heart. The children merely looked.

The housekeeper stood there, like a monk, in her brown dress. She frowned. "There's been a change of plans. I'm afraid the doctor has been unexpectedly detained. You'll have to come another time."

That was that. The whole afternoon for nothing, and now Sylvia was going to have to herd the children back outside, and back to the car for the ride home.

But they left the parlor quietly, single-file by height and age. Outside, on the front steps, they halted in a row, like little soldiers, while the car pulled around. They got in, sat quietly, and stayed that way until the car left the grounds of Lambshead's manor. Then, they burst into screams, the boys hit the girls, the girls pinched the boys, and everybody bounced against the ceiling. She could only watch. They were spring toys that had been let loose.

Terrifying.

The Girl at the Fountain

A week later, Jerome returned to the manor in a hopeful mood, eager, prepared. His newspaper had agreed that a second trip to Lambshead's manor was worth it, for the chance to recoup some of the expenses with an actual story. This attempt couldn't possibly go any worse than the last. He knocked on the door, which the scowling housekeeper opened, showing him into the foyer and pointing him to the library.

The lady reporter was in the library, standing before the tapestry of a girl at a fountain, nestled amid the staring portraits.

"Not you again!" he blurted, and she turned on him, gaze fierce. She had the most extraordinary green eyes, he noticed.

"Oh, give me a break!" she said.

"What are you doing here?"

"I'm here for my interview—what are you doing here?"

"*Your* interview, this is supposed to be *my* interview. How did you manage this?"

"Don't lay this on me, this isn't my fault!" She stepped toward him, pointing, and he took a step forward to keep her from getting the upper hand.

"You're trying to tell me that you aren't following me?" he said. "That you didn't arrange to be here simply to aggravate me?"

"Wait a minute—I was here first this time! Are *you* following *me*?"

"What? No!"

She was only slightly shorter than he was, but the heels of her shoes may have made her appear taller, just as they accentuated the curve of her calves and the slope of her hips inside their clinging skirt. Today, she wore navy blue, a well-tailored and flattering suit, a cream-colored blouse contrasting with the flush of the skin at her throat.

"I don't care who screwed up and who double-booked us," she said. "I'm getting my interview and you can't stop me." Her lips were parted, her eyes shining, and her hair seemed soft as velvet.

"I don't want to stop you," he said, and realized that he really didn't.

"Then you'll turn around and walk out of here right now?"

"I don't know that I'm ready to do that."

She tilted her head, her fury giving way to confusion, which softened her mouth and forehead and made her eyes wide and sweet. "But you won't stand in my way?"

"Well, I might stand in your way."

In fact, they had moved close enough together that they were only inches apart, gazing into each other's eyes, feeling the heat of each other's bodies.

"And why would you do that?" she said, her voice low.

"I think—to get a better look at you."

"Really?"

"Yeah." He couldn't see the rest of the room anymore.

"I have to admit, you're an interesting man— I . . . I don't even know your name."

"Jerome. Yours?"

"Elaine."

They kissed.

The shock that passed from his lips through his nerves to the tips of his toes came not only from the pressure of her mouth, the weight and warmth of her body pressed against him, her hands wrapped around the hem of his jacket to pull him closer—but also from the fact that he was kissing her at all. It should never have happened. It was meant to be.

The kiss lasted for what seemed a very long time, lips working between gasps for breath, hands on each other's arms. This, he thought, this was what he had come for.

Finally, they broke apart and stared at each other in wonder.

"What was that?" she—Elaine—said. Her cheeks were pink, and her breathing came quickly.

"It was perfect," he breathed.

"God, it was, wasn't it?" she whispered.

"Oh yes." He leaned forward for another kiss, but she interrupted the gesture. "Let's go. The two of us, together, let's leave, go somewhere and never look back."

"What about your interview?" he said.

"What interview? Who?"

He could hardly remember himself. They were in this archaic parlor filled with artifacts, books, carved fireplace, stern portraits, and that faded tapestry, which hardly seemed a setting for passion—his heart was suddenly filled with fragrant gardens and winding paths where he could hold her hand and walk with her for hours.

He took both her hands and pulled her toward the door. "You're right, let's go."

A wide, glorious smile broke on her face, a flower unfolding, opening to him, filling him with joy, unbridled and bursting. Hand in hand, they left the parlor, breezed past the scowling housekeeper, and burst through the front doors to the outside, where the sun was shining gloriously and the shrubs seemed filled with singing larks. Jerome had an urge to sing along with them. Elaine was grinning just as wide as he was, and he'd never felt so much . . . *rightness* in being with someone.

They had to step aside for a passing car filled with countless children, whose screams were audible through the glass.

"Can I ask you a question?" Elaine asked.

"Of course." He would do anything for her.

"Do you want children?"

He thought a moment; he'd never really considered, and found he didn't much need to now. "No, not really."

"Good. Excellent." She smiled at him, and his heart nearly burst.

At the end of the drive, the boundary to the property, Elaine stopped. Her tug on his hand made Jerome stop as well. He blinked at her; her frown gave him the sense of a balloon deflating, of a recording of birdsong winding down to the speed of a dirge.

They dropped each other's hands. He was rather startled that he'd been holding it at all.

"What are we doing?" she asked. "We can't just run off like a couple of teenagers. This isn't like me *at all*."

"Nor me," Jerome said. "But . . . perhaps if you think that I simply couldn't help myself." That was true enough—whatever had happened, it was a surge of passion that seemed to have vanished, much to his regret. He wanted it back.

He tried on an awkward smile for her, and if she didn't return it, she at least didn't scowl.

"There's something really weird about that house," she said, looking back to the manor.

"Agreed," he said. "I find I don't want the interview so much after all."

"Yeah. You said it."

"Elaine, would you like to have dinner with me?" he asked impulsively, sure she would rail at him for it and not caring.

She studied him a moment, then said, "You know? I think I would."

The Hunt

The doctor's manor was an edifice of terror. The foundation stones exuded a fog of trepidation. Knowing that the children would be horrible would be easier than not knowing at all what they would do this time.

For yes, Doctor Lambshead had sent a note to Lady Smythe-Helsing, apologizing profusely for cutting short their previous tour and offering a second opportunity, which the lady accepted. Once again, Sylvia rode in the Bentley with the angry chauffeur and four screaming children. The housekeeper was waiting for them at the front doors. Once again, she directed them to the parlor. The children lined up next to her, and the doors closed.

Sylvia closed her eyes, held her breath. Waited for screams or sighs or giggles. Or quiet, obedient breathing. As it happened, she didn't hear anything. So she opened her eyes.

The children were gone.

She had no idea where to look for them, and studied the walls as if the children had melted into the wallpaper, as if she might see their faces staring out of the portraits or stitched into the threads of the tapestry, among the hunters and their spears surrounding the poor unicorn at bay.

A snap of a breeze touched her, and she flinched as something tugged at her hair. Reaching up, she picked at the curl tucked behind her ear and felt some foreign object. She untangled it and looked—a toothpick, perhaps. Or a tiny dart.

She looked to where it had come from and saw Andrew, the older boy, with none other than a blowgun in his hands. And the empty spot on the wall where he'd taken it from. Dear God, the heathen had fired at her.

He ducked behind the sofa and ran.

That was it. She'd had enough. She went after him, with every intention of laying a hand on him—only for as long as it took to throw him out of the house. All of them. Let Lady Smythe-Helsing fire her. Let the doctor report what an awful governess she was.

As she chased Andrew through the doorway from the parlor to the library, she tripped. Looking back, she saw why—Alice and Arthur, crouched on either side of the doorway, had pulled a length of rope across the passage, just as she stepped into it. Good heavens, what had gotten into them? They'd always been holy terrors but never truly malicious. The injuries they inflicted were usually accidental.

The two of them scrambled to their feet and ran back toward the parlor.

Rubbing a bruised elbow, she went to follow them. Four against one was terrible odds. Especially those four. How had she gotten into this? Oh yes, she needed a job. She had too much education for scut work but not enough for anything professional. Be a governess, that was the solution. Some of the very wealthy families still had them. What an opportunity. Better than regular teaching, and maybe she'd catch the eye of some wealthy gentleman who would take her away from all this.

Bollocks. All of it. This wasn't a job, it was a war.

She entered the parlor and paused—they'd hidden, and were being very quiet for once.

Several more weapons seemed to have vanished from their places on the wall, and she had a sinking feeling. She had already started backing away, step by step, when Arthur came at her with a spear that was larger than he was. Alice had a bow and quiver of arrows.

Sylvia turned and ran. Out of the parlor, through the kitchen, where she nearly collided with Andrew, who was now wielding an axe as well as the blowgun. Changing direction mid-stride, she made her way through a pantry to a scullery and then to a workroom, and from there to the foyer again, and to a second library, where she slammed shut the door and bolted it.

There, next to the wall, stood Anne. She'd been hiding behind the door, and Sylvia hadn't looked. Anne stared at her. In her hands, clutched to her chest, she held a cage the size of a shoebox, made of sticks tied together with twine. In the cage was a mouse, the small, brown kind that invaded pantries and scurried across kitchen floors. The creature huddled in the corner, sitting on its haunches, its front paws pressed to its chest, trembling. Its large and liquid eyes seemed to be pleading. Sylvia understood how it felt.

On the other hand, the girl's gaze was challenging. She looked up at Sylvia, who somehow felt shorter. Her breath caught, and when she tried to draw another, she choked. The corner of the girl's lips turned up.

Meanwhile, little hands had begun pounding on the door.

"All right," Sylvia said. "That's how it is, is it?" She unbolted the doors and flung them open. The other three children—spears, blowguns, axes, arrows, daggers, and scalpels in hand—were waiting for her. Little Anne stood behind her, wearing an expression of utter malice, like she was thinking of how to build a larger cage. "You lot will have to catch me, first," Sylvia said.

She shoved past them with enough force to startle them into stillness, just for a moment. Then, they pelted after her. This time, Sylvia made for the front door, breezing past the startled housekeeper. She wrestled opened the heavy front doors, didn't say a word to the chauffeur who was leaning on the hood of the Bentley and smoking a pipe. He stared after her wonderingly, but she didn't have time to explain, because the four little Smythe-Helsings were charging after her, silent and determined, weapons held to the ready. As she'd hoped they would.

The end of the drive was perhaps a hundred yards away. Sylvia wasn't an athlete, by any means, but she was no slouch, either, and herding these children for the last year had certainly kept her fit. All she had to do was reach the end of the property and not look back. But she could hear their footsteps kicking up gravel, gaining on her.

Then she was across the line marked by the brick columns at the end of the drive. If this didn't work, she was lost. She stopped and turned to see the four children running after her, murder hollowing their expressions. First Alice, then Andrew, then Anne, then little Arthur crossed the invisible line, and they all stopped and stared, bewildered, at the weapons in their hands.

Arthur dropped the spear and started crying.

"Oh, Arthur, hush now, it's all over now, it's all right." Sylvia knelt beside him and gathered him in her arms, holding him while he sobbed against her shoulder. Then all the children were crying, clinging to her, and she spread her arms to encompass them.

She made them wait by one of the brick columns while she went to fetch the car. They stayed right where she told them to, hand in hand, watching her with swollen red eyes her entire way back to the manor, where she told the chauffeur that they'd like to go home now, and didn't answer any of his brusque questions. The housekeeper watched her from the front steps, a glare in her eye and a sneer on her lips. Sylvia paid her no mind.

BACK AT THE Smythe-Helsing estate, the children were exhausted, and Sylvia gave them each a glass of water and a biscuit and put them to bed. She then went to see Lady Smythe-Helsing, who had returned from her watercolor class and was sitting in her parlor taking tea.

Sylvia approached. "Lady Smythe-Helsing, ma'am?"

"Yes, what is it?" She set aside her cup and scowled at the interruption.

Taking a deep breath, Sylvia said, "I quit."

The woman blinked, transforming her native-born elegance into a fish-like gawping. It made Sylvia stand a little taller. Without her furs and title, the lady was no better than her governess.

"What?" she finally said.

"I quit. I'm leaving. I've had enough. I quit." She felt like a general who'd won a battle.

"This is outrageous."

"This is not the Middle Ages," she said, imagining tearing that medieval tapestry to bits. "I can leave when I like."

"But what will you do? I certainly won't be writing you a referral after this."

"Anything I want," she shot back without thinking, then tilted her head, considering. "Maybe I'll go to America. Hollywood. I'll be a movie star."

"You're delusional."

"Perhaps. Perhaps not."

"You'll fail. And you'll never find another position as a governess."

"Thank God," Sylvia said, and went to fetch her things.

SYLVIA REACHED THE stairs that led down from the children's wing to the back door when a figure stopped her. Little Anne in her nightgown, hugging her flaxen-haired doll.

"Anne. Hello."

"Hello."

"And then good-bye, rather. I'm leaving."

"I know," the girl said. "I'll miss you."

"Pardon? Really?"

"You're the best governess we've ever had. You listen."

"Oh, Anne. But you understand that I have to leave."

"Oh yes. It's the only sane choice."

Sylvia smiled. "There's a good girl, Anne."

Anne smiled, too, and wandered back to bed.

Suitcase in hand, Sylvia left through the back door and walked away from the Smythe-Hesling manor with a spring in her step.

Storage

The housekeeper watched the Smythe-Helsing children and their governess depart, then went to the parlor, to the tapestry hanging in the center of a group of portraits. Odd, faded, ambiguous, it seemed to change shape based on how one tilted one's head when looking at it. A fascinating piece. The housekeeper took it down off its nail, rolled it up, and carried it to a downstairs room, to put with other ambiguous experiments. On the way, Lambshead removed the wig and false nose, and dispensed with the stooped posture that had transformed him.

There was nothing, he considered, like a little firsthand observation in one's own home.

Ambrose and the Ancient Spirits of East and West

By Garth Nix

Ambrose Farnington was not particularly well-equipped to live an ordinary life. An adventurer in the Near East before the Great War, the war itself had seen him variously engaged in clandestine and very cold operations in the mountains between Turkey and Russia; commanding an infantry battalion in France and Belgium; and then, after almost a day buried in his headquarters dugout in the company of several dead and dismembered companions, as a very fragile convalescent in a nursing home called Grandway House, in Lancashire.

Most recently, a year of fishing and walking near Fort William had assisted the recovery begun under the care of the neurasthenic specialists at Grandway, and by the early months of 1920, the former temporary Lieutenant Colonel Farnington felt that he was almost ready to reemerge into the world. The only question was in what capacity. The year in the Scottish bothy with only his fishing gear, guns, and a borrowed dog for company had also largely exhausted his ready funds, which had been stricken by his remaining parent's ill-timed death, his father putting the capstone on a lifetime of setting a very bad example by leaving a great deal of debt fraudulently incurred in his only child's name.

Ambrose considered the question of his finances and employment as he sorted through the very thin pile of correspondence on the end of the kitchen table he was using as a writing desk. The bothy had been lent to him with the dog, and though both belonged to Robert Cameron, a very close friend from his days at Peterhouse College in Cambridge, his continued presence there prevented the employment of bothy and dog by a gamekeeper who would usually patrol the western borders of Robert's estate. Besides, Ambrose did not wish to remain a burden on one of the few of his friends who was still alive.

It was time to move on, but the question was: on to what and where?

"I should make an appreciation of my situation and set out my qualities and achievements, Nellie," said Ambrose to the dog, who was lying down with her shaggy head on his left foot. Nellie raised one ear, but made no other movement, as Ambrose unscrewed his pen and set out to write on the back of a bill for a bamboo fishing rod supplied by T. H. Sowerbutt's of London.

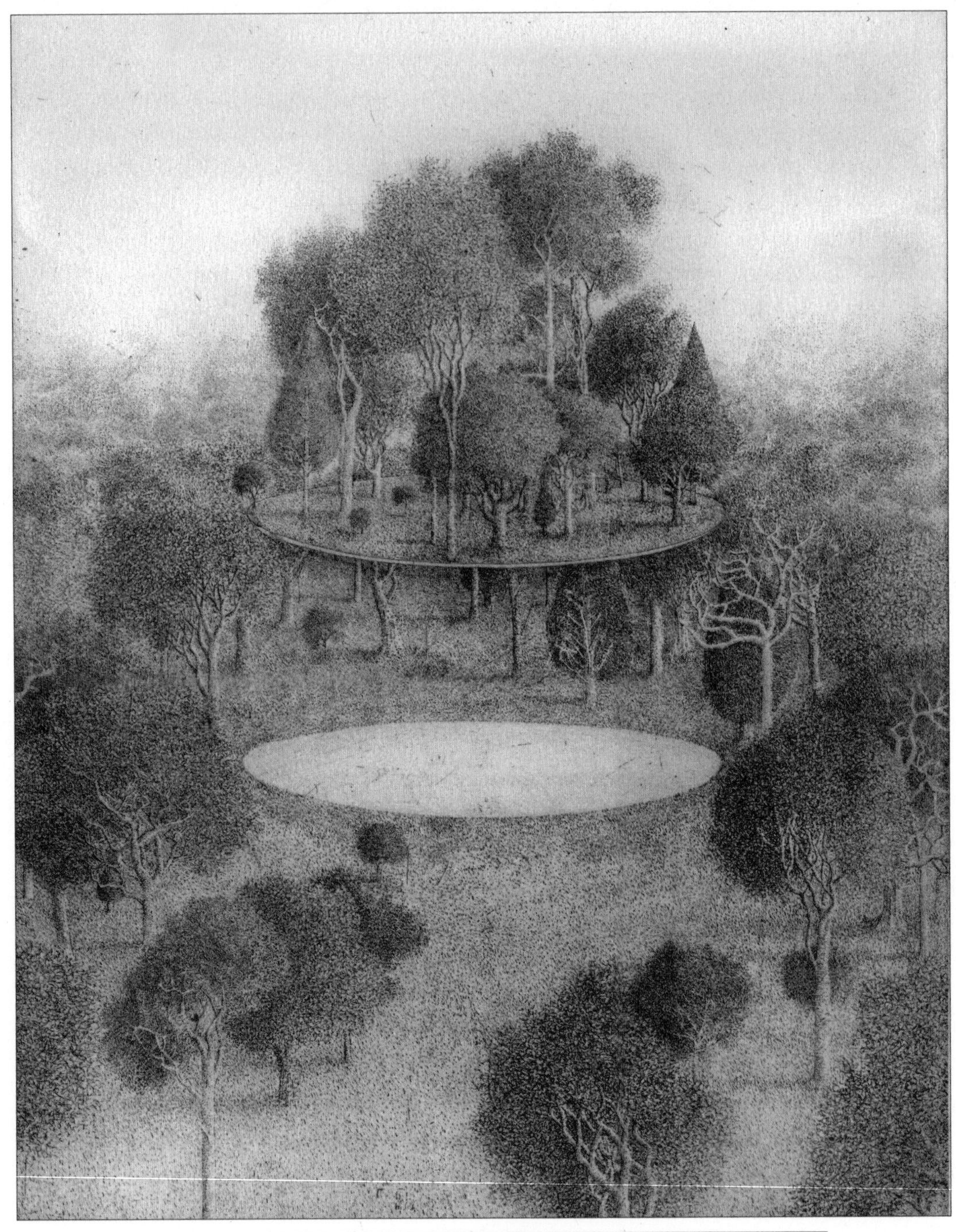

Jonathan Nix's etching "Tree Spirits Rising," honoring Dr. Lambshead's period of interest in "bushes, bramble, herbs, and eccentric ground cover."

"Item one," said Ambrose aloud. "At twenty-nine, not excessively aged, at least by time. Item two, in possession of rude physical health and . . . let us say . . . in a stable mental condition, provided no underground exercise is contemplated. Item three, a double-starred first in Latin and Greek, fluent in Urdu, classical Persian, Arabic, Spanish, French, German; conversant with numerous other languages, etc. Item four, have travelled and lived extensively in the Near East, particularly Turkey and Persia. Item five, war service . . ."

Ambrose put down his pen and wondered what he should write. Even though he would burn his initial draft on completion, he was still reluctant to mention his work for D-Arc. Even the bare facts were secret, and as for the details, very few people would believe them. Those people who would believe were the ones he was most worried about. If certain practitioners of some ancient and occult studies discovered that he was Agent çobanaldatan, the man who had so catastrophically halted that ceremony high on the slopes of Ziyaret Daği, then . . .

"I suppose if I am not too specific, it can't matter," Ambrose said to Nellie. He picked up the pen again, and continued to speak aloud as he wrote.

"Where was I . . . war service . . . 1914–1915. Engaged by a department of the War Office in reconnaissance operations in the region of . . . no, best make it 'the East.' Returned in 1916, posted to KRRC, rose to brevet lieutenant colonel by May 1918, commanded the Eighth Battalion, wounded 21 September 1918, convalescent leave through to 5 March 1919 . . . no, that looks bad, far too long, will just make it 'after convalescent leave' resigned temporary commission . . . how do I explain this last year? Writing a paper on the Greek inscriptions near Erzerum or something, I suppose, I do have one I started in '09 . . . let's move on . . ."

He paused as Nellie raised both ears and tilted her head towards the door. When she gave a soft whine and stood up, Ambrose pushed his chair back and went to the window. Gently easing the rather grimy curtain aside, he looked out, up towards the rough track that wound down from the main road high on the ridge above.

A car was gingerly making its way down towards the bothy, proceeding slowly and relatively quietly in low gear, though not quietly enough to fool Nellie. It was a maroon sedan of recent European make, and it was not a car that he knew. To get here, the driver had either picked or more likely cut off the bronze Bramah padlocks on both the upper gate to the road and the one in the wall of the middle field.

Quickly, but with measured actions, Ambrose went to the gun cabinet, unlocked it with one of the keys that hung on his heavy silver watch-chain, and took out his service revolver. He quickly loaded it and put the weapon and another five cartridges in the voluminous right pocket of his coat, his father's sole useful legacy, an ugly purple-and-green tweed shooting jacket that was slightly too large.

He hesitated in front of the cabinet, then, after a glance at Nellie and at a very old pierced bronze lantern that hung from a ceiling beam, he reached back into the cabinet for a shotgun. He chose the lightest of the four weapons there, a double-barrel four-ten. Unlike the other guns, and against all his usual principles, it was already loaded, with rather special shot. Ambrose broke it, whispered, *"melek kiliç şimdi bana yardum"* close to the breech, and snapped it closed.

The incantation would wake the spirits that animated the ammunition, but only for a short time. If whoever came in the maroon car was an ordinary visitor, the magic would be wasted, and he only had half a box of the shells left. But he did not think it was an ordinary visitor, though he was by no means sure it was an enemy.

Certainly, Nellie was growling, the hair up all along her back, and that indicated trouble. But the bronze lamp that Ambrose had found in the strange little booth in the narrowest alley of the Damascus bazaar, while it had lit of its own accord, was not burning with black fire. The flame that flickered inside was green. Ambrose did not yet know the full vocabulary of the oracular lantern, but he knew that green was an equivocal colour. It signified the advent of some occult power, but not necessarily an inimical force.

Readying the shotgun, Ambrose went to the door. Lifting the bar with his left hand, he nudged the door open with his foot, allowing himself a gap just wide enough to see and shoot through. The car was negotiating the last turn down from the middle field, splashing through the permanent mud puddle as it negotiated the open gate and the narrow way between the partly fallen stone walls that once upon a time had surrounded the bothy's kitchen garden.

Ambrose could only see a driver in the vehicle, but that didn't mean there wouldn't be others lying low. He raised the shotgun and thumbed back both hammers, suddenly aware of a pulsing in his eardrums that came from his own, racing heart. Nellie, next to his leg, snarled, but well trained as she was, did not bark or lunge forward.

The maroon sedan stopped a dozen yards away. Past the gate, and within the walls of the garden, which might or might not be significant. When he had first moved in, Ambrose had planted silver sixpences in every seventh stone, and buried three horseshoes in the gateway. That would deter most of the lesser powers, particularly those already distressed at being so far west of the old Giza meridian. Which meant that his visitor was either mundane or not one of the *lesser* powers that stalked the earth. . . .

The car door creaked open, backwards, and a tall man in a long, camel-coloured coat with the collar up and a dark trilby pulled down over his ears hunched himself out, his arms and legs moving very oddly—a telltale sign that told Ambrose all he needed to know. As the curious figure lurched forward, Ambrose fired the left barrel at the man's chest, and a split-second later, the right barrel at his knees.

Salt splattered across the target and burst into flame where it hit. Hat and coat fell to the ground, and two waist-high creatures of shifting darkness sprang forward, salt-fires burning on and in their mutable flesh.

Ambrose pulled the door shut with one swift motion and slammed down the bar. Retreating to the gun cabinet, he reloaded the shotgun, this time speaking the incantation in a loud and almost steady voice.

A hissing outside indicated that the demons had heard the incantation, and did not like it. For his part, Ambrose was deeply concerned that his first two shots had not disincorporated his foes; that they had freely crossed his boundary markers; and that they had got to his home without any sign of having aroused the ire of any of the local entities that would take exception to such an Eastern presence.

He looked around the single room of the bothy. The windows, though shut, were not shuttered, and there was probably not enough sunshine for the glass to act as mirrors and distract the demons. If they were strong enough to cross a silver and cold-iron border, they would be strong enough to enter the house uninvited, though not eager, which was probably the only reason they had not yet broken down the door or smashed in a window—

Nellie barked and pointed to the fireplace. Ambrose spun around and fired both barrels as the demons came roaring out of the chimney. But even riddled with ensorcelled salt, the demons came on, shadowy maws snapping and talons reaching. Ambrose threw the now-useless shotgun at them and dived to one side, towards the golf bag perched by his bed, as Nellie snarled and bit at the demons' heels.

Demon teeth closed on his calf as his hands closed on his weapon of last resort. Between the irons and the woods, Ambrose's fingers closed on the bone-inlaid hilt of the yataghan that bore the maker's mark of Osman Bey. Tumbling the golf bag over, he drew the sword, and with two swift strokes, neatly severed the faint red threads that stood in the place of backbones in the demons, the silvered blade cutting through the creatures' infernal salt-pocked flesh as if it were no more than smoke.

The demons popped out of existence, leaving only a pair of three-foot lengths of scarlet cord. Nellie sniffed at them cautiously, then went to nose at Ambrose's leg.

"Yes, it got me, damn it," cursed Ambrose. "My own fault, mind you. Should have had the sword to hand, never mind how ridiculous it might have looked."

Ambrose looked over at the oracular lantern, which had gone out.

"Possibly inimical, my sweet giddy aunt," he muttered as he pushed down the sock and rolled up the leg of his plus fours. The skin was not broken, but there was a crescent-shaped bruise on his calf. Next to the bruise, the closest half-inch of vein was turning dark and beginning to obtrude from the skin, and a shadow was branching out into the lesser blood vessels all around.

Ambrose cursed again, then levered himself upright and hobbled over to the large, leather-strapped portmanteau at the end of his bed. Flinging it open, he rummaged about inside, eventually bringing out a long strip of linen that was covered in tiny Egyptian hieroglyphics drawn in some dark red ink. Ambrose wrapped this around his calf, tapped it thrice, and spoke the revered name of Sekhmet, at which the hieroglyphics faded from the bandage and entered into his flesh, there to fight a holding battle against the demonic incursion, though it was unlikely that they would entirely vanquish the enemy without additional sorcerous assistance. Egyptian magic was older and thus more faded from the world, and though Ambrose had immersed the bandage on his last visit to the Nile, that had been many years before, so the hermetic connection was no longer strong.

Ambrose had nothing else that might work. Nor was there anyone he could easily turn to for assistance. In fact, he thought wretchedly, there were only two possible sources of the kind of help he needed within a thousand miles. One he had hoped to stay away from, and the other was very difficult to reach without extensive and unusual preparations that would simply take too long.

"First things first," muttered Ambrose. Using the yataghan as a crutch, but also to keep it close to hand, he limped to the table. Lighting a match against the back of his chair, he applied it to the bill for the fishing rod, and watched his recent appreciation crumble into ash, dousing the blaze with the last half-inch of cold tea from his mug when it threatened to spread to the other papers.

"Just like the war," he said wearily to Nelly. "Bloody thing was obsolete as soon as I wrote it. I suppose I shall have to—"

Nellie lifted her ears.

Ambrose whipped around to check the oracular lantern. The flame had relit and was even higher now, burning red and gold, signifying danger, but not immediate, and allies. Not friends, but allies.

“I’m not trusting you,” Ambrose said to the lantern. Still leaning on the yataghan, he retrieved his shotgun and reloaded it, though this time he did not speak the words. Nellie stayed by his side, her ears up and intent, but she was not growling.

As the sound of a car being driven a shade too fast for the rough track grew louder, Ambrose cautiously opened the door and looked out.

He was not very much surprised to see that the second car was a green Crossley 20/25, the usual choice of the Secret Service Bureau and so also of its even lesser-known offshoot, D-Arc. He even recognized the two men in the front, and could guess at the other two in the backseat. Nevertheless, he kept the shotgun ready as the Crossley skidded to a halt behind the maroon sedan and the men got out. Three of them, two with revolvers by their sides and one with a curiously archaic, bell-mouthed musketoon, stayed close to the car, watching the bothy, the maroon car, and the hillside. The fourth, a man Ambrose knew as Major Kennett, though that was almost certainly not his real name, advanced towards the bothy’s front door. The quartet were dressed for the city, not the country, and Ambrose suppressed a smile as Kennett lost a shoe in the mud and had to pause to fish around for it with a stockinged foot.

“I see we’re a little late,” said Kennett, as he pulled at the heel of his shoe. He was a handsome man, made far less so by the chill that always dwelt in his eyes. “Sorry about that.”

“Late for what?” asked Ambrose.

“Your earlier guests,” answered Kennett. He held out his hand. After a moment, Ambrose balanced the shotgun over the crook of his left arm and shook hands.

“You knew they were coming?” asked Ambrose.

Kennett shook his head. “We knew something was coming. Quite clever really. We’ve been keeping tabs on a private vessel for days, a very large motor yacht owned by our old friend the emir and captained by Vladimir Roop. It docked at Fort William, the car was lowered, and off it went. Nothing . . . unwelcome . . . touched the earth, you see, and it’s a hardtop, windows shut, keeping out all that Scottish air and lovely mist and those who travel with it.”

“Did you know I was here?”

“Oh yes,” said Kennett. He looked past Ambrose, into the simple, single room of the bothy. “Rather basic, old boy. Takes you back, I suppose?”

“Yes it does,” said Ambrose, without rancour. Kennett, like most D-Arc operatives, was from an old and very upper-class family. Ambrose was not. Everything he had achieved had come despite his more difficult start in life. He had taken a long series of steps that had begun with a scholarship to Bristol Grammar at the age of seven, the first part of a challenging journey that had taken him far, far away from the ever-changing temporary accommodations shared with his father, at least when that worthy was not in prison for his various "no-risk lottery" and "gifting circle" frauds.

"Each to his own," remarked Kennett. "I take it you've dealt with the visitors?"

"Yes."

"We'd best take you away then," said Kennett. "Lady S wants to have a word, and I expect you'll need that leg looked at. Demon bite is it?"

"Lady S can go—" Ambrose bit back his words with an effort.

"Quite likely," replied Kennett. "I wouldn't be at all surprised. But I don't see the relevance. Lady S wants to see you, therefore you will be seen by her. Unless, of course, you want to stay here and turn into something that will have every Gaelic-speaking entity of wood, air, and river rising up to assail?"

"No," replied Ambrose. He knew when it was pointless to rail against fate. "I don't want that. Do we have to go all the way to London? I don't think I can make—"

"No, not at all," said Kennett. "Lady S is on a progress through the far-flung parts of the D-Arc realm. She's in Edinburgh, taking stock of our new medical advisor."

"New medical advisor?" asked Ambrose. "What happened to Shivinder?"

Kennett turned his cold, cold eyes to meet Ambrose's gaze, and held it for a second, which was sufficient reply. Whatever had happened to Dr. Shivinder, Ambrose would likely never know, and if he did find out, by some accident of information, he would be best to keep it to himself.

"The new chap is quite the prodigy," said Kennett. "Oxford, of course, like all the best people."

Ambrose sighed and limped a step forward towards the car. There were tiny wisps of smoke issuing from under the hieroglyphic bandage, as the small angels of Sekhmet fought the demonic infestation. While it wouldn't actually catch alight, the pain was quite intense, which was another sign that the demons were winning.

"Spare me the jibes," he said. "Can we just go?"

"Yes, we should toodle along, I suppose," said Kennett. "Jones and Jones will stay to secure the place, and they can bring your gear along later and so forth. Do we need to shoot the dog?"

Ambrose bent down, gasping with the pain, and took Nellie by the collar.

Turning her head, he looked deeply into her trusting brown eyes, and then ran his hand over her back and legs, carefully checking for bites.

"No, she's clear," he said. "She can go back to the big house. Nellie! Big house!"

He pointed to the garden gate as he spoke. Nellie cocked her head at him, to make sure he was serious, yawned, to show her lolloping red tongue, and slowly began to pick her way through the mud.

She had only gone a few yards when Kennett shot her in the back of the head with his revolver. The heavy Webley .455 boomed twice. The dog was shoved into the puddle by the force of the impact, her legs continuing to twitch and jerk there, even though she must have been killed instantly. Blood slowly swirled into the muddy water, steam rising as it spread.

Ambrose fumbled with his shotgun, swinging it to cover Kennett. But it was broken open, and Kennett was watching him, the revolver still in his hand.

"There was demon-taint in her mouth," said Kennett, very matter-of-fact. "She wouldn't have lasted a day."

Ambrose shut his eyes for a moment. Then he nodded dully. Kennett stepped in and took the shotgun, but did not try to remove the yataghan that Ambrose used to lever himself upright.

"You're all right?" asked Kennett. "Operational? Capable?"

"I suppose so," said Ambrose, his voice almost as detached as Kennett's. He looked down at Nellie's body. Dead, just like so many of his friends, but life continued and he must make the best of it. That was the litany he had learned at Grandway House. He owed it to the dead, the dead that now included Nellie, to live on as best he could.

"Did you do that to test me? Did Lady S tell you to shoot my dog?"

"No," replied Kennett calmly. "I had no orders. But there was demon-taint."

Ambrose nodded again. Kennett could lie better than almost anyone he knew, so well that it was impossible to know whether he spoke the truth or not, unless there was some undeniable evidence to the contrary. And there could have been demon-taint. Of course, with the dog's head shattered by hexed silver fulminate exploding rounds, there was no possible way to check that now.

Leaning on his yataghan, Ambrose trudged to the standard-issue departmental car. He had hoped to avoid any further involvement with D-Arc, but he had always known that this was a vain hope. Even when he had left the section the first time in 1916, escaping to regular service on the Western Front, there had still been occasional reminders that D-Arc was watching him and might reel him in at any time. Like the odd staff officer with the mismatched eyes, one blue and one green, who never visited anyone else's battalion in the brigade but often dropped in on Ambrose. Always on one of the old, old festival days, sporting a fresh-cut willow crop, a spray of holly, or bearing some odd bottle of mead or elderberry wine. Ambrose's adjutant and the battalion's second-in-command called him "the botanist" and thought he was just another red-tabbed idiot wandering about. But Ambrose knew better.

Once in the car, Ambrose retreated almost immediately into a yogic trance state, to slow the effects of the demon bite. Possibly even more helpfully, it stopped him thinking about Nellie and the long roll-call of dead friends, and as it was not sleep, he did not dream. Instead, he experienced himself travelling without movement over an endless illusory landscape made up of Buddhist sutras.

Ambrose came out of this trance to find that the car had stopped. He looked out the window and saw that the sun was setting. The gas lamps had just been lit, but it was still quite bright enough for him to work out that they had reached Edinburgh, and after a moment, he recognized the street. They were in South Charlotte Square, outside what, at first glance, appeared to be a hotel, till he saw a small brass plate by the front door, which read ST. AGNES NURSING HOME.

"New Scottish office, more discreet," grunted Kennett, correctly interpreting Ambrose's expression. D-Arc's previous Scottish office had been co-located with the SSB, tucked away in a temporary building on the outer perimeter of Redford Barracks, a position that provided physical security but made more arcane measures difficult to employ.

Kennett led Ambrose quickly inside, through the oak-and-silver outer doors, past the mirrored inner doors, and across the tessellated, eye-catching tiled floor of the atrium, all useful architectural defences against malignant spirits. The demon had grown enough in Ambrose's leg for him to feel its attention drawn by the mirrors, and his leg twitched and twisted of its own accord as he crossed the patterned maze of the floor.

Kennett signed them into the book at the front desk, at which point Ambrose was relieved of his yataghan and revolver in return for a claim ticket, before being helped upstairs.

"Lady S will see you first," said Kennett. "Afterwards . . . I suppose the medico can sort out your leg."

Ambrose caught the implication of that phrasing very well. Any treatment would be dependent on Lady S and how Ambrose responded to whatever she wanted him to do: which was almost certainly about him returning to active duty with D-Arc again.

"In you go," said Kennett. He rapped on the double door, turned the knob to push it open a fraction, and released his supporting grip on Ambrose's elbow.

Ambrose limped in, wishing he was elsewhere. Kennett did not follow him, the door shutting hard on Ambrose's heels with a definitive click.

The room was dark, and smelled of orange zest and the sickly honey-scent of myrrh, which was normal for any chamber that had Lady S in it. Ambrose peered into the darkness, but did not move forward. It was better to stay near the exit, since he knew that only a small part of this room was actually connected to the building and to Edinburgh itself. The rest of the room was . . . somewhere else.

He heard a rustling in the dark, and swallowed nervously as the strange smell grew stronger. A candle flared, the light suddenly bright. Ambrose hooded his eyes and looked off to one side.

Lady S was there, some feet away from the candle, again as expected. He could see only her vague outline, swathed as she was in gauzy silks that moved about her in answer to some breeze that did reach the door.

"Dear Ambrose!" exclaimed the apparition, her voice that of some kindly but aged female relative welcoming a close but morally strayed junior connection. "How kind of you to call upon me in my hour of need."

"Yes," agreed Ambrose. "I could not, of course, resist."

Lady S laughed a hearty laugh that belonged to a far more full-fleshed person, someone who might have triple chins to wobble as they guffawed. The laugh did not match the narrow, dimly perceived silhouette in her fluttering shrouds.

"Oh you always could make me laugh," she said. "I don't laugh as much as I should, you know."

"Who does?" asked Ambrose, unable to keep the bitterness from his voice.

"Now, now, Ambrose," said Lady S. Something that might be a finger wagged in the air some distance in front of his face. "No petulance. I can't abide petulance. Tell me—your father, he of many names and aliases, may he rest in peace—his birth name was really Farnowitz and he *was* born in Germany?"

"You know he was," said Ambrose tightly. "It's in my file and always has been. My mother was English, I was born in Bristol, and what's more I have served my country more than—"

"Yes, yes dear," comforted Lady S. "We're not holding it against you. Quite the contrary. We need someone with a modicum of the art who also has German blood. Apart from the king, who naturally isn't available to us, the combination is rather scarce among our ranks."

"What do you need me to do, and what do I get out of it?"

"Oh, my dear young man, such impatience and, dare I say, rudeness will not serve you well. But perhaps it is the demon that is gnawing its way up your leg? I will make some allowance for that."

"I beg your pardon, Lady S," muttered Ambrose. Even at the best of times, it did not pay to offend Lady S, and this was far from the best of times.

"Oh, do call me Auntie Hester," cooed the apparition in the darkness. "You know I do like all my young men to call me Auntie Hester."

"Yes, Auntie Hester," said Ambrose reluctantly. He could not suppress a shiver, as he knew exactly what she was: a revenant who survived only thanks to powerful magic, numerous blood sacrifices, and a budget appropriation that was never examined in Parliament. Lady Hester Stanhope had been dead for eighty years, but that had not ended her career in one of the predecessor organizations of D-Arc. She had gone from strength to strength in both bureaucratic and sorcerous terms since then. Though she was severely limited in her physical interaction with the world, she had many other advantages. Not least were her unrivalled political connexions, which ran all the way back to the early nineteenth century, when she had managed the household of her uncle William Pitt the Younger, then prime minister of Britain.

"Very good. Now, it has come to our attention that someone exceedingly naughty in Solingen . . . the Rhineland, you know . . . is trying to raise a *Waldgeist,* and not just any sixpence-ha'penny forest spirit, but a great old one of the primeval wood. They've got hold of the ritual and three days from now they're going to summon up the old tree-beastie and set it on our occupying forces—and we can't allow that, can we? Therefore, Ambrose my darling, you will dash over to Solingen, call up this *Waldgeist* first, and bind it to our service, then have it destroy the second summoner. Are you with me so far?"

"I know very little Teutonic magic," said Ambrose. "Surely there must be someone else better—"

"You'll have a *grimoire,* dear," said Lady S. "You *can* read Old High German?"

"Yes, but—"

"That's settled then!" exclaimed Lady S. "Our new doctor will cut that demon out for you, he's a darling boy and such a fine hand with the blade. Major Kennett will accompany you to Solingen, by the way. In case you need . . . assistance."

"What about the attack on me today?" asked Ambrose quickly. The wind-swept figure was retreating further into the dark, and the candle was guttering. "They were Anatolian demons! Why would the emir be sending them against me now?"

“You will be protected,” said Lady S. Her voice was distant now. “D-Arc takes care of its own.”

“I know it does!” shouted Ambrose. “That’s why I want to know who really sent those demons! Did you set this all in train—”

“Au revoir, my dear,” said a very remote voice, no more than a whisper on the wind.

The door behind him snapped open, and an inexorable force propelled Ambrose back out through the doorway. Landing on his injured leg, he fell and sprawled lengthways across the carpeted hall. Kennett looked down at him for a moment, sniffed, and helped him up.

“Doctor Lambshead is all ready for you,” he said. “Gunderbeg is standing by to eat the demon when it’s cut out, and we have all the recuperative apparatus prepared. Best we get a move on, I think.”

Ambrose looked down at his leg. The bandage of Sekhmet was now just a few strands of rag, and it was being chewed on by a mouth that had grown in his calf muscle, a black-lipped, razor-fanged mouth that was trying to turn itself upwards, towards his knee.

“Yes,” said Ambrose faintly. “If you don’t mind.”

AT NOON THE next day, his leg salved, bandaged, and entirely demon-free, Ambrose was on the boat train to Dover and thence to Calais, with Kennett keeping company. An uneventful channel crossing was complete by midnight, and after only changing trains twice, they were in Solingen the following morning.

Ambrose spent a good part of their travelling time reading the *grimoire* that Kennett had handed to him in Edinburgh. The book had come wrapped in a piece of winding cloth cut from the burial shroud of the Scottish sorcerer Thomas Weir, a fabric made to stifle sorcery, indicating that the D-Arc librarian believed the *grimoire* had the potential to act of its own volition. Accordingly, Ambrose treated it with care, using reversed gloves to turn its pages and marking his place with a ribbon torn from a child’s bonnet.

The *grimoire* was a typeset version of a much older text. It had been printed in the late sixteenth century, and a note with it attributed the book to the German sorcerer and botanomancer Bertin Zierer, though, as the flyleaf was missing and the original binding has been replaced several times, this was noted as being speculation rather than fact.

The section of the *grimoire* dealing with the *Waldgeist* of the Primeval Wood that had once stretched across much of modern Germany was, as per usual, couched in rather vague language, apart from the description of the actual ritual. It did not describe the form the *Waldgeist* usually took, or go into any details of its powers, beyond a warning that these would be employed against anyone who dared wake it who was "not of the blood of Wotan." The only clue to the nature of the *Waldgeist* came from an etching that showed a disc of ground covered in trees rising from a forest. Titled, in rough translation, "Tree Spirits Rising," it did not help Ambrose very much, though it did make him wonder if the *Waldgeist* manifested as some sort of gestalt entity composed of a whole section of modern forest.

Apart from the *grimoire,* the duty librarian had also included a large-scale map of the area around Solingen and some typed pages of research and observation. The map indicated that the locus of the *Waldgeist* was in the middle of a small but very old wood some twenty kilometers south of Solingen. The notes cross-referenced the ritual cited in the *grimoire* with other known practices of Teutonic magic, and affirmed that it looked to be complete and not designed to trap or harm the caster by some omission or intentional change.

Shortly before their arrival, both men assumed their appointed disguises, which had been placed by unseen hands in the next-door compartment. Ambrose became a full colonel from the staff sent to join the British forces of occupation on some mission that was not to be denied or enquired about by anyone. Kennett, on the other hand, simply put on a different and more conservative suit, topped with a grey homburg identical to that worn by the late King Edward, and thus assumed the appearance of a mysterious civilian from the upper echelons of Whitehall.

They were met at the Ohligs Wald station in Solingen by a young subaltern of the Black Watch, whose attempt at an introduction was immediately quashed by Kennett.

"You don't need to know our names and we don't want to know yours," he snapped. "Is the car waiting? And our escort?"

"Yes, sir," replied the young second lieutenant, a blush as red as the tabs on Ambrose's collar spreading across his cheeks. "As per the telegraph message."

"Lead on then," said Kennett. "The sooner we take care of this the better."

The car, commandeered from the divisional general, was accompanied by four motorcycle outriders and three Peerless trucks carrying the nameless subaltern's infantry platoon and a machine gun section.

"We hardly need all this carry-on," protested Ambrose as he settled into the grandly upholstered backseat of the general's car, and Kennett climbed in next to him. "Surely it would be better for me to get changed and just walk into the wood as a tourist or something?"

"I don't think so," replied Kennett. "The fellow who is hoping to . . . carry out his deed . . . is the leader of a gang of militants called Die Schwarze Fahne and they have quite a membership of former soldiers and the like. We'll have these lads establish a cordon around the wood, then you and I will go in."

"You're coming with me?" asked Ambrose. "The *grim—*"

He stopped himself, aware that the driver and the subaltern in the front seat were so obviously trying to not listen that they must be able to hear everything, even over the noise of the engines as the whole convoy got under way. "That is, the reference is specific about German heritage and the . . . subject's response if . . . ah . . . in contact with others."

"M' grandmother was Edith Adler, the opera singer," drawled Kennett out of the side of his mouth, so only Ambrose could hear. "So I have a drop or two of the blood. But I'll keep well back, just the same."

Ambrose nodded slightly and tried not to show how much he was discomfited by Kennett's disclosure. Even from such slight information, he would now be able to positively identify the man. Which meant that Kennett was either taking him into some inner echelon of trust, or he didn't think Ambrose would be around long enough for it to matter.

It only took forty minutes to reach the fringes of the wood. Ambrose sat in the car for a few minutes while everyone else got out, and read the relevant pages of the *grimoire* for perhaps the twentieth or thirtieth time. The ritual was not complex, but he had to memorise it. It would not be possible to refer to the book in the middle of the process.

He felt quite calm as he slipped the *grimoire* inside his tunic and did up the buttons. They looked like the usual brass, but were, in fact, silver-gilt, part of the sorcerous protection that Ambrose hoped would help him if things went only slightly awry. Of course, when dealing with an entity like a primeval tree spirit, it was far more likely that if something did go wrong, it would be on a scale so immense that no amount of sorcerous protection would make the slightest difference.

The lieutenant's platoon, under the direction more of a leather-lunged sergeant than the pink-faced officer, were forming up in three ranks on the verge. The trucks were parked across the road to block other vehicular traffic, and the Vickers machine gun was in the process of being emplaced on its tripod some way off, up a slight rise, to enfilade the road.

Ambrose got out and orientated the map to north by the sun, shifting it slightly to get the road in the right relationship, map to real topography. The map indicated the beginning of a footpath a dozen or so yards beyond the machine-gun position, and sure enough, there was a stone cairn there and a rotting wooden signpost that once upon a time had something written on it.

"We'll follow the footpath," said Ambrose, indicating the way. He folded the map and slipped it in with the *grimoire*. "It goes to the . . . the agreed rendezvous."

Kennett nodded and turned to the anxiously waiting lieutenant.

"Send one section to patrol the perimeter of the wood to the west and one section to the east. Keep one section here. Your men are not to enter the wood, no matter what you hear. Cries for help, orders that sound like they come from me or the colonel, all are to be ignored unless we are actually in front of you. If we do not come out within three hours—my watch says ten twenty-two, set yours now—return to Solingen, report to your CO, and tell him to immediately contact General Spencer Ewart at the War Office and relay the code phrase *'defectus omnes mortui.'*"

"But that's . . . uh . . . fail . . . failing . . . failure . . . all dead," said the lieutenant, busy trying to scribble the phrase in his notebook and set his watch, all at the same time.

"Did I ask you to translate?" snapped Kennett. "Do you have the code phrase?"

"Yes, sir!" replied the lieutenant. He closed his notebook and managed to successfully set his watch, his platoon sergeant surreptitiously leaning in to make sure he'd got it right.

"Finally, fire two warning shots over the heads of anyone approaching. If they continue, shoot to kill. It doesn't matter who they are. Civilians, women, children, whoever. Here is a written order to that effect."

"Yes, sir," said the lieutenant. There was considerable doubt in his voice and his hand shook a little as he unfolded the letter, his eyes flickering across the typewritten lines before widening enormously as they came to the short signature—just a first name and a capital letter—at the bottom of the page.

"Yes, sir!" he repeated, much more vigorously.

"Presuming we return, I'll want that back," said Kennett. "Carry on."

The lieutenant saluted and whirled about, speaking quickly to his sergeant, who a moment later began to bellow orders. Ambrose ignored the sudden bustle of military activity and began to walk towards the footpath. His eyes were on the fringes of the wood, looking for signs of arcane disturbance. But there were none visible. This part of the wood was composed of beech trees, their trunks green and mossy, their foliage a darker green. The light changed under the trees, gaining a soft, green tinge, but this was the natural magic of leaves and sun, not anything sorcerous.

It was also cooler under the canopy of the forest. Ambrose led the way with Kennett a dozen yards behind. They walked in silence, save for the occasional squelch of soft ground, or the snapping of a fallen twig where the footpath wound through higher, drier ground.

A half-mile or so in, the beeches began to give way to oaks. They were much older, and grew closer together, the footpath leading into relative darkness. As they left the beech forest behind, Ambrose noticed that it was quieter among the oaks as well. All the bird-sound had vanished, and all he could hear were his own and Kennett's footsteps. Then, not much farther on, Kennett's footsteps stopped.

Ambrose looked back. Kennett was leaning against the broad trunk of one of the ancient oaks. He nodded and waved Ambrose on. Clearly, this was as far as Kennett cared to go into the heart of the wood, and, as he was far more in practice and so currently more attuned to the occult than Ambrose, this probably meant he had sensed the locus of the *Waldgeist* somewhere close ahead.

Indeed, no more than fifty yards ahead, there was a forest glade where the oaks parted around a clear expanse of grass. In the middle of this small clearing was an incredibly ancient, stunted tree, a king-oak that could well be thousands of years old. Blown over by some long-forgotten storm, it still lived, its branches spreading horizontally, its trunk twisted and gnarled, its bark as hard as iron.

Ambrose could feel the *Waldgeist* now, the sense of the sleeping spirit that had been born of thirty million trees, and would not fade until the last of those trees was gone. Humans had decimated the primeval forest, but the spirit still remained. It only slept, and in Ambrose's opinion, it would be best left to do so. But he knew he had no real choice. If Lady S wanted the *Waldgeist* awoken, then it had to be awoken.

He knelt by the trunk of the king-oak, and paused, just for a moment, to gather his thoughts, mentally going through each step of the ritual. Satisifed that he had remembered it all, he laid out everything he needed on the forest floor.

First of all was the silver *athame,* his sacred knife, the one he had used in Turkey and thought lost when he was at the Front, only to find it had been stored away in the D-Arc armoury against his later use. They had always presumed he would come back.

Second was an acorn from this same wood, though from long ago. It was so old it was almost petrified, and though he had been assured its origin had been checked by thaumaturgic assay, as well as in the D-Arc records, it was the one element that he doubted. If it was from somewhere else, it might well help to raise the *Waldgeist,* but it would not be a friendly awakening.

The third thing was not in the ritual. Ambrose took his revolver from its holster and laid it down, to be ready at hand. If things went very badly wrong, he intended to shoot himself. It would be a far quicker and kinder way to die. Ancient spirits were not known for their sense of mercy.

That done, it was time to start. Ambrose began to recite the words of the waking ritual. His voice was steady, and he spoke carefully, as he sliced the end of his left thumb with the *athame* and let the bright blood drip onto the ancient acorn. As the blood dripped, the words became a chant, rhythmically repeated over and over again.

The acorn soaked up the blood like a sponge. When nine drops had fallen, Ambrose cut his right thumb and let another nine drops fall, without faltering in his chant. The guttural Old High German words sounded very loud in the stillness of the wood, but Ambrose knew it wasn't so much the words themselves that mattered. It was the thoughts behind them, the blood, and the aged seed.

He finished the chant at exactly the same time he pushed the acorn into the soil with both his bleeding thumbs, and sat back.

Nothing happened. Ambrose waited, sitting cross-legged next to the ancient oak, his hand on the butt of the revolver, ready to lift it up to his temple and fire.

A slight breeze swooped down and rustled the leaves on the low, spreading branches. It was cold, ice-laden, and out of time and place, in this splendid German summer.

"So it begins," whispered Ambrose. He could feel the *Waldgeist* stirring all around, the spirit waking in the wood. He looked up and saw the branches of the king-oak lifting, and then a moment later the trunk groaned and creaked, as it began to straighten up. It was becoming the great tree of old, when it had stood sixty feet high or more, tall and straight and strong.

If it was a typical manifestation of a tree spirit, the tree itself would respond to Ambrose's summoning, either to whisper with the soft sussuration of leaves, or to pin him down with a heavy branch and send a thousand green shoots to penetrate his body, slowly growing through skin and flesh until they did fatal damage to some vital organ. Or, even worse in some ways, the *Waldgeist* might force itself into Ambrose's mind, remove everything of his personality, and create for itself a human puppet. That was likely one of Kennett's main reasons for accompanying him, to guard against this eventuality with his revolver and its exploding silver bullets.

The wind blew stronger, and the tree grew taller. Ambrose made his fingers uncurl from the revolver, though he kept his hand close. It was important not to appear with weapons in hand, for that in itself might sway the *Waldgeist* to enmity.

Then the ground shivered and sank beneath Ambrose. It was an unwelcome sensation, delivering sudden uncertainty, and even worse, the sharp memory of being buried alive. Wildly, he looked around, and saw that just as in the etching in the *grimoire*, the king-oak and all the trees around the glade had risen from the surrounding forest, as if a disc had been cored out and lifted straight up.

Ambrose looked down, and saw the earth crumbling beneath him. His fingers closed on the revolver and he managed to get it halfway to his head before he was suddenly pulled down, taken into the earth as a shark drags down a swimmer, without mercy or any possibility of resistance.

The ground closed over Ambrose's head, the revolver landing with a thud to mark the spot. Grass grew in an instant through the bare soil, eager tendrils of green wrapping around the blued metal of the gun, until in a moment it was covered in green and lost to sight.

Deep underground, Ambrose screamed and screamed and screamed, all inside his head, for his mouth was shut with soil. He relived the sudden concussion of the German shell, the blankness in his ears, the earth silently cascading into the dug-out, the last glimpse of Peter's terrified face, the lantern snuffed out in an instant... and then the darkness, the pressure of the earth, everywhere about him save for a tiny air pocket between two fallen beams, where he had pressed his face.

Then there had been the terrible, never-ending time of being trapped, not knowing whether he would ever see daylight again, or breathe the clean air, untainted by earth and fumes and the slowly building stench of the corpses of his friends as they began to rot around him. Alone in the earth, held in an implacable grasp and wreathed in silence. Slowly dying, but not quickly enough for it to be an escape.

Now it was all happening again.

But it was not the same, some fragment of Ambrose's still-screaming mind observed. He was completely buried in the earth, this time, and so should already be well on the way to asphyxiation. But he felt no need to breathe.

Also, he could hear. He could hear his own heartbeat, beating a sharp tattoo of panic, but he could also hear the movement of the earth. But there was something else, as well, something that, as his panic lessened, he realised was a voice, the voice of the *Waldgeist*.

What he heard was not words, at least not in any human language. It was the sound of the forest, of the wind, and the trees, and the birds and the insects, somehow ordered and structured to become something that he could understand.

The *Waldgeist* of the primeval forest was whispering to him, as it took him into its embrace. Its true heart was down in the tangled roots where he lay, not in the tree above. He could feel those roots now, twining around him, gripping him lightly, but ready to rend him apart should the spirit's feelings change.

It wanted to know why he had awoken it, and for what purpose.

Ambrose told it, not bothering to open his mouth. It took his explanation and went into his mind for more, its presence like a sudden shadow on a summer's day, cool and crisp as it slowly spread through his memories and mind. Ambrose's panic shrank before this shadowy touch, and he grew quiet, almost asleep himself, the *Waldgeist* growing more awake.

As the tree spirit wandered in his thoughts, Ambrose relived them, too, slowly and sleepily. All the wonders and horrors of his life, from his earliest recollections to the events of the last few days. All were examined by the tree spirit, and as they progressed, in no particular order, Ambrose felt that each memory, and everything he had done or not done, was being weighed up and catalogued, added to the *Waldgeist*'s careful inventory of all the other living things in its forest domain.

Eventually, it finished looking. Ambrose was very tired by then, so tired that he could barely formulate the question that constituted his mission, visualising each word in his mind as if he were writing it down on an order pad, the question carefully contained within the rectangular grid.

So	**you**	**will**	**not**	**answer**	**this**	**other sum-moner**
in	**the**	**days**	**to**	**come?**	**and you**	**will**
be	**content**	**to**	**rest**	**until I**	**call**	**you**
from	**your**	**sleep**	**again?**			

No answer came. Ambrose tried to ask the question again, but he was too tired. Fear and panic had exhausted him, but now he felt a different weariness. He was warm, and comfortable, and the tree roots that cradled him felt as familiar as the ancient armchair by the fire in the bothy, the one with the sheepskins laid over its creased and faded leather upholstery.

Ambrose slept, and did not dream.

When he awoke, it was with a start. There was bright sunshine on his face, making him blink, and the blue sky above was bordered with green. He sat up and saw that he was at the foot of the king-oak, which was once again bent and bowed by the passage of time. There was no sign of his revolver or *athame,* but when he stood up, and checked himself over, everything else seemed to be unchanged. The *grimoire* was still in his tunic, as was the map. There was some earth caught under his Sam Browne belt, and his uniform was somewhat mussed, but that was all.

Everything else looked normal. There was no risen disc of trees, and though he could feel the *Waldgeist,* it was very faint. It slept again, and was sleeping very deep. Whether he had convinced it or not to remain quiescent, it would take far more than the blood of two thumbs and the ritual he had used to wake it now.

Ambrose frowned, but it was a merry frown. He didn't really understand what had happened, but he knew his object had been achieved. He also felt surprisingly good, almost as happy in himself as he had been in the far-off, golden days before the War.

He clapped his hand against the king-oak in friendly farewell, and set off along the path. Several paces along, he was surprised to find himself whistling. He frowned again, and stopped, standing still on the path. He couldn't remember when he had last felt like whistling.

There was a rustle up ahead. Ambrose's attention immediately returned to the present. He snuck off the path and crouched down behind a lesser but still substantial oak, regretting the loss of his revolver. Someone was coming very cautiously up the path, and it could be a German anarchist as easily as Kennett, and even if it was Kennett, Ambrose couldn't be sure of his intentions, and he was no longer so ready to just let Kennett kill him. There would be time enough to join his friends.

"Ambrose?"

It was Kennett. Ambrose peered around the trunk. Kennett was coming along the path, and he wasn't brandishing a weapon. But very strangely, he was no longer wearing the same suit with the grey homburg. He was in tweeds, with a deerstalker cap, and there was something about his face . . . a partially healed scar under his eye that hadn't been there . . .

"Ah," said Ambrose. He stepped out from behind the tree and raised his hand. "Hello, Kennett. How long have I been away?"

Kennett smiled, a smile that, as always, contained no warmth whatsoever, and was more an indication of sardonic superiority than any sense of humour.

"A year and a day," he said. "Just as the *grimoire* said."

"Not the copy you gave me," said Ambrose.

"Naturally," replied Kennett. "You might have refused to go. But from the whistling, the general spring of the step, and so forth, I presume the cure has been efficacious?"

"I do feel . . . whole," admitted Ambrose. He paused for a moment, eyes downcast, thinking of his own reactions. "And I believe . . . I am no longer afraid to be underground."

"That's good," said Kennett. "Because we have a job to do, and I'm afraid a great deal of it is deep under the earth. High, but deep. I'm not fond of the Himalayas myself, but what can you do?"

"Was there actually a German adept who wanted to raise the spirit?" asked Ambrose, as they began to walk together back along the path.

"Oh yes," said Kennett. "It's doubtful if he would have succeeded, and the timing was not quite what we said, but Lady S thought we might as well try to get two birds with one stone. The new doctor brought it to her attention that this old spirit had a twofold nature, that as well as trampling the undeserving and so on, it also traditionally sometimes healed the sick and those of 'broken mind.' "

"Broken mind," repeated Ambrose. "Yes. I suppose that I wasn't really getting any better where I was. But those demons—"

"They *were* the emir's," interrupted Kennett. "Forced our hand. Couldn't be helped."

"I see," said Ambrose, with a swift sideways glance at Kennett's face. He still couldn't tell if the man was lying.

They walked the rest of the way out of the wood in silence. At the road, there was a green Crossley 20/25 waiting, with Jones and Jones leaning on opposite sides of the bonnet, each carefully watching the surrounding countryside. They nodded to Ambrose as he walked up, and he thought that Jones the Larger might even have given him the merest shadow of a wink.

Ambrose's yataghan was on the floor behind the front seat, and there was a large cardboard box tied with a red ribbon sitting in the middle of the backseat. Kennett indicated the box with an inclination of his head.

"For you," he said. "Present from Lady S."

Ambrose undid the ribbon and opened the box. There was a velvet medal case inside, which he did not open; a silver hip flask engraved with his name beneath a testimonial of thanks from an obscure manufacturer of scientific instruments in Nottingham; and a card with a picture of a mountaineer waving the Union Jack atop a snow-covered mountain.

Ambrose flipped open the card.

"Welcome back," he read aloud. "With love from Auntie Hester."

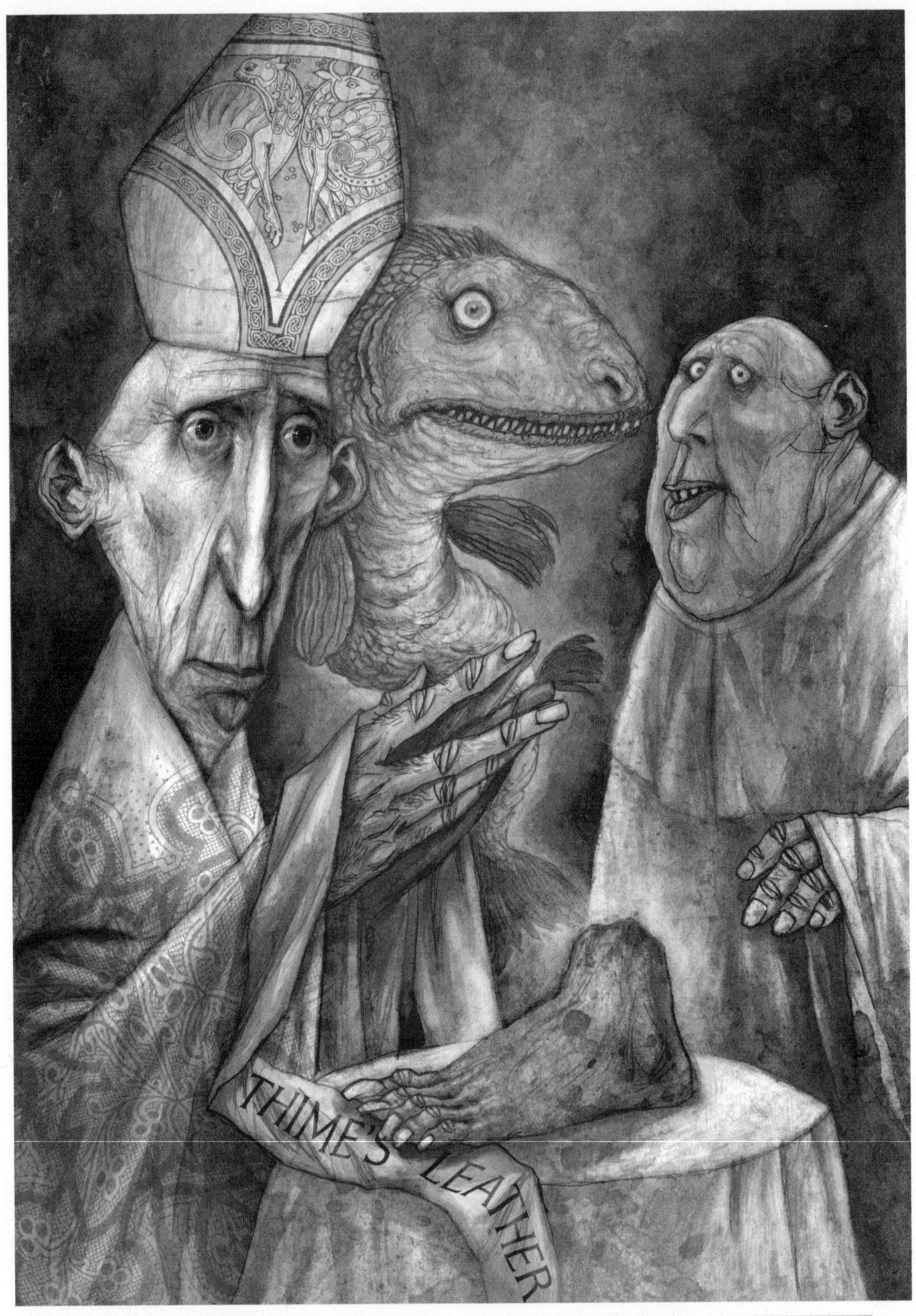

Ivica Stevanovic's "Relic with Fish," part of his series "The Silence of Many Pattering Feet: Saints and the Bits They Leave Behind."

Relic

By Jeffrey Ford

Out at the end of the world, on a long spit of land like a finger poking into oblivion, nestled in a valley among the dunes, sat the Church of Saint Ifritia, constructed from twisted driftwood and the battered hulls of ships. There was one tall, arched window composed of the round bottoms of blue bottles. The sun shone through it, submerging altar and pews. There was room for twenty inside, but the most ever gathered for a sermon was eleven. Atop its crooked steeple jutted a spiraled tusk some creature had abandoned on the beach.

The church's walls had a thousand holes, and so every morning Father Walter said his prayers while shoveling sand from the sanctuary. He referred to himself as "father" but he wasn't a priest. He used the title because it was what he remembered the holy men were called in the town he came from. Wanderers to the end of the world sometimes inquired of him as to the church's denomination. He was confused by these questions. "A basic church, you know," he'd say. "I talk God and salvation with anyone interested." Usually the pilgrims would turn away, but occasionally one stayed on and listened.

Being that the Church of Saint Ifritia could have as few as three visitors a month, Father Walter didn't feel inclined to give a sermon once a week. "My flock would be only the sand fleas," he said to Sister North. "Then preach to the fleas," she replied. "Four sermons a year is plenty," he said. "One for each season. Nobody should need more than four sermons a year." They were a labor for him to write, and he considered the task as a kind of penance. Why he gave sermons, he wasn't sure. Their purpose was elusive, and yet he knew it was something the holy men did. His earliest ones were about the waves, the dunes, the sky, the wind, and when he ran out of natural phenomena to serve as topics, he moved inward and began mining memory for something to write.

Father Walter lived behind the whalebone altar in a small room with a bed, a chair, a desk, and a stove. Sister North, who attended a summer sermon one year, the subject of which was The Wind, and stayed on to serve Saint Ifritia, lived in her own small shack behind the church. She kept it tidy, decorated with shells and strung with tattered fishing nets, a space no bigger than Father Walter's quarters. In the warm months, she kept a garden in the sand, dedicated to her saint. Although he never remembered having invited her to stay on, Father Walter proclaimed her flowers and tomatoes miracles, a cornucopia from dry sand and salt air, and recorded them in the official church record.

Sister North was a short, brown woman with long, dark hair streaked with grey, and an expression of determination. Her irises were almost yellow, cat-like, in her wide face. On her first night amid the dunes, she shared Father Walter's bed. He came to realize that she would share it again as long as there was no mention of it during the light of day. Once a season, she'd travel ten miles inland by foot to the towns and give word that a sermon was planned for the following Monday. The towns she visited scared her, and only occasionally would she meet a pilgrim who'd take note of her message.

In addition to the church and Sister North's shack, there were two other structures in the sand-dune valley. One was an outhouse built of red ship's wood with a tarpaulin flap for a door and a toilet seat made of abalone. The other was a shrine that housed the holy relic of Saint Ifritia. The latter building was woven from reeds by Sister North and her sisters. She'd sent a letter and they'd come, three of them. They were all short and brown, with long, dark hair streaked with grey. None had yellow eyes, though. They harvested reeds from the sunken meadow, an overgrown square mile set below sea level among the dunes two miles east of the church. They sang while they wove the strands into walls and window holes and a roof. Father Walter watched the whole thing from a distance. He felt he should have some opinion about it, but couldn't muster one. When the shrine began to take form, he knew it was a good thing.

Before Sister North's sisters left to return to their lives, Father Walter planned a dedication for the relic's new home. He brought the holy item to the service wrapped in a dirty old towel, the way he'd kept it for the past thirty years. Its unveiling brought sighs from the sisters, although at first they were unsure what they were looking at. A dark lumpen object, its skin like that of an overripe banana. There were toes and even orange, shattered toenails. It was assumed a blade had severed it just above the ankle, and the wound had, by miracle or fire, been cauterized. "Time's leather" was the phrase Father Walter bestowed upon the state of its preservation. It smelled of wild violets.

There was no golden reliquary to house it; he simply placed it in the bare niche built into the altar, toes jutting slightly beyond the edge of their new den. He turned and explained to the assembled, "You must not touch it with your hands, but fold them in front of you, lean forward, and kiss the toes. In this manner, the power of the saint will be yours for a short time and you'll be protected and made lucky."

Each of them present, the father, Sister North and her sisters, and a young man and woman on their honeymoon, who wandered into the churchyard just before the ceremony got under way, stepped up with folded hands and kissed the foot. Then they sat, and Father Walter paced back and forth, whispering to himself, as was his ritual prior to delivering a sermon. He'd written a new one for the event, a fifth sermon for the year. Sister North was pleased with his industry and had visited his bed the night he'd completed it. He stopped pacing eventually and pointed at the ancient foot. The wind moaned outside. Sand sifted through the reeds.

Father Walter's Sermon

When I was a young man, I was made a soldier. It wasn't my choosing, I don't know. They put a gun to my head. We marched through the mud into a rainy country. I was young and I saw people die all around me. Some were only wounded but drowned in the muddy puddles. It rained past forty days and forty nights and the earth had had its fill. Rivers flooded their banks and the water spilled in torrents from the bleak mountains. I killed a few close-up with a bayonet and I felt their life rush out. Some I shot at a distance and watched them suddenly drop like children at a game. In two months time I was savage.

We had a commanding officer who'd become fond of killing. He could easily have stayed behind the lines and directed the attack, but, with saber drawn, he'd lead every charge and shoot and hack to pieces more of the enemy than the next five men. Once I fought near him in a hand-to-hand melee against a band of enemy scouts. The noises he made while doing his work were ungodly. Strange animal cries. He scared me. And I was not alone. This Colonel Hempfil took no prisoners and would dispatch civilians as well as members of his own squad on the merest whim. I swear I thought I'd somehow gone to hell. The sun never shone.

And then one night we sat in ambush in the trees on either side of a dirt road. The rain, of course, was coming down hard and it was cold, moving into autumn. The night was an eternity I think. I nodded off and then there came some action. The colonel kicked me where I sat and pointed at the road. I looked and could barely make out a hay cart creaking slowly by. The colonel kicked me again and indicated with hand signals that I was to go and check out the wagon.

My heart dropped. I started instantly crying, but as not to let the colonel see me sobbing, I ran to it. There could easily have been enemy soldiers beneath the hay, with guns at the ready. I ran onto the road in front of the wagon and raised my weapon. "Halt," I said. The tall man holding the reins pulled up and brought the horses to a stop. I told him to get down from his seat. As he climbed onto the road, I asked him, "What are you carrying?" "Hay," he replied, and then the colonel and the rest of our men stormed the wagon. Hempfil gave orders to clear the hay. Beneath it was discovered the driver's wife and two daughters. Orders were given to line them all up. As the driver was being escorted away by two soldiers, he turned to me and said, "I have something to trade for our freedom. Something valuable."

The colonel was organizing a firing squad, when I went up to him and told him what the driver had said to me. He thanked me for the information, and then ordered that the tall man be brought to him. I stood close to hear what he could possibly have to offer for the lives of his family. The man leaned over Hempfil and whispered something I could not make out. The colonel then ordered him, "Go get it."

The driver brought back something wrapped in a dirty towel. He unwrapped the bundle and, whisking away the cloth, held a form the size of a small rabbit up to the colonel. "Bring a light," cried Hempfil. "I can't see a damn thing." A soldier lit a lantern and brought it. I leaned in close to see what was revealed. It was an old foot, wrinkled like a purse and dark with age. The sight of the toenails gave me a shiver.

"This is what you will trade for your life and the lives of your family? This ancient bowel movement of a foot? Shall I give you change?" said the colonel and that's when I knew all of them would die. The driver spoke quickly. "It is the foot of a saint," he said. "It has power. Miracles."

"What saint?" asked the colonel.

"Saint Ifritia."

"That's a new one," said Hempfil and laughed. "Bring me the chaplain," he called over his shoulder.

The chaplain stepped up. "Have you ever heard of Saint Ifritia?" asked the colonel.

"She's not a real saint," said the priest. "She is only referred to as a saint in parts of the Holy Writing that have been forbidden."

Hempfil turned and gave orders for the driver's wife and daughters to be shot. When the volley sounded, the driver dropped to his knees and hugged the desiccated foot to him as if for comfort. I saw the woman and girls, in their pale dresses, fall at the side of the road. The colonel turned to me and told me to give him my rifle. I did. He took his pistol from its holster at his side and handed it to me. "Take the prisoner off into the woods where it's darker, give him a ten-yard head start, and then kill him. If he can elude you for fifteen minutes, let him go with his life."

"Yes, sir," I said, but I had no desire to kill the driver. I led him at gunpoint up the small embankment and into the woods. We walked slowly forward into darkness. He whispered to me so rapidly, "Soldier, I still hold the sacred foot of Ifritia. Let me trade you it for my life. Miracles." As he continued to pester me with his promises of blessings and wonders, the thought of killing him began to appeal to me. I don't know what it was that came over me. It came from deep within, but in an instant his death had become for me a foregone conclusion. After walking for ten minutes, I told him to stop. He did. I said nothing for a while, and the silence prompted him to say, "I get ten yards, do I not?"

"Yes," I said.

With his first step, I lifted the pistol and shot him in the back of the head. He was dead before he hit the ground, although his body shook twice as I reached down to turn him over. His face was blown out the front, a dark, smoking hole above a toothful grimace. I took the foot, felt its slick hide in my grasp, and wrapped it in the dirty towel. Shoving it into my jacket, I buttoned up against the rain and set off deeper into the woods. I fled like a frightened deer through the night, and all around me was the aroma of wild violets.

It's a long story, but I escaped the war, the foot of Saint Ifritia producing subtle miracles at every turn, and once it made me invisible as I passed through an occupied town. I left the country of rain, pursued by the ghost of the wagon driver. Every other minute, behind my eyes, the driver's wife and daughters fell in their pale dresses by the side of the road in the rain, and nearly every night he would appear from my meager campfire, rise up in smoke, and take form. "Why?" he always asked. "Why?"

I found that laughter dispersed him more quickly. One night I told the spirit I had plans the next day to travel west. But in the morning, I packed my things up quickly and headed due south toward the end of the world. I tricked him. Eventually, the ghost found me here, and I see him every great while, pacing along the tops of the dunes that surround the valley. He can't descend to haunt me, for the church I built protects me and the power of Saint Ifritia keeps him at bay. Every time I see him his image is dimmer, and before long he will become salt in the wind.

The impromptu congregation was speechless. Father Walter slowly became aware of it as he stood, swaying slightly to and fro. "The Lord works in mysterious ways," he said, a phrase he'd actually heard from Colonel Hempfil. There was a pause after his delivery of it, during which he waved his hands back and forth in the air like a magician distracting an audience. Eventually, two of the sisters nodded and the honeymoon couple shrugged and applauded the sermon.

Father Walter took this as a cue to move on, and he left the altar of the shrine and ran back to the church to fetch a case of whiskey that the Lord had recently delivered onto the beach after a terrific thunderstorm. The young couple produced a hash pipe and a tarry ball of the drug, which bore a striking resemblance to the last knuckle of the middle toe of Saint Ifritia's foot.

Late that night, high as the tern flies, the young man and woman left and headed out toward the end of the world, and Sister North's sisters loaded into their wagon and left for their respective homes. Father Walter sat on the sand near the bell in the churchyard, a bottle to his lips, staring up at the stars. Sister North stood over him, the hem of her habit, as she called the simple grey shift she wore every day, flapping in the wind.

"None would stay the night after your story of murder," she said to him. "They drank your whiskey, but they wouldn't close their eyes and sleep here with you drunk."

"Foolishness," he said. "There's plenty still left for all. Loaves and fishes of whiskey. And what do you mean by murder?"

"The driver in your sermon. You could have let him live."

He laughed. "I did. In real life, I let him go. A sermon is something different, though."

"You mean you lied?"

"If I shot him, I thought it would make a better story."

"But where's the Lord's place in a story of cold-blooded murder?"

"That's for Him to decide."

Sister North took to her shack for a week, and he rarely saw her. Only in the morning and late in the afternoon would he catch sight of her entering and leaving the shrine. She mumbled madly as she walked, eyes down. She moved her hands as if explaining to someone. Father Walter feared the ghost of the driver had somehow slipped into the churchyard and she was conversing with it. "Because I lied?" he wondered.

During the time of Sister North's retreat to her shack, a visitor came one afternoon. Out of a fierce sandstorm, materializing in the churchyard like a ghost herself, stepped a young woman wearing a hat with flowers and carrying a travel bag. Father Walter caught sight of her through blue glass. He went to the church's high doors, opened one slightly to keep the sand out, and called to her to enter. She came to him, holding the hat down with one hand and lugging the heavy bag with the other. "Smartly dressed" was the term the father vaguely remembered from his life inland. She wore a white shirt buttoned at the collar, with a dark string tie. Her black skirt and jacket matched, and she somehow made her way through the sand without much trouble in a pair of high heels.

Father Walter slammed shut the church door once she was inside. For a moment, he and his guest stood still and listened to the wind, beneath it the distant rhythm of the surf. The church was damp and cold. He told the young lady to accompany him to his room where he could make a fire in the stove. She followed him behind the altar, and as he broke sticks of driftwood, she removed her hat and took a seat at his desk.

"My name is Mina GilCragson," she said.

"Father Walter," he replied over his shoulder.

"I've come from the Theological University to see your church. I'm a student. I'm writing a thesis on Saint Ifritia."

"Who told you about us?" he asked, lighting the kindling.

"A colleague who'd been to the end of the world and back. He told me last month, 'You know, there's a church down south that bears your saint's name.' And so I was resolved to see it."

Father Walter turned to face her. "Can you tell me what you know of the saint? I am the father here, but I know so little, though the holy Ifritia saved my life."

The young woman asked for something to drink. Since the rainwater barrel had been tainted by the blowing sand that day, he poured her a glass of whiskey and one for himself. After serving his guest, he sat on the floor, his legs crossed. She dashed her drink off quickly, as he remembered was the fashion in the big cities. Wiping her lips with the back of her hand, she said, "What do you know of her so far?"

"Little," he said and listened, pleased to be, for once, on the other end of a sermon.

Mina GilCragson's Sermon

She was born in a village in the rainy country eighty-some odd years ago. Her father was a powerful man, and he oversaw the collective commerce of their village, Dubron, which devoted itself to raising plum fish for the tables of the wealthy. The village was surrounded by fifty ponds, each stocked with a slightly different variety of the beautiful, fantailed species. It's a violet fish. Tender and sweet when broiled.

Ifritia, called "If" by her family, wanted for nothing. She was the plum of her father's eye, her wishes taking precedence over those of her mother and siblings. He even placed her desires above the good of the village. When she was sixteen, she asked that she be given her own pond and be allowed to raise one single fish in it that would be her pet. No matter the cost of clearing the pond, one of the larger ones, she was granted her wish. To be sure, there was much grumbling among the other villagers and even among If's siblings and mother, but none was voiced in the presence of her father. He was a proud and vindictive man, and it didn't pay to cross him.

She was given a hatchling from the strongest stock to raise. From early on, she fed the fish by hand. When she approached the pond, the creature would surface and swim to where she leaned above the water. Fish, to the people of Dubron, were no more than swimming money, so that when Ifritia bequeathed a name on her sole charge, it was a scandal. Unheard of. Beyond the limit. A name denotes individuality, personality, something dangerously more than swimming money. A brave few balked in public, but If's father made their lives unhappy and they fell back to silence.

Lord Jon, the plum fish, with enough room to spread out in his own pond and fed nothing but table scraps, potatoes, and red meat, grew to inordinate dimensions. As the creature swelled in size, its sidereal fish face fleshed out, pressing the eyes forward, redefining the snout as a nose, and puffing the cheeks. It was said Jon's face was the portrait of a wealthy landowner, and that his smile, now wide where it once was pinched, showed rows of sharp, white teeth. A fish with a human face was believed by all but the girl and her father to be a sign of evil. But she never stopped feeding it and it never stopped growing until it became the size of a bull hog. Ifritia would talk to the creature, tell it her deepest secrets. If she told something good, it would break out into its huge, biting smile; something sad, and it would shut its mouth and tears would fill its saucer-wide eyes.

And then, out of the blue, for no known reason, the fish became angry with her. When she came to the edge of the pond, after it took the food from her hand, it splashed her and made horrid, grunting noises. The fish doctor was called for and his diagnosis was quickly rendered. The plum fish was not supposed to grow to Lord Jon's outsized dimensions, the excess of flesh and the effects of the red meat had made the creature insane. "My dear," said the doctor in his kindest voice, "you've squandered your time creating a large purple madness and that is the long and short of it." The girl's father was about to take exception with the doctor and box his ears, but in that instant she saw the selfish error of her ways.

After convincing her father of the immorality of what they'd done, she walked the village and apologized to each person privately, from the old matrons to the smallest babies. Then she took a rifle from the wall of her father's hunting room and went to the pond. A crowd gathered behind her as she made her way to the water's edge. Her change was as out of the blue as that of Lord Jon's, and they were curious about her and happy that she was on the way to becoming a good person. She took up a position at the edge of the water, and whistled to the giant plum fish to come for a feeding. The crowd hung back, fearful of the thing's human countenance. All watched its fin, like a purple fan, disappear beneath the water.

Ifritia pushed the bolt of the rifle forward and then sighted the weapon upon a spot where Jon usually surfaced. Everyone waited. The fish didn't come up. A flock of geese flew overhead, and it started to rain. Attention wandered, and just when the crowd began murmuring, the water beneath where Ifritia leaned over the pond exploded and the fish came up a blur of violet, launching itself the height of the girl. Using its tail, it slapped her mightily across the face. Ifritia went over backwards and her feet flew out from under her. In his descent, Jon turned in midair, opened his wide mouth, and bit through her leg. The bone shattered, the flesh tore, blood burst forth, and he was gone, out of sight, to the bottom of the big pond, with her foot.

She survived the grim amputation. While she lay in the hospital, her father had the pond drained. Eventually, the enormous fish was stranded in only inches of water. Ifritia's father descended a long ladder to the pond bed and sloshed halfway across it to reach Lord Jon. The creature flapped and wheezed. Her father took out a pistol and shot the fat, odious face between the eyes. He reported to others later that the fish began to cry when it saw the gun.

The immense plum fish was gutted and Ifritia's foot was found in its third stomach. Her father forbade anyone to tell her that her foot had been rescued from the fish. She never knew that it stood in a glass case in the cedar attic atop her family home. As the days wore on and her affliction made her more holy every minute, the foot simmered in Time, turning dark and dry. She learned to walk with a crutch, and became pious to a degree that put off the village. They whispered that she was a spy for God. Dressing in pure white, she appeared around every corner with strict moral advice. They believed her to be insane and knew her to be death to any good time.

Mina held her glass out to Father Walter. He slowly rose, grabbed the bottle, and filled it. He poured himself another and sat again.

"Did she make a miracle at all?" he asked.

"A few," said Mina and dashed off her drink.

"Can you tell me one?"

"At a big wedding feast, she turned everybody's wine to water. She flew once, and she set fire to a tree with her thoughts."

"Amazing," said Father Walter. He stood and put his drink on the desk. "Come with me," he said. "There's something I think you'll want to see." She rose and followed him out the back door of the church. The sand was blowing hard, and he had to raise his arm in front of his eyes as he leaned into the wind. He looked back and Mina GilCragson was right behind him, holding her hat on with one hand. He led her to the shrine.

Inside, he moved toward the altar, pointing. "There it is. Saint Ifritia's foot," he said.

"What are you talking about?" said Mina, stepping up beside him.

"Right there," he said and pointed again.

She looked, and an instant later went weak. Father Walter caught her by the arm. She shook her head and took a deep breath. "I can't believe it," she said.

"I know," he said. "But there it is. You mustn't touch it with your hands. You must only kiss the toes. I'll stand outside. You can have a few minutes alone with it."

"Thank you so much," she said, tears in her eyes.

He went outside. Leaning against the buffeting wind, he pushed aside the bamboo curtain that protected the shrine's one window. Through the sliver of space, he watched Mina approach the altar. Her hands were folded piously in front of her, as he'd instructed. He realized that if she'd not worn the heels, she'd never have been able to reach the foot with her lips. As it was, she had to go up on her toes. Her head bobbed forward to the relic, but it wasn't a quick kiss she gave. Her head moved slightly forward and back, and Father Walter pictured her tongue passionately laving the rotten toes. It both gave him a thrill and made him queasy. He had a premonition that he'd be drinking hard into the night.

After the longest time, Mina suddenly turned away from the foot. Father Walter let the bamboo curtain slide back into place and waited to greet her. She exited the shrine, and he said, "How was that? Did you feel the spirit?" but she never slowed to answer. Walking right past him, she headed toward the outhouse. The sand blew fiercely, but she didn't bother to hold her hat and it flew from her head. Mina walked as if in a trance. Father Walter was surprised when she didn't go to the outhouse, but passed it and headed up out of the valley in the dunes. On the beach, the wind would have been ten times worse. As she ascended, he called to her to come back.

She passed over the rim, out of sight, and he was reluctant to follow her, knowing the ghost of the driver might be lurking in the blinding sandstorm. He turned back toward the church, his mind a knot of thoughts. Was she having a holy experience? Had he offended her? Was she poisoned by the old foot? He stopped to fetch her hat, which had blown up against the side of the outhouse.

That night, his premonition came true, and the whiskey flowed. He opened Mina GilCragson's travel bag and went through her things. By candlelight, whiskey in one hand, he inspected each of her articles of clothing. When holding them up, he recognized the faint scent of wild violets. He wondered if she was a saint. While he was searching for evidence in the aroma of a pair of her underpants, Sister North appeared out of the shadows.

"What are you up to?" she asked.

"Sniffing out a holy bouquet. I believe our visitor today may have been a saint."

"She was nothing of the sort," said Sister North, who stepped forward and backhanded Father Walter hard across the face. His whiskey glass flew from his grasp and he dropped the underpants. Consciousness blinked off momentarily and then back on. He stared at her angry, yellow eyes as she reached out, grabbed his shirt, and pulled him to his feet. "Come with me," she said.

Outside, the sandstorm had abated and the night was clear and cool and still. Not letting go, she pulled Father Walter toward the shrine. He stumbled once and almost fell, and for his trouble, she kicked him in the rear end. Candlelight shone out from the shrine's one window, its bamboo curtain now rolled up. Sister North marched the father up to the altar and said to him, "Look at that."

"Look at what?" he said, stunned by drink and surprise.

"What else?" she asked.

And, upon noticing, he became instantly sober, for the big toe of the holy foot was missing. "My God," he said, moving closer to it. Where the toe had been was a knuckle-stump of sheered gristle. "I thought she was sucking on it, but in fact she was chewing off the toe," he said, turning to face Sister North.

"You thought she was sucking on it . . ." she said. "Since when is sucking the holy toes allowed?"

"She was a scholar of Saint Ifritia. I never suspected she was a thief."

Sister North took a seat and gave herself up to tears. He sat down beside her and put his arm around her shoulders. They stayed in the shrine until the candles melted down and the dawn brought bird calls. Then they went to his bed. Before she fell asleep, the sister said to him, "It happened because you lied."

He thought about it. "Nahh," he said. "It was bound to happen someday." He slept and dreamt of the driver's wife and daughters. When he woke, Sister North was gone.

Sister North's Sermon

Father—By the time you find this, I'll already be four miles inland, heading for the city. I mean to bring back the stolen toe and make amends to Saint Ifritia. She's angry that we let this happen. You, of course, bear most of the responsibility, but I, too, own a piece of the guilt. It may take me a time to hunt down Mina GilCragson. I'll try the university first, but if she's not a scholar, I fear she might be a trader on the black market, trafficking in religious relics. If that's the case, the toe could at this moment be packed on the back of a mule, climbing the northern road into the mountains and on through the clouds to the very beginning of the world. If so, I will follow it. If I fail, I won't be back. One thing I've seen in my sleep is that at the exact halfway point of my journey, a man will visit the church and bring you news of me. If he tells you I am dead, then burn my shack and all my things and scatter the ashes over the sea, but if the last he's seen of me I'm alive, then that means I will return. That, I'm sure of. Wake up and guard the foot with your very life. If I return after years with a toe and there is no foot, I'll strangle you in your sleep. Think of me in bed, and in the morning, when you shovel sand, pray for me. There are four bottles of whiskey under the mattress in my shack. You can have three of them. I spent a week of solitude contemplating your sermon and realized that you didn't lie. That you actually killed the driver of the hay wagon. Which is worse? May the sweet saint have mercy on you.

—Sister

TWO DAYS LATER, Father Walter realized he'd taken Sister North for granted, and she was right, he had killed the driver just as he'd described in his sermon. Without her there, in her shack, in the shrine, in his bed, the loneliness crept into the sand dune valley and he couldn't shake it. Time became a sermon, preaching itself. The sand and sun and sand and wind and sand and every now and then a visitor, whose presence seemed to last forever until vanishing into sand, a pilgrim with whom to fill the long hours, chatting.

Every one of the strangers, maybe four a year and one year only two, was asked if they brought word from Sister North. He served them whiskey and let them preach their sermons before blessing them on their journeys to the end of the world. Sometimes an old man, moving slowly, bent, mumbling, sometimes a young woman, once a child on the run. None of them had word from her. In between these occasional visits from strangers lay long stretches of days and seasons, full of silence and wind and shifting sand. To pass the long nights, he took to counting the stars.

One evening, he went to her shack to fetch the second bottle of her whiskey and fell asleep on her bed. In the morning, there was a visitor in the church when he went in to shovel. A young man sat in the first pew. He wore a bow tie and white shirt, and even though it was in the heart of the summer season, a jacket as well. His hair was perfectly combed. Father Walter showed him behind the altar and they sat sipping whiskey well into the afternoon as the young man spoke his sermon. The father had heard it all before, but one thing caught his interest. In the midst of a tale of sorrows, the boy spoke about a place he'd visited in the north where one of the attractions was a fish with a human face.

Father Walter halted the sermon and asked, "Lord Jon?"

"The same," said the young man. "An enormous plum fish."

"I'd heard he'd been killed, shot by the father of the girl whose leg he'd severed."

"Nonsense. There are so many fanciful stories told of this remarkable fish. What is true, something I witnessed, the scientists are training Lord Jon to speak. I tipped my hat to him at the aquarium and he said, in a voice as clear as day, 'How do you do?' "

"You've never heard of a connection between Saint Ifritia and the fish?" asked Father Walter.

The young man took a sip, cocked his head, and thought. "Well, if I may speak frankly . . ."

"You must, we're in a church," said the Father.

"What I remember of Saint Ifritia from Monday Afternoon Club, is that she was a prostitute who was impregnated by the Lord. As her time came to give birth, her foot darkened and fell off just above the ankle and the child came out through her leg, the head appearing where the foot had been. The miracle was recorded by Charles the Bald. The boy grew up to be some war hero, a colonel in the war for the country of rain."

The young man left as the sun was going down and the sky was red. Father Walter had enjoyed talking to him, learning of the exploits of the real Lord Jon, but some hint of fear in the young man's expression said the poor fellow was headed all the way to the end, and then one more step into oblivion. That night, the father sat in the churchyard near the bell and didn't drink, but pictured Sister North, struggling upward through the clouds to the beginning of the world. He wished they were in his bed, listening to the wind and the cries of the beach owl. He'd tell her the young man's version of the life of Saint Ifritia. They'd talk about it till dawn.

For the longest time, Father Walter gave up writing sermons. With the way everything had transpired, the theft of the toe, the absence of Sister North, he felt it would be better for the world if he held his tongue and simply listened. Then, deep in one autumn season, when snow had already fallen, he decided to leave the sand dune valley and go to see the ocean. He feared the ghost of the driver every step beyond the rim but slowly continued forward. Eventually, he made his way over the dunes to the beach and sat at the water's edge. Watching the waves roll in, he gave himself up to his plans to finally set forth in search of Sister North. He thought for a long time until his attention was diverted by a fish brought before him in the surf. He looked up, startled by it. When he saw its violet color, he knew immediately what it was.

The fish opened its mouth and spoke. "A message from my liege, Lord Jon. He's told me to tell you he'd overheard a wonderful conversation with your Sister North at the Aquarium restaurant one evening a few years ago, and she wanted to relay the message to you that you should write a new sermon for her."

Father Walter was stunned at first by the talking fish, but after hearing what it had to say, he laughed. "Very well," he said and lifted the fish and helped it back into the waves. When he turned to head toward the church, the driver stood before him, a vague phantom, bowing slightly and proffering with both hands a ghostly foot. "Miracles . . ." said a voice in the wind. The father was determined to walk right through the spirit if need be. He set off at a quick pace toward the sand dune valley. Just as he thought he would collide with the ethereal driver, the fellow turned and walked, only a few feet ahead of him, just as they had walked through the dark forest in rain country. In the wind, the holy man heard the words, "I get ten yards, do I not?" repeated again and again, and he knew that if he had the pistol in his hand, he'd have fired it again and again.

With a sudden shiver, he finally passed through the halted ghost of the driver and descended the tall dune toward the church. The words in the wind grew fainter. By the time he reached the church door and looked back, the driver was nowhere to be seen along the rim of the valley. He went immediately to his room, took off his coat, poured a glass of whiskey, and sat at his desk. Lifting his pen, he scratched across the top of a sheet of paper the title: "Every Grain of Sand, a Minute."

When he finished writing the sermon, it was late in the night and, well into his cups, he decided on the spot to deliver it. Stumbling and mumbling, he went around the church and lit candles, fired up the pots of wisteria incense. As he moved through the shadows, the thought came to him that with the harsh cold of recent days, even the sand fleas, fast asleep in hibernation, would not be listening. He gathered up the pages of the sermon and went to the altar. He cleared his throat, adjusted the height of the pages to catch the candlelight, and began.

"Every grain of sand, a minute," he said in a weary voice. With that phrase out, there immediately came a rapping at the church door. He looked up and froze. His first thought was of the driver. The rapping came again and he yelled out, "Who's there?"

"A traveler with news from Sister North," called a male voice. Father Walter left the altar and ran down the aisle to the door. He pushed it open and said, "Come in, come in." A tall man stepped out of the darkness and into the church's glow. Seeing the stranger's height, he remembered the driver's, and took a sudden step backward. It wasn't the ghost, though, it was a real man with thick sideburns, a serious gaze, a top hat. He carried a small black bag. "Thank you," he said and removed his overcoat and gloves, handing them to Father Walter. "I was lost among the dunes and then I saw a faint light issuing up from what appeared in the dark to be a small crater. I thought a falling star had struck the earth."

"It's just the church of Saint Ifritia," said the father. "You have news of Sister North?"

"Yes, Father, I have a confession to make."

Father Walter led the pilgrim to the front pew and motioned for the gentleman to sit while he took a seat on the steps of the altar. "Okay," he said, "out with it."

"My name is Ironton," said the gentleman, removing his hat and setting it and his black bag on the seat next to him. "I'm a traveling businessman," he said. "My work takes me everywhere in the world."

"What is your business?" asked the father.

"Trade," said Ironton. "And that's what I was engaged in at Hotel Lacrimose, up in the north country. I was telling an associate at breakfast one morning that I had plans to travel next to the end of the world. The waitress, who'd just then brought our coffee, introduced herself and begged me, since I was travelling to the end of the world, to bring you a message."

"Sister North is a waitress?"

"She'd sadly run out of funds, but intended to continue on to the beginning of the world once she'd saved enough money. In any event, I was busy at the moment, having to run off to close a deal, and I couldn't hear her out. I could, though, sense her desperation, and so I suggested we meet that night for dinner at the Aquarium.

"We met in that fantastic dining hall, surrounded by hundred-foot-high glass tanks populated by fierce leviathans and brightly colored swarms of lesser fish. There was a waterfall at one end of the enormous room, and a man-made river that ran nearly its entire length with a small wooden bridge arching up over the flow in one spot to offer egress to either side of the dining area. We dined on *fez-menuth* flambé and consumed any number of bottles of sparkling Lilac water. She told me her tale, your tale, about the sacred foot in your possession.

"Allow me to correct for you your impressions of Saint Ifritia. This may be difficult, but being a rationalist, I'm afraid I can only offer you what I perceive to be the facts. This Saint Ifritia, whose foot you apparently have, was more a folk hero than a religious saint. To be frank, she went to the grave with both feet. She never lost a foot by any means. She was considered miraculous for no better reason than because she was known to frequently practice small acts of human kindness for friends and often strangers. Her life was quiet, small, but I suppose, no less heroic in a sense. Her neighbors missed her when she passed on and took to referring to her as Saint Ifritia. It caught on and legends attached themselves to her memory like bright streamers on a humble hay wagon."

"The foot is nothing?" asked Father Walter.

"It's an old rotten foot," said Ironton.

"What did Sister North say to your news?"

Ironton looked down and clasped his hands in his lap. "This is where I must offer my confession," he said.

"You didn't tell her, did you?"

"The story of her search for the missing toe was so pathetic I didn't have the heart to tell her the facts. And yet, still, I was going to. But just as I was about to speak, beside our table, from out of the man-made river, there surfaced an enormous purple fish with a human face. It bobbed on the surface, remaining stationary in the flow, and its large eyes filled with tears. Its gaze pierced my flesh and burrowed into my heart to turn off my ability to tell Sister North her arduous search had been pointless."

Father Walter shook his head in disgust. "What is it she wanted you to tell me?"

"She wants you to write a sermon for her," said Ironton.

"Yes," said the father, "the news preceded you. I finished it this evening just before your arrival."

"Well," said the businessman, "I do promise, should I see her on my return trip, I will tell her the truth, and give her train fare home."

For the remaining hours of the night, Father Walter and his visitor sat in the church and drank whiskey. In their far-flung conversation, Ironton admitted to being a great collector of curios and oddities. In the morning, when the visitor was taking his leave, the father wrapped up the foot of Saint Ifritia in its original soiled towel and bestowed it upon his guest. "For your collection," he said. "Miracles."

They laughed and Ironton received the gift warmly. Then, touching his index finger and thumb to the brim of his hat, he bowed slightly and disappeared up over the rim of the dune.

More time passed. Every grain of sand, a minute. Days, weeks, seasons. Eventually, one night, Father Walter woke from troubling dreams to find Sister North in bed beside him. At first, he thought he was still dreaming. She was smiling, though, and her cat eyes caught what little light pervaded his room and glowed softly. "Is it you?" he asked.

"Almost," she said, "but I've left parts of me between here and the beginning of the world."

"A toe?"

Sister North's Sermon

No, only pieces of my spirit, torn out by pity, shame, guilt, and fear. I tracked Mina GilCragson. She's no scholar, but an agent from a ring of female thieves who specialize in religious relics. The toe was sent along the secret Contraband Road, north, to the beginning of the world. I travelled that road, packing a pistol and cutlass. And I let the life out of certain men and women who thought they had some claim on me. I slept at the side of the road in the rain and snow. I climbed the rugged path into the cloud country.

In the thin atmosphere of the Haunted Mountains, I'd run out of food and was starving. Unfortunately for him, an old man, heading north, leading a donkey with a heavy load, was the first to pass my ambush. I told him I wanted something to eat, but he went for his throwing dagger, and I was forced to shoot him in the face. I freed the donkey of its burden and went through the old man's wares. I found food, some smoked meat, leg bones of cattle, and pickled plum fish. While

I ate, I inspected the rest of the goods, and among them I discovered a small silver box. I held it up, pressed a hidden latch on the bottom, and the top flipped back. A mechanical plinking music, the harmony of Duesgruel's *Last Movement,* played, and I beheld the severed toe.

I had it in my possession and I felt the spirit move through me. All I wanted was to get back to the church. Taking as much of the booty from the donkey's pack as I could carry, I travelled to the closest city. There I sold my twice-stolen treasures and was paid well for them. I bought new clothes and took a room in a fine place, the Hotel Lacrimose.

I spent a few days and nights at the amazing hotel, trying to relax before beginning the long journey home. One afternoon, while sitting on the main veranda, watching the clouds twirl, contemplating the glory of Saint Ifritia, I made the acquaintance of an interesting gentleman. Mr. Ironton was his name and he had an incredible memory for historical facts and unusual opinons on the news of the day. Having travelled for years among paupers and thieves, I was unused to speaking with someone so intelligent as Ironton. We had a delightful conversation. Somewhere in his talk, he mentioned that he was travelling to the end of the world. At our parting, he requested that I join him for dinner at the Aquarium that evening.

That night at dinner, I told Ironton our story. I showed him the toe in its small silver case. He lifted the thing to his nose and announced that he smelled wild violets. But then he put the toe on the table between us and said, "This Saint Ifritia, you speak of. It has recently been discovered by the Holy of the Holy See that she is in fact a demon, not a saint. She's a powerful demon. I propose you allow me to dispose of that toe for you. Every minute you have it with you you're in terrible danger." He nodded after speaking.

I told him, "No thank you. I'll take my chances with it."

"You're a brave woman, Ms. North," he said. "Now what was the message you had for your Father Walter?"

As I told him that I wanted you to know I was on my way, and to write a sermon for me, an enormous violet fish with a human face rose out of the water of the decorative river that ran through the restaurant next to our table. It startled me. Its face was repulsive. I recalled you telling me something about a giant plum fish, Lord Jon, and I spoke the name aloud. "At your service," the fish said and then dove into the flow. When I managed to overcome my shock at the fish's voice, I looked back to the table and discovered both Ironton and the toe had vanished.

I had it and I lost it. I felt the grace of Saint Ifritia for a brief few days at the Hotel Lacrimose and then it was stolen away. I've wondered all along my journey home if that's the best life offers.

SISTER NORTH YAWNED and turned on her side. "And what of the foot? Is it safe?" she asked.

He put his arm around her. "No," he said. "Some seasons back I was robbed at gunpoint. A whole troop of bandits on horses. They took everything. I begged them to leave the foot. I explained it was a holy relic, but they laughed and told me they would cook it and eat it on the beach that night. It's gone."

"I'm so tired," she said. "I could sleep forever."

Father Walter drew close to her, closed his eyes, and listened to the sand sifting in through the walls.

Lord Dunsany's Teapot

By Naomi Novik

The accidental harmony of the trenches during the war produced, sometimes, odd acquaintances. It was impossible not to feel a certain kinship with a man having lain huddled and nameless in the dirt beside him for hours, sharing the dubious comfort of a woolen scarf pressed over the mouth and nose while eyes streamed, stinging, and gunpowder bursts from time to time illuminated the crawling smoke in colors: did it have a greenish cast? And between the moments of fireworks, whispering to one another too low and too hoarsely to hear even unconsciously the accents of the barn or the gutter or the halls of the public school.

What became remarkable about Russell, in the trenches, was his smile: or rather that he smiled, with death walking overhead like the tread of heavy boots on a wooden floor above a cellar. Not a wild or wandering smile, reckless and ready to meet the end, or a trembling rictus; an ordinary smile to go with the whispered, "Another one coming, I think," as if speaking of a cricket ball instead of an incendiary; only friendly, with nothing to remark upon.

The trench had scarcely been dug. Dirt shook loose down upon them, until they might have been part of the earth, and when the all-clear sounded at last out of a long silence, they stood up still equals under a coat of mud, until Russell bent down and picked up the shovel, discarded, and they were again officer and man.

But this came too late: Edward trudged back with him, side by side, to the more populated regions of the labyrinth, still talking, and when they had reached Russell's bivouac, he looked at Edward and said, "Would you have a cup of tea?"

The taste of the smoke was still thick on Edward's tongue, in his throat, and the night had curled up like a tiger and gone to sleep around them. They sat on Russell's cot while the kettle boiled, and he poured the hot water into a fat old teapot made of iron, knobby, over the cheap and bitter tea leaves from the ration. Then he set it on the little camp stool and watched it steep, a thin thread of steam climbing out of the spout and dancing around itself in the cold air.

Yishan Li's depiction of Lord Dunsany's Teapot, from the forthcoming Novik-Li graphic novel "Ten Days to Glory: Demon Tea and Lord Dunsany."

The rest of his company were sleeping, but Edward noticed their cots were placed away, as much as they could be in such a confined space; Russell had a little room around his. He looked at Russell: under the smudges and dirt, weathering; not a young face. The nose was a little crooked and so was the mouth, and the hair brushed over the forehead was sandy brown and wispy in a vicarish way, with several years of thinning gone.

"A kindness to the old-timer, I suppose," Russell said. "Been here—five years now, or near enough. So they don't ask me to shift around."

"They haven't made you lance-jack," Edward said, the words coming out before he could consider all the reasons a man might not have received promotion, of which he would not care to speak.

"I couldn't," Russell said, apologetic. "Who am I, to be sending off other fellows, and treating them sharp if they don't?"

"Their corporal, or their sergeant," Edward said, a little impatient with the objection, "going in with them, not hanging back."

"O, well," Russell said, still looking at the teapot. "It's not the same for me to go."

He poured out the tea, and offered some shavings off a small, brown block of sugar. Edward drank: strong and bittersweet, somehow better than the usual. The teapot was homely and common. Russell laid a hand on its side as if it were precious, and said it had come to him from an old sailor, coming home at last to rest from traveling.

"Do you ever wonder, are there wars under the sea?" Russell said. His eyes had gone distant. "If all those serpents and the kraken down there, or some other things we haven't names for, go to battle over the ships that have sunk, and all their treasure?"

"And mermen dive down among them, to be counted brave," Edward said, softly, not to disturb the image that had built clear in his mind: the great writhing beasts, tangled masses striving against one another in the endless cold, dark depths, over broken ships and golden hoards, spilled upon the sand, trying to catch the faintest gleam of light. "To snatch some jewel to carry back, for a courting gift or an heirloom of their house."

Russell nodded, as if to a commonplace remark. "I suppose it's how they choose their lords," he said, "the ones that go down and come back; and their king came up from the dark once with a crown—beautiful thing, rubies and pearls like eggs, in gold."

The tea grew cold before they finished building the undersea court, turn and turn about, in low voices barely above the nasal breathing of the men around them.

IT SKIRTED THE lines of fraternization, certainly; but it could not have been called deliberate. There was always some duty or excuse which brought them into one another's company to begin with, and at no regular interval. Of course, even granting this, there was no denying it would have been more appropriate for Edward to refuse the invitation, or for Russell not to have made it in the first place. Yet, somehow, each time tea was offered, and accepted.

The hour was always late, and if Russell's fellows had doubts about his company, they never raised their heads from their cots to express it either by word or look. Russell made the tea, and began the storytelling, and Edward cobbled together castles with him, shaped of steam and fancy, drifting upwards and away from the trenches.

He would walk back to his own cot afterwards still warm through and lightened. He had come to do his duty, and he would do it, but there was something so much *vaster* and more dreadful than he had expected in the wanton waste upon the fields, in the smothered silence of the trenches: all of them already in the grave and merely awaiting a final confirmation. But Russell was still alive, so Edward might be as well. It was worth a little skirting of regulations.

HE ONLY HALF-HEARD Russell's battalion mentioned in the staff meeting, with one corner of his preoccupied mind; afterwards, he looked at the assignment: a push to try and open a new trench, advancing the line.

It was no more than might be and would be asked of any man, eventually; it was no excuse to go by the bivouac that night with a tin of his own tea, all the more precious because Beatrice somehow managed to arrange for it to win through to him, through some perhaps questionable back channel. Russell said nothing of the assignment, though Edward could read the knowledge of it around them: for once, not all the other men were sleeping, a few curled protectively around their scratching hands, writing letters in their cots.

"Well, that's a proper cup," Russell said softly, as the smell climbed out of the teapot, fragrant and fragile. The brew, when he poured it, was clear amber-gold, and made Edward think of peaches hanging in a garden of shining, fruit-heavy trees, a great, sighing breath of wind stirring all the branches to a shake.

For once, Russell did not speak as they drank the tea. One after another, the men around them put down their pens and went to sleep. The peaches swung from the branches, very clear and golden in Edward's mind. He kept his hands close around his cup.

"That's stirred him a bit, it has," Russell said, peering under the lid of the teapot; he poured in some more water. For a moment, Edward thought he saw mountains, too, beyond the orchard-garden: green-furred peaks with clouds clinging to their sides like loose eiderdown. A great wave of homesickness struck him very nearly like a blow, though he had never seen such mountains. He looked at Russell, wondering.

"It'll be all right, you know," Russell said.

"Of course," Edward said: the only thing that could be said, prosaic and untruthful; the words tasted sour in his mouth after the clean taste of the tea.

"No, what I mean is, it'll be all right," Russell said. He rubbed a hand over the teapot. "I don't like to say, because the fellows don't understand, but you see him, too; or at least as much of him as I do."

"Him," Edward repeated.

"I don't know his name," Russell said thoughtfully. "I've never managed to find out; I don't know that he hears us at all, or thinks of us. I suppose if he ever woke up, he might be right annoyed with us, sitting here drinking up his dreams. But he never has."

It was not their usual storytelling, but something with the uncomfortable savor of truth. Edward felt as though he had caught a glimpse from the corner of his eye of something too vast to be looked at directly or all at once: a tail shining silver-green sliding through the trees; a great green eye, like oceans, peering back with drowsy curiosity. "But he's not *in* there," he said involuntarily.

Russell shrugged expressively. He lifted off the lid and showed Edward: a lump fixed to the bottom of the pot, smooth, white, glimmering like a pearl, irregular yet beautiful, even with the swollen tea-leaves like kelp strewn over and around it.

He put the lid back on, and poured out the rest of the pot. "So it's all right," he said. "I'll be all right, while I have him. But you see why I couldn't send other fellows out. Not while I'm safe from all this, and they aren't."

An old and battered teapot made talisman of safety, inhabited by some mystical guardian: it ought to have provoked the same awkward sensation as speaking to an earnest spiritualist, or an excessively devoted missionary; it called for polite agreement and withdrawal. "Thank you," Edward said instead; he was comforted, and glad to be so.

Whatever virtue lived there in the pitted iron, it was no more difficult to believe in than the blighted landscape above their trenches, the coils of hungry, barbed, black wire snaking upon the ground, and the creeping poisonous smoke that covered the endless bodies of the dead. Something bright and shining ought not to be more impossible than that; and even if it was not strong enough to stand against all devastation, there was pleasure in thinking one life might be spared by its power.

THEY BROUGHT HIM the teapot three days later: Russell had no next of kin with a greater claim. Edward thanked them and left the teapot in a corner of his bag, and did not take it out again. Many men he knew had died, comrades in arms, friends; but Russell lying on the spiked and poisoned ground, breath seared and blood draining, hurt the worse for seeming wrong.

Edward dreamed of sitting with Russell: the dead man's skin clammy-grey, blood streaking the earthenware where his fingers cupped it, where his lips touched the rim, and floating over the surface of the tea. "Well, and I was safe, like I said," Russell said. Edward shuddered out of the dream, and washed his face in the cold water in his jug; there were flakes of ice on the surface.

He went forward himself, twice, and was not killed; he shot several men, and sent others to die. There was a commendation, at one point. He accepted it without any sense of pride. In the evenings, he played cards with a handful of other officers, where they talked desultorily of plans, and the weather, and a few of the more crude of conquests either real or hoped-for in the French villages behind the lines. His letters to Beatrice grew shorter. His supply of words seemed to have leached away into the dirt.

His own teapot was on his small burner to keep warm when the air raid sounded; an hour later, after the all-clear, it was a smoking cinder, the smell so very much like the acrid bite of gas that he flung it as far up over the edge of the trench as he could manage, to get it away, and took out the other teapot, to make a fresh cup and wash away the taste.

And it was only a teapot: squat and unlovely except for the smooth, pearlescent lump inside, some accident of its casting. He put in the leaves and poured the water from the kettle. He was no longer angry with himself for believing, only distantly amused, remembering; and sorry, with that same distance, for Russell, who had swallowed illusions for comfort.

He poured his cup and raised it and drank without stopping to inhale the scent or to think of home; and the pain startled him for being so vivid. He worked his mouth as though he had only burned his tongue and not some unprepared and numbed corner of his self. He found himself staring blindly at the small, friendly blue flame beneath the teapot. The color was the same as a flower that grew only on the slopes of a valley on the other side of the world, where no man had ever walked, which a bird with white feathers picked to line its nest so the young, when they were born, were soft grey and tinted blue, with pale yellow beaks held wide to call for food in voices that chimed like bells.

The ringing in his ears from the sirens went quiet. He understood Russell then finally; and wept a little, without putting down the cup. He held it between his hands while the heat but not the scent faded, and sipped peace as long as it lasted.

The teapot is unremarkable in itself: a roundbellied, squat thing of black, enameled iron, with the common nail-head pattern rubbed down low over the years and a spout perhaps a little short for its width; the handle has been broken and mended, and the lid has only a small, stubby knob. Dr. Lambshead is not known to have used the teapot, which wears a thin layer of grey dust, but a small attached label indicates it was acquired at an estate auction held in Ireland circa 1957.

Lot 558: *Shadow of My Nephew* by Wells, Charlotte

By Holly Black

As an auctioneer, I can tell you that there are only two things that make buyers bid on a piece. They want it for the money or they want it for the story.

And even when they want it for the money, it's the story that keeps them bidding as the numbers spiral higher and higher, past the reasonable limit they set, upward, to sweaty and exultant triumph. A young man looking to invest in an artist whose name he mispronounces—but knows is worth a lot—might actually be sold on his own story. Born in a grubby apartment to parents who never finished college, but look at him now—look at all that art on his walls—what a man of taste he must be! Or maybe he's sold on the story of the artist himself, who died young and in debt—a tragedy that our investor finds romantic from his penthouse apartment with park views. Or perhaps it is the story of the piece itself that evokes a single memory—the tilt of the neck on a beautiful girl our investor never got the courage to approach but still burns for in his fitful dreams.

Well, take a look at this next piece and see if its story appeals to you.

Take a good, long look.

It might appear to be a contemporary found-object sculpture, with its speaker-heart and diamond eyes. You might guess it came from a gallery in SoHo, but this piece actually dates from the turn of the century.

The artist, Charlotte Wells, was born in a logging camp in the northeastern part of Maine. Her father was a cook. He and his wife lived in a ramshackle cabin with their three children—John, Toby, and baby Charlotte.

In the winter, food was scarce, and that February had been worse than most. When a black bear was spotted, the loggers tracked it back to its lair and shot it for meat and the warmth of its pelt. As they made ready to drag the dead bear's body back to camp for butchering, they realized it wasn't alone in the cave. A bear cub cried weakly for its mother.

Not sure what to do with it, the men brought the cub back to camp and dumped it in the snow outside the cook's cabin. The bloody flesh of its mother

Eric Orchard's "Portrait of a Bear Unbound (with speaker)"

was brought inside, along with her pelt. Young Toby and John found it and begged their mother to let them keep the little bear.

"There's no food to spare," her husband warned.

"Nonetheless," said Mrs. Wells and nursed the bear cub along with Charlotte.

Mrs. Wells would rest each of them on opposite hips, as though they were twins. It got to be that the bear seemed like just another baby, even sleeping beside Charlotte in her crib, thick fur tickling her nose and teaching her his bestial scent.

They had to call him something, so Mrs. Wells named the bear Liam, after a cousin of whom she'd always been fond.

Liam followed Charlotte around, never wanting to be parted from her side. When she began to crawl, he tottered around on all fours. When she began to walk, he stood up, too, much to the consternation of Mr. and Mrs. Wells.

Charlotte's first word was "Mama."

Liam's first word was "Lottie."

Mr. and Mrs. Wells were surprised, but pleased. Liam turned out to be a quick learner. He had trouble holding an ink pen, and although his penmanship was to be despaired of, he was very good with sums.

And when Charlotte was given a bear-fur cape, made from the pelt of Liam's bear mother and lined in velvet as bright red as droplets of blood in snow, he did not mourn. He barely seemed to recall another life. And if sometimes he grew silent or withdrawn, Charlotte quickly jollied him out of his sulks with some new game.

If Liam and Charlotte were inseparable as children, they were even closer in adolescence, always climbing trees and playing games and pulling at one another's hair. But Liam never seemed to stop growing. Mrs. Wells had to use curtains and bedsheets sewn together for his shirts and trousers. Shoes were hopeless. And no matter how much food he ate, Liam's stomach was always growling for want of enough. He gulped down huge portions of soup, drank the whole kettle's worth of tea, ate an entire loaf of bread at a time, and, on at least one holiday, devoured an entire haunch of salt-cured venison.

By the time he was fifteen, he towered over Mr. Wells and could carry a felled tree on his back. His strength was so great he could no longer control it. One afternoon, while playing a game of tag, he reached for Charlotte, and instead of touching her shoulder lightly with the pad of his paw, he slashed her cheek with his nails.

She screamed, blood soaking her dress, and soon the whole camp was gathered around Liam, looking at him through narrowed eyes. A few had brought rifles.

"He didn't mean to," Charlotte shouted, burying her face against his fur.

The crowd dispersed slowly as she wept, but not before Liam saw in each of their faces that they were afraid, that they had been afraid for a long time. He would never be one of them. Mrs. Wells saw it, too.

"Liam," Mrs. Wells said, later that night. "You can't stay here anymore. It's not safe."

"But Mother," said the bear. "Where will I go?"

"Perhaps it is time for you to be among your own people," said Mrs. Wells.

He looked around the far-too-small kitchen, where even if he hunched over, the tips of his ears scraped the ceiling. He touched the stool that creaked underneath him and glanced across the table at the tiny, bird-boned woman with the silvering hair. "I do not know their ways," said Liam.

Mrs. Wells stroked his cheek like she had when he was small. "Then go to the big city down east. All manner of folk live there. All manner of different customs. Maybe there'll be a place for you, too."

Liam nodded, knowing that she was right. "I will leave in the morning," he said.

Mrs. Wells packed up cheese, bread, apples, preserves, and sausages for his journey. Mr. Wells gave Liam five shiny dollar coins to get him started. John gave him a fishing pole so he'd be able to catch some lunch any time he wanted. Toby gave him a Bible and a flask of the strong liquor they distilled from potato peels. It wasn't a small flask, but in Liam's paw, it might as well have been a thimble.

"Where's Charlotte?" Liam asked. "Won't she come and kiss me good-bye?"

"She's taking this very hard," Mr. Wells said. "Feels responsible."

"Is she very hurt?" asked Liam, thinking of the marks on her face. Wondering if they would scar. Wondering how it would be for her if they did, for she was thought of as a great beauty and much admired. Would that change?

"She'll get better," said John. "Lottie knows you didn't mean to hurt her."

"And we all know she's not vain," said Toby, which made Liam feel even worse. Toby's mouth lifted on one side. "I wager you'll always be her favorite."

"Tell her," Liam said in his deep, growling voice. "Tell her that I will write."

"Of course," said Mrs. Wells, neither of them mentioning that mail took ages to find its way up to their town.

He embraced them, one by one. He tried to be as gentle as he could, tried not to crush them against him, tried not to press his nose against their necks as he drew the scent of them into his lungs one final time.

Then, sack of food tied to the fishing pole, fishing pole slung over his shoulder, Liam started the long journey south.

He walked for half the day, stopping to eat everything Mrs. Wells had packed for him. His stomach hurt less, but self-pity still gnawed at his gut.

That night, he slept under the stars. A cool breeze tickled his fur, his ears twitched, and he could almost imagine that he had always lived this way. He was tempted to throw away his rod and flask, to strip off his clothes, and never to walk upright again.

It thrilled him and made him afraid, all at once.

For three days and three nights, he journeyed thus. He spoke no words on his journey—there was no one to speak to—and although sometimes the smells of humans and woodsmoke gusted toward him, they were being replaced with the vivid smells of crushed pine needles and the clotted sap of trees.

One morning, he stopped at a river to catch his breakfast. Slowly, he waded into the water on all fours, the bright, bubbling river shockingly, joyously cold. He felt every pebble against the pads of his paws. He reached out to sweep a silvery fish into the air, where he knew he would catch it between his teeth. Just then, the wind changed directions, blowing a familiar scent to his twitching nose.

He stood and lumbered into the woods.

Charlotte was running toward him, wrapped in the fur of his mother, the cloak's lining as bright as blood. A dirty and tear-stained bandage still covered her face.

Her eyes went wide.

For a moment, he imagined roaring up and striking her down. He imagined chewing her up, sinew and bones. He imagined being a bear and nothing more.

Then he remembered himself.

"Charlotte," he said, his voice cracking with disuse. Three long days in the forest had almost made him lose his human speech.

She was shivering with cold. She went to him and pressed herself against him, so that, with her cloak, he didn't know where he ended and she began.

"I'm sorry," he said gruffly, trying not to rest his claws against her, even gently. He was apologizing for what was beneath the bandages, but also for the terrible thoughts he tried to put out of his mind. "Very, truly sorry."

"What you are is wet," she said, with a laugh. "And your nose is cold."

With those words, he knew he was forgiven.

He gathered wood and Charlotte made a fire, talking the whole time. She told him about her plan to sneak out and come with him. She told him how cleverly she'd snuck out of the house with her little suitcase and waited for him by the ford in the road. But, as time passed, she realized he must have taken a different road entirely. She headed out after him, thinking she might yet catch him, but by nightfall, although she was sure she was following the right road, there was no sign of Liam.

"And such sounds the night makes!" she told him. "I was sure I was going to be eaten up by wolves. I barely slept a wink!"

Her relief was so great that she couldn't stop talking. His happiness was so great that he was content to listen.

"But why did you come?" he asked finally.

"I can't let you have all the adventures," she told him. "The world is bigger than one logging town, big enough for you. And since I am so small, I figure I might be able to fit in it, too."

He smiled big enough to show a row of white teeth.

And so, together, they journeyed south. Charlotte picked berries from bushes and Liam fished from streams and lakes without his rod, wading in and tossing gleaming trout onto the bank.

Sometimes Charlotte set traps and caught tiny birds that crunched between Liam's teeth.

At night, Charlotte and Liam covered themselves in a blanket of leaves and curled up together, telling stories until they fell asleep.

Finally, they saw the city in the hazy distance. It seemed to be sculpted from red brick and chimney smoke. As they drew closer, they passed more and bigger houses. Motorcars whizzed by, ladies turning their scarved heads to stare at the bear and his sister.

Liam stared back, full of awe.

"We will make our fortunes here," Charlotte said, dancing her way across the cobblestones, her scuffed boots as elegant on her as any slipper. "Here, everything is going to happen."

They were poor, but they managed to rent a little apartment, and when Liam's head brushed the lintel, it made them smile.

Liam got work loading boxes along the docks while Charlotte made a little money by sweeping up for a taxidermist whose office was a few streets over. He specialized in creating curiosities like fishes covered in fur, chimeras, tiny griffins, and fossilized fairies. Sometimes he let her stroke her finger carefully across a fox pelt before attaching chicken wings to the creature's back.

Sometimes, too, they would go to the cinema, where movie villains tied bow-lipped starlets to the tracks. Liam had to sit in the back, because he was so large, but Charlotte sat with him and they shared candy corn in little funnel cups.

Liam loved the city. He was strange, but in a place that delighted in strangeness. Everywhere that Liam turned, there were odd fashions, unfamiliar foods, and stores selling things of which he never could have dreamed. And he loved his job—unloading and loading exotic things heading from and to far-off places. Occasionally, one of the boxes didn't make it to its destination, and those nights Liam brought home a cloudy bottle of bourbon or a pound of coffee beans so strong that they woke the whole building when they were brewed. Just the scent of them was enough to make your heart race.

And, heart already racing, Liam met a girl. Her name was Rose, and the first time he saw her, she'd just broken the heel off of one dove-grey shoe. He carried her all the way to the boardinghouse where she lived. The other girls giggled when they spotted the bear lumbering up the steps, and the stern woman running the place even let him take a cup of tea in the kitchen, remarking that she'd never seen shoulders as broad or teeth as white on Rose's other suitors.

Turned out, Rose was a seamstress. When her long hours in the factory were over, she sewed herself smart dresses, each more beautiful than the last.

By the time he got back to their apartment, Charlotte could see that Liam was in love.

All he talked about was Rose. He told Charlotte about her soft hands, the way her bright blond hair fell around her face in soft curls, the way her clothes were always stiff with starch and freshly pressed, the no-nonsense way she told him about nearly getting arrested for smoking. She and her friends had to run away from a policeman, in their stiff corsets, ducking into a sweet shop and hiding in the bathroom. According to Rose, it had been a near thing.

Rose was always getting into scrapes. She had dozens of friends, most of them male. And she always had perfume to dot behind her ears and at the pulse points of her wrists.

Charlotte didn't like Rose, but she bit her tongue to keep from saying so. For so long it had just been Charlotte and Liam in the world, but though they had endured all other things together, love was something they must each endure alone.

"I want to marry her," Liam said.

Charlotte just nodded as she rolled out dough for pie. Cooked all together with gravy, the bits and pieces of the week's meals tasted just fine. She made two—a generous slice for her and the rest for Liam—then, as an afterthought, sliced a piece that he could take to Rose.

"She will be like a sister for you," Liam said.

Charlotte nodded again. The taste of copper pennies flooded her mouth, she was biting her tongue so hard.

Sometimes, when he was with Rose, Liam wished he could open up his fur like it was a cloak and wrap it around her.

But he did what he thought was expected of him. He looked for a better job and found one—as a stonemason, lifting slabs of marble and setting them with precision. He took Rose to his apartment, where Charlotte cooked them a whole ham. He bought her a pair of gloves sewn of lace so fine he was afraid his claws would pull it. When he asked Rose to marry him, he went to one knee, although he still towered over her chair, and shut his eyes. He could not bear to see her expression.

In lieu of a ring, he had scrimped and saved to buy her a pair of diamond earrings. They sparkled in their box like tiny stars. His palm quavered with nerves.

"I cannot marry you," Rose said, "for you are a bear and I am a woman."

And so he went away and wept. Charlotte made him a gooseberry pie, but he wouldn't eat it.

When he returned, he brought with him a long strand of pearls, each one fat and perfect as the moon.

Although Rose wrapped the strand around her neck three times, she replied again, "I cannot marry you. You are a bear and I am a woman."

Again he went away and wept. This time, Charlotte baked him scones. He picked at a few of the raisins.

"If she doesn't love you," said Charlotte, "she will only bring you sorrow."

"I love her enough for us both," said Liam and Charlotte could say no more.

The third time he went to Rose, he brought with him a golden ring as bright as the sun.

This time, greed and desire overtook her, and she said, "Even though you are a bear and I am a woman, I will marry you."

The bear's happiness was so vast and great that he wanted to roar. Instead, he took her little hands in his and promised her that he would put aside his bear nature and be like other men for as long as they were wed.

This time, Charlotte baked them a wedding cake, and Liam and Rose ate it together, slice by slice.

After Liam and Rose married, Charlotte moved out of the little apartment and took a room above the taxidermist's shop.

She had more time to help out, and so the taxidermist showed her how to cut wires and wrap them in perfumed cotton to give life to the skins. He showed her how to choose glass eyes that fit snugly in the sockets. He told her about Martha Maxwell, one of the founders of modern taxidermy, whose work he had once seen.

Time passed and Liam seemed happy as ever, doting on Rose. But Rose grew distant and vague. She stopped sewing and sat around the house in a dressing gown, plates piling up in the sink.

"What's wrong?" Charlotte asked, when she came over to bring them her very first attempt at taxidermy—a tiny bird with black eyes and feathers it had taken her a whole day to arrange. The taxidermist had told Charlotte that she had the touch, nodding approvingly as he walked around the piece.

Rose curled her lip at the sight of it. "Liam's not home."

"Can I leave it for him?" Charlotte asked.

Rose looked resigned, but allowed her into the house. As Rose turned, Charlotte saw the swell of her stomach.

She grinned and would have embraced Rose, would have babbled on with congratulations, would have offered to knit blankets and pick out ribbons, but Rose gave her such a look that Charlotte hesitated and only set the little bird down very carefully on the arm of Liam's chair.

Two nights later, Liam roused Charlotte from her bed in the middle of the night.

"There's something wrong with her," the bear said. "She's dying, Charlotte."

"What happened?" Charlotte said.

He shook his massive head. "She took something—I found the vial. To get rid of the baby. She said she could feel the little claws scratching at her insides. She said she dreamed of sharp teeth."

There was no doctor for many streets, so Charlotte woke the taxidermist from his bed, thinking he might know what to do. Rose had gone into labor by the time they got there.

All night long they laid cold compresses on her brow and grabbed her hands as she screamed through contractions. But the poison in the vial had stained her tongue black and robbed her of strength.

After hours of struggle, the child was born. A small bear child, already dead.

Rose died soon after.

Liam fell to all fours. "I tried to live as a man," he said, "but I am a bear in my blood."

"Liam!" Charlotte called, running to him and touching his back, sinking her fingers into his fur. "Bear or man, you are my brother."

But he turned away, lumbering down the stairs. He cast away his clothes and his boots as he came to the outskirts of the city. He entered the forest and would never walk upright or speak again.

Charlotte held the bear child to her, though it was cold as snow.

"I will call the necessary people," said the taxidermist. He looked uncomfortably at Rose's body, growing pale and strange. Death was something he was used to seeing at a remove. "You shouldn't have to see this—a young lady like you—"

But Charlotte ignored him. She recognized the scent of the child, the smell of Liam, as familiar as her own. "He's warming up," said Charlotte.

The taxidermist frowned. "The child is dead."

"Can't you hear him?" she asked. "He's crying for his father."

"Please, Charlotte, you must—" began the taxidermist, but then he paused. He could hear a low, thready sound, like weeping.

Closer and closer he came, until he was sure the sound came from the body in her hands.

"We will save him," Charlotte said.

They made this piece together, imbedding a speaker in the little bear's chest to amplify the sound and giving him Rose's diamond earrings in place of eyes. This, the first of many marvelous and wonderful creations by Charlotte Wells. Each one, it is said, came nearly alive under her touch. Nearly.

But does it still cry? I'm sure that's what you're wondering. Come closer, lean in. The little bear has something different to tell each one of you.

Lottery ticket numbers.

Messages from lost lovers.

Predictions for the future.

Oh, you want to know what *I* heard when I leaned near the speaker? Only this—that whomsoever is the next buyer will have luck and fortune for the rest of his days!

Think of the story.

I believe it's time for the bidding to begin.

A Short History of Dunkelblau's Meistergarten

By Tad Williams

One of the more unusual education devices ever designed was the Meistergarten of Ernst Dunkelblau, the "Pedagogue of Linz." When it was first presented to the public in 1905, it was called "The Eighth Wonder of the World" by some newspapers of the day, "The Devil's Carousel" by others. All agreed, however, that its like had never been seen before.

"It resembles a Lazy Susan," commented a reporter for America's *New York World,* "but instead of spinning to present dishes to be served, its revolutionary motion is meant to deliver children to Scholarship."

The Inventor: Ernst A. Dunkelblau

Little can be understood of either the Meistergarten or its products without first examining the life of its creator, Ernst Adelbert Dunkelblau.

Dunkelblau was born in a suburb of Linz, Austria, in 1859. His father was one of the engineers who designed and built the first iron bridge over the Danube, but his mother, Heilwig, had even bigger plans for her only child, and from a very early age little Ernst was given the benefit of her fascination with childhood learning. The acknowledged star of European education at the time was Friedrich Fröbel, famous for his ideas of the kindergarten—a place where children would learn through play. Frau Dunkelblau, however, was a stern woman who felt that the currently fashionable dogma was totally reversed—that children should learn by suffering, not play. She developed her own method, which she called *"Arbeit und Verletzung,"* or "Work and Injury," and employed it along with a very ambitious curriculum for her infant son, which she had determined would prepare him to enter a good Austrian university by the time he was twelve years old. In fact, Ernst Dunkelblau was accepted to the Karl-Franzens-Universität, better known today as the University of Graz, at the prodigious age of ten.

Young Dunkelblau never graduated from the university, however. Rumors of the day linked him to a scandal with a much older woman, the wife of a university custodian, who claimed that young Dunkelblau offered her a florin to "nap upon her bosom." Accounts subsequent to his death suggest that Dunkelblau never entirely overcame this troubling propensity for offering money to women not of his own family; in later years the significance of this weakness became so divisive among European Freudians that there were violent differences of opinion about it—indeed, there are reports of a famous fight in a London café between Otto Rank and Melanie Klein, in which Klein was said to have slapped Rank so hard and so often that he was led away weeping and for weeks would only see patients with a scarf draped over his face.

Much of Ernst Dunkelblau's personal history between the years of 1871 and 1899 is hazy, little more than rumor and innuendo. It is known that he served briefly in the Austro-Hungarian army as a telegrapher, but was discharged because so many of his messages contained interpolated phrases such as "Ernst is scared," "sleepy dumplings," or simply the word *"Mutti"* ("Mommy") typed over and over, none of which bore any relationship to the military messages young Dunkelblau had been tasked with sending.

Apparently, he also found time during these years to finish his education, graduating from a small university in Triesen, Liechtenstein, called the Todkrank-Igil Institute. Little more is known, because the university was subsequently burned to the ground by local villagers and its records lost.

Many of Dunkelblau's later experiments in pedagogy, including the famous Meistergarten, seem to have roots in his Liechtenstein student period, because his adult writings on the subject of educational psychology frequently contain phrases, such as "two-schilling Vaduz Mustache" and "bloody Triesen pitchforks ouch ouch," which seem to trace to this time.

However, with 1899 and his return to Linz, we see the triumphant execution of designs and ideas that had obviously been building in Dunkelblau's mind for some time, culminating that year in the opening of the St. Agnes Blannbekin Private School for Boys and Girls, an institute under Dunkelblau's personal supervision. The doctor was described by one of the school's first students as "a great, smiling, bearded Father Christmas of a man" and "a performing bear, quick to growl, quick to eat off the plates of others, but also swift with a booming laugh or a sudden storm of tears caused by the frustrations of his work."

In 1905, after some period of experimentation with mechanical equipment and the selection of a first set of human test subjects, Dunkelblau unveiled his magnum opus to the Austrian and international press: the Meistergarten.

John Coulthart's painstaking reconstruction of the Meistergarten.

The Meistergarten

The machine itself was described in a subsequent legal deposition by a lawyer for the family of one of the children:

> It was the size of a very small fairground ride, and, in fact, bore much of the appearance of a children's carousel, being circular, a little less than three meters in diameter, and profusely decorated in the very ornamented style of the time with baroque leaves and vines. At the center, a bit larger than the human original it sought to emulate, was the bronze head that contained the speaking tube and the audio tubes and various other bits of the mechanism that would allow it to interact with the youthful subjects.

The machine itself (although most of the gears and tubes were hidden from view by the panels on the outside of the Meistergarten) was designed as both a teaching resource and a self-contained supply of everything by way of health and nurture that the child subjects would need. The bronze head that took pride of place at the center of the Meistergarten, perched much as a bride and groom might stand in the middle of a wedding cake, was created in the image of a classical sculpture of a goddess, but with a hinged jaw and small lightbulbs behind the isinglass of the eyes. It would turn on a swivel to listen or speak to the children in turn. A correct answer would solicit a mechanical smile (signaled by a grinding noise as the jaws rubbed together) and various invisible caresses on the student's unprotected skin within the body of the machine. A wrong answer would cause the automaton's eyes to flash red and its mouth to gape widely as it gave forth a loud klaxon that some observers called "horrifying," but Doktor Dunkelblau called "usefully arresting."

Other facilities for the better promotion of learning had been built into the Meistergarten but were not immediately revealed by the staff of the St. Agnes Blannbekin school.

The Subjects

"Die Berühmten Fünf," or "The Famous Five," as the first child subjects were known, had been handpicked by Dunkelblau himself because he felt they would be "uniquely susceptible" to this new kind of learning, which he sometimes referred to as his *"Automatische* Super-Mama," but more often as simply "The System."

The names of these first volunteers, or at least the names by which they were known in the literature surrounding the experiment, were:

Trudl K., 7 years old, from Linz
Wouter S., 9 years old, from Passau
Franz F., 8 years old, from Linz
Helga W., 8 years old, from Scherding
Lorenz D., 7 years old, from Radstadt

These students (or, rather, their parents) had agreed that they would spend at least the next three years as part of Dunkelblau's experiment—joined to the apparatus, with all their needs satisfied by the machine while they received the most complete and thorough education of any human child ever. Or so was Dunkelblau's assertion; the results of his groundbreaking experiment and the value of his data are still in dispute to this very day.

Some later researchers have claimed that Ernst Dunkelblau chose his subjects by nonstandard criteria that included "interesting distress noises," "shape of feet and nose," and, in one case, that of Helga W., because the young girl had "a tantalizingly brilliant future in Music or the Arts," epitomized by her singing voice and early grace at the Austrian *Boarischer*, the polka, and other folk dances.

The Experiment

The name of Dunkelblau's invention, Der Meistergarten, was a play on Fröber's famous "kindergarten"—a children's garden. Ernst Dunkelblau, though, did not plan simply to educate children, but to create "masters," students who would be superior to ordinary children in every way, as Dunkelblau had felt himself to be.

"I was a nightingale in a cage full of croaking ravens" is how he once described his time at the University of Graz. "My little, sweet, and sensible voice could not be heard above the cacophonous din of the other so-called scholars. . . ."

So it was that the Famous Five were "assigned to the System," in Dunkelblau's phrase, in September 1905 at his school in Linz. Completely immobilized by machinery from the neck down, the children were catheterized for waste disposal and fitted with feeding tubes that periodically pumped meals (a slurry of oats, root vegetables, and some meat products) directly into their stomachs. The inside of the Meistergarten device also contained a number of specialty appendages, which were not displayed to the children, capable of administering to their hidden bodies comforting pats and caresses as well as pinches and slaps.

The Meistergarten was then closed and the neck-rings sealed, so that all that could be seen of the subjects were their heads, all facing in toward the center of the circular Meistergarten, which was set in an otherwise empty, mirrored hall specially prepared by Dunkelblau at the St. Agnes Blannbekin school. Observers watched the experiment from behind the one-way mirrors lining the large room. From that moment on, the subjects had no other direct human contact. The machinery of the Meistergarten itself was serviced during the subjects' sleeping period by silent custodial workers and mechanics dressed in black robes and hoods. If the children seemed restless on service nights, a mixture of nitrous oxide and chloroform was pumped into the System Hall so that they would not be unduly bothered by the presence of the dark figures.

From the moment of their introduction into the Meistergarten until their release, the subjects interacted only with the bronze head at the center of the machine, nicknamed Minerva. In an effort not to confuse the subjects with old associations, Dunkelblau decided against an overly sympathetic "female presence" for his invention: at the last moment, he cancelled a contract with well-known stage actress Lottelore Eisenbaum, who would have contributed Minerva's voice, and took on the role himself, speaking to the students in a strained, falsetto, "female" voice with as little emotional inflection as possible, attempting to create what he called "a true Machine Mother Sound." One of his research assistants said that twenty years later she still "woke up wailing and weeping" after dreaming of the Minerva voice.

The children were roused from sleep each morning by the sound of Minerva's wake-up call, a loud, ratcheting shriek based on Dunkelblau's idea that, of all noises, the most perfect focus of attention could be created by the sound of an industrial accident coupled with an expression of human terror. After the previous night's meal had been pumped out of their system and a new meal pumped in, the students began a long and rigorous day of history, mathematics, natural sciences, Greek and Latin, and some unusual coursework of Dunkelblau's own devising, including Lesion Studies, Practical Engorgement, and Social Attack Theory. They were taught by the rote method, instructed by "Minerva" (in reality, Dunkelblau, of course, watching from the far side of a one-way mirror and speaking into a tube) and immediately corrected for each error on a rising scale of reprisal that began at "Lightly Bruising Pinch with Flashing Eyes" and peaked at "Flare, Shriek, and Scourge" (at which point, the subject usually had to be sedated for at least twenty-four hours to allow recovery and what Dunkelblau termed "deeper learning").

Correct answers received praise from "Minerva" and sometimes also the singing of a verse of *"Hejo, Spann den Wagen an,"* one of Dunkelblau's favorite songs from his childhood:

Hey ho! Hitch up the cart,
For the wind brings rain over the land.
Fetch the golden sheaves,
Fetch the golden sheaves . . .

The student who answered Minerva correctly was also rewarded by the activation of certain bladders within the machinery that, when inflated, gave a pleasurable sensation.

Problems

The first real controversy about Dunkelblau's experiment came in December 1905, when the parents of Trudl K. asked that their daughter be released from the System for the Christmas holidays and were refused. They were denied a similar request at Easter as well. In her unhappy missive to the doctor, Frau K. wrote, "Our daughter's letters appear to be written by someone other than our daughter. The last three have all said exactly the same thing, 'Do not come visit—it will interrupt the important work we are doing here, work that will forever confound the servile devotees of that ape Fröbel and his "Child-Garden"!' We find it hard to believe," Mrs. K continued, "that our daughter cares greatly about Friedrich Fröbel, who died almost a half century before she was born, and we have also heard disquieting rumors from neighbors of the St. Agnes school that children can be heard throughout the day and night, moaning, weeping, and even barking like distressed dogs. . . ."

A year later her parents were given permission by the Bildungsministerium, the Austrian educational authority, to remove their daughter from Dunkelblau's machine. Perhaps piqued by their withdrawal from the experiment, Herr Doktor Dunkelblau ordered that Trudl be delivered to her parents' house at night in a device he called an "Egress Chrysalis," which the K. family claimed was little more than a conventional straitjacket augmented with a canvas sack over the patient's head.

Schooling continued for the other four subjects despite some odd malfunctions from the Meistergarten, in which Minerva continued to speak as though the missing child was still part of the experiment and would even dole out stinging electrical shocks to the remaining subjects for "teasing poor little Trudl."

The End of the Experiment

The remaining four children all stayed in the Meistergarten for the duration of the planned three-year period, without parental interference. In fact, by the time the Meistergarten was opened and the students removed, the parents of Franz F. and Lorenz D. could not be easily located. The family of Franz F. proved to have moved to Swabia in Germany and at first maintained that they had no child. The D. family, still in Linz, did not deny young Lorenz was theirs, but argued that they had "sold" him to Dunkelblau and that, by giving him back, Dunkelblau was reneging on their agreement.

The scandal over Trudl K. had died down at last, but when little Franz F., now almost eleven years old and newly returned home, attacked and bit a postman so badly that the man nearly bled to death, the newspapers again picked up the story, many of them painting Dunkelblau as "irresponsible" and "unscientific." Dunkelblau responded in a famous letter to the editor of the *Linzer Volksblatt,* stating "the hounds of Conventionality can sniff my arse to their hearts' content—all they will discover is the scent of Genius leaving them far behind!"

The Aftermath

Ernst A. Dunkelblau never published his results of his experiment, claiming that "the general population is not capable of understanding the sublime heights of Truth we have scaled here." In later years, the St. Agnes Blannbekin school was closed by the Linz authorities. A special squadron of Bundesheer troops took away the Meistergarten itself, which had fallen into disrepair—the head of Minerva was currently being used by the school as a gramophone horn for folk-dancing practice—but the final disposition of the rest of the famous device is unknown. The Minerva head was reportedly displayed in a 1938 British auction house catalog, listed as "macabre pseudo-classical ash tray," but its current whereabouts are also a mystery.

Dunkelblau himself died in Linz in 1932, in the Altstadt apartment of a "working woman," murdered by parties unknown. At the time of his death by strangulation, the doctor was dressed in the costume of a nineteenth-century schoolboy, complete with rucksack (which, for some reason, was stuffed full of boiled eggplant) and a false mustache. The false mustache was a particularly odd detail, because it was smaller than the doctor's own mustache, over which it had been affixed.

The Lives of the "Famous Five"

TRUDL K.: After she was removed from the Meistergarten and the school, little is known about this subject. In the 1920s, when Dunkelblau was much in the news, various stories appeared in the newspapers to suggest she had become a (not very successful) music-hall performer or acrobat in Vienna. None of this was ever proved, although to this day, in Austria, a street mime is still called a "Shrieking Trudl." When she died in 1948 in a Graz hospital, her obituary noted only that she had "been part of a famous educational experiment, and later married a Polish animal trainer."

FRANZ F.: Although best known for his attack on a postman in 1908, Franz F. had perhaps the most unusual history of any of the Meistergarten subjects. When the Great War began, he enlisted under an assumed name in the Austro-Hungarian army and rose through the ranks by dint of almost heedless courage under fire. He was nicknamed *Der Werwolf* by his comrades and reputedly crossed no-man's-land every night to bedevil the enemy, dressed only in a kilt made from the scalps of his victims. In fact, a vast collection of body parts in glass jars, known as "Franz's Toys," is reportedly still hidden in a back room of the Museum of Military History in Vienna. After the war, Franz F. disappeared from public view, although a few historians insist he was eventually hunted down and killed in the Bohemian Forest by a specially trained team of Austrian police led by an American Cherokee Indian tracker, William First Bear.

LORENZ D., described by Dunkelblau as "a quiet, unassuming child," never spoke a distinguishable word after being part of the Meistergarten system, although he sang wordlessly and laughed and even screamed without visible cause for the rest of his life. He was institutionalized in 1916 and began to paint, primarily "huge, barren landscapes peopled by burning mice and human-headed octopuses," as a nurse described them. He also climbed walls with great skill, and was often to be found by his caretakers curled up in the institution's overhead light fixtures, asleep. Lorenz D.'s family never questioned their own judgement in letting him be part of Dunkelblau's experiment, and described those who criticized their choice as "pitiful" and "jealous," despite their own lack of interest in visiting Lorenz after he was institutionalized.

HELGA W., whose "brilliant future" in the arts never materialized, nevertheless did become a performer of sorts. Witnesses in the 1930s identified her as the "Hard-Boiled Egg Woman" in Berlin's infamous Der Eigenartige Wandschrank club, who was said to be able to fling an egg fifteen meters with her reproductive parts while leading the crowd in singing *"Wir Wollen Alle Kinder Sein!"*

WOUTER K., the most materially successful of the doctor's subjects, founded a number of private hospitals for the care of "difficult children" (which, some alleged, were merely "holding cells" for the unwanted offspring of the wealthy) and then funneled the profits into the manufacture of chemical agents such as mustard gas, which was banned after the Great War by all sides but still bought and stockpiled by many nations for years after, so that Wouter K. became known in international military circles as "Meister Senf," or "Mister Mustard." Soon his factories were making many other kinds of poisons as well, and his scientists are linked to the discovery of the infamous G-series poison gases, including sarin, tabun, and cyclosarin. Wouter K. made millions but used the money primarily to shield himself from the public eye, and was not heard from again until he issued the following "proclamation" to the world's leading newspapers in early 1939:

> The work of Doktor Adelbert Dunkelblau has been much maligned in the international press, especially by those whose minds are too small to understand his vision. What his work proved was not that the Meistergarten was unworkable, or a "crackpot" scheme, as some have termed it, but simply that the experimental sample was too small. I was one of five subjects, and I have become one of the world's most successful and richest men. Surely a success rate of twenty percent is not to be mocked, especially with a discovery that will *literally change the world.* A generation of supermen is a goal that no one can fault, and I will provide the first seeds for that wondrous human accomplishment. Twenty percent. It is something to think about—something to thrill the human soul!
>
> I have purchased a quantity of land—no one will know where!—and on that site I shall build Dunkelblau's Meistergarten anew. But instead of five, I shall commit five hundred or even five thousand subjects to the test (there are orphanages the world over that will happily contribute their superfluity), and from these humble materials will our first generation of *"Meistermenschen"* be born. But unlike the clownish National Socialists of the current German government, our gifted ones will not reveal themselves, let alone brag of their superiority, but instead they will turn around and create newer, larger generations of others like them, until one day we shall emerge from the wild places where we have hidden ourselves and take our true place as leaders of a fallen, but not entirely hopeless, world. Be warned! On that day, *everything* will change.

It was rumored in some circles that throughout the 1920s and 1930s "Wouter K." secretly bought extensive tracts of land in the largely unexplored Chaco Boreal region on the border between Paraguay and Bolivia. Others claim his major holdings were uninhabited volcanic islands in the South Atlantic and Southern Ocean. In either case, to this day, nothing definitive has ever been heard of the last Dunkelblau test subject, and although a few businesses with the name "Meistergarten" have shown up in international registries from places as distantly separated as Franz Joseph Land in the Arctic and Dar Es Salaam, Tanzania, no sign of the promised "first generation of *Meistermenschen*" has yet been seen. However, it is clear that even at this late date, the book on Dunkelblau's experiment cannot quite be closed for good.

MICROBIAL ALCHEMY
and Demented Machinery
The Mignola Exhibits

The Mignola Exhibits

The artifacts researched as part of the Mignola Exhibits tend to reflect *Hellboy* creator Mike Mignola's own fascination with Lambshead's cabinet. Mignola says he first remembers reading about Lambshead "in a comic when I was nine—it was one of those two-page spreads they used to fill space, with a title like 'Strange but True.' It might've been a *Tales from the Crypt*."

The images of such iconic Lambshead pieces as the Clockroach were originally intended for an abandoned Mignola project titled *Subsequently Lost at Sea,* which would have been a detailed illustrated chronicle of, as Mignola puts it, "important stuff that got lost at sea." The book would have reached back as far as the Romans with their "often unreliable galleys." Mignola feels the results "would've been as important to the study of all kinds of crap lost at sea as Alasdair Gray's *Book of Prefaces* is to the study of the English language."

The pieces documented herein were initially lost at sea in the spring of 2003, following an urgent directive from Lambshead that rescinded the museum loans on the Clockroach, Roboticus mask, Shamalung, and Pulvadmonitor.

Lambshead's directive sent the exhibits to the Museum of Further Study in Jakarta, Indonesia, all by circuitous routes. Roboticus and Shamalung left via the HMS *Dorsal Fin of God,* which disappeared seventy miles west of the Canary Islands. The USS *Jeraboam II,* carrying the Clockroach, was captured by pirates off the coast of Somalia, led by, as the BBC put it, "What looked like someone's Greek great-grandmother with a knife in her teeth," who managed to elude U.S. and British naval units during a heavy storm. *The Baalbek,* flying the Libyan flag and carrying a twice-hermetically sealed Pulvadmonitor, vanished off the Horn of Africa. (Some—specifically, Caitlín R. Kiernan—have suggested that the route of the freighters and the points at which they disappeared form a complex message from Lambshead "to parties unknown," if we could only interpret it.)

By then, the good doctor's heart had finally given out and his heirs countermanded his orders, an act that seemed to have no agency. However, astoundingly enough, Roboticus, Shamalung, and the Pulvadmonitor (babbling incoherently) turned up at Lord Balfoy's Antiques on London's Portobello Road two years later, selling for fifty pounds apiece. The artifacts were turned over to the Museum of Intangible Arts and Objects in Saragossa, Spain, where experts eventually confirmed that all three pieces now met "all of our requirements regarding Immateriality, Intangibility, Elusiveness, and the Ephemeral." When the objects were returned to their respective museums, the attendants therein seemed united behind Billy Quirt—thirty-year velvet-rope veteran of Imperial War exhibits—in believing that the artifacts are "a bloody lot more and a bloody lot less than they were before they went traveling."

The predicament does underscore one reason Mignola abandoned the book: "Too much stuff eventually washes up. Sometimes just when you'd like it to stay lost. I'd rather just draw stuff that's always there, like monsters."

Addison Howell and the Clockroach

Documented by Cherie Priest

Museum Name and Location: The Stackpole Museum of Prototypical Industry; Port Angeles, Washington

Name of Exhibit: Pioneer Myths and Lore in Peninsular Victoriana

Category information

Creator: Addison Sobiesky Howell (alleged); American, born 1828 in Chicago, Illnois. Died 1899 in Humptulips, Washington

Title: "Clockroach," built 1878(?)

Medium: Mixed, primarily steel, cast iron, rubber tubing, and glass

Source: Donated in 1953 by the Museum of History and Industry in Seattle, Washington, at cost of transportation—and a gentleman's agreement with regards to subsequent restoration and display

Accession number: 1953.99

Exhibit Introduction Panel: Pioneer Myths and Lore in Peninsular Victoriana

The Olympic Peninsula has long been home to a number of Native American tribes, including the Hoh, Makah, and the Quileute; but it was not until the second half of the nineteenth century that it became settled by white homesteaders. Primarily, these homesteaders were farmers and loggers, lured by the Homestead Act of 1862 and the promise of a temperate climate.

Though much can be said about the Native traditions and myths, this exhibit focuses on the rural homesteaders and their inevitable bedtime or campfire stories—some of which were regarded with a seriousness that borders on the charmingly naïve or dangerously optimistic, as evidenced by the items on display.

Highlights of the collection include:

(1908.32, items a-g) Filbert Seyfarth's assortment of "vampire-killing" poisons. These anti-undead concoctions were understandably unpopular—considering that, given a vampire's traditional diet, the poisons must first be consumed by a potential victim (presumably, of the suicidally game-for-anything variety).

(1912.11) Earl Lenning's Skoocooms Mesmerizing Ray (patent no. D224,997), a trigger-operated light-projecting contraption intended to befuddle a creature now better known as "Sasquatch." The existence of this device leads some researchers to suspect that a Native American practical joker enjoyed a hearty laugh at Mr. Lenning's expense.

(1953.99) Addison Howell's "Clockroach," a one-man, quasi-lobster-shaped vehicle allegedly designed and driven by an aloof, peculiar craftsman who was rumored to be the devil himself.

We at the Stackpole Museum of Prototypical Industry would like to welcome you to this exhibit and invite you to ask questions. However, we ask that you not touch the Clockroach—nor allow children to climb upon it and make the *choo-choo* noise, as this is both contextually inappropriate and bound to result in tetanus shots for all concerned.

Clockroach: The Legend

(Oral tradition transcribed by UW graduate student Gregory Blum from an interview with Petra Oberg [1902–1996], daughter of Isac and Emma Johnson—two of Humptulips' original settlers.)

Addison Howell didn't so much arrive in Humptulips as appear there sometime around 1875. He had money, which set him apart from everybody else—because everybody else was working for the logging company, and mostly they didn't have a pot to piss in, as my daddy put it.[1]

Mr. Howell built himself a house, way outside of town, a big three-story place set back in the hills—and you couldn't see it until you were right on top of it, what with all the trees.

He had a wife with him at one point, but she died up there. Folks said he'd murdered her with an ax, but there was never any proof of that and we didn't have any law at the time nohow, not a sheriff or anything, much less a jail. We had a mayor, though—a fellow named Herp Jones—and I think if Herp could've rounded up enough warm bodies, he would've seen to a lynch mob.[2] But everyone he might've asked was either working or drinking, so I guess that didn't happen.

The town gave Mrs. Howell a Christian burial in a little plot back behind the only church we had, and her guilty-as-sin husband paid a pretty penny to have a crypt built up around her. It was a real big deal, because nobody else in town had ever gotten a crypt, and only about half the folks who ever died even got a tomb

Addison Howell on his Clockroach

stone.[3] Then Mr. Howell went back to his house in the trees, and, for the most part, nobody hardly ever saw him again.

A few years later, as I heard it, Addison Howell was out and about doing whatever it is a wicked man does on a Sunday, and he came across a homesteader's camp just off the old logging road. There was a wagon with a broken axle, and two dead men lying beside a campfire. It looked like they'd been tore up by wolves, or maybe mountain lions, or somesuch creature. But inside the wagon he heard a little girl crying. He looked inside and she screamed, and she bit him—because like attracts like, I suppose, and the girl had a bad streak in her, too. That's why he took her home with him.

She was maybe eight or nine when he brought her inside, and legend has it she was mute. Or maybe she didn't feel like talking, I couldn't say. . . . [4] . . . Anyway, he raised her as his own, and they lived together in the house in the hills, and nobody ever visited them because everybody knew they were doing evil things up there.[5]

But people started telling stories about hearing strange noises out there at night, like someone was whacking on metal with a hammer, or sawing through steel. Word got around that he was building a machine that looked like a big bug, or a lobster, or something. It had a big stack on top and it was steam-powered, or coal-powered, or anyway it was supposed to move around when he was sitting inside it.

I don't know who was fool-headed enough to get close enough to listen, but somebody did, and somebody talked.

And later on, the mayor and some friends of his, all of them with guns and itchy trigger fingers, went up to that house and demanded to know what was going on up there. For all they knew, he was summoning Satan,[6] or beating up that girl,[7] or raising whatever kind of hell I just don't know.

Addison Howell told them they were welcome to look around, so they did. They didn't find anything, and they were mad about it. They asked the girl what was going on, but she wouldn't say nothing and they thought maybe she was scared of Howell, and that's why she wasn't being helpful. But she was a teenager by then, or old enough that she could live there with a dirty old man if she felt like it, and people'd look askance, but no one would take her away.

Not long after that, Addison Howell went into town to do some business—he was over at the logging foreman's place, and nobody has any idea why, or what they were talking about. They got into some kind of fight—the foreman's wife overheard it and she came out and saw them struggling, so she took her husband's shotgun and she blew the back of Addison Howell's head clean off, and he died right then and there.

The foreman went and got Herp Jones, and between 'em, they figured it was good riddance. They decided they should just leave him in the crypt with his wife, since there was a slot for him and everything, and that's what they did. They wrapped up his body and carried it off.

When they got to the crypt, they found that one of the doors was hanging open—and that was odd, but they didn't make nothing of it. They thought maybe there'd been an earthquake, a little one that wasn't much noticed, and the place had gone a little crooked. It happens all the time. But inside the thing, they found the floor all tore up. There used to be marble tiles down there, and now they were gone. Nothing but dirt was left.

I expect they wondered if someone hadn't gotten inside and stolen them. Marble might've been worth something.

They didn't worry about it much, though. They just dumped old Addison Howell into his slot, scooted the lid over him, and shut the place up behind them. Then they remembered the girl who lived at Howell's place—nobody knew her name, on account of she'd never said it—and they headed up there to let her know what had happened.

I think privately they thought maybe now she'd come into town and pick a husband, somebody normal and good for her. There weren't enough women to go around as it was, and she was pretty enough to get a lot of interest.

When they told her the news she started screaming. They dragged her into town to try and calm her down, but she wasn't having any of it. Around that time there was a doctor passing through, or maybe Humptulips had gotten one of its own. Regardless, this doctor gave her something to make her sleep, trying to settle her. They left her in the back room of the general store, passed out on a cot.

And that night, the town woke up to a terrible commotion coming from the cemetery behind Saint Hubert's. Everybody jumped out of bed, and people grabbed their guns and their logging axes, and they went running down to the church to see what was happening—and the whole place was just in ruins. The church was on fire, and the cemetery looked like someone had set off a bunch of dynamite all over it. The Howell crypt was just a bunch of rubble, and there was a big old crater where it used to be.

And by the light of the burning church, the mayor and the logging foreman and about a dozen other people all swear by the saints and Jesus, too . . . they saw a big machine with a tall black stack crawling away—and sitting inside it was the demon

Addison Howell, driving the thing straight back to hell. Some said he was laughing, some said he was crying. Most everyone said they were glad he was gone.

ENDNOTES

1. Colloquialism for severe poverty. I offered to amend the "i" in "piss" to an asterisk for the sake of decency, but head of antiquities Dr. Meagher said to leave it alone, surprising no one even a little bit.
2. Census records for this region are all but nonexistent until well into the twentieth century, so little is officially known about the town's population; but anecdotal evidence and extensive, thankless, unpaid legwork by a graduate student (who is poor enough to warrant an analogy in need of an asterisk) suggests that fewer than three hundred people were in residence at the time.
3. Records kept at Saint Hubert's Church imply an average of half a dozen deaths per year—startling only if one fails to consider that Humptulips was a logging town. As a side note, it turns out that St. Hubert is the patron saint of woodsmen.
4. Mrs. Oberg took this opportunity to speculate with regards to what wild animals might have eaten the girl's family, and then suggested that maybe she was too traumatized to speak thereafter. She also brought up the possibility that Mr. Howell was a pedophile, though that isn't the term she used. As Mrs. Oberg went on at great length upon the subject, her digression has been edited out. After all, an endnote is in better taste, unless Dr. Meagher wants a protracted diatribe about body parts and their respective fluids described with a good number of Anglo-Saxon, consonant-heavy words engraved on a plaque right there on the exhibit, surely prompting a number of embarrassed parents[4a] to answer many awkward questions on the way back to the car.

4a. Do they still let children scale the Clockroach and pretend it's a train? That was always my favorite part of school field trips to the SMPI, until one day I fell off and impaled my foot on a rusty spring. They made me get a tetanus shot.

5. When asked precisely how everybody knew this if no one ever visited them, Mrs. Oberg's ironclad logic went as follows: "If they weren't up to any mischief, they would've just moved to town like civilized people."
6. This seems rather unlikely.
7. The interviewer considered the wisdom of interrupting to ask if the girl was made of metal, given Mrs. Oberg's previous statement, but resolved instead to save his breath. After all, he wasn't getting paid by the word. Or at all.

Clockroach: The Facts

(Fact-checking provided courtesy of Julia Frimpendump, professor emeritus of regional history, University of Washington. Sponsored in part by the West Coast Pioneer Bibliography Project, but not sponsored so extensively that the graduate student who was stuck typing out Dr. Frimpendump's notes was compensated one red cent for his efforts.)

Though Saint Hubert's church was, in fact, subjected to a fire in 1889, it did not burn in its entirety, and most of its records were preserved. There is a record of burial for a woman named "Rose M. Howell" on October 2, 1878, lending credence that the story of Addison Howell may hold a grain of truth; but there is no record for Mr. Howell's death, nor any subsequent burial.

After consulting with an archeo-industrialist in Cincinnati, I have concluded that the peculiar device known locally as "the clockroach" is very likely intended for use in the logging industry. Its forward claws suggest a machine capable of carrying tremendous weight, and the multiple legs imply that it could have traversed difficult terrain while successfully bearing a load.

Based on this information, one could speculate a kinder story for the tragic Addison Howell. It's reasonable to guess that he might have been a lonely man who adopted an orphaned girl, and in his spare time he devoted himself to tinkering . . . eventually coming up with this peculiar engine that might have revolutionized the industry, had it been adopted and mass-produced. His conversation-turned-argument with the logging foreman may have been some patent dispute, or an altercation over the invention's worth—there's no way to know.

The casual record-keeping and insular nature of a tiny homesteader's town has left us little with which to speculate.

However, the remains of a marble crypt can be found in Saint Hubert's churchyard. The church's present minister, Father Frowd, says that it collapsed during an earthquake well before his time—and to the best of his knowledge, it was salvaged for materials.

As for the wagon with the murdered occupants and the sole surviving child, evidence suggests that a family by the name of Sanders left Olympia, Washington, intending to homestead near Humptulips in 1881. This family consisted of a widower Jacob and his brother Daniel, and his brother's daughter Emily. The small family never reached Humptulips, and no record of their demise or reappearance has ever been found.

In one tantalizing clue located (once again) via Saint Hubert's, a spinster named "Emily Howell" reportedly passed away in 1931, at the estimated age of sixty. Her age was merely estimated because she never gave it, and she passed away without family members or identification. She was found dead alone in the large home she kept outside the city limits—her cause of death unknown.

But she is buried behind the church, and her tombstone reads simply, EMILY HOWELL, D. 1931. SHE NEVER FORGOT HIM, AND NEVER FORGAVE US.

Sir Ranulph Wykeham-Rackham, GBE, a.k.a. Roboticus the All-Knowing

Documented by Lev Grossman

Museum: Imperial War Museum, London

Exhibit: Military Miracles! Medical Innovation and the Great Wars

Category: Full-body prosthetic

Creator: Diverse hands, including Marcel Duchamp, Pablo Picasso, Thackery T. Lambshead, Adolf Hitler, and Andy Warhol

Medium: Stainless steel, rubber, enameled copper, textile

Sir Ranulph Wykeham-Rackham was born in 1877. As heir to the legendary Wykeham-Rackham wainscoting fortune, he was assured a life of leisure and privilege, if not any particular utility. But no one suspected that his life would still be going on 130 years later, after a fashion.

A brilliant student, he went up to Oxford at the age of sixteen and was sent down again almost immediately for drunkenness, card-playing, and lewdness. Given the popularity of these pastimes among the undergraduate body, one can only imagine the energy and initiative with which young Ranulph pursued them.

Although he had no artistic talent himself, Wykeham-Rackham preferred the company of artists, who appreciated his caustic wit, his exquisite wardrobe, and his significant annual allowance. He moved to London and rapidly descended into dissipation in the company of the members of the Aesthetes, chief among them Oscar Wilde. Wykeham-Rackham was a regular presence in the gallery during Wilde's trial for gross indecency, and after Wilde's release from prison, it is strongly suspected that wainscoting money bankrolled the elaborate ruse surrounding Wilde's supposed death, and his actual relocation to a comfortable island in the remote West Indies where such advanced Victorian ideas as "gross indecency" did not exist.

The real Wilde died in 1914, leaving Wykeham-Rackham alone and feeling, at thirty-seven, that his era was already passing away. Pater and Swinburne and Burne-Jones and the other aesthetes were long gone. The outbreak of World War

I further deepened his pessimism about the future of modern civilization. Rich, bored, and extravagantly melancholy, he enlisted in the Twenty-eighth Battalion of the London Regiment, popularly known as the "Artists Rifles," because, as he said, he "liked the uniform, and hated life." One can only imagine his surprise when the Artists Rifles were retained as an active fighting force and sent on a tour of the war's most viciously contested battlefields, including Ypres, the Somme, and Passchendaele. All told, the Artists Rifles would sustain more personnel killed in World War I than any other British battalion.

But Wykeham-Rackham survived, and not only survived but flourished. He discovered within himself either an inner wellspring of bravery or a stylish indifference to his own fate—the line between them is a fine one—and, over the course of three years of trench combat, he was awarded a raft of medals, including the Military Cross for gallantry in the face of the enemy at Bapaume.

His luck ran out in 1918, during the infamous hundred-days assault on Germany's Hindenburg line. Wykeham-Rackham was attempting to negotiate a barbed-wire barrier when a sharpshooter's bullet clipped a white phosphorus grenade that he carried on his belt. White phosphorus, then the cutting edge of anti-personnel weaponry, offered one of the grimmest deaths available to a soldier in the Great War. In short order, the chemical had burned away much of Wykeham-Rackham's lower body, from the hips down. As he writhed in agony, the German sharpshooter, evidently not satisfied with his work, fired twice more, removing the bridge of Wykeham-Rackham's nose, his left cheekbone, and half his lower jaw.

But not, strangely, ending his life. The former dandy's soul clung tenaciously to his ruined body, even as it was trundled from aid station to field hospital to Paris and then across the channel to London. There he became the focus of one of the strangest collaborations to which the twentieth century would bear witness.

At that time, the allied fields of prosthetics and cosmesis were being marched rapidly out of their infancy and into a painful adolescence in order to cope with the shocking wounds being inflicted on the human body by the new mechanized weaponry of World War I. Soldiers were returning from the battlefield with disfigurements of a severity undreamt of by earlier generations. When word of Wykeham-Rackham's grievous injury reached his family, from whom he had long been estranged, rather than attend his bedside personally, they opted to send a great deal of money. It was just as well.

In short order, Wykeham-Rackham's feet, legs, and hips had been rebuilt, in skeletal form, out of a new martensitic alloy known as stainless steel, which had just been invented in nearby Sheffield. They were provided with rudimentary muscular power by a hydraulic network fashioned out of gutta-percha tubing. The whole contraption was then fused to the base of Wykeham-Rackham's spine.

It was a groundbreaking achievement, of course, but not without precedent. The field of robotics did not yet exist—the word "robot" would not be coined till 1920—but the history of prosthetic automata went back at least as far as the sixteenth century and the legendary German mercenary Götz von Berlichingen, who lost his right arm in a freak accident when a stray cannonball caused it to be cut off with his own sword. The spring-loaded mechanical iron arm he caused to be built as a replacement could grip a lance and write with a quill. (Wykeham-Rackham was fond of quoting from Goethe's *Goetz von Berlichingen,* based on von Berlichingen's life, in which the playwright coined a useful phrase: *"Leck mich am Arsch,"* or, loosely, "Kiss my ass.")

To replace Wykeham-Rackham's shattered face, a wholly different approach was required. When he was sufficiently recovered from his first operation, Wykeham-Rackham was removed to Sidcup, a suburb of London, home to a special hospital dedicated to the care of those with grotesque facial injuries. It was an eerie place. Mirrors were forbidden. Throughout the town were placed special benches, painted blue, where it was understood that the townspeople should expect that anyone sitting there would present a gravely disturbing appearance.

Wykeham-Rackham's old artist friends, those who were left, rallied around him. Facial reconstruction at that time was accomplished by means of masks. A plaster cast was made of the wounded man's face, a process that brought the patient to within seconds of suffocation. The cast was then used to make a mask of paper-thin galvanized copper. Prominent painters competed with one another to produce the most lifelike reproduction of Wykeham-Rackham's vanished features, which were then reproduced in enamel that was bonded to the copper.

In all, twelve such masks were produced, suitable for various occasions and displaying a range of facial expressions. On seeing them for the first time, Wykeham-Rackham held one up, like Hamlet holding up Yorick's skull, and quoted from his old friend Wilde: "Man is least himself when he talks in his own person. Give him a *mask,* and he will tell you the *truth.*"

Following the end of the war, Wykeham-Rackham enjoyed a second heyday. His fantastical appearance made him the toast of the European avant-garde. A pioneer of kinetic sculpture, Marcel Duchamp was enraptured by Wykeham-Rackham, who agreed to be exhibited alongside Duchamp's other "ready-mades"; he even allowed Duchamp to sign his steel calf with his distinctive "R. Mutt."

Man Ray photographed him. Cocteau filmed him. Stravinsky wrote a ballet based on his life, choreographed by Nijinsky.

Picasso created a special mask for him, a Cubist nightmare that he never wore. (Wykeham-Rackham remarked that Picasso seemed to have missed the point, as the mask was more grotesque than what lay beneath it, not less.) Prosthetics became increasingly fashionable, and not a few deaths and grievous injuries among the fashionable set were explained as attempts to reproduce Wykeham-Rackham's distinctive "look."

Meanwhile, he was continuously undergoing mechanical upgrades and improvements as the available technology progressed. He regularly entertained whole salons of inventors and engineers who vied to try out their innovations on him. Nikola Tesla submitted an elaborate, wildly visionary set of schematics for powering his movements electrically. They were, characteristically for Tesla, the subject of a defamation campaign by Edison, then a blizzard of lawsuits by others who claimed credit for them, and then, finally and decisively, lost in a fire.

But as time wore on, Wykeham-Rackham became increasingly aware that while his metal parts were largely unscathed by the passage of time, his human parts were not. At a scandalous fiftieth birthday party thrown for him by the infamous Bright Young Things of London, Evelyn Waugh among them, Wykeham-Rackham was heard to remark that he was both picture and Dorian Gray in one man.

It was not long afterwards, in 1932, that Wykeham-Rackham opted to have the remainder of his face removed. He was tired, he said, of having his mask touched up to look older, to match his surviving features. Why not become all-mask, and look however he wished? It is not known with any certainty who performed this "voluntary disfigurement" operation, but it is strongly suspected that Lambshead's steady if not overly fastidious hand held the scalpel, judging by the fact that Wykeham-Rackham took a sub-rosa trip to Madagascar at around this time.

Meanwhile, storm clouds of international tension were once again massing. For a brief period, Wykeham-Rackham's lower limbs were declared a state secret, and he was required to wear specially designed pantaloons to conceal them. There were numerous attempts by Soviet emissaries to lure Wykeham-Rackham to Moscow—Stalin was said to have been obsessed with the idea of acquiring a literal "man of steel" to lead the glorious proletariat revolution.

No one was wholly surprised when Wykeham-Rackham reenlisted following Germany's invasion of Poland in 1939. He had grown increasingly disenchanted with twentieth-century urban life, with its buzzing electric lights, blaring radios, and roaring automobiles, even though he himself existed as its living, walking avatar. (He had reluctantly submitted to the electrification of his nether regions in the mid-1920s, after a series of messy, embarrassing hydraulic failures at public functions.) He mourned the elegance of his vanished late-Victorian world.

He was also lonely. His romantic life had stalled, in part because he lacked anything in the way of genitals. (It is rumored, although not confirmed, that attempts to add sexual functionality to Wykeham-Rackham's steel groin had to be abandoned after a catastrophic injury to a test partner.) At one time, he had hoped that the same procedure that made him what he was would be performed on others, who would share his strange predicament. But all attempts to repeat the experiment failed. It has been argued, most notably in Dominic Fibrous's definitive *Wykeham-Rackham: Awesome or Hokum?,* that this is because Wykeham-Rackham's condition was "medically impossible" and "made utterly no sense at all."

His one, platonic, romance seems to have been with a young mathematician and computer scientist named Alan Turing. Their dalliance led to the latter's formulation of his famous Wykeham-Rackham Test, which raised the question of whether it would be possible to devise a robot so lifelike that it would be impossible to tell it apart from a human being while making love to it.

Now in his sixties, Wykeham-Rackham was far too old for active service, but the physical stamina resulting from his unusual physical make-up, and his value to the troops as a source of morale, made him indispensable. For public-relations purposes, he joined the invasion of Normandy on D-Day, and the famous photograph of him striding from the surf onto Omaha Beach, his steel pelvis dripping sea foam, a bullet pinging off his enamel face, remains one of the iconic images of World War II. The American GIs cheered him on and called him "Tin Man."

But Wykeham-Rackham's excessive bravery was again his downfall. Emboldened by this taste of his former glory, he refused the offer of transport back to England and stayed with the Allied forces pressing forward through the Norman hedgerows. A close-range encounter with the infamous German *Flammenwerfer* seared his arms and torso almost to the bone. Once again, he made the perilous journey back across the Channel to the hospitals of London. This time, it was necessary to replace almost his entire upper body, leaving only his head and major organs in place.

Astoundingly, he lived on.

Indeed, some began to speculate that out of the crucible of the world wars, humanity's first immortal being had emerged. Wykeham-Rackham showed no obvious signs of aging, apart from his mane of white hair, which he took to dyeing to match its original lustrous black.

But inside, his soul was wasting away. A dark time began for Wykeham-Rackham. Owing to the precipitous decline in sales of wainscoting and wainscoting accessories since the Victorian period, his family fortune had dwindled almost to nothing. He was able to survive only on his military pension, and whatever he received making promotional appearances for the British Armed Forces. Twice he was caught stealing lubricants for his joints and convicted of petty larceny. He became silent and morose. He sold off eleven of his masks, and the Picasso, leaving only the one titled "Melancholia." It was, he said, the only one he needed.

Wykeham-Rackham's last moment in the spotlight came in the 1960s, when he became one of the oddities and grotesques taken up by Andy Warhol and the Factory scene in New York. He appeared in several of Warhol's movies, to the lasting detriment of his dignity, and was, of course, the subject of Warhol's seminal silkscreen *Wykeham-Rackham Triptych.* It was at Warhol's suggestion that Wykeham-Rackham commissioned the final surgery that turned him into an entirely synthetic being: the replacement of his skull with a steel casing, and his brain with a large lightbulb.

Conventional wisdom would argue that this was the end of Wykeham-Rackham's existence as a sentient being, but in truth, it was difficult to tell. As the 1960s wound down, he had spoken and moved less and less. One Warhol hanger-on remarked, in a display of sub-Wildean wit, that after the operation his conversation was "more brilliant than ever."

But Warhol cast Wykeham-Rackham off as lightly as he took him up, and the old soldier passed the 1970s and 1980s in obscurity. It's difficult to track his movements during this lost period, but curatorial notes found in Lambshead's basement suggest that some of Warhol's junkie friends eventually sold him to a traveling carnival, where he was put to use as a fortune-telling machine.

Even there, he was exiled to a gloomy corner of the midway. The proprietors despaired of ever making money off him, because, they said, no matter how they fiddled with his settings, he only ever predicted the imminent and painful demise of whoever consulted him.

His glorious past had been entirely forgotten but for a single trace. On the sign above his booth was painted, in swirly circus calligraphy, a quotation from Oscar Wilde:

"A mask tells us more than a face."

Sir Ranulph Wykeham-Rackham in his full sartorial (and metallic) splendor

Shamalung (The Diminutions)

Documented by Michael Moorcock

SIR JOHN SOANE'S MUSEUM

13 Lincoln's Inn Fields, London, England

St. Odhran's coll

Reverend Orlando Bannister 1800–1900

Miniaturisation experiment? (c. 1899)

Organic material (wood, etc.) plus metals (various)

Loaned by the Barbican Begg Bequest at the City Museum (note, proprietorship challenged by Battersea Municipal Museum, by the Lambshead Trust, and by Greyfriars School, Kent)

L1922.11. bmm/LT/GFS

(Private viewing and reading of associated notes by appointment only.)

Notes

Greyfriars School in Kent claims this odd piece on the grounds that (a) Reverend Bannister was an ex-pupil still funded by the school to perform certain scientific investigations and experiments, and (b) the piece is possibly the work of another of its alumni, the sculptor and scientist John Wolt. Wolt disappeared from his lodgings in 1899, leaving only a brief note suggesting that he intended to take his own life ("My final journey, undertaken voluntarily, should not prove a difficult one, and I could ultimately come face to face with my Creator. Even if a little discomfort is felt, it will be as nothing compared to the joy of bringing the word of Our Saviour to God's tiniest creatures. B. has convinced me of their intelligence and individuality, and therefore they must be possessed of souls, just as St. Francis, apparently, believed that animals, too, have souls. I am filled with humility and ecstasy when I consider that I was their first missionary. Though the transition be painful and not a little difficult, I am assured by B. that all will be well in the ultimate."). This note and others are attached. In Reverend Bannister's remaining journal fragments (the majority were eaten by rats while in storage), he writes for January 1, 1900: "W. proves to be an enthusiast, perfectly willing to aid me in my work. We both feel God has chosen us."

One of the early cases of Seaton Begg ("Sexton Blake," as he was known to readers of detective fiction) was reported as "The Fairy Murders" in the *Union Jack* magazine, a patriotic weekly, of February 16, 1901, featuring Griff the Man-Tracker, probably an invented creature.

This manuscript being by far the most complete, believed the work of Sir David Garnett Blake, great-great-grandson of Sir Sexton Blake of Erring Grange, Erring, Sussex.

The bare facts of the case were as bizarre as they were brief: The small daughter of a Bermondsey tailor claimed that her half-grown cat, Mimi, had eaten a fairy. Of course, no one would believe her, even though she insisted she had seen Mimi nosing around a tiny leg. Rebecca, of course, was rightly punished for telling stories. But a few days later, she came to her mother holding triumphantly a little human ear. The Rabinowitzes, her parents, were unusual in those days in that they were vegetarians. The only meat they bought was for their cat. It came from their local butcher, Jacob "Cocky" Cohen. They inspected the ear and decided it was not human. When they went to Cocky's next, they would complain that monkeys and possibly other animals had been used in the preparation of his cats' meat.

Then Rebecca found part of a miniature arm, dressed in what appeared to be a tiny silk blouse sleeve, and brought this to her horrified parents, who could no longer hide the truth from themselves. The following Tuesday, they confronted the butcher.

Suspecting them of an extortion plan, so before witnesses, including PC Michael McCormac, Cocky began to sort through his supply of cats' meat in order to prove the Rabinowitzes wrong.

To his shocked astonishment, he discovered several items of what could only be human remains, but of such tiny proportions, they were immediately called "Lilliputian," by one of his witnesses, a Dr. Jelinek, Bohemian music teacher, originally of Prague, who would later give his part of the story in German to his sister. Upon informing the police, the witnesses were sworn to secrecy and made to sign Her Majesty's Official Secrets Act, but this did not stop the disgusted Cocky Cohen from taking the case to a young consulting detective who had recently set up practise in Norfolk Street, London E.

Seaton Begg (not yet knighted) would become famous under another name when his adventures were sensationalised and written up for a popular weekly,

An unfortunate participant in an ill-fated conversion

but in those days, he was scarcely a household name. He worked at that time with a gigantic creature of no known breed, whom he had raised and trained and named "Griff," or sometimes "Man-Tracker." An invaluable asset. Begg eagerly undertook to investigate the case, and within hours, Griff had found the source of the butcher's meat. A Battersea slaughterhouse advertised as The Metropolitan Meat Supply Co., which supplied sausages, animal food, fertilizer, and pie-filling to the trade, the firm seemed conscientious as far as its sanitary arrangements were concerned, and had passed its recent inspection with colours flying. When he confronted them, Begg himself considered their professional ethics beyond reproach.

With the help of his strange, unhuman assistant, Griff, Begg next discovered that Metropolitan Meat was being used by a corrupt entrepreneur known as Moses Monk to get rid of unwanted flesh. Aided by an accomplice on the premises, he introduced the meat into MMP's supply. Monk made most of his money by working as a "waste-disposal merchant," employed by unscrupulous merchants to get rid of organic material local councils refused to handle. However, Monk had a rather grislier arrangement with the Brookgate undertakers Ecker and Ecker to dispose of what they termed their "overspill"—paupers who had died without relatives in surrounding London boroughs. The council paid the Eckers by the corpse, supposedly buried in consecrated ground in simple lead coffins. It was far more profitable to let Monk handle the business, no questions asked, and sell the spare plots to grieving relatives. Yet this still did not explain the tiny "fairy" body parts discovered in Bermondsey. Under threat from young Begg and his strange assistant, Griff, Monk eventually confessed.

Of course, it was completely against the law to mix human remains with meat sold for consumption by animals, so Begg was at least responsible for bringing that filthy practise to an end.

The central mystery remained. Who were the "Lilliputians" and why was the government covering up their existence? Once again, Begg decided to put Griff the Man-Tracker on the case. Here is a description of Griff from the original fictionalised report in *Union Jack* no. 356, quoted on the Blakiana Web site:

> Can it be a man—this strange, repulsive creature so stealthily stealing along? Surely no human being was ever so repulsively formed as this? Yet it is garbed as a man!
>
> A bowler hat, long, loosely fitting black overcoat, baggy trousers, tan-coloured spats, and great, ill-shaped boots. But the face! How can we possibly

> describe it—or, rather, the little that can be seen of it? The bowler hat is full large for the head, and is drawn down over the forehead and skull, and rests upon large, outstanding, and hair-covered ears. Great blue spectacles, of double lens, cover the eyes and some portion of the visage. The nose is very flat, and of great width of nostrils. The unusual sight of a "respirator" can be seen well covering up the mouth. A great and light-coloured muffler also is so arranged that chin and jaws are both concealed; but what little of the face that can be detected is covered to the cheekbones with short and stiff-looking hair of a dull-brownish colour.
>
> There is something strangely inhuman in the general expression, while the small, round eyes peer through the deep blue glasses like two brilliant sparks of fire.
>
> Of wonderful breadth of shoulder, girth of chest, and length of arm, this is an individual who must be endowed with prodigious strength. A crooked back and bowed legs greatly add to the general grotesque hideousness of the figure as a whole.

This would be the first time that the government stepped in to dissuade Begg from unleashing his horrid assistant (ultimately, Griff would be housed at a facility—he died some time in 1918, where he had been employed in the bloody trench fighting which developed during the first world war), for, within an hour or two of putting Griff on the scene, Begg was summoned to the offices of the Home Secretary Lord Mauleverer, who told him that, since he could not put Begg (younger son of his good friend General Sir Henry Begg) *off* the scent, then he had better put him *on* it. There were two conditions: (1) Griff must be "retired" as soon as possible, and (2) Begg must sign the Official Secrets Act and consider himself to be working not for Cocky, the Bermondsey butcher, but for His Majesty the King. Begg agreed. Turning over all available evidence in the case, Mauleverer commissioned Begg, under oath to the monarch, to investigate the matter as discreetly as possible.

The fictional version is, of course, well known. Clue by clue, Begg tracked down the fairy murderer to a deserted mill in the heart of Kent, where, with a secret grant from "Blackmonk Academy" (easily identified as Greyfriars School), mad scientist "Professor Maxwell Moore" had found a way to grow plants so much like human beings they deceived everyone. His aim was to breed a race of "peace-loving plant people," who would eventually take over from the human race. Begg's first clue was in the cat's refusal to eat vegetable matter.

Typical story-paper rubbish, of course, which satisfied the rumour-mongers when inevitably the tale got out in a garbled form. The truth was far more startling.

At this stage, we must introduce one of the key players—if not *the* key player—in this melodrama:

Orlando Bannister, D.D., the so-called Barmy Vicar of Battersea, at that time enjoying the living of St. Odhrán's, a Methodist and a master of the Portable Harmonium, also amateur inventor, had successfully weighed the human soul but not the mind. As a missionary, he had served for some years in the jungles of Guatemala, where he had become known for his unorthodox views concerning the nature of both dumb animals and even dumber plants. His scientific investigations informed the nature of his theological views. His book *Our Lord in All Things,* in which he argued that every individual blade of grass, every leaf or flower, possessed a rudimentary soul, went into many editions and was in the library of every sentimental lady in the land. The Blavatskyians embraced him. Sales from his book funded his travels and his scientific investigations. A devout Methodist, he was of a missionary disposition and had travelled everywhere on what he amiably called "the Lord's work."

With a fellow evangelist Sir Ranald Frieze-Botham, D.D. founded missions not only in several leading zoological gardens but also a score or so of botanical gardens, most of them in New Zealand.

Having done all he could do for the creatures of the land, at least for the moment, Bannister turned his attention to the deep. He built his rather spectacular Underwater Tramway, or Submersible Juggernaut, in order to carry the story of Creation to the creatures of the sea. He had pretty much exhausted his attempts to bring the Gospel to the Goldfish (as the vulgar press had it) when he happened upon Pasteur's study of microbes and realized his work had hardly begun.

Bannister and Frieze-Botham spent long hours discussing what means they could employ to isolate and introduce the word of God to the world of microorganisms. They did, in fact, receive some funding from Bannister's old school after he had persuaded the board of governors that, if a will to do evil motivated those microbes, then the influence of the Christian religion was bound to have an influence for good. This meant, logically, that fewer boys would be in the infirmary and that, ultimately, shamed by the consequences of their actions, the germs causing, say, tuberculosis would cease to spread.

The crucial step, of course, was how to reduce a missionary, complete with all necessary paraphernalia, to a size tiny enough to contact individual—or, at any rate, small groups of—microbes.

As it happened, Frieze-Botham was in regular correspondence with the inventor Nikola Tesla, who at that point had lost his faith in his adopted homeland of the United States and planned to emigrate to England, where he felt his less conservative ideas would find more fruitful ground. Upon disembarking from the S.S. *Ruritania,* he was at once met by the two divines, who hurried him off to Bannister's vicarage in leafy Balham.

There, Tesla was allowed to set up his Atomic Diminution Engine in what had been the vaults of an old abbey created on the site by the so-called Doubting Friars, or Quasi-Carmelites, in the thirteenth century.

Tesla needed an assistant, so the obvious person was John Wolt, who had been at school with Bannister and Frieze-Botham and was a great admirer of Tesla. He had already read his hero's paper *On Preparing a True Atomic Diminution Engine,* printed privately in Chicago, and could think of no better way of serving both God and Science than helping carry the scriptures to the germs. "Better than trying to persuade the Germans," he quipped, referring to Tesla's humiliating experience in Berlin, which had rejected his electric recoilless gun, among other inventions.

Their work began apace.

Tesla, Wolt, and Frieze-Botham set to work unpacking and assembling the massive crates as they turned up from America. Soon an entire machine took shape in the church basement, and Tesla's mood became increasingly elevated as his dynamos set to mumbling and whistling, then yelped into sudden life, drowning all other sound before being brought under purring control by their master.

"Messieurs, we have our power," declared Tesla in his preferred language. His wife had always preferred it, too.

From what Begg pieced together and lodged under the "50 Years Act," we can see that only Tesla, and perhaps Bannister, survived their attempts to shrink through what Tesla named "metamultiversal plates" down through the alternative universes to near-infinity. Practicing first on dead animals, then on human corpses obtained from Monk (which was what was turning up as parts of "fairies" or "Lilliputians" in the "meat" Monk disposed of through his usual means), the inventor and his colleagues were soon prepared to experiment on living animals and eventually on human subjects—and then themselves. All human subjects were volunteers and paid well, but only advanced to the first and second levels. Four died, all at what was called "the first level of descent." Which was when Monk, who had supplied the corpses, now offered to take them off the vicar's hands. He was growing rich on what they paid him and rather neglecting his usual dumping business.

When Tesla was satisfied that no harm could possibly come to human organs subjected to his electrics, he announced that he was ready to send a living creature straight through into what he termed the Intra-Universe, or Second Aether, down to worlds subtly different but ranged according to scale and mass so that the smaller one became the denser one, and the larger the more amorphous. The process had to be endured by degrees, stepping down a level at a time. All the laboratory guinea pigs used returned safely and indicated what was likely to happen to a human subject. At the first level, one remained small but visible and yet one's normal weight. At the second level, one vanished from human sight, though one's weight could still be measured as identical and the subject could be observed through a microscope; and at the third level, far more powerful instruments were needed until the traveller vanished completely from the scale, and weight became meaningless in the context. Wolt would, at his own request, be the first to be sent "downscale."

Tesla was by no means oblivious of concern. He was nervous. He asked Wolt over and over if he felt ready. He received a steady affirmative. And so, the process began as Wolt stepped into the apparatus and the tall bell jar was lowered over him until it came to rest on the sturdy mahogany plinth. Lights and gauges let into the wood indicated the progress as Tesla's dials and graphs began precise measurement of the man's molecular structure before sending him on the first stage of his journey. Wolt carried with him portable versions of the crucial instruments, together with Dr. Bannister's patented Portable Harmonium and a case of Bibles. On his left were the controls he would use for his return through five groups of six levels. Before returning, however, he would establish a base camp, where, before he returned, he planned to leave the majority of items he took with him.

The others watched eagerly and with concern the first transition, which the guinea pigs were known to have survived. Before their eyes, within a glorious, pale green aura, Wolt grew smaller and smaller until, triumphantly brandishing his Bible, he disappeared from view—to reappear in the viewing screen of the electric microscope still waving, evidently in good health. Another stage, and Wolt could be observed staring in awe at the lush, almost infinite world of the Submicroscopic.

He could be seen to consult his Bible at this point, and begin to preach. He was still preaching when he vanished at last from human ken, beyond the range of all Tesla's detection devices.

Now the men waited impatiently. Would Wolt return safely?

Hours went by. Tesla, who always ate voraciously when nervous, sent out for sandwiches.

And then, as dawn began to touch the horizon with a delicate grey, Wolt's image popped onto the microscope lens, and soon he was looking up at them and showing them that apart from his crucifix, he was empty-handed.

Another ten minutes, and a breathless, grinning Wolt stepped from his plinth with stories of wonderful landscapes, new spectra, and sometimes dangerous types of flora and fauna—all, he felt sure, waiting to be instructed in the ways of the Bible. He was full of the emotions and feelings he had experienced in the other world. He had feared he might be descending into Hell, but instead he had been close to Heaven. "Ah, the ecstasy." He had felt at one with the raw stuff with which God made the world. Far from reporting failure, Wolt was almost raving about his success. There were intelligent creatures in our bloodstreams, discussing ideology that could destroy or save our world, and when their fight was decided, so our fate was decided. Not only could these creatures learn from the Bible; it was a matter of grave urgency that they be converted to the Christian faith as quickly as possible. "Whole armies of missionaries are needed down there!" Wolt insisted. He would help train them, perhaps draw maps from the sketches he had made.

Overjoyed, the three Methodists congratulated Tesla, who was anxious to remind them that the work was still at an early stage. Privately, he wondered if Wolt had experienced a series of delusions and was merely mad.

As Begg wrote in his report to the Home Office: "They did not know what the effects on a living human brain might be, let alone to what harm his body had been exposed. There could be terrible side-effects, which might materialise in days or even years, produced by the rapid change of size while retaining the same mass."

Wolt spoke of "making holes in the cosmos," and nobody was sure what that meant. Nonetheless, the experiment seemed to have proven everything they had considered in theory. Bannister, in particular, was anxious to make the next trip. Wolt drew him a map, showing where, protected from the strange elements of the submicroscopic world, he had left the Bibles, the Portable Harmonium, and all the other materials that had accompanied him. With more Bibles, perhaps some firearms for self-defence, and provided with food and a few other necessities, they could probably remain in the Second Aether for months. The four men celebrated, inflamed by the knowledge that they had found new worlds to conquer for their beloved Saviour.

Although Wolt was anxious to return, they decided to send another of their company and drew lots, Frieze-Botham winning the right to be the next to descend. He took another case of Bibles, more supplies of soap, tinned butter, bully beef and so forth, ammunition and firearms. His experience was pretty much identical to Wolt's. He reported a rather peaceful scene, with herds of oddly shaped herbivores moving placidly through dimensionless veldts and forests whose crowns were invisible. More like fresh coral than anything above the waves, said Frieze-Botham on his return. He said he felt like some heavy sea-beast brought by gravity to the only depths it could comfortably negotiate. And, at last, it was the eager cleric's turn to experience what he had, after all, first sought to explore. Equipping himself with more Bibles, bully beef, and bullets, he gave the signal to Tesla and ultimately was gone.

This time, however, the hours became slow days as the trio prayed that no accident had come to Bannister. Tesla cursed himself for not rigging up some kind of subatomic telephone. A week was to pass before the apparatus began to flicker and spark, and still the men did not dare to hope. When all was over, they stared into an empty stage. Only the controls and wires were to be seen, perfectly intact, as also were the levers and gauges.

Before the others could stop him, Wolt had vaulted the brass rail and given the signal to raise the bell. "It's up to me to find him. Don't try to stop me. I know those timeless, dimensionless spaces like the back of my hand." He then remembered to call for the last Portable Harmonium, the only instrument to send out sounds loud enough for the reverend to hear. His crucifix clutched to his chest, Wolt gave the signal to begin the descent across the planes of the multiverse into what were essentially alternate worlds. Tesla and Frieze-Botham remained to operate the equipment and rack their brains for further means of communicating with the micronauts.

This time, the apparatus was back in minutes, rocking crazily and empty of most supplies. A crazed and battered Wolt, his clothing in shreds, fell from the gigantic bell and reeled to the rail of the crypt, mouthing a single word: *"Shamalung."* And that was all. Next, he seemed to remind himself of something and, reaching into the jar, clambered back aboard the machine. He pulled two levers, then waved from the apparatus as it disappeared on another journey down the dimensions. The two observers were at a loss to control what was happening.

But the next time it returned, it came bearing a different passenger successfully up through stage five and four, and made it shakily through three before jamming at two, showing a small Orlando Bannister, brass crucifix in one hand, a Bible lying on the surrounds of the ruined electrics next to some loose notes,[1] as if from a book,[2] and a small Portable Harmonium, which, on further inspection, proved to be a perfect working model. The figure of Bannister appeared to be made of a very heavy metal, so far unidentified, and was exquisitely carved, impossible to tell from its original.

Tesla and the others knew exactly what had happened, realising the effect of repeated atomic shifts on a living creature, especially a creature of Bannister's venerable years. His atoms had atrophied, as the few knowledgeable scientists of the day described the process. What was a lifelike statue to the world, was really the last remains of a brilliant scientific mind and a man of almost childlike faith in the workings of his Maker. The apparatus was eventually dismantled, after Tesla and Frieze-Botham had worked for almost a year attempting to reverse time and to rescue Wolt, but it was as if, said Frieze-Botham, growing increasingly spiritual, the Almighty had made it clear that these experiments, however innocent and moved by faith, were to cease.

To this day, people interested in such things continue to debate the meaning of the word "Shamalung," but, as yet, no credible interpretation has been offered. It could be from any one of millions of microbe languages.

ENDNOTES

1. Subsequently much enlarged, each a perfect page of writing, sadly not sequential, in OB's hand.
2. See above.

Pulvadmonitor: The Dust's Warning

Researched and Documented by China Miéville

British Dental Association Museum
64 Wimpole Street, London

Xanthe Serkis (British, 1903–1953), Thomas Thomas (British, 1890–1964)
Pulvadmonitor; the Dust's Warning (c. 1937–1952, 1952–1986)
Glass, wood, brass, leather, wire, mechanisms, dentures, dust
Undocumented (twice)

To be discovered is the task and telos of an artefact. Its historic mission is to be born, midwifed into the light like any other whelp, pulled out of the earth or delivered from a long-forgotten cupboard womb. It dies when it is born, of course: and its post-birth duties in the museum where we trap it are an afterlife in a most literal sense, and as drab, doubtless, as quotidianly dull as the afterlives that await us. It is best to avoid consideration of what it is we commit when we investigate: curation is an unkindness we perpetrate against objects and we must hope their revenge is endlessly deferred. After all, we must do it. To be themselves, all artefact are born once.

—Thackery T. Lambshead, "The Violent Philosophy of the Archive"

when because it comes and
what may we say among those things
shall not be if we have shame enough for truth
that we were not warned

—Unknown, "Ode to Everything"

1. The Second Birth

In 1986, under a brisk new administration, the British Dental Association Museum, until then an institution that had been allowed to tick over in a relatively sedate manner, somewhat insulated from the ravages of visitors, was subjected to a vigorous clearout and cleaning. What, in their later paper, the Trades Union Congress called "this notorious Cleansing Event" was conducted in an atmosphere of laissez-faire vim, blamed by some participants for several breakages and the disappearances of at least four artefacts. Considerably less discussed—meriting only an oblique and en passant mention in *Thatcher's Mops,* Cecily Fetchpaw's otherwise exhaustive book on the subject—is what was uncovered in the museum attic as it was emptied of cardboard boxes, spider corpses, and long-ossified cleaning products.

The agency staff, they later testified, hesitated as they ascended the stepladders at a sound they thought was a gas leak. When, gingerly, their team-leader raised her head through the hatch and scanned the area with her torch, she was shocked initially to realise how much further the unlit room extended. Immediately, she was shocked, and much more violently, again, when the light reached into a low triangular nook below a staircase at the windowless chamber's rear, onto the heads of a sarcophagus and an antique Anubis, various other items of Egyptiana, and a bell jar containing a head, on the floor, eyes at the level of her eyes. What caused her, it emerged, to stagger on her precarious perch, fall, and break her hip, was when the ash-coloured lips behind the glass moved.

Word spread, of course. A number of staff bypassed the inefficient, jury-rigged security and went to look. This was an age before camera phones, but someone procured the Polaroid used for artefact records, and there exist three bad pictures of inquisitive students of dental surgery and museum workers ranged around the bell jar in what looks like worship. Even such inadequate still images give a sense of the atmosphere at the scene. According to those present, the head, though it did not at any point open its eyes, moved its mouth and bit startlingly white teeth, hard enough that the chattering was audible through the bell-jar glass. Next to it, wired up to it, hissing faintly and clattering like a telegraph machine, was a battery or engine, with gently pulsing gauges.

"We didn't shine the lights on it too hard," according to one of the cleaners. "Not too often. It seemed like that might be a bit . . . much for its eyes." "It definitely wasn't alive," according to the Head of Dentures. "No way. Yes, I know it was moving. But it was grey, grey, grey. And dry. Mummified or saponified or something. No, I don't know how it was moving. Electricity or something. No, I don't know. I have nothing more to say."

Even by the indirect light, the extraordinary texture of the head was clear. It moved in small spasms, creasing its dun self in unnatural directions. "Not like a head," one witness said. Its teeth, gleaming from behind dirt-coloured lips,

Another unfortunate participant

ceramic-white and vivid, look in the photographs overlaid on the picture like a crude collage, part of a wholly different image with a quite different palate. At seconds when the dials on the little motor twitched, the face might slightly crease its eyes or wince as if in pain, in response or cause, it was impossible to say.

It was not long until a small team of uniformed men and women arrived and declared the attic out of bounds. They hauled equipment up the ladder and in, and the staff on duty on the floor below grew used to the scuffing sounds of whatever their investigations were. It was two days before anyone from the museum realised that what the visitors wore were not scene-of-crime police overalls, although similar. The women and men who had received the information about the find and were performing their forensics in the attic were not police. (It was, indeed, for exactly such exigencies as this accidental discovery, and not for the spurious reasons set out elsewhere in this volume, that Professor Lambshead kept his extensive network of sleeper agents on retainer at most museums worldwide.) Before any scandal could ensue, Lambshead himself had arrived from his Polish trip and arranged a private meeting with the head of the Dental Museum, in the aftermath of which the police were never called and the cut of the director's clothes improved.

it is not through pages turning to elements
nor through liminals nor tumbling streets
and there is no etherized sky above us as we
that we walk only rather by this cleanest
steel yet this steel glass this tough clean material
also sheds time's exhaust

—Unknown, "Ode to Everything"

1.2. The Damascene Moment

The famous Lambshead passage at the start of this entry, from the "Violent Philosophy . . . ," has been repeatedly parsed and interpreted, according to most hermeneutics going. What had, until the discovery in the Dental Museum attic, been less universally considered was the asterisk that beckoned at that paragraph's end, to whisper its content from page bottom: "*At least* once, we should say. And what of the artefact that is born twice? What of such ontological profligacy? Deep understanding seems to slide with appearance, reappearance; now inspiring, now gone."

The existence of the object in the museum attic was no secret from Lambsheadians from the time of its discovery, but it was not considered a major piece, and was not much studied (even allowing for difficulties of access), until events at the notorious 2005 Conference on Lambshead Studies drew researchers' attention to it. Auto-argumentative footnotes such as the one quoted here have always commanded the attention of a small subgroup of specialist Lambsheadologists; dissidents among dissidents, the Digressionists, who insisted that these were the keys, bloated with import, master codes, the texts to which they pretended to be adjuncts, messages to be unpicked. Condemned by more traditional textualists as tendentious, they insisted that this particular passage, for example, must refer to an artefact known not merely to have been found and lost again, but to have been discovered twice, unique and different each time.

Determined to humiliate them and destroy the credibility of these avant-garde heretics, the leading scholars of mainstream Lambsheadianism invited Simone Mukhopadhay, the most eloquent of the Digressionists, to a debate with Alan Demont, secretary of Lambshead Studies. As Demont started his careful demolition job, focusing on what he insisted was the lack of deep meaning in the "Twice-born Footnote" above, as it was called, from "The Violent Philosophy of the Archive," his eight-year-old daughter (who was present at the session, crèche facilities unavailable, and who was drawing a tiger on the back of, and a forest in the margins of a printout of his paper) interrupted him, in front of the audience, to point out that the first letters of the last, oddly syntaxed sentence of that footnote spelled out a message. (She had picked out the relevant letters with crayoned flowers.)

Lambshead, it transpired, was more than a curator of this piece; he was, indeed, unusually active in its creation. From that Rosetta-stone footnote moment, identifying as it did the object of its own attention, it was a relatively short time until, by dint of intense and sometimes destructive rummaging through the doctor's effects, papers, and above all his diaries, first the identity, then the story of the twice-found object and, to a limited extent, Lambshead's peripheral and unclear role in its creation, came out. So many mentions of so many objects litter those extraordinarily extensive records that it is often only with such external prods that the distinctions between items of importance, and pretty rocks or banged together bits of wood with which Lambshead was momentarily taken, can be ascertained. These passages had been read many times, but no one had put them together, until that acronym came to light, and the memory of the attic, and the specific anecdote became important.

Here the focus must be on the reconstructed story: the history, prehistory, and two births of the artefact itself, the Pulvadmonitor. Or, in the name given it by Lambshead's acronym, about the deep understanding that seems to slide with appearance, and so on: the Dust's Warning.

will you your will?
will it to me.
I will you mine.

—Unknown, "Ode to Everything"

2. The First Birth

The professor, though a man of science, was a polymath. He enjoyed the company of, and endeavoured to participate in salons and discussion groups with, artists, writers, poets, and various other representatives of *La bohème*. One from such a milieu was the literary critic Thomas Thomas. It was to Lambshead that Thomas came in 1952, begging his help, bearing a large box and several books. Lambshead was surprised to see him, as their particular circle had mostly attenuated by the mid-1940s, and it was some years since he and Thomas had been in each other's company.

After abbreviated pleasantries, Thomas explained his message and presence. He had been put in an awkward position, he explained, by Xanthe Serkis, and seeking Lambshead's advice. Serkis was a critic, known to the professor, but only very slightly, a good decade previously. When he had met her, she had been working on a book about David Gascoyne and other British surrealists.

"That's correct," Thomas told him. "She still is. That's rather the point."

In a pre-echo of Thomas's approach to Lambshead, Serkis, who had absented herself from the poetic and critical scene for several months, had recently and aggressively contacted Thomas, demanding to see him. Some months earlier, Serkis had received, she told him, a copy of Gascoyne's *Man's Life Is This Meat*, preceding the 1936 Parton Press edition. She had shown it to him, and he described it to Lambshead: imperfectly printed, the publisher Down-Dandelion Press, its colophon showing a stylised upside-down flower, its roots above the earth, its bloom below. In content, it was largely the same as the later official editions, except for a few differences of punctuation, and, the one substantial difference, a whole extra poem inserted into the text. Its title was "Ode to Everything."

Serkis had received the book in the post. That she did not remember ordering it did not surprise her overmuch: as a critic of solid though unorthodox reputation, she received a good deal of material unsolicited, most of it from small presses anxious to gain her mention. There was, however, no return address, no covering note, no enclosure of any kind. She could find no details on Down-Dandelion Press from any of her usual sources, and later and exhaustive searches failed to turn up any more copies of the book. Gascoyne himself, whom she knew though not well, denied any knowledge of the copy or the poem, and seemed mildly amused but not very interested by them.

In truth, Serkis hadn't felt much different at first, thinking the book some illicit curio, a mischievous thing put together from a proof, leaked to her with, she vaguely assumed, the "Ode . . ." inserted to draw attention—camouflaged by Gascoyne's minor but real reputation—to another, shyer poet's work. "She told Thomas," Lambshead's journals read, "that she had included a one-line mention of the odd edition in her monograph. Then padded that one line with another. Returned again, to add some few words, on the subject of the ode itself, interpreting it, with a tendentious and provocative heuristic, as if it *were,* in fact, one of Gascoyne's, to see what it told us about the rest of his corpus."

The teleology is clear. Lambshead recounts Thomas's recollections. "What started as that mention became a paragraph, then a chapter—a chapter devoted to an interloping poem!—then a whole section. Abruptly, it was the subject of her book, still at first, in an increasingly absurd pretence, discussed as if Gascoyne had written it, until the title had been changed to *Anon's Ode*. But that was not the end of it, either. Her focus did not stop. Had continued down like the switching and switching of a microscope's field of focus, probing no longer the whole poem but one section, stanza, on down."

Thomas had brought a copy of the "Ode to Everything," the initial stanzas of which read to Lambshead, he tells us, like a rather too-unreconstructed riff on one thing or another, though here and there, a turn of phrase—"this minatory summer," he mentions; "your felt-silenced castanets"; "the slander that a lizard feels no love"—startled him. (The few snips and stanzas that he reproduces, in passing praise, reproduced again here, are all we have. The poem, indeed the book, the few details available, are untraceable. Nor does the Internet help us, whatever the search string.)

Months of research, she had told Thomas; hundreds of pages of notes; reams of started, interrupted, and restarted chapters—all of which she brought out in sheaves and bundles and laid across his desk to prove her point—and Serkis had been moved to write her monograph entirely on one line: "What does the dust wish to tell us?"

"That's the question," she told Thomas. "That's the only question."

Thomas, quailing, had gently prodded, offered to read her book, and she had looked at him with bewildered anger. She swept her papers off his table. Forget the book, she said. The book, she assured him, was no longer the focus of her work. Thomas had understood abruptly that what had been a project of interpretation had become one of lunatic detection. She was not, as he had thought at first, applying her considerable critical skills to the eight-word question: she was, rather, attempting to answer it. What does the dust wish to tell us?

She had opened her box. She had brought out for Thomas a glass dome, its base connected to that mockery of a battery. From the front of the dome jutted a flared tube, and rattling around within the glass, unsecured, were a pair of dentures. The two of them had regarded the collection of equipment for some time, in silence. "It took me three years of physics," Serkis said, "but I worked out how to build it."

"I need you to look after it," Serkis said. "I have a fear."

"'By this time, old man, as you can imagine,' Thomas said to me, 'I had my doubts about poor old Xanthe's sanity,'" Lambshead wrote. "'And where are you going?' I asked her. Answer, as she left, came there none." Thomas, aware in vague terms of his friend's interests and predilections, had immediately decided to bring it to Lambshead. As for Xanthe, neither Thomas, nor Lambshead saw her again.

What would have looked to the nonspecialist like a disconnected pile of rubbish was not something Lambshead, with his considerable experience, would ever dismiss out of hand, of course. For two weeks, he fiddled. He put his ear close to the speaking tube. He tinkered with the battery. When one combination of switches were switched, he records, he heard a tiny hiss: pushed another way, he heard nothing. What the dials measured remained opaque to him, but measure it they did, tweaking and jumping in response to he knew not what. He, attuned to the importance of time, left the bell jar alone for several days. He waited, one of his assistants reported, "with more than mere patience." On his return, all was as it had been.

"I gave it one last shake," he writes, "listened to the rattle of the teeth through that upturned speaking trumpet, and nothing else."

A year and three months after his visit from Thomas—during one of his periodic clear-outs of artefacts for which he no longer had space, or in which he no longer had interest, or which were "not working"—the professor is believed to have given what we later came to know as the Pulvadmonitor to the Dental Museum; on the grounds, presumably, that what it appeared to be designed to showcase, if for reasons beyond him, were the disaggregated dentures. In the museum itself, sterling detective work has uncovered an acquisition note for what is recorded simply as "Item," on which note is an irate scribbled exchange in two hands: "What the hell am I supposed to do with this?" "Bung it in the bloody attic."

Where, undisturbed, it did not so much languish as prepare itself for its second birth, for more than thirty years.

beyond any fog
in which copyright has been asserted
is where the geese live

—Unknown, "Ode to Everything"

3. The Internatal Decades

Lambshead quickly ascertained, after the second birth of what was later named Pulvadmonitor, that it was too fragile to be moved. It remained, and remains, in the attic of the Dental Museum. It was simple, with the resources and unorthodox measuring equipment to which Lambshead had access, to ascertain that, contrary to the assumption made by all other observers in the team, no long-mummified head had been placed within the container to be minutely animated by current from the battery. There was no residue of any matter transference. The head was not a speaker of, or for, the dead.

The realisation came, at last, according to the simpler exigency of placing a hand over the mouth of the trumpet, and observing the start of a slow collapse and agitation in the face within, that rather than a speaking tube leading out, it was a funnel drawing in.

A little super-gentle unscrewing of the outer rim, and Lambshead uncovered a filter like a finely holed sieve, clogged by now with three decades of hairs and larger airborne particles. This he cleaned and replaced. There was another, finer-grained filter further down the tube. The inside of the bell jar was under constant negative pressure. Air emerged from the grille at its base, but it was sucked in fractionally quicker through the trumpet, and from it was removed in stages the larger scobs of airborne debris, so that what it deposited at last within the long-undisturbed glass was a constant, extraordinarily slow, stream of London dust.

And it was from thirty-plus years of that dust that the head within had slowly self-organised. Around the palate and fake gums and teeth from which it could make a mouth.

"She did it," Lambshead was to write. "My poor lost friend Serkis. She found a means to give the dust a voice."

neither lens nor cheque can clear for you
nor shall this cat and nor shall these beaked bones intervene

—Unknown, "Ode to Everything"

4. The Dust's Warning

With this realisation, it became doubly imperative that the object not be moved, the battery not turned off (not that any researcher knew what combination of dials and switches might perform that action, nor how it had been left in an "on" position initially). The tiny chatterings and whisperings of the head were already enough to strain the integrity of the desiccated coagulum, held together by air pressure and the willpower of dust clearly desperate to communicate a message.

If the mouth opens—for it opens still now—more than the tiniest crack, the lines of the face go deep, and a little avalanche of mouse-back-coloured substance spills away. Its shape is constantly replenished by the slow intake from the funnel, and so long as the losses occasioned by such linguistic exigencies are in balance with that new matter, the head can sustain itself. A sudden movement, a loss of power, and the face-slide would be catastrophic.

Anyone who wishes to study or learn from the Pulvadmonitor must scooch uncomfortably down on the attic floor, to its eye level, more or less, making their notes in the dim illumination of field lights (more permanent alterations to the room to accommodate a better display would cause vibrations that might destroy the emissary).

Almost all our questions remain unanswered. Why does the dust not open its eyes? What nature of eyes exist, indeed, if any, below those powder lids? Was it some sense of propriety that led the dust to construct the top of a collar, as if it was the bust only of a full person? As if, having decided to mimic our shape to make the transmission of information easier, in consideration for our psychology, there was no point in doing less than a thorough job. And, on the other side, what uncanny intuition for transubstantial courtesy was it that led Xanthe Serkis to place teeth ready for the soft-palateless dust, that it had grown around and constructed its dust-lips around, to ease its shaping of our words?

Of course, the main question has always been, what is the dust's warning?

no
no no no
o really?
yes no

—Unknown, "Ode to Everything"

5. The Tragedy of Design

There can be no doubting the urgency of whatever message it is the dust wishes to convey. Whenever footprints, be they ever so careful, cross the floor towards it, it appears to become aware that it has watchers. Its mouth moves as quickly as it dares, it speaks as eagerly as its substance allows, its teeth, those little ceramic flashes in otherwise quite matt, quite indistinguishable dun skin, chatter like a telegraph operator. It wants to tell us something.

The funnel is just in front of its lips, so tantalisingly like the speaking tube we know it is not. It might even operate like one, amplifying its breathless voice enough for us to hear, but that the soft current of air from *out to in* effaces whatever minutely whispered phrases the head might speak. Its voice is so faint that not even stethoscopes on the glass can help. It is simply inaudible. Only the click of those teeth can be heard, and if they tap in code, it is not one amenable to our codebreakers.

Of course, lip-readers of countless languages have been brought to watch the head, to decipher its words. What is most frustrating of all to dust-watchers is not that none of them can discern any meaning but rather that they often see a few phrases, always disputed, never quite clear.

Two English-speaking lip-readers have claimed the dust said *this dog will never be your friend* amid a stream of meaningless syllables. An Italianophone claimed that it told her three times to *cross the bridge. It is too late for the light* has been seen spoken in four languages. In 2002, a Hindi reader and a Finnish one both claimed to have read the lips *at the same moment,* the first seeing *stop up all these gaps before it comes,* the latter *consider where your own bones go.*

Opinion is divided as to how to proceed. Lambshead was a pessimist on this issue. "As Lichtenberg said of angels," he wrote in one of his last letters, "so I say of dust. If they, or it, ever could speak to us, why in God's name should we understand?"

Two things remain unclear, and intemperately debated. One is the origin of the quiet Egyptian heads that watch the Pulvadmonitor, the Dust's Warning, approvingly. They were not a gift from Lambshead. No one knows their provenance, and there is no record of their arrival.

The second concerns the "Violent Philosophy of the Archive." This essay, in which is the footnote where first is mentioned the Dust's Warning, and which hints at the importance of its (second) birth, was found in a sheaf of Lambshead's papers dating from the mid-1980s and published posthumously. What is controversial is precisely when it was written. Textual evidence suggests that while it might have been just after, it could very well have been just before, the nook in the museum attic was uncovered. The question is whether, in other words, Lambshead was musing on something recently discovered; or was waiting impatiently for something that he had prepared to be found again.

The dust doubtless knows the answer, and its agitated efforts notwithstanding, can tell us, and warn us of, nothing.

THE MIÉVILLE ANOMALIES
ZARAGOZA
РУБ 5 ЛЕЙ

The Miéville Anomalies

The following art from China Miéville and accompanying descriptions by writer Helen Oyeyemi and "philosopher prince" Reza Negarestani first came to our attention by an exceedingly circuitous route that started with an anonymous e-mail that linked to a long article on Lambshead's "secret past" published by an Athens newspaper. A week later, a letter with a Malaysian postmark arrived from someone named only "Incognitum," who claimed to belong to a secret radical society devoted to change "through extreme re-contextualization and cross-pollination." The envelope contained a key to decode the article. Two weeks after that development, the editors of this volume had an unpleasant encounter with a masked stranger who shadowed the house for two weeks before leaving a rather less encrypted message on the garage door.

Decoding the article revealed the text for "The Very Shoe" and "The Gallows-horse." Photographs of the crudely related pictographs on the garage door with the initials "CM" scrawled beside them were sent to the agent of China Miéville, whose sole response was to provide the two images reproduced herein. Failed attempts were made to telephone both Helen Oyeyemi and the Philosopher Army or "Shield Wall" dedicated to preventing Reza Negarestani from being contaminated by the world.

Although these inquiries yielded no direct results, we subsequently received permissions to reprint from the same Malaysian address, which a Google Earth search revealed to be an empty lot in Kuala Lumpur. Thus, while we present this material as "in the spirit" of the cabinet, we cannot verify that Dr. Lambshead ever possessed such a shoe, or such a gallows-horse. As of this writing, there seem few options for obtaining further information. (It was a condition of Miéville's participation in this compilation "and any future project that you may wish to pursue with him until either his demise or your own," per telephone conversations with his designated "metamorphosis attaché," that we not question him further on the subject.)

The Very Shoe

As Told to and Compiled by Helen Oyeyemi

Created: circa 1940–1941

Creator: Radim Kasparek (1901–1971) of Bohumil, Moravia

Materials: Silk and canvas, with leather uppers, glass strip (3 cm), pinewood heel. Antenna: galvanized steel. Inner compartment (low-grade balsa wood, cotton lining) and accompanying window (low-grade balsa wood, 10 denier nylon) at the front of the outer sole added at a later date by person/s unknown

Property of: Petra Neumann née Tichy (1970–), legal owner of shoe as per inheritance. Lambshead's diary notes that "the most curious shoe" arrived in the first post on September 28, 1995, in a box postmarked Lausanne, accompanied by a note dated "October 1990": "I trust you, Lambshead—inasmuch as I can be bothered to trust anybody. We are forbidden to bring material possessions to the monastery, so I leave this in your hands. Its value is beyond measure to me. It is my great-aunt's shoe—the other one is lost, but the story in the family is that when Ludmila first saw the pair she was absolutely thrilled, clasped her hands together, and said in her best English: 'They're just too very very!' So I call it 'the Very Shoe.' This thing is a witness, my friend. It stands by and it does not change its story. Extend the antenna and listen. Then tell me: am I mad, or are there still miracles in the world?" It can be seen that the doctor underlined the words "the monastery" and surrounded them with red exclamation marks, and indeed, the location and affiliation of this "monastery" Neumann mentions is unknown; subsequently, so are Neumann's current whereabouts. The only other extant note from Neumann to Lambshead mentioning this institution is found among his papers—Neumann describes "the monastery" as "a place you go to learn conversation with stones, to find out what it is stones know."

Accession number: L1990.43

The story of this shoe is quite a plain one, I'm afraid—the shoe has no ethnographic significance, nor does it have anything as exciting as a curse or a long-standing feud associated with it. It was made by a man who was not exactly poor, but close enough. He was awkward-looking, and he stammered because he was shy, and he always said the wrong thing to women, so they didn't like him. He believed that he was born to loneliness. He ended up alone, so maybe he was. There was a William Blake poem that he muttered to himself as he worked, joining soles and heels:

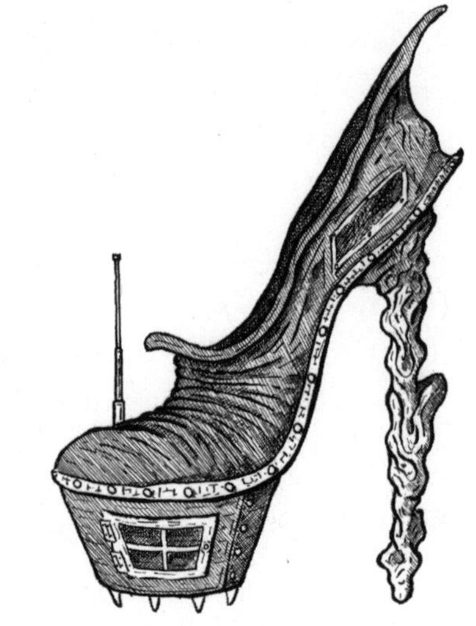

Man was made for joy and woe;
And when this we rightly know
Through the world we safely go . . .

(there's more but it is a long poem)

. . . Every night and every morn
Some to misery are born.
Every morn and every night
Some are born to sweet delight.
Some are born to sweet delight,
Some are born to endless night.

And yet, and yet, Radim got a wife. A woman of elegance, a dancer. Ludmila. She had dainty, beautiful feet, with the highest and most pliant arches Radim had ever seen. The glass panel on the side of the shoe is titillation, designed to show a mere hint of a beautiful curve. Ludmila was of the Romani. One day, some soldiers and some doctors came to Bohumil, and they separated the Romani men from the Romani women, and made inspections of their health. The soldiers and the doctors found Ludmila even though she lived in a house with Radim—vigilant neighbours informed them that some of the Romani lived in houses now, so they knocked on doors. Ludmila's health was excellent, and the following week she was sent a letter, ordering her to settle her affairs before a certain date, twenty-eight days away. Then, on the date given, she must go to a camp at Lety and serve as a labourer. Radim began to make plans for the two of them to run away together, but Ludmila would not run. Radim applied to go to the labour camp with her, but his application was refused. So he made her a pair of shoes, because he didn't know what else to do. Ludmila danced for him the night before she went to the camp, and he was afraid that he'd made the heel too high. The next afternoon, Radim's younger brother, Artur, went around to Radim's shop to see how he was holding up after Ludmila's departure. Radim told him about the dancing: "At one point she was simply spinning, round and round. And so fast, her face was a blur. It looked dangerous. And she said—*I can't stop! Catch me!* And I did. But what about when she's over there? What if—"

(What if she can't stop? It was silly to ask such a question. That would be the least of her worries; even a fool could see that.)

Years later, Radim and Artur Kasparek went to that camp at Lety, where many, many Czech Romani were sent—the brothers went down on their knees amongst others who were also on their knees, and they searched a great hill of shoes, listening to cries of grief and cries of dismay: "They all look the same. . . ."

When they found this shoe, the brothers knew that Ludmila had died at Lety. They would not have to go to Auschwitz, where some five hundred of the labourers had been sent, and search the shoes there. Radim and Artur puzzled over the addition of the window to the structure of the shoe; then, with a finger, Radim pierced the scraps of stocking that hung over the window and brushed gnawed bits of newspaper out of the compartment, newspaper and breadcrumbs and little bits of crumbled sugar. A mouse had been nesting in there. A pet—Ludmila had had a pet, at least. Radim looked for the second shoe. He looked and looked, but he couldn't find it. Night came, and he and Artur slept beside the pile, woke at dawn and kept searching, but by the end of the second day, they knew the other shoe was gone.

(For validation purposes, I should perhaps say something about who I am, and how I have come by this information. I am Antonin Neumann, Petra Neumann's husband. The first time I took her to dinner, she told me she could never love anyone who ate their soup the way I did. I didn't see anything wrong with the way I ate my soup, but I tried to change it. She laughed, and repeated herself. It demoralized me. I was reduced to asking for a very simple thing: her friendship, her respect. Then she made a U-turn and said she didn't care either way, but we could get married if I liked.

I am a jeweller by trade, and I can say, without overstating my situation in any respect, that I am a rich man. Still, I have not known happiness for many years. Petra went off on her wild-goose chase without doing me the courtesy of announcing her plans, and I haven't heard from her since. Talking to stones . . .

I suppose I could fall in love with someone else, or, at the very least, distract myself with some other love, but I don't want to. I've been tracing Petra's family tree instead. With money, you can buy whole lives; you have only to wait until they have been lived. I've been reading diaries, reading letters of the most trivial kind, travelling, looking into the faces of her forebears and finding her there. I don't think I'll show her anger when she returns: my time has not been wasted. Somehow we've grown closer, much closer than we could have grown if she had been sat by my side all these years, much closer than most lovers ever get. Needless to say, I'm grateful to have been asked to produce the notes on this item.)

I'll get on with it now.

Radim Kasparek's younger brother, Artur, is still living. The things I have written are things he dictated to me. He says that Radim first saw Ludmila at a bonfire—there was a fiddler there, and he saw her at the edge of the crowd, knee-deep in shadow, and she chose his shadow, Radim's shadow, and she danced with it, and she came near . . . and he thought—"Is it *me* she's coming to? Can she mean it? She cannot mean it." Radim wrote this down. His thoughts about Ludmila. She was like a reed—when she moved, you saw her and you saw what moved her. She opened her hand to him. Here is the wind. She came still nearer, and Radim offered her his cup, and she drank mead from it, and she greeted him in a language he didn't understand.

Artur says he didn't talk to Ludmila much. She was only interested in Radim, and dancing, and her people.

"Want to know what that brother of mine spent his life savings on?" Artur asked when I visited him. He still lives in Bohumil with his wife, two doors away from the shop and the flat above it, where Radim and Ludmila lived for two years. He showed me a blackened patch on the roof, where lightning had struck years ago; he showed me two blocks of space that were lighter than the tile that surrounded them. At first, I didn't really take in what he was telling me, because I was nervous that he should fall or injure himself in some other mysterious way that only those over eighty are capable of.

But the gist of the matter is this: Radim Kasparek bought two wide-ranging transmitters, hi-tech stuff back then, though it looks almost pre-mechanical now. He placed the transmitters on the roof, and he played music for Ludmila to dance to. Nothing especially tasteful, or sophisticated, nothing that outlasted the era—saccharine waltzes, mainly. And he recorded his voice, and he transmitted that, too. He'd only say a couple of things—he was none too imaginative, and he was unsure that the messages would really go from Bohumil to Lety, and he was wary, too, of saying too much, of his voice being heard by others tuned into that frequency. Still, it was a nice idea. When he returned from his trip to the camp of Lety, he stopped the transmissions, though he left the transmitters on the roof, left everything in place until the storm that finished it all off six or seven years later.

That's the story of the Very Shoe—but there's just one thing more. On the back of one of my Petra's letters to him, Lambshead scrawled some words I recognize.

Ludmila, jsem s tebou.
Miluju tě, Ludmila, víc než kdy jindy . . . víc než kdy jindy.

How do I recognize these words?

I have heard them.

Don't ask me how this works, reader, when the transmitters are gone, and the man and the woman involved are deep in the ground, miles and miles apart. And anyway, even if the transmitters were still there, they would be in Moravia, and this shoe is now in Wimpering-on-the-Brook! I don't know how this works, and it's a headache even trying to think my way around it, but—pick up this shoe, reader, this pretty, sturdy thing. You've picked up the Very Shoe? You're holding it? Good. Now—extend the antenna—slowly, carefully, so that it will continue to work for the next listener, and the next. First, you will only hear crackling; almost deafening white noise. Then you will hear some music . . . something silly and light, just barely melodic, in three-quarter time. Then you will hear a voice—deep and strong, speaking phrases broken with emotion. The man stammers. Allow me to translate for you:

> Ludmila, I am with you.
> I love you, Ludmila, more than ever . . . more than ever.

We cannot truly know what happened to Ludmila at Lety, how much she suffered, whether she danced there at all, whether she heard the music or the words. We don't know anything about Ludmila Kasparek, not even what her surname was before she married. We just have one of her shoes, one transmission—we don't even know the content of the other transmission. We only know that Ludmila Kasparek could dance, and that she inspired a devotion that lasted a long time. From then until now, and who knows how much longer . . .

Yes, that's all we know about her. But I think she would have liked that.

The Gallows-horse

Documented by Reza Negarestani

Museum: Museum of Intangible Arts and Objects, Saragossa, Spain
Exhibitions: The Secret History of Objects; The Center for Catoptrics and Optical Illusions; Hall of the Man-Object
Creators and Causes: Objects themselves; Deviant phenomenal models of reality; Neurolinguistic and cognitive distortions
Dates of manifestation: May 4, 1808–1820(?); July 1936–January 1961; January 2003
Title: The Gallows-horse
Objectal mediums: Gaspar Bermudez (Spanish, 1759–1820), Thackery T. Lambshead (British, 1900–2003)

Also known as the Edifice of the Weird, the gallows-horse is the highlight of the Museum of Intangible Arts and Objects. Simultaneously being displayed in three distinct and permanent exhibitions, the gallows-horse presents the four basic criteria of the museum—Immateriality, Intangibility, Elusiveness, and Ephemeral Manifestations. Gallows-horse was first brought to the attention of the museum's board of experts and trustees by an international collective of researchers consisting of art and science historians, linguists, and philosophers, who were commissioned by the Universities of Oxford and Exeter to index and organize the notes and memoirs of the late Dr. Thackery T. Lambshead, a prominent British medical scientist, explorer, and collector of esoteric arts and exotic objects. These notes, according to the research collective, include references to various objects and artworks collected by Dr. Lambshead during his lifetime. Whilst the majority of these references have been traced to tangible corporeal objects currently on display in various international museums, there were also scattered allusions to objects that did not have any record in museums or private collections. Either ravaged by a fire that broke out in Dr. Lambshead's private residential collection, or lost during his lifetime, nearly all of these objects—thanks to engineering and technological interventions—are now visually reconstructed through digital simulation.

In the late stages of documentation, however, the research collective came upon a concluding remark written by Dr. Lambshead regarding an alleged and final item added to the collection before his death. In a presumably closing remark marking the completion of the collection, Dr. Lambshead writes:

> January 28, 2003: It is not about the question of part-whole relationships, it is not even about the question of possible combinations of different objects, it is about the self-improvising reality of objects—unapproachable and incommensurable with our perception—that could give rise to gallows-horse just as it could rise to either horse or gallows, or something fundamentally different, or nothing at all. Even in its most kitsch material forms, the gallows-horse rises from the pandemonium of objects. A collection without such a thing is simply a tawdry carnival that spotlights human perception and displays our mental bravado instead of objects themselves. [. . .] Today I erected the gallows-horse as the final and crowning piece of the wonder-room.

"It is this emphatic reference to the *final* and *crowning* piece that made us reexamine [his] notes in search of the gallows-horse," says Professor Rachel Pollack, one of the researchers appointed to index and categorize the bulk of writings penned by Dr. Lambshead. The first reference to the gallows-horse dates back to January 10, 1936, when Dr. Thackery T. Lambshead writes in his journal: "The sky is clear and the gallows-horse reigns; canaries sing from crogdaene." For more than two decades, references to the gallows-horse persist always in the context of such enigmatic sentences that undulate between brief cryptic notes and self-invented semantic structures, and are always preceded by an exact date. For example, a note from July 15, 1953, reads, "The Salamian began to sink Ariabignes' boat. When a man runs out of the steam of history, it is in our best interest to restore the history to a previous state, when that man did not exist, or make that man mount the gallows-horse." Or "December 3, 1958: In the wake of recent incidents, my pain is rekindled every night either by the fear of death or even worse, by the fear of riding the gallows-horse at a gallop."

I. Gallows-horse at The Secret History of Objects (second floor, room 6)

The letter to the Museum of Intangible Arts and Objects states that none of the early references to the gallows-horse written between 1936 and 1959 described or even identified it as an object or a *thing*. During this period, the gallows-horse continually appeared in the form of a chameleonic crypt or a cipher that opportunistically mimicked the semantic context of the sentence or the phrase it inhabited. It has been unanimously confirmed by the members of the research collective that, in its larval stage of development between 1936 and 1959, before it began to fully appear as an object—at least as objects are commonly known—the gallows-horse has been a linguistic crypto-object with parasitic behaviors. "Like a menace that must be assimilated by its foes to defeat them from within," the research collective emphasizes, "the early form of the gallows-horse tends to adapt—in the most esoteric way—whatever meaning the sentence that hosts it conveys. This uncanny linguistic crypto-object demonstrates its independent reality by moulding the world of the conscious and thinking subject around itself, literally thinking the subject that thinks it."

During its incubation period, the gallows-horse was simply feeding off of contexts and linguistic connections in Dr. Lambshead's notes and memories in order to build an empty cognitive carapace around itself. In this period, therefore, the gallows-horse cannot be understood in terms of an emerging thing, whether this new thing would be an idea, a thought, or a corporeal object. Adamantly refusing to be considered as something (let alone a unified thing made of a gallows and a horse), the gallows-horse is *the very personification of the primordial death of all meaning par excellence* that oscillates between sense and non-sense, depending on its mode of deployment against the parameters of human perception. In this early linguistic incubation period, the deeper you dig into the context where the gallows-horse is buried, the more promiscuous you find the gallows-horse is in relation to its semantic and semiotic neighbors. In digging for the true gallows-horse, you simply dig out nothing. In its basal form—that is, before it is born as a distinct idea and is manifestly imagined—the gallows-horse can be anything precisely because it is nothing.[1]

The Secret History of Objects is proud to present *Naught-horse-Naught-gallows,* an equivocally inexistent object that linguistically manifested as the gallows-horse from 1936 and 1959 throughout notes attributed to Thackery T. Lambshead—a meaning-feigning crypto-object that not only reveals a tenaciously alien yet meaningless expanse behind its ideated components, which are "horse" and "gallows," but also worms itself into the semantic foundation of its context, eroding it so thoroughly that only a depth devoid of meaning, significance, and ghosts remains.[2]

II. Gallows-horse at the Center for Catoptrics and Optical Illusions (second floor, room 9)

The second life of the gallows-horse as an intangible object began December 15, 1959, when for the first time Dr. Lambshead directly addressed the gallows-horse as an object by obliquely writing on the ambivalent aspects of the gallows-horse:

> I dreamed of myself dancing on the gallows-horse, hanging to its neck, swaying on its back, trotting with the rest of the herd. How can a horse take you to the gallows when the gallows is the horse? It is not a euphemism for death nor does it realize the literality of a horse carrying the convict to the gallows. As far as the nomenclature is concerned, it can be the horse-gallows as much as it can be the gallows-horse. There is no distance between the gallows and the horse to be either stretched or traversed. Yet despite the absence of such a distance, the gallows and the horse retain their distinct identities, the horse is still a horse and the gallows is still an inanimate edifice. But the curious aspect of this object is how can the horse and the gallows be united as one without one being the extension of the other or without a substantial change in their nature so as to make the intimacy and entanglement of the animate with the inanimate possible?

For less than two years, a scarce number of comments on the gallows-horse were made by Dr. Lambshead. These comments have frequently been presented in the form of bewildering riddles regarding the unified nature of the gallows-horse as one object in which both the gallows and the horse retain their distinct identities in one way or another without veering toward monstrous or marvelous categories. This "period of second advent" (as it is stated in the letter to the Museum of Intangible Arts and Objects) lead the research collective to believe that what Dr. Lambshead was calling the gallows-horse should be none other than the Equcrux, which is also known as the cross-horse or the Spanish sphinx.

During the Spanish War of Independence (1808–1814), two days after civilian residents of Madrid stood in rebellion against the occupation of the ruthless

French army and one day after the massacre of the same Spanish civilians by Bonaparte's army, on May 4, 1808, on a hilltop outside of Madrid, a small French task force handpicked by Marshal Joachim "Dandy King" Murat had prepared the gallows for hanging a Spanish traitor who was also a renowned and talented portraitist named Gaspar Bermudez. Being an artist friend of Francisco Goya, Bermudez certainly did not share Goya's more patriotic sentiments. He had been providing the French troops with vital military and inside-palace information since the beginning of war. But on the first of May, he had inadvertently given erroneous information to the French army stationed in Madrid, contributing to the rebellion of the second of May and the flowing of French blood in the streets of Madrid. Marshal Murat had ordered the execution of Bermudez immediately after repressing the uprising, but he later changed his mind and decided to subject the Spanish artist to a humiliating mock execution instead. This was mainly due to the popularity of Bermudez as a gifted portraitist among royal and wealthy French patrons, including Murat, who had Bermudez paint seven different portraits of himself.

Reportedly, minutes before sunrise, the French soldiers take Bermudez to the gallows riding on a horse; they perform their short everyday ritual by putting the noose around Bermudez's neck and charging the horse. The gallows having been manipulated by the French soldiers possessed two adjacent nooses, a fake and a real noose. Once the horse leaps forward, Bermudez finds himself—perhaps after a minute or two lost in terror—with a second noose around his neck, fallen on his chest on the ground. As he raises his head, he sees the sun dawning and an opaque light that permeates between the gallows, the neighing horse, and a patch of swampy ground in which the horse is rearing, transiently filling the gap between all three objects (that is, the waterlogged patch of earth, the horse, and the gallows). And Gaspar Bermudez beholds what he later calls the Equcrux, a spectral object consisting of three distinct identities (the soggy earth, the horse, and the gallows) seamlessly fixed upon each other in a fashion that the horse was beheaded by the gallows and the quaggy patch of earth was inseparable yet categorically distinct from the hooves. The Equcrux, according to the Spaniard himself, was an object that had been created outside of the infinite possibilities given to the worlds of the horse, the gallows, the waterlogged earth, and even the aurora as separate objects; it was a spectral gradient between the animate and the inanimate, a frozen instance of transgression from the realm of the individual objects toward a universe in which things were always anonymous until now.

The figure of the Equcrux enjoyed a brief popularity after the war, when Bermudez claimed himself as a war hero and mass-produced the spectral object as a kitsch symbol of the horrors of war branded as the Spanish sphinx, an object made of stuffed leather and wood in the form of a horse in rearing position, whose body was attached to a modeled gallows from the base of the neck so that it had as its head, literally, the gallows. However, due to production constraints and additional costs, it had been decided by Bermudez himself to abandon the third object, the quaggy patch of water, which in the first models was unsuccessfully made of straw mixed with resin. In the course of a few years, the Spanish sphinx lost its national popularity after Gaspar Bermudez was finally brought to the Spanish court as a traitor and a national shame. The last vestiges of the Spanish sphinx as a figure of terror were erased from memories and flea markets when Francisco Goya's *Disasters of War* was finally published in 1863.

As a part of the Center for Catoptrics and Optical Illusions, an inoperative replica of the Spanish sphinx has been installed with a patch of wet soil, a taxidermized horse, and a wooden gallows brought together in an illuminated cubicle, where these objects can no longer be conceived as the gallows-horse.

III. Gallows-horse in the Hall of the Man-Object (third floor)

In 1920, an unpublished essay by the Russian psychoanalyst Sabina Spielrein, titled "Gaspar Bermudez: A Case Study in the Spontaneous Shape of Trauma," recounts a different analysis of the Spaniard's spectral object. As Spielrein writes in the introduction to her essay, through a German collector she came across a surprisingly well-preserved copy of a personal diary attributed to a Spanish portraitist named Gaspar Bermudez and became increasingly interested in the life of this obscure artist and his vision of the cross-horse. The diary, as Spielrein remarks, opens a secret passageway into the life of this enigmatic Spanish artist. A major portion of the diary deals with Bermudez's intimate fascination with horses, which obsessively asserts itself as a form of identification of his self with a horse or a drove of horses. The diary reveals that in conjunction with his main profession as the portraitist of Spanish and French nobles, yet hidden from the eyes of the public, Bermudez had the habit of making self-portraits of himself as horses with different—subtly human—postures and facial expressions. This complete identification of his self and ego with a horse, Spielrein argues, eventually became a mental basis for the figure of the Equcrux, or the cross-horse. During the mock execution, the humiliating blow that was inflicted on Bermudez's outgrown and mutated ego forced the self—that is, the Spaniard's self—to shed part of itself in order to cope with the extreme and unbidden force of trauma that asserted itself not as a French executioner but as the gallows that firmly stood before his overthrown self and prostrate ego.

The act of shedding a part of the self in order to save the rest is, in fact, common among organisms (such as lizards shedding their tails or the so-called scratching tic) as a primitive yet powerful means of self-preservation. The curious and interesting aspect of Bermudez's traumatic experience is that while he was degraded at the foot of the gallows, it was not his human self that cut off a part of itself but his earlier identification of his *self* with a horse. Since Bermudez's ego had already fully identified with a horse, at the moment of the traumatizing blow, it was his equine self that cut parts of itself in order to save the integrity of the rest of the horse (or, more accurately, Bermudez's full mental identification with a horse). When Bermudez's ego dismembered itself to ensure the survival of the greater part, a void was left in his nervous system, a deep hole punctured in the horse that had already replaced the mental human image of the self. Knocked down at the foot of the gallows and his ego dismembered, Bermudez's equine self had no option to restore its "lost chunk" (Spielrein) other than by filling in the new cavity with the invasive force of trauma that could neither be expelled nor be allowed to shatter the entire nervous system. The cross-horse is precisely the mental object created by these traumatic tensions and breaches in Bermudez's psychic structure, the beheaded horse was permanently trephinated by the gallows, which was but the mental identification of the traumatic force. Spielrein writes that not only the damaged cervical vertebrae of the horse tightly locked into the wooden end of the gallows but also the intrusive traumatic force of the gallows impaled the horse from precisely where it had already torn off one of its parts. The upright pole of the gallows was re-erected as the restored cervical vertebrae of the horse, the triangle formed by the cross-beam its new cranium and the noose-hole the space between the mandible and the higher jaw.

An offspring of a traumatic invasion, a traumatic object with a spontaneous anatomical structure, the Equcrux intriguingly does not signify a receding tendency toward earlier states of the evolutionary chain. In other words, for Bermudez, the trauma of the mock execution did not—unlike other instances of trauma and toppling of the ego—cause the individual to relapse into an earlier state of evolution when the species was still crawling, due to the lack of spinal developments. On the contrary, the Equcrux melds the bestial locomotion or four-legged model of walking with the anatomy of a straightened spine, which characterizes the bipedal species. The quadrupedal horse gets a new spine that exhibits the traits of a straightened—perhaps even too straightened—spinal curvature that has been transplanted by the L-shaped and the obsessively perpendicular composition of the gallows. For this reason alone, the spinal anatomy of the Equcrux cannot be compared with the spinal formations in monstrous mental categories, such as that of a centaur, in which the curved spine of the horse shifts to the less curved spine of the human. In the Equcrux, the spinal curvature is not produced by extending a more curved spine to a less curved one; it is the creation of a mathematical marriage between a curve (the quadrupedal spine) and a straight line (the gallows).

Spielrein continues by stating that from the day of the great humiliation onward, the Equcrux became the sole mental and artistic image of the Spanish portraitist, for it was not really a passing traumatic object anymore but his very self and psychic structure that had turned into a full-fledged object. After a month-long pause, Bermudez recommenced writing his diaries, which were, this time, exclusively dominated by his ambitious rants about replicating the Equcrux by any means or method of fabrication, and his immutable and recurring dreams, wherein he was always a drove of gallows-horses rushing down in great numbers from a hilltop toward a city.

The Equcrux, or Gaspar Bermudez, as he was traumatically conceived in the form of the gallows-horse, is currently kept in the Hall of the Man-Object in an empty vitrine labeled *Gaspar Bermudez, the gallows-horse.* A motto runs under the label: *¡Suelta a los raros!*

ENDNOTES

1. "It has been suggested that mimicry such as that of a chameleon is an impulse for dissolving back to the environment from which the individual was once relatively segregated; it is a force that is temporarily lent to the individual entity by nature. In using mimicry, the individual unconsciously utilizes the impulse for dissolution (or death) in order to gain some kind of profit (surviving, preying, or living in harmony with something else). But in reality, in using mimicry, the individual exercises the indifference of its environment to meaningful change and intention, that nature does not have any interest or motive to create meaningful differences, and that even in its most cunning and meaningful acts, the individual affirms the dissolution whereby all differences (including its own) and meanings are eradicated. The semantic mimicry that the gallows-horse undertakes is, in the same vein, neither a tendency to return to a meaningful semantic environment nor a meaningful yet cryptic act in itself. Instead, it is an act that reveals the fragile construction of meaning as the aftereffect of a compulsion to return to a meaningless abyss that precedes all patterns, signs, and signifiers. The gallows-horse communicates a meaning by mimicking its sentential environment, and in doing so, it demonstrates how meaning is the result of mimicry, which is, in fact, a compulsion to flatten all semantic differences and return once again to the meaningless abyss that lingers behind the words *horse* and *gallows*, as well as any other word, sign, idea, or image." (Richard Graansvort, *From Cryptography to*

Neurolinguistic Mimicry in Thackery T. Lambshead's Memoirs, London: Samuel Buscard Institute, 2009)

2. Shortly after the death of Dr. Thackery T. Lambshead and the publication of a number of his memoirs, the pseudonymous Pravda Online columnist Novena Brines published an exposé on the life of the British scientist. According to Brines, Lambshead was an overseas coordinating officer of MI6, whose scientific journeys and seemingly scandalous Communist sympathies were only shields to protect his true identity. Among the documents and sources that Brines cites as evidences and clues, are Lambshead's memoirs. Brines particularly focuses on the name "gallows-horse." She considers gallows-horse as a codename or what she calls an operation-marker. Brines argues that in the majority of cases, the name "gallows-horse" marks an imminent launch of an operation. In her exposé, Brines cites as an example the note "January 10, 1936: The sky is clear and the gallows-horse reigns; canaries sing from crogdaene." She explains that the note is dated one day before the British MI6 officers departed from Croydon Airport toward the Canary Islands in order to move and protect General Francisco Franco for the nationalist military coup that began with the code "Over all of Spain, the sky is clear" and ignited the Spanish Civil War. Brines, however, fails to provide any more convincing examples or concrete documents and mostly resorts to rumors to the extent that, in a public apology, *Pravda*'s editor in chief called Brine's speculation "a wild conspiracy theory more fitting for an American gossip column than *Pravda*."

FURTHER
ODDITIES

Further Oddities

Through the catalyst of a generous grant from the Institute for Further Study, additional research into Lambshead's cabinet was undertaken expressly for this volume. Each item selected has been the subject of intense debate by Lambsheadeans and Lambsheadologists for years, while Lambshead's own attachment to these items varied from indifference to obsession.

For example, although Lambshead took it upon himself to document (admittedly, in a sardonic mood) the provenance of the Sir Locust armor, it was found upon his death in his clothes closet—wearing lingerie and a sunflower hat, with an Oxford jacket draped over it. One armhole had been turned upward and blocked off with an ashtray that overflowed with Punch cigar stubs. *The Thing in the Jar*, on the other hand, as chronicled by Michael Cisco, seemed to inspire not just a flurry of speculation as to its origins, but also a pervasive emotion of profound regret, along with bald-faced fictions of a sort not displayed by Lambshead elsewhere in his long recorded history. Items like the two art pieces, *The Singing Fish* and *Taking the Rats to Riga,* Lambshead kept in a small locked room, along with a scandalous Chagall and a Picasso titled *Quarantine for the Infected.* The two times Lambshead possessed *The Book of Categories,* it also resided therein. The room could only be opened using the Castleblakeney key, which tended to discourage idle curiosity.

Some might question the editorial decision to include research from Amal El-Mohtar and Caitlín R. Kiernan, given their criticism of, and wild theories about, Lambshead. However, it should be noted that the doctor himself, in his will, cited both "as members of the loyal opposition" who should be given "as much equal opportunity to feast on my corpse as anyone else. They've earned it."

The Thing in the Jar

Researched and Documented by Michael Cisco

The Thing in the Jar was presented to Dr. Lambshead by an African anthropologist specializing in the study of Europeans, one Prof. Manjakanony Ramahefajonatana, of the University of Antananarivo, Antananarivo, Madagascar, in exchange for some assistance rendered in accumulating a representative collection of items of contemporary everyday English use. The object was discovered by Prof. Ramahefajonatana's principal research assistant, Vololoniaina Rasendranoro, who, owing to a condition of amnesia brought on by a clout she received on the head as she was escaping from a burning barn in Essex, was entirely unable ever to account for how she came across it. The only definitely known fact about the jar's past is that it was found in England, and does not appear to have originated elsewhere.

The object is a cylindrical glass jar, fifteen inches tall and six inches in diameter, weighing about twenty-five pounds, with a bronze base and lid. The bottom is wrapped in a fringed skirt of faded red velvet with gold tassels, and bears at its center an engraving of an owl in semi-profile and the legend "Griscyple Bros.—1737." The top is hermetically sealed with black wax.

The jar contains an anthropic creature.

This object is associated with a manuscript in Dr. Lambshead's own hand, consisting of a great many sheets of different hotel stationery, contained in a manila file folder. The folder's projecting tab is covered with a stack of adhesive labels, one laid atop another. The exposed, uppermost label had something written on it which was then aggressively scribbled over, and the rest of the folder is leopard-spotted with scribbled-out words or phrases. The only unmarred writing on the folder itself consists of three words inscribed in a column on the inner surface of the front, or untabbed, half of the folder. They are, from top to bottom: MUSHROOMS, BACON, OVALTINE.

Not unlike the folder, the manuscript is also heavily emended, with many strikethroughs and insertions. The battered, fraying pages show signs of having been much handled. Not only are all the pages from different hotels, but they are written and marked in a variety of media, including ink, pencil, lipstick, crayon, pastels, and, in one case, a dry and crusty reddish-brown fluid that has the characteristics of blood. The alterations are, more often than not, written in a medium different from that of the older text. The implements used also must have been highly varied, ranging from rare and expensive Sheaffer or Pelikan fountain pens to the quills of exotic birds to ordinary run-of-the-mill ballpoint pens and No. 2 pencils to sharpened fragments of bone or medical implements dipped in ink or stain. In one case, a correction is actually cut into the paper with a sharp instrument, perhaps a scalpel, and there are minute discolorations around the incisions suggesting the scalpel had been in surgical use quite recently when the correction was made, or, perhaps, that Dr. Lambshead had been struck by an idea in the very midst of performing an operation, and had paused to make the change in the text using literally what he had in his hand just at that moment.

In content, the manuscript consists of a list and seven fragmentary narratives or descriptions, all of which seem intended to account for the existence of the Thing in the Jar. All of them are, also, mutually exclusive, and it is impossible to ascertain which of them, if any, is the true explanation.

The list reads, in part, as follows:

imp / witch's brat
immature yeti
immature yama / yamantaka
buffalo spirit
buffalo minotaur
hoax by M.
motile fruiting body from enormous Kamchatkan mycelium
found in meteor / chrysolite
automaton replacement for lost child, abused, becomes monster
Japanese legend: pregnant mother murdered, stillborn child avenger
stillborn specimen, ankylopsoriasis
found blocking sewer drain under big city
infant gorilla raised by crocodiles
wandered into small German town in 1762 with note
discovered in exhumed coffin in place of body: cadaver changeling
conceit of insane taxidermist
small island North Atlantic where wrecked Vikings married wolves
mature specimen of gnome

"Thing in Jar" as first reproduced within Ramahefajonatana's dissertation, *Les Articles des Usages Quotidiens des Communautes Rurales et Semi-Rurales de l'Angleterre du milieu du Siècle Vingtième* (Paris: Plon, 1957)

According to the first narrative, the Thing is a fetish, created for some religious purpose. A sentence to the effect that it was made by the Akimel O'odham people of the American Southwest is struck out and somewhat ambiguously modified to mean something else that isn't exactly clear. The intention seems to be that this fetish was found among or traded from, or possibly to, the Akimel O'odham, and/or might be Aztec in origin. The text does clearly state that the fetish was placed in the jar by a white American individual who acquired it by theft. Many possible names for this recipient, or thief, are given, all of them crossed out: Buckwaldo Mudthumper, Eustace Bucke, Cornelius Abereustace, Haldernablou Yuchachev, Steven Williams, Shi Mu-ke, Beldu Terrance, Josephine Mouse, Melinda Postoffice, Macfitzhugh O'Donaldin, Wigberto Fuentes, Mustafa Mukhtar al Kateb, Bradford Frederic. The story breaks off after mention of this person, with no indication of its intended ending.

The second manuscript bluntly identifies the Thing as an aborted minotaur. This is cancelled and replaced with the phrase "reverse minotaur," meaning not the offspring of a bull and a woman, as in the fable, but of a man and a cow. A partial list of the less well-known of the Greek islands is included; most likely, Dr. Lambshead intended to select one of these as the setting for his story, but abandoned it altogether before doing so.

The third and longest fragment is a rambling narrative, based on documented events, of an expedition to Saibai in the Torres Strait, and the Biak-Numfoor rain forests of the Schouten Islands. After many pages of laborious description mainly devoted to detailing their efforts to capture a living specimen of the Biak Naked-backed Fruit Bat (*Dobsonia emersaa*), Dr. Lambshead turns his attention to the island of Saibai and the Zaman Wislin cargo cult he and his companions discovered there. One practitioner in particular, a "pariah" who was compelled to live apart from the other inhabitants of the island, was rumored to have made strange use of an infant for magical purposes. Deleted segments of the story made this person a member of the cult in good standing at first, then "a demented European convert," but in the end Dr. Lambshead chose the native pariah variant. It was said that this man ["woman" was written first, then struck out] used to put a baby in a pot of boiling elixir ["water" had been written first, then struck out]. There is a careted phrase for insertion that indicates this was to be after incantations had been chanted over the baby for . . . and then this is followed by only a blank, presumably to be filled in later, but which remains empty.

When the enchanted baby would be placed in the pot, the boiling fluid would recoil away from the baby's body. Unharmed in any way, the baby would go to sleep in the warm pot, "in a kind of magnetic bubble" that prevented the fluid from injuring it. Meanwhile, "the crazed practitioner would solemnly open an elaborately carved box, and, with many gestures of sanctification and holiness, take out from the box a battered, ramshackle pair of aviator headphones. Handling them with exaggerated care, he would insert the plug at the end of the headphone cable into a crude, jury-rigged jack, basically just a hole cut into a large, hollow nut, affixed to the side of the pot by a stinking lump of coal tar. Then, placing the headphones on his own head, this man would pantomime efforts to 'tune' the pot by turning knobs he'd fashioned out of spools, and attached to a board. Through these headphones, the man claimed to be able to hear the voices of ancestral spirits, and of the gods themselves, talking to him. When asked what they sounded like, he raised his voice to a high falsetto and faintly repeated distinct phrases, much separated in time. While some were in Kalau Kauau Ya [the native language], most were American English. I plainly heard him say, 'I am the one who does not come when called.' What could be discerned of the remainder in English consisted of fragments: '. . . the water of skulls . . .' '. . . too much is happening when I try to sleep . . . sleep . . . sleep . . . in my sleep . . .' '. . . anyone dead must be treated or they may do more . . .' With this last, he began to shake violently, and threw a fit that seemed to me to have no obvious somatic cause."

The rest of the account slides back and forth; in some passages, it seems the doctor continues, as in the above quotation, to put himself on the scene observing the practitioner at work. In others, however, he comes to the island only after the death of the outcast, and receives the entire story secondhand. In both versions, however, the infant is initially normal, becoming less and less normal, more and more inhuman as the rituals are repeated, finally dying of an excess of mutation, at which point it is collected or traded for by Dr. Lambshead.

The fourth story is the outline of a work that, had it been written, would have run as long as a good-size novel. It was set on a farm in Indiana around the first few decades of the twentieth century, and was permeated with "a bittersweet air of nostalgia, the haunting poignancy of remembered youth, the amber radiance of sanctified recollection, the gentle grief of hindsight softened by the passing of time, the tender longing for bygone scenes, the pathos of enduring love devoted to people and things that have yielded themselves unto the Destroyer, the ghostly romance of innocent boyhood fantasy, the eerie melancholy of brooding and incommunicable childhood secrecy, and the wistfully spectral yearning for unseen and beautiful things that abide beyond the limits of life."

The main character, a boy of about nine, has an imaginary friend who "may be more than mere imagination," and which corresponds in description to the Thing in the Jar. Interspersed among typical domestic and rural scenes, "tinged ever with a foreboding of darker things," and described in lofty, high-minded prose poetry, are a series of lethal mishaps that would appear to be revenge for slights against the boy, although he is always obviously innocent of any connection to these suspiciously frequent and numerous accidents. Whatever his other reasons for not undertaking the composition of this novel, the notes show clearly Dr. Lambshead's indecision about the outcome of the story. The imaginary friend is now a disowned, disfigured twin brother—presumed dead, now a creation of the boy's own mind—a figure so intensely visualized and otherwise invested in by the boy as to take on physical, independent form, as a kind of projection of the boy's unconscious, yet now the imaginary friend is an alternate personality, and yet now it is a demon, now a ghost.

The fifth story is a terse, telegraphic account of an earthquake in Mexico, and is the only really complete piece in the folder. The setting is an ancient Olmec ritual center, only recently uncovered by archaeologists. Twenty minutes or so before the earthquake hits, the carvings ornamenting certain of the site's structures begin to come to life. They flee the site, crawling, flying, hopping, slithering, burrowing, throwing themselves into a swiftly flowing river nearby, flapping off among the clouds, or creeping hurriedly away toward the distant mountains. The carvings all escape except one, which is killed when a piece of debris dislodged from a hillside falls, striking it. This creature, collected by the archaeological team, is the Thing in the Jar.

The sixth item is lengthy and so extensively revised that it is very difficult to read. In it, Dr. Lambshead, or his source, lays out a theory of modified reincarnation redefining the idea of the *"bardo"* condition, originally found in the spiritual teachings of Tibetan Buddhism. By tradition, the *bardo* is a sort of pause between incarnations, where the souls of the dead linger for a time. The theory set down by Dr. Lambshead is that, under certain circumstances, some souls enter into a physical *bardo* condition involving the organic remains of their former bodies, although the process often introduces strange alterations in these bodies, coupled with some kind of machinery. Neither the provenance of the machinery nor the details or causes of the "process" alluded to can be made out in the garbled text of the description. The result is a hybrid being, part cadaver, part machine, which houses the soul during its *bardo* period. Dr. Lambshead calls these beings *"sarkoforms."* The only further information that can be extracted from this text is that the Thing is believed to be a bungled *sarkoform*, consisting of weirdly mutated and miniaturized remains drifting through time until they find their correlative machinery.

The seventh and final manuscript in the folder is included here in its entirety, as a sample of the general condition of the whole of the folder's contents.

The Seventh Manuscript

Once upon a time there was a man who loved volcanoes. ~~From birth or not~~. At first, his instincts were innocent. ~~His father his mother his uncle Brobisher~~ His father had told him once of a volcanic eruption ~~of Kraka of Herac Pomp~~ of Krakatoa, and he'd done a book report in school in grammar school that had been well received that had won him his first real praise in school. ~~He became a vulcanologist~~. ~~Amateur~~. When he went to university he devoted himself to the study of vulcanology and in time became a professor of that subject, although his chief love was not in teaching about volcanoes in the classroom nor even of lecturing on volcanoes or conducting most forms of research into, for example, the history of volcanoes ~~of volcanic of vulcanic vucl~~ vulcanism and humans in human history. His great love was in visiting volcanoes and it was during one such visit that he realized his interest was sexual. When in the presence of erupting volcano he would experience all symptoms of intense arousal, including tumescence, tension in the groin, shortness of breath, an increase in temperature, a flush in the face, anxious nervous excite intension tension in the thorax. He often found that he'd be so lost in amorous contemplation of the gushing crater that he had made no observations of any scientific ~~use~~ utility. But only had penned such empty chestnuts as magnificent, breathtaking, beautiful, thrilling etc.

Finally taken aside by so-called "friend" and colleague.

"You had better be careful," his friend said. "Now, you wouldn't want to be catching 'volcano fever.'"

"Why is now a bad time to catch 'volcano fever'?"

"It happens to every vulcanologist, sooner or later," he ~~added~~ muttered a moment later ~~after a long pause~~ hastily. "The intellectual ~~intelligentsual~~ passion spontaneously develops a sensual dimension, the dense, shielding foam that protects the gem facet of eroticism lamentably dissolves to expose the bare and tinglingly sensitized surface to the ~~polyfluous exagamies of hermitanical and phantasmic erotimoids~~ . . ."

"I gather your meaning—[Here is interposed a long list of possible names for the interlocutor of the stricken vulcanologist. In the interests of economizing our use of space, only a few examples will be given: "Earthflounder . . . Soildozer . . .

Marldozer . . . Dozemarl . . . Claybeater . . . etc."]—Your prognosis is ~~a fetishistic transference~~ a common, everyday ~~fetishistic~~ transference."

"I'm glad we had this little talk, DAQUIRI." ["DAQUIRI" being the name attributed to the afflicted vulcanologist, in this line only. The paper shows signs of a name that was written, erased, and rewritten again and again, until the name DAQUIRI was allowed to remain on the smudged and badly roughened paper.]

Finally, on occasion of witnessing eruption and heavy flow at close hand, perfectly understandable given the circumstances loses all self control and experiences spontaneous orgasm ~~deliberately gets no accidentally~~—somehow ejaculates copiously into lava torrent before dragged away by hysterical, overreacting and narrow-minded assistant ~~who's too busy prying into other people's affairs to mind his own bloody business~~.

Few years later ~~stories~~ local legends begin to be told about a curious little man-like figure observed gamboling on slopes. Volcano's slopes. Thought to be a child in outfit. Costume. Very young. Too young for costumes really. At play unattended, dangerous locations. Virtually in the flames at times, untroubled. Found eventually curled in blazing hot alcove, in softened recess, sucking at unusually rounded ~~stalagmite tite mite TITE damn~~ stalagTITE. Netted. Snared. Resemblance. Faint. Distorted. Yet, somehow plain. Unmistakable. Creature radiates fantastic heat. Handler must wear aluminium suit.

Recognition mutual?

Escapes.

Winter. Volcano enters less active stage, coincidence.

Child found dead. Hypothermia.

Cools to room temperature.

Transferred to jar. Former contents, a salted lammergeier chick, sent to taxidermist [seven pounds ten shillings] for stuffing never retrieved. Jar sent to the farmhouse in Essex.

Grief of the father.

The Singing Fish

Researched and Documented by Amal El-Mohtar

This exciting find, titled *Der singende Fisch* ("The Singing Fish," pen and ink with watercolour, circa 1860), is a rare reproduction of the last known work of artist, artisan, and poet Edith Abendroth. She created *Der singende Fisch* during her incarceration in the Lunatic Asylum at Eberbach Abbey from 1861 until her death in 1869. Until now, only scattered descriptions of the piece were available, reproductions suppressed by the unusual events following Abendroth's death, which resulted in the superstition that surrounds *Der singende Fisch* to the present day.

The image contains the distorted proportions characteristic of all Ms. Abendroth's work, but there are more symbols at work here: consider that the critic is cock-eyed, seen in profile, which associates him with the noble figure of one-eyed Odin, the Norse God of the gallows, who sacrificed an eye in order to gain all the world's wisdom. Yet instead of Huginn and Muninn, Odin's twin ravens named Thought and Memory, two parrots perch on his shoulders, symbolic of meaningless chatter and thoughtless repetition. Still there are ravens in the image, after a fashion: two raven feathers (one from Thought, one from Memory?) peek out of the well of Imperial Ink at the critic's feet, suggesting that he has sacrificed Thought and Memory to produce the ink with which he will write his vicious tracts.

The fact that the critic leans against a stack of books could indicate any number of things: that he leans on the works of his betters without understanding them; that all his learning is useless to him as a means of understanding the singing fish; that all he can do is parrot the words of his educators without contributing thoughts of his own. Consider that he covers his mouth with his hand, and that he is dressed all in black—almost as if he had bathed himself in the death of Thought and Memory.

But where the critic's mouth is covered, the fish's mouth is wide-open; where the critic is silent, the fish sings.

What bait could hook such a throat?

Early Portrait of the Artist

Ms. Abendroth was born in Berlin in 1821 to Karl and Frieda Abendroth, who kept a prosperous print shop in the city, out of which they also taught drawing, painting, and etching. She showed a keen interest in these arts from an early age, and quickly grew quite skilled, in spite of—or perhaps partly due to—suffering from severe migraines. During such episodes she sometimes claimed to perceive things as larger or smaller than they truly were, and described the sensation in detail:

> It is as if the pain in my head comes from the swelling of the object in my sight—as if the table captured by my eye has grown too big for my head to contain without agony. Yet while these things grow, I think surely I must shrink, must be dwindling to a speck, and tremble to look at my hands for fear of seeing them become either a bird's or a giantess's. It hurts—and yet I think there must be something terribly splendid in being able to see the world as in a story book, that perhaps I am a heroine of some sort, yet to discover my purpose. It is all terribly interesting.[1]

The uniqueness of her perspective can be readily appreciated in her work, and is perhaps what suited it to the entertainment of children: giant frogs squat in well-upholstered seats, tiny horses pull carriages for damsel-fly nobility, and enormous mice-gentlemen dance with delicate ladies at a masque. She wrote

Edith Abendroth's "The Singing Fish"

charming books of fairy-tale verse in which such animals spoke and had adventures; these she illustrated herself, most often working in a combination of pen, ink, and watercolours, materials she had mastered by the time she composed *Der singende Fisch.* She sometimes turned toy-maker when a story became particularly popular: resin castings of Gren Ouille, hero of *Der stolze kleine Frosch* ("The Proud Little Frog"), and his good friend Hop, still command high prices at antique auctions. Happily, Dr. Lambshead's cabinet includes a model of her *Die Auferstehung des Frosches* ("Frog Resurrection"), which captures in surprising detail the most poignant moment of little Gren Ouille's struggle with pride, when he must humbly harness himself to a wagon in order to carry Hop's coffin into the revivifying light of Venus.

Ms. Abendroth's ability to mine her own work for inspiration was admirable, as was her skill at using it to generate multiple streams of revenue. She never married, but from her twenties on she was able to support herself comfortably without recourse to her parents' estate, though she continued to live with them until their death. She participated in Berlin's high society and was modestly admired and respected as a lady of good breeding; she enjoyed a passionate friendship with actress Gertrude Nadel, a woman renowned for her controversial portrayals of Dr. Faustus on stage. Ms. Nadel would later be instrumental in the preservation and presentation of Ms. Abendroth's oeuvre—however, it is ironically thanks to Ms. Nadel that Ms. Abendroth's renown in artistic and literary circles is less for her published material than for the rumour of a small satirical manuscript, *Leitfaden der Kritik* ("The Manual of Criticism"), of which *Der singende Fisch* would have been the final illustration.

The Regrettable Influence of Klaus Mehler

It was at one of Ms. Nadel's salons that Ms. Abendroth met Klaus Mehler, the man who would have an incalculable influence on her life and work. Nine years her junior, he was a former student of the Royal Prussian Academy of Arts turned critic, and was, according to Ms. Abendroth, very forceful in his interactions with her:

> I cannot say for certain how tall he is, and I think perhaps this infuriates him; sometimes he seems a comically little man, and I must squint to see him clearly in the shadow of a chair or soup tureen—yet at other times I feel like a beetle beneath the heel of his gaze. I do not like him—Gertrude does not like him, only she sighs and says his sister has influence at court and she simply *must* invite him

> to her every gathering. He does not leave me alone, he does not even ask me to dance, but will insist instead upon debating my opinions on the merits of aquatint and Imperial Ink. I think I would be more interested in his conversation if he ever seemed to listen to what I had to say, but he does not—it is as if he listens with his eyes, watches my mouth to grasp my arguments, and so does not make any *sense* when he says I am wrong, wrong, wrong. I wonder if it is all women he dislikes, or all women artists, or me alone.[2]

It was not long after meeting Mehler that Ms. Abendroth ceased to write in her diary. Stephen Kurtz, who up until quite recently was the leading authority on Ms. Abendroth's career, suggests that her thoughts with regard to him were of so intense a nature that she recoiled even from articulating them to herself, preferring to retreat into increasingly escapist art. Helena Rothschild, however, disagrees, saying that the cessation of her diaries after keeping them meticulously for twenty years was a clear symptom of her growing terror of the man; Ursula Nussbaum suggests that Ms. Abendroth did keep writing, but later destroyed her journals to prevent them from falling into Mehler's hands while she was incarcerated.

The latter two conclusions are no doubt unnecessarily alarmist, but what little we do have of Ms. Abendroth's thoughts on Mehler indicates beyond any

Ron Pippin's model of Abendroth's *Die Auferstehung des Frosches* (Frog Resurrection)

doubt that she found him unsettling and relentless in his attention—behaviour that would only intensify when he began publicly criticising her work:

> Ms. Abendroth is certainly talented, and it is therefore all the more lamentable that she should turn her not inconsiderable skill to grotesque drolleries and fantastical nonsense. Her lines bespeak a steady hand, but her vision is wobbly; her choice of subjects speaks clearly of an immaturity of spirit, a child's mind in a woman's body. In this, it is true, she is not far different from most of her sex, but progress being what it is one has come to expect better of our city's women, and consequently one holds them to the highest possible standard.[3]

Taken alone, such comments might not, perhaps, have had quite the effect they did on Ms. Abendroth—but it was sadly at this time that her mother passed away, likely from some form of cancer, and was followed shortly thereafter by her father. Not very long afterwards, Ms. Abendroth moved into Ms. Nadel's home (as she, too, was unmarried), which should have been a comfort to the newly orphaned artist but made her rather an easier target for Mehler's savagery:

> One could perhaps surmise that Ms. Abendroth's art is the stunted result of a woman kept incomplete: were she to marry, to have a child of her own, it is possible that she would no longer present herself as one in her work. One suspects, however, that Ms. Abendroth thumbs her nose at such decency, preferring her twilight world of mannish actresses, spear-shaking frogs, and singing fish to the land of the living.[4]

It seems likely that Mehler was jealous of Ms. Nadel and Ms. Abendroth's intimacy, though Nussbaum's suggestion that he was a rejected suitor of one or both of them seems to err on the side of sensationalism.[5]

Effects on Abendroth and Her Work: A Mysterious End Game

At any rate, it was Ms. Abendroth who received Mehler's vitriol in public, and suffered from it tremendously. Her migraines grew more frequent and more pronounced; she restricted herself to her rooms when company called; she grew thin and listless, though she continued to produce work. Ms. Nadel was clearly anxious with concern, as evidenced by the number of doctor's bills in her household accounts for the years between 1857 and 1861; sadly, the numerous physicians she engaged proved to be of little help. In 1861, Ms. Abendroth's sensory uniqueness progressed into full-blown hallucinations, and she began to stab her pens into the wallpaper of her rooms, her bed, her paintings, and her own skin. One doctor's account suggested that she had taken to drinking her ink.[6] It was agreed that it would be best for all concerned if Ms. Abendroth should retire to the countryside and avail herself of the high standard of care for which Eberbach Abbey was renowned.

After a year of treatment—and, one suspects, protection from Mehler's constant attacks—Ms. Abendroth's condition improved to the point that the sisters of the abbey cautiously allowed her access to the tools of her trade, though always under their supervision. According to Kurtz, all the material she produced while incarcerated had one driving idea behind it, one unifying theme:

> *Leitfaden der Kritik* was to be Ms. Abendroth's opus, the last word in her seemingly relentless feud with Mr. Klaus Mehler. In it, she told Gertrude Nadel, she would create something so perfect, so pure, so unassailable that Mehler would be forced to put aside his scalpel of a pen and concede it unimprovable, a job well done. That she told Gertrude this from within the sanatorium at Eberbach Abbey did nothing to dampen her enthusiasm, though it did somewhat dim her loved one's confidence in her ability. Nevertheless, from 1862 until her death, most of her waking hours at Eberbach were spent in producing material for it.[7]

And yet, *Leitfaden der Kritik* never saw print; to this day, it exists only as a series of scattered papers that have yet to be assembled into one coherent whole. Kurtz reproduces some in support of his thesis: illustrations include savage caricatures of Mehler as a little teapot spewing tar, a Mehler-faced cushion being kneaded by a cat's extended claws, and a rather distressingly graphic image of Gren Ouille committing seppuku with a nib pen while Hop weeps over him. But the fact that Kurtz's selections are so limited speaks volumes about the morass of mixed metaphors and half-remembered French from which he chose them, and certainly Rothschild and Nussbaum don't consider the bulk of her creations during the Eberbach period to be anything more than the expiation of her tormented thoughts, finding the whole to be decidedly less than the sum of its remarkable parts.

Der singende Fisch, however, is not reproduced in Kurtz's book, and has never appeared in print until now.

According to Ms. Abendroth's will, only one copy was to be made of the image: the original was to be kept by Ms. Nadel, while the print was to be delivered, with compliments, to Mr. Klaus Mehler, beseeching his thoughts. Mehler received the letter and the print on Monday, May 10, 1869; by Monday, May 17, he had committed suicide. He was found slumped over a mess of illegible, blood-spattered notes, a pen embedded in his left eye, the copy of *Der singende Fisch* torn to shreds. An autopsy later found pieces of it lodged in his trachea. Gouged into the polished surface of his mahogany desk were the words *Die Palette hat keine Farbe,* which translates to "the palette has no colour."

Publicly, Ms. Nadel declared that his guilt over destroying Ms. Abendroth's mind and health had consumed him; privately, she insisted to friends and family members that *Der singende Fisch* was a curse eight years in the making, that Edith had confided in her the instrument of her revenge, and instructed her to produce copies for whichever critic should desire one. We must recall, however, that Ms. Nadel was a consummate actress, and her grief may have led to undue dramatization of the facts.

Still, it is surprising that there is no record of anyone publishing their thoughts on *Der singende Fisch;* Rothschild and Nussbaum remain far more interested in the facts of Abendroth's private life and analysis of her journals, and in the wake of Mehler's suicide, very few individuals applied to Ms. Nadel for copies, perhaps feeling that to succeed where he had so spectacularly failed would be unseemly. Nevertheless, it was rumoured that Stephen Kurtz had intended to produce a monograph focusing on *Leitfaden der Kritik* and *Der singende Fisch* alone, and had even applied to Ms. Nadel's estate for permission to see the original—but that project, like many others since the publication of *Frogs, Frocks, and Fol-de-Rol,* has fallen by the wayside while he recovers from his unfortunate boating accident.

Further Examination of *The Singing Fish*

Why, then, is the fish singing?

Certainly, divorced from its incredible history, *Der singende Fisch* is not particularly noteworthy: its lines are simple, its subject odd, if charming. All its cleverness lies in the recursivity of the meta-narrative—the fact that we, as critics, are observing a critic observing a fairly absurd creature, trying desperately to puzzle out its meaning. Just as the critic in the image is stymied by observing the fish, so must we be momentarily stymied by observing him observing the fish, and the dissonance produced by observing the fish in our turn, with all the calculated detail surrounding it.

Notice, for example, the thorns. Observe how one's gaze moves from left to right, to begin at the roses, tempting in the gentle wash of the watercolour, before thickening into thorns the closer one approaches the fish. Surely this symbolises the inaccessibility of the art object, the difficulty facing any critic who attempts to penetrate its mystery. Again, why is the fish singing? Why is it performing an act we cannot apprehend without the frame of the title? Is it triumphant? One could argue that its triumph is in its inscrutability, in the impossibility of seeing it as anything but what it is.

But the critic does not look cowed, only frowning in thought; he is sainted, even, he wears a halo! Could that indicate that the critic is dead? Is the Singing of the Fish synonymous with the Death of the Critic? Can the one exist without the other? *Finale,* spell the ribbons—or are they scarves? The looping of the letters is rather noose-like—hearkening back, perhaps, to Odin's gallows-heritage? The more answers one finds, the more thorns, or questions, one encounters!

This is terribly exciting work, you must understand. There is a terrible burden to be shouldered here, in being the first to offer a detailed analysis of the fish in print. Mehler's death-desk scribbles offer little in the way of illumination, except for his gouged-out exclamations about palettes and colour. These are useless. Of course the palette has colour on it—the whole piece is washed in a pale rose watercolour, and the palette is shaped for holding oils or acrylic. Ah, but is that irony at work? Oh, of course! It is a pen-and-ink drawing—and look, there, the inkwell and the feathers! She has *appropriated the critic's tools*! That is why the palette has no colour on it—the palette is her vulnerability, the colours her Achilles' heel! *The palette has no colour on it.* The fish has sprung fully formed from it—the fish *is* the palette's colour! The only colour is in the end—*Finale,* in colour, in the colour that the palette lacks—the colour the fish brings! The devilish detail of it! *Frogs begin as fish! They die and are resurrected as singing fish!* Oh, I see it all, Ms. Abendroth, I do, I see! I can hear it clear as a bell!

Such, at any rate, would likely have been Mehler's statements, had he been able to communicate them in something other than the blood and wood-dust beneath his fingernails. The piece seems very nice, and it is testament to Dr. Lambshead's discerning taste that he sought to preserve so excellent a thing in his Cabinet.[8]

ENDNOTES

1. Stephen Kurtz, ed. *The Early Journals of Edith Abendroth,* vol. III, p. 67 (Routledge, 1959)
2. Ibid., vol. VI, p. 98

3. *Die Spitzer Feder,* April 1856, p. 24
4. Ibid., October 1856, p. 32
5. Nussbaum, Ursula. *Loves That Did Not Know Their Names: Lesbian Desire in Edith Abendroth's Early Journals*, p. 134 (Ashgate, 1979)
6. Kurtz, Stephen. *Frogs, Frocks, and Fol-de-Rol: The Mirth and Madness of Edith Abendroth*, p. 91 (Routledge, 1961)
7. Ibid., p. 113
8. While the main body of this essay and all previous endnotes were the work of Amal El-Mohtar, the final paragraph was appended by a friend who has chosen to remain anonymous. This friend would like to make clear that Ms. El-Mohtar's unorthodox approach to the essay's conclusion is to be read as ironic, and certainly has nothing to do with the fact that she has since withdrawn into the seclusion afforded by a village in the southwest of Cornwall, where she spends her days in pursuit of garden fairies to dissect for her doctoral thesis, and her nights in tormented, guilt-wracked sobs for subjecting them to the cruelty of iron.

The Armor of Sir Locust

As Dictated to Stepan Chapman by Dr. Thackery Lambshead, 1998

Until recently, I looked forward to cataloging my collection of souvenirs and curios. Now, in retirement, I finally have the time, and it turns out that the job is an endless drudgery. It further turns out that I know nothing worth recording about my possessions. I only know that I acquired some of these things during my years of constant travel. Others could explicate them with better success than I. My memory is not what it was.

This thing, for example. I had to wire it together from various pieces. Bought it in a canvas box from an antique store in Cairo. Got it for peanuts. Had it appraised at the London Natural History. The docent said it was priceless. Hard to know what that means, coming from a docent.

It's unusual, these days, to own a suit of medieval armor, but this specimen is more than unusual, it's downright peculiar. The metal's been assayed. I'm assured that it's an alloy of tin and bronze characteristic of the Second Crusade. Copper grommets—probably a later addition. Scraps of leather, hung with buckles.

Ivica Stevanovic's "Armor Montage" incorporating Dr. Lambshead, as first published along with the doctor's account in the magazine *Armor & Codpiece Quarterly* (Winter 2000).

The first time you see this thing, a series of questions enter your mind. Such as: Is it armor for a man or for a horse? And if it's for a man, why has it got armor for four arms? And if it's for a horse, why has it got armor for six legs? That's three questions already, and they just keep coming. For as long as the legend of Sir Locust has been recited, there have been variants, and the variants raise questions of their own. Was he originally a soldier? Was he a priest? Was he a locust that grew and grew and somehow, by some bizarre spontaneous recombinant mutation, took on human attributes? Was he a man who was cursed, at puberty perhaps, with the attributes of a locust? Too many questions.

Sometimes I entertain the ghoulish notion that perhaps this armor is no artifact at all, but rather a mummified skeleton, scooped out subsequent to burial and grave robbery. But then I look closely at the hooks and loops and chain mail, and I remember that insects, of whatever size, are not made of metal. But a custom-forged spring-wound machine, an engine of war disguised as a person, *that* would be made of metal. Speculation is impossible. Let's examine the written records.

Sir Locust appears in several of the illuminated annals of the Second Crusade. His presence is noted at certain battles. One such text, which still exists in scattered fragments, is *The True Chronicle of Sir Locust the Unlikely*. It reports that Sir Locust had a nemesis, an opposite number on the Saracen side of the conflict, who was called the Mullah Barleyworm. This priest of Allah, so we're told, sent a series of three assassins against Sir Locust. None returned. At this juncture, the mullah confronted the French knight directly. They joined combat, and neither survived. I'm leaving out all the good parts. My time is limited, and my collection is extensive.

For instance, I'm leaving out the love interest. Evangelette of Lombardy was Sir Locust's lady. After his death, she cherished a bloodstained silk scarf, and so on. I'm sure that he wrote her countless sonnets from the front. If the Second Crusade *had* a front. The Christians lost that crusade, as you may recall.

So now we have a cast of characters all constellated around this dented suit of giant insect armor. Once, the Mullah Barleyworm traveled to France in disguise and kidnapped the Lady Evangelette. Word reached our hero. What a kick in the head for him. He followed his archenemy to Syria but could only effect his lady's release by giving himself into Barleyworm's power, as they say in gothic novels. Torture followed, and rooms filling with water, walls sprouting spikes, bottomless chasms, impregnable towers, the jaws of death, all the usual flummery. Also there was some question as to whether the lady actually *wanted* to be rescued, having fallen in love with her captor in the time-honored masochistic tradition. Legend has it she was drugged. That's just what Crusaders would expect from an infidel.

I remember one last thing about Sir Locust. I almost left this out. It's an alternative-origin story, which hinges on the third-century Syrian mystic, Saint Simeon Stylites.

Saint Simeon, as everyone knows, mortified his flesh by living for thirty-seven years at the top of a pillar. They say he subsisted on honey-dipped locusts, provided, I suppose, by respectful local peasants. I always wondered how the locusts got to the top of the pillar. Perhaps he had a bucket on a rope. I don't see why not. Simeon was so holy, they say, that even the fleas and horseflies refrained from biting him.

But one day, a great grey locust lighted on his sun-blistered nose, as bold as you please. This locust called out to Simeon. "Now I shall bite you, old hermit," it told him, "for excellent reasons. I can ignore your incessant consumption of my brethren bugs, soaked in the baby food of my cousin bugs, for such is the way of nature. But why should I excuse you from reciprocation? You may very well be considered a candidate for sainthood amongst the benighted Christians. But I, I'll have you know, am a good *Mussulman* locust." Whereupon the locust bit Simeon's nose, drank his blood, and flew away.

The saint might have been excused for cursing the locust. Being a saint, he did the opposite. He *prayed* for the proud heathen insect, and God was so impressed that He followed the saint's suggestions and blessed the locust with three boons. First, it grew as large as a horse—a miracle! Then it grew a human face on its head—an egregious miracle! The third boon, longevity, would only become apparent as the years went on. Saint Simeon had assumed that the locust would be grateful for its transformation. He hoped that it would convert to the true faith and save its tiny soul. (Saint Simeon didn't get out much.) The locust remained an unrepentant Muslim, and to compound its ingratitude, it outlived the saint by decades.

In fact, it lived in Syria for eight centuries, doing whatever it did without making any impression on the historical record. Then came 1144, the fall of Edessa, and the Second Crusade. The ancient creaking locust purchased a sword, commissioned a fine suit of armor, and joined the army of defense. It marched into legend as an illustrious soldier of Islam and died, in due course, a soldier's death.

The Christians, far from home, heard the story of the pious old locust from their wretched prisoners of war. And one Frenchman liked the story so well he stole it.

A Key to the Castleblakeney Key

Researched and Documented by Caitlín R. Kiernan

Excerpt from a postcard found among the correspondence of the late Dr. Thackery T. Lambshead, from Ms. Margaret H. Jacobs (7 Exegesis Street, Cincinnati, Ohio) to Lambshead; undated but postmarked January 16, 1979:

> . . . kind of you to give me access to the collection. Such marvels, assembled all in one place! It was like my first visit to the Mütter, so crammed with revelation. But the hand, the hand—well, I'll have to write you at length about the hand. I had a dream . . .

Excerpt from *Archaeological Marvels of the Irish Midlands* by Hortense Elaine Evangelistica (2009; Dublin, Mercier Press):

> . . . and is undoubtedly one of the more curious and, indeed, grisly side notes to the discovery of the "Gallagh Man" bog mummy. The hand clutching the key is severed just behind the wrist, bisecting the radius and ulna bones (short sections of which protrude from the desiccated flesh). The bronze skeleton key is held firmly between the thumb and forefinger in such a way as to give one the impression that the hand was lobbed off only moments before the key would have been inserted into the lock for which it must have been fashioned. The key measures just under seven centimeters, from the tip end of the shank all the way back across the diameter of the bow, and the bit has three prongs. As mentioned earlier, the hand clutching the key is exceptionally small, measuring not much more than nine centimeters, diminutive even for a small child.
>
> Littleway (2006) suggested the hand was not human at all, but, in fact, belonged to a species of Old World monkey (*Cercopithecidae*), probably a baboon or mangabey. This suggestion was subsequently rejected by Davenport (2007), who noted that no species of Old World monkey possesses claws, and even those few primitive New World species that do (*Callitrichidae*, the marmosets, and tama-

rins) lack opposable thumbs. Certainly, the sharply recurved claws at the end of each finger remind one more of the claws of a cat or bird of prey than anything even remotely human. After his thorough examination of the hand, Davenport (ibid) concluded it to be a hoax, a taxidermied chimera fashioned from the right hand of a primate and the talons of a barn owl, then treated with various acids, salts, and dyes so as to give it the appearance of having been excavated from the peat deposits at Castleblakeney. Prout (2007) agreed with Davenport that the hand wasn't that of a primate, but insisted it belonged to a three-toed sloth (despite the presence of five digits). Regardless, Davenport's hoax explanation appears to have run afoul of carbon-dating carried out at Brown University (Chambers and Burleson, 2009b), which indicated the hand likely dates from between 300–400 B.C.E., which would make it much older than "Gallagh Man." Also, a biochemical analysis of tissue samples taken from the hand reveal that it differs in no significant way from bog mummies known from Ireland and other locations across Northern Europe.

However, even if we accept that the strange hand from the late Dr. Lambshead's cabinet is almost twenty-five hundred years old, we're left with still another conundrum: the oldest known metal skeleton key (or passkey) dates back no farther than 900 C.E. Also, as Davenport was quick to point out, the only indication that the hand was recovered from the vicinity of Castleblakeney is a charred and faded label apparently written in Thackery Lambshead's hand.

As it stands, the matter may likely never be resolved to anyone's satisfaction.

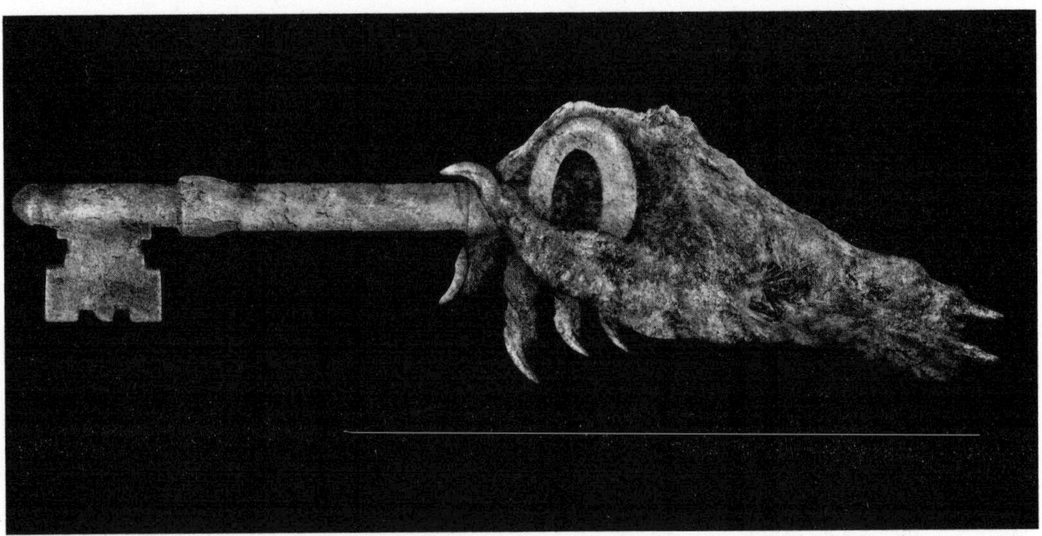

Aeron Alfrey's eerie rendering of the Castleblakeney Key

Following a break-in on the evening of April 12, 2010, the hand and key were discovered to be missing from the collection of Brown University's Department of Anthropology, where the artifact was on long-term loan from the National Museum of Ireland (*Ard-Mhúsaem na hÉireann*). Reports indicate that the thieves took nothing else. . . .

Excerpt from "An Act of Rogue Taxidermy? Preliminary Report on the Morphology and Osteology of the 'Castleblakeney Hand,'" P. O. Davenport, *American Journal of Zooarchaeology,* vol. 112, no. 1 (2007):

. . . that evidence provided by these high-resolution X-ray CT images leads the author to the conclusion that the artifact is no more representative of the remains of a single animal than are other chimeric forgeries, including jackalopes, Barnum's "Feejee mermaids," the Minnesota iceman, the Bavarian Wolpertinger, Rudolf Granberg's skvader, or the fur-bearing trout of Canada and the American West. As will be demonstrated, these X-rays reveal fully intact terminal ungual phalanxes (bones and keratin sheaths) indistinguishable from those of members of the family Tytonidae (barn owls), articulated to the proximal metacarpophalangeal and ginglymoid surfaces of the phalanges of an adult Barbary macaque (*Macaca sylvanus*). It is not possible, at this time, to determine whether or not Lambshead himself was involved in fashioning the hand or whether he believed it to be authentic, having been duped by its creator, but that question is irrelevant to the current investigation.

The form and function of claws varies significantly among vertebrate species, though the composition of the claw sheath does not. Claw sheaths, nails, and hooves are comprised of an exceptionally tough class of fibrous structural protein monomers known as keratin (Raven and Johnson, 1992), which protects the bone of the terminal phalanx and assists in providing traction during such activities as climbing, defense, prey acquisition, and intraspecific combat associated with mating (brief review in Manning et al., [2006]). Mammalian claw sheaths are composed of a-keratin (helical), while those of avians, nonavian archosaurs, and non-archosaurian reptiles are composed of β-keratins (pleated-sheet) (Fraser and MacRae, 1980). The results of this study leave no doubt that the claw sheaths associated with the Castleblakeney artifact are composed of β-keratin and so cannot have originated from any primate or other mammal. Before addressing . . .

Excerpt from a letter found among the correspondence of the late Dr. Thackery T. Lambshead, from M. Camille Dussubieux (n°50, Rue Lepic, Paris) to Lambshead, dated November 17, 1957):

... do hope that your time abroad in the States was not in any way especially inconvenient, and that it proved helpful and productive in all your various researches. I hope to one day see Chicago and Manhattan for myself.

Setting aside casual pleasantries for another day and another letter, I am writing this evening to inform you that Monsieur Valadon and his circle of associates continue to press the matter of——, that *objet curieux* now residing in your care. Indeed, I begin to believe that you may have made a terrible error in taking the thing from *les carrières de Paris*. As you well know, I'm not a superstitious man, nor am I even particularly religious. But my concern is that Valadon's "warnings" that you may be visited by some mystic, infernal retribution are, in fact, thinly veiled threats of physical violence by members of his order now residing in Britain. If there's any truth to his unsavory reputation (and I have no reason to believe otherwise), these threats should be taken with the utmost seriousness. I would caution you to make such precautions as you may, if, indeed, I cannot persuade you to immediately divest yourself of that abominable relic.

It is beyond me what you hope to learn from ——, and seems far more likely, my dear friend, that you have merely convinced yourself it has added an additional measure of mystique to your cabinet. By now, I know you well enough to feel confident in drawing such a conclusion, and I hope you won't find it too presumptuous. You must not consider possession of —— to be a privilege or to carry any prestige. It is, at best, a burden.

I have taken the liberty of contacting our mutual acquaintance at the Musée Calvet à Avignon, who assures me that —— would be safe in that institution's care, even from the likes of Valadon, Provoyeur, and Rykner. She is also willing to travel to England to receive —— in person, rather than entrusting it to any courier or post. She only awaits word from me that you are agreeable to this arrangement.

Those passages you quoted from Balfour's *Cultes des Goules* are grim enough to rattle the nerves of even an old skeptic like myself. . . .

Excerpt from "Artifact, Artifice, and Innuendo" by Tyrus Jovanovich, *Art Lies: A Contemporary Art Quarterly* (no. 62, Summer 2009):

. . . and so have allowed questions of biological and historical "authenticity" to dominate the discussion. Insistent, unrelenting authority intervenes, and we are not allowed to view an *object* as a *work.* The potential for message is denied by the empirical demand for objective meaning. If we are to gain access to the intriguing conceptual dimensions and dialectics presented by this *hand* and this *key,* by the unity of hand *with* key, key *with* hand, it becomes necessary for us to invert, or entirely disregard, the inherent limitations of that scientific enterprise and its attendant paradigms. First off, we must cease to view the work—as it is now reconsidered, rescuing it from the mundane—as fragmentary or in any other sense lacking in fundamental wholeness, though questions of fundamental [un]whole[some]ness will be evaluated in light of complexities of the object-subject relationship.

As we refocus our attention from a normative default, it is neither the hand nor the key that consumes our need for understanding. Rather, we find, literally, new direction by *implication.* The hand holds the key, and the key moves our eyes from the visible towards the invisible. Here, a moment is brilliantly captured, and yet entirely escapes stasis. The hand is always and forever acting upon the key, and the key is ever pointing, moving, urging us towards the implicit *lock,* which is the truest *locus* in this configuration, even if the lock exists only by implication. So, too, the existence of a mind behind the hand and key and lock is unspoken, but no less essential. Finally, the efficacy and undeniable kinetics make themselves known, and we are drawn away. . . .

Excerpt from a letter found among the correspondence of the late Dr. Thackery T. Lambshead, from Ms. Margaret H. Jacobs (7 Exegesis Street, Cincinnati, Ohio) to Lambshead; undated but postmarked May 4, 1979:

. . . to put it out of my mind. But the dreams return night after night, each incarnation almost identical to every other, except that they grow worse, more horrifying. They're unrelenting. I've never suffered insomnia, but now I find myself afraid to sleep. I put off going to bed as long as possible. The thought of a catnap is enough to make me anxious.

As I've said, the dreams didn't begin until shortly after my visit with you last December. Don't get me wrong, Dr. Thackerey [sic]. I'm still grateful for having been allowed to view your collection and photograph the key. But I'm beginning to think I'm paying an awful price for that opportunity. Yes, I know how that must sound to a man of science such as yourself. By divulging my situation, I more than half-suspect I might find myself described in some future edition of your medical guide. But I don't know who else I would tell this to. Friends or family? No, they all think me odd enough already. They would dismiss it all, and ridicule me in the bargain. A psychiatrist? A priest? I can't abide the former, and, despite my Catholicism, have always been unable to open up to the latter.

That leaves just you, Doctor. I suppose it's like they say, and no good deed goes unpunished.

Please don't feel obligated to read what follows. Just because I had to write it down and send it to you doesn't mean you have to subject yourself to these grotesque, absurd ramblings. But I implore you again, please, *please* destroy the key (as I have destroyed the pictures I took). If I am certain of anything at all (and I doubt that more each day), I'm certain that the destruction of that thing will stop the nightmares, just as I believe my lifting it from its box, and daring to hold it, triggered them. And I suspect, too, there's something greater than my sanity at stake. How can I convince you that what you're harboring beneath your roof is more virulent than any disease? Burn it, Doctor. Melt the damned key to slag, and scatter the ashes of that mummified claw to the four winds.

The dream always begins with me looking out to . . .

Excerpt from "The Monkey's Paw Redux," Jones, Z . L . I. *Skeptical Inquirer,* vol. 30, no. 3 (May/June 2006):

. . . that has yet to be addressed by any of these investigators is the inconsistent nature of the second digit, even though it is obvious from the most cursory glance at photographs of the "Castleblakeney hand." On the thumb, and digits three, four, and five, the nails curve downward, exhibiting the normal condition for primates (and, for that matter, the ungues of all tetrapods). Yet, on the second digit, the nail displays a feat of anatomical gymnastics and curves *upwards.* Three possible explanations for this irregularity come to mind: (1) sloppiness on the part of the hoaxer; (2) a simple and intentional signal that the hand is indeed a hoax; (3) an attempt by the perpetrator of the hoax to make the hand/key contrivance seem even more bizarre.

For the moment, I'll focus on the second option, though it is probably the least likely of the three. I'll assume, for the sake of argument, that the hoaxer is an educated individual who would be well aware of the faux pas presented by the upturned nail. I will even go so far as to consider the possibility that it was his or her intent to embed in this intentional mistake some hidden meaning. Pause to consider the significance of the index finger in Western art and culture. For example, in Leonardo da Vinci's *St. John the Baptist* (c. 1513–1516), the right hand of the subject is raised, pointing heavenward, the index finger extended. In Michelangelo's *The Creation of Adam* (c. 1511), it is the index finger of the creator's right hand (*digitus paternae dexterae*) that is shown delivering the spark of life to the index finger of Adam's left hand. Comparable instances from Christian iconography are too numerous to list, though it is worth noting an altarpiece in the basilica of . . .

Excerpt from a letter found among the correspondence of the late Dr. Thackery T. Lambshead, from M. Camille Dussubieux (n°50, Rue Lepic, Paris) to Lambshead, dated January 23, 1954):

. . . only tell you what little I know of this odious thing, though surely there must be far less repellent subjects upon which you could fixate. It is a mummified hand, as small as a child's, gripping a bronze key. The fingers bear long talons, and the hand is so shriveled the bones show through. Both the hand and key are mottled with rot and verdigris, with a scab of long ages hidden away in darkness and damp. As for its provenance, I have heard a story told that it was discovered by Howard Carter in the spring of 1903, during his initial excavations at the entrance of the tomb of Thutmose I and his daughter Hatshepsut, though the key is clearly not of ancient Egyptian origin. I have also heard a claim that the hand is the remains of an homunculus created by John Dee, for Robert Dudley, 1st Earl of Leicester, and also that it came to France from China, and even that it was found in an Irish peat bog. I see no reason to give credence to any one of the tales; they seem equally outlandish.

I first saw it seven years ago, when it was very briefly on display in the Galeries de Paléontologie et d'Anatomie comparée on the rue Buffon. However, the Muséum national's former director, Achille Urbain, apparently ordered its deaccession from the museum's catalog, following a scandal of some sort (I confess, I do not follow such sordid affairs). In 1952, it resurfaced in a peculiar little antiquities shop on the rue de Richelieu, near the Bibliothèque nationale. Though some say this hand was no more than a clever counterfeit of the original. Either way, it was purchased by a Mlle. Dominique Provoyeur, an occultist who, in her younger days, is said to have had dealings with Crowley and others of his ilk. At this point, I caution you, we must descend into the sheerest sort of hearsay, but it may be that Provoyeur made a gift of the hand to another black magician, Erik Valadon.

There are rumors that the pair used it during profane rituals somewhere within the catacombs, perhaps l'Ossuaire Municipal.

By all accounts, Valadon is an especially execrable fellow, a drunkard and heroin addict, obsessed with various arcane texts and the notion that these texts contain rituals capable of summoning some manner of prehistoric deities, banished from the world before the evolution of mankind. Indeed, it is all quite completely ridiculous. Which is why I suggest you focus your energies elsewhere, Thackery. Your prodigious intellect should not be squandered on this sort of foolery. Let us speak no more of any . . .

Excerpt from a letter found among the correspondence of the late Dr. Thackery T. Lambshead, from Ms. Margaret H. Jacobs (7 Exegesis Street, Cincinnati, Ohio) to Lambshead; undated but postmarked March 12, 1981:

. . . by now, you must have stopped even opening my letters. I wouldn't blame you if that's the case. I wouldn't blame you if you write back and tell me please never send another. I think you've been too patient with me, too lenient, Doctor, these last two years, and it's difficult for me to imagine why. It must be wearing thin, and I picture you rolling your eyes at the arrival of every envelope bearing my name.

"Oh, good heavens. It's that dreadful woman from Ohio," you might say. Something like that. I truly have become "that dreadful woman," here in my own mind. That woman filled with little but dread.

Still and all, here I am, regular as clockwork, writing you again. Writing you again about my dream, my nightmare, which I cannot ever stop believing began with my visit to your home more than two years ago. But at least, this time, I'm writing to say that something has *changed*. Beginning last week, last Wednesday, a new wrinkle has been added to the dream narrative, which by now has become so threadbare and monotonous (but has lost none of its nerve-racking hold over me) any change is welcome.

It starts as it always does. Me waiting on the shore for the ferry, looking out across the sea, the waves thundering against the rocky jetty. The ferry arrives, and it delivers me to the island where the sickly yellow house stands alone amid that shaggy grove of hemlocks and the overgrown rose garden. Nothing's any different until after I've spoken with the ravens and the silver-eyed women and the Bailiff, until after the cannibalistic banquet and the disturbing images that old film projector spits out onto the parlor wall. But then, when I'm lead [sic] to the cellar door, the women both turn back and leave me to make the descent alone! Never before have they done this, but you know that. They shut the door behind me, and bolt it, and I go by myself down those creaking wooden steps.

I think, at least for a few moments, that I'm less afraid of what I'll see down there than I am surprised that they've allowed me to go without a chaperone. It'll sound strange, no doubt, but it makes me proud, as if I have been accepted as an equal, as one of the house's monstrous inhabitants. There is a sense of belonging. How can there be any comfort in such a thought? I can't say, only that this is what I feel.

As always, I reach the bottom of the stairs and find the cellar flooded by several inches of stagnant saltwater. The odor is overwhelming, and bloated fish and tangles of seaweed float all about me. Tiny crabs scuttle across the submerged cellar floor. This part is the same as always, of course. I try not to smell the rot, and splash between those moldering brickwork arches until I have come to the wall of grey granite blocks and grey mortar. Like always, it's encrusted with slimy moss and barnacles. Like always, the moss and barnacles have grown in patterns that make them look like leering skulls. All of this is the same.

But when I reach into my pocket for the skeleton key the Bailiff always gives me, it isn't there. There's nothing there, and for a moment I panic. They've trusted me to go down to this place *alone,* and I've managed to lose the damned key! I stop, trying hard to remember each step across the cellar, each step down, everything that occurred before the silver-eyed women lead [sic] me to the cellar door, how I might have possibly mislaid the key (which I always put in my dress pocket immediately, the moment the Bailiff places it in my palm). My mouth goes dry. My heart is hammering in my chest. They'll make me leave and never ask me back again, never again send the ferry for me (and, I know, I know, I should be glad, but in the dream I am mortified).

Then I look down, and there's something hideous crouched in the water not far from me. It's not much larger than a very large rat, and *it* has the key, clutched tightly in one hand. It isn't human, the thing with the key, and immediately I turn away, the sight of it enough to make me feel ill. Gone are those feelings that I've disappointed the Bailiff and his pale companions, that I *belong* here, below the yellow house. I only want to run back to the stairs and hammer on the door until they let me out again.

"Too late for that, Missy," the crouched thing with the key says. I don't look at it. I can't bear the thought of ever setting eyes on it again.

"Daresay, took you long enough to puzzle it out. Been waiting here so long

I've memorized the names of all the crayfish, and I think I might be waterlogged."

"I don't want to see any more," I say, and it laughs at me. Or maybe it doesn't laugh *at* me, but it laughs. It's a small laugh, very small, and the sound makes me think of burning paper.

"Best be minding your P's and Q's, Missy. Come too far to go lily-livered on us now, don't you reckon?"

And I hear a clattering noise that I know is the crouched thing fitting the skeleton key into the keyhole in the granite wall. And I'm thinking how all this is wrong, that I should be at the keyhole, that the women should be with me, when the granite wall swings open wide, and the barnacles scream, and . . .

Excerpt from *Darkening Horizons: The American Supernatural Novel During the 1980s* by Gerald Hopkins (Austin: University of Texas Press, 1993):

. . . and, regrettably, the unjustly celebrated "Evil God, Out of Words" (*Twilight Zone* magazine #8, November 1981) isn't much better than Chalmers's earlier attempts to update the weird tale. Like Klein's *The Ceremonies,* this story adopts the basic framework and themes of Arthur Machen's "The White People"—a loss of innocence and the corruption of the untainted by way of induction into a secret witch cult—but does so far less effectively than Klein's revisiting of Machen's premise. And, to make matters worse, somehow, Chalmers has managed to write a story of only some eight thousand or so words that seems to go on forever, heedless of its size, not unlike the cursed real estate of Joseph Payne Brennan's "Canavan's Backyard."

The genesis of "Evil God, Out of Words" proves a good deal more intriguing than the story itself:

> The entire plot coalesced indirectly around a single childhood memory, something I saw when I was ten years old. This would have been 1946 or '47. My mother and I accompanied my father on a business trip to Paris. We rarely took proper vacations, and I think he was trying to make up for that. Anyway, we saw the usual sights one sees in Paris, but we also visited a natural history museum, which delighted me far more than all the Eiffel Towers and Arcs de Triomphe combined. There was an enormous Victorian gallery filled with dinosaur skeletons! For a ten-year-old boy, how could the Louvre ever possibly hope to compete with *Diplodocus,*

Allosaurus, and *Iguanodon*? Of course, though, none of these served as the story's inspiration. But there was also a small glass case containing a sort of mummified hand, and the hand was gripping an old-fashioned key. I believe it was an Egyptian artifact of some sort, and it seemed entirely out of place there among the dinosaurs and mastodons. Perhaps this is *why* I recall it so clearly. The fingers had hooked nails or talons, and it reminded me immediately of W. W. Jacobs's "The Monkey's Paw," which I'd read by then, naturally. The odd thing is, decades later, I wrote the museum to inquire about the hand, wishing to compare my memories with the reality of what I'd seen. I received a somewhat terse response to the effect that there had never been any such artifact displayed at the museum. Now, I knew better. I'd seen it with my own eyes, hadn't I? I wrote a second time, and they didn't even bother to answer me. But what's important here is that it set me on the path leading to "Evil God, Out of Words."

Though the relic Chalmers may or may not have seen while in Paris as a child doesn't appear in the story, it is plainly echoed in the recurring motif of keys, both literal and figurative. Most notably, the terrible old man who first speaks to the story's *l'enfant innocent* of "the mysteries of the worm" describes nine magical keys. Each key bears the name of one of the muses of Greek mythology, as set forth in Cesare Ripa's *Iconologia* (1593). The old man tells the girl that the two most powerful keys, Polyhymnia and Calliope, are required for the ritual of resurrection ("shredding the veil, casting back, fetching up"). If Chalmers's choice of these two muses is meant to hold a particular symbolic meaning, it escapes repeated . . .

Excerpt from "The Thousand and Third Tale of Scheherazade: A Survey of the Arabian Ghûl in Popular Culture," Esther Kensky, *The Journal of Popular Culture,* vol. 42, no. 6 (December 2009):

. . . will, instead, quote at length from the summary provided by Niederhausen and Flaschka (1992): "This was the time before the war between the Ghûl (plural, Arabic لوغ) and the other races of the Djinn (يّنج)—the Ifrit, the Sila, and the Marid. In those days, the men of the desert still looked upon all the Djinn as gods, though they'd already learned to fear the night shades, the *Ghûl,* and guarded their children and the graves of their dead against them. Among the fates that could befall the soul of a man or woman, to have one's corpse stolen and then devoured by the *Ghûl* was counted as one of the most gruesome and tragic conceivable. It was thought that to be so consumed would mean that the deceased would be taken from the cold sleep of *barzakh,* never to meet with the angels Nakir and Munkar, and so never be interrogated and prepared for Paradise (جنّة, Hebrew cognate *jannah*).

"It is said that these demons fear both steel and iron, like the other Djinn, and so people wear steel rings or place steel daggers where protection from Djinn and ghouls is needed. Salt is another means of protection, since ghouls hate it. The names of God, Qur'anic verses, magic squares (Muska), or that group of magical symbols known as 'the seven seals' are frequently worn by people or attached to their property to ward off the demons.

"One of the more obscure customs meant to provide a ward against the *Ghûl* is mentioned briefly in Jorge Luis Borges's *The Book of Imaginary Beings* (*Manual de zoología fantástica,* 1957). According to Borges, these creatures have an obsession with keys and locks, and can be thwarted by scattering a dozen or so keys near a locked door or gate, none of which actually fit the lock in question. The ghoul will try each key repeatedly (despite its purported fear of iron), so doggedly determined to find the correct match that it immediately forgets a given key has already been tested. It may continue this for hours, neglecting to watch for dawn, and be destroyed by the rising sun. It's believed that the severed hand of a ghoul dispatched in this manner, still holding tight to the last key it tried, is a powerful talisman against all manner of evils and misfortune. Interestingly, a similar predilection to arithmomania is ascribed to vampires in certain Chinese and European traditions, and to witches and other mischievous . . ."

Excerpt from a letter found among the correspondence of the late Dr. Thackery T. Lambshead, from Ms. Margaret H. Jacobs (7 Exegesis Street, Cincinnati, Ohio) to Lambshead; undated but postmarked May 25, 1981:

. . . the crouching thing, that goddamned horrid thing like a huge rat, and it scampers over the threshold that hadn't been there before it used the key. Its tiny claws scritch, scritch, scritch against the granite, a sound that makes me shudder whenever I remember it. I can be wide awake and driving to work, on a sunny day, and I recall that scratching noise and shudder. So, it crosses the threshold and calls for me to follow. I glance back at the flooded cellar, and see that the stairs have vanished, that it's not even a cellar anymore. It's a cave opening out onto the sea, a sea cave.

This is one of the new twists, Dr. Lambshead. Always before, always, when I'd pause and look back over my shoulder, the stairs would still be there. And they were a comfort to me, because the stairs implied a way out, that I could escape simply by retracing my steps. I could run back and hammer at the locked door until the silver-eyed women or the Bailiff came to let me out. It's awful, just awful, not having the reassurance of those stairs. I look at the entrance of the cave, and it's night outside, but I can see the water gets deep very fast out there. I've never been a very strong swimmer, Doctor.

"Stop dawdling," says the thing with the key. Its voice is as wretched as everything else about it. Have I ever mentioned that before? "Maybe you want to get yourself left behind, is that it? Maybe you want to be around for high tide and the sharks?" It has a dozen of these "maybe" questions. At least a dozen and sometimes a lot more than that. "Maybe you got gills I can't see?"

I tell it I'm coming, and I cross the threshold, too. This part's like before. But on the other side of the granite wall, everything's changed, the same way the cellar became a sea cave. Now, beyond the wall, where before there were only the winding tunnels, the Minoan maze where I used to wander for what seemed like hours before finding my way out into the cellar again, now there's an enormous chamber. We're still underground. That's obvious. The air is dank, musty, foul, but dry after the sea cave.

"This is the place it all begins," the wretched rat thing says. It sounds *proud,* like it's declaring some grand accomplishment, as if whatever begins here is *its* doing. Like that. "Now, was this anything that man, that Doc Sheepshead, ever told you about?" it asks me.

I know that it's getting your name wrong on purpose, but I correct it anyway. "Lambshead," I say, and it replies, in a singsong sort of way, "Shut up, Maggie. Sheep or lamb, ram or ewe, it hardly matters to me."

Yes, it knows my *name.* It knows my name, and it *speaks* my name. Surely, that should be enough to shock me awake, but I never wake until farther along.

"Beginnings are just as important as whatever comes along and happens after," it says. I want to cut its throat so I'll never have to hear that wretched voice again, but I look at the chamber, instead. It's an ossuary. I've never been inside an ossuary, but of course I've seen photographs of them. The floor below me is earthen, and there are two square pillars supporting the earthen roof. Between the pillars is a third column, made of blocks of granite held together with mortar and crowned with something like a huge bowl or basin or baptismal font or birdbath. I don't know the word for what it is, and it's not always the same. The wall beyond the three pillars is built entirely of the skulls and thighbones of human beings. The bones are very old. I know that just from looking at them.

"You pay close attention to all this," says the wretched not-rat thing. I tell it I want to go back. I ask it to take me back, but it doesn't reply. I think it is selectively deaf, if you get my drift.

And I realize there are two other people in the ossuary chamber with us. A man and a woman. Both are wearing heavy black robes with hoods. The robes and hoods are lined with purple silk. The man is holding an open book in his right hand and a silver cup in his left. The woman is holding a dagger of some sort. There's something dead on the floor between them, but I turn away before I can see what it might be. I don't want to know. I can't be blamed for not wanting to know that, can I?

The man and the woman are chanting. It might be Latin, but I'm not sure. I've never studied . . .

Excerpt from "The Castleblakeney Key: Unlocking an Example of the Importance of Uncertainty to Ontological Processes in Social Constructionism," Siegfried Glaserfeld, *Psyche: Journal of the Association for the Scientific Study of Consciousness,* vol. 12 (2006):

. . . the unfortunate case of Margaret Jacobs, that we quickly arrive at a position where it becomes obvious that the important questions here have nothing to do with the objective origins of the hand and whether or not it's genuine or a hoax. It makes no difference whether we say it came from an Irish peat bog or the Parisian catacombs, whether it belongs to a child, a monster, or a monkey. It doesn't matter if Lambshead knew it was a hoax or was duped by Dussubieux (or anyone else). Any answer regarding its "authenticity" is, by necessity, only provisional, open to correction or revision at any time, and, hence, far from being a direct representation of a preexisting singularity. All answers retain an inherently experimental character. Regardless of the hand/key's status as virtual construct/s, they remain, however, selections from our sensory fields that are causally linked to the real and, therefore, may surprise us at any time and without . . .

Excerpt from a letter found among the correspondence of the late Dr. Thackery T. Lambshead, from M. Camille Dussubieux (n°20, rue de la Chaussée-d'Antin, Paris) to Lambshead, dated August 2, 1961:

. . . that it pains me. The offer seemed more than equitable, considering you paid a mere 200 francs for ——. And to accuse me of secretly acting as an agent for Valadon and Provoyeur! Such an allegation strikes at the core of all our years of friendship and trust, and yet you make it so lightly. Am I supposed to put that out of my mind now?

Likewise, to accuse me of lying, when you can have no foreknowledge of my dreams, excepting to the degree I may divulge them. I tell you, Thackery, with no guile in my heart, that I *did* stand there in l'Ossuaire, at Crypte de la lampe sépulcrale, and I saw the foul beast come trundling through an opening in the wall, which it clearly used the key to fashion. I did not in the least exaggerate the repellent nature of the dwarfish creature, nor did I exaggerate the fear and confusion in the eyes of the poor woman who followed it through that doorway. She never once looked directly at me, but kept her eyes on the obscene ritual being performed (except once, when she glanced over her shoulder). But enough. I've told you this already, and in exacting detail. You may choose to believe me or not. The offer stands. And I will endeavor to set aside your last letter, in hopes of preserving our friendship. I pray you will do . . .

Excerpt from a letter found among the correspondence of the late Dr. Thackery T. Lambshead, from Ms. Margaret H. Jacobs (7 Exegesis Street, Cincinnati, Ohio) to Lambshead; undated but postmarked June 7, 1981:

. . . I can't imagine I'll ever write you again. Not because the psychiatrist has advised me to stop, and because of that very rude letter from your lawyer (if that's really who he is), but because I'm losing heart at your persistent refusal to respond. When we met, you seemed like such a good man, so forthright and generous. But now, I don't know.

So, probably this is the last time I'll bother you. I'm sure you're relieved at that news. Maybe I don't blame you for being relieved. If I were you, I might feel the same way. Only, I'm *not* you.

The dream has a new bit at the end. Toward the place I usually wake up, which I think of as the end. I've followed the wretched not-rat beast into the ossuary, and the two robed figures are waiting there. We've interrupted them again. I try not to dwell on what manner of witchcraft they might be up to. They don't look at me. They don't look at the wretched thing with the key. They turn and look at a man who has just entered (stage left).

He's a painfully thin man, and he looks like someone only half-awake, or like a sleepwalker, maybe. A somnambulist. He's barefoot. He's come down a flight of earthen stares [sic] at [sic] stands at the bottom, gazing directly at me and the wretched thing. He says something, but it's all French, and I'm not very good with

French. I only catch a few words. I'm almost pretty sure he says, *"Ne prenez pas cette route, Madame."* It's happened twice now, and I wrote that down as soon as I woke the second time. He also says, in English, "Please, turn around, go back!" He's very upset, and points at the hole the wretched thing made in the wall with the key. The robed figures are glaring at him now. The woman raises her dagger, taking a step towards him. The somnambulist turns and dashes back up the steps.

When he's gone, the wretched not-rat beast scrambles up to the man with the open book, and they whisper to one another. Then the man looks directly at me, and his eyes flash red-gold in the gloom, the way a cat's eyes will. He says, in English, "Heaven dost provide for all its children." I'm so scared, I finally do turn around, meaning to run back to the cellar or sea cave, whichever, because anything's better than this. But the hole in the granite wall is gone, and I'm *trapped* there. I slam my fists against the rock, over and over.

It shouldn't surprise you that I hardly sleep. . . .

Excerpt from a postcard found among the effects of Ms. Margaret H. Jacobs (7 Exegesis Street, Cincinnati, Ohio) following her suicide, from Lambshead, dated July 10, 1981 (postmarked July 13):

. . . can assure you, Ms. Jacobs, the letter in question did not come from my solicitors. I've inquired regarding this matter, and they've sent no such letter to you. Which is not surprising, as they aren't in the habit of taking such action unless I've requested that they do so. However, this said, I do think we might both be happier if these reports of yours ceased. I don't know what to make of them, and while I am obviously sorry if your visit set these unpleasant dreams in motion, I am not trained in psychoanalysis, and you'd be better served . . .

Excerpt from the obituary of Margaret Harriet Jacobs, *The Cincinnati Post,* July 8, 1981:

. . . a respected teacher and scholar, she was a tenured professor of Political Science at the McMicken College of Arts and Sciences, University of Cincinnati. She is survived by her sister, Dorothy Frost (née Jacobs), and her brother, Harold Jacobs. In lieu of flowers the family prefers memorial donations in the deceased's name to the Cincinnati chapter of the American Foundation for Suicide Prevention. Condolences may be expressed at . . .

Taking the Rats to Riga

A Critical Examination of Stigmata's Print

By Jay Lake

Perhaps the most quotidian detail of the print *Taking the Rats to Riga* (1969) is the eponymous rats themselves. This is somewhat uncharacteristic of the work of the artist Stigmata (b. Crispus Chang-Evans, Nanking, China, 1942; d. Khyber Pass, Pakistan, 1992). The artist was notorious for eschewing both representation and naturalism, noting in a 1967 interview with Andy Warhol, "The dial ain't set on sketch, and I'll never be a d**ned camera" (*artINterCHANGE;* vol. III, no. 4; 1968).

The unusual inclusion of such readily identifiable elements strongly hints that *Rats* is based on an actual event. The precise nature of this event is obscured by our distance in time from the origins of this print, as well as Stigmata's notoriously poor record-keeping. Lambshead's own acquisition notes on the print are strangely sparse as well. Art world rumor whispers that the print depicts a scene from *Karneval der Naviscaputer,* an occasional festival of deviant performance art held within East Berlin's underground club culture during the mid-to-late 1960s.

The astute observer would do well to attempt deconstruction of some of the other elements in *Rats.* Art unexamined is, after all, art unexperienced. In this case, even a close examination is unlikely to reveal the mundane truths behind the print. The emotive truths are, however, most certainly available.

Consider the chain that the rats are climbing. Why do they ascend? From where have they come? A hook dangles or swings not far below the lower rat. It appears ornamented in both shape and detail. Bejeweled, this cannot be an artefact of the working man. Nor does it conform to the Continental notion of *kunstbrukt,* that design should be both beautiful and functional. This hook is curious and attractive, but hardly something to lift a bale of opium from the decks of a shabby Ceylonese trawler. One must also consider the possibility hinted at in the print's title, that these are the plague rats Renfield carries into the world for his master Dracula, as depicted repeatedly in cinema.

Examine the chain itself. In Stigmata's rendering, this could just as easily be a motorcycle chain as a cargo chain or an anchor chain. Were that to be the case,

Taking the Rats to Riga, by Stigmata (1969); image from the collection of Eric Schaller.

we might assume the rats were being drawn upward, toward the top verge of the image. The dynamism of their forms suggests that they are more than mere passengers. Still, is that no different from a man walking up an escalator?

Once we have evaluated the context in which the rats appear, the image begins to lose its coherence. Most observers consider the smaller lines in the background to be more distant chains of the same sort the rats are climbing, but Priest has advanced the argument that those may be strings of lightbulbs (*Struggles in European Aesthetics,* Eden Moore Press, London, 1978). Her assertion is undercut by the strong front lighting on the primary figures in the composition, but given Stigmata's well-documented disregard for artistic convention, this is an inherently irresolvable issue.

The most visually dominant element in *Rats* is the tentacled skeleton in the left side of the image. Sarcastically dubbed "The Devil Dog" in a critical essay by Robyn (*Contemporary Images,* Malachite Books, Ann Arbor, 1975), this name has stuck, and is sometimes misattributed as Stigmata's title for the work. In stark contrast with the climbing rats, there is nothing natural or realistic about the Devil Dog. Rather, it combines elements of fictional nightmare ranging from Lovecraft's imaginary Cthulhu mythos to the classic Satanic imagery of Christian art.

Priest (op. cit.) nevertheless suggests that the Devil Dog may, in fact, be representational. Presuming even a grain of truth, this theory could represent the source of Lambshead's interest in acquiring *Rats* for his collection, given the doctor's well-known dedication to his own extensive *wunderkammer.* It is difficult for the observer to seriously credit Priest's notion, however, as she advances no reasonable theory as to what creature or artefact the Devil Dog could represent. She simply uses scare words such as "mutant" and "chimera" without substantiation. The burden of proof for such an outlandish assertion lies very strongly with the theorist, not with her critics.

Robyn and other observers have offered the far simpler hypothesis that the Devil Dog is an expression of Stigmata's own deeper fears. The open jaw seems almost to have been caught in the act of speech. While the eyes are vacant, the detail along the center line of the skull and above the orbitals can be interpreted as flames rather than horns or spurs. For a deep analysis of this interpretation, see Abraham (*Oops, I Ate the Rainbow: Challenges of Visual Metaphor,* University of New Mexico Press, Albuquerque, 1986). The tentacles dangle, horrifying yet not precisely threatening to either the artist or the observer. Rising above and behind is an empty rib cage—heartless, gutless, a body devoid of those things that make us real. This is a monster that shames but does not shamble, that bites but does not shit, that writhes but does not grasp.

The most important element in *Rats* is, without a doubt, the hand rising up to brush at the Devil Dog's prominent, stabbing beak. It is undeniably primate, and equally so undeniably inhuman. Still, a strong critical consensus prevails that this is Stigmata's own hand intruding to touch the engine of his fear. While the rats seek to escape up their chain, this long-fingered ape reaches deeper into the illuminated shadows, touching the locus of terror without quite grasping it.

The parallels to Michelangelo's *Creation of Adam* (ca. 1511) are inescapable and disturbing. Who is creating whom here? Is Stigmata being brought to life by his own fears? Or does he birth them into this print, as so many artists do, to release his creation on an unsuspecting world?

We can never answer those questions for Stigmata. Reticent in life, he, like all who have gone before, is thoroughly silent in death. Each of us can answer those questions for ourselves, however, seeing deeper into this print than the casual horror and blatant surrealism to what lies beneath. Much as Lambshead must have done when he bought the piece from the court-appointed master liquidating Stigmata's troubled estate, via telephone auction in 1993.

What wonder lies in yonder cabinet? *Taking the Rats to Riga* is a door to open the eyes of the mind. Like all worthwhile art, the piece invites us on a journey that has no path nor map, nor even an endpoint. Only a process, footsteps through the mind of an artist now forever lost to us.

The Book of Categories

Handled, Damaged, Partially Repaired, Damaged Again, and Then Documented by Charles Yu

0 What there is

1 Proper name

The full name for *The Book of Categories*[1] is as follows:

THE BOOK OF CATEGORIES
(A CATALOG OF CATALOGS
(BEING ITSELF A VOLUME ENCLOSING
A CONCEPTUAL STRUCTURE
(SUCH STRUCTURE BEING
COMMONLY REFERRED TO AS AN
(IDEA)-CAGE)))

2 Nature of

2.1 Basic properties of

The Book of Categories is composed of two books, one placed inside the other.

The outer book (formally known as *The Outer Book*) is a kind of frame wrapped around the inner book, which is known as, uh, *The Inner Book.*

2.1.1 Paper

The Inner Book's pages are made of a highly unusual type of paper, which is made of a substance known as (A)CTE, so-called because of its (apocrypha)-chemical-thermo-ephemeral properties, the underlying chemistry of which is not well understood, but the practical significance of which is a peculiar characteristic: with the proper instrument, (A)CTE can be sliced and re-sliced again, page-wise, an indefinite number of times.

2.1.1.1 Method for creation of new pages

Each cut must be swift and precise, and the angle must be metaphysically exact, but if the operation is per-

1 Which itself is listed in *The Book of Books of Categories*, vol. III, p. 21573, row K, column FF.

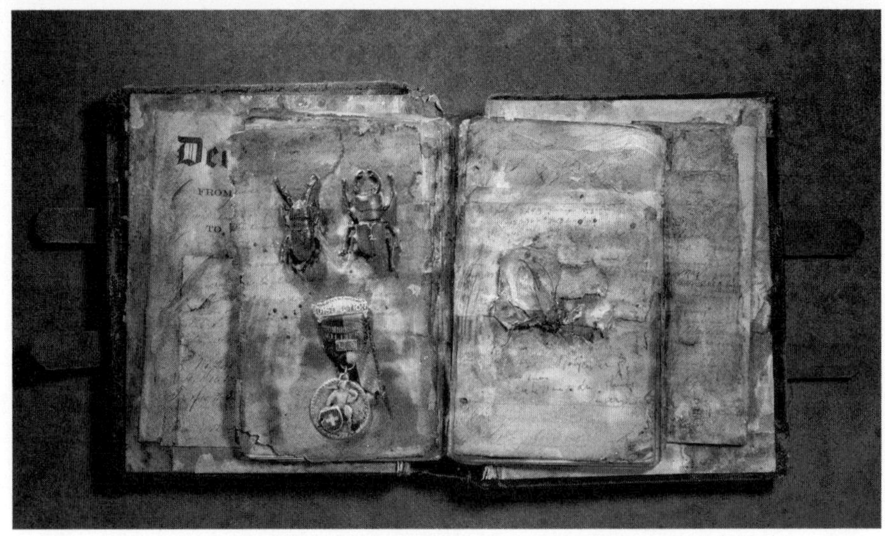

A photograph of pages from *The Book of Categories*, origin unknown.

formed correctly, there is no known lower bound to the possible thinness of a single sheet of (A)CTE paper.

2.1.1.1.1 Page count

To wit, as of the time of this writing, despite having total thickness (in a closed position) of just over two inches, *The Book of Categories* contains no less than 3,739,164 pages.[2]

3 Intended Purpose

3.1 Conjecture

This property of repeated divisibility is believed to be necessary for *The Book of Categories* to function in its intended purpose (the Intended Purpose).[3]

3.2 Theories regarding Intended Purpose

There are four major theories on what the Intended Purpose is. The first three are unknown. The fourth theory is known but is wrong.

The fifth theory of the Intended Purpose (the Fifth Theory) is not yet a theory, it's still more of a conjecture, but it has a lot of things going for it and everyone's really pulling for the Fifth Theory and thinks it's well on its way to theory-hood.

2 And counting.

3 The Intended Purpose is unknown, so this is basically just a wild-assed guess.

3.2.1 Unsubstantiated assertion (status: in dispute)

Whatever the Intended Purpose may be, this much is clear: the book is a system, method, and space for a comprehensive categorization of all objects, categories of objects, categories of categories of objects, etc.

4 What there is not

5 Mode of propagation

5.1 How the book changes hands

On the left-facing inside cover of The Framing Book, we find the word "DEDICATED," and underneath, two lines labeled

"From: ______________________________ "

and

"To: ______________________________ ".

5.2 Each possessor of the book

attempts to impose his numbered ordering of the world by adding categories.

5.3 At some point whether out of frustration or a sense of completion, or a desire to impose such system on others,

a possessor will pass the book on to another user, by excising his or her name from the To line, placing the name in the From line, and then writing in the name of the next possessor of the book in the To line. The excision should be performed with the same instrument used to cut new pages.

6 As you may have realized

6.1 What this means is

The Book of Categories contains what is, in essence, its own chain of title. It is a system of world-ordering, which has, encoded into itself, a history of its own revision and is, in that sense, the opposite of a palimpsest. Nothing is ever overwritten in *The Book of Categories,* only interspersed, interlineated, or, to be more precise, inter-*paginated.*

7 Why

7.1 Why

would someone ever give this book away?

8 A man

8.1 Looking for what was there

8.1.1 Trying to name it

8.1.1.1 **Naming being one way**

to locate something not quite lost, and not quite found

8.1.1.1.1 **A name also seeming**

to be a necessary AND sufficient condition to possession of an idea, a name being a kind of idea-cage.

9 Something else you need to realize about the book

9.1 **Is that**

The sheer number of pages in the book is such that ordinary human fingers cannot turn the pages in a reliably repeatable fashion. Simply breathing in the same room as the book will cause the book's pages to flail about wildly. Even the Brownian motion of particles has been known to move several hundred pages at a time.

9.2 **In fact, if you ever lose your place in the book,**

it is unlikely that you will ever be able to return to the same page again in your lifetime

[INSERTED]

6.1.1 **One reason**

why someone would give this book away: at some point, whether out of frustration or a sense of completion, or a desire to impose such system on others, a possessor will pass the book on to another user, by excising his or her name from the To line on the

[INSERTED]

5.2.1 Each possessor of the book [4]

The various possessors of the book can be traced, from which[4]

4 Lambshead himself has been the caretaker of the book on two separate occasions, each time receiving it from Bertrand Russell, and each time passing it to Alfred North Whitehead.

10 A man named Chang Hsueh-liang

has possessed the book seventy-three times. No other individual has owned it more than six times.

10.1 Little is known about Chang, a general in the Chinese army,

except that he is believed to have lost a child, a newborn daughter, in a freak accident while on a brief holiday with his family.

10.1.1 The incident

Onlookers who witnessed the incident say there were no words in their language to describe what occurred, only that "the water took her" and that although "nothing impossible happened," it was, statistically speaking, a "once in a universe event."

10.1.1.1 His daughter

was five weeks old when she died. For reasons unknown, she had yet to be named.

10.2 It is unclear whether Chang

was repeatedly seeking out the book, or it kept finding its way back to him.

10.3 A medal of some sort, and two insects

are believed to have been placed inside the book by Chang.

10.3.1 The general problem of categorization

Although it is worth noting that the location of these objects is unstable, due to a phenomenon particular to *The Book of Categories* known as "wobbling," which can result from stored conceptual potential energy escaping through the frame of *The Inner Book* and resonating with *The Outer Book*.

10.5 It is clear from certain sites in the book

that Chang remained obsessed with naming what had happened to his child.

10.5.1 Chang's last entry

is a clump of (A)CTE paper consisting of hundreds of thousands, maybe millions of blank pages, known as The Chang Region. On each page of The Chang Region of the book is written what appears to be an ancient form of a Chinese character. Scholars disagree as to the identity of the character.

11 Eventually, a possessor of the book comes to realize

how hard it is to find any given page, lost among the pages. Trying to find that slice, to cut through it on either side, before the page has been lost.

[INSERTED]

8.1.1.1.1.1 **A name actually being**
a memorial to the site where an idea once rested, momentarily, before moving on.

8.1.1.1.1.1.1 **If you listen carefully,**
you can hear it in there, but when you look inside, the idea-cage is always empty, and in its place, the concrete, the particular, something formerly alive,

now dead and smashed.

Objects Discovered in a Novel Under Construction

Documented by Alan Moore

The following items have been retrieved from the construction site of an uncompleted novel, *Jerusalem,* where completion of the structure's uppermost level has been delayed by unanticipated setbacks that are unrelated to the project.

The site itself is gigantic in its dimensions, with more than half a million words already in place and the three-tier edifice as yet only a little more than two-thirds of the way into its lengthy building process. The intimidating silence that pervades the vast and temporarily abandoned landscape is exacerbated by the absence of the novel's characters and by the lack of any background noise resulting from the engineering and the excavation usually associated with such ventures.

Making a considerable contribution to the already unsettling ambience is the anomalous (and even dangerous) approach to architecture that is evident in the unfinished work: the lowest floor, responsible for bearing the immense load of the weightier passages and chambers overhead, seems to be built entirely of distressed red brick and grey slate roofing tiles with much of it already derelict or in a state of imminent collapse. Resting on this, the massive second tier would seem to be constructed mostly out of wood and has been brightly decorated with painted motifs that would appear to be more suited to a nursery or school environment, contrasted with the bleak and even brutal social realism that's suggested by the weathered brickwork and decrepit terraces immediately below.

The topmost storey, where work has been halted, seems again to be accomplished in a style that is entirely unrelated to the floors beneath. The building's lines and sweeping curves are unresolved, curtailed in jutting spars or girders that stand enigmatically against the skyline. Amidst these skeletal protrusions are two or three relatively finished works of decorative statuary, the most notable being a winged stone figure representing the archangel Michael, who is depicted

A book discovered in Dr. Lambshead's cabinet, the bulk of it taken up by a false bottom, inside of which researchers found the text by Alan Moore and a tiny architectural structure consisting of several floors, somewhat akin to a doll's house, with a variety of odd objects inside each compartment or room.

standing with a shield held in his left hand and what seems to be a snooker cue clutched in his right.

The oddities listed below were all discovered in the confines of the structure's bottom two floors, and are labelled with an indication of which level and which individual chamber or compartment they were found in.

1. Deathmonger's aprons, two in number. Found on ground floor; chamber 10.

These two aprons, which have been dated as originating from the first years of the twentieth century, have stitched-in tags identifying them as property of one Mrs. Belinda Gibbs. Supporting evidence suggests that Mrs. Gibbs's profession was that of an unofficial midwife/undertaker working in a badly disadvantaged neighbourhood located in the English midlands, persons of her calling being locally referred to as a "deathmonger."

One of the aprons is entirely black, being apparently the mode of dress appropriate for "laying out," or dealing with the bodies of the recently deceased. The other apron, meant for use on the occasion of a birth, is mostly white and yet around its edge is decorated with embroidered bees and butterflies in vivid, naturalistic colours.

In an inside pocket of the jet-black funeral apron, a discoloured handkerchief was found. Its sepia and burnt-umber stains suggest that Mrs. Gibbs was a habitual snuff-user, possibly as a precautionary measure to alleviate any olfactory distress occasioned by her work with cadavers.

2. Children's toys from dream, anagrammatically derived. Found on first floor; chamber 13.

The second storey of the structure seems, from the inside, to border on the infinitely large, in terms of area, being much bigger than the floor below on which it somehow stands. Also, the actual substance of this second tier seems to be constantly in flux, with details of the landscape metamorphosing and shifting like the details of a dream. The overall appearance of this chamber is of an enormously wide wooden hallway or arcade, immeasurably long and with a grid of rectangular apertures set in its wooden flooring at regular intervals. These apertures look down upon the rooms and alleys of the floor immediately below, although for reasons that are as yet unexplained the holes are not apparent from beneath. Some of the spaces have entire (and massively expanded) trees growing up through them from the ground floor, with their upper branches reaching to the arcade's ceiling, a glass roof supported by Victorian ironwork beyond which vast geometric clouds, more like a diagram of weather than weather itself, appear to drift. The giant thoroughfare is thought to be known by its currently absented population as "The Attics of the Breath."

The hallway seems to be a magnified reflection of an ordinary shopping arcade found on the more naturalistic bottom level. Its endless walls are lined with shops, above which there are numerous wooden balconies. One of the businesses in the much smaller precinct on the lowest floor is a shop known as Chasterlaine's, dealing in toys and novelties. In the exploded reaches of the upper storey, though, this enterprise is subject to the creeping, dreamlike transformations that seem to afflict the second floor, its name moving through various anagrams to finally express itself as "The Snail Races" by the point at which work on the structure halted. In the window, displayed resting on their cardboard boxes in the manner of miniature 1950s Matchbox reproduction cars, was found a range of die-cast metal molluscs that were manufactured to incorporate the features of the scaled-down vehicles which they resembled: one snail has been painted white and has a red cross stencilled on its shell so that it calls to mind an English ambulance of the same vintage. Another has been liveried in navy blue with white calligraphy along its side, identifying it as a Pickford's removal van. A third has the snail's body dyed a brilliant post-box scarlet, while its spiral shell has been replaced by a tightly wound fireman's hose. All of the specimens discovered were roughly two inches long, two inches high, and an inch wide. Their value on the collector's market, if any, has proven impossible to calculate.

3. Solidified puddle of gold, three feet in diameter. Found on first floor; chamber 18.

Discovered in a typically oversized arena-like construction (which once more appears to be a massively expanded version of a site existing on the bottom floor), this smooth and flat ellipse of precious metal is reputedly a pool of scabbed, coagulated blood remaining from a brawl between two of the so-called Builders that are to be found amongst the structure's wildly variegated populace. According to reliable accounts, the Builders, upon this occasion, were perceived as being well over a hundred feet in height and were each armed with a proportionately massive snooker cue, their altercation having started in a nearby gaming parlour given over to the play of "trilliards," apparently a form of billiards undertaken by four players upon an impractically vast table with perhaps a thousand balls but just four pockets, situated at the corners. It would seem that local trilliards champion "Mighty Mike" emerged victorious from the colossal scrap, but since both combatants were wounded in the course of the engagement, it is not known from which Builder this specific pool of priceless blood was spilled.

4. Unusual fungal growths, found on ground floor in chamber 4; found widely distributed across first floor with specimens discovered in most of this second storey's chambers.

This peculiar variety of fungus seems to be a type that roots itself in higher mathematical dimensions, with the actual growth protruding down into the three-dimensional continuum below, where they are sometimes fleetingly apparent to a human viewer, despite being perceived very differently from a lower-dimensional perspective.

When viewed in their own environment, these growths have an attractive radiating symmetry, at first glance looking like some complex, delicately coloured form of starfish. Upon close inspection, though, it is apparent that the fungal bloom has taken the appearance of an interwoven ring of tiny naked women, all joined at the head with a communal tuft of "hair" (usually red, but sometimes black or blond) protruding from the centre of this strange, symmetrical arrangement. The bodies and the faces of these exquisite homunculi are overlapped in something of the manner of an optical illusion, so that three eyes will share two separate noses and two sets of rosebud lips, and that two distinct torsos will have only three legs with one limb shared by both.

Therefore, seen from above, these "fruit" have the communal tuft of usually crimson fibres at their centres, with a ring of glittering miniature eyes arranged around it, then a ring of noses, then lips, breasts, navels, and even dots of fibrous "pubic hair" set at the junctions of the radiating petal "legs." Turning the fungus over to inspect its underside, we have a scaled-down rear view of the conjoined female bodies with the decorative addition of small and translucent insect wings growing out from the beautifully sculpted miniature shoulder-blades. This would seem to explain why this form of the fungus is referred to as the "fairy" type, and would appear to represent the riper, more mature stage of the fungus's development. In its colouration, this mature form is astonishingly naturalistic in its mimicry of the nude human body, with a slightly carmine flush in the minuscule "cheeks" and bright green pinprick irises in the unusually animated-looking ring of eyes. The subtly graded pinks and creams have an appearance that is almost appetising, and the scent detectable upon the specimen is sweet and heavy, having notes of cardamom.

This is not true of the fungal growth's unripe or less mature form, known colloquially as the "spaceman" type. These growths are typified by a mildly unpleasant blue-grey colouring and an aroma that is sour and bitter, almost acrid. Rather than the visually pleasing ring of conjoined fairy figures found in more developed specimens, the miniaturised figures here are sinister and unappealing: spindly humanoids of no apparent gender, the smooth heads are disproportionately large and bulbous, and if these possess lips, ears, or noses, then these features are at best vestigial and practically unnoticeable. The eyes, however, are much bigger than those found in the mature and fully ripened "fairy" specimens, being a uniform and glassy black in colour, noticeably slanted and entirely lidless.

Where they are rooted on the building's second level, these growths are entirely visible and tangible. In the one instance where a specimen was found upon the ground floor, it was hidden to the ordinary senses and appeared to only manifest itself in brief consciousness-spasms that afflicted certain individuals, causing hallucinations where the compound figures of the higher-dimensional growth were perceived as independent tiny females in the manner of a fairy visitation. It may be imagined that the less-mature "spaceman" variety might bring about comparable dreams or mirages, but with black-eyed goblins substituted for wing-sporting naked women.

On the structure's upper floor, where the starfish-like blooms are easily detectable, they are known variously as Puck's Hats, Bedlam Jennies, Hag's Teats, or Mad Apples. It seems that the most important quality of these intriguing fungi is that they are the one foodstuff that such insubstantial and higher-dimensional beings as ghosts find edible. According to reports from these dimensionally displaced inhabitants of the unfinished structure's second storey, while the ripe "fairy" variety are the most flavoursome and sought-after, the "spaceman" form may be resorted to at times for want of any other sustenance. In either instance, the growth's "eyes" turn out to be small pips or seeds, hard and inedible, that must be spat out or excreted, thus ensuring that the growth . . . obviously not a fungus in the strict terrestrial sense . . . can propagate itself.

There are also reports that structures exist on some mezzanine level that's halfway between the ground and first floors, these being effectively the "ghosts" of long-demolished public houses. In these, revenant drinkers are alleged to congregate in mutual enjoyment of a form of alcohol that can be by some means fermented from the fungus to produce a rough home-made concoction known as Puck's Hat Punch. While enjoyably intoxicating in small quantities, it is believed that a prolonged exposure can wreak havoc with the mostly psychologically based "substance" of the phantom form, resulting in unstable physiologies that the sufferer will then have to endure perpetually. A local "character" known as Tommy Mangle-the-Cat is cited as evidence of this effect.

Down on the ground floor, where there may be many dozens of these growths existing undetected by the more prosaic population, it is said that the fungi prefer to root in places that have been associated either with intoxication or with mental illness. Public houses, drug dens, and, above all, psychiatric institutions are thus more than usually prone to infestation, and there have been anecdotal cases of the growths attaching themselves to a living human being's head, where they can bloom unseen by all but the afflicted party, while that party's consciousness is horribly afflicted by the visions that the fungus generates. Reportedly, Victorian patricide and fairy-painter Richard Dadd had an enormous "Puck's Hat" sprouting from his temple and affecting his behaviour tremendously, while it remained predictably invisible to Dadd's doctors and captors.

The display case containing these specimens appears to be empty, with its contents only viewable when situated on the structure's upper level.

5. Miscellaneous; found upon both completed floors, in various chambers.

One piece of burned cork, dated around 1910, supposedly used by Charles Chaplin as part of the makeup for his character "The Inebriate," performed with travelling comedy troupe Fred Karno's Army during that same year.

One gentleman's bicycle and two-wheeled trailer, also circa 1910, having no working brakes and being fitted with thick lengths of rope around the wheel-rims rather than the usual rubber tyres.

One printed pamphlet dating from 1738, titled "Submission to Divine Providence in the Death of Children recommended and enforced in a SERMON preached at NORTHAMPTON on the DEATH Of a very amiable and hopeful CHILD about Five Years old."

Imaginary children's book retrieved from dream of school, with green cloth boards and gold inlay illustration depicting a group of children including an older boy wearing a bowler hat. The book is titled *The Dead Dead Gang,* and its author is, apparently, one Marjorie Miranda Driscoll, a ten-year-old known more usually as "Drowned Marjorie."

Scrapbook of Princess Diana memorabilia, covering the period 1997–2005, belonging to Roberta Marla Stiles, an eighteen-year-old sex worker and crack cocaine addict who has decorated the book's cover with a collage of her own design, combining a sunset scene from a Sunday colour supplement with a picture of the late Diana Spencer's face pasted inexpertly onto the sun.

Artists' materials, circa 1865, thought to belong to Ernest Vernall, a worker employed in retouching the frescoes decorating the interior of the dome of London's St. Paul's Cathedral.

Artist's materials, circa 2015, belonging to Ernest Vernall's great-great-granddaughter, illustrator Alma Warren.

Sledgehammer, used in steel-drum reconditioning by Ernest Vernall's great-great-grandson and Alma Warren's younger brother, Michael.

THE ABOVE EXHIBITS, after cataloguing, have all been returned to the locations where they were discovered, ready and in place for when work once again resumes upon the structure, progressing towards its revised completion date of 2013.

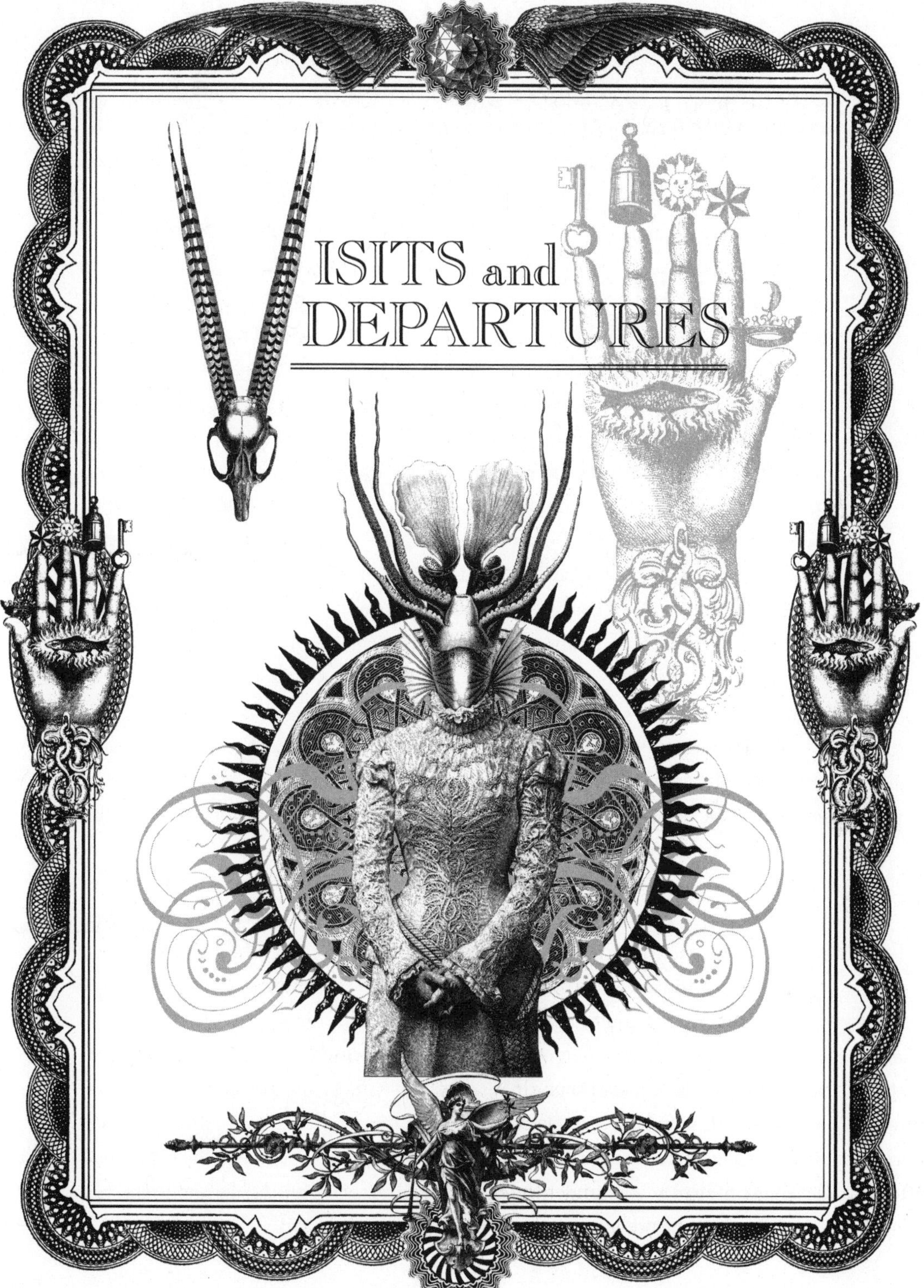
VISITS and
DEPARTURES

Visits

Over the years, several people visited Dr. Lambshead, and saw his cabinet. Few, however, can agree on its dimensions, exact location, or its contents. Sometimes, it isn't even clear that these visitors actually saw the core collection rather than just an overflow room on the first floor of the house. In three separate journal entries, Lambshead alludes to "a special room for the rubes," which he set up out of frustration at the number of requests to visit his cabinet. Many times he would relent and allow a visit, only to have his housekeeper lead the party in question to "the Rube Room" and then out the front door again.

A few notes on these entries, regardless of their accuracy. First, there is no truth to the claim that the chronicler of "The Singular Taffy Puller" simply "mistook Lambshead's kitchen for his cabinet," as put forward by Poe scholar S. J. Chambers. Nor is Mur Lafferty's failure to pass a polygraph test in 1965 relevant to her account. Those who doubt the testimony of Rachel Swirsky, meanwhile, should note that in 1994 she underwent a five-hour polygraph interrogation about her visit as part of misguided therapy for her "condition."

Finally, better investigators than the current editors have come up with inconclusive evidence as to the veracity of Lambshead's housekeeper, Paulette, whose account ends this section. Certainly, it's as good a story as any, even if it paints a rather narrow portrait of the good doctor.

As for more personal "visits and departures," Lambshead wrote on the subject in his journal while visiting newly independent Algiers in the late 1960s. He was no doubt thinking back to his involvement on the side of the National Liberation Front during the fight against the French a decade earlier.

"A visit presages its own departure, and almost no one makes it out," he wrote. "There's a hideous truth hidden in there—that sometimes *things* do the visiting for you and sometimes they're the message. Sometimes, too, whether it's a bullet or a collapsed roof or a fire or some other act of fate or chance, you don't always get to take out what you brought with you—even your own life."

Reports that a Greek woman, about a decade younger than Lambshead, was seen with him in Algiers that year, much as his wife, Helen, had in the 1950s, are entirely apocryphal. Certainly, no one matching the description appears in any of the official state footage of various public events. Indeed, Lambshead himself is rarely on display in these films—a matter of a few seconds here and there, his image soon gone and fading.

1929: The Singular Taffy Puller

As Told to N. K. Jemisin

I had traveled far—along the bustling coast by rail, then across the Atlantic by steamship, at great expense, I might add—on a matter of pride. Or, more specifically, dessert. You see, the cobbled and sweaty streets of my city would reek but for the exquisite aromas that offer relief from horse manure and overindulgence. Wrinkle your nose and you might miss the scent of the most delicate amaretto fondant, or creamy divinities solidifying to tooth-tenderness. And when the pecan harvest is brought—ah, me! You never tasted pralines like mine.

But those selfsame streets are crowded with eateries these days, and an old octoroon spinster looking to make a name for herself must employ more than the braggadocio that paler, maler chefs may indulge. Especially given that, of late, my business had suffered by its proximity to a flashy new restaurant next door. It was for this reason that I traveled to the house of the esteemed doctor, and was ushered into the renowned cabinet, so that I could at last behold the item that might—I hoped—save my business.

On entry to the doctor's home, I was momentarily stunned by the profusion of wonders within. These included the cabinet itself: a room of what had been handsome walnut wainscott and elaborately worked moulding (French rosettes and Egyptian cartouches, of all the mad combinations), though the lingering evidence of half-finished reorganization obscured the best of it. What remained of the chamber's treasures had been tossed, with no apparent regard for further cataloguing or even convenience, onto bookshelves, plinths, and racks, which quite crowded the space. Someone, however, had at least made an effort to group the items by purpose, so after some searching, I discovered the relevant rack. This was a baker's rack, naturally: three shelves of well-made ironwork fashioned into the most peculiar decorative geometries—what might have been lettering in some tongue of the far Orient, or the lost Toltec. But I will admit I spared less attention for the rack itself than for what it held.

All of the items were cooking implements of some sort: tongs for cooks lacking thumbs; an exceptionally large corkscrew; a strainer that, to all appearances, was solid but whose label indicated it could sift out bacterial particulates if given several days to work. There was also a fine Dutch oven, rather plainly enameled in white, whose lid had been securely tied with twine, then glued-and-papered over at each knot, then clamped with three vices, each of which appeared to have been welded so as not to turn. Like all the scions of Pandora who encompass my sex, I was most tempted to peel back at least one of the taped-over bits. My hand was stayed not by prudence, however, but by greed and impatience; the oven was not what I had come for.

At last I found it, behind a half-melted waffle iron: the Singular Taffy Puller.

Not much to look at, after all the effort I'd expended! The thing resembled nothing so much as an old-fashioned box iron of the sort my mother used when she took to laundering, after my father grew tired of keeping a *placée*. But where irons had a flat, tapered plate on the business end, this device had an irising cover that could be retracted by means of a clever mechanism on the handle. With the iris closed, the device was inert. When I opened it, however, and looked within the Puller, I beheld . . . nothing. No surface. Nothing

that I could see, as I turned it to the light, save an unblemished, undifferentiated deepness of black. It was rather like a yawning, shadowless hole—but as I brought my free hand near it, I felt the powerful tug of the Puller's force. It was, for one moment, as though the Puller, not the ground beneath my feet, exerted the greater force of gravity. . . . Per my researches, I knew better than to move my hand much closer. And every journal I'd read on the object contained large-writ, dire warnings against ever breaching the horizon of its opening.

You may ask: of what use is such an item in taffy pulling? Well, as any confectioner can tell you, taffy must be pulled to achieve its proper consistency. When air bubbles are incorporated into the sugar matrix—yes, yes, science is of great relevance to cooking, but let us return to the matter of *taste*—the taffy becomes lighter, softer, chewable rather than a jawbreaking knot. Unfortunately, when one pulls taffy with hands or even a standard machine, it is almost impossible to keep contaminants from affecting the resulting substance. One of my best batches of Atlantic City Strawberry was utterly ruined when the stupid young potager of that damnable restaurant next door made a batch of gumbo with too much garlic. Just the scent of the stuff invaded my shop, but that was enough: invisible particulates of garlic worked their way into my candy, which I had flavored with real dried strawberries, and . . . Well, preventing such disasters was precisely why I had come all this way.

The Puller was capable of removing such particulates from the air. It would remove the air itself, if one pressed a different button on the handle, but as I fancied breathing, I resolved to test that one later. More important, my researches intimated that the Puller might improve my taffy in other ways. For the Puller did not just *draw in*. As I tilted the device, I noted a small glowing light near its tip. This was not part of the device, strictly speaking; rather, it was a sort of vent, covered over with leaded glass for safety's sake. However the Puller worked—and the books I'd found were as vague on its mechanics as they were regarding its origins—the by-products of its internal processes were said to include a peculiar form of emission, which appeared here as radiant light. If one could remove the glass and find a way to safely harness the emitted energy . . .

I make other sweets besides taffy, after all, and unique heat sources make for unique flavors. I would have to be careful regardless, as the Puller had had many, many owners over the years, some for ominously brief periods. One fact stood clear through all its shadowed history, though: those who mastered the Puller's secrets ranked among the greatest chefs and innovators of our art.

So I would test, and take great care in the testing. I would use every bit of knowledge and skill that I possessed, and some that I did not yet, to determine how best to employ this marvelous device. And if that thrice-damned potager next door ever again abused a bushel of garlic . . . Well, then I would have myself a fine new guinea pig.

So. When next you visit the city of the crescent, be certain that you come to the Vieux Carre, Toulouse Street, and ask for my shop. You will find the finest taffy in the city, to be sure—but if you find *new* desserts, then you will know my experiments have been successful. I shall owe it all, or at least its beginnings, to the good professor.

1943: A Brief Note Pertaining to the Absence of One Olivaceous Cormorant, Stuffed

By Dr. Rachel Swirsky

It was some sort of stuffed sea bird. A pelican or puffin or penguin . . . I'd never been good at birds. It stood with its feet awkwardly splayed and its wings raised in a threat display, neck curved and beak hissing. Black glass eyes shone murderously.

Dr. Lambshead (Thackery T.) thrust the dead thing forward. "This is it, you see! What did I tell you?"

"Doctor, I don't understand," I said. "What makes you think this seagull is the source of the phoenix mythology?"

"Gull? This is no gull!"

"I don't really do birds . . ."

"Note the slender body and long tail. This is a Brazilian olivaceous cormorant." He paused meaningfully. "Or looks superficially like one."

It was late 1943. I prickled in my cardigan suit and d'Orsay pumps; Dr. Lambshead looked breezy in his linen jacket and geometric tie. We stood in the basement of his Whimpering-on-the-Brook home, where he'd received me for the weekend, temporarily abandoning his post tending war wounded at the Combustipol General Hospital of Devon.

Readers who recognize me as a contemporary science fiction writer may be confused by my claims of visiting Dr. Lambshead in 1943. It's true, my body has only aged twenty-eight years at the time of this writing. This seeming contradiction is the result of a rare biological ailment, the nature of which Dr. Lambshead had been secretly helping me investigate, this comprising the bulk of our acquaintance.

You see, when I experience particularly extreme emotional states—sometimes joy, though usually pain or fear—my condition triggers a painful chemical process wherein I stiffen, contract, and shrink in on myself until I am reduced to infancy, and must re-embark upon the tiresome process of growing.

You must not take this for some airy supernaturalism. The matter is simple biology.

I maintain strict secrecy about my affliction; the world has always been hostile toward the unusual, and for centuries I've feared the historical equivalent of "alien autopsies." For this reason, I pressed Dr. Lambshead to keep his research confidential, which is why my affliction does not appear in any edition of his rare disease guide.

Dr. Lambshead was well aware that my condition had made me obsessed with legends of immortality, particularly those relating to the mythical phoenix, who—like me, and unlike the equally mythical vampire—must suffer periodic rebirth (with its loathsome necessity of periodic adolescence). Therefore, he had been sure to include the word "phoenix" in his invitation, knowing I would hasten to meet him immediately.

With this background, you may understand my disappointment as the distinguished scientific gentleman did nothing more dramatic than wave about the avian corpse while lecturing me on taxonomy.

"Of what possible interest," I asked with exasperation, "is this dead, grey thing?"

"That's just it!" he replied, excitement undimmed. "It's not grey at all!"

He pulled me nearer. Despite my natural disinclination toward being in such proximity to a corpse, I gasped—the feathers shone a strangely inorganic, metallic silver. Dr. Lambshead plucked one feather loose and held it to my eye. Even more remarkable! It shimmered with intense, beautiful colors that did not merely change in reaction to the light, but seemed to alter of their own accord. Gold, white, orange, rose, violet, and crimson danced together like the heart of a flame.

"Where did you find this?" I murmured.

The cabinet had a Victorian stiffness and eclecticism; I expected an answer in keeping with the air of pith helmets and mosquito nets. However, I must also report that I later felt that this was just a front or disguise of some sort for a more profound and eclectic collection.

"Some sprog found it in Gurney Slade. Sold it for thruppence."

"It's beautiful . . . but surely only superficially related to the phoenix mythos."

"You might think so! But my experiments have yielded other data . . ." Here, he digressed into such specialized, technical vocabulary that I cannot hope to repeat his lecture. At the completion of this torrent of obscurantism, he said, "I'll go fetch my notes."

Without further niceties, the doctor withdrew, taking the bird's corpse with him. Abruptly, I found myself alone in Dr. Lambshead's cabinet of curiosities.

A great deal of wordage has been spent describing the cabinet, but I will add my own. I've already mentioned that the rooms exuded a dark, musty air, crowded as they were with objects ranging from exquisite to disposable. A large number of preserved animal parts were affixed to brown velvet drapes that hung from the ceiling: malformed antlers, jagged horns, monstrous fish, paws and pelts and glowering heads. Bookcases crowded the walls, some filled with actual books, others piled high with specimen jars and music boxes and inscrutable devices.

My meandering took me to an archway blocked by a heavy, green-gold curtain. I admit I should not have swept it aside, but curiosity overcame my sense. As the fabric shifted, I saw a gleam in the shadows—something enormous and mechanical.

It will not surprise you that Dr. Lambshead attracted a great deal of gossip. In my social circle, it had long been suspected that Dr. L. was building some sort of war machine with which to aid the British effort. None of us doubted he could build such things; it was clear his genius extended beyond the medical.

It was such an armored monstrosity I expected to encounter when I stepped into the room. Imagine my surprise when I found myself nose to nose with a mechanical bull.

Don't mistake me. I don't mean the sort of crass rodeo relic on which inebriated young people struggle to maintain their equilibrium. This was a colossal bronze and silver construction, so large that its wickedly curved horns swept the ceiling. It was worked in excruciating detail, from muscular neck to powerful haunches. Only on close examination did I discern the evidence of clockwork mechanisms beneath its metal "skin."

I found myself drawn to the creature. I extended my hand, longing to stroke that vast, smooth muzzle.

At that moment, I heard Dr. Lambshead's returning footsteps. I snatched back my hand and turned toward the entryway. I expected him to be angry; instead, Dr. Lambshead seemed thoughtful as he looked between me and the bull.

He tucked the papers from upstairs under his arm. "My latest acquisition," he said. "More precisely, a loan from the Greek government. They want me to determine how it works."

"They don't know?"

"It was found at a recently discovered archaeological site containing a number of items typically used in the worship of Zeus. The bull appears to represent the god himself, who took a bull's form for seducing maidens. It's a sophisticated clockwork automaton and seems capable of independent motion, but I have not yet ascertained how to activate it."

"Archaeological site? This thing can't be more than a hundred years old!"

"The ancients appear to have possessed a great deal more technology than is commonly understood. For example, consider the Antikythera Mechanism, recovered at the beginning of the century from a shipwreck site. My more radical colleagues hypothesize it's a sophisticated clockwork-powered calendar, though they lack verification."

He paused to give me a significant look.

"Don't you remember?" he asked.

Dr. Lambshead was perpetually trying to discern when I'd contracted my ailment. "I may be old," I said, "but not that old."

The doctor gave me another strange look. "Sometimes you look quite young."

His gaze traveled briefly down my body. With a jolt, I realized the bull's allure had done more than draw me closer. Without noticing, I'd undone my jacket's top button. I ran my fingers through my hair; it tumbled untidily from my French twist.

"It's strangely beautiful," I said. "It seems so polished, so smooth." I reached toward its muzzle again. This time, my fingertips connected.

The bull blinked.

It let out an enormous snort. Metal rasped against wood as it pawed the floor. Its head swung back and forth, horns lowered and pointing straight toward us.

For a moment, we stood, stunned and still.

Then Dr. Lambshead screamed: "Run!"

Dr. Lambshead's papers tumbled to the ground as we bolted past the green-gold curtains, through the crowded rooms, up the basement stairs and out into the road. The bull crashed through walls as he barreled after us, the steam from his nostrils acrid in the air.

Our feet pounded the mud. "What happened?" I shouted, breathing hard as I ran.

"There must have been a chemical catalyst! Tell me, are you menstruating?"

"What a question!"

"I know the trigger can't be touch, because I've touched it. It can't be a woman's touch because I asked my cook downstairs for such an experiment. Are you a virgin?"

"An even worse question!"

"Zeus used his bull form to seduce maidens. Some womanly attribute must be key."

"If the bull seduced maidens, why is it trying to kill us?"

"Now *that* is a good question!"

We rounded past the hedge maze, pushing toward the chapel on the hill. The bull's footsteps thundered close behind. And yet Dr. Lambshead continued to ruminate aloud.

"The catalyst must be a complicated chemical interaction. Perhaps pheromonal. I've been experimenting with such things for treating Recursive Wife Blindness. I think—"

I was not to know his thoughts, for the bull had finally caught us. It reared, massive golden hooves raking the sky. I knew with sinking certainty that my long life would end there, trampled by those hooves and then gored for good measure by those horribly curved horns—

—as the terror overcame me, I felt the familiar shrinking sensation that meant only one thing.

I was about to be reborn.

Through my narrowing vision, I saw that, against all odds, Dr. Lambshead had rallied, having dredged up a square of red fabric from who knows where. He rounded on the bull with a wide, confident stance, flag rippling behind him.

I laughed. How could I have doubted a man like Doctor Thackery T. Lambshead? But the shrinking accelerated and I knew I would not see his victory, at least not in a way I could comprehend. Oh damn, I was going to have to be thirteen again. Oh damn, oh damn, oh damn.

I know not what happened next, only that Dr. Lambshead survived the encounter. That was the last I saw of the Grecian bull.

I have some suspicions, however. It is my belief that Dr. Lambshead bested the thing and then disassembled it, using the intricate technological secrets he derived to begin what's now known as the Information Age.

Don't scoff. As I've mentioned, Dr. Lambshead was clearly capable of such scientific feats. My explanation is at least as plausible as the traditional one that hypothesizes an exponentially accelerating pace of technological invention.

ALL THIS HAPPENED nearly seventy years ago. I've lived two lives since then. Nevertheless, there are two things I wish made known about the incident before I complete my notes.

First: Don't allow superstitions to cloud what I've written. Everything that occurred had a mundane, natural explanation. Honor Dr. Lambshead's memory. He would not want you engaging in tempting flights of fancy.

Second: There is no way to prove my assertions. I admit this suits my purposes as I remain dedicated to protecting my secrecy. It's only because of the recent conventions merging memoir and fiction that I can tell this story at all. I hide behind the edifice of literary convention, and its helpful construction of the unreliable narrator.

As for objects that might substantiate my claims, there are only two. One, the bull, was long ago disassembled. Two, the stuffed corpse of a mysterious sea bird, such as the one listed in your exhibit's inventory as One Tern, Stuffed, Moderate Condition—as to this latter item, I hope you will forgive me. I cannot risk you examining its feathers and concluding my claims are true. Therefore, I've relieved your exhibit of one stuffed bird, though I hope you will equally enjoy the plastic flamingo I've left in its place.

Of course that's not my only reason for making off with your treasure. After being reborn in 1943, I was understandably too preoccupied to track down Dr. Lambshead for several years. I was unable to investigate as an adult, either, for reasons too complicated and personal to note here. I did attempt to pilfer both bird and notes after Dr. Lambshead's death, but the collapsed basement thwarted my attempts.

Thus it was with great pleasure that I received my invitation to preview the exhibit. It was with even greater pleasure that I discovered your security guards to be both affable and susceptible to drugs.

My consolations for your loss—and thank you for the bird.

1963: The Argument Against Louis Pasteur

By Mur Lafferty

Is it odd that my clearest memory about Dr. Lambshead, world traveler, collector, and chronicler of the obscure, was his hatred of Louis Pasteur? I suppose when you connect a gastronomically violent reaction to a memory, that particular recollection sticks longer than others do.

It was 1963. I remember because I was to have been in Dallas to cover Kennedy's visit the following week, but I was unable to go because I was too weak due to my visit with Dr. Lambshead.

I had gotten a choice assignment to interview Dr. Lambshead, who agreed to meet me in his own home. I brought three notebooks and three pencils, but never thought to bring my own cream.

The doctor was polite yet distracted, as he poured my tea and added a dollop of cream without asking me if I preferred it (I didn't). I was focusing on my books and idle chitchat with Lambshead (I don't remember what about; that was erased by the next forty minutes), I took a large gulp of the Earl Grey. When the curdled cream hit my system, my skin broke out in a cold sweat and I found myself in the profoundly embarrassing position of needing, if not a toilet, a chamber pot where I could be politely ill.

The doctor took my request in stride, pointing me to the head and saying

Louis Pasteur, 1822–95

through the door that it was "only a bit of food poisoning, [I] should get over it posthaste and we can start the interview."

I'm sure I would have enjoyed looking at the fascinating drawings and pieces of art, including an odd anatomy chart that hung, water-wrinkled, in the curtainless shower, but I was too busy voiding the very fine salmon I'd just had for lunch. And the tea. And the wretched cream. And possibly some stomach lining.

When I returned to him, shaky and pale, but confident I could at least finish this rarest of rare interview opportunities (Lambshead was not often at home in the sixties), he started talking, not about his research but about Louis Pasteur. He derided the French scientist, saying that the world honored him for pasteurization, but Lambshead could easily name fourteen strains of bacteria that could figure out how to maneuver Pasteur's innovative S-shaped flask.

"You can't even call that a maze," he said, laughing.

I glanced at my teacup, with little lumps of curdled cream floating in it, and asked if that was why he refused to use pasteurized milk.

He waved me off, not answering, and motioned me to stand. "If you want to see a way to battle bacteria, come with me."

He led me back to the kitchen (the cream bottle sat on the counter, the cream clearly separated. I looked away) and out the back door. A cellar door sat flat in the lawn, surrounded by odd purple plants and prickly flowers. I was no botanist, but I was pretty sure they weren't native to England. I had no chance to ask about them, as he quickly hefted the door open and led me to the basement.

"There's no light right now, so just give me a second," Lambshead said. "Pasteur would have killed to see this. He would have eaten his *hat*."

There was indeed no light, but the basement was oddly dry and warm, something you didn't really see in an underground, English room made of stone. The dim daylight that dared to follow us into the basement tentatively touched a couple of shelves, and I gasped. The doctor had taken me to his cabinet, and I could see almost nothing! I could make out a large table in the corner with a single chair, both table and chair covered with various books, maps, and, I think, a taxidermed three-legged platypus.

One shelf had stuffed (although I could swear I saw one move, but it was dark) tropical birds. I tried to make out what was in some glass globes that looked as if they were full of mist and fireflies. Lambshead rummaged in a corner, murmuring to himself. I could make out, "If he'd just held out five years, we could have done so much together, but he died a moron."

(I later checked on this: Lambshead was born in 1900, and Pasteur died in 1895. I knew Lambshead was a child prodigy, but what he thought a seventy-eight-year-old man would have learned from a newborn, I did not ask.)

I reached out my finger to touch what looked like a finely crafted wooden horse, but then pulled back. Something had shifted, almost imperceptibly, inside.

An ancient spear sat propped in the corner opposite the door, and I peered at it. The spear was filthy, still bloody from the poor victim that had been pierced last. I shook my head. On the floor next to the spear lay at least twenty pots, most of them closed, but one on its side, shattered, with dust spilling out everywhere.

Something that looked like a bouquet of dried scorpions stuck up from another urn, and I decided I would not try to touch anything else.

Then Lambshead made an "aha!" sound, and I heard a crash as he tried to extricate something from a pile. He looked down at the floor and frowned. He said, "That was unfortunate, I should get Paulette to clean that up before it spreads," and then took my arm. I followed him reluctantly out to the sunny afternoon and watched as he closed the door.

But then I saw what he held, and the mysteries under the floor seemed unimportant. It was a most curious item; a flask, like Pasteur had created, but that was like saying a Chevy Sedan is a carriage much like Maximus Creed from Rome had cobbled together in 200 B.C. A large bulb at the bottom held a clear, broth-like liquid, but the neck of the flask swooped down in Pasteur's S shape, and then split in three, one swooping back up into a spiral that nearly reached two feet high, and then ended at a sealed glass nipple. Another branch of glass wound round itself, creating knots and curlicues; I counted at least three different sailor's knots and one Celtic knot, and seven more I couldn't identify, some seeming to actually have glass tubes entwined with it that started nowhere and ended nowhere. This whole complex mess wound round the bulb in a spiral, swooping back up to form the open mouth of the flask. The third branch was the strangest, stretching up and then coming back down to go back into the bottle, and, as far as I could tell, back out the bottom, only to fold back and actually form the bulb of the jar itself. This made it a Klein bottle (named for Felix Klein, d. 1882, and, unlike Pasteur, apparently a man *not* to be derided by Dr. Lambshead), sharing its inner and outer side.

I stared at it, flabbergasted by the sheer mastery of workmanship. It could have been my previous unfortunate upchucking situation, as I rarely find myself at a loss for words, but I simply looked from the flask to the doctor, and waited.

"You see, Pasteur managed a reasonable solution for everyday basic bacteria, proving that they can't pass a normal S bend. But you know he was killed by bacteria? Some say it was a stroke, but it was a bacterium with skilled navigational instincts, the kind of thing that laughs at the S bend, and is capable of trekking the fine capillaries, avoiding white blood cells, to attack at the most vulnerable areas in the brain. If he'd developed and learned about this flask in the years before I was born, he could have flummoxed the bacterium and lived longer." He pointed to one of the sailor's knots in the flask. "Here's where they usually get caught, in the Figure of Eight Stopper. Just get outright lost. They rarely make it to the Angler's Loop," he pointed to the final knot.

It was true, the open tubes had varying amounts of grime near the opening, with dead bugs caught in the knots, and some even having followed the dead-end tube and gathered in the nipple, but all of the glass near the bulb to the flask was perfectly clean. It was even clean on the outside.

I pointed to the bulb. "What do you have in there?"

He waved his hand again, and I wondered how many of my interview questions he would brush away. "Something pure, I can tell you that, untouched by neither smart nor ignorant bacteria. I'm saving it for a special occasion." He winked at me.

He took the flask with us inside and then offered me more tea, which I politely refused. We went on with the interview, not mentioning the cabinet again.

When I heard of his death in 2003, I wondered if he'd ever used what was in the flask, or if any of his journals would detail its contents. I also wondered if, perhaps, the flask died the same death as whatever crashed to the ground during my visit, and went from "something pure" to "something Paulette has to clean up before it spreads."

Regardless, in perusing the recent auction catalog for the few unearthed cabinet items that survived the fire, I was struck by the following description: "*Glass abstract sculpture*. Unknown origin. Composed of several curving and circular parts. Badly scorched and melted." Unfortunately, the item had already been bought, and I could not act on my sudden impulse to own it.

1972: The Lichenologist's Visit

As Told to Ekaterina Sedia by S. B. Potter, Lichenologist

As many readers of my novels know, I am also a professional lichenologist, and as such also part of a select and small community of fellow researchers. A few years back, when lichen taxonomy was revised based on new molecular data, it caused quite an upheaval—meaning that among fifteen people who've heard about it, ten cared. One of more vocal critics of the new taxonomic system was one S. B. Potter (not his/her real name), who has been active in the field for years, and who vigorously objected to redefining of some lichen genera. After one particularly heated Internet discussion, I received a snail-mail letter from S. B., containing the following story about a visit to Dr. Lambshead back in the 1970s. I'm afraid Potter has not communicated with me since, and I have no further information to offer. Although I do often wonder about the hand.—E. S.

I first visited Dr. Lambshead under a purely professional set of circumstances: I was recommended to him as the main lichenology expert of the area. At the time, Dr. Lambshead was just beginning to acquire a reputation for his acumen in the unusual diseases, and, like most men who are out to establish themselves, he was particularly impatient with anything that threatened to thwart his progress.

He called on me in secrecy, as if sharing his befuddlement would somehow diminish his stature: he had sent his letter with a messenger, the red wax of the seal reflecting the monogram of his signet ring, pressed with unnecessary vigor.

"Dear Dr. Potter," he wrote in his meticulous, small and square letters, "I loathe to impose on your time, but I suspect that I'm in need of your expertise. I have a patient, one Mrs. Longford, who has developed a persistent cough, and then, a week later, strange greenish-grey splotches on the backs of her hands. I took a sample of the tissue and subjected it to microscopic examination, and to my surprise, the tissue appeared to be of a plant origin. I sent samples to my friends in Oxford, and they confirmed that the sample is indeed a lichen. They also forwarded your name and address to me, and in that regard I am now seeking your advice.

"Would you be able to identify the specimen, and possibly suggest the ways to alleviate my patient's suffering? As time goes on, she is getting worse, with lichen now covering most of her extremities and spreading to her neck. Her cough has become rather fitful as well, and the sputum contains blood as well as lichen tissues. Yours sincerely, Dr. Thackery Lambshead."

At the time, I had just begun to stumble toward the discovery of the link between seemingly innocuous lichens and the disease, but I was still ignorant of the darker nature of this connection; despite my ignorance, however, I had developed a sense of foreboding, as if the part of me that was more perspicacious than the rest was trying to warn me of some unknown danger. However, being a man of

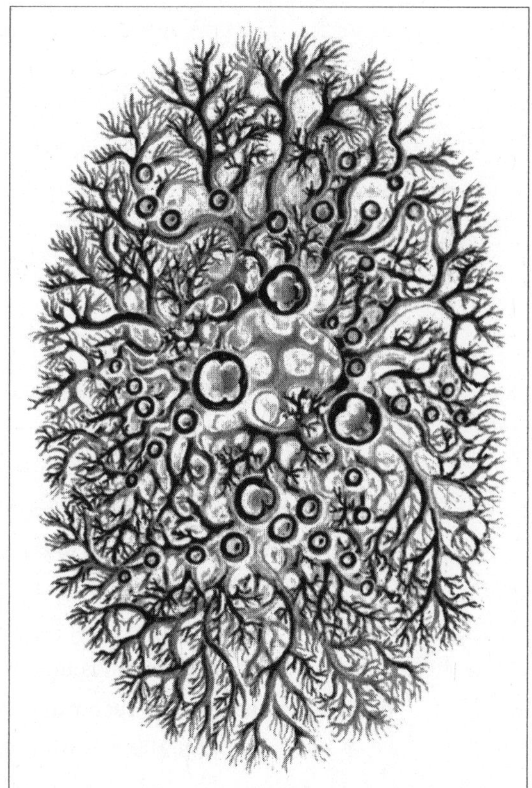

Lichen or Lambshead's new fingerprint?

science, I had dismissed such irrational thoughts and decided to travel to Dr. Lambshead's abode.

He resided in a large house, old and broad, fitting for a family doctor, I thought. The stones that composed its walls bore green and grey splotches, familiar to me—out of the habit, I gauged the age of the house by the lichen size. You see, lichens grow so slowly that many only increase their diameter by one millimeter a year; a lichen blemish the size of a penny is usually a hundred years old. The lichens on Lambshead's home, however, were enormous—if I was to believe them, his house was much older than Hadrian's Wall. Or at least the stones that composed it were—which was rather easier to believe, and I accepted this supposition as truth, reluctant (or unable) to continue thinking about the alternatives.

My next (unnoticed, unheeded!) warning came when the door swung open—it was a massive iron contraption, painted russet-red—and revealed a small man, his grey hair crusting over the dome of his variegated skull. His small eyes looked at me dully.

I asked to see the master of the house, and the man who answered the door turned, exposing the same powdery, unhealthily greenish aspect on the back of his neck as I had previously noted on his head.

Dr. Lambshead himself didn't seem to belong in the foreboding and dark atmosphere of the house—he, as you would well know, was a jovial, hearty man, and his appearance dispelled any doubts I might have had about coming there. He had not a trace of the sickly pallor about him, and at once I scolded myself for my overly active imagination.

I looked at the samples and was able to confirm that they were indeed soredia (asexual reproductive structures) of a lichen; I was even able to guess its genus as *Caloplaca*, but the species eluded me. I promised to conduct additional chemical tests to tease out the exact nature of the specimen, and, with the business concluded, agreed to join my host for tea.

Over tea, I started to feel mildly ill, and was unable to much concentrate on the words of Dr. Lambshead. Blood pounded in my ears, muffling his voice, and my right hand was throbbing. I glanced at my fingers holding the teacup, and noticed that they had grown swollen and powdery; moreover, small brown fruiting bodies were staring to open on my fingertips, like tiny ulcers.

I kept staring at my hand, paralyzed—the speed with which the lichen was growing was shocking, and I could not decide how I had managed to get myself exposed. I did not handle the specimen; it was presented to me on a glass slide. In fact, the only thing I had touched in that whole house was Dr. Lambshead's hand when I shook it—and the teacup.

A sudden realization shifted inside me, snapping like a string, forcing everything into focus. The butler, the blotches of lichen on the house itself . . . "Excuse me," I asked my host then in a trembling voice. "But that patient of yours . . . did you know her before she fell ill?"

Dr. Lambshead nodded. "Yes," he said, after a brief hesitation that told me that he was acquainted with the woman rather more than he wanted anyone to know. "I am friendly with the entire family." During this exchange, he looked straight at me, at my disfigured, bloated hand, and there was no possibility that he didn't see its state. And yet, he didn't make the slightest show of concern. "Is that important?"

"My hand is bothering me," I said, and splayed my blotchy fingers on the white tablecloth.

"It seems to be in order," he said. "Why do you think that my previous familiarity with the patient is relevant?"

His calm tone was the last shred of conviction I needed. I now knew—and I also knew the only reasonable thing to do. I grabbed the bread knife off the table and brought it hard over my wrist, for it is better to amputate one's appendage than to let the terrible contagion spread. The pain was surprisingly dull, even as I cringed at the impossible cracking of the bone and snapping of cartilage, as my blood stained the tablecloth and my host stumbled backward away from the table, his eyes and mouth opening wide.

I do not remember how I fled—the loss of blood weakened me, and I recovered my memory only a few days later, when I discovered myself in my own bed, light-headed but lucid. A neatly bandaged stump of my wrist proved that the events were not my imagination, and my renewed horror was soon soothed by relief once I discovered that *Caloplaca* or whatever accursed genus it was had not spread to the rest of my arm—I had acted just in time.

Despite the time that passed and the pestering questions of friends and relatives who wanted to know what happened to my hand, I have kept these events private until now. As much as I wanted to alert others to the danger, I also feared that my sanity would be questioned, and I did not relish the thought of involuntary commitment to the asylum. My story was as implausible as it was truthful, and really, who in their right mind would believe my discovery—that the man of such knowledge and medical expertise is not what he claims to be at all. You see, that day I realized that Dr. Thackery Lambshead was nothing more than a novel species of lichen, which somehow managed to impersonate a human being. I still believe that it belongs to *Caloplaca* genus.

1995: Kneel

By Brian Evenson

It should be no surprise that, in addition to his catalog of discredited diseases, Dr. Thackery T. Lambshead's collecting impulse extended to art, as exemplified by the galleries that form part of his cabinet of curiosities. His taste here ran to the mad and the mystical: at its best, *brut*ists like Adolph Wölfli and William Kurelek on the one hand, symbolists such as Carlos Schwabe and Mikalojus Konstantinas Ciurlionis on the other. In his galleries, I noted several pieces likely to cause a connoisseur's eye to glisten—for instance, a previously unknown minor Einar Jónsson sculpture or a particularly luminous landscape by Lars Hertervig. But for the most part, the work is mystical in a stately, dignified way, rarely shocking or surprising.

Or at least that is the case with the pieces most readily on display. If you navigate the twists and turns of Lambshead's galleries, if you begin to pay as much attention to your surroundings as to the work itself, you might stumble upon a certain plain white wall. If you take the time, as I did, to look carefully at this wall, you might glimpse a thin filament of light, nearly invisible, crossing it at about the level of your hips. And if you, intrigued, approach this wall and push at it and prod at it, you might well be rewarded, as I was, by the sound of a slight click and the opening of a panel.

An ordinary visitor to Lambshead's home might not be tempted to take the next steps: to fall to his hands and knees, peer into the opening revealed, and then crawl in. But I, as a trusted member of the organization hired by Lambshead to evaluate the artistic portion of his collection while he was away (an organization which, for the purposes of this report, must remain nameless), did take these next steps. On my knees, I peered into darkness. And then, taking a deep breath, I crawled in.

AT FIRST, I thought I had entered some sort of ventilation shaft. The passage was square, the floor and walls made of polished concrete, surprisingly warm to the touch. I was puzzled not to detect the fusty scent I often associate with such places; indeed, there was no smell to it at all. The passage itself sloped very slowly down, just enough that I could feel it. Glancing behind me, at first I could see the opening I had come through, but soon the passage had slanted enough that even that had vanished.

How long I crawled I cannot say. It seemed like some time: I had the impression that I had journeyed outside the confines of the house proper, down into the soil of the grounds surrounding it, but perhaps it was no more than a few dozen meters. Several times I nearly turned back—and indeed would have if the passage had not been too tight to negotiate turning around.

Then, abruptly, the passage reached its termination, concluding in a blank wall, a fact which, I have to admit, caused a certain amount of panic to well up within me. I pawed at the wall, looking for some hidden lever or some sign that what I was facing was not a wall but a door.

But I found nothing.

I AM GENERALLY not the sort to lose my composure. I am, in fact, known among my associates for my sangfroid, my ability to remain cool as a corpse no matter what difficulty I confront. I have no doubt that, despite my panic and the strangeness of the situation, I would have soon succeeded in mastering myself and proceeding in a calm and orderly fashion toward the nearest exit, backing my way slowly out. But in this task, I immediately encountered a complication. For as soon as I began to move backward, I discovered that not only was there a wall in front of me, but now a wall behind me as well.

THERE FOLLOWED A period that I cannot account for, in which I lost track of myself. Perhaps I lost consciousness. Perhaps in my panic I became, for a few seconds, for a few hours, another person entirely. I cannot account for this period. This fact troubles me more than any other.

Suffice it to say that, when I found myself again, my situation had changed. I was lying on the floor of a small, surprisingly modern room, architecturally dissimilar to the rest of the Lambshead residence. The contents of the room seemed to be an artistic installation. There was a painting hanging on the wall, with what I at first interpreted to be a sculptural object just before it, the word KNEEL inscribed in gothic script along the object's base.

Perhaps I was wrong in judging it to be an art installation, I thought, seeing this word. It had a dark, religious feel to it. Perhaps rather than a sculpture, this was an altar.

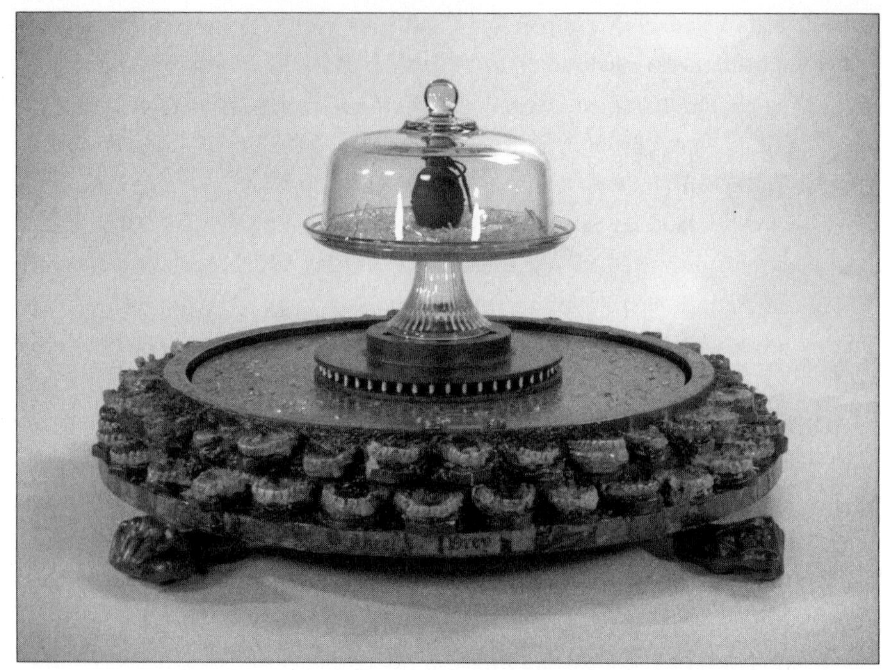

A rare view from inside Dr. Lambshead's cabinet, ca. 1995, showing Scott Eagle's art installation.

But, I wondered, *an altar to what?* I shook my head, told myself I was letting my time in the darkness get the better of me. Of course it was an art object, and I, as a member of the organization, was here to evaluate it.

The painting associated with the installation depicted a teapot, flame spurting from its spout, its body seemingly bloody. It rested on a mound of what might be tentacles or intestines, though they had a machinic aspect as well, and at least one of them terminated in a long-fingered, sharp-clawed hand. There was no signature that I could see, though the technique recalled for me the work of Scott Eagle, or Scott Aigle (as the French call him). The frame was irregular, strangely patched on one side. The longer I looked at it, the more I came to feel that the artwork did not end with the painting proper but extended into this frame. I heard, when I approached the painting, a strange humming, as if I might turn it over to find its reverse swarming with bees. But perhaps this was a quality of the room tone and not of the painting itself.

THERE WAS, BELOW the painting, what at first appeared to be a poem. A series of words, in any case. I read it, but once I had finished, found that I could not remember what it had said, nor, indeed, make any proper sense of it. I read it again, and a pressure began within my head, which, rightly or wrongly, I ascribed to the poem. I was tempted to read it a third time, this time aloud, but resisted, vaguely afraid of what might happen to me if I did.

And what was that at the bottom of the wall, that strange grouping of blood-red, unidentifiable objects? I crouched and examined them, picked one up and turned it round and about in my hand. It was like a small stone, but soft, and made of a substance I did not recognize.

I followed the line of objects back to the altar, for I had now begun in earnest to think of it as an altar. In the place of wooden spindles or legs, it rested on four simulacra of arms, lacquered. These supported a bottom platter, round, upon which rested sets of false (so I assumed) teeth, arranged in two rows. A top platter was cracquelured over with dried blood, and on this, other platters, other inexplicable disks, and finally, at the top, a glass bell, containing flecks of something like ice. Riding within the ice was an object of uncertain design.

What was the object? I could make out aspects of it, had something of a grasp of its shape and color, but still could not determine what it was. Truth be told, I remained unsure whether it should be considered art or something else, something ritualized and potentially threatening.

Kneel, the base of the altar commanded me. But I did not kneel. Instead I

Detail shot of Eagle's art installation

remained standing, hunched and leaning over the altar, my face nearly touching the glass bell. And then, on a whim, I reached up and lifted it away.

And here, I am afraid to admit, I suffered another lacuna, another moment of loss. There are things I remember. A roaring sound, but distant, as if miles away, as if there were still time to find shelter from whatever was coming. A horrible stench, like the air itself had been scorched. Brief flashes of motion and light, coming initially from the painting but quickly spreading all around me. And then nothing.

I returned to consciousness in the bushes next to one wall of the estate, unsure of how I had arrived there. One side of my body was sore, covered with scratch marks and scabs. My earlobe was stiff with dried blood, though I found no sign of any injury or wound. My tongue was scraped raw and sat heavy in my mouth.

When I stumbled back into the house, I discovered several days had passed and I had been replaced in my project of evaluating the collection.

When asked to justify my absence, first by my replacement and then by my betters in the organization, I recounted all that had happened. And yet, no matter how I searched, no matter where I looked in the galleries, I could find no hidden entry or door. I did my best to draw what I had seen, what I had perceived, but my interlocutors remained incredulous. There was, they told me, no secret room, no private altar of forearms and blood and teeth; I had dreamed it; I had imagined it.

When they told me this enough times, I stopped trying to convince them. Yes, I conceded, it was not real. I had merely fallen and hit my head. Nothing happened. I saw nothing.

BUT, OF COURSE, I had seen what I had seen, and as time went on, I found the memory of what I had seen working away at me. I saw it there before me: a painting of tubes and tentacles, an unknown object on a strange altar, balanced atop teeth and arms. And sometimes, in my thoughts, the teeth begin to chatter and the arms flex and stretch, the fingers moving, calling me, beckoning me. And though I had originally been repulsed, I now found myself more and more attracted, more and more drawn in.

Tonight I will break into the estate and then, with a sledgehammer, strike wall after wall until I find the vanished door. Once found, I will open it and again follow the passage slowly down until I find myself standing before the altar. This time, I will heed its advice and kneel. It will, I am certain, reward me. But how, and with what, and whether for better or worse, I do not know.

I am writing this record to stand in my place in case I do not return.

2000: Dr. Lambshead's Dark Room

By S. J. Chambers

About ten years ago, Dr. Lambshead published an article in the *Psychomesmeric Quarterly* about hypnotic techniques inherited from his grandfather, a great confidant of Monsieur Mesmer. Among Lambshead's mesmeric family legacy was the Valdemar Method, which enabled the doctor, so he claimed, "to extract from even the most cavernous subconscious those diseases that afflicted the soul, as demonstrated in the mesmeric stories of Edgar Allan Poe."

As I am a Poe scholar, the doctor's claims intrigued me and I wrote him requesting a demonstration. I knew the good doctor could not resist a challenge, so to further intrigue him, I mentioned that I felt riddled with a disease of influence that was affecting my work and love life, and offered myself up as the proverbial guinea pig. Within a fortnight, I received an invitation to his house, "the only place," he wrote, "where the Valdemar Method could be manifested."

Surprisingly, Dr. Lambshead appeared to have no maid or butler, and was already waiting at the door when I arrived. An ancient but spry man in a tailored silk bathrobe, he was headed down the hallway before I could put my bags down and greet him.

"To the matter at hand," he said. "Don't tell me a thing. That is for the Dark Room to show."

He waved me inside and led me to the back of the house, where he pulled aside a faded Turkish rug to reveal a trap door that fell open into a dark and dusty staircase. He descended into that darkness, and I followed him down several flights, feeling my way around the rocky walls, until he suddenly halted and clapped his hands repeatedly. When he stopped clapping, several floating orbs illuminated the basement.

"Will-o'-the-wisps," Lambshead said, "from the Iberian Coast. I caught them with one of Nabokov's butterfly nets." I looked at the floating lights, which graduated from green to purple, blue to red, like childhood's LED sparklers. I held out my hand and one alighted on my finger—its touch cool as the Mediterranean.

"How . . . how do they . . ."

"Float? Live? Glow?" He shrugged. "Curious, no?" This response disappointed me. It was unlike a man of science to pass up a chance to explain away the world. As if he knew my thoughts, he smiled. "Even in this century, there are still wonders beyond explanation. They are rare, but they do exist, and it has been my hobby, I suppose you could say, to collect all the world's true curios, as you will see. But no more words for now unless prompted; it disrupts the process!"

We continued through the hallway, and the will-o'-the-wisps grew brighter as we walked through the cabinet until we entered a dark chamber, empty but with the exception of two worn Louis XVI chairs.

"Ah, now we can really begin."

He sat in one chair and gestured for me to occupy the other. The will-o'-the-wisps floated out of our hands and hovered between our eyes. They undulated, glowing and dimming in tune with my heartbeat that swooshed through my ears.

"I want you to watch the wisps," he whispered, "and tell me: have you experienced these following symptoms: soaring soul, existential exigency, speaking in cryptically symbolic metaphor, vertigo caused by sublimity, vision heightened by chiaroscuro, dead-dwelling, or head-swelling?"

"Yes," I said.

"To all?"

"Yes."

"Hmmmm . . ." His disbelieving expression ebbed into a dare-to-hope.

The two will-o'-the-wisps glowed blindingly blue and I became dizzy and hot, and the doctor and the wisps became double-exposed, and somehow I was split twain by the sides until there were two of me. One sat in front of Lambshead and the undulating wisps, while the other, conscious and seeing, was free to traverse the room.

"Do you suffer from daydreaming reflex with reveries that include blackbirds, scents of an unseen censor, or aberrant alliterative applications?"

Beady eyes glowed from the wisps, and wings fluttered by my ears. I smelled dried flowers and cut grass, upturned earth and the fading waft of fabric softener. I looked at my sitting-self in the chair and heard her indolent "Yes."

"What else do you see?"

The wisps left Lambshead and my sitting-self to illuminate the corners of the empty room where ebon bookcases grew from the walls and within them appeared objects that my sitting-self described:

Jaundiced blueprints of a non-Euclidian pendulum; a stuffed cat with a hissing throat encircled in white fur; a fractured skull chilling a broken bottle of blood-thick sherry; a tailor's mannequin wearing a white, blood-soaked and dirt-streaked dressing gown, its neck a splintered pine plank engraved with claw marks.

Beside the cases stood a stuffed gorilla. I couldn't help but touch its fur, which turned to feathers and fluttered to the ground, revealing the tarred and malformed skeleton of a dwarf. Through its eye socket, a gold beetle climbed out and over to a shelf that held a jar of putrescence and nestled itself in an open locket containing a strand of blond hair speckled black.

At the very bottom of the bookshelves were several jorums filled with animated landscapes: tiny ships thrusting within a maelstrom pint; a littoral liter with a weeping willow tree overlooking a craggy shore; and a quart of electrified clouds in the shape of women hovering over an abandoned manse, crying dust and leaves.

"What are these?" I asked Lambshead. From his chair, he looked up to the ceiling, unsure of my voice's source.

"What do they look like?" he asked my sitting-self. I heard her describe the jorums, and he smiled.

"Mood," he spoke into the ether. "They are jars of mood."

I squatted at the bookshelf and selected one containing the cosmos. Several minute stars swam like strawberry seeds in a phosphorescent jam that churned and congealed into a sun that heated the glass. It burned my hand and I dropped it, and, with a loud bang, it exploded on the floor, incinerating all within the jar and melting the glass, which pooled and cooled into a Bristol blue fetus.

Before I could retrieve it, I heard Lambshead command me awake, and suddenly I was back in the chair—whole—and subject to his sherry-sweet breath. The bookshelves, the taxidermy, curios, and jars were all gone, but on the ground remained the glass fetus, which the doctor rushed to rescue.

He coddled it in his palm. "This—this is what ails you!"

"A child?"

"Of the imagination, yes. You thought you had a disease of influence, but it is much, much worse. You have a disease of the *imagination,* probably from too much Poe. But don't worry, this here is your cure."

"I thought you said it was what ails me?"

"You *are* cured," he said. "And I have another child for my cabinet!" He waved the wisps away and they dimmed in rejection. Before I could ask what the other children were, he all but rushed me from the basement and out of his house.

I did not see where he kept the Dark Room's offspring, and I suppose now I never will, but after I left Lambshead and his curious cabinet, I admit I felt a lot lighter. Before booting me off the steps, he gave me permission to write of my disease, which seemed to ameliorate my condition more.

Having been able to resume a normal, perhaps even an extra-normal life, I am forever indebted to that cabinet and to Dr. Lambshead. When I read of his death, just three years later, I mourned not only the loss of that great man but also of his Dark Room and its soul-ware nursery that has inevitably become overexposed and returned to the ether.

2003: The Pea

Related to Gio Clairval in 2008 at a Parisan Café, by Dr. Lambshead's Housekeeper

Dr. Lambshead had told me not to dust the object resting on the third shelf from the floor, a collector's item hidden behind a maroon curtain. In my twenty years at the doctor's service, I had never contravened an order.

Nevertheless, my employer's days being numbered, it seemed to me that I should redouble my efforts in keeping the basement spotless.

Behind the curtain stood a bell jar of oxide-stained glass, iridescent with blues, pinks, and greens, as tall as my forearm, protecting a Smyrna-red velvet cushion the size of a full-blossomed rose. Golden tassels hanging from a crown of braided trimmings strangled the cushion into the shape of a muffin, the top of which appeared to be decorated with an embroidery of silver-coloured human hair stitched at regular intervals to form a lozenge pattern.

On the cushion sat a perfectly preserved pea.

I gasped, suddenly aware of my staring at a piece of Dr. Lambshead's secret collection, and lowered my gaze to examine the elegant pedestal. It was made of grey-veined marble carved into ovals framed by acanthus leaves. A slight suspicion of dust filled the carvings. After five seconds, I looked at the item again. How could a pea not shrink and shrivel, unless it was preserved in oil or in a vacuum? To judge by the colour, it was a young pea freshly spilled from its pod, full of water and life that made its skin turgid, ready to burst if squeezed between index finger and thumb.

My stomach clenched at the unprofessional thought. I concentrated on my task, passing my feather duster with the greatest attention on the delicate pedestal carvings, but my gaze wandered back to the pea. It had never happened before. In all those years, never had one single question about any of the objects crossed my mind. My deference to the doctor's wishes had always been absolute.

Dr. Lambshead had become all my family after my parents died. No sensible person can lend credence to the cook's rants; he attributes a selfish intent to each of the doctor's good actions. It is untrue that my legal guardian discouraged my interest in humanities to secure the services of an unpaid employee. When a paralysing timidity forced me to abandon my studies at Oxford, the doctor restored my self-esteem by assuring me I was the only person he could trust to keep his ever-growing collection mildew-free. He had always treated me with consideration. And dust was our enemy.

Dust, Paulette, dust hard and true, he used to say. Blessed be the stutter that forced you to forgo your wish to become a teacher. Dusting is a greater responsibility. Dusting must be your obsession. The professional Duster's mission is to make a stand against the particles that come out of the ether, the first step taken by Mother Nature in the process of smothering her children. Entropy, the doctor said, erases all differences, deconstructing complex matter into simple elements. Dust, full of vile microorganisms, is the harbinger of entropy and must be confronted with unrelenting determination. Forget the wonders gathered in this basement room. See only concave shapes and recesses and carvings as receptacles to choking death, headquarters where the enemy prepares for sorties. Don't let the soldiers of entropy regroup to launch the next offensive. Destroy them with your feather duster, moist rag, and badger-bristle brush. Wage war against the blanket of oblivion, Paulette. Make these shelves a testimony to Man's struggle for eternity.

With these words in mind, I would spend my days in the doctor's cabinet of curiosities, stroking precious items with my instruments. Never seeing the items themselves. Always considering these disparate objects in their mere quality of innocent victims to dust.

So why was I fascinated by the most humble among the doctor's treasures? Despite the glamorous presentation on the tasselled cushion, it was a simple pea—so round, so green, so impossibly glossy within the confined space of the bell.

It struck me that the pea, like other items protected by cloths, jars, bottles, cases, and sandalwood- or stone-inlaid boxes, didn't need me. Surely enough, the outer shell, the glass bell that protected it, would soon be marred by layers of particles, without my repeated interventions. But the pea itself flaunted its perfect round shape unblemished by the agents of annihilation. My chest ached as I realized how peripheral I was in the pea's destiny.

Dr. Lambshead's cook, a retired professor who philosophised while stirring sauces, once said my job epitomised the concept of empty instrumentality. He meant that once I had finished dusting, I would have to start it over again and there could be no lasting result of my toiling, ever. You're like the dust you fight, Paulette, a monument to impermanence. But I saw no problem in being a modest tool. Day after day, I won my battle against the dancing motes and went home happy, knowing that the enemy would infiltrate the basement during the night, laying a thin sheet of powdery specks on everything, but I would counter the attack the following day, and again, and I'd never be unemployed.

An immutable ritual. I wore a pristine white apron. Washed my hands at the sink concealed behind a drape in a corner of the one-room basement. Seized my instruments. Dusting, I crossed the strokes, swivelled before stepping toward the next spot, dedicated an entrechat to the smallest pieces and bowed to the tallest, seeing them as a continuum of surfaces to dust. I worked with enthusiasm, disputing my protégés to my opponent's domination. I was proud of my mission. I was content. Above everything, I was useful.

Until I saw the pea and its uncaring perfection.

The most fragile of pieces owed its safety to a transparent dome, an inanimate device, not to me. The doctor believed my work insufficient. He displayed the pea to prove the inanity of my task, and the cruel man had expected my curiosity to take over. He had wanted me to see the pea.

Brass clasps held the rim of the bell jar fixed to the marble pedestal. I fingered one, jerked my hand away. Overwhelmed by my audacity, I forced myself to step out of range, and glanced at other pieces that rested under their glass shields, forever impervious to the impalpable powders of time. One of the bells protecting a gilded mask had a spidery crack at the base that ended with a chink in the glass rim. The enemy had defeated all defences and penetrated the sanctuary. Trails of insectile feet crisscrossed the ebony floor around the mask. A fly had traced a series of doodling circles in the dust before extending its six legs in the rigour of death. What could my honest work do against such power of insinuation?

I spun other bells around and examined them under every angle. A few clasps were open or not fully cinched over the small indents in the pedestals. Worse still, I discovered a greater number of subtly broken glass surfaces. Bent on ignoring the pieces themselves, concentrating on the dust, I had never noticed any blemishes. Fear scratched tiny claws at my heart. At least one third of the stored bell jars had flaws that allowed decay to invade them. They were sly traitors collaborating with the armies of dissolution. I gripped the edge of the nearest table. Dr. Lambshead knew the shelves like his pockets. He had known the truth all the time. I was his alibi in an illusory resistance. I clenched my fists, fingernails digging into my palms.

And the pea, the only ordinary piece in that unbelievable collection. . . . The doctor couldn't trust a fragile glass case to protect it. To showcase a perfectly preserved specimen, he surely replaced it at the first sign of corruption, as a statement of short-lived flawlessness.

I went to fetch one of the tallow candles from the pantry. Back in the basement, I drew the drapes that concealed the sink and pushed the candle into the plastic siphon. I struck a long match used for the hearth and lit the wick. I counted on the flame to consume the plastic siphon and create a cloud of soot. It had happened to my cousin once removed when she had inadvertently dropped a candle in the sink after cleaning up the dinner table. The wick was still burning and the siphon had simmered all night, along with the plastic pipe, spitting out particles of soot. She and her husband had awoken to an apartment covered in a layer of greasy black stuff that stuck to every object.

The pea of record. On a cushion.

For the first time since I had begun working there, I opened jars, bottles, boxes, and set the objects free. The tour of the shelves took more than the usual three hours. By then, black particles fluttered about, spurting from the slow-burning plastic under the drain, blackening the unprotected pieces with myriad new soldiers of doom.

I rolled up my sleeves, plunged my rag into a bucket of soapy water, and smiled. Let the best one win.

My plan did not include sparks shooting out of the carbonized siphon. The drape took fire, which I noticed only when the fire reached an electric socket and the light went out. The auxiliary lighting bathed the basement in red. Petrified, I watched the flames lick a nearby shelf.

The side effect of my experiment shocked me at first and then thrilled me. I had intended to measure my skills against a formidable greasy black dust, but I had acted as an agent of purification by creating a cleansing fire.

I unclasped the bell, lifted it, and snatched the pea from under the protective dome. Now I held the doctor's most precious item between my index finger and thumb—the only symbol of life in a collection of dead objects. I pictured myself slipping the pea into an envelope, along with my resignation.

The pea was very heavy. The skin had lost its glossy polish, growing rough, lumpy. Unnaturally warm.

I threw the thing into the flames. It exploded like a firecracker, in a spray of blue sparks. I ran to the basement door and slammed it behind me.

Like every day before, I went home happy.

Happier.

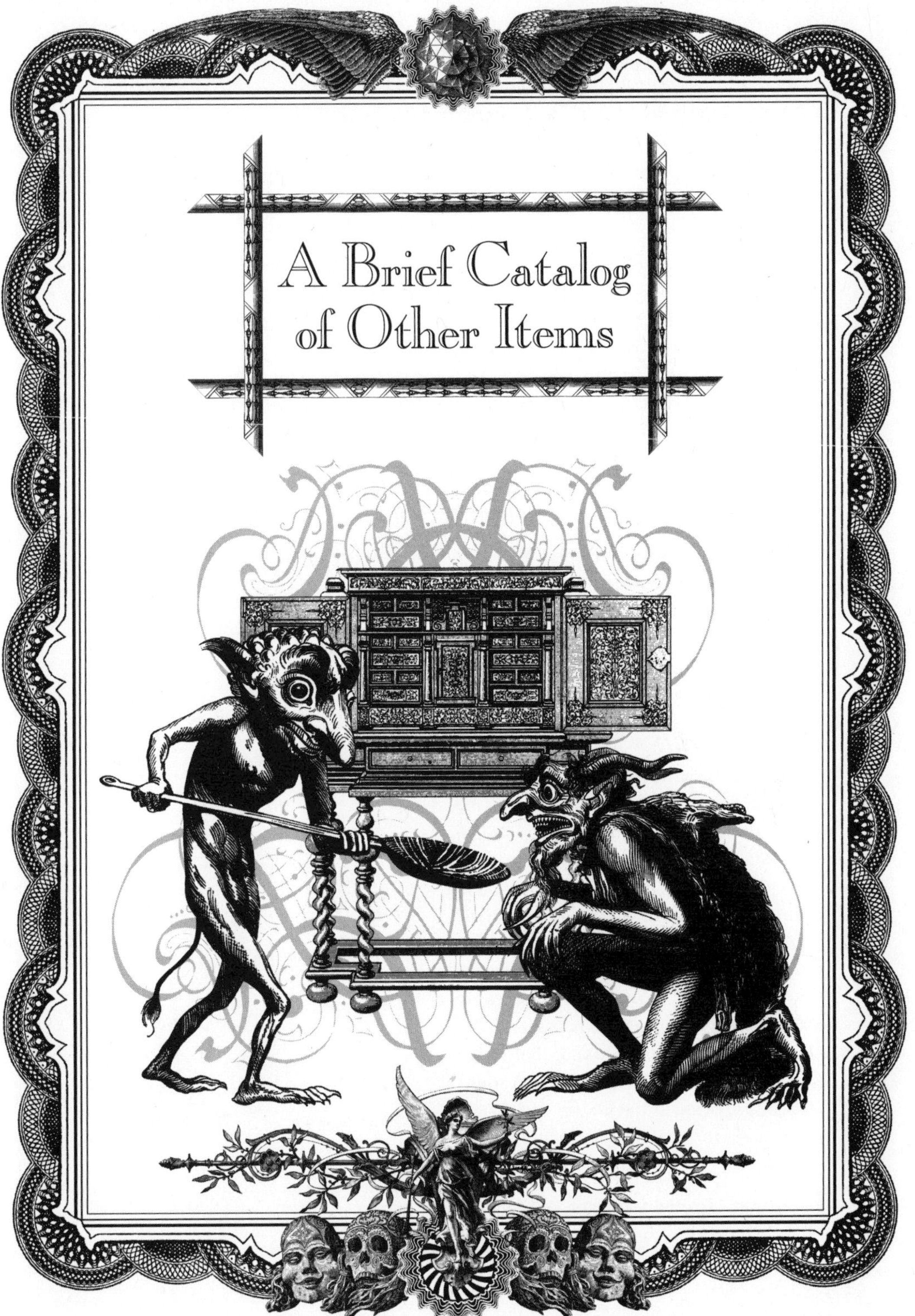
A Brief Catalog
of Other Items

The discovery of the half-burned subterranean space devoted to Dr. Lambshead's cabinet of curiosities created an urgent need to sort through the wreckage and document "survivors." A number of experts helped catalog both the remains and the occasional miraculous find of an undamaged object. The most interesting of these items have been described below by the experts who discovered, cleaned, and researched them. Where appropriate, we have also included photographs, illustrations, and diagrams in support of these findings. Not every conclusion reached herein has been verified independently.

Bear Gun—Long-barreled flintlock rifle, four feet butt to muzzle, made from timber that traces back to a species of hickory previously abundant in the Appalachians and long thought to be extinct. When fired, it releases a live bear as a projectile. The bear expands in a matter of seconds from the size of a musket ball to full size, at which point it latches onto its target and devours it noisily. Documents found partly scorched in Dr. Lambshead's cabinet claim the use of the gun in the American Civil War for political assassinations. The scene of a vicious bear attack often permitted assassins an avenue for escape, while journalists and the government revised the facts of such events due to their absurd nature. A receipt wrapped around the barrel carries the signature of one John T. Ford, but the fire left the cost and date of the transaction unknown. (Adam Mills)

Bullet Menagerie—A clear surface two feet square and one inch in thickness, with the consistency of cold Vaseline. Metal shutters on each side, labeled A and B, may be opened or closed by button-press. When the A shutter is open, a projectile fired at the pane with a velocity greater than ten feet per second will remain trapped within the medium. Opening the B shutter will cause it to exit with its original length and velocity. Inscribed by the inventor: Chas. Shallowvat, 1788. An inventory sheet indicates that the menagerie preserves live bullets fired by French, Prussian, Ottoman, Hanoverian, Etrurian, Swedish, and unidentified forces, which Shallowvat managed to capture while traveling during the Napoleonic Wars. Upon acquiring the menagerie, Dr. Lambshead, perhaps thinking that opening the B shutter would also reopen an infelicitous period in the history of Europe, neglected to verify its contents. (Nick Tramdack)

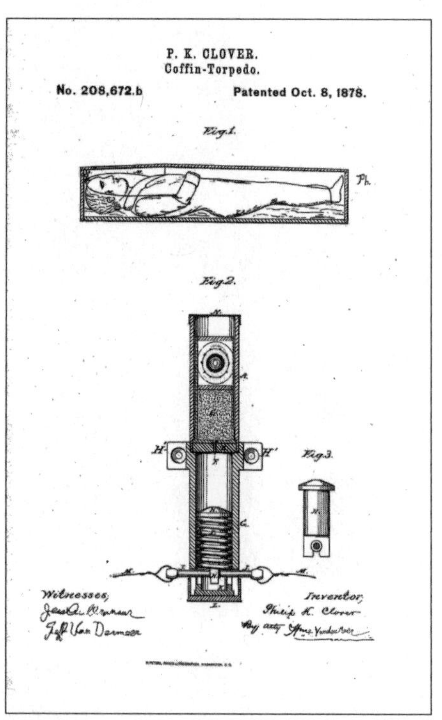

The very coffin torpedo from Lambshead's collection.

Coffin Torpedo—Ostensibly of the Clover type, though considerably smaller

"This is one of only several existing images of a bear rumored to have been fired from a bear gun. That this bear was thus fired is assumed based on visible friction burns in its fur, most notably on one of its front legs and its back (the latter is evident in an accompanying photograph, not reprinted due to permission issues). The bear seems to have been shot with a taxidermy gun postmortem, as evidenced by stitches visible in hairless patches on its body. The bear's owner has so far ignored requests for fur samples, despite the need for carbon dating." (Adam Mills)

than other unexploded specimens originating in the latter half of the nineteenth century. Devices like these were used to discourage the very real threat of grave-violation by Resurrectionists, and their armament packages typically contained powder, shot, chain, etc. The triggering lever on this item is removed, thankfully, but it should be noted that the munition here is not of any recognizable type—warm to the touch, and emitting a surprising amount of detectable radiation for so small an object. (Jess Gulbranson)

Czerwatenko Whelk in Olive Oil—Preserved specimen of *Turpis pallidus,* a small whelk that once dominated the littoral fauna of the Czerwatenko Sea. The species disappeared when that body of water was drained in 1917 to create the International Saltworks Project. Within months, sixty-five salt-scrapers died, and company scientists traced the cause to the whelks. Upon desiccating, the delicate snails had crumbled—shell and all—into a highly toxic powder and mixed with the precipitated Czerwatenko sea salt, rendering it deadly. The saltworks was abandoned. In the 1920s, anthropologists discovered a group of indigenes who had once eaten the whelks as part of their staple diet. When asked how they had survived ingesting the toxic snails, they replied that any sort of oil or fat would neutralize the poison. The specimen in Lambshead's collection was purchased from a centenarian villager who claimed she had never developed a taste for the snails. (Therese Littleton)

Dander of Melville, The—Small crimson phial of biological ejecta sloughed from beard and waistcoat of one Herman M., inspector of customs. In cities prone to ship-rot and oracular drifters, admixture of same with barnacle flower was briefly regarded as a palliative for Vesuvian angers and scrimshaw-related injuries. In street parlance, more commonly referred to as "Red-burn's Rake" or godflake. (Brian Thill)

Decanter of Everlasting Sadness, The (*La decanter de tristesse qui dure pour toujours*)—Acquired in 1928 by Thackery T. Lambshead during an outbreak of blood poisoning at Le Moulin Rouge, this crystalline bottle includes a glass stopper in which an earlobe, purportedly that of Vincent van Gogh, has been chambered. An accompanying tag, attached to the neck of the bottle with braided cornsilk, indicates that imbibing any aperitif, properly aged within, will induce visions of a universe writ large. Earthy notes of potato, almond, and sunflower accompany a spectral show—in which the appetitive soul is riddled with starry starlight. On the base of the decanter, curving gracefully about the punt (and most easily read when the bottle is empty), a cursive admonishment is etched: *Use judiciously. The yeast of life's melancholy rises in proportion to the sedimentation of posthumous renown.* (William T. Vandemark)

Dinner Bell of the *Mary Celeste,* The—The bell, which was present when the *Mary Celeste* was towed into Genoa, was found to be absent when the ship was inspected in Gibraltar. The couple who presented the bell for auction in 1893 claimed to have snuck aboard the derelict ship as children, and to have taken the artifact as a memento. They asserted that ringing the bell caused a curious sensation in the back of the head, as well as a desire to go swimming, and as such was unsuitable as a dinner bell due to the dangers of swimming immediately after a meal. Experimentation at a boy's school next to a lake in the summer provided inconclusive data about the bell's efficacy in this regard, though it has been theorized by some that there must be a meal present to cause the bell's unusual effect. (Jennifer Harwood-Smith)

Dracula's Testicles—Unusual in size (they have a diameter of five inches apiece), these were a donation by Jonathan Van Helsing Jr. It is believed that the gigantic size of the testicles is due to their use while they were still attached to the body. According to Dr. Lambshead's hypothesis—enounced in a note glued to the jar filled with clear garlic juice in which the exhibits are stored—the testicles were used as reservoirs for the extra blood that the vampire had to suck before travelling, so as to be able to survive longer without drinking blood. According to the donor, the famous vampire-hunter's son, the testicles were a gift by Count Dracula's twenty-second wife to his father, in exchange for being allowed to collect and enjoy the vampire's life insurance (a fabulous sum, or so the rumors of the period said) after Dr. Van Helsing Sr. performed the staking of the four-hundred-year-old vampire. (Horia Ursu)

Ear Eye—This instrument functions in the same way as a periscope but is in the shape of a C, and therefore requires many more mirrors. It is apparently designed for looking into one's own ear. A transparent casing displays the mirrors inside. Inexplicably, one of them is tinted so dark as to be minimally reflective. According to Lambshead's journal, an employee of the caretakers of the doctor's house was testing the Ear Eye when he dropped it (fortunately, it doesn't appear to have been damaged) and ran away, yelling inarticulately and covering the ear he had just been looking into. He seemed to want no one to see into it. He has not reported back. No one has yet been found willing to further investigate the Ear Eye. (Graham Lowther)

Fort Chaffee Polyhedral Deck, The—This item consists of fifty-four uncoated paper playing cards in a cardboard sleeve printed with the slogan KNOW YOUR ENEMY. The cards resemble spotter decks used to train World War II pilots, but in place of aircraft silhouettes, each card is illustrated with a different stellated polyhedron and its Schläfli symbol. This is the only known copy of the Fort Chaffee deck and it is regrettably incomplete: the ace of spades was replaced with an ordinary playing card with a similar backing. It was discovered by Dr. Lambshead at a poker tourney hosted by an acquaintance, a professor of high-energy physics tenured at Los Alamos. According to his personal correspondence, Lambshead procured the Fort Chaffee deck with "haste and discretion," which may explain both his lack of inquiry into this apparent geometric incursion and the sudden end of his career as a cardsharp. (Nickolas Brienza)

A card carrier of the type used with the Fort Chaffee deck.

Harness & Leash for Fly—Harness fashioned from newspaper. Coiled, grey-colored leash of undetermined material. Possibly a relic from the Cult of the Fly, an obscure movement originating in the workingmen's clubs of nineteenth-century Lancashire. What little we know about the cult comes from a letter by a Miss Phyllis Grimshaw of Oswaldtwistle to a Mrs. Evelyn Hunt of Crewe (currently on display in the MOSI). She states: "Father has taken up with those ridiculous fly men and is growing a beard, to his knees, he says, so he can pluck a hair from it. Mrs. Cackett, at the shop, says some never-sweats have been plucking the tail hairs from passing horses." The precise nature of the ritual involving the flies is unknown, although it is unlikely the incumbent of this harness lived a full life: a fragment of wing remains attached to the newspaper. (Claire Massey)

Human Skeleton, Irregular—Adult male, 20th c. European, identity unknown. Acquired from the estate of noted dog breeder and occult hobbyist Mr. Comfort of Derbyshire, whose widow sold his collection and prized Schnauzers after his fatal hunting accident in 1952, the skeleton may be an example of an unclassified bone disorder or an elaborate anatomical hoax; Dr. Lambshead's records are inconclusive. Curious features include pronounced phalangeal keratin structures, twelve coccygeal vertebrae, rotated scapula and absent clavicle, convex frontal bone, and an elongated mandible with overlarge canines. A small hole in the occipital bone along with traces of silver and indentations in the cervical vertebrae suggest death by foul play rather than disease; scorching indicates posthumous exposure to fire. Mr. Comfort's journals contain no mention of the specimen and disclose no provenance. Mrs. Comfort's auction notes are brief: "Skeleton, male, possible medical interest. Nobody important. £3 starting bid." (Kali Wallace)

Ichor Whorl—Small, coarse, black object suspended in a yet-to-be-analyzed solution. Object is variable in size—averaging one cubic inch—and vortical in shape. Date of manufacture unknown. Lambshead journal fragment 729 notes the item's place of origin as "a polluted shoreline of a former Soviet republic." Dr. Lambshead sent the item to Tillinghast Laboratories, which provided the following report: "Keep organic matter one meter from contents. Empirical tests reveal living tissue placed within one meter is remotely hollowed (by undetermined means) to the limit of solidity without liquefying. Spectroscopic results inconclusive. Presence of organic matter within one-meter orbit is accompanied by slight phase change in object, from solid to non-Newtonian fluid, and extension of one spiral arm to three centimeters covered in half-centimeter protrusions. Authorization for further tests required." Donated to Dr. Lambshead by Maximilian Crabbe, 1989. (Ben Woodward)

Rikki Ducornet's still-life mug shots, drawn from her encounters with disgruntled artifacts

Jug, Disgruntled, et al.—A series of cabinet artifacts, generally from antiquity, depicting human facial features that appear to differ in expression following the cabinet fire, based on records of their expressions prior to the fire. While the catalyst for the change may be apparent, the agency is not. (Art by Rikki Ducornet)

Kepler the Clock—Franz Kepler's rigorous attention to his many appointments made him susceptible to Chronometrophilia. Initially, the disease manifested in twitches of his right hand, as if he were reaching for a pocket watch. Had he sought treatment then, he may have been cured. But Kepler had no time for illness. Gradually, his features began to resemble a clock face. Within a month, his moustache would rotate to indicate the time. When his legs became mahogany, he adjusted by scheduling meetings in his office, ensuring none would fall on the hour, whereupon he would utter a loud "bong." One Monday, Kepler's colleagues arrived at work to find a grandfather clock behind his desk. Dr. Lambshead purchased the clock some years later from a private collector. Kepler is, we assume, still alive. He keeps excellent time and should continue to do so if he is regularly wound. (Grant Stone)

Kris ("The Assassin's Twist")—A kris whose every turn and twist on the blade is supposed to inflict a certain wound or an affliction upon the victim. However, unlike in all other krises, the twists in this one have been forged in a way that any attack by the tip or part of the blade will surely kill the target, yet when the large kris is pushed into one's body up to the hilt, it will leave the person alive (owing to a secret twist devised on the blade below the hilt). This geometric weapon increases the assassin's chance of killing the target (for even a single scratch would be enough) yet introduces a final plot twist to the weapon by leaving the target alive once it is pushed up to its hilt to the body. (Incognitum)

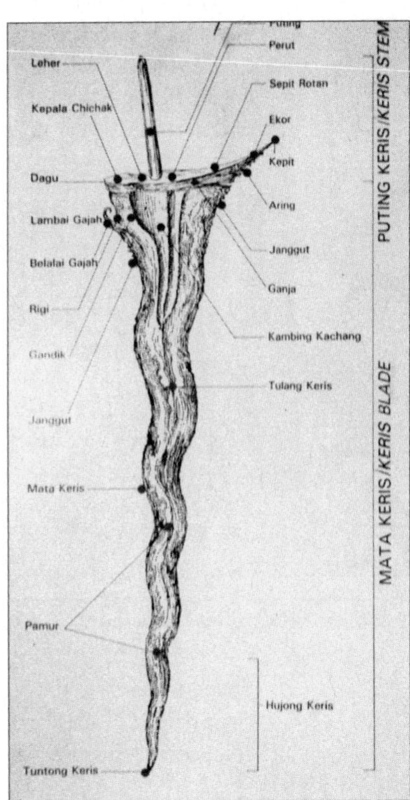

The map for creating an Assassin's Twist (plot twist included).

Leary's Pineal Body—This *epiphysis cerebri* was pickled in vivo by the late American psychologist most famous for his mantra "Turn on, tune in, drop out." Dr. Leary opened gates heretofore unknown beyond the speculations of H. P. Lovecraft, and this gland is noteworthy for its ability to have survived multiple encounters with beings from beyond—and otherwise. Research is pending on a way to safely experiment on it; the Stanford Asylum has a special wing for those who have attempted, to date. (Kaolin Imago Fire)

Mellified Alien—The enlarged head and oversized eyes of this diminutive, mummified humanoid creature would indicate that it is of the Grey type of extraterrestrial. That it has been preserved in honey is clear. What is less clear is if it feasted upon, willingly or unwillingly, "the golden stuff," before it died. For only if it had ingested honey in sufficient quantities over a number of days would its remains be truly mellified and impart their healing properties to whoever had been nibbling on it. The application of forensic dentistry may confirm the conjecture that this sweet confection once belonged to Sir Arthur Conan Doyle before coming into Dr. Lambshead's possession. (Julie Andrews)

Mooney & Finch Somnotrope—These sleep simulators (pictured on page 301) have become rare artifacts; even though they were mass-produced in the Mooney & Finch Sheffield facility, each one of them emerged as a unique object due to the pressures of the oneiric centrifuge. However, they were only sold for three months, prior to the first reports of somnambulance addiction and peripatetic insomnia. The idea of experiencing four or five hours of sleep within a mere few minutes held almost unlimited allure for the world's busiest captains of industry and harried matrons. But few were prepared for the intoxication of the Somnotrope's soothing buzz, the sheer pleasure of watching its central piston raise and lower, gently at first and then with increasing vigor, until your mind flooded with dream fragments and impression of having sailed to the nether kingdom and back, all in a few minutes. It only took a few unfortunate deaths for the whole line to be recalled. (Charlie Jane Anders)

Mother of Spirits—Drab olive in color, with copper flecking, this three-inch-long sessile organism resembles a desiccated asparagus spear mated with a tiny artichoke. Once rehydrated in a suitable measure of clean water, it manifests a most peculiar phenomenon. When placed into a vessel containing fermented alcoholic beverage—beer, wine, mead, etc.—the Mother of Spirits catalyzes a secondary fermentation up to 120 proof (provided sufficient sugars are available). The Mother extrudes rootlike growth during this process, which can last several months, and it is speculated these function in a symbiotic relationship with residual yeasts to effect the unusually high secondary fermentation. Daughters form at the root nodes once alcohol content surpasses 50 percent, as the Mother is spent during the process. The resulting liquor is of fine quality, but a distinct aroma and flavor of cilantro renders it unpalatable to some. (Jayme Lynne Blaschke)

Ron Pippin's optimistic vision of the Much Smaller Cabinet's contents.

Much Smaller Cabinet—This miniature cabinet is a duplicate of Dr. Lambshead's in nearly every respect, a 1/1000th-scale model incorporating scorch marks and splintered frame down to the smallest detail. A single variation: the door remains locked. The doctor dropped the diminutive key in his squid tank and failed to retrieve it before Longfellow's greedy tentacles snatched it from view. Peering through the keyhole—itself no wider than the head of a pin, with no room to spare for dancing angels or other divine revelers—one can glimpse a mere hint of the curios stored inside. Perhaps someday a scholar of all things underestimated will write a short story seeking to describe and comprehend the dwarf contents. (Paul Kirsch)

Night Quilt, American—A notable example of a hand-stitched night quilt featuring unusual subject matter: smallpox, penury, and death by hanging. The thread and dye indicate the quilt originated in the small farming communities of east-central Wisconsin around 1850.

The quilt was purchased during the 1902 decommissioning of Lake Covenant Church near Oostburg, Wisconsin. "Absolutely no return" is handwritten on the receipt. Two

The Steampunk Workshop/Jake von Slatt re-build of a Mooney & Finch Somnotrope

newspaper articles are attached to the receipt. The first, from the July 19, 1871, *Plymouth Herald,* reports on the acquittal of Samuel Ronde in his trial for the brutal murder of the Denne family in Oostburg and his unlikely escape from mob justice following his release. The second article is from the November 13, 1871, issue of the *Sheboygan Courier.* In reporting the great Peshtigo fire the previous month, the article reports that one S. Ronde, lately of Oostburg, is among those missing since the conflagration.

All three of the quilt's existing panels show exquisite and extensive detailing and remain in remarkable condition. Based on cut work, threading, and style, each of the panels was created by a different family member. The quilt's blue border is worked with alternating white stars and black circles, probably by the creator of the third panel.

In clockwise order, the appliqué panels show: first, a naked boy, covered in small sores, asleep atop a rough pine bed. The bed covering in the panel is worked with miniature red versions of the stars and circles that line the quilt's borders.

Second, a blond man at night, his felt pockets turned inside-out, standing in a fallow field. He appears to be holding a jug. A plow with empty traces is visible in the background. There is a waning quarter-moon visible in the night sky, but no stars.

Third, the same blond man from panel two, hanging from a leafless tree. On the right side of this panel, three women (wearing matching red bonnets) weep vibrant cloth tears. On the left side of the panel, a stout preacher wearing a black felt hat watches. What appears to be a sliver of moon is visible through the tree branches. Again, there are no stars.

The fourth panel is missing. (Tom Underberg)

Oneyroscope—A device designed by French inventor Louis Lumière after the invention of the cinematograph. His purpose was to record dream experiences, showing them on a screen, like motion pictures. Lumière's brother, Auguste, was the first subject of the experiment, and there is a silent movie directed by George Méliès registering the entire process. In the film, August Lumière is lying on his bed wearing a steel helmet on his head, connected by a bunch of wires to a strange machine operated by his own brother. Behind them, a silver screen is showing us what he's dreaming: a flock of clay pigeons flying underwater. On April 15, 1900, the first public demonstration of a prototype Oneyroscope was given at the Exposition Universelle held in Paris, France, becoming a huge success. At the time, Sigmund Freud, the father of the psychoanalysis, reportedly said that the Oneyroscope could be "the most revolutionary discovery in history." (Ignacio Sanz)

"Our Greatest President," Reel 3—A single reel of film with a yellowing, typewritten label that reads OUR GREATEST PRESIDENT—1939—REEL 3 OF 5. Notable for its size (38 millimeter instead of the standard 35 millimeter), the aging film is of interest for two other reasons. First, the movie features performances by Sarah Bernhardt, Marilyn Monroe, and someone who bears a striking resemblance to Steve Guttenberg. Second, and most intriguing, the plot of the movie seems to revolve around America's seventh president: a man called Ronald Smith Washington, purportedly the son of George Washington. The third reel tracks his last term in office and his struggle against the Japanese in the War of 1812. Despite the strange nature of the film's content, preliminary lab results have indicated the reel itself is consistent with other prints from the late 1930s. The other four reels have yet to surface. (Tucker Cummings)

Reversed Commas (box of)—The ordinary comma creates pauses in text; it logically follows that the reversed comma gives prose a push, accelerating it sometimes beyond the point of breathlessness into a blur or scream. A full box of these extremely rare punctuation marks turned up inside a volume on the laws of motion: the pages of that tome had been cut away to make a secret hollow space sufficiently large to securely hold the box. Dr. Lambshead does not remember how the book and thus the box came into his possession. He once sprinkled a handful of reversed commas into a copy of the *Highway Code*: the text immediately broke its own laws by exceeding the mandatory speed-limit in an urban zone. Reversed commas are more properly known as *ammocs*, hence the phrase "to run ammoc." Serious attempts to create interstellar engines by composing entire books exclusively with reversed commas are destined to fail: nothing can exceed the speed of lightheartedness. (Rhys Hughes)

Sea Scroll, The—A live spiny eel (*Mastacembelus mastacembelus*) 40 centimeters long, the Sea Scroll has puzzled mystics and biologists alike. The scales' coloration and shape produce visible text in Akkadian cuneiform; more unusual yet, the fish continues to flop about in its small glass-and-teak aquarium, apparently unhindered by the absence of water and food for some years. Somehow imperishable, the eel shows no sign of age or illness, apart from its atypically molting scales. The message it bears changes regularly as new scales grow, attested to by accompanying diaries with nine centuries of transcriptions. The text has proven untranslatable thus far into Akkadian or any other language, and marginalia indicate that previous owners believed the writing was a divinely encrypted mystery time might uncover. Dr. Lambshead offers a different conjecture: "What if," the last entry in the notes reads, "the fish is merely illiterate?" (Hugh Alter)

Silence, One Ounce—Origins unknown. Found amongst the possessions of the recently deceased Frank Hayes, thirty-four, who tragically lost his life when he stepped in front of a public bus that failed to stop. Its provenance is thought to include M. Twain, W. Wilson, and the Marquis de Sade. Handle with care, not to be administered more than one drop at a time. Silence is golden, but too much will kill you. (Willow Holster)

Skull—Human, probably male. Physically unremarkable. Attached tag reads B. S. LONDON, 20/4/1912. The skull appears normal in all respects except during the new moon of every month, when it screams uncontrollably. (Amy Willats)

A Decadent-era example from Lambshead's prodigious and largely anonymous skull collection.

Skull, Parsimonious—The foul-smelling skull of a large owl, albeit with three eye-sockets, reputed to be of sentimental value to the doctor because of his dear departed mother's fondness for owls, particularly those possessing unusual congenital characteristics. Tufted with feathers and a patch of moldering owl flesh, the skull was lost on the moorlands of Tasmania after Lambshead's porter, a drunkard named Hendrick Carmichael, gambled it away on a wager with an unnamed fellow traveler. According to Carmichael's widow, the skull answered yes/no questions with astonishing accuracy and foresight, blinking with eerie illumination from within, once for yes and twice for no; this amounted to a useful basis for gambling and drinking games. Found unharmed in Lambshead's cabinet neatly wrapped in a pair of striped shorts thought to belong to legendary pugilist Gerald Jenkins, known to be on walkabout in Australia at the time of the doctor's travels to Tasmania. (Tracie Welser)

South American Insult Stone—This item came into the doctor's possession by way of his drawing-room window, through which the stone was hurled one evening. Six inches in diameter and almost perfectly spherical, one side of the stone had been carved into a stylized face reminiscent of Incan art. Upon picking up the stone, Dr. Lambshead was greeted by a voice emanating from within, which addressed him gruffly and at length in an obscure South American dialect, centuries dead. Transcribing and translating the words took over a week. It turned out that the stone had, in fact, been insulting the doctor, calling into question both his parentage and personal hygiene, among other things. Though the stone had obviously been thrown by a rival or malcontent, Dr. Lambshead was far too enamored of the device to dispose of it. (Nicholas Troy)

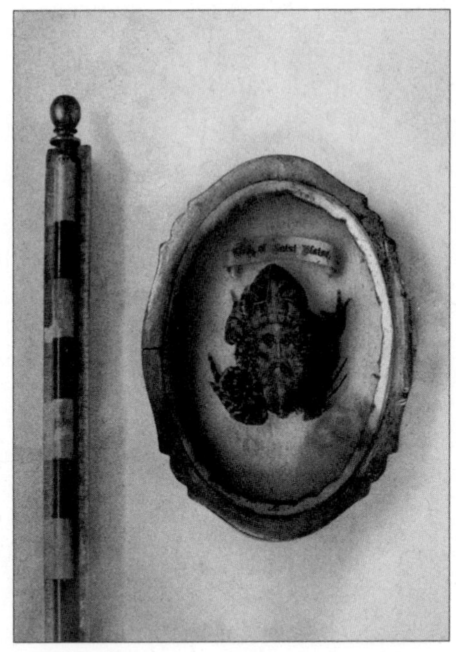

The St. Blais Toad at rest, as photographed by Dr. Galubrious.

St. Blaise's Toad—A 6-inch × 6-inch × 3-inch plastered and gilded wood, glass-and-taxidermied common toad. Referred to as "the miracle of the toad." In 1431, a vision of St. Blaise appeared to a farm boy catching toads near a spring in Bromley,

Kent. The saint called upon the boy to be kind to all amphibians. After the vision, an image of St. Blaise appeared on the back of a toad near the edge of the pool. The creature was skinned, stuffed, and enshrined by the church. This gilded toad reliquary was decommissioned by the church during the Calvinist reformation. The toad remained in the collection of Rawsthorne Family of Denbies Hall, Dorking, until won from Lord Rawsthorne by Dr. Lambshead in a game of skittles. Glass damaged in lower right corner resulting in mild molding and mouse damage to the epidermis. Papal seal on verso, canceled promissory note pasted on side. (Dr. Galubrious)

Tomb-Matches—Half a dozen square-stick lucifers, secured in a waxed-paper wrapping. The attached card indicates, in slightly shaky, faded handwriting, that these matches, when struck, produce not light, nor a means of igniting a cigarette, pipe, candle, or lamp, but instead a bloom of impenetrable, sound-muffling darkness. This darkness lasts for as long as the match burns. If, the card notes, members of the match-striker's party are missing when the light returns, it is only to be expected. (Nadine Wilson)

Tycho's Astronomical Support Garment—Designed by the sixteenth-century astronomer Tycho Brahe (1546–1601) as a device to combat chronic neck and back pain caused by years of stooping over observational instruments. The garment resembles an oversized corset stiffened by stays of horn, buckram, and whalebone. The center front is further reinforced by a busk made of ivory. The garment was fastened to the body via a complicated system of leather straps. How this was done remains a subject of controversy, as it is not obvious how certain straps were used. Tycho was not wearing the garment on October 13, 1601, when his bladder burst after he drank too much wine at a dinner party, which resulted in his eventual death. It is not clear that the abdominal support afforded by the garment could have prevented this tragedy. (Steven M. Schmidt)

Unhcegila's Scales—Vacillating between sickly virescent and rotted plum hues, these peculiar lamina are rumored to be found in the darkest corners of the North American Badlands' caverns. Thirty were found in Lambshead's cabinet, with each being roughly the size of a fig leaf. He said that he won them in a poker game with a hand of aces and eights in the Berlin Hellfire Club on April 28, 1945. The graybeard he won them from claimed to be the bastard son of Jesse James and said that he stole them from Bill Hickock as a boy. Hickock had told the boy that Sitting Bull gave them to him when they toured together in Buffalo Bill's Wild West shows. The scales are said to allow a man to make his enemies mysteriously disappear, when ground up and put into their food or drink. Curiously, his ledger shows he sold some to gangsters with connections to both Jimmy Hoffa and Elvis. (Christopher Begley)

Untitled Booklet—Consists of six bound pages obtained by Dr. Lambshead from a Prague antiquarian bookshop in January 1948, one month before the Czechoslovak coup d'état, donated to him for safekeeping. The booklet appeared to contain a short story in a Central Moravian Czech dialect. Dr. Lambshead, however, was assured the booklet was not what it appeared to be, but an insect able, through mimicry, to imitate any inorganic object placed within a short distance (including its smell). The creature was discovered in one of the "Stránska Skála" Upper Paleolithic caves in the northern outskirts of Brno not long after Professor Svoboda's archaeological excavations in the

Tartarus Press edition of Jean Lorrain's *Nightmares of an Ether-Drinker.* In this instance, the insect documented by Tony Mileman had insinuated itself under the dust jacket and wrapped itself around the pages, replacing the boards and simulating a cloth binding.

summer of 1946. Despite attempting escape many times, the insect was finally secured amongst a collection of obscure short stories by forgotten Czechoslovak writers of early twentieth-century Weird Fiction. The insect (booklet) is presumed dead. (Tony Mileman)

Von Slatt Harmonization Device—A system and method for cultural transmission scrambling, patent application number 15/603976. Assignee: Harmonization Incorporated. Summary of the Invention from the patent application: "Very soon, science will confirm that cultural information passes from one entity to another using devices accessed psionically via instructional facilities. It is the object of this device to locate, demodulate, and scramble cultural transmissions passing between hostile social formations. This novel device allows operators to inject false vernacular and traditions into cultural signals as they pass between entities. It can also hijack signals carrying historical intelligence by providing a stronger signal on the same frequency." (Annalee Newitz)

Wax Phonograph Cylinder, Unlabeled—Object appears to be over a century old, but is still functional. When played, the sound of a percussive instrument, possibly a large tubular drum, can be heard for approximately the first forty seconds of recording time. During this sound, the murmurings of a man's voice become interpolated with the beat. The syllables are indistinguishable, but as the drumbeat continues, the voice rises until it becomes a series of shouted plosives. At around the four-minute mark, both sounds stop completely and are replaced by a series of high-pitched cries, from which can be gleaned the only coherent word of the entire piece: "Alley-Caster," or perhaps "Snally-Gaster." The final sound heard on the recording is an extremely loud screeching whistle, which sounds reptilian in origin. An attached note indicates that Dr. Lambshead acquired the object from a motel-room drawer in Braddock Heights, Maryland. (Michael J. Larson)

An unprecedented panoramic view of the East End of Lambshead's cabinet, taken surreptitiously by photographer Bruce Ecker in 1999.

Artist and Author Notes

Story Contributors

Kelly Barnhill has had fiction published in *Fantasy, Weird Tales, Clockwork Phoenix,* and many other publications. Her first novel, *The Mostly True Story of Jack*—a lyrical fantasy for middle-grade readers—is set for a 2011 release by Little, Brown.

Holly Black is a best-selling author of contemporary fantasy novels for teens and children, including *The Spiderwick Chronicles* and the *Curse Workers* series.

S. J. Chambers has had fiction and nonfiction published by *Fantasy,* the *Baltimore Sun's Read Street Blog, Yankee Pot Roast,* and Tor.com. Her most recent projects include *The Steampunk Bible,* a coffee-table book coauthored with Jeff VanderMeer.

Stepan Chapman is the author of *The Troika,* which won the Philip K. Dick Award. His short fiction can be found in magazines and anthologies such as *Analog, Lady Churchill's Rosebud Wristlet, Leviathan, Polyphony,* and *Album Zutique.*

Ted Chiang is a multiple award–winning short story writer. His work has won the Nebula, the Hugo, the Locus Award, and others. His latest book is the novella *The Lifecycle of Software Objects,* published by Subterranean Press in 2010.

Michael Cisco's novels include *The Divinity Student, The Traitor,* and, most recently, *The Narrator.* His stories have appeared in *Leviathan 3, Leviathan 4, Lovecraft Unbound,* and many other anthologies.

Gio Clairval is an Italian-born speculative fiction writer who commutes between Paris and Lake Como. Several of her translations of iconic stories will appear in *The Weird: A Compendium of Strange and Dark Fictions* from Atlantic in 2011.

Amal El-Mohtar is currently pursuing a Ph.D. in Cornwall, England. Her poetry has won the Rhysling Award, and her fiction and nonfiction have appeared in *Weird Tales, Cabinet des Fées,* and *Shimmer.* She also coedits *Goblin Fruit,* an online quarterly of fantastical poetry.

Brian Evenson is the author of nine books, most recently the novel *Last Days* and the short story collection *Fugue State.* He directs Brown University's Creative Writing program.

Minister Faust is an Edmontonian writer, high school English teacher, union delegate, broadcaster, community activist, and novelist. His latest book is titled *From the Notebooks of Doctor Brain* and he is a past finalist for the Philip K. Dick Award.

Jeffrey Ford lives in South Jersey and is a multiple World Fantasy Award winner. His latest novel is *The Shadow Year,* and his latest collection of stories is *The Drowned Life* (both from HarperCollins).

Lev Grossman is a journalist for *Time* magazine and novelist living in New York City. His latest book is *The Magicians,* and the sequel is expected in 2011.

Will Hindmarch is a writer and graphic designer, with work published in various books, games, and magazines. Some of his work has appeared in *The Escapist, Atlanta* magazine, *Geek Monthly,* and *Everywhere.*

N. K. Jemisin is a Brooklyn-based author. Her short fiction has been published in *Clarkesworld, Baen's Universe, Strange Horizons, Postscripts, Weird Tales,* and many others. Her first two novels, *The Hundred Thousand Kingdoms* and its sequel, *The Broken Kingdoms,* have been published by Orbit Books.

Caitlín R. Kiernan was born in Ireland, raised in the southeastern United States, and now lives in Providence, Rhode Island. Her short fiction has been collected in several volumes, most recently *A Is for Alien,* and she's published eight novels, including *Daughter of Hounds* and *The Red Tree.*

Mur Lafferty is a writer, podcaster, and blogger. She has written for various RPGs, Tor.com, *Scrybe Press, Murky Depths,* and *Hub Magazine.*

Jay Lake lives in Portand, Oregon, where he writes, edits, and generally misbehaves. His latest novels are *Green* and *Madness of Flowers.*

China Miéville lives and works in London. He is three-time winner of the prestigious Arthur C. Clarke Award. His novel *The City & The City* recently won the British Science Fiction Award, the Arthur C. Clarke Award, the World Fantasy Award, and the Hugo Award. In addition to fiction, he has also contributed his art to this book.

Michael Moorcock is an iconic figure in literature, having written in perhaps every genre as well as published such classics as *Mother London.* A multiple-award winner, he lives in Texas with his wife, Linda, and several cats.

Alan Moore is an English writer primarily known for his work in graphic novels. Some of his more well-known series include *Watchmen, From Hell, V Is for Vendetta,* and *The League of Extraordinary Gentlemen.*

Reza Negarestani is an Iranian writer working in diverse fields of contemporary theory, ancient Greek and contemporary philosophy, and politics. His latest novel is *Cyclonopedia: Complicities with Anonymous Materials.*

Garth Nix is a best-selling, multiple award–winning Australian writer best known for his young adult fantasy novels. He has also written for RPGs and magazines and journals. His latest book is *Lord Sunday.*

Naomi Novik is a *New York Times* best-selling writer. She was awarded the John W. Campbell Award for Best New Writer in 2007. Her latest book is *Tongues of Serpents.*

Helen Oyeyemi is a Nigerian writer living in the United Kingdom. Her latest novel, *White Is for Witching,* was nominated for the Shirley Jackson award.

Cherie Priest is the author of seven novels published by Tor and Subterranean Press, including the Nebula Award nominee *Boneshaker, Dreadful Skin,* and the Eden Moore trilogy. Her short stories and nonfiction articles have appeared in such fine publications as *Weird Tales, Subterranean Magazine, Publishers Weekly,* and the Stoker-nominated anthology *Aegri Somnia* published by Apex.

Ekaterina Sedia has published three novels—*The Secret History of Moscow, The Alchemy of Stone,* and *The House of Discarded Dreams.* Her short stories have been published in *Analog, Baen's Universe,* and *Clarkesworld.*

Rachel Swirsky has had short fiction appear in venues including Tor.com, *Subterranean Magazine, Fantasy Magazine, Weird Tales,* and the *Konundrum Engine Literary Review.* Her latest book, *Through the Drowsy Dark,* is a mini-collection of feminist poems and short stories, available from Aqueduct Press.

Carrie Vaughn is the author of the popular urban fantasy Kitty Norville series. She has published over forty short stories in magazines such as *Weird Tales, Strange Horizons, Realms of Fantasy,* and *Asimov's Science Fiction.*

Tad Williams is a best-selling writer who lives in California. His latest book is *Shadowheart,* the fourth book in his Shadowmarch series.

Charles Yu is an American writer whose first novel, *How to Live Safely in a Science Fictional Universe,* has been added to many year's best lists for 2010. His short fiction has been published in a number of magazines and literary journals, including *Oxford American, The Gettysburg Review, Harvard Review, Mid-American Review, Mississippi Review,* and *Alaska Quarterly Review.*

Artists

Aeron Alfrey creates unique imagery inspired by strange fantasy worlds filled with monsters, magic, and death. His art has been published in numerous books and shown in galleries around the world.

Kristen Alvanson is an American artist based in Malaysia and Iran. She has participated in group/solo shows in New York, Tehran, London, Istanbul, Berlin, Belgium, and Vilnius, including a solo exhibition of her work at Azad Gallery (Tehran) and at the International Roaming Biennial of Tehran.

Greg Broadmore is a New Zealand illustrator, writer, and conceptual designer for Weta Workshop and has designed for the motion pictures *District 9, King Kong, The Lion, the Witch and the Wardrobe,* and *Black Sheep,* among many, many others.

John Coulthart is a world-recognized illustrator, graphic designer, and comic artist, who lives in Manchester, England. He has designed and provided art for several classic books, including *The Thackery T. Lambshead Pocket Guide to Eccentric & Discredited Diseases.* Find more of his work at johncoulthart.com.

Scott Eagle is a professor of painting and drawing at East Carolina University in Greenville, North Carolina. His paintings have graced the covers of many books, including *City of Saints and Madmen* and *Secret Life* by Jeff VanderMeer. His illustrations have appeared in a number of national magazines.

Vladimir Gvozdariki, a Russian artist who also works under the moniker Gvozd (which means "Iron"), is known for his whimsical and mechanical illustrations and sculptures. His Web museum can be found at gvozdariki.ru.

Yishan Li is a professional manga artist living in Edinburgh, Scotland. She has been published internationally, including in China, the United States, France, and the United Kingdom. Her latest book is *The Complete Shojo Art Kit.*

Mike Mignola is an artist known for graphic novels such as *Hellboy* and *The Amazing Screw-on Head.* He was also the production designer for the Disney feature film *Atlantis: The Lost Empire.*

Jonathan Nix is an award-winning director, animator, artist, and musician. He lives in Sydney, Australia.

Eric Orchard is an award-winning illustrator and cartoonist living in Canada. He most recently illustrated the children's book *The Terrible, Horrible, Smelly Pirate.* His work has been recognized in the Spectrum Annual of Fantastic Art and the Society of Illustrators annual exhibit.

James A. Owen is an American comic book artist, publisher, and writer. He is the author of the popular Chronicles of the Imaginarium Geographica series and the creator of the critically acclaimed *Starchild* graphic novel series. His most recent book is *The Dragon's Apprentice.*

Ron Pippin's artwork has been shown around the world in solo shows as well as group exhibitions. His art has also been seen in various movies and TV shows such as *Spider-Man.*

J. K. Potter is an iconic photographer known mostly for his work in the horror, science fiction, and fantasy world, as well as his album/CD covers. He has produced art for many book covers, including the recent Subterranean Press limited editions of *Ebb Tide* by James Blaylock and *Last Call* by Tim Powers.

Eric Schaller is an artist, writer, and scientist. His stories have appeared in *Postscripts, New Genre,* and *Nemonymous,* and his artwork in *The White Buffalo Gazette, Lady Churchill's Rosebud Wristlet,* and Jeff VanderMeer's mosaic novel *City of Saints and Madmen.*

Ivica Stevanovic is a Serbian artist. He has won several prizes in the fields of design, illustrations, cartoons, and comics. His specialty is graphic novels and art book projects. His latest book is *Katil* (Bloodthirsty Man) and he also recently contributed to the anthology *Steampunk Reloaded.*

Jan Svankmajer is a famous Czech surrealist artist and filmmaker. His first feature film in 1987 was *Alice,* based on Lewis Carroll's *Alice in Wonderland.* His most recent film is the Czech comedy *Surviving Life* (2010), which he claims will be his last.

Sam Van Olffen is a French artist best known for his surreal depictions of steampunk and/or dieselpunk images. His work has been featured in many books as well as gallery exhibits around the world.

Myrtle von Damitz III is a painter living in New Orleans who sees her work as a form of storytelling. She has had numerous solo exhibits as well as group gallery showings around the country. She is the founder and curator of Babylon Lexicon, an annual exhibition of artists' books and local independent presses.

Jake von Slatt is a steampunk contraptor and proprietor of the popular Web site The Steampunk Workshop (steampunkworkshop.com); he lives in Boston. He and his projects have been featured in Boing Boing, *WIRED, Nature, Newsweek,* and the *New York Times.*

Catalog Contributors

Hugh Alter is currently working on novels that you will recognize as award-winning best-sellers from the future. He is also working on retrieving coins from inside his couch. **Charlie Jane Anders** blogs at io9.com and organizes the Writers with Drinks reading series. Her work has also appeared at Tor.com and the *McSweeney's Joke Book of Book Jokes.* **Julie Andrews** is a 2007 graduate of the Clarion Writers' Workshop and is a member of both Broad Universe and The Outer Alliance. **Christopher Begley** is thirty and lives in Worcester, Massachusetts. This is his first published work. He wouldn't call his writing Moore-ish or Gaiman-esque but will not stop others from doing so. **Jayme Lynn Blaschke** writes science fiction, fantasy, and related nonfiction. He has authored a book of genre-themed interviews, titled *Voices of Vision: Creators of Science Fiction & Fantasy Speak.* **Nickolas Brienza** is a Seattle resident; all further CV may be confidently extrapolated via the usual statistical methods. **Tucker Cummings** has been writing strange stories since the day she developed sufficient hand-eye coordination to hold a crayon. Previous microfiction efforts garnered accolades during competitions held by HiLoBrow.com and MassTwitFic. **Rikki Ducornet** is one of her generation's best surrealists, with books including *The Word Desire* and *The Fountains of Neptune.* She is also the Rikki in the Steely Dan song "Rikki Don't Lose That Number." **Kaolin Imago Fire** is a conglomeration of ideas, side projects, and experiments. He has had short fiction published in *Strange Horizons, Crossed Genres, Escape Velocity,* and *M-Brane SF,* among others. **Jess Gulbranson**, a hyperminimal neoplastic bricoleur from Portland, Oregon, is an author, musician, critic, artist, and family man. He has swell hair. **Jennifer Harwood-Smith** is a Ph.D. student at Trinity College Dublin. She won the 2006 James White Award and has been published in *Interzone* magazine. **Willow Holser** is a twenty-six-year-old daydreamer with delusions of adulthood, gainful employment, and grammatical correctness. However, she does have what has been called a "Quite Suitable Hat." **Rhys Hughes** is a writer of absurdist fantasy; he lives in Wales. His most recent book is the novel *Twisthorn Bellow,* and he contributed to the first Lambshead anthology. **Incognitum** has long been part of a secret society dedicated to the subversion of reality through the recontextualization of museum exhibits and various other contaminations of meat-minds through subtextual viruses. **Paul Kirsch** grew up on an unhealthy diet of grilled cheese and ghost stories. He's been tinkering with a steampunk/fantasy series, and writes book reviews at paul-kirsch.com. He lives in Los Angeles. **Michael J. Larson** lives in Minneapolis when he's not on his private dirigible, holding wild midair parties and getting involved in international intrigue. **Therese Littleton** is a curator and writer who lives in Seattle, Washington. **Graham Lowther**, born in Vermont, now lives in Maine, where he is building his own house. He has long been a fan of horror and surreal fiction, and sometimes writes it. This is his first appearance in print. **Claire Massey** lives in Lancashire with her husband and two young sons. Her short stories have been published in a variety of places and she is the founding editor of online magazine *New Fairy Tales.* **Tony Mileman** lives and works in the Czech city of Brno. His pleasures include translating Czech supernatural fiction. His previous short fiction has appeared in *Nemonymous.* **Adam Mills** lives in a town in the Missouri Ozarks, one you can only see if you pay attention and pass by at the right time of night. He writes coded messages, teaches college English, and lives in a bowling alley. **Annalee Newitz** is the editor in chief of io9.com. She's published her work in *Wired,* the *Washington Post, Flurb,* and *2600.* She used to be a professor who studied monsters. **Ignacio Sanz** was born in Madrid, Spain, in 1977, and is a sci-fi and fantasy aficionado. Until now, he has written some short pieces, but this is the first time he has competed in an international writing contest. **Steven M. Schmidt** is a person of no importance whatsoever. He is working to correct this appalling state of affairs but it may take some time. **Grant Stone**'s stories have appeared in *Shimmer, Andromeda Spaceways Inflight Magazine,* and *Semaphore.* He lives in Auckland, New Zealand. Which is handy, since that's where all his stuff is. **Norman Taber** (aka Dr. Galubrious) teaches graduate studies in ethereal anthropology and at Exeter University in Putney, Vermont. He is the world's foremost expert on toad-scrapings. Galubrious is represented in the United States by Norman Taber, a professor of design at SUNY Plattsburgh. **Brian Thill** is the director of the Humanities Core Writing Program at UC Irvine, where he completed his Ph.D. in English. His research focuses include American literature, art, and politics. **Nick Tramdack** was born in 1985 and grew up in New Jersey. He works in the stacks of a Chicago library, where he has developed a Grendel-like hatred for noise. **Nicholas Troy** was born in Washington, D.C., grew up a bit in Germany, then grew up some more in Boston. He has always loved stories, and is currently a part of the Illiterati writing group. **Tom Underberg** lives with his wife and children in an old house. Standing on his roof, you can see Lake Michigan. He has been an economic consultant (excellent), bartender (disastrous), and dishwasher (promising). **Horia Ursu** is a Romanian publisher, translator, and (sometimes) writer of science fiction and fantasy. He is also senior editor of *Galileo,* a digest-size F&SF magazine. He lives in Satu Mare with his wife and daughter. **William T. Vandemark** can be found wandering the backroads of America in a pickup truck. His fiction has appeared in *Apex Magazine, InterGalactic Medicine Show,* and in several anthologies. **Kali Wallace** is inconveniently overeducated and underemployed. She lives in Colorado with her family, four cats, and a turtle. **Tracie Welser** is a speculative fiction writer and instructor of women's studies. She's quite fond of owls. In 2010, she was fortunate enough to survive the Clarion West Writers' Workshop. **Amy Willats** is originally from California, although she has also been seen in Texas and Maryland. Currently residing in the San Francisco Bay Area, she tries not to scream uncontrollably, although sometimes she just can't help herself. **Nadine Wilson** is a reader of books, scribbler of stories, taker of photographs, mother of one, big sister to many, pet of cats, lover of oddities, seminomadic and vaguely ambitious. She loves the world, even you. Especially you. **Ben Woodard** recently completed a master's in philosophy at the European Graduate School. He blogs at naughtthought.wordpress.com, and his first monograph, *Slime Dynamics: Generation, Mutation, and the Creep of Life,* is forthcoming from Zer0 Books.

About the Editors

Hugo Award–winner Ann VanderMeer and World Fantasy Award–winner Jeff VanderMeer have recently coedited such anthologies as *Best American Fantasy #1 & 2, Steampunk, Steampunk Reloaded, The New Weird, Last Drink Bird Head,* and *Fast Ships, Black Sails.* They are the coauthors of *The Kosher Guide to Imaginary Animals.* Future projects include *The Weird: A Compendium of Strange and Dark Fictions,* for Atlantic. Jeff's latest books are the novel *Finch,* a World Fantasy Award and Nebula Award finalist; the story collection *The Third Bear*; the nonfiction collection *Monstrous Creatures*; the coffee-table book *The Steampunk Bible* (with S. J. Chambers); and the writing strategy guide *Booklife.* Ann is the editor in chief of *Weird Tales* magazine and has a regular art column on the popular SF/fantasy Web site io9. Together, they have been profiled by National Public Radio and the *New York Times'* Papercuts blog. They are active teachers, and have taught at Clarion San Diego, Odyssey, and the teen writing camp Shared Worlds, for which Jeff serves as the assistant director. They live in Tallahassee, Florida, with too many books and four cats. For more information, visit jeffvandermeer.com.

Acknowledgments

First and foremost, a huge thank-you to Diana Gill, our editor, for being wonderfully supportive of this project and letting this three-ring circus reach its full potential. Thanks also to Will Hinton at Harper Voyager, who put up with a constant stream of e-mails and image downloads, among other impositions—as well as everyone else involved in this project, including the book designer. Huge thanks as well to John Coulthart for acting as an image consultant to this anthology, while also providing his own art/design and found art—you're the best and we couldn't have done it without you. Thanks to the gang at Brueggers, Hopkins, and Monks for good company, and for keeping us fed and caffeinated during the process. Thanks to our friends at the Leon Station post office for laughs and over twenty years of great service. We would also like to thank Myra Miller and Arthur Burns at Alpha Data Systems for continuing support (and a special shoutout to Arthur for keeping all our technology running smoothly).

We're also indebted to Stepan Chapman and Michael Cisco's contributions to *The Thackery T. Lambshead Pocket Guide to Eccentric & Discredited Diseases,* as this volume makes use of some of their ideas and writings from that prior volume. We're also forever indebted to our *New Weird* editor in the Czech Republic, Martin Šust, for his help in acquiring art from Jan Svankmajer. Finally, thanks to all of the contributors for making this anthology so special for us.

Credits

ARTISTS

All images copyright 2011 to the individual creators and original to this anthology, unless otherwise noted. All public-domain art and photography provided by and/or Photoshopped by John Coulthart. All title pages copyright 2011 John Coulthart.

"Mecha-frog" and "Mecha-fish" on pages 18 and 19, Vladimir Gvozdev, copyright © 2008

Introduction

"just one shelf in Lambshead's study"—Jennifer and J. K. Potter, photograph from their "knickknack collection," as arranged by Jennifer

"stage set for musical of Dr. Lambshead . . ."—Sam Van Olffen, "Travailleurs de lacier," copyright © 2008

"secret medical laboratory stage set . . ."—Sam Van Olffen, "Dissecator," copyright © 2007

"One of Lambshead's few attempts at art . . ."—Myrtle von Damitz III, detail shot from "Family Portrait" with Michael, Michelle, and Sydney Holdman pictured, copyright © 2010

"One of the few museum exhibit loans . . ."—Vladimir Gvozdev, "Mecha-Rhino," copyright © 2008

"Spell or secret communication?"—Kristen Alvanson, "Constructing an Elysian Pod for the Last Journey," copyright © 2007

"so-called 'Skull Cucumber' hoax . . ."—Jan Svankmajer, cryptozoology print, copyright © 1975

"demonstrating the doctor's commitment to the future . . ."—Jake von Slatt, "Bassington & Smith Electro-Mechanical Analog Brain," copyright © 2010, first publication herein

"More evidence of the disarray . . ."—J. K. Potter, originally end papers for James Blaylock's *The Adventures of Langdon St. Ives* from Subterranean Press, copyright © 2008

The Broadmore Exhibits

"Electrical Neurheographiton," "St. Brendan's Shank," "The Auble Gun," and *"Dacey's Patent Automatic Nanny"*—Greg Broadmore

"Nikola Tesla ca. 1890"—Wikipedia Commons

"The Tasker Battle Carriage"—Sam Van Olffen, "Cours Lapin, cours!" copyright © 2008

Honoring Lambshead

"medieval tapestry . . ."—James A. Owen

"Tree Spirits Rising"—Jonathan Nix, copyright © 2006

"Relic with Fish"—Ivica Stevanovic

"Lord Dunsany's Teapot"—Yishan Li

"Portrait of a Bear Unbound (with speaker)"—Eric Orchard

"The Meistergarten"—John Coulthart

The Mignola Exhibits

"Addison Howell on his Clockroach," "Sir Ranulph Wykeham-Rackham," "Shamalung," and *"Pulvadmonitor"*—Mike Mignola

The Miéville Anomalies

"The Very Shoe" and *"Gallows-horse"*—China Miéville

The Further Oddities

"Thing in Jar"—Aeron Alfrey

"Frog Resurrection"—Ron Pippin, copyright © 2008

"Armor Montage"—Ivica Stevanovic

"Castleblakeney Key"—Aeron Alfrey, copyright © 2009

"Taking the Rats to Riga"—Eric Schaller

"The Book of Categories"—Ron Pippin, copyright © 2008

"The Dead Dead Gang book cover"—John Coulthart

Visits and Departures

"Kneel" (full and detail views)—Scott Eagle, "Meditation on Power" installation, copyright © 2009

Catalog of Additional Items

"Bear Gun/Taxidermy Gun"—Eric Orchard

"Coffin Torpedo"—Jess Gulbranson

"Disgruntled Artifacts"—Rikki Ducornet

"Mooney & Finch Somnotrope"—Jake von Slatt, "Chronoclasmic Inhibitor," copyright © 2010, first publication herein

"Much Smaller Cabinet"—Ron Pippin, Archive Box #2, copyright © 1999

"Skull"—John Coulthart, copyright © 1995

"The St. Blais Toad"—Norman Tabor

"Jean Lorrain's Nightmares of an Ether-Drinker*"*—R. B. Russell, Tartarus Press designer/artist for dust jacket and boards, copyright © 2003

"Panoramic view of the Lambshead's cabinet"—Bruce Ecker, The Obsolete Gallery, copyright © 2007

Text

"Introduction: The Contradictions of a Collection, Dr. Lambshead's Cabinet" and all image captions, unless otherwise noted, copyright © 2011 Jeff & Ann VanderMeer. The character of Thackery T. Lambshead is a creation of Ann & Jeff VanderMeer, copyright © 2003.

The following subsection introductory text copyright © 2011 Jeff VanderMeer: "Holy Devices and Infernal Duds: The Broadmore Exhibits," "Honoring Lambshead: Stories Inspired by the Cabinet," "Microbial Alchemy and Demented Machinery: The Mignola Exhibits," "The Miéville Anomalies," "Further Oddities," "Visits and Departures," and "A Brief Catalog of Additional Items."

Additional text: caption for Jake von Slatt image in the introduction, *"demonstrating the doctor's commitment to the future,"* copyright © 2011 Annalee Newitz; caption for *"Bear Gun/Taxidermy Gun"* at beginning of "A Brief Catalog" copyright © by Adam Mills. *"Disgruntled Artifacts"* text attributed to Rikki Ducornet (with her permission) in "A Brief Catalog" copyright © 2011 Jeff VanderMeer.

In order of appearance in the anthology:

"The Electrical Neurheographiton" copyright © 2011 by Minister Faust
"St. Brendan's Shank" copyright © 2011 by Kelly Barnhill
"The Auble Gun" copyright © 2011 by Will Hindmarch
"Dacey's Patent Automatic Nanny" copyright © 2011 by Ted Chiang
"Threads" copyright © 2011 by Carrie Vaughn
"Ambrose and the Ancient Spirits of East and West" by Garth Nix
"Relic" copyright © 2011 by Jeffrey Ford
"Lord Dunsany's Teapot" copyright © 2011 by Naomi Novik
"Lot 558: *Shadow of My Nephew* by Wells, Charlotte" copyright © 2011 by Holly Black
"A Short History of Dunkelblau's Meistergarten" copyright © 2011 by Tad Williams
"Addison Howell and the Clockroach" copyright © 2011 by Cherie Priest
"Sir Ranulph Wykeham-Rackham, GBE, a.k.a. Roboticus the All-Knowing" copyright © 2011 by Lev Grossman
"Shamalung (The Diminutions)" copyright © 2011 by Michael Moorcock
"Pulvadmonitor: The Dust's Warning" copyright © 2011 by China Miéville
"The Very Shoe" copyright © 2011 by Helen Oyeyemi
"The Gallows-horse" copyright © 2011 by Reza Negarestani
"The Thing in the Jar" copyright © 2011 by Michael Cisco
"The Singing Fish" copyright © 2011 by Amal El-Mohtar
"The Armor of Sir Locust" copyright © 2011 by Stepan Chapman
"A Key to the Castleblakeney Key" copyright © 2011 by Caitlín R. Kiernan
"Taking the Rats to Riga" copyright © 2011 by Jay Lake
"The Book of Categories" copyright © 2011 by Charles Yu
"Objects Discovered in a Novel Under Construction" copyright © 2011 by Alan Moore
"1929: The Singular Taffy Puller" copyright © 2011 by N. K. Jemisin
"1943: A Brief Note Pertaining to the Absence of One Olivaceous Cormorant, Stuffed" copyright © 2011 by Rachel Swirsky
"1963: The Argument Against Louis Pasteur" copyright © 2011 by Mur Lafferty
"1972: The Lichenologist's Visit" copyright © 2011 by Ekaterina Sedia

"1995: Kneel" copyright © 2011 by Brian Evenson

"2000: Dr. Lambshead's Dark Room" copyright © 2011 by S. J. Chambers

"2003: The Pea" copyright © 2011 by Gio Clairval

The flash fictions in "A Brief Catalog of Additional Items" are copyright © 2011 to the writer noted in parentheses at the end of each entry: Hugh Alter, Charlie Jane Anders, Julie Andrews, Christopher Begley, Jayme Lynn Blaschke, Nickolas Brienza, Tucker Cummings, Kaolin Imago Fire, Jess Gulbranson, Jennifer Harwood-Smith, Willow Holser, Rhys Hughes, Incognitum (aka Reza Negarestani), Paul Kirsch, Michael J. Larson, Graham Lowther, Claire Massey, Tony Mileman, Adam Mills, Annalee Newitz, Ignacio Sanz, Steven M. Schmidt, Grant Stone, Norman Taber (aka Dr. Galubrious), Brian Thill, Nick Tramdack, Nicholas Troy, Tom Underberg, Horia Ursu, William T. Vandemark, Kali Wallace, Tracie Welser, Amy Willats, Nadine Wilson, Ben Woodard.

W9-CDV-947

Existential Foundations of Psychology

DUQUESNE STUDIES
Psychological Series
3

Existential Foundations Of Psychology

by

ADRIAN VAN KAAM

DUQUESNE UNIVERSITY PRESS
Pittsburgh, Pa.
Editions E. Nauwelaerts, Louvain
1966

DUQUESNE STUDIES

Psychological Series

Adrian van Kaam, Ph.D., and Edward H. Hogan, Ph.D., editors.

Volume One—Stephen Strasser, PHENOMENOLOGY AND THE HUMAN SCIENCES. *A Contribution to New Scientific Ideal.* XIII and 339 pages. Price: $6.00.

Volume Two—Aron Gurwitsch, THE FIELD OF CONSCIOUSNESS. XIV and 427 pages. Price: $7.95.

Volume Three—Adrian van Kaam, EXISTENTIAL FOUNDATIONS OF PSYCHOLOGY. XIV and 386 pages. Price: $7.95.

Library of Congress Catalog Card Number 66-16065

Printed in the United States of America

TABLE OF CONTENTS

INTRODUCTION

The following study is a dialogue between the field of scientific psychology and the newly emerging awareness of the structure of man in relation to his world. All science evolves in the light of the implicit view of reality which imposes itself on man as an inevitable result of his evolution in knowledge and experience. The science of psychology, in order to keep in harmony with this evolution, must continually re-examine its foundations, investigating whether or not its structure of fundamental constructs has assimilated the new attitudes toward reality developed by humanity in evolution. Such an expansion and deepening of the fundamental structures at the basis of scientific psychology does not necessarily mean that the traditional theories, data, and methods of psychology will be eliminated or even changed. It means that they will be seen in a new perspective, that their position within the total structure of the science of psychology will undergo a re-evaluation.

Originally, man's awareness of himself and his world is pre-reflective, pre-philosophical, and pre-scientific. Sooner or later, however, scholars and scientists reflect on this pre-reflective insight in the light of their own fields of specialization, such as physics, physiology, philosophy, psychology, and psychiatry. The author of the present work believes that one central aspect of the new view of man is the radical perspectivity of his knowledge. This insight can be made explicit in a psychological, philosophical, sociological, anthropological or any other reflective elaboration. This book attempts to make explicit in terms of scientific theoretical psychology the meaning and implications of this insight.

It is the conviction of the writer that psychology will be forced to assimilate perspectivity and its implications into the fundamental structure of psychology. He does not believe that other developments of the science of psychology as a whole can survive because the awareness of man's perspectivistic or existential structure of knowledge is already too strongly alive in contemporary awareness to be either eradicated or dismissed. Two other possible directions of development are the one school (one method) approach or the totally disintegrated approach to psychology. The one school approach cannot be maintained, for perspectivity demonstrates only too clearly that a science can advance only by means of the development of an increasingly wide variety of perspectives. Therefore, the existential or perspectivistic view of psychology subscribes to the necessity for a continual multiplication of methods and viewpoints.

Concomitantly, the existential approach maintains that psychology can be made serviceable to man's practical interest only if the results of perspectivistic research are constantly integrated so as to contribute to the solution of the concrete problems which man faces in his concrete life situations. This integration is not a philosophical but a scientific theoretical integration in the light of practical problems confronting psychology and challenging it to shed light on man's life situation. Scientific theoretical integration demands, however, hypothetical constructs which can serve as a framework for this integration. Man's philosophical reflection on his implicit awareness of the perspectivity of his knowledge preceded, on a historical level, his scientific psychological reflection on this same awareness. Therefore, philosophers have been able to develop concepts that are useful for the integration of the results of perspectivistic psychological research in the light of the practical questions which the psychologist attempts to answer from the limited viewpoint of his specialization. Thus the psychologist sometimes finds it practical to borrow such philosophical concepts and to utilize them as quasi-hypothetical constructs.

Obviously, these constructs acquire a different meaning in the science of psychology than they have in the context of philosophy. The reader should be aware of this distinction while reading the following chapters. Even when certain terms used are similar to those found in existential philosophy, they do not always have the same meaning in the context of psychology. Because of the danger of misunderstanding, the author has felt obliged to refer as little as possible to existential philosophers who may have influenced his thought: they might rightly protest the alteration of the meaning of their concepts in the new context, as it were, of the scientific theoretical discourse of psychology. The following exposition is guided necessarily by the peculiar traditions, methods of exploration, experimentation, and theory construction proper to the science of psychology. Psychology incorporates man's emerging pre-reflective awareness of his perspectivity within the traditional dialogue of its own field of competence. Therefore psychology, when it has absorbed the implications of man's insight into its existential structure, must still be fundamentally separate from philosophy, physics, sociology, or physiology even when these disciplines have also assimilated the implications of the new awareness of perspectivity insofar as it is relevant to their special fields.

The expression "existential psychology" should not be misunderstood. It does not mean a new school or area of psychology comparable to other schools of psychology. Existential psychology is a temporary movement within the field of psychology as a whole that attempts to assimilate into the field of psychology the implicit awareness that man's knowledge is perspectivistic. As soon as the science of psychology has discovered and totally assimilated this newly emerging awareness, we shall no longer speak of existential psychology, for psychology as such will then be existential: it will be in harmony with the latest phase of the evolution of human insight. After this assimilation has been achieved, psychology will again await its further fundamental enrichment through assimilation of the next development of our view of man, which may emerge as a result of the next phase of the human evolution.

Existential psychology is thus an attempt to assimilate into the science of psychology the implications of the contemporary perspectivistic view of man insofar as it is directly relevant for the evolvement of empirical, clinical, and theoretical psychology. This movement toward reconstruction of psychological science by assimilation will become superfluous as soon as psychology has fundamentally restructured, deepened, and expanded itself through integration of the insight into man's radical perspectivity which has recently emerged in Western humanity as an inescapable result of its cultural and historical development. Because the present work is a first attempt to explicate this unavoidable task of assimilation, it cannot be the final word on the subject. The author will feel deeply rewarded if he is able to raise important questions and propose problems. Though he has attempted to answer some of them, he is aware that he must rely on the constructive criticism and help of all his colleagues concerned with the same basic problems that face us at this moment of crisis in psychology. Because his subject matter is so profound and complex, the author did not hesitate to be repetitious in the hope that repitition might keep clearly before his own eyes and those of his readers the course of his thought.

ADRIAN VAN KAAM

January 17, 1966

CHAPTER ONE

THE NATURE AND MEANING OF SCIENCE

Man may seek the meaning of science by approaching it as a typically human endeavor and asking: What is it in human nature that leads to the emergence of the scientific attitude? In what sense is human existence itself a foundation of scientific interest? Once I have the answer to this question and understand how the scientific attitude is rooted in the very nature of man, I may begin to grasp what science really means. From that moment on, I may be able to trace back to man's existence all forms, aims, and methods of science and to demonstrate that they are manifestations of his nature.

Thus I may hope to arrive at an understanding of the nature and meaning of science by exploring how science is rooted in my own nature. In order to do so, I must first of all know my own nature. Is my nature different from the nature of the things around me? Many thinkers have attempted to find an answer to this question. I can hear three different voices of humanity explicating the nature of man: the positivist, the rationalist, and the existential voice.

The Positivist View of Man

When I consider the positivist explanation of man's being, I discover that positivists do not distinguish fundamentally between man and the things that surround him. They state that man and other things are basically the same, differing only in appearance, that both are outcomes of the same processes and forces which blindly play in the cosmos. According to this view, I am in the world as a complex piece of matter among numerous more or less similar pieces. It would be sheer arrogance for me to pretend that I differ basically from the things around me. I am a fragile fragment of nature, a trifle, an incident, a minute moment in the vast ocean of changing matter; I am in the world along with other things, such as a stone in the river, a weed in the garden, a speck of dust in expanding space.

This point of view as adopted by thoughtful people cannot be dismissed lightly, nor can I say that their perception is based on mere imagination. There must be something in human appearance that leads to the notion that I am like the things around me. Indeed, when I think about myself and others, I must admit that I am also in a certain sense a thing and that I also display the features of a process. This is so true that disciplines such as physiology, biology, biochemistry, and neurology are able to identify and describe a multitude of processes in my organism. While I recognize this fact, I am also aware, however, that only man develops sciences about his own mechanisms. I never saw a stone, cactus, or crystal reflect on its chemistry. As a human being, however, I can establish a science concerning my biophysical attributes because I can perceive them intelligently, because they really have meaning for me. My being has meaning for me, processes have meaning for me, and the things around me have meaning for me. But things and processes have no meaning either for themselves or for one another. If there were nothing else but things and processes, nothing would have any meaning; there would be nobody for whom they could *mean* processes or things.

When I consider the many processes that govern my organism, I feel that I am related to them differently than oil, wine, or vinegar, for example, are related to their chemical structures. Oil, wine, and vinegar are identified with their mechanisms; they cannot distance themselves from these mechanisms. I experience, however, that I depend on my organismic properties in one way while I escape them in another; that I adapt to them faithfully and yet in a certain sense withstand them with facility; that I am absorbed by them and yet take a stand toward them. Even under the overpowering impact of a painful or exciting biophysical process, I am still able to experience that it is I who undergoes this event; I can still impose a variety of meanings on this physical performance of my organism; I can still experience that I accept or reject, like or dislike, adapt unhesitantly or withhold a wholehearted assent to my bodily conduct. When I take a stand in respect to the processes of my body, I already go beyond them, I transcend them, I experience that I am more than they are. No thing or process is able to spontaneously take a stand toward itself or toward other things or processes. Only man can take such initiative.

It is true that I may be able to build into a machine or robot the practical implications of original and spontaneous perspectives of reality. I may devise a computer, a teaching machine, or a robot which—within the range determined by me—may make technical "choices" among different possible courses of action. These selections, however, will be mechanical variations of the pragmatic implications of the fundamental choice originally made by me and embodied afterward in my technical creation. The robot, moreover, can never become really like me so long as it retains its machine-like qualities. It can never uncover spontaneously a total new meaning in people, nature, and things nor take a stand wholly in and by itself in a creative, unpredictable, or surprising human fashion. Imagine, for example, a mechanical hair stylist devised to care for women's hair and to adapt itself selectively to the inexhaustible variety of female heads and hairdo's. Such an amazing robot could never of itself change its perspective and—let us say—fall passionately in love with the attractive subject of its care!

I must even say that the meaningful "thing" or "process" is possible only with the emergence of man in the cosmos. Even the verb "to be" in the statement, "there are things and processes," is meaningful to me only when I recognize that other men and myself are present in the world as subjects who discover such meaning. For whom would the verb "to be" exist if there were only things and processes? I may conclude that the process-like aspect is only one important aspect of my human nature. Positivism has splendidly explored and elaborated this essential feature of man's nature, while neglecting other fundamental aspects. It has carefully investigated the organismic participation of man in the world of things. The positivist rightly demonstrates how the human organism shares somehow in the multitude of processes and laws which are formulated by biology, biochemistry, physics, physiology, and other sciences. In consequence, positivism has stimulated the biophysiological sciences to explore diligently the degree to which human behavior remains subjected to the measurable impact of a universe of matter. This magnificent and massive exploration will continue, for science will never exhaust the richness, subtlety, and complexity of this particular profile of man's being.

The Rationalist View of Man

This one fundamental perspective alone, however, cannot provide for me a full account of my unique human situation as I experience it in my daily life. For my biochemical processes do not fully explain to me the fact that I know myself as existing for myself, while at the same time I spontaneously experience things and processes as having meaning for me. I experience this aspect of "meaning-giving" as a profile of my life which is at least as essential and original as my organismic participation in biochemical laws. My nature reveals to me that I am involved in the world not only in an organismic but also in a meaning-giving way.

I may even become so overwhelmingly aware of this meaning-giving aspect of my life that I forget about the organismic processes which also belong to my nature. When I describe the nature of man, I may then be tempted to ignore his bodily-organismic aspects. In this case, my description is again one-sided because I have stressed only one aspect and concealed another. To omit the contribution of positivist thought on man is just as pernicious as the omission of the "meaning-giving" attribute of human existence.

It is the rationalist and idealist thinkers who fall into this biased view. They inflate unduly the subjectivity of man; they overemphasize his power of giving meaning to the world. Their slanted considerations regard his limited, embodied subjectivity as an absolute and sovereign subjectivity, restricted in no way by his biophysical conditions, by his sense information, and by his being bound to the world. It is true that without man's subjectivity, without his capacity to discover sense and meaning, nature would have no meaning; things and processes would simply not exist for him. Without man, who is the discoverer of meaning, the universe would be meaningless and empty. Even the meaning "universe" could not exist without someone for whom it means "universe". When I affirm things and processes, I affirm them in their being for me and for all other men; outside this affirmation, there is no human meaning in the cosmos.

A rationalist or idealist view of man, however, places extreme stress on this specific human aspect. Such exclusive preoccupation leads to a distorted view of my nature; it makes me—the thinking subject—the supreme source, the independent creator, the mysterious spring, the hidden well of all processes and things which I experience. All of them are considered as mere productions of my inventive thought. I do not even know whether things in nature correspond with them. In such a subjectivistic approach, the scientific designs which I, the subject, invent and project are considered to be more dependable and trustworthy than the things "out there" which they capture under some of their aspects. The real things out there, however, actually reveal more aspects, views, or profiles than any scientific design can cover. If I am a subjectivistic scientist, however, I may simply assert that those aspects do not exist at all, or that they are unreal, insignificant, and unimportant because the rational measurements invented by my thinking subjectivity cannot be applied to them. In short, that which does not fit my subjective, rational, mathematical creation should be disregarded. Faced with a choice, I shall enhance my inventive subjectivity at the expense of the richness and density of reality.

Such subjectivism, while most conspicuous in scientism, reaches its extremes in idealistic philosophy. Subjectivism, if pushed to the limit, leads to the conviction that all my experience is merely the reflection of my isolated, self-sufficient, inventive intellect; everything is nothing but a mirage of what I think, feel, wish, and imagine; the reality and density of the world evaporates into the mere contents of my consciousness. So-called "things" and "processes" are pure products of my thought without correlates in reality. My knowledge is nothing but the lonely presence of my thought to itself. Such a sterile subjectivity, imprisoned in itself and fully self-sufficient, is not a human kind of subjectivity; it contradicts my spontaneous perception in daily life. Therefore, I cannot really believe in it. Deep down, I am forced to admit that things are real and not merely my invention and imagination. Even if I loudly declare that nothing is real except my thought, I still manifest in my very behavior the fact that I do not really believe what I say. For in my daily actions I clearly take into account that the world in which I live, move, and labor is real and unescapable, is density and resistance. If I did not behave in accordance with the reality of the world, I would be the constant victim of serious accidents. If I really lived in my behavior what some idealistic thinkers believe in their isolated rationality, I would destroy myself.

The Existential View of Man

Neither the positivist nor the rationalist view fully represents man as I actually experience him in daily life, although each of these perspectives uncovers real insights into essential aspects of his nature.

When I observe man as I meet him in reality, I realize that he is neither a mere thing like other things in the universe nor self-sufficient subjectivity which maintains itself in splendid isolation from the world. He is not locked up within himself as mere thought and worldless self-presence. Instead he is always already outside himself and in the world, he involves himself continuously in the density of reality in and around him: he *is* a dialogue with things and processes in his own organism and in his surroundings. At the same time, he remains a subject in the world and *lets the world be for him* by steadily uncovering its manifold meanings.

In short, I really experience myself as a being-in-the-world, an ex-sistence, a presence, an encounter, and an involvement. I am inconceivable without my human world. Conversely, the human world as I experience it is inconceivable, imperceptible, and unimaginable without me, without man. Man's world reveals itself as sky, mountains, valleys, forests, streams, and oceans. But without man there would not be the human meaning of sky, mountain, valley, forest, stream, and ocean. I cannot even imagine what they would be like without their specific meaning for man in a humanized universe.

To be man is thus fundamentally and essentially to exist, and to exist means to-be-in-the-world. The subject which is man simply does not happen without being involved in the world; it presents itself only in relation to the world. The subject "I", the self that I am, cannot occur other than as the source of activity which is in some way oriented to the world as it appears. The self cannot be conceived, affirmed, experienced, or imagined without the world or some aspect of the world to which the self is directed or in which it is involved. Expressions such as I think, I do, I feel, I imagine, I anticipate, I dream, and I own all imply a being-in-the-world, always presuppose something which is more than the isolated self alone.

The assertion that the subjectivity of man presents itself only in relation to the world cannot be precisely demonstrated, for it cannot be derived with certainty from another and more fundamental insight. If it could be derived from a more basic insight into man's nature, then the assertion that "being-man" is "being-in-the-world" would no longer be the most fundamental description of man. Since there is no formal proof for this assertion, its truth can be *indicated* only by demonstrating that no mode of being man can be conceived, perceived, or imagined which is not at the same time a mode of being-in-the-world. It is indeed impossible to fully describe any mode of being-man without implying some aspect of the world in the description. In our daily parlance, this aspect is usually only implicit in our statements. I may say that I walk, talk, imagine, or fear, but these declarations always imply that I walk somewhere in the world, that I talk to somebody or about something, that I imagine or fear something, no matter how vague and indefinite it may be.

In other words, human consciousness is always consciousness of something which is not consciousness itself. It is a being together with the world, an encounter with, an orientation to, a directedness, an intentionality. Consciousness is an orientation to what it is not; it is always consciousness *of*; a consciousness of nothing is not imaginable for it would no longer be consciousness. Consciousness is not a "thing" closed in upon itself; it is an act, an act of revealing, the act of man that reveals the world; it is a radical openness for all that may manifest itself to man.

This balanced view of man unites the two aspects of man's being which have been explored one-sidedly by positivism and rationalism, by objectivism and subjectivism, by naive realism and idealism. Centuries of intense thought, of fierce intellectual struggle were required of Western humanity before this precarious balance between the subjective and the objective was won.

The existential view thus sees me, man, as a being-in-the-world. I am not in the world, however, in the same way that chairs are in a room, cigarettes in a package, or candy in a box. These things are not affected meaningfully by other things which surround them, and they in turn do not affect other things meaningfully. I am influenced, however, by the world in which I dwell and I influence this world. I "dwell," "inhabit," "sojourn" in the world; I "cultivate," "transform," "humanize," "personalize" the world by my simple human presence. I am not in the world as a stone is in a wall, a broom in a closet, or a vegetable in a freezer; they are contained in the wall, the closet, the freezer in a spatial manner, side by side with other motionless things. But I am involved, engaged in my world; I am preoccupied with my world in many ways; I am concerned, I care as no stone, broom, or vegetables can care. I am acquainted, familiar with the world; I am at home in the world. I find myself irritated, annoyed, fascinated, depressed, bored, excited by the world. I find myself using, developing, organizing, accepting, rejecting, explaining, fostering, cultivating, questioning, searching, and discussing the world. The stone, the broom, the vegetable never find themselves in any of these attitudes or activities with regard to the things that surround them. They are merely "side by side" with other things in the same container. But I as man really encounter the world in these many attitudes and operations. The world reveals itself to me in its manifold lived concreteness when I am with the world in these many modes of daily "lived" encounter.

Science and the Existential Nature of Man

The original, spontaneous way of being-in-the-world is thus not the scientific mode; my concrete daily experience is not scientific. My first, natural experience is spontaneous, multi-dimensional, unorganized, somewhat vague and undetermined, while my later scientific experience may be planned, strictly defined, well designed, systematized, and logically formulated. I can easily observe this difference between my spontaneous and my scientific experience when I compare, for example, my spontaneous and my scientific experience of a rat in motion. As a child I may have seen a rat suddenly run away when my father switched on the light in the basement. This experience was quite different from my present experience as a scientist when I observe, in terms of operationally defined categories, the response of a carefully selected laboratory rat to a measured stimulus in a scientifically designed experimental situation. However, I should not therefore jump to the conclusion that the world of my spontaneous experiences is nothing more than a senseless chaos of incoherent impressions that tumble after one another without rhyme or reason. The world of spontaneous experience has its own design, its own language, its own "logic", its own coherent pattern of meaning, its own "Gestalt." Sigmund Freud, for example, already attempted to penetrate into the pre-logical language of infantile experience when he studied the world of meaning structured by the child's experience of his body.

All later language of science is derived from the typical language of primary experience which it presupposes as its point of departure. The world of my first experience shows spatial, temporal, intentional, and dynamic characteristics of its own which are quite distinct but not separated from the constructs of time, space, and dynamics in science. The abstract space spoken of by Newton, for example, presupposes the concrete space in which I live. The idea of an endless space, which is the container of everything situated within it, is an abstract idea, largely a product of subsequent thought. But I form this idea on the basis of my experience of concrete space as an endless container in which things are placed. In this space which I "live" in my spontaneous experience, things are far-away or close-by, high or low, right or left. This space is thus given to me as already oriented. The orientation of this space apparently does not exist independently of me. For in absolute space it would be meaningless to speak in such terms as far-away or close-by, high or low, which refer to space only as it exists for me, the subject. In my concrete existence, therefore, I am bound by spatial dimensions from which I cannot escape. Regardless of my thoughts, scientific constructs, and abstractions, the road on which I walk is low for me and the sky is high. In the production of instruments such as forks, spoons, knives, and rakes, I have to adapt myself to a spatiality that is simply given. Thus there is an oriented space of primary experience which imposes itself on me as an undeniable necessity. It is only on the basis of this primary experience that I can arrive, by a process of abstraction, at the scientific construct of space as an endless container without orientation.

It may be clear from this example that my world of primary experience, from which science emerges and on which it is nourished, is constituted by a different kind of fact and meaning than science itself. However, I can fully understand my scientific mode of existence only if I grasp first of all my primary mode-of-being-in-the-world. For the very possibility of the development of any science whatsoever is based on this natural primordial way of existence. Being a scientist presupposes being a man in daily life.

The above statement is more specifically true of the human sciences because of their specific subject matter. For human sciences will never present us with a full understanding of man so long as they are pure speculative knowledge or mere laboratory knowledge without reference to the real, lived world of man. In this case, they would be nothing more than splendid logical structures, experimentally validated but irrelevant to the actual "lived" human situation. Psychology would become merely a sophisticated exercise in systematic and statistical thought, magnificently illustrated by carefully selected, well-controlled experiments beautifully adjusted to an impressive system, related perhaps to some measurable features of behavior, but having little to do with the "lived" human reality. Human behavior as it really appears in its fullness would evaporate and finally disappear in the rarefied heights of technical, statistical, and experimental abstractions. Such a system would quantify certain relations between measurable aspects of behavior only to lose in the end the behaving man. Psychology would become a satire on the psychologist himself, for it would become an impressive feat of experimental, intellectual construction in which even the psychologist as a living person would find neither an explanation, a hearing, an understanding, nor a place. For there would be no relationship between the intellectual-experimental structure and the actual human life of the man who devised the structure.

The scientific psychologist is capable of devising relevant empirical research if he remains present to human behavior as it appears in real life situations. In other words, his scientific mode of existence should never lose contact with his spontaneous "lived" mode of life. Human science should never replace, erase, or distort human experience. The degree to which this happens determines the degree of the irrelevancy of psychology to human life. Therefore the human scientist should not restrict himself to only objective and detached measurement and observation. To be sure, a necessary scientific detachment should dominate the second phase of his scientific research, a phase which succeeds and presupposes his immersion in the world of experienced behavior itself, where he has already discovered the relevant questions and problems. However, he should continually recover the immediate experiences of human behavior which preceded his experiments, his empirical research, and his scientific constructs. For the human scientist is not simply, nor first and foremost, a scientist but a human being. The foundations of the human sciences, therefore, cannot be reduced to a collection of objectifying, experimental, measuring, and theorizing manipulations.

This does not mean, to be sure, that the human sciences should be limited to the description and analysis of the spontaneous natural experience of human behavior. On the contrary, they should be strictly scientific about human behavior, but about human behavior as it really appears in the lived world of man. Human scientists should adapt their methods to behavior as it appears instead of arbitrarily adapting behavior under all its possible aspects to a few methods borrowed from physics or physiology. The task of the human scientist is to explore "lived" human behavior scientifically in its fundaments, conditions, and implications. He must penetrate particular, concrete human behavior with the light of scientific constructs of universal validity from which testable hypotheses can be derived.

The empirical and scientific attitudes of the human scientist do not at all exclude his attentive presence to human behavior as it appears in meaningful life situations. A distinction must be made here between empirical research which is relevant and that which is irrelevant to the understanding of behavior. Irrelevant empirical research is produced by the totally detached, abstract, and isolated investigation carried on by the neutral spectator of behavior who is indifferent to the relationship between his abstract game and the life situation of man. Relevant research is that which explores, describes, and empirically tests human behavior while preserving a "lived" relationship with it in the reality of life. Of course, all empirical research, relevant or irrelevant, necessarily presupposes a temporary detachment from actually lived behavior. Otherwise, no research would be possible. But relevant research *starts out* from an involvement in reality as it is lived, and it recovers this relationship after obtaining its scientific results.

Thus the human scientist must understand behavior as lived in the daily situation before his abstracting intellect can devise scientific constructs, empirical and experimental designs which are truly relevant to the understanding of this behavior. Indeed, scientific, abstract, empirical knowledge appears relatively late in man's experience. When it does appear, it already constitutes a thematization of particular kinds of immediate, spontaneous, "lived" experience. The immediate understanding of human behavior, on the other hand, occurs on a level of experience which exists in advance of any type of objectifying, whether rational or scientific. For this reason, the human scientist cannot express the results of his experiential, pre-empirical exploration of behavior in a manner which is rationally convincing or experimentally verifiable. The logically convincing and experimentally testable mode is necessary in science, but possible only in the second, empirical phase of scientific endeavor. So long as the human scientist works in the fundamental or experiential phase of human science, he can only elucidate his immediate perception of behavior by means of description.

Even in this fundamental phase of science, however, some type of intersubjective affirmation is possible. The scientist may invite his fellow scientists to interrogate their own perception to discover whether they find a topography of human behavior similar to his own. In this way, the pre-empirical elucidations of behavior which are originally personal may attain intersubjective affirmation. Such elucidations are the indispensable matrix of relevant scientific constructs and hypotheses, and of subsequent empirical and experimental research. Thus the experiential elucidation of the spontaneous perception of behavior is the missing link between the spontaneous and the scientific modes of existence of the human scientist.

A human scientist who has lost his roots and is no longer in touch with the spontaneous natural perception of behavior will easily ascribe a priority to scientific methodology. He will often conceal, because of his methodological preconceptions, relevant human behavior which is waiting for exploration. He may even lose himself in methodological analysis at the expense of never arriving at relevant human behavior itself. A continual preoccupation with scientific methodology leads to sterility. Moreover, a preconceived empirical, experimental, or statistical method may distort rather than disclose a given behavior through an imposition of restricted theoretical constructs on the full meaning and richness of human behavior. Such a situation becomes even more precarious when the human scientist blindly borrows scientific methods from the physical or physiological sciences. The methods of physics undoubtedly disclose certain measurable properties of human behavior, but beyond this they conceal more than they reveal. Unfortunately, the imperialism of the physical method may even cut human science off from relevant human behavior as it is revealed in the spontaneous, experiential mode of existence.

This caution against the premature introduction of scientific methodology does not in the least mean that the human scientist in the pre-empirical phase of his research should approach human behavior in a haphazard, random, aimless way. Although he does not give priority to methodological formulation in his pre-empirical elucidation of actual behavior, he does approach it in a certain mode, style, or manner. He seeks to maintain such unity between actual behavior and his psychological descriptions of it that the very meaning and structure of behavior itself is immediately revealed in his descriptions. This approach in the first, fundamental phase of psychological research is called phenomenological psychology.

Phenomenological psychology, in its broadest definition, is an attempt to return to the immediate meaning and structure of behavior as it actually presents itself. Phenomenology as a method in psychology thus seeks to disclose and elucidate the phenomena of behavior as they manifest themselves in their perceived immediacy. The human scientist, in this fundamental phase of his research, must thoughtfully penetrate his concrete lived perception of behavior and describe this behavior in its immediate disclosure. It is precisely the phenomenological method which allows him to penetrate to the structures of human behavior. At this pre-experimental and pre-theoretical level, the human scientist precludes all scientific constructs, methods, and theories. His immediate task is to make explicit, describe, and interpret the originally given behavior. The original datum of psychology is behavior itself, and the function of this fundamental phase of scientific exploration is to provide a conceptual clarification of behavior by making explicit its constitutive structures.

The phenomenological procedure in fundamental psychological research demands emancipation from all scientific-theoretical prejudgments, from all methodological and statistical limitations, which can only distort or conceal original behavior in its givenness. For the datum or phenomenon of behavior is always prior to any experiment, measurement, or theory *about* behavior. Therefore measurement, experiment, or scientific theory can never provide a sound point of departure in psychology. They are important and necessary modes of scientific exploration, but by their very nature they are always secondary, subsequent, and subordinate to phenomenological elucidation. Human scientists who preoccupy themselves exclusively with secondary scientific theory and subordinate laboratory experiments seldom arrive at a full understanding of relevant human behavior as it appears in daily life. For the road which they follow does not lead to actual, significant behavior. Having lost access to real human behavior, they may become preoccupied with an endless refinement, perfection, and sophistication of operational methods. But no refinement of method in the second phase of psychological research can make up for the lack of the phenomenological approach in the first, fundamental phase. What actually results is an increase in knowledge of the subtleties of operationalism and a decrease in knowledge of relevant human behavior. No method of the second phase of scientific research in psychology can of itself lead the psychologist to relevant behavior if he does not start from such behavior in its original appearance. The main purpose of the phenomenological phase in psychology, therefore, is to return to actual "lived" behavior as it manifests itself and in the manner in which it manifests itself: phenomenological psychology examines behavior as it is given.

Man as Being In the World In and Through His Body

If I desire to know how science is rooted in my nature, I must try to grasp not only that I am in the world as an "act-of-revealing," but also *how* I am in the world as an act of revealing. This knowledge may help me to understand what specific "mode-of-my-revealing-of-the-world" science is.

I am always in the world in and through my body: I am an embodied consciousness, an incarnated subjectivity. *All* my modes of existence are fundamentally modes of existence in and through my body. I am neither a disembodied self nor a mechanical organism, but a living unity, a body permeated by self. Because I am a bodily self, I experience myself in my behavior as an orientation to the world; I sense my outgoing self, my intentionality, at least implicitly and pre-reflectively. And this tending presence of my subjectivity to the world is always bodily presence. My body belongs to me, the tending, outgoing subject; I experience my body as that in, with, and through which I am present to the world; I "live" my body as that which grasps and seizes the world. My body is my spontaneous, unpremeditated entrance into the dense reality which permeates and surrounds me. I could not feel, grasp, assimilate, understand, perceive, elucidate anything in the world without this bridge which is my body, a bridge that is never absent but always present, a bridge which I truly am. My body makes the world available to me; it is in and through my body that the world becomes-for-me, becomes mine, my world. The total destruction or disintegration of my body is also the destruction or disintegration of my world. At the moment that I and my world are both ended, I shall no longer be ex-sistence, which is being-in-the-world. In daily life I know this fateful agent as the death of man.

My bodily presence to reality makes the world exist for me pre-reflectively before I think about it, probe it intellectually, reflect on it. The world is already there for me even before my reflection. For my body is my spontaneous lived presence to the world, obscure but real, vague but factual.

The fact that I am a bodily act of revealing the world has various implications. The first is that my actual presence to the world will always be necessarily a limited presence, and my actual revelation of reality a limited revelation. For my body not only makes the world available to my subjectivity, but also defines my limited position or situation in that world and consequently the limited availability of the world to me. My body makes my existence situated existence, my openness limited openness. The field of my bodily presence, of my senses and movements, is limited in time and space. I cannot see and touch at once everything that is visible and touchable in the world. How much of an object I can see depends on the actual position of my body. When I see something from the back, I cannot at the same time see its front. The reverse would be true if I were to find myself in front of the same object. Thus the various bodily positions which I assume give rise to various viewpoints or limited visions of reality.

When I, for example, study the behavior of a person who moves into my field of vision, I cannot escape the limitations of my bodily position. I may successively assume different bodily positions, shifting from one to another, but I can take only one position at a time. Every position which I assume will make available to me a different aspect of the moving person, such as his side view, his back, or his front. Every one of my positions will present me with a different perspective of his behavior. But ultimately I must make up my mind and select one of these many possible positions at any given moment of observation. My bodily position thus determines which view of the moving person will reveal itself to me within a confined field of perception, and my field of perception is always limited because of my being an *embodied* subjectivity.

This positional limitation of my perception is not the only one imposed on me by my body. My bodily existence differentiates the presence of my subjectivity in many modalities such as seeing, touching, hearing, smelling, and tasting. I cannot perceive a person or thing with all my sense modalities at the same time. At least, I cannot do so in a concentrated, intense way which will reveal to me all that can be revealed by each specific modality of presence alone. Each bodily modality of existence reveals a different aspect of the perceived world than other modalities. When I "look" at a person, I experience primarily other aspects than those perceived when I "touch" or embrace him. I say "primarily" for I am aware that by some kind of synesthesia the other aspects are at least implicitly present in my perception. For example, in looking at the fine texture of a silk shirt, I am implicitly aware of its soft tactile qualities. Or when my fingers feel the soft, smooth folds of this shirt in the darkness, I am implicitly aware that it will not appear to my eyes as heavy or rough. The basic quality of my perception, however, and therefore the basic revelation of what a silk shirt is like, depends on the specific bodily modality of existence in and through which my body relates to this object.

I may attempt to transcend both limitations of my embodied subjectivity, that of restricted bodily position and that of single modality. I may, for example, walk around a person who moves into my field of vision in order to see him from all sides, and I may even try to be present to him in all of my bodily modalities. I may touch, smell, see, hear, and even taste him. I may ask him how he himself feels about his movements, what makes him behave as he does, what he is attempting to communicate in his actions. In this way, I may try to build up a full understanding of his concrete behavior. However, even this knowledge will never be a complete *immediate* knowledge of this living person; even this comprehensive cognition cannot escape my bodily limitations. Because of my own shifting bodily positions in the world, I shall have obtained this knowledge primarily by a variety of shifting perspectives. The assemblage, montage, or aggregate of these perspectives will lead to a knowledge that will remain fundamentally fragmentary and retain the character of a collection of partial perceptions. It will not provide an immediate, integral understanding of the moving person, but a notion made up of numerous fragments of perceptions representing the results of my various bodily positions and modalities. Indeed, my bodily existence compels me to perceive the world always in limited ways. Consequently, my knowledge of the world is always originally fragmentary knowledge.

This limitation of knowledge by bodily position and modality seems evident enough in my perceptual mode of existence, which necessarily implies my assumption of a particular bodily position and my selection of one or the other sensuous modality in my presence to the world. But is my thought limited as my perception is? Is my thought about the moving person absolutely free from limitation? Or does my embodied existence limit not only my perceiving but also my thinking?

My thought is necessarily co-original with my perception. My thought about a moving person, for example, cannot be dreamed up arbitrarily; it necessarily originates with my perception of his behavior. All my ideas about this moving person, all my statements about him, are finally dependent on my bodily-perceptual presence to him in various bodily positions and modalities. Therefore my thinking approach to reality is also fundamentally fragmentary. My bodily being in the world makes it impossible for me ever to achieve a moment in which I can maintain all possible viewpoints in thought at the same time. The actual availability of the world to me is forever limited by the finiteness of my corporeal situation.

This human situation has far-reaching implications for the nature of the development of science: it explains first of all the differentiation of science into many sciences, and more specifically the differentiation of psychology into many differential psychologies, each one opening up its own perspective. This same insight provides the basis for the task of comprehensive psychology, which is an attempt to integrate the perspectives developed by the differential psychologies.

Finally, my body enables me to exist in a *social* world. I do not experience myself as an isolated discoverer of meaning. I do not perceive myself as the only man on earth, lonely and lost in an overwhelming multitude of blind processes and opaque lumps of matter, for which I do not exist as a meaningful other and which cannot discover meaning in me. I meet other men, other embodied subjectivities, who in and through their bodily presence to the world uncover meaning in the world as I do. I am even acutely aware of the fact that they judge me, that they are aware of me and impose meaning on me, that I belong to their field of meaning. I thus discover that I am not the only openness in the world, but that there are others like me who in and through their bodies are outgoing, meaning-giving subjectivities in the midst of people, animals, things, and processes.

The others communicate to me, in and through their bodies, their own uncovering of meaning in the world, and I respond to their communications. We may join one another in a community of men who decide to explore together, by means of certain methods, selected profiles of the world. This community of specialists in a specific area of discovery may stretch itself over cultures and generations. The social aspect of our embodiment, namely the bodily presence of our subjectivity to one another, is the condition for the possibility of science as an organized endeavor over generations of men.

Body as Revealing Behavior

Behavior is the bodily presence in the world of the revealing, existing movement which I am. My bodily behavior reveals the world to me. My moving hands reveal to me a basketball as spherical, solid, and leathery; my throwing hands unveil to me its bouncing quality; my pressing hands discover its elasticity. The same behavior in others reveals to me how they too discover, in and through their behavior, the meaning, the sense of a basketball. Behavior as gestures, movements, and language is my being-in-the-world, my immediate presence to reality.

Thus behavior is not a mediatization or a symbolization of my intentionality or subjectivity, but rather my intentionality itself, my existing itself. In our consideration of the science of psychology as the study of behavior, we shall see how this fact enables psychology to declare itself the empirical science of behavior while at the same time the science of the *whole man* in so far as he appears in behavior.

I am in the world through my body, and as such I am a behaving subjectivity. The perceived world is relative to my behaving intentionality, for it is always a world for me as a behaving subjectivity. Behavior, therefore, cannot be studied by itself, for it is fundamentally a revealing act and can be understood only in terms of my world which I as behavior reveal around myself. The behaving body-which-I-am is the *original* locus for the appropriation of sense and meaning. Behavior is the original existential presence by which my body makes the world be for me.

Meaning is thus not ready-given in the world as a being-in-itself; sense and meaning are not "out there," clear-cut like a map or photograph. If such were the case, I would have only to take in passively a representation of the things out there. On the other hand, sense is not merely an arbitrary invention of my mind or my creative imagination; sense is born in and through my life, which is bodily being and behaving in the world. Sense emerges in and through the dialectic relation between me and my world. The notion of body-subject developed by Maurice Merleau-Ponty helps to clarify the statement that my body is revealing behavior.

I must strive, first of all, to understand something of the original, obscure field of my existence from which science emerges. Science itself operates with clear, well-defined constructs and concepts. But the emergence of science presupposes spontaneous experience, and the emergence of the scientist presupposes the spontaneously living human being. While I can be perfectly clear about a scientific system which I have developed, I cannot be so clear about my initial "lived" experience of the world which preceded my scientific development, and which is the original source of any scientific concept that I may elaborate in precise ways. Nevertheless, I am interested not only in the exact and logical development of scientific systems, but also in their initial origin in spontaneous human existence. My original, spontaneous interaction with the world before I approach it as a scientist is not a presence to things which are already sharply delineated and categorized; it is rather my being involved in a field of existence in which everything is interwoven with everything else, in which everything points to every other thing. It is a movable, fluid field, vastly different from my precisely organized collection of scientific constructs.

I should anticipate, therefore, that it will be impossible for me to view my original human field of lived experience in full precision and clarity. I cannot transcribe this region of prime experience into systematic constructs which together form a tight, theoretical, scientific system. For as soon as I begin to build a scientific system, I have already ceased to consider my primary field of spontaneous being in the world. In spite of these reservations and restrictions, I can still express coherently my growing insight into this pre-reflective, spontaneous realm of my existence. At the same time I remain aware that I do not and cannot know distinctly and exhaustively this obscure, original root of my scientific life. My understanding of the realm in which all science begins will always be blended with not-understanding; my perception of it will be permeated by blind spots. While it is crucial for me to devise precise constructs when I build a scientific system, it is also essential to recognize the obscurity of my primordial field of "lived" knowledge from which my scientific theory emerges and to which it points. Such a recognition will prevent me from making my theory of behavior inflexible, closed, and immutable; it will keep it open, hypothetical, and provisional.

This pre-conscious, pre-objective field of my original perception is thus so obscure that ordinary reflection cannot really penetrate it. My body, according to Merleau-Ponty, is a subject or, in other words, a meaning-giving existence, even if I am not yet conscious of its meaning-giving activity. My body has already invested my world with meaning before I think about this meaning. It is not the same as the imposition of meaning on the world by my consciousness. Certain things in the world, for example, already mean shelter, food, or obstacle for me as body-subject before I am consciously aware of it. I am thus already a meaning-giving existence on the pre-conscious and not-yet-free level of my bodily existence. Numerous examples demonstrate that my body exists as a giver of meanings. I see colors, I hear sounds, I feel with my fingers the roughness and smoothness of things, I smell odors, and I taste flavors. Sounds, odors, flavors, and colors do not exist as such completely in themselves "out there" in the world, independent of my bodily presence to the world. Without man, without me, there would be no sights, sounds, and flavors but only some unknown substratum that can appear as sounds, flavors, and colors as soon as I am present to it.

My experience tells me, on the other hand, that sounds, colors, flavors, and tactile qualities do not exist only in me and not in reality. I experience that the sunshine itself is warm, the grass green, and the rose fragrant. All these sensitive meanings are, as it were, the face which the world shows to me. I am in my bodily behavior a manifold question, and I make the world reply in many ways. The world itself is color and shape in reply to my seeing; it is a field of sound in answer to my hearing; it is savory in response to my tasting. But it is clearly not my conscious free ego which questions the world in this way. I do not willingly and consciously ask the world to reveal itself to me in color, sound, taste, touch, or smell. This interplay between the questioning me and the replying world takes place before I consciously think about it, or before I make a conscious, free decision to interrogate the world. This original dialogue between me and the world is preconscious; it takes place on the level of my bodily existence and is connected with the structure of my body. Here I do not "choose," but I "find" something that is already given before any choice.

I am thus already a meaning-giving existence on a level on which I am not yet conscious of myself, and on which I am not yet free. The sensitive meaning, therefore, of color, taste, smell, and sound is a result of a pre-conscious dialogue with the world. This dialogue takes place at such depth that I am unable to penetrate it through my reflective consciousness. Neither am I able to influence this dialogue by means of my free decisions. Below me, therefore, as conscious subject, is another subject that is pre-conscious and pre-personal. This subject is my body itself, for all forms of meaning which emerge on this level appear to be related to the structure of my body. Consequently, I should not identify my meaning-giving subjectivity with my conscious and free thought only. I should recognize that my body itself is already a subject.

At the same time, I should realize that meaning originates in a dialogue. In a real dialogue both partners are active. This implies that I, as a behaving body-subject, must be somehow active in my encounter with the world. My body is not passive in this dialogue. On the contrary, it assumes spontaneously and actively a position which makes this dialogue possible and facilitates it. For example, if my body wants to see something, it must assume the correct ocular position. The pupils of my eyes, for instance, must be dilated according to the darkness of the field of vision. In other words, my body has to situate itself if a certain sensitive meaning is to emerge. My freedom and consciousness are not involved in this spontaneous assumption of a position. I do not know at all what happens in and through my body while I am seeing.

In my scientific life I take up again and continue my pre-conscious existence, my pre-reflexive way of being in the world. As a scientist, I am able to devise well-defined scientific constructs and impressive experimental designs. On closer inspection, however, I realize that these designs and constructs presuppose the meaning which originated in my pre-conscious bodily presence to the world. An experiment that measures, for example, to what degree a certain behavior of rats is reinforced by certain types of rewards, is steeped in preconscious bodily knowledge of the world. For I presuppose that rats react when properly stimulated, that their body is a possibility of movement, that there is an oriented space inseparably and naturally bound up with their possibility of limited bodily movements. I presume, moreover, that rats have built-in needs to respond to rewarding stimulations if exposed to them under the appropriate conditions. I spontaneously incorporate this assumed need into my experimental design. I never attempt to demonstrate these presuppositions experimentally. In any case, such a demonstration would be impossible. I cannot discover experimentally that a rat is a rat, for such an experiment would already presuppose what I am trying to prove. If I did not know rats at all in my daily experiential life, I could not initiate any experiment whatever concerning them. My scientific life never begins with zero; as a scientist, I always start from a meaning which I find already there. This meaning, however, originates within the dialogue of body and world. The conscious scientific mode of existence, then, always refers to the preconscious bodily mode of existence.

The scientific mode of existence is a conscious, free, planned, and selective "taking up" of meanings and relations already given in the preconscious dialogue of my behaving body. My body *gives* me the world through an interplay with the world, but in such a way that my bodily behavior organizes the world. The world's structure thus depends on the structures of my body. My body is a possibility of meaning-giving activity, and the so-called natural world is the whole of the meanings resulting from the dialogue between my body and the world. As a scientist I take up this world in a conscious, reflective, selective, abstractive way, but I do not constitute it, for it is already there for my taking. The "natural" world is the result of the dialogue between my body and the world: a dialogue which precedes existence-insofar-as-it-is-scientific and a world which antedates the abstract world of science. My body already dwells in the world before my scientific-dwelling-in-the-world can take up my pre-conscious bodily dwelling.

The pre-conscious behaving body is thus the ultimate source of my scientific designs, theories, and constructs.

The Behaving Body on the Conscious Level of Existence

Is my role as behaving body completed when I transpose my pre-scientific, spontaneous existence in a scientific, abstractive, experimenting existence? Every mode of my existence is embodied, for I *am* bodily behaving presence to reality. Therefore, the role of my behaving body is different but still paramount on the scientific level of existence. I must realize that my pre-conscious bodily dialogue with the world becomes gradually permeated by my consciousness, that I assume my bodily behaving more and more in a conscious manner, that my conscious self is increasingly present in my bodily behavior. This does not mean that I shall ever be able to penetrate the deepest original, spontaneous, pre-conscious dialogue between my body and the world. I shall never know in a clear and distinct way, for example, how this dialogue leads to the sight of color, the scent of a rose, and the taste of honey. But I am able gradually to organize, expand, foster, limit, and concentrate my bodily, behavioral presence to the world. I can do this in a fruitful fashion, however, only when I take into account the data presented to me in my pre-conscious dialogue with the world, which is the always present, unescapable basis of my life, my thought, and my science. Its total disappearance is the disappearance of me, is my death.

The increasing permeation of my behavior by my consciousness also leads to a fuller expression of my reflective and pre-reflective self in my bodily behavior. For "expression" is an indispensable and deeply influential mode of being in the world. My presence to the world in and through my behaving body can thus be more or less conscious, more or less concentrated, intense, full, and rich. My capacity for intense personal presence increases with my growth and maturation. In other words, my organism becomes more and more my personalized body during the course of my existence.

My movements as an infant, for example, were somewhat wild, jerky, and disorganized. My anger was expressed in a primitive way; my little body squirmed, kicked, and screamed; my face became purple and my breathing was impaired. As I grew older, however, I manifested in my behavior that I was more fully present in my bodily senses, postures, and movements than I was as an infant. This increasing emergence of consciousness enabled me, among other things, to express my anger more efficiently. And this effectual, socially acceptable, bodily expression of my anger made me adept in dealing with my neighbors and proficient in my conquest of reality.

I have sometimes seen, on the other hand, a drunken man who is enraged because he cannot fit his key in the keyhole. His fury, instead of leading him to experimental probing of the keyhole, erupts in unadapted movements directed against the house as a whole. I can observe comparable reactions in an adult who becomes panic-stricken or loses control in an emergency. People may say that such a person forgets him*self* or is beyond him*self*. The bodily behaviors of infants, drunkards, and panic-stricken people are thus similarly ill-adapted modes of involvement with reality.

The increasing presence of the conscious self in human behavior can be observed in many bodily expressions. The face of an infant is somewhat empty in expression. Painters prefer to depict the faces and figures of older people. In the mature personalized human body, the face, hands, movements, and posture radiate the presence of a self much more fully than in the immature body of the child. For this reason a clergyman, a musician, or a wrestler may sometimes be spotted by a sensitive observer of the human scene even if he has little information as a clue. Their professional modes of existence are inherent in all their behavior. Even the manner in which they move reveals them.

This progressive incarnation of the conscious self is observable even in the young child. When I compare carefully the movements of the hands of a child and those of the paws of a monkey, I note a striking fundamental difference. The functional and expressive quality of the paw of a monkey is basically limited by biological needs and stimulations, while the spontaneous functions and expressions of the hand of a child are of a virtually infinite variety and refinement. This is one possible explanation of why there are no painters or sculptors who dedicate their artistic lives to the recreation of the paws of animals. A great number of artists, however, have painted and sculptured over and over again the human hands. The visitor to the Museum Rodin in Paris is struck by the amazing variety of human hands in which Rodin expressed the profound and dramatic presence of the human self.

The human self permeates not only the functional and expressive movements, the mimics and postures of man, but also the physical and chemical surroundings in which he moves and lives. The whole man as embodied self leaves his mark wherever and whenever he emerges in nature and in culture. Man influences, masters, takes hold of, embodies his surroundings; he transforms them into his world through his bodily being in reality. This is true not only of the individual man but of mankind as a whole. The human race as a community of men develops by being present together to reality as it unveils itself in millennia of evolution and human history. It is in such creative, historical community that man constitutes the numerous cultural worlds of meaning which mark his erratic, frequently interrupted ascent and enlightenment.

The way in which we structure our hearths and homes today, for example, is the outgrowth of a long history of bodily perception and manipulation of the world. By the acts of seeing, touching, and using, we have uncovered in reality the meaning of stone, wood, glass, and tools, of protective walls and roofs against rain, snowfall, and burning sunshine. In this sense, our existence is fundamentally co-existence, vertically in history, horizontally in contemporary culture. Vertical co-existence means that we assimilate what others have unveiled before us, while horizontal co-existence implies that we are influenced by the insights and experiences of those who presently live with us. Not only our forebears but also our contemporaries unveil in bodily behaving, in sensing and moving, aspects of reality which are relevant, for example, to the construction of the place in which we live; and we profit from sharing in this movement of their existence. Even rebellion against the points of view of other men is elicited by the ideas against which our revolt is directed and cannot be understood without the view which it attempts to correct.

When I understand that my exploration of the world is fundamentally a bodily exploration, I realize at once that science is not only a mode of existence but also one of the central modes of human existence. For the scientific attitude is a way of concretizing in an effective and organized manner my bodily encounter with reality. This is eminently true of experimental science. For authentic experimentation implies an efficient and well-organized embodiment of my searching insight. This insight is embodied in my sense observation and in the manipulation of reality by means of my experimenting hands.

Technology also means the organized embodiment of my involvement in reality. This technical embodiment changes reality and subdues it, as it were, to my conscious human self. In other words, I embody not only my own organism, but also the world. My culture becomes my second body. Consequently, also, the world of science and technology is an unique expression of the emotional, intellectual, and spiritual presence of man. Suppose that a sole survivor of a shipwreck is stranded on an island and feels himself to be completely alone and forlorn. Suddenly he spies, at the other side of the island, a small house with a garden; a spiral of smoke rises from the chimney on the roof. He is overjoyed and deeply moved, for this home and garden are the very embodiment of a human presence. At this fateful moment, the island is changed for him totally; it becomes at once a human world.

Everywhere in human history we find traces of this embodiment of man. It enables us to reconstruct the psychology of a prehistoric tribe on the basis of the behavioral creations in which they embodied their human selves. Prehistoric grottoes covered with the wall paintings of our ancestors hold a peculiar fascination for us. For we realize that there we communicate with our co-existents who lived thousands of years ago. They are present to us in the rocks and stone in which they embodied their human selves. These human selves are not strange to us but deeply familiar.

Bodily presence to the world means primordially a presence by means of bodily senses and movements. When a man changes an acre of wild prairie into a lovely garden, he is present to the earth, the weeds, and the stones by means of his eyes, his sense of touch, and his ears, all of which are aware of the grit that grinds under his footsteps. He is also present to the earth by means of his measuring walk and his digging, weeding, planting hands. In such ways man and mankind are always embodied and embodying.. It is this continual event of incarnation which changes the world. The active embodiment of the conscious human self by the human race appears to men most strikingly in our own day. Science and technology as the incarnation of human skill and knowledge transform the world at a pace never dreamt of before in the course of our evolution.

To be sure, science is only one mode of existence. Art, for example, is another bodily mode of existence. A striking example is the dance. When I study the development of the dance in primitive tribes, I realize that these people expressively embodied their thoughts, feelings, and attitudes regarding religion, war, childbirth, weddings, rain, and agriculture in their bodily movements. They attempted, moreover, to influence in a magical way the course of events in their world by means of these bodily manifestations. Emotional, experiential uncovering of the world always prevails in the dance as it does in other artistic endeavors. For this reason, art loses its character when it becomes too intellectual, pragmatic, or technical.

As a scientist, however, I aim primordially not at an emotional-experiential uncovering of the world, but at the unveiling of my surroundings by means of a well-organized, planned, and controlled use of bodily senses and movements. When I reflect on this scientific uncovering of reality in the light of what I have already explicated, I realize at once that my empirical, scientific mode of existence is a most human way of being in the world. For it is now clear to me that scientific existence is rooted in the very structure of my nature and my primordial situation. First of all, I am a self-body unity. Therefore, my human way of learning is by means of bodily senses and movements. Even as an infant I tried out all things by tasting, chewing, touching, throwing, looking, hearing. I experimented all day long and mastered my world in the course of this process. I was an incipient scientist. Science is always a controlled, planned, and organized bodily participation in that which is bodily given. On the other hand, that which is in no way observable can be made an object of science only when it is made observable. Scientific knowledge, therefore, remains in principle dependent on externally observable data.

This necessity of bodily mediation moves the scientist to invent instruments which expand the power of his bodily senses and movements. Such expansion is the necessary condition for new discoveries and for new forms of cultivation and utilization of reality. The scientist invents microscopes to increase the power of his eyes so that he may knowingly embody himself in the microcosmos. He constructs telescopes as a prolongation of his seeing organism so that he may be present in space. He develops space craft to prolong his bodily movements so that he may dwell in thoughtful observation among the stars.

This tremendous development of observational power is inspired and maintained by the most fundamental drive in man, the drive to exist, to participate in being, to embody himself in reality. Embodiment, incarnation, bodily participation, is a very deep urge in mankind. All human activities and inventions are its expression.

The Scientific Mode of Existence

If I wish to understand my scientific mode of being, I must first of all clarify the similarities and dissimilarities between my original and my scientific existence. Second, I must demonstrate precisely how I change from an original to a scientific attitude.

Pre-Reflective and Reflective Mode of Living

I am necessarily and spontaneously oriented toward the world. Through my presence to the world, the veils of reality are removed; in this sense, existence is unveiling and revealing. It is my essence, my very nature to be a revealer of reality. In my encounter with the world, reality is revealed and made meaningful to me. My every encounter with a person, a dog, a tree, a desk, or even a stick brings to light some aspect of reality. I call such revealing encounter experience. Experience is thus any revealing presence to any reality whatsoever. The expressions, "I experienced cold and hunger," "It was a great experience," and "I experienced the dullness of a rainy day," all imply perception of some reality, a presence to some manifestation of all that is. In this perception, meaning is unveiled: experience is my revealing presence to the world.

This primary awareness, this meaning-giving experience, is pre-reflective. Pre-reflective means that I am familiar with a person or thing as a part of my lived world, as something that belongs to my spontaneous experience. I have not yet thought about what this person or thing that I am meeting *is*. If I do think about it, my pre-reflective knowledge becomes reflective.

Reflective knowledge arises from a consideration of, or bending-back upon, my experience. For example, during a single day I may move my car out of the garage, shovel snow, say "Hello" to a neighbor, and feel shocked by news of the stock market. Each of these incidents leads to meaningful behavior on my part. I know each one of these situations because they belong to my world and I respond to them spontaneously. But it is only in reflection on the experience of these situations that I know them fully and clearly and that I am able to communicate this knowledge verbally.

In my reflection on experience I "thematize" it. That is, I direct my conscious *attention* toward a particular experience. In this reflection I become more fully present to the meaning of the reality which is revealed to me in my experience. Only now I am able to express to *myself* and to others the meaning which I unveiled in my meeting with reality.

Interrelationships of the Pre-Reflective and Reflective Modes of Being

My pre-reflective and reflective modes of being in the world are interconnected. For I can reflect only on what I have experienced. This is also true of my scientific knowledge, which is a special mode of reflective existence. Science necessarily presupposes experience and is always concerned with some aspect of it. In scientific reflection I place myself at a distance from that particular aspect of the world about which I am thinking. But I am at the same time the person who first discovered this aspect by being in the world and with this aspect of it. Moreover, when I am no longer involved in scientific reflection, I fall back into this original mode of being in reality; I continue to live in my everyday world as I did before my scientific study. As a scientist, I objectify, I thematize certain aspects of my experience; but in living my daily life, I am involved in the world and my life merges with it. For example, as a medical diagnostician I thematize and objectify that aspect of my perception of the hand of a patient that reveals it as a vulnerable structure of bones, nerves, joints, and muscles. I do so by using a system of abstract physiological categories. After my scientific work is finished, however, I fall back into my original daily mode of existence. While I tenderly caress the hand of my wife or sweetheart, I do not reflect on its muscular composition and its innervation by blood vessels and nerves.

Let us cite another example. In my everyday life I participate in my family situation and engage spontaneously in behavior which will motivate my boisterous offspring to go to bed at the proper hour. My personal participation in the situation teaches me how to handle it adroitly. As a psychologist, however, when I begin to think about effective relationships between parents and children, I may turn into an object of scientific reflection the spontaneous manner in which I persuade my children to sleep. Such scientific psychology is not given with my experience of life; it is the analysis, the unfolding, the objectification of a certain aspect of my experience of life. Psychology, like the other sciences, is ultimately rooted in my situated experience, which is related to my being a behaving body.

Therefore, I can devise scientific psychological constructs and theories only by virtue of an analogy with, or opposition to, the pre-reflective psychological relationships in which I have lived. Even when I do so, I remain rooted in my original mode of being in the world. My scientific view, therefore, always remains a view taken from a particular situation. I who make scientific statements about the world am the same person who lives perceptively and experimentally in the world. I seek light in both ways. My scientific constructs, judgments, and theories cannot substitute for the experience which emerges in my original presence in the world. Consequently, it is not so-called "bare facts" which are the starting point of science, but my pre-scientific experience. Thus there should exist a unity of reciprocal implication between my scientific and pre-scientific modes of being. When my scientific statements are totally divorced from my primary perception, they no longer make sense. For all scientific reflection is a reflection on my experience and my world. As a scientist I attempt within certain limits to understand something of the world in which I live, and I form scientific concepts which throw light on this world. Therefore, science can be made intelligible only from the standpoint of my original field of experience. For all my scintific and reflective knowledge is rooted in the dialogue between reality and me, and therefore presupposes the fundamental fact of my existence as a giver of meaning. This original field of awareness is the origin and purpose of all science.

For example, structures of behavior are available to me as a scientific psychologist because I myself, as a bodily behaving subject, am involved in intentional behavior in daily life. Therefore, the way in which I behave intentionally in the world cannot be irrelevant to the way in which I pursue psychology. My attitude toward behavior arises somehow from my pre-reflective existence. I experience behavior in myself and in others in a certain way; it reveals itself to me under certain aspects. All this is still prior to my explicit psychological judgments. However, these judgments have roots only when they are related to my original experience. I can be a scientific psychologist only from the standpoint of my particular situation. A psychologist today may consider the same behavior as the psychologist of fifty years ago, but he does so in a different historical and cultural situation. Consequently, the intentional behavior itself in its concrete form and appearance becomes different. For example, since Western humanity has learned much about unconscious influences on behavior from psychoanalysis, intentional behavior itself appears different to man than it did before the historical emphasis on unconscious drives.

Theory: Pre-Reflective and Reflective

The shift from original to scientific existence is not a change from "pure" unstructured experience to structure or theory. Primary experience itself already implies pre-reflective, spontaneous theorizing. In my daily dealings with reality I am guided by certain spontaneous considerations; in pre-reflective life I am not only a doer but also a planner. When I am forced to park my car in a small area, I move smoothly and carefully. As an experienced driver I do not sit down and reflect on the exact distance between the cars, on the measurements of my car, on the speed of my wheels. I am immediately present to the situation: I plan my practical movements pre-reflectively. This designing, projecting, and maneuvering is implicit in my practical behavior and characterizes my daily dealing with life situations. My immediate view of the parking situation transforms itself into a pre-reflective design or theory. Guided by a spontaneous scanning of the mutual relationships between such elements as the number of cars, the size of the parking area, the traffic situation, and the manipulation of the steering wheel, I know how to move in without scratching paint or fenders. The scheme according to which my pre-scientific theorizing develops may be characterized by the conditional relation: if . . . then . . . *If* I want to park between these two cars, *then* I must turn my wheel thus in this direction. Through such pre-scientific planning, I become clearly aware of my situation. Thus, the intention of my pre-theoretical planning is not to know the characteristics of cars, parking areas, and steering wheels as such, but rather to know them as they are practically relevant to my efficient orientation. Pre-reflective theory is thus praxis-oriented. Such practical theorizing involves my past experience. I have parked my car before, I have observed other people parking cars, and I have heard about the parking of cars. This past experience is made available to me in my pre-reflective theorizing.

Such implicit, pre-reflective surveying of daily life situations is also characteristic of pre-reflective psychology. When I need to obtain some immediate service from a moody person, I do not make a reflective analysis of his temperament and the possible factors in his past which led up to his disagreeable disposition. My practical need for immediate service mobilizes not only my present perception of the situation but also my *past* experience with moody fellowmen and my *future* possibility of obtaining the service required within the next moment. Before I know it reflectively, I find myself already engaged in behavior that placates the moody person and stimulates his willingness to be of service. My practical lived psychology is thus functional and praxis-oriented rather than speculative and insight-oriented. The difference between the two is striking when an emergency situation suddenly compels me to shift back from a scientific-theoretical to a pre-reflective, practical-theoretical attitude.

Suppose, for example, I am studying scientifically the nature and number of hallucinations in hospitalized patients. When a disturbed patient unexpectedly attacks me with a knife, I shift suddenly from theoretical reflection on hallucinations to a rapid pre-reflective scanning of the situation. This spontaneous survey guides my immediate, efficient handling of the emergency. In this case the reflective, scientific approach could mean the end of both me and the situation! While the ineffectiveness of reflective theory in this situation is too obvious to be stated, it should be noted that it is basically impractical because it takes me partly out of the situation, because I am not totally involved in it. Instead, I confine myself to observation of only certain aspects of it, such as the scientific nature and number of hallucinations. I see the situation only from a specific viewpoint, in this case that of the categories of psychopathology. This attitude in psychological research reveals to me only one area of reality and leaves out all other aspects. In a practical life situation, however, I can plan efficiently only when I spontaneously take into account all aspects which are relevant to my practical purpose, which in the case above is the immediate escape from a dangerous threat.

I have made a distinction in the example given between an efficient presence to the situation as a whole in the light of a practical purpose, and my presence to certain aspects detached from the situation in the light of abstract scientific categories. When I am engaged in scientific, psychopathological research which aims at the identification of certain categories, I abstract from the person as a whole and from his life situation. I am not concerned with his worries, hopes, dreams, his appearance, or his dislike of the situation. I detach from this whole human situation only those aspects which are relevant to my psychopathological study of the scientific nature and frequency of hallucinatory symptoms in a certain group of patients. All other aspects are left out of consideration. In daily life, however, when I interact with my friend, my wife, or my child I am spontaneously open to many other aspects, and it is almost impossible for me to abstract from them. This is one of the reasons why medical doctors and psychotherapists do not usually treat the members of their own families. It is almost impossible for them to shift from their daily involved attitude to the detached scientific one in regard to the same persons.

In the reflective-theoretical as well as in the scientific attitude, I adopt an entirely new standpoint with regard to people, whereby I acquire a totally new viewpoint about their behavior. This viewpoint in turn produces a completely new type of comprehension by which certain types of behavior are seen simply and solely as given incidences of psychopathological categories which may be computed statistically. This shift in comprehension consists in the act of detaching these aspects of behavior from their natural context by no longer conceiving them in their relation to the whole of the particular life situation of the unique, individual person.

When I enumerate incidences of hallucinatory behavior in a statistical survey, I disregard not only any possible application of these incidences to the behavior of the person and of the people related to him in everyday life, but also the relative position which this behavior might have within the psychological make-up of the person as a whole. For my research, the life situation as a whole does not matter. The aspect of behavior which I am studying is for me no longer within the life situation; it has become a statistical moment, an incident which is in no way distinguished from similar incidents recorded in books in my library. In this way behavior is stripped of its concrete situational determinations. I no longer consider a particular aspect of behavior in the perspective of an application based on a given life situation. The advantage of this attitude is that I am able to describe and determine with precision the structural moments of simply-and-solely given psychopathological behavior.

Let us take another example. I am learning the Greek alphabet. I can express this experience of learning in two ways which are fundamentally different. I may say, "It is fascinating to learn that intriguing alphabet from that encouraging teacher whom I like so much." So speaking, I experience my learning as my lived relationship to a meaningful situation with many elements which appeal to me. On the other hand, I may say, "Learning is a function of reinforcement." In this case I no longer consider my personal learning as a lived role within a full life situation brimming with a variety of meanings. I see it rather as a psychological construct which is subject to psychological laws and which fits into a neatly defined theoretical-psychological system. Compared to the first statement, the second one represents a shift in standpoint: my learning has been detached from the whole of a life situation within which it emerged; now it is considered as nothing but a psychological event which is simply-and-solely given, independent of any individual life situation.

In this latter perspective it no longer makes sense to state that learning is fascinating and that a teacher is encouraging. The only meaningful statement which can now be made is a statistical expression of the degree of reinforcement needed for a certain degree of increase in retention. This shift of standpoint is neither the outcome of the fact that I have actually ceased to learn the Greek alphabet, nor of the fact that I have abstracted from such possible practical learning. The only possible explanation is that I have assumed an entirely new standpoint with regard to my learning, whereby I acquire a totally new viewpoint toward it. This viewpoint in turn leads to a completely new type of comprehension by which learning is seen as a quantifiable process of behavior, as simply-and-solely given. This shift in my comprehension is the act of detaching the behavior of learning from the lived learning situation by no longer conceiving it in its concrete relationship to the whole situation.

When I express in statistics or graphs that a certain degree of retention is correlated with a certain degree of reinforcement, I disregard not only the possible application of this fact to personal situations like learning the Greek alphabet from an encouraging teacher, but also the position which learning might have within my particular life situation. In my scientific research, the possible application and concrete position of learning behavior have no significance, for behavior is no longer perceived within the world of everyday life. I may also reverse this statement and say that the position of learning behavior has become a theoretical construct within a theory of learning related to other theoretical constructs. It is no longer posited in a real lived world, but in an ideal, intellectual, abstract world, a man-made universe of discourse. The reflective theoretical mode of existence thus differs greatly from the pre-reflective theoretical one. The reflective-theoretical mode is no longer an implicit, spontaneous guide to practical behavior in a life situation as pre-reflective theory was.

Reflective theory implies an explicit, systematic attention to a selected aspect of a situation. It thus presupposes a shift of attitude, a second look. In behavioral science this means that I take behavior out of its natural lived context, out of the frame of my original world, and that I separate it from its life situation. From that moment on, this behavior appears as no longer related to the individual living person. I can now manipulate it experimentally, empirically, and statistically within the artificial situation of a theoretical system or experimental design. I establish as it were a new abstract context, a world of constructs, an artificial space for this incident of behavior that I have lifted out of its situation. I can now relate it to other similar incidences of behavior which have been isolated in the same way.

My scientific-theoretical approach always implies a certain viewpoint. As a scientist I see people, animals, plants, and minerals differently than I do as a spontaneous, unreflective participant in daily life. The reality encountered in my original mode of existence is brimming with meaning, but as a scientist I select only certain meanings of reality as the focus of my investigations. These objective meanings of reality which I can select as matter for study are manifold. Thus I can develop a wide range of scientific concerns, each of which is related to a different objective meaning of reality. Each one leads, therefore, to a specific well-organized system of thought and perception. As a scientist I thus restrict my perception of reality by asking only certain well-defined questions. The possible replies of "what-is" to these specific questions are correspondingly limited by the specificity of the questions asked. Consequently, the answers of reality will reveal only certain of its manifold aspects. Finally, all these specific answers together will be gradually integrated within a specific system of meaning, a comprehensive theory, a body of scientific truth, a science.

In other words, a specific science does not reveal "all-that-is" but only one realm of objectivity. This area of being is defined by the fundamental concern of the science in question. Therefore, every science constitutes its own objective world which is different from that of all other sciences. The differences between the sciences are thus based on the differences between the questions asked and the correspondingly isolated profiles of reality. Therefore, a complete conformity in aim, method, or results of the various sciences is in principle and in fact impossible. Fundamentally different questions lead to fundamentally different answers or systems of meaning. And fundamentally different systems of meaning cannot be added together, just as we cannot add cows, cobwebs, rivers, and rockets together with any meaning. For the same reason, it is unthinkable and even impossible to reduce one system of meaning to another system of meaning; for example, psychology to physiology, or biology to physics. Such a reduction would be as impossible as the transformation of tulips to dresses, or vegetables to glass. If the reduction of one science to another is successful, it proves only that the science which is reduced either has not yet found itself as a particular quest for reality or has abandoned its own quest. In such a case, it is not yet a differential science in its own right with its own system of meaning, with its own inalienable methods which are the subtle elaborations of the unique questions asked by the representatives of the science in question.

I may conclude that the characteristic property of my theoretical-scientific existence is that I confine myself to an observation of the world without thereby being totally involved in the world. This reflective theoretical observation always implies that I take a specific attitude toward reality. Correspondingly, reality that is encountered in this way is always seen from a specific viewpoint. Which of its aspects reality will reveal to me as a reflective theoretical observer depends on my attitude with regard to reality. If I select a certain aspect or profile as the object of critical and methodical investigation, I lay the foundations of a specific science. By my attitude towards reality, I as a scientist begin to delimit an area of reality as the domain of my research. The precise differentiation of such a well-defined area from every other domain of investigation is my first step in scientific research.

The objective of every science thus represents a separated and well delineated domain that in turn is differentiated in sub-domains. These differentiations of a science are constituted by various perspectives which are taken in regard to the common objective of the science; they thus imply a differentiation of the common perspective. For example, the objective of psychology as a whole is intentional-functional behavior, while differential psychologies such as learning theory, psychoanalysis, and introspectionism approach this common objective from various viewpoints which are still possible within the common perspective.

Every new phenomenon which emerges in a science is examined to the degree that it conforms to the normative object-coherence of the specific science. For example, the phenomenon of religion is examined in psychology to the degree of its relevance for the understanding of intentional-functional behavior; beyond this, the study of religion is left to theology and other disciplines. Similarly, the phenomenon of brain waves is studied in psychology only insofar as it reveals intentional-functional behavior; beyond this, it is the domain of neurophysiology, biochemistry, and related sciences.

Criterion of Selection

As a scientist, I restrict myself necessarily to one of many possible viewpoints which emerge in my encounter with reality. Through my selection of a specific viewpoint, I limit that which was originally given in my experience. My objects in science are not objects which are given to me as such in primary perception; they are the results of my specific selective orientation toward reality. My original perception does not know about the objects of science, about H_2O, atoms, molecules, reinforcement, and Oedipal constellations; it does know about rivers, houses, trees, birds, flowers, love, hate, jealousy, and anxiety.

When I decide to consider certain realities from specific scientific viewpoints, I limit my perception of them by my scientific frame of reference. They are no longer what they were. So-called exact data are rather scientific interpretations of my primary experience. Scientific thinking foregoes primary experience instead of penetrating it. The scientific view of man and the world is thus the result of a certain modification of the human attitude. Science modifies my primary perception fundamentally. This selection of a certain viewpoint in my encounter with reality is dependent on me and on the community of scientists. I am not forced by reality to change my original mode of being into a scientific concentration on only this or that aspect of reality. It is I who decide to prefer one objective aspect of reality to other aspects as the focus of my methodical investigation. There are many factors involved in the selection of a scientific viewpoint, such as an implicit or explicit philosophy, the "Zeit Geist", the practical needs of society, the temperament and disposition of the scientist concerned, social pressures, and the cultural language with its built-in preference for certain phenomena, values, and goals.

This selection of a specific objective moment of man's perception as a focus of intellectual attention is not yet a science, but only the possible beginning of a science. The delineation of the field of inquiry, however, is of the utmost importance and must be repeated many times during the development of the science in question. For it is not always clear in the beginning what the exact aims and proper methods of a specific science are. A science is fully established in its own right when its scientists have discovered which objective and which corresponding methodology make their science fundamentally different from all other actual and possible sciences. As long as this delineation is not yet achieved by a science, there is always the danger that its scientists may exceed the limits of their proper interest and competence. If a science does not clearly comprehend its own proper mode of questioning reality, it will be unaware of its own limits. Consequently, it may become involved in questions which do not pertain to its primary interest and which transcend its competence. This happened, for example, when theologians attempted to tell scientists that the earth was the center of the universe. It happened again when Sigmund Freud insisted that religion was only a neurosis.

Every science, then, should discover and make explicit the object of its fundamental interest. In this way, it will avoid intruding upon other special modes of grasping reality. Outside the boundaries of its own special interest, a science is not able to speak with authority. It may happen that, as the representative of a new science, I am not yet clear about the special interest, method, and area of investigation of my science. As a result, I and my fellow scientists may be attracted by the concerns, aims, and methods of another successful science which reveals a quite different profile of reality. I do not refer merely to being enlightened by the methods of another science or attempting to adapt them to my own domain of exploration. This is commendable and fruitful. Nor do I refer to the obvious fact that my research benefits from information obtained by other sciences. I have in mind the situation in which I, as the insecure representative of a young science, am absorbed by the objectives and methodology of an established older science to such a degree that I lose sight of the objectivated profile of my own scientific endeavor. Early physicists, for example, were at times philosophers of nature; alchemists became mythologists; and psychologists sometimes slipped into physiology or biology.

There is nothing blameworthy about shifting from one area of scientific investigation to another so long as the scientists are aware that they are leaving their former field of concentration. They should then make it explicit to themselves and to others that they are no longer speaking as, say, physicists or psychologists. However, they may mistakenly believe that they are still speaking as physicists or psychologists while they are in fact revealing philosophical, mythological, physiological, or biological aspects of reality. To be sure, what they reveal in this way may be extremely valuable for humanity and for the development of philosophy, mythology, physiology, and biology.

However, when psychologists who shift to another science stubbornly insist that in doing so they are revealing the psychological or behavioral aspect of human reality, they may considerably delay the development of psychology itself. This insistence is especially harmful when their methods are valid and impressive, when their findings foster scientific understanding of non-psychological aspects of man, when their communication of methods and results is lucid, convincing, and clear. The measure of their achievement may be the measure of postponement of the day on which psychology will discover itself as a science in its own right, with its own unambiguous fundamental interest which will render it irreducibly different from any other science of man. Many psychologists may give up the arduous endeavor of establishing the identity of their own science. They may lose the courage to bear the ambiguities, uncertainties, and awkward beginnings which are unavoidable when humanity embarks on a new science, a new adventure of exploration.

It is in a formal definition that a science explicitly states its own unique perception of reality, the object of its fundamental interest, and its proper mode of questioning the world. By discovering its own limits, a science not only avoids trespassing on the proper concern of another science, but also uncovers the specific area in which it should concentrate its effort. A clear awareness of their fundamental interest prevents scientists from dissipating their talents and energies in areas which do not pertain to their field.

Further Conditions of Scientific Development

A science is formed originally by a specific attitude of man toward a particular aspect of reality, but this attitude alone does not constitute a science. For it is quite possible for man to question an aspect of reality in a specific way without doing so in a scientific way. For example, a child acts in a naïve and primitive manner when he explores the mechanism of his father's watch, but no one would say that his efforts constitute a science.

At least four conditions must be fulfilled before I can dignify a specific mode of questioning reality with the name of science. In order that a way of knowing be considered scientific, it must be methodical, critical, communal, and integrational. A fifth condition must be added for the empirical sciences, namely observation and experience. Only when these conditions are present does a science exist in the proper sense of the term. Let us consider these five conditions briefly.

My scientific concentration on a profile or aspect of reality differs from my casual, haphazard, or incidental attention in that it is planned, systematic, orderly, and coherent. It develops methods, tools, and techniques with which I can handle systematically the special profile of my scientific attention. My every-day knowledge is frequently naïve, inexact, and influenced by myth, folklore, and superstition. In daily life I have neither the time nor the ability to subject all my knowledge to critical evaluation. As a scientist, however, I critically evaluate every step in the process which leads to the uncovering of the aspect of reality I have selected.

As a scientist, moreover, I am not engaged in an isolated effort. I share in the fruits of the efforts of countless dedicated men of the past and the present. This communal aspect of science also makes possible the necessary inter-subjective check on my scientific work. I need this possibility of control and correction in order to prevent or to rectify the influence of my personal bias. My scientific endeavor also has an integrational aspect. I strive by nature for a coherent and orderly comprehension of the manifold discoveries of the community of scientists. The ultimate objective of every science is understanding and explanation. This is possible only on the basis of an explicit discovery and formulation of the unifying factors and universal characteristics which bind the disconnected facts related to the science into an ordered and comprehensive system. In every science, it is theory which performs this task of unification.

Psychology, for example, reveals two types of scientific theory, namely differential and comprehensive theories. A differential theory aims to bind together the data and insights which are discovered in a differential psychology such as psychoanalysis, behaviorism, or introspectionism. Comprehensive theory, in turn, integrates the theories and discoveries of the various differential psychologies. Every science is thus a methodical, critical, communal, and integrational investigation of certain well-defined moments of experience.

For the empirical sciences we must add the specific condition that the moment of perception selected as a focus of attention must always be observable by the senses. An empirical science may become predominantly theoretical, abstract, and quantifying, as in the case of quantum physics or learning theory in psychology. Yet it always starts from some original sense perception of my world or of my body as I find them in everyday life. There is no other basis from which science can arise. All that I know "scientifically" about the physical world is inferred from certain selected phenomena in the perceived world. This world remains my ultimate and only basis for statements about physical facts. My only way of exploring quantifiable, physical aspects of reality is that of observing objective perceptions and inferring from them the proper conclusions. This is true not only of physics but of all empirical sciences. My knowledge of physiology, for instance, depends upon my observations of what I call a body in direct perceptual experience. All my scientific constructs and observations are somehow contained in or derived from direct perception, and all scientific terms which I use in agreement with my fellow scientists ultimately refer to the same source. Immediate perception is the raw material of all sciences.

We may conclude that science is developed by methodical investigation of selected observable moments of perception; by critical evaluation of every one of its scientific procedures and discoveries; by the subjection of its results to the test of intersubjective agreement in the community of scientists; and finally by the integration of its insights and discoveries in differential and comprehensive theories.

CHAPTER TWO

THE SCIENCE OF PSYCHOLOGY

To discover what the science of psychology is, we must uncover the specific human interest which distinguishes it. Inseparably linked with this interest is the field of investigation which it constitutes. A precise view of this field will prevent the confusion of the specific object pole of psychology with that of any other science.

Our search for what psychology fundamentally is, however, can lead only to provisional conclusions. We can discover only what psychology is at the present stage of its historical development. No scientist knows *a priori* precisely how new discoveries may change our conception of psychology. A premature fixation concerning what this science should be would paralyze its spontaneous growth. In fact, any fixation at any time is premature insofar as the human existent can reach a relative but never a full and final maturity. This general statement is true of psychology as well as all modes of human existence.

The seemingly obvious method of discovering how psychology reveals itself today is observation of the activities of psychologists followed by explication of the specific common interest implicit in their scientific endeavors. It is really not surprising that the theoretical delineation of psychology as a specific mode of interest has been so long delayed by psychologists. It is not necessary for the work of the individual psychologist that he perceive clearly the viewpoint which he takes when he investigates behavior. His specific interest may remain almost totally implicit, absorbed as he is in his experiments or in the diagnosis and treatment of patients. His concrete empirical task itself may leave no time for reflection on what constitutes the essential direction of psychology as a whole.

The same observations may be made of any empirical science. Only when it is well established does it develop an explicit, general, theoretical branch which reflects on its foundations and integrates the activities and data of its scientists in the light of this reflection. The appearance of this unifying, theoretical reflection implies that a science has attained relative autonomy and become aware of itself. Only such a self-conscious science can clarify the confusing interests which obscured its identity during the earlier phases of its hesitant emergence. Many physicists of the past, for example, confused their science with a philosophy of nature which could not be proved or disproved by empirical methods. The coming of age of physics in theoretical physics has lessened this confusion.

Thus it is important for scientific psychology to make explicit the common viewpoint which is implicit in the endeavors of its scientists and which constitutes the science of psychology in the present phase of its evolution. When we observe psychologists in laboratories, clinics, and consulting rooms we become easily aware that they investigate the behavior of animal and man in various situations. Every empirical science requires an externally observable datum as its primary object pole of investigation; behavior is undoubtedly such a datum. When we analyze certain definitions of behavior critically, however, we perceive a contradiction between what psychologists do, or their "lived" psychology, and what some scientific theorists say that psychologists are doing.

Some theoretical scientists, for example, define behavior so comprehensively that any series of externally observable changes in any patricular object falls under their definition. In this case, one may speak indiscriminately of the behavior of molecules, snow, tulip bulbs, or children, a procedure which makes it difficult to distinguish psychology from any other science. A few scientific theorists, such as Harry Hollingworth and Rudolf Carnap, have been aware of this inference and consequently have defined many or even all sciences as sciences of behavior. Evidently, such a definition confuses psychology with other sciences; it does not describe the actual involvements of psychologists today. When we carefully observe the manifold activities of psychologists, we become aware that they almost invariabily study the behavior of animal or man in their laboratories and consulting rooms. No psychologist or psychiatrist up to the present has studied the "behavior" of stars or trees. However, even the restriction of the object of psychology to the behavior of animal and man is not sufficiently exact to prevent the possibility of a confusion of the object pole of psychology with that of other sciences; nor does it make explicit in a precise way the specific interest implicit in the activities of contemporary psychologists.

Behavior, to be sure, is an object of interest for persons as diverse as the beautician, the athletic trainer, the moralist, the philosopher, and the physiologist, as well as the psychologist. They all observe behavior, but their ways of perceiving it are indeed different. The beautician may observe that a certain manner of walking enhances the charm of a lady, while the athletic trainer may note that similar movements facilitate the development of certain muscles. The physiologist may focus his attention on the processes he observes in nerves, muscles, and organs, while the student of ethics may be interested in the moral intentions possibly implied in certain ways of walking. The philosopher, on the other hand, will establish what the behavior of walking is as behavior. The psychologist, finally, will concentrate his interest on that aspect of the activity of walking which we shall later clarify as intentional-functional-behavioral.

The example just given illustrates that our spontaneous, prereflective experience of any behavior implies the awareness of a variety of aspects of this behavior. Each of these aspects can be made explicit by a process of reflection and abstraction. Thus we can set a certain aspect of behavior apart, as it were, from the others in our experience. A scientist can select one of those aspects which he has abstracted from his experience of behavior and make it a specific object of study. Each aspect of behavior selected in this way points potentially to a new science of behavior. Every new science of behavior is thus necessarily different from every other science because it concentrates on a totally different feature. Moreover, it is determined in the development of its language, method, and frame of reference by the specific interest which constitutes this unique feature.

The various sciences of behavior are therefore so distinct that it is impossible for them to oppose one another so long as they remain within their own domains. It is obvious that observers can disagree with one another only when they speak about the same object of observation. When one observer is interested in rockets and another in rivers, there is no possibility of their contradicting each other so long as one reports on rockets and the other on rivers. These two observers move in different phenomenological worlds, in different universes of thought where they will never meet and therefore never confute each other. The same may be said of any two scientists pursuing different sciences of behavior.

Because these diverse perceptions of behavior are based on different points of view, they necessarily create different phenomenological worlds or systems of meaning. Every new manner of perception makes for a new world of meaning which remains inseparably linked to this perception and to the fundamental interest which underlies it. The beautician *as beautician,* therefore, can never affirm something which the athletic trainer denies; nor can the physiologist, so long as he remains within the limits of his special field, pronounce a judgment which the student of ethics, the philosopher, or the psychologist can refute from his respective point of view. Such a contradiction is in principle unthinkable. It is possible only when one of these experts, because of lack of clarity regarding his fundamental object of study, goes beyond the limits of his specialty, confusing two entirely different worlds of meaning. A psychologist who *as psychologist* makes physiological or philosophical statements about behavior can and should be refuted by physiological or philsophical experts. Similarly, a philosopher of behavior who ventures unwittingly into psychological explications of behavior may find himself in disagreement with the psychologist. Contradiction, however, remains impossible in principle so long as each expert moves only in his own field of scientific perception.

The Object Pole of Psychology: Intentional-Functional Behavior

Our spontaneous experience of the behavior of animal and man implies an inexhaustible variety of aspects. Which of these aspects constitutes the object pole of psychology? When we make explicit the various interests of psychologists today in order to uncover those aspects of behavior toward which they implicitly direct themselves, the common object we discover is intentional-functional behavior.

The expression intentional-functional behavior represents *one Gestalt* abstracted from our spontaneous experience of the behavior of animal and man; it constitutes one unified object of investigation for the empirical psychologist. Therefore the intentional, functional, and behavioral aspects should never be perceived as if they were isolated entities. On the contrary, they are interdependent features of the one undivided object pole of psychology. These essential aspects of the object pole influence one another mutually and constantly. They represent an internal differentiation or articulation—not a separation—of one and the same object pole of psychology.

Even though there is no separation of these aspects of behavior, distinction among them is a necessary intellectual operation. Because of the limited, abstract nature of man's intellect, he can obtain a thorough scientific understanding of these aspects only by concentrating his research on one of them at a time. Therefore, the distinction among these aspects is due more to the limitation of man's intellect than to the object pole of his study.

This same innate limitation of the approach to scientific knowledge accounts for the fact that an individual psychologist or a certain group of psychologists may be predominantly interested in the intentional, or the functional, or the behavioral aspects of human and animal behavior as a specialized object of study. Every empirical psychologist studies intentional-functional behavior in at least one of these perspectives.

Some psychologists, however, such as the comprehensive-theoretical and the practicing psychologists, are concerned with all three aspects of the object of psychology in their concrete living unity. Comprehensive theoretical psychology strives for an integrating, over-all view of behavior. Therefore, it is concerned precisely with the unity of and the relations among the intentional, functional, and behavioral aspects. It presents the unity of human behavior. The theoretical psychologist develops scientific constructs in a constant dialogue with the data provided by phenomenological, functional, and behavioral psychology.

It is clear that behavior as a field of study for the contemporary psychologist requires more precise definition in order to distinguish it from behavior as an object of study for other scientists. We have proposed, therefore, to define the specific object of study for the psychologist as intentional-functional behavior of animal and man. We have suggested that this qualified object pole of study corresponds with that in which the majority of recognized psychologists are daily engaged. The behavioral aspect of psychology may be defined as *an essential aspect of the object pole of psychology, consisting of the whole of objectively observable modes of animal and of human response to situations, which manifests the intentionality and functionality of the subject.* The meaning of this definition will be clarified in the following discussion of the terms "intentionality" and "functionality".

Intentionality

The first part of our definition of the behavioral aspect of the object pole of psychology describes behavior as the whole of objectively observable modes of animal and of human response to a situation. Many psychologists would consider this part of our definition as the complete definition of psychology.

They would find it unnecessary and even undesirable to add that observable responses should in some way manifest intentionality and functionality. This addition, however, we maintain to be crucial for the validity of the definition of behavior as the specific field of study for the psychologist. Spasmodic vomiting, for example, when *merely* a consequence and a symptom of food poisoning, would be an objectively observable mode of animal or of human response to a situation. Yet such a response is of interest to the physiologist or medical expert, but not to the psychologist. In other words, not all kinds of observable responses lend themselves to psychological investigation. Only that kind of behavior can be the object pole of scientific psychology which is open to study not only by means of biological, physiological, physical, or philosophical methods, but also by means of typical psychological methods. Precisely what kind of behavior would this be?

Let us cite a simple case. A monkey attempts to reach a banana near its cage. After trial and error, it obtains the banana by the manipulation of an iron rod which has been placed in its cage by an experimenter. This behavior of the monkey affects us immediately as being different in kind from the spasmodic vomiting behavior of an animal after food poisoning. One of the characteristics which we perceive in the food-getting behavior of the monkey is that the whole animal, the animal as tending subject, is involved in this behavior. Another feature is that the animal as subject is tending toward something that is not yet itself, something that promises to fulfill certain needs and therefore acquires the character of a goal of behavior. An attitude of food-directedness is embodied and manifested in the behavior of grasping for food.

We may change this experimental situation by placing the iron rod under an electric charge. The monkey suffers shock when touching the rod and now manifests avoidance behavior in regard to it. A new mode of behavior has been evoked as a response to this threatening situation. This behavior, however, is again characterized by a directedness or orientation. In this case, it is a tending away from the object concerned.

In neither case does the orientation of the monkey reveal itself to our immediate experience as blind, automatic, mechanical, relatively static, or built-in directedness as in the case of the vomiting responses of a food-poisoned animal. The orientation represented by the experiments with the monkey is highly variable; it changes with the varying experience of the striving animal. In other words, some kind of "lived" experience appears in the changing modes of directedness which are exteriorized in the tending behavior. Whether this experience is conscious or only "lived", the experiential quality is present.

We may conclude that the typical behavior which forms the field of study for the psychologist always implies a directing experience of the subject toward some reality, or its engagement in some reality that is not itself. We shall call this quality of directing experience or involvement *intentionality*, and the behavior that demonstrates this quality *intentional behavior*.

This intentionality seems to be present in animal behavior in a different way than it is present in man. The animal behaves *as if* it has recognized certain realities as such in an explicit way. But the animal cannot recognize these realities in an explicit human way. The tending experience of the animal is only toward biologically meaningful Gestalts of stimuli which are given in its biological world and which evoke certain responses based on aroused instinctual needs. Therefore, intentionality in animal and in man is not similar but analogous. Man is intentional in the most proper and the deepest sense. The intentionality of the animal seems to be a shadow or an image of man's intentionality.

Intentionality and the Nature of Man

Intentionality in man seems to be so bound up with his very essence that a deep phenomenological insight into his nature is necessary to clarify the character and scope of his intentionality. Therefore, we shall discuss intentionality as a fundamental feature of human existence. As we shall demonstrate later, no science is developed without a basis of axiomatic assumptions which can be neither proved nor disproved by the empirical methods of the science itself. These assumptions are usually built-in, as it were, in the methodology of the science, which always implies a certain axiomatic view of nature and of knowledge. A comparatively new science, such as psychology, must make explicit its implicit assumptions in order to expose them to critical evaluation.

One of the implicit assumptions of psychology is that man is born with a potential openness or perceptivity for reality as it manifests itself in him and his surroundings. This natural dynamic perceptivity enables man to discover a variety of meanings in the manifold life situations within which he encounters reality under its many aspects. These meanings are dynamic, that is, they tend to initiate psychological functioning and behaving. A man who perceives a situation as threatening, for example, will feel and act differently from one who understands a situation as pleasant or amusing. Therefore, the study of perception of reality, of meanings and intentions, is of central importance for the understanding of behavior. The fact that man tends to discover varied aspects and concrete meanings in reality is due to his very nature: man *is* always and necessarily intentional; he *is* orientation, directedness to the world; he *is* potential openness for all-that-is.

The very possibility of hallucinations, illusions, and delusions confirms this basic fact of human existence. It is so essential for man to "intend" a reality, a world, that he is forced to create some kind of delusional universe if the surrounding world becomes too threatening for him because of his emotional problems. This reality-directed involvement which man *is,* is not necessarily an *explicit* awareness of his "lived" reality. For man usually experiences reality initially in a pre-reflective or preconscious way. In other words, the actualized intentionality of man is first of all "lived" experience. Man may express this primary "lived" experience in judgments. When he does so, he makes expressly conscious that which was at first implicit awareness. We may call this experience reflective intentionality. Thus man is always basically intentional, either implicitly or explicitly.

This fundamental intentionality of man actualizes itself, however, in many and varied involvements in his encounter with the world. For reality itself manifests innumerable aspects giving rise to a potentially infinite number of meanings. No man, therefore, can perceive all the aspects of reality or exhaust all its possible meanings. Actually, man is always limited in his presence to reality. He is restricted in his modes of perception by the structure of his body and his senses. He is also circumscribed by time and space because he belongs to a specific culture, which is in a certain phase of its development, and which has embodied its traditional intentionalities in a specific language. He is constricted, moreover, in his locations and surroundings. In addition, he himself limits his actual perception by the individual *interests* which he chooses and develops in his personal history. His actual intentionality is further restricted by his practical commitment to a world of work or a profession. Finally, man is limited by reflective or pre-reflective needs, desires, drives, and conflicts and by the particular phase of psycho-physiological development which he has reached at any given moment.

In short, man *is* a radical or fundamental intentionality directed toward all reality. His actual intentions, however, are always limited though amazing in variety. It is the business of the philosopher to dwell on the characteristic openness of man for being. The psychologist, however, studies the forms and contents of actual intentions as they appear in the functioning and behavior of man.

We are now ready to define precisely the term *intentional* as it is used within the context of our definition of psychology. *Intentional refers to those reflective and pre-reflective modes of experiential involvement in any reality whatsoever which are somehow manifest in behavior.* The latter part of our definition, which states that the modes of intentionality which the psychologist studies should be in some way "manifest in behavior" requires a brief clarification.

We have already seen in our discussion of science that an empirical science is concerned with data which are given in sense perception. Therefore, intentionality can be an object of empirical psychology only if it is present in some way in patterns of behavior which can be observed by the senses; or in observable products of this behavior such as language, literature, art, social institutions, and cultural customs. These latter bear within themselves the *sediments* of past intentional behavior. Psychology as an empirical science aims at the understanding of all sense-perceived behavior by the investigation of its determinants. The chief determinant of behavior is intentionality; for behavior without intentionality is not behavior but a mechanical process. Consequently, the specific object of the empirical science of psychology is not intentionality as such, but intentional behavior whether manifest in patterns of behavior or in their observable products.

Intentionality as such is an object of study for the philosopher. The theorist in psychology is naturally interested, however, in the ideas of the philosopher who explores the essence of human intentionality in the light of his study of being. The theoretical psychologist considers the relevance of these philosophical concepts for his own theoretical constructs, which he develops in a dialogue with the data of empirical psychology. At times, he may even borrow some of the concepts of the philosopher if these are in conspicuous harmony with the data and laws discovered by the empiricist. But these philosophical views remain for him only assumptions or borrowed hypothetical constructs, which he *as a psychologist* can neither prove nor disprove by means of his own empirical methods. Similarly, he is interested in the studies of the physiologist, which throw light on other conditions of intentional behavior which lie outside the proper domain of psychology. Here, too, he may borrow some of the findings of the physiologist, which likewise remain for him only assumptions which he can neither prove nor disprove through his own science of psychology.

Certain psychologists specialize in the study of the intentional aspect of behavior. They become experts in the methodical and critical explication of the experiences which appear in behavior, and they attempt to establish their intersubjective validity. This special field of psychology is called *phenomenological psychology.*

FUNCTIONALITY

The second essential aspect of the object pole of psychology is functionality which, together with the intentional and behavioral aspects, co-constitutes concrete animal and human behavior. The fact that functionality is a fundamental element in the actual areas of interest of psychologists may be illustrated by the experiment with the monkey cited above. The food-getting behavior of the animal implies an intentionality, an experiential involvement in securing a certain kind of food. The psychologist, however, is interested in much more than this intentionality. He may ask himself many other questions: "How is the intentional behavior of this animal related to outside stimulation, physio-psychological conditions, past behavior, instinctual-biological makeup, and spatial and temporal conditions? By means of what processes and functional structures does this intentionality become observable behavior? How is this intentionality related to other intentionalities? How does behavior reinforce the intentionality? How does intentionality realize itself by changing the environment of the animal? How does this environment, while changing under the impact of intentional behavior, in turn influence further behavior?" These are only a few of a potentially endless series of *how* problems evoked in the student of intentional behavior.

This wide breadth of interest of the empirical psychologist is even more evident in his study of man. The psychologist is better acquainted with the intentional and functional behavior of man because it is his own behavior. When a psychologist studies the intentionality of human love, for example, he first observes its presence in certain perceived or recorded patterns of behavior with which love is identified. His explication of the love which is implicitly present in the behavior of people may presuppose a verbal or even written description of his own love experience. Through such an account, the psychologist transforms his own experience of love into an observable behavioral product which can be compared methodically and critically with exteriorizations of similar intentionalities of love in other people. But the empirical psychologist will not stop here. He will ask himself how the intentionality of love came about. How does it develop under certain conditions in the environment? What does it mean for the other intentionalities of the subject, such as his anxiety, hate, fear, shyness, happiness, sexuality, and emotionality? How does it affect his behavior in various situations in the family, school, office, and places of entertainment? In this case, also, there emerges a never finished series of *how* questions which the psychologist attempts to answer by means of experiments, questionnaires, tests, clinical observations, analyses—in short, by all observational and experimental methods which are available to him or which he himself develops, if necessary, for the research in question.

The search for intentional behavior is predominantly a *what* question. The search for the relationships between various intentional patterns of behavior; between intentional behavior and situations; between intentionality and the other two essential aspects of behavior; between intentionalities themselves; and between past, present, and future patterns of intentional behavior, situations, and intentionalities is not primarily a *what* question. It is predominantly a *how* question, a search for working relationships. In other words, the psychologist is interested not only in the *what* of intentional behavior, but also in its functional aspect.

Functionality, to be sure, is only one aspect of the object pole of psychology. Because it is merged inseparably with the intentional aspect of behavior, we use a hyphen between the terms "intentional" and "functional" to express their essential unity. This unity explains why psychological functioning is always dynamically present in its functional-behavioral realization in a situation. There is no real separation between the two, but only an intellectual distinction which is dependent on the presence of certain articulations in behavior.

Similarly, the psychological functional structures which enable man to realize his intentionality in behavior are essentially different from physical, physiological, and biological functional structures. Numerous philosophers and psychologists—Bergson, Husserl, Heidegger, Merleau-Ponty, Lavelle, Nogue, von Weiszäcker, Minkowski, Strasser, Buytendijk, Straus, Linschoten, Graumann, Plessner, James, Stern, Hönigswald, Pradines, Koffka, and Van der Horst—have demonstrated that the "lived" space and the "lived" time structures which enable the intentional subject to function psychologically are essentially different from geometrical space and mathematical time structures in the framework of which the objects of physics and technology function.

Functionality and the Nature of Man

We have related the various intentionalities of man to one another and integrated them in one hypothetical basic construct, namely the fundamental intentionality which we assume to be identified with man's essence. An analogous statement may be made concerning man's psychological functionality. For when we attempt to discover just how this functionality is rooted in man's nature, we are no longer in the purely empirical stage of psychology. We are moving into the area of fundamental assumptions which are made explicit in that branch of comprehensive-theoretical psychology which we call theory of foundations.

Let us assume that man *is* intentional functionality. This hypothetical assumption provides us with a useful explanatory foundation for the unity of intentionality and functionality in his behavior. For man's intentionality is not devoid of dynamism. The hypothetical construct of intentionality means not only that man is "*in*-the-world" but also that he is "*at*-the-world." Man's intentionality is not a static quality but a dynamic tendency. Therefore, man's subjective experiential involvement in reality implies that he, as selfbody unity, tends toward reality in a behavioral way. His intentionality constantly spurs him on to realize himself by partaking in reality as it manifests itself, assimilating and appropriating it. On the other hand, the same dynamic intentionality drives him to express himself in his surrounding reality, to insert himself meaningfully in the world, to humanize the world.

According to this assumption, man's functionality is the essential dynamic aspect of his intentionality. And because of the fact that man *is* always a bodily subjectivity, both intentionality and functionality are inseparably present in behavior, which is a bodily mode of being in the world.

To be sure, psychology does not dwell on intentional functionality insofar as it is an essential feature of man's nature. Psychology is not philosophy. However, theoretical psychology may use the philosophical concept of "essential functionality" as one of its hypothetical explanatory principles. Such a concept may be useful for the theoretical integration of the concrete intentional-functional-behavioral relationships which the psychologist discovers in his empirical research. What the psychologist as empiricist is chiefly concerned with, however, is man's concrete intentional-behavioral functioning in family, school, business, church, and other life situations. He is interested in the concrete normal and abnormal developments of this functioning and in the development of psychological functional structures. He is also concerned with the organismic and environmental conditions of this development.

Experimental psychologists specialize in the study of these functional relationships. Some of them are interested predominantly in the functional relationships between stimulating situation and behavior. We may call them behavioral-experimental psychologists insofar as their interest emphasizes the behavioral aspect. Other experimental psychologists search primarily for the functional relationships between the intentional aspect of behavior and the situation, or between the intentional aspects of various kinds of behavior. We may identify this group as clinical, social, or humanistic experimental psychologists. The specialized interests and endeavors of both groups of functional psychologists are necessary for the progress of their science. The same may be said of the scientific endeavors of phenomenological psychologists. The essential limitation of man's scientific way of knowing—which is always knowledge by abstraction—makes it necessary for psychology to evolve by differentiating itself in specialties.

At times, the expert who is committed to one or the other abstract aspect of behavior may lose sight of the whole. But even the overestimation of the value of his own specialty may be advantageous for the development of psychology as a whole insofar as it stimulates his complete dedication to his own field of study. However, this one-sidedness will remain fruitful for the development of psychology only when it is balanced by a well-developed branch of comprehensive theoretical psychology. The latter specializes in the whole, and keeps the dialogue open between comprehensive theoretical constructs and assumptions on the one hand, and differential theories and data of phenomenological, experimental, and clinical psychologists on the other.

We are now prepared to define precisely the functional component of behavior. *The functional aspect of behavior is an essential aspect of the object pole of psychology which refers to an individual totality of changes elicited by a reflective or pre-reflective intentionality, and which co-constitutes with this intentionality certain objectively observable modes of behavior.*

Applied Psychology

The common denominator of basic interest implicitly present in the scientific endeavors of recognized empirical psychologists is incorporated in the statement that psychology is the science of intentional-functional behavior. The practice of applied psychology is specifically related to this definition.

We use the term *applied psychology* to refer to the work of psychiatrists and psychotherapists and of clinical, educational, and industrial psychologists. An efficient application of the science of psychology to the problems of daily life presupposes an understanding of the intentionality and functionality of the individuals concerned and of the embodiment of these characteristics in patterns of behavior. It is clear that the methods and findings of phenomenological, functional, and behavioral psychologies facilitate this kind of understanding. For example, the discoveries of these psychologies concerning the intentionality, functionality, and behavioral patterns of specific age and cultural groups can obviously enlighten the practicing psychologist in his observation of human beings.

The practicing psychologist, however, does not restrict himself to the application of the methods and findings of academic psychology. He frequently involves himself in a type of research which is more directly related to the understanding of particular individuals and groups. He may also dedicate himself to the development of instruments and techniques. Some of these psychological techniques aim at the exteriorization of inner experiences; others foster change in the behavior of animal and man. An example of the first is the evolvement of techniques for interviewing and testing; examples of the latter are the development of therapeutic techniques and of machines for programmed learning.

When we first consider the highly individualized type of research which aims at clarification of the behavior of patients and clients, it may seem that such individual understanding does not relate to the object pole of psychology as it has been defined. A large number of psychiatrists, as well as clinical and analytical psychologists, daily study the disturbed experiences of patients. It seems to the casual observer that these clinicians are interested in unperceivable experiences and not in the behavior which expresses these intentionalities. A closer observation, however, reveals that they too study the experience and functionality of man insofar as these are objectivated in the observable behavior or in behavioral products such as free associations, test protocols, narration of dreams, facial and postural expressions, play behavior, role playing, oral or written reports of experiencing, and other exteriorizations of intentional-functional involvement.

The other type of research in applied psychology, as stated above, is the development of instruments and techniques for the behavioral exteriorization of inner experiences, or for the promotion of change in the intentional-functional behavior of individuals and groups. It is our contention not only that this type of research is proper to psychology, but also that it contributes at least as much to the growth of the science as academic research does, although in a different fashion.

Academic research in its pure form discovers and makes explicit intentional-functional-behavioral relationships already implicit in animal and human behavior. Applied research, on the other hand, is concerned with the invention of instruments and techniques which will change behavior. Thus academic psychology and applied psychology appear as two distinct and complementary areas of one science. While academic research refers primarily to the uncovering of the innumerable features and implicit relationships of intentional-functional behavior, applied psychology as research aims at the discovery of methods of combining these features and relationships in such a way that new constellations may arise which will promote change in behavior.

For example, the development of an efficient psychological technique for animal conditioning in a zoo or circus implies the combination of certain elements already discovered in animal behavior, such as need for certain rewards, fear of certain punishments, and typical relationships to the person who feeds the animal. These characteristics of animal behavior may be combined in such a way that a new constellation arises which cannot be found as such in nature. Particular rewards and punishments administered by a certain trainer who daily feeds the animal are associated, for example, with specific performances of the animal. This new constellation promotes changes in the behavior of the animal, which can now learn to exhibit a certain behavior when the trainer uses a particular technique.

Again, the discovery of a new constellation may refer to the invention of a psychological *instrument* which cannot be found as such in intentional-functional behavior; for example, a teaching machine or a brain computer. It may also refer to a *process* or technique which promotes intentional-functional-behavioral changes more efficiently and rapidly than psychological forces as given in man's nature. An example might be a psychological technique of salesmanship or of efficient management which is a new constellation of human characteristics and their relationships. Such a technique may depend, for example, on the arousal of certain basic human needs which could not be achieved so quickly without the planned psychological stimulation.

The distinction between academic and applied research in psychology, however, is relative. For the progress of the science of psychology is promoted by the discovery not only of hitherto unknown features of intentional-functional behavior, but also of new aspects of those already known. The two are closely connected. The discovery of new phenomena in academic psychology is almost always the result of taking a fresh look at what is already known. For example, the new view that behavior *is* at the same time both intentionality and functionality gave rise to the discovery that phenomenological and experimental psychology should be integrated as mutually complementary sources of the understanding of behavior.

An original approach to behavior also lies at the basis of the discovery of new psychological instruments and techniques in applied psychology. The invention of the practicing psychologist consists in the discovery of previously unknown possibilities in the patterns of intentional-functional behavior in concrete problem situations. A case in point is that of the industrial psychologist who develops a system of personal rewards for dedicated workers which enhances their feeling of being personally appreciated and thereby improves their motivation for work, which in turn increases the quality and quantity of their output. The first industrial psychologist who conceived of this efficient system may have been a practicing scientist who utilized the well known law of intentional-functional behavior that man is motivated by personal appreciation of his performance. He saw the possibility of a "built-in" appreciation in the form of a system of typical rewards applied in the industrial setting.

He tested this hypothesis scientifically and discovered that it worked in a significant number of cases.

It may have happened, however, that this working system was discovered first as a result of trial and error; and that only later, as a consequence of this development, the functional relation between personal reward and enhanced performance was discovered. There are numerous examples of the latter process in the development of psychoanalysis and psychotherapy. For example, methods of changing pre-reflective experiences into verbalized, reflective ones were at first discovered during the practice of therapy; only later, as a consequence of these discoveries, were the functional relationships between repression and forgetting uncovered. Another example, which in this case refers to a psychological instrument rather than a technique, is the invention of the brain computer. The use of this instrument, and especially its feedback circuits, led indirectly to a new view on certain neural processes.

Discovery in academic research and invention in applied research, therefore, are closely connected, or rather, they compenetrate each other. The inventions of the applied psychologist require new modes of seeing intentional-functional behavior in certain life situations. The discoveries of the academic psychologist, in turn, demand the invention of technical psychological methods. These technical means required by the academic psychologist are not only those which have a material character, such as laboratory instruments. Discovery in psychology requires not only empirical instruments to make new observations possible and to test and analyze the functional relationships of behavior, but also conceptual instruments or constructs, models by which newly acquired knowledge of behavior can be properly represented.

Academic psychology is always directed to the understanding of the intentional-functional behavior of animal and man. Applied psychology, on the other hand, aims at organizing the data of this behavior in concrete situations, in such a way that they facilitate an effective control of the behavior with respect to the needs and desires of man. The preceding discussion demonstrates, however, that there is an essential interconnection and interdependence of academic and applied research in psychology.

We may conclude that applied psychology is in conformity with our definition of the science of psychology, not only because it adapts the methods and findings of psychology to the problems of life, but also because it contributes in an original way to the growth of this science.

Theoretical Psychology

The aim of this chapter has been to uncover and define the specific fundamental interest of man which constitutes the science of psychology. The criterion for the validity of our definition has been the explicit or implicit presence of this interest as the common denominator in the various recognized areas of psychology. As a result of our investigation, we have arrived at the conclusion that psychology, at least at the present stage of its historical development, is the science of intentional-functional behavior.

We are now ready to consider psychology from the genetic point of view, to ask ourselves precisely how such a science of behavior unfolds itself. What are its phases? The science of psychology is a mode of human existence; it is a special mode of a more general mode of existence which is the pursuit of abstract knowledge. Science as an abstract human mode of knowing necessarily implies a process of becoming, during which the scientific endeavor differentiates itself in phases. Starting from the experience of single data and their immediate interrelationships, science develops in theoretical complexity in its explication of the increasing multiplicity of relationships which it discovers in an underlying unity. This complex activity of science is unavoidable because the human mode of knowing reality is not one single, intuitive, and comprehensive act which grasps reality at once; it is a gradual, slow uncovering of reality by means of a process of repeated abstraction and synthesis of the knowledge obtained in abstraction. For psychology, this principle implies that the reality of intentional-functional behavior is revealed to the scientist only through a step by step process.

One of the first necessary steps to be taken in the science of psychology is the observation of behavior. But human observation itself is a complex act. It is not the pure sense activity which at first sight it seems to be. A minimum of rational thought or theory is always implied in observation as its core and guiding principle. This theory may be hidden from the reflective awareness of the observer. He may have absorbed his naïve theory pre-reflectively while he assimilated the cultural views permeating the language and the customs which he adopted from early childhood. Nevertheless, some theory is always present—no matter how implicit—guiding all his observations.

The original theoretical-empirical observation of intentional-functional behavior is only a first phase in the development of the science of psychology. This natural observation must be extended and perfected by the use of instruments which extend the power of human observation, and by the performance of experiments which open up new areas of controlled observation not directly given as such in the appearance of behavior in daily life. Another early step in the practice of psychology is the phenomenological explication of the experiences evoked during natural and controlled observation. Following this analysis, further theoretical reflection and observation lead to the establishment of psychological hypotheses which can be verified in controlled observation or experimentation.

At the same time, this vertical differentiation of psychology into many phases, each with its own methods of research, is accompanied by a horizontal differentiation into many single areas limited by special fields of concentration, such as animal psychology, physiological psychology, and developmental psychology. These single areas of psychology are differentiated in turn into special domains. Developmental psychology, for example, becomes child, adolescent, adult, and old age psychology.

Moreover, each of these single domains may differentiate further into new fields. Also, we may find in each of them a variety of specialized theories which direct observational and experimental research within the domain concerned.

Finally, the rich accumulation of observations, phenomenological explications, functional relationships, and differential theories, which are developed in the many areas of psychology and accepted by the significant majority of experts in these fields, must be integrated into a general, provisional theory of psychology.

Every one of the developmental phases of psychology has a necessary dynamic function in the evolution of this science. Moreover, none of the research activities pertaining to any one phase can be disregarded without distorting the science of psychology as a whole. None of the phases is ever completed, for man will never exhaust the reality of intentional-functional behavior. If there is any hierarchy among these phases of development, it is only one of natural priority by which one kind of research is necessarily presupposed by another, the results of which it utilizes. Direct or implicit phenomenological explication, for example, necessarily precedes a scientifically responsible formulation of hypotheses concerning the impact of social factors on the response of subjects to a specific stimulus presented to them in a certain social situation. The necessary function of each phase in the dynamic evolution of psychology defines the value of its careful study. Our purpose is not, however, a detailed study of the science of psychology in all its necessary phases of development, but the exposition of the nature, aim, meaning, and function of existential and of anthropological psychology. These belong primarily to only one developmental phase of empirical psychology, namely comprehensive theoretical psychology.

Consequently, following the discussion of science in general in our first chapter and of the science of psychology in particular in the present chapter, we shall next consider one specific phase of the science of intentional-functional behavior, that is, comprehensive theoretical psychology. Just as some grasp of the meaning of science and of scientific psychology is necessary in order to understand theoretical psychology, so a clear conception of theoretical psychology is necessary in order to comprehend the existential and anthropological developments of theoretical psychology. The understanding of these recent developments of theoretical psychology is the final aim of this book.

CHAPTER THREE

PSYCHOLOGY AND THEORY

To clarify the theoretical mode of existence in the science of psychology, we must first of all consider the role of theory in science in general. Science, as a universal human enterprise, must be rooted somehow in the possibilities of the existence of man the scientist. If there were no potentiality for science in man's existence, science could not emerge in his evolution. But precisely how is the scientific attitude rooted in the existence of man? An answer to this question may constitute a fundamental insight into the role that theory plays in all science.

Science falls among those activities of man which are called "cultural" as distinguished from "biological." The cultural modes of the life of man are rooted in his existence, that is, in his basic characteristic of standing out in reality as it reveals itself. Every cultural enterprise can be traced, therefore, to some interest inherent in man's existence. Such interests are activated when existence differentiates itself in various modes of involvement during man's many encounters, or dialogues, with concrete situations. To ex-ist or to stand out is to be in *interested* contact with the world. Thus, man's cultural activities are the development of various possibilities of *interested* involvement.

We may speak of such modalities of contact as perceiving, feeling, loving, striving, hearing, acting, contemplating, touching, thinking, experimenting, and expressing. Almost every integrated appearance of human behavior is a combination of various modalities of contact. Medical behavior, for example, integrates the modalities of observing the patient, touching him, considering his symptoms, asking relevant questions, recalling and applying medical knowledge and experience, and verbalizing meaningful advice. These modalities constitute the structural unity of medical behavior. In other words, various modalities of existence are incorporated in the medical mode. A common purpose organizes these modalities in such a way that they constitute one mode of existence. All modalities that make up the medical mode of existence, therefore, are directed by the common medical project of diagnosing and curing the patient. *A mode of existence is thus a special structure of the modalities of existence. The unifying character of this structure is determined by a specific interest developed by the existent in the course of his existing.*

In almost any society, one finds individuals who have developed similar modes of existence. These persons feel attracted to one another because of their common interests. They consider the possibility of pooling their potentialities and developing together the mode of existence which they have in common. Man's existence is coexistence. This implies, among other things, that man seeks fellowship with those in whom he discovers kindred interests. The evolution of human existence is accelerated by the fact that men thus discover one another in the cultivation of common concerns.

Science is a mode of contacting reality. A man may specialize his existence or his being in contact with the world in such a manner that the scientific way of contacting reality becomes a predominant mode of existence for him. Other men may join him in this specialization of existence in the scientific mode. At such a moment of human evolution, science is manifested as a cultural enterprise. This pooling of potentialities leads to an accelerated evolution of the scientific dimension of human existence.

Attitudinal Constituents of the Scientific Mode of Existence

Scientific knowledge depends on the perception of the phenomena which are given to the senses. This does not mean that naïve seeing, hearing, or touching is sufficient for the development of science, which presupposes *thoughtful* observation and manipulation. It is precisely thought or theory which changes naïve, spontaneous sensing into scientific attention. Thoughtless awareness can never be called science. Therefore, thought or theory is as essential to the scientific mode of existence as is bodily perception. Thought embodies itself in the searching hands and eyes of the scientist.

Thought or naïve theory is already present in the child in his quest for knowledge. The attempts of the child to stand out knowingly in the world gradually become organized and meaningful. His curiosity, his inner seeking, manifest themselves in the manner in which he handles his toys and other objects that come his way. His behavior reveals to the observer that he is developing a certain effective way of acting. We may even say that primitive, prescientific theories inform and direct the searching movement and observation of the curious child. These naïve bits of theory are based on his experiences. They are, as such, a far cry from the well-organized theories of contemporary science, which are continually put to the empirical test. But, despite the differences, the theoretical attitudes of the scientist and the child are basically identical. Scientific theory is nothing other than the critical development, organization, and specialization of the naïve theoretical attitude which we observe in the child—the attitude of bodily observation and manipulation of reality. The two attitudes are inseparable. Man *is* an experimenter by nature, and man *is* by nature a theorist.

We may add that the technical attitude, too, is a characteristic manifestation of man's being. Man's thoughtful standing-out into reality, his observation and manipulation of the world, enables him to perceive things as actual or potential tools. Observe, for example, the naïve technical attitude of the child who discovers with delight that he can use one toy to fashion another and who proudly applies his thoughtful observation. He changes his little world intelligently while embodying his insight in a technical operation.

We may conclude that thoughtful observation, empirical manipulation, and technical application are rooted in the fundamental structure of man, which is his existence, or his being involved with others bodily in the world. It is for this reason that we find manifestations of these fundamental attitudes in men of all times and in cultures at all stages of development.

I have stated that man stands out in the world together with all other men who coexist with him. Man's natural coexistence explains the heights reached by science and technology in our day. Generations of men have cooperated in the gradual development and the critical refinement of the scientific attitude—a growing mastery of the world of mankind. Science and technology today embody the impressive acquisitions of the evolution of the human race.

It is not impossible that mankind may stand today at the threshold of a golden age. A prerequisite for such a unique period of harmonious progress would be the reintegration of the scientific attitude as a whole. With all its potentiality for integration, the scientific attitude is still split into one-sided components.

Reintegration of Attitudinal Constituents

The scientific attitude consists of various constituents, such as the theoretical, observational, manipulative, and effectuating attitudes. We may call these necessary and sufficient constituents. When one of them is totally lacking, we do not have the scientific attitude in its fullness. In this sense, every attitudinal constituent is *necessary*. On the other hand, these constituents are *sufficient* for the makeup of the fundamental scientific mode of existence. To be sure, other special attitudes may be adopted for certain kinds of science, for example, the mathematical attitude for physics. The mathematical attitude, however, is not a necessary constituent of the scientific mode of existence as such.

The scientific attitude necessarily contains various attitudinal constituents. This does not imply, however, that all these constituents are at all times equally and fully present. Ordinarily, one of the attitudinal constituents is dominant, while other constituents remain implicit. The attitude of scientific application, for example, is explicit in the engineer who constructs a bridge. At the same time, however, theoretical and empirical attitudes are implicit in his engineering insofar as the engineer draws on the theoretical and empirical findings of physics.

The history of science in Western culture is the history of the changing prevalence of the various attitudinal constituents of the scientific mode of existence. In the course of this history, every attitudinal constituent of the scientific mode of existence has had an opportunity to differentiate itself during its prevalence in the culture.

The irregular development of each constituent of the scientific mode of existence is due in part to the primordial situation of man. Even a casual view of the historical evolution of science reveals that the development of one constituent has always presupposed the development of another. Technical appliances for airplanes, for example, were elaborated only after a period of one-sided development of theoretical-empirical physics. The latter, in turn, developed only after a long process of one-sided philosophical theorizing on the nature of knowledge and matter.

A more basic reason for this irregular, though lawful, development of the scientific mode of existence, however, is the typical primordial structure of man himself. Man's existence is a bodily one. He is necessarily limited in space and time. He is limited in his energy, his insight, and his historical situation, which forces him to specialized preoccupations. A primitive tribe which must survive in the jungle has neither time nor energy for philosophical theorizing; a differentiated civilization which must develop complicated techniques to ensure its survival is also limited in philosophical theorizing. Man's bodily limitations allow historical situations to play an important role in the evolution of science. Therefore, the demands of historical situations have initiated, accelerated, or retarded developments in the scientific mode of existence.

This historical influence does not, however, explain a certain lawfulness observable in the development of science. We note, for example, that accelerated development of efficient observation and manipulative intervention is regularly preceded by the development of scientific theorizing. Such lawfulness in the characteristic evolution of science is due to the inner structure of the scientific mode of existence. The latter, in turn, is dependent on the primordial structure of man. There is only one order in which empirical science can be pursued: philosophical and scientific theorizing; sense observation; and concrete, manipulative intervention. These three together form the characteristic mode of man's scientific standing-out in the world. There exists, moreover, a hierarchical order within this triad insofar as a considerable development of the second or third phase presupposes a certain development of the first or second.

We may conclude that the evolution of the scientific mode of existence necessarily requires a temporary distinction of its attitudinal constituents. This distinction leads to the specialized and concentrated evolution of each constituent. Several stages must be passed before the attitudinal constituents of the scientific mode of existence can be reunited. In the naïve scientific mode of existence the three phases of theory, sense observation, and concrete manipulation developed together as a natural unity. But, in the course of history, these attitudinal constituents had to develop separately before they could again be reunited.

The Prescientific Mode of Existence

A deeper insight into the prescientific view of prehistoric man may help us to understand more clearly the meaning and development of science. We need to be precisely aware of the differences between our daily postscientific perception of reality and the prescientific views which dominated primitive existence, for our seemingly "spontaneous" perception is indeed pervaded by unconsciously assimilated scientific views which are embodied in our culture.

When we inquire how primitive man looked at reality, we are impressed by the fact that his view of "what is" lacked the kind of critical objectivity which prevails in our scientific and postscientific perceptions. The absence of this kind of scientific objectivity does not, however, imply the absence of all objectivity, for even primitive man thought and talked about nature in abstract concepts and categories. Every abstraction presupposes some objectification. Without abstraction, primitive man would have been overwhelmed by a rushing stream of consciousness in which he would not have been able to isolate any point of orientation. Consequently, he could not have said anything about experience; he could not have construed a language, as he actually did.

The objectification of primitive man is, however, not the critical kind which is typical of modern man. Therefore, we characterize the prescientific stage of existence as naïve, uncritical, or prereflective. Our forebears did not reflect critically on the spontaneous notions which emerged when faced with reality, nor did they test those notions in experimental ways.

When we consider the subject matter of their spontaneous, untested views of reality, we discover that their vision of life was mythological. They did not develop a critical philosophy, physics, or theology. The vision of primitive man was bound to the legends and traditions of his clan. It was influenced by his spontaneous, immediate impressions of nature as it appeared in his peculiar local situation. His view of reality was also linked to the symbols perpetuated by his tribe. These influences were, to be sure, outside agents. The fact that prehistoric man was bound to these external manifestations of reality demonstrates again that his world was not merely a subjective creation of his own. He based his vision of reality on customs, traditions, and manifestations of nature which revealed themselves to him as "objective" necessities imposed on his subjectivity.

On the other hand, the objectivity of the primitive view differs greatly from the objectivity of our scientific and postscientific vision. First of all, each prescientific, mythical view of reality was shared by only a relatively small, isolated group. The clan or tribe perpetuated a traditional mythological vision among its members. This view was related to a limited number of life situations typical for a specific tribe; with a peculiar tradition; living in special surroundings; and surviving by means of specific kinds of hunting, fishing, farming, searches for shelter, and preparation of food. Our own scientific or postscientific view, on the contrary, tends toward universality. In other words, we strive consciously for a vision which may prove true for all people everywhere. We approximate this aim by constant reflection on our impressions of reality. This reflection enables us to question these impressions and to devise experiments to test their validity. Testing purifies our primordial impressions.

Primitive, prescientific existence, on the other hand, was characterized by the absence of reflection. But it is precisely reflective knowledge which makes us aware that we are the source of our own thoughts and feelings. Such awareness leads us necessarily to the knowledge that we differ from the situation about which we think and feel. In other words, it makes us cognizant of our limited, but real, freedom. The same reflective knowledge enables us to question our spontaneous, uncritical notions of nature, people, things, and events. It also enables us to be critical of the ideas which we ourselves have introjected during our dialogue with our culture. Reflective knowledge is knowledge about our own knowledge.

The condition of a scientific view of the world is thus the emergence of critical reflection on one's spontaneous vision of the world. Such critical reflection implies, however, a negation, doubt, or suspension of the primitive view. As long as we experience our primitive view of reality as absolute, we cannot be critical about it. We cannot be convinced of the certitude of our view of reality and at the same time genuinely doubtful about it.

We may apply this rule of logic to the history of scientific and postscientific existence in the Western world. The reflective critical attitude could emerge in the West only on the basis of the dissolution of the primitive vision of reality. Stephan Strasser compares this historical disintegration of the primitive world to an explosion. Primitive man did not develop well-differentiated physical, metaphysical, or religious views of reality. His mythical perception took the place, as it were, of our physical, metaphysical, and theological comprehension. The dissolution of the primitive view of reality was, however, like an explosion of the mythical perception into its physical, metaphysical, and theological components. After this explosion, the primitive physical view of reality gradually developed into science. The primitive metaphysical view of the world, indistinguishably blended with the physical perception of prehistoric man, evolved by degrees into independent, systematic philosophy. The primitive religious view, which permeated physical and metaphysical perceptions, became theology in its own right.

Dissolution of the Prehistoric Visions of Reality

An attempt at a universal view of reality succeeded the primitive views of the isolated societies which made up prehistoric humanity. The necessary condition of such a universal cognitive mode of existence was the disintegration of the primitive views of reality.

The occasion for this breakdown was the primitive societies' being thrown together in new empires. Such encounters familiarized the tribes with one another's mythological views. Each tribe discovered that other tribes also experienced their own mythologies as the only possible explanation of all that manifests itself in nature. Until this fateful moment of ideological collusion, each isolated society was convinced that its own was necessarily *the* view of reality. The close interaction with members of other tribes, however, led each society to the discovery that the others' myths and traditions differed. Their modes of existence, their existential positions, or their ways of standing-out into reality revealed themselves as strange and different, yet effective. The tribe with the different mode of existence also survived and maintained itself as an organized unity which coped successfully with untamed nature and with interpersonal problems among its members.

Such observation made it impossible for each society to experience the mythical existential position of its own tribe as the only possible one. Doubt, criticism, skepticism, and nihilism took the place of naïve certainty. Doubt forced the members of each tribe to reflect on their spontaneous impressions and notions of nature. As a consequence, reflective knowledge developed rapidly. Critical reflection led finally to an attempt to reconstruct the original, isolated views of the various societies into a philosophical-theoretical vision that would be universally valid.

The universal-theoretical view in turn led people to question reality to discover whether it was in all conditions in correspondence with the new theoretical vision. At this moment, science was born. The questions of society were translated into the empirical, operational idiom. Nature answered these empirical questions positively or negatively. The answers led to the elaboration or transformation of the theoretical position.

In early Western culture, we find philosophical reflection first of all in the writings of such men as Heraclitus and Parmenides. They were among the first to escape the limited mythological vision. They uncovered general validities in the appearance of nature. They studied the possibilities of human knowledge and the structure of nature and of man. Plato, Socrates, and Aristotle advanced this early philosophy. The Greek philosophical vision of reality became the basis of Western science. The philosophical-theoretical view of the Greek thinkers was, in fact, the necessary condition of the emergence of science. Therefore, we do not find science in early cultures other than the Greek, for the emergence of experimental science is dependent on scientific theory. Scientific theory of man and nature can arise only on the basis of a more general theory of reality.

Aristotle, for example, reflected on the species-individual structure. He discovered that man can say about the individual members of a species or class that which he can say about the species. This discovery awakened the insights that one may study a sampling of the individual members of one class of objects. The qualities which are discovered to be common among the members of this sampling of objects may then be predicated of the whole class of objects. For example, when one discovers that a hundred identical pieces of iron melt in fire, he may suppose that all identical pieces of iron will melt when exposed to fire of the same intensity. Such a conclusion leads to a scientific law. A mythological view of reality would not have opened man's mind to such a discovery.

Eastern and Western Developments after the Breakdown of Mythological Existence

We have said that the emergence of empires in the Western world threw isolated tribes together. The collision of isolated tribes demolished their mythologies. As a result, a more universal view of reality emerged. But what about such Eastern empires as the Indian and Chinese? They did not develop natural sciences as did the West. But this does not imply that they did not attempt to establish universally valid views transcending the particular mythologies of their tribes. They did hold universal views, though they did not take the form of categorical views of nature. On the contrary, the Eastern universal view is embedded in the wisdom of living.

Eastern thinkers transcended mythology by establishing universal rules of wise conduct, such as we find in Hebrew writings, in Taoism, and in Buddhism. While the Greeks concentrated on external nature, Eastern thinkers concentrated on the subject and on the relations of the subject to his fellow man, his home, and his life task. We do not suggest that Eastern thinkers showed no interest in nature nor that Western philosophers gave no attention to the subject, man. But, in terms of emphasis, objectified nature prevails in the thought of the later Greeks, whereas the development and growth of the subject is the dominant theme in the Eastern theory of existence.

One cannot express a universally valid thought about reality without the use of categories. Such accepted categories, then, have a determining influence within a culture on all subsequent appreciation of the nature of reality. The later Greek thinkers adopted their basic categories—such as substance, accident, quality, and quantity—from the observation of external nature. Man is a substance, but he is a substance in a different way than a stone, a rock, or a ship is. The early Greek thinkers were well aware of this difference. The "objectivist" origin of the category subsequently proved poisonous, however, to the thought of Western man. In the course of the centuries, he developed an objectivist attitude in his understanding of the human condition. The Judeo-Christian heritage of the West temporarily balanced the objectivist slant of Greek speculation. This truce between the Judeo-Christian and the Greek vision of man promised a harmonious blend of civilization and culture. The decline of the Judeo-Christian influence, however, gave free play to the objectivist tendencies in Western humanity. Before the Western world realized this clearly, it was caught up in an objectivism which expanded until it forced even the subject into categories. As a result, Western thinkers often attempt to deal with man as though he were merely a measurable substance to be organized into objective units.

Such objectivism makes for an advance in civilization and a decline in culture. "Civilization" in this sense is the objectivist organization of matter in such a way that it enables man to function more effectively. Civilization produces bridges, air conditioners, refrigerators, mills, labor unions, and functional university buildings. Culture, on the other hand, is the development and expression of the personal qualities of the human subject. Culture promotes music, paintings, poetry, novels, creative science, a beautiful and harmonious manner of living, and imaginative intellectual encounters within the universities. When civilization and culture are wedded harmoniously, a well-integrated society is born. But when one of the two prevails, society suffers.

Certain contemporary Western societies reveal a rapid advance in civilization among the mass of the population while the same majority is not developing so intensively in personal culture. We can observe efforts to balance this dominant objectivism by a new humanism and even by the introduction of Eastern wisdom. These isolated attempts do not, however, appear to be greatly successful thus far.

To be sure, the scientific mode of existence of the West remained predominantly theoretical-philosophical up to the Renaissance. Even mythological motives did not disappear all at once. They permeated and sometimes colored philosophical theory. Medieval alchemy, for example, was a curious blend of philosophical and scientific theorizing permeated by mythological motives.

The late Middle Ages and the Renaissance saw the gradual split of the Western cognitive mode of existence into philosophical-theoretical, empirical-theoretical, observational, experimental, and applied modes of knowledge. Such distinctions were a methodological necessity. It would have been impossible for these modes of knowledge to develop in their own right had it not been for these actual distinctions. In reality, of course, these modes of knowledge cannot be separated absolutely. They always influence one another. But their temporary methodological distinction was a necessary condition for the growth of the scientific mode of existence. Such distinctions promoted a necessary division of labor. Various experts could now concentrate exclusively on certain aspects of the scientific way of life. A full differentiation of the various attitudinal constituents of the scientific mode was now possible.

One danger was inherent in this split. The expert in one of the differentiated attitudes of the scientific mode of existence might be carried away by his specialty. He might then be inclined to forget his dependency on other aspects of the scientific way of life developed by other experts. He might claim that his own approach to reality was "the" scientific one. And this is precisely what did happen. The tremendous growth of science, however, compelled the scientist to realize that his problems were closely linked with theoretical-empirical thought and even with philosophical theorizing. Moreover, the tremendous differentiation in the scientific realm itself offered a challenge for integration. Added to this challenge, as we have already seen, was the demand in Western thought for a recognition of the unique place of the *subject.*

Briefly, the differentiation of the scientific mode of existence has now reached a point where reintegration seems to be an inescapable task. We may conclude that this reintegration comprehends three aspects:

1. Reintegration of the constituent attitudes of the scientific modes of existence.

2. Reintegration within each field of scientific endeavor of the various differential theories and correlated data. This reintegration would lead to a comprehensive theory of the science itself.

3. Reintegration, especially in the human sciences, of the subjective and the objective realms of reality.

It is impossible for one person to be a complete expert in every phase of the scientific mode of existence. This impossibility implies that the integrative task will lead to a new branch of science in every field, namely, that of the comprehensive theorist. This phase of the evolution of science is most clear in physics. Theoretical physics as a specialty actually does exist. The same development must necessarily take place in psychology, for the development of comprehensive theory is not a question of choice or interest, but the necessary result of the inner structure of the scientific mode of existence. This structure, in turn, follows necessarily from the existential structure of man, the scientist, for there is only one way in which the scientific mode of existence can be developed: theoretical thinking, sensitive experiencing, and concrete manipulative intervention. Every new step in the development of a science necessarily requires renewed theoretical reflection on what has already been learned by sense observation and experimentation.

The Relationship Between Observation and Theory in the Scientific Mode of Existence

The aim of this chapter is to clarify the role of the theoretical attitude in the scientific mode of existence. As already indicated, the theoretical attitude is essentially human. If this is true, theorizing should manifest itself even on the level of prescientific observation. A close consideration of the essential relationship between observation and theory will demonstrate that they imply each other mutually.

Man is basically existence. His involvement in the world can be viewed under various perspectives or dimensions. One of these is the observational mode of existence, which implies the sensuous standing-out of a subject into the observable reality which reveals itself to him. The subject's taking a stand manifests itself, among other ways, in his theoretical attitude, for to theorize is to adopt a certain way of looking at something. The objective aspect reveals itself in that which is observed.

Observation is thus really preceiving what is "out there." But observation is also perceiving according to a theory of an observing subject. Therefore, existence as observation is necessarily theoretical and empirical at the same time.

We may illustrate this conclusion with an example from daily life. As I walk down the street, I see a child playing, and I make the observation to myself or to my companion that this child moves rather slowly. When I reflect, however, on my observation and my expression of this "fact," I realize that they are one-sided and selective, for this child is an inexhaustible source of meanings. To enumerate only a few: the traffic around the playing child is moving rapidly; the weather is hot and humid; he has blond hair; he looks weak and tired; he seems to be about eight years old; two men next to him are arguing about politics; the high, dark wall of a house narrows his horizon. We could go on and list an indefinite number of circumstances surrounding this child and his play.

As the observing subject, however, I select only a single characteristic, namely, the slow movement of the child. In reality, however, all these circumstances are in some way related and create the situation in its realistic totality. I have no right to say that circumstances other than the child's movement are irrelevant. Maybe the child is afraid of the other children; maybe he is awed by the somber wall of the high building; maybe he is confused by the men who shout mysterious phrases about politics in incomprehensible agitation; maybe the child's fatigue is far more relevant than his being slow. But I, the observing subject, abstract from all these other appearances of the child and his situation. I select only one phenomenon, namely, his slowness.

How do I abstract this one phenomenon from the whole phenomenological situation? I do so by placing the reality of the child-in-his-situation in a specific context. In this case, the context is that of speed of movement. I look through this frame, as it were, and, while doing so, I do not consider blue eyes, blond hair, the age of the child, or his being awed by the wall, but only the phenomenon of his slowness. Against the background of the meanings of "fast," "slow," and "movement," he appears to be moving slowly. I could have chosen another world of meaning, for example, the meaning of age. Then I should have observed, not his slowness, but his probable age, based on a system of meaning developed in my culture regarding age levels and their appearances.

But where do I obtain these theoretical frames of reference through which I may observe the child? Like every other theoretical frame, they are composed of many elements. One fundamental theoretical component is the language which I inherited through my culture. I am, in fact, inserted in my language. Language embodies a certain view of the world. It represents the modes of existence of the generations which lived before me in my country. Every language is a theoretical frame of reference which helps man to uncover various aspects of reality in and around himself. The same is true of such artificial languages as statistics, mathematics, psychoanalysis, learning theory, and physics.

Therefore, when I say that this child moves slowly, I express a fact, but I express it in a selective, abstract, or theoretical way. My experiences, my specialized interests, and my language are influential in my choice of a definite system of meanings. The "fact" of slowness is, therefore, the product of two main factors. One building block of this "fact" is an event that happens; the other is my theoretical frame of reference. The two are inseparably blended in what I call my observation. If I used no frame of reference, that is, if I took no stand, I should not ex-ist, I should not stand out in any way, and I should experience nothing. Therefore, whenever I observe, I always do so within at least a naïve theoretical frame of reference.

Every mode of existence corresponds with a world of meanings. My culture has embodied these modes of perception with their corresponding worlds in the natural or scientific language which I use. Only by this existential or selective expression is a fact a fact. Only in this way can facts be incorporated in human existence, find their place in it, renew, reinforce, and enrich it.

Sense observation can take place only when one or more of my senses are stimulated. Sense stimulation alone, however, is not yet observation of a fact. We experience that we are observing only when sense stimulation becomes meaningful in some theoretical frame of reference. A nontheoretical expression of a stimulation of our external senses would indeed be unthinkable and even impossible.

On the other hand, the term "existence" always implies two poles—the existent or the subject and that reality toward which he exists. Therefore, the observational mode of existence also implies a subject pole and an object pole. The object pole of my observation reveals itself to me as an experience of "being-found-there," of "being-not-me." I call this the experience of objectivity. As soon as I take some stand toward the stimulation of my senses, then sense data impose themselves on me within my theoretical frame as reality, that is, as object pole. At the same time, I, the observing subject, the existent, am in some way present in that which is given in my mode of existing. It is precisely the human light of my knowing which translates the sense stimulations into something intelligible and meaningful. The specific kind of intelligibility and meaningfulness is again codetermined by the theoretical frame of reference of me, the subject.

Meanwhile, the experience that the data are given, that they are object pole, that they are not me, never disappears totally. This remains true even when I leave behind prescientific, naïve theories and begin to develop complex, scientific–theoretical frames of reference. The theory which guides prescientific observation is usually so simple that the presence of the observational data is quite clear and convincing. As soon as observation becomes scientific, however, the theoretical frame of reference (for example, the theory of relativity or the stimulus-response theory) is so subtle and ingenious that the object pole seems to disappear. Of course, this is never really the case.

Even such a highly abstract theory as the stimulus-response theory refers in some way to some given reality. Indeed, the whole scientific mode of existence is built on the inseparable relatedness of subject pole and object pole within every so-called datum of science.

To clarify the role of the theoretical attitude within the scientific way of life, we have considered, first of all, the nature and development of the various existential attitudes which constitute this scientific mode. One of these is the theoretical attitude. We have also investigated the relationship between observation and theory in the scientific mode of existence. Beginning with a consideration of the mutual implications of prescientific observation and prescientific theory in human existence, we have sought the root of the relationship between scientific observation and theory in the nature of man himself.

We have concluded that, even on the prescientific level of existence, a moment of meaningfulness and intelligibility occurs in every observation. This implies, as we have seen, a moment of theory in every observation, for sense stimulation as such cannot explain the variety of meanings which emerge even when the same sense is stimulated by the same stimuli. We speak of people, for example, as nasty, kind, stupid, clever, polite, awkward, strong, or weak. Then we make statements concerning properties related to these behaviors, such as the statement that a stupid man should not be a professor. In other words, when we observe behavior, we are implicitly aware that there are different theoretical, abstract categories. We know this without studying scientific psychology. Thus there is a theoretically organized way of existence even on the prescientific level of human life.

The essence of human life *is* existence. It excludes the possibility of a purely sensuous givenness, of purely being-a-fact. Every so-called fact is embedded in some kind of theoretical context. It is always and necessarily embedded in some world. This world is constituted by some mode of existence, of taking a stand. Human ex-istence is never terminated. Even on the prescientific level, it is a constant attempt to assimilate reality; it is always a theoretical endeavor to make reality transparent. It is a theorizing existence insofar as it perceives concrete realities in intelligible contexts of phenomenological worlds or systems of meaning.

Implications of Observation and Theory in the Scientific Mode of Existence

The mutual implications of observation and theory manifest themselves in the scientific, as well as in the prescientific, mode of existence. The empirical, scientific mode is a methodical, critical, organized mode of standing-out into a selected area of reality which is given to the senses. In science, the theoretical context and its embodiment in terminology are more refined, complex, and exact. The area of reality in which a specific mode of scientific existence stands out is more strictly delineated. Furthermore, the observations which result from this involvement in a specific area are more coherently organized in an open scientific system. Nevertheless, there is no fundamental difference between the prescientific and the scientific modes of cognitive existence. We may demonstrate this by applying the same theoretical process to the scientific mode of existence as we did to the prescientific mode.

One scientific mode of life—the psychological—will serve our purpose. The theoretical frames and the terminologies of psychology are, to be sure, more subtle and complex than the naïve, prescientific frames of reference. The specific area of this mode of existence is also more sharply delineated. We have already investigated this delineation in Chapter Two, in which we concluded that psychology's area of reality is intentional-functional behavior. Certain experiences or observations resulting from involvement in the reality of this behavior are organized in differentiated, internally consistent, theoretical systems. The organization of all these differential theories and their corresponding data within a comprehensive theory, however, has not yet been attempted on as large a scale in psychology as in physics.

We may apply to scientific psychology all the essential characteristics of the prescientific relationship between behavior and observation. Therefore, when a psychologist speaks of data of intentional-functional behavior, his statement should never be considered a mirror or a picture of that behavior. Every behavioral fact is only a fact within one or the other system of meaning, within one or the other theoretical context used by the psychologist. This framework may be, for example, learning theory, psychoanalytic theory, *Gestalt* theory, or any other psychological system of ideas. The psychological fact, like every other scientific fact, can never be a pure fact or merely a fact. Facts exist only in a theoretical frame of reference. Consequently, when a scientific psychologist uses the word "fact" or "datum," we should be aware that the terms always refer to a factual-theoretical aspect of the whole of intentional-functional behavior.

The Increasingly Theoretical Character of Science and Its Continual Relationship to Observation

The development of psychology implies that it acquires an increasingly scientific, theoretical character. Thus it is distinguished from prescientific, everyday psychology, in which the theoretical aspect is less developed. Science in general may be aptly described as that mode of cognitive existence which implies a continually developing theoretical explanation of phenomena. The same phenomena were once less accurately defined in original, prescientific theoretical explanations. This increasingly theoretical development is most striking in contemporary physics. But it becomes more and more evident in psychology.

In spite of the inescapable evolution of science toward an expanding system of theoretical constructs, however, it must remain thoroughly empirical. This implies that the science of behavior, in spite of the primacy of the theoretical, must remain bound to behavior that is given to the observing senses. As we have seen in the earlier part of this chapter, the scientifically theorizing subject reaches out to perceptible reality in and through his senses and bodily movement.

If the primary theoretical aspect of a science were to lose all implicit reference to the data which are given to the senses, then it would no longer be science, but philosophy. The philosopher begins with immediate, empirical experience, about which he speculates. His abstract speculation removes him further and further from the immediate data. Finally, he arrives at statements, which are of such a nature that they cannot be verified by empirical operations directly or indirectly. Empirical operations are those which are basically bound to bodily sensing and moving.

Statements of comprehensive scientific theory, however, must be verifiable, at least indirectly, by empirical operations. The theory of relativity, for example, cannot be verified directly by such operations. But the scientist can deduce postulates from the theory of relativity which can be verified by empirical operations. The ontological truth that man is existence, however, cannot be proven *as ontological truth* by empirical sense operations. For this reason, psychology cannot borrow this ontological statement *as ontological statement* in scientific theory. The theoretical psychologist, however, may borrow the concept and change it to a hypothetical theoretical construct. The scientific theorist neither affirms nor denies the ontological truth of the statement. But he gives it the same status in psychological science as the constructs of the theory of relativity are given in physics. He cannot prove directly that the broad theoretical construct that man is existence is ontologically true; but he can deduce verifiable postulates from this theoretical statement.

For example, the theoretical psychologist may hypothesize that man on the proper level of his being always "ex-ists," or uncovers some meaningful world. Then he may suggest to "differential psychologists" that they deduce operational postulates from this statement. If the comprehensive theoretical statement is valid, one postulate might be, for example, that a man who is exposed to sensory deprivation will invent some imaginary kind of world. The differential operational psychologist can test this postulate by empirical operations. Experiments in sensory deprivation have indeed affirmed this postulate and, therefore, indirectly affirmed this hypothetical construct.

Why is it that every science becomes increasingly theoretical? We have seen that scientific existence is an observant existence. It is a standing-out boldly into reality that is given to the senses of the scientist. The psychologist stands out in this way into a specific area of reality, namely, the area of behavior. Doing so, he observes a tremendous number of behavioral phenomena. He observes people learning, playing, arguing, working, writing, and so on. Observation of any one of these behavioral phenomena on the prescientific level of existence already presupposes a prescientific theoretical frame of reference. Therefore, we might imagine that the psychologist could make it his task to simply investigate a great number of prescientific theories in which he discovers numerous phenomena. He could thus reduce psychology to a description of every behavioral phenomenon caught in every prescientific theory. Such a purpose, however, would involve the psychologist in an extremely complicated and, in the end, impossible enterprise, for he would inevitably bog down in the multiplicity of singular phenomena which he would uncover in the behavior of animals and people.

In other words, psychology, to be effective and manageable, cannot be concerned only with the observation and description of phenomena. It is theory which enables the psychologist to reduce to a few fundamental properties the many which have appeared to his sense observation. The theoretical psychologist develops a structure of ideas through which he attempts to express behavioral relationships. This texture of ideas helps him to structure behavioral phenomena. These phenomena then become intelligible in their interrelationships.

Therefore, the psychologist does not observe and describe phenomena of behavior merely for the sake of inventory. He assembles behavioral phenomena to construct theories which reveal something about the structure of behavior. One differential theory of behavior, for example, structures a group of behavioral phenomena by the construct of reinforcement. This is, of course, only a theory and, therefore, hypothetical. But this theory makes intelligible to a degree a certain number of behavioral phenomena which are observable. It does so by theorizing about behavioral phenomena which manifest themselves in numerous experiments in learning.

The structures which bind phenomena together, to be sure, are not immediately observable by the senses. Therefore, the psychologist can only devise hypothetical theories which approximate the nature, properties, and relationships of these structures. He can experimentally demonstrate only that his theoretical model is coherent with the observable behavioral phenomena. In other words, he can only test whether this theoretical structure is a model that points to what actually appears in the observable phenomena. Thus, all science remains bound to observable appearances.

Science, therefore, fosters the careful study of observable sense appearances which are directly available for observation or empirically evoked to test postulates deduced from scientific theory. The sense observation affirms or negates the intellectual structure which has been devised by scientific theory. In the beginning of the development of a science, one and the same scientist may possess the required knowledge, time, and energy to commit himself to observation, theorizing, and experimentation. When a science develops further, however, it becomes so complex that specialists are needed for each of these phases.

This development is especially manifest at the crucial moment when differential theory requires the supplement of comprehensive theory. Differential theory devises a conceptual structure which explains a particular group of phenomena studied by specialists in a given area of behavior. Comprehensive theory develops a structure of ideas which explains the variety of phenomena which are described in the various differential theories, for science necessarily leads to the attempt to understand the many phenomena and differential theories in their unity.

The scientific mode of existence by its very nature seeks unity in multiplicity. Both elements are necessary. The comprehensive-theoretical approach emphasizes the unity of science whereas the differential-theoretical approach guards the openness of science. If the comprehensive-theoretical psychologist were not to accept the findings of the differential psychologists, he would create a unity at the expense of the multiplicity of phenomena. His theory would lose contact with reality. On the other hand, if there were no comprehensive theory, psychology would be lost in the multiplicity of recorded phenomena and differential theories. The dialogue between observation and theory commands respect for behavioral appearances. The theoretical psychologist, for example, should never discard an exception in behavioral appearances which does not conform to his hypothetical theory. It is exactly this exceptional behavior which may become the starting point for crucial corrections or developments in psychological theory. The openness to behavior which does not fit the hypothesis is the guarantee of the multiplicity which must be integrated into a unity without being distorted in the process.

The preference of the psychologist for the scientific mode of existence is not for the behavioral phenomena as many, but for the many as integrated into a unity. The psychologist is interested in behavioral appearances in their endless plurality and multiformity. Whatever behavior appears he wishes to make his own by investigating it and adding it to the phenomena he has observed. The psychologist, however, is not interested only in bringing together the many behavioral phenomena. He also wishes to *com*prehend the many from a single or from several points of view. These integrating, comprehensive, theoretical viewpoints are attempts to approximate the basic structure that appears in the phenomena.

Although this preference of the scientific psychologist is understandable, it should not cause him to lose sight of the absolute necessity for the experimental and clinical search for the many behavioral appearances. Otherwise, the desire for integration may lead to an inauthentic simplification and distortion of the given plurality. For this reason, the aspect of the scientific mode of existence which impels the scientist to explore as many behavioral appearances as possible is indispensable for the growth of the science. Equally indispensable, however, is the theoretical aspect of standing-out toward the fundamental structure which integrates and explains these phenomena as a unity.

The Theoretical-Observational Structure of Science Is Rooted in Man's Existence

The theoretical-observational structure of science is not a result of arbitrary choice. It is rooted in the scientific mode of existence. The latter, in turn, is rooted in the primordial structure and situation of man. Therefore, there is no other possible way for the development of science. According to his primordial structure, man experiences himself as an unlimited dynamic intentionality. He experiences his subjectivity as an urge to stand out toward all that is. On the other hand, his subjectivity is an embodied subjectivity. Therefore, he has to stand out toward all that is in and through his bodily senses and movements. Furthermore, his embodiment restricts him to a certain place and a temporary phase in the historical development of mankind. Consequently, his actual, concrete standing-out is limited.

This necessity of standing-out bodily in a limited way compels the psychologist to develop differential-operational and experimental psychology first of all. This is the only road to behavior available to him as a bodily existent. His awareness of his unlimited dynamic intentionality, however, leads to his theoretical quest for a unifying structure of ideas which will enable him to *com*prehend behavior as an intelligible unity. Therefore, the constant tension, or dialogue, between theory and observation is unavoidable in human science and will never be resolved. It is rooted in the very structure of man. This tension is, however, at the same time the dynamic, propelling force which keeps science alive and growing.

The Theoretical and Experimental Constituents of the Scientific Mode of Existence

Most important in the development of psychology is the experimental constituent of the scientific psychological mode of existence. As we have already seen, the experimental mode of being is a proper mode of being man, for it pertains to man's nature to ex-ist bodily in the world and to unveil this world. The theoretical psychologist cannot perform his comprehensive task without the experiments of the empirical psychologist. This is especially true when he wishes to develop a system of ideas which will help him to comprehend behavior as it manifests itself in behavioral phenomena. Therefore, the extension of the experimental mode of being to as many realms of psychology as possible is a definite necessity for the development of theoretical psychology.

Unfortunately, not every area of psychological interest is as manageable by the experimental psychologist as every other area. The study of the intentional component of behavior, for example, often seems to require methods other than the experimental. Even here, however, the differential psychologist should use the experimental method as far as possible. Thus he will be able to provide the comprehensive theoretical psychologist with more reliable data and more adequately tested differential theories.

Another problem with regard to the unlimited use of the experimental method is the ethical principle that the fundamental human rights of the individual should not be jeopardized even to obtain valuable psychological knowledge. For example, it would be interesting and worthwhile from the viewpoint of psychological knowledge to expose human subjects to clearly defined injuries of the brain. Psychologists could then study the impact of these injuries on behavior. The study of the results of brain injury in war casualties has already been undertaken. But a well-planned gradation of brain injuries inflicted on a large sampling of, say, a prison population, would provide a more exact design and a better control of the variables. It seems certain that valuable information regarding behavior would be gained. This would be especially true if brain surgery were performed on hundreds of confined subjects who could be observed over a long period. The subjects would suffer lasting impairment, but mankind as a whole might profit from the experimentation. So would the development of theoretical psychology. Despite the value of this procedure from the viewpoint of theoretical and clinical psychology, however, it could not be carried out because of ethical principles regarding the human rights of the individual.

Despite limitations, the theoretical psychologist is optimistic about the development of his field because of the advance of the experimental method in an increasing number of areas of animal and human psychology.

The Existential Character of Scientific Theory

We have investigated the scientific mode of existence, its attitudinal constituents, and their relationships. These observations enable us to perceive more clearly the existential view of scientific theory, which differs from the positivist and rationalist ones. I have emphasized that the scientific mode of existence implies a unity between the subject pole, or the scientific psychologist, and his object pole, behavior. The theoretical constituent of the scientific mode is predominantly subjective, but not only subjective. It is true that this theoretical constituent steadily increases in importance with the development of the science. The object pole of the psychological mode of existence, however, will never be totally absent.

Psychology and Theory

Psychology in its advanced state is a flexible, open structure of an ever-changing number of ideas which enable us to comprehend the phenomena of behavior. These theoretical structures thus refer in principle to the phenomenal appearances given to our senses. The theoretical ideas that make up the science of psychology are, therefore, not merely arbitrary, imaginative configurations. These structures always point to the phenomena. They are in some way imposed on the psychologist by his perception of behavior. Therefore, the object pole to which psychological theory refers always remains in some way present in the theory itself. At the same time, the theory represents, however, more than the phenomena which the psychologist perceives when he looks at behavior from differing perspectives.

This existential conception of science and, more especially, of scientific theory differs from the two chief pre-existential views of scientific theory—the positivist and the rationalist. Each of these isolates one of the constituents of scientific theory which are in the existential view inseparable. Positivism places everything, as it were, at the object pole, whereas rationalism considers only the subject pole.

The initial conception of positivism in psychology is that theory exactly mirrors the structure of behavior and that the observed behavioral phenomena are the effects of this underlying real structure. According to this view, such concepts as libido, id, ego, and superego mirror a hidden reality which underlies certain groups of behavioral phenomena. The phenomena are the effects of this dynamic structure. They stand in a causal relationship to the concrete reality of libido, id, ego, and superego. Similarly, the concept of stimulus in an original, positivist learning theory mirrors a reality that causes certain behavior in animals and men. This was the initial view of positivism. The unavoidable evolution in Western thought, however, quite naturally affected the positivist position in psychology. Therefore, new concepts and formulations have emerged in positivist psychology itself which manifest a new conception of science approximating the existential position.

Rationalism, on the other hand, fosters a view of scientific theory which is the opposite of the objectivist conception that dominated positivism. For the rationalist or the idealist, theory is nothing but a logical system of classifications. The psychologist developed this categorical structure as a tool for summarizing information about behavior. In the idealistic view, this system is merely subjective, and we cannot know whether the thing "out there" corresponds to our conception of it. The concepts of libido, id, ego, superego, stimulus, and reinforcement are merely subjective. They are only in the mind. We do not know whether they represent actual behavior. Here, again, we must add that the existential evolution of Western thought has finally led many rationalists and idealists to concepts and formulations which reveal the impact of the new cultural development.

Finally, the existential view of scientific theory unites the positivist and rationalist views in a flexible synthesis. According to this concept, theory is a subjective-objective creation of the scientist. Theory is subjective insofar as it is a creation of the scientific thinker. It is objective insofar as it represents *in principle* structural properties and relationships among the behavioral phenomena. Theory is thus a subjective frame of reference created by the scientific thinker to represent structural properties and relationships which he observes in the appearances of behavior.

CHAPTER FOUR

DIFFERENTIAL THEORETICAL MODES OF EXISTENCE IN PSYCHOLOGY

Differential Theories

All theories and possibilities of theory in science can be reduced to two main groups, comprehensive and differential. A theory in one single field of physics concerned with the properties of electricity, for example, differs from the comprehensive theory of relativity or of quantum physics. This distinction is evident to one who compares the uses, methods, developments, and scope of both kinds of theories. We shall later discuss some of the divergent characteristics of comprehensive and differential theories notable in psychology. But before doing so, we should like to point out how this self-evident distinction is rooted in the very existence of man.

Is there some differentiation in the primordial structure of existence itself which explains why all scientific theory is either comprehensive or differential? We cannot find the answer to this question by means of the empirical methods of psychology. Empirical observation teaches us that the distinction exists, but it does not tell why. The only method open to us is to make explicit our assumptions regarding man's nature. As we have already seen, psychology borrows such assumptions from contemporary philosophy, but deals with them as hypothetical constructs.

According to our hypothetical assumption, then, man finds himself as an existent subjectivity in the world. He is vaguely aware of the totality of all that is. His dynamic intentionality urges him to comprehend all being. But reality does not reveal itself to him immediately as a clearly structured whole, but as a vague aggregate of singular phenomena. Every new manifestation of knowledge regarding a particular phenomenon teaches man something about the whole of reality. Therefore, when man grasps, appropriates, and understands one single, particular, phenomenal appearance, he grows at the same time in the knowledge of the whole insofar as it manifests itself in this particular phenomenon. Man thus strives for a knowledge of the whole by seeking a knowledge of singular concrete appearances. Briefly, the primordial structure of man seems to be such that he tends at the same time toward a knowledge of both the whole of reality and of particular phenomena.

Why is it that the restless intentionality of man toward the comprehension of the whole must make a detour, as it were, through individual phenomena? The most fundamental reason seems to be that man's subjectivity is bodily. This means that man's actual concrete existence is always limited in time and space. Therefore he must encounter the whole of reality in its separate, material, palpable manifestations which present themselves to his senses. Only by growth in the clear knowledge of particular appearances can man grow in the knowledge of the whole.

As a result, the knowledge of man is dialectical. We use the term "dialectical" in the present context to indicate the polar relationship between the knowledge of particular phenomena and that of the whole. Man's knowledge shifts continuously, as it were, from an accurate, observational-experimental-theoretical knowledge of a specific phenomenon to a deeper, universal, theoretical knowledge of the whole group of phenomena to which it belongs. Then, from his new theoretical knowledge of the whole, man shifts back again to a renewed, deeper investigation of the singular phenomenon with the aid of his newly learned hypotheses. This dialectical nature of man's knowledge explains the constant tension between the comprehensive theories and the differential theories which are immediately bound to empirical observation of particular groups of phenomena. To be sure, there is no essential opposition between a comprehensive theory and the various differential theories with their experimental-observational components. The two approaches to knowledge necessarily compenetrate, sustain, and stimulate each other. For they are two essential experiences of one and the same bodily existence. The vague knowledge of the whole is primary. Then, differentiation takes place when man concentrates his attention on particular phenomena. This differentiated knowledge leads back to a deeper, more structured knowledge of the whole.

The primordial structure of the cognitive activity of man thus urges him in two directions. These two theoretical modes of knowing interact not only on the scientific but also on the pre-scientific level of his existence. When we observe people in the act of understanding their experience, we note their natural, spontaneous tendency to unite their individual experiences into wholes which are meaningful to them. They shift continually from a special attention to the phenomena of their daily lives to an interest in comprehensive naïve theory which gives meaning to this variety of otherwise isolated appearances. As we have already seen, their observation of particular phenomena already implies a theoretical movement. We may call this theoretical movement inherent in every observation a naïve differential theory.

A mother, for example, accepts implicitly the differential theory that her child should eat a sufficient amount of food. This theory enables her to be perceptive of the phenomena of refusal of food by her child. She may also have developed another naïve differential theory regarding her relationship to the child, which may be formulated as: "When I am disturbed, my child is less cooperative." This pre-scientific theory enables her to observe in the child various phenomena of refusal to cooperate. Her tendency to understand the possible relatedness of the variety of phenomena may lead her to combine her two differential theories. She may theorize that the refusal of food by her child is a sign of refusal of cooperation because she herself is upset. In the meantime, and in the same manner, she may have developed a variety of other pre-scientific theories concerned with other phenomena. All of these may lead to a whole network of observations which reinforce her naïve theories. Finally, when she has a sufficient number of differential theories and their corresponding phenomena at her disposal, her restless striving for total knowledge about her child may urge her to construct a comprehensive theory. She has observed, let us say, that she is upset when the child does not live up to her expectations. She has discovered in other situations that these expectations are due to criteria prevalent in her social circle. Ultimately, she formulates the comprehensive theory that parental preoccupation with social demands leads to bad eating habits in children. Of course, this whole process it at least partly unconscious, pre-scientific, and uncontrolled. Therefore, this particular comprehensive theory may be faulty. But it demonstrates that all the essential constituents of the scientific theoretical process are already present in the pre-scientific theoretical mode of man's existence.

The process of psychotherapy provides another example of a situation which enables man to become aware of spontaneous new differential theories. The patient ordinarily becomes conscious of phenomena in his life which he has previously been unable to observe. Moreover, the therapeutic process enables him to formulate a variety of possible comprehensive theories which may integrate his new differential theories and the phenomena he observes by means of them. Therapy thus facilipitates the emergence of a spontaneous dialogue between pre-scientific comprehensive and differential theories. This process may enable the patient to create a world of meaning which is more congruent with his actual everyday experience.

Human existence, moreover, is essentially co-existence. Therefore, the task of uncovering reality is shared by many. One of the innumerable manifestations of this cooperation of persons who want to know is the development of science. Every science is an organized attempt of many individuals to understand a particular area of reality. The methods used to increase knowledge in every science necessarily conform to the existential structure of man as scientist. As we have seen, man involves himself in the whole of reality by taking a stand toward the particulars that make up this whole. Therefore, we find in every science the development of differential theories immediately related to observation of and experimentation with a limited number of phenomena. We also find in every science the development of comprehensive theories just as soon as a number of isolated differential theories sufficient to demand integration have been developed. Man's co-existence implies specialization in various sciences. Efficient co-existence also leads to specialization within each science. When each phase of a science has its own specialists, a more rapid and efficient development of this science as a whole becomes possible. When a science becomes complex, it is impossible for one man to be excellent in all of its phases. For this reason, the various sciences produce both specialized differential theorists and specialized comprehensive theorists. Such a development is now taking place in the science of psychology.

Mutually Exclusive Quality of Differential Theoretical Constructs

We have already discussed the fragmentary approach to the object pole of psychology. We have pointed out that it may be explained by the bodily character of man's existence. And we have concluded that this fragmentary approach cannot result in a total construct or model of behavior even if we combine the outcomes of all our observations. The rationale for our conclusion is the fact that we can never achieve a moment in which all possible viewpoints can be maintained simultaneously.

However, this is not the only reason why it is impossible to obtain a total construct through the multiplication of differential theories. Another reason is that the partial constructs, or aggregates of ideas, of these theories have meanings which are mutually exclusive. Even when the same terms are used, these constructs do not have the same meanings within the various differential theories. Therefore, we cannot combine them to form a homogeneous unity.

To understand this concretely, we may consider a psychologist who specializes in a differential theory, for example, the physiological psychologist. He has developed a solid theoretical, empirical, and experimental knowledge of physiology. Let us say that he is observing a moving hand from a specific theoretical frame of reference of interconnected physiological constructs. This texture of physiological ideas leads him to perceive certain appearances while not perceiving others at the same time. Certain phenomena of the moving hand reveal themselves to him; others do not. The theoretical stand which he takes determines what kind of phenomena reveal themselves to his perception. He does not perceive in the moving hand the phenomena, let us say, of reaching out for an object, of external behavioral characteristics, or of cultural expression. He is aware only of the phenomena which are revealed in the light of an aggregate of physiological ideas.

There are, however, other specialists in psychology who perceive quite different phenomena because they use different theoretical approaches. These psychologists might observe one and the same moving hand in many different ways. The theoretical constructs which are developed and applied by these various experts are also necessarily different. For the physiological psychologist, the moving hand is a manifestation of phenomena which are in harmony or disharmony with ideas proposed by physiological thinkers. For the social psychologist, the appearance of the moving hand expresses certain cultural influences whch may or may not correspond with ideas developed by theorists in his field. For the psychologist of learning, the movement of the hand reflects processes of conditioning and reinforcement. He discovers phenomena which are related to the elaborate system of ideas which is called learning theory.

The psychoanalytically oriented psychologist sees in the moving hand an expression of feelings and tendencies determined by a genetic process in the early history of the subject. He questions whether the phenomena observed correspond to a refined texture of psychoanalytic ideas spun out in years of intensive theorizing.

In other words, all behavioral phenomena can be inserted, as it were, into various differential theories of psychology. Every single differential theory is a frame of reference in which behavior is approached and known in one of its manifold aspects. Every single area in psychology is constituted by a specific fundamental interest of the observing psychologist. Each interest reveals one perspective of the total object pole of psychology which is intentional-functional behavior. These specific interests constitute the single fields of psychology. We may say that they are the differentiations of the over-all psychological mode of existence. The latter is in turn a differentiation of total human existence or involvement in the world.

We may conclude that every differential theory in psychology is essentially limited: only certain constructs belong to its frame of reference while others are necessarily excluded. Even when differential theories of psychology use the same constructs, they are integrated into different tissues of ideas. Such integration necessarily changes the original meaning of these constructs. For example, the idea of "energy" has different meanings when used in the differential theories of psychoanalysis and of physiological psychology. The same is true of the idea of "learning" when integrated within the differential theory of strict behaviorism and that of client-centered therapy.

From all we have said, it becomes more and more clear that science is fundamentally a well-organized aggregate of ideas, a theoretical structure, and that the scientist is basically a thinker, a theorist, and only secondarily an observer. All that precedes this state of theoretical organization of phenomena is pre-scientific.

Differential-Theoretical and Experimental Modes of Existence

We have seen that the experimental mode of existence is a necessary constituent of the general scientific mode. How is this experimental component related to the differential-theoretical one which we have been analyzing?

The experimental is a proper mode of existence for man. It is man's nature to be involved bodily in the world and to unveil the world gradually by bodily observation and manipulation. Thus the scientist's own nature impels him to develop the experimental method. The structure of intentional-functional behavior and the possibilities implied in this structure are uncovered by the experimental psychologist, therefore, in an experimental way. He is not satisfied merely with the observation of behavior as it presents itself to him; he organizes experimental situations in which he can propose certain questions about behavior. The answers presented to him during the experiment confirm or challenge directly the differential theoretical structures, and indirectly the comprehensive theoretical structures, which make up the science of psychology. Therefore, theoretical psychologists require the experiments of empirical and applied psychologists in order to develop theoretical structures which will organize as adequately as possible the phenomena observed in behavior. For this reason, the extension of the experimental mode of existence to as many areas of psychology as possible is a necessity.

When a psychologist devises an experiment, he begins with a differential theoretical point of view concerning behavior. This attitude may have been developed in a dialogue with comprehensive-theoretical psychologists. In this case, we may say that the differential-theoretical view is a postulate derived from the comprehensive-theoretical vision of psychology. But it is not uniquely characteristic of a differential-theoretical view that it be hypothetical. What makes a theory differential in the strict sense is its quality of being translatable into operational terms. The experimental psychologist thus devises an experiment on the basis of a differential-theoretical view in the strict sense. The outcome of the experiment affirms or challenges totally or partially the differential theory of the psychologist. The experimental results, therefore, may give rise to a new differential theory concerning the aspect of behavior under study.

A somewhat similar situation exists in applied psychology. Though the latter is experimental in a far looser sense than psychology pursued in the laboratory, one cannot deny its experimental aspect. For the applied psychologist aims at the solution of certain problems in human life, for example, in industry or in education. He does this only by utilizing certain possibilities of human behavior within given situations. He develops of necessity some differential theory which guides his attempts to utilize these possibilities in a way which will produce the desired effects. While doing so, he discovers that this differential theory is valid, invalid, or only partially valid. This knowledge may restructure his differential theory. New possibilities in behavior within a given situation may reveal themselves to him. His new differential theory in turn calls for experiment with the new possibilities which he has discovered. In this sense, we may say that the applied psychologist also engages in experiments which arise from and lead to differential theories.

It is clear that every experiment is rooted in an operational theory. Later in our discussion, we shall demonstrate that this operational theory may be rooted in turn in a phenomenological description of the situation under study.

Individual operational theories, when translated into actual observation, experimentation, or application within a certain area, give rise to a more complex operational theory. That is, the results of different operational theories within the same area of investigation give rise to the structure of a differential theory which integrates them. This differential theory, to be sure, must be broken up again into its constituent operational theories when the psychologist wishes to translate it into concrete operational procedures. Examples of more complex differential theories are learning theory, field theory, and Gestalt theory.

The comparatively new science of psychology, like physical science in its beginnings, is still largely a collection of differential-operational theories. The psychologist cannot build at once a structure of ideas which presents a comprehensive theory of intentionl-functional behavior. It is mainly through phenomenological descriptions and through experiments which test operational differential theories that the psychologist obtains the numerous fragmentary pieces of knowledge which will enable him ultimately to form a comprehensive theoretical structure. Early psychologists were forced to grope for understanding through phenomenological descriptions, observations, and experiments. This research enabled them to expand their store of fragmentary but nonetheless effective theoretical constructs. As we shall see later, the fragmentary nature of these constructs does not mean that psychology must abandon the quest for the understanding of the whole of intentional-functional behavior. Rather, the universality of man's existential quest implies that he will necessarily strive for a comprehensive theoretical view of psychology which will integrate partial discoveries and fill the gaps left by differential-theoretical structures. This new comprehensive structure of ideas will, in turn, illuminate and stimulate further development of the differential and operational psychological theories.

Characteristics of Differential Theories

When we examine the characteristics of differential theories, we discover that they are not primordially reflective in the proper sense, that they are limited in comprehension, and that they are mastered by the actual performance of the operations concerned. We shall examine these three characteristics more or less in detail.

Reflection in the proper sense mans that man "bends back" on his own existence. When the psychologist reflects in this sense, he shifts his attention from the behavior which he has under observation to his own behavior as a psychologist. He then makes his own psychological mode of existence the object-pole of his investigation, and he develops a psychology of the psychologist. This reflection also enables him to hypothesize about the relationships between the psychological mode of existence, other modes of existence, and the primordial structure of existence itself. To further his understanding he may borrow comprehensive concepts from philosophers. He uses these as hypothetical constructs in his sytsem of ideas, suspending belief or disbelief in their ontological status. Moreover, he keeps his reflection on his psychological mode of existence in constant dialogue with the phenomena and the theoretical constructs developed by differential theorists. If the result of his reflection is clearly inconsistent with the phenomena, he rejects the borrowed constructs and revises his theory.

As we shall see later in our analysis, this theory of the psychological mode of existence is not the whole of comprehensive psychological theory. It is its necessary foundation. It may be called, therefore, fundamental or foundational theory.

In the strict or proper sense, differential and operational theories in psychology are not reflective. Differential theorists are not primordially interested in the psychological mode of existence as a whole. Reflection on the psychological mode and all its differentiations is not a study which lies within the realm of one or the other differential theory. On the contrary, it implies of necessity a study *about* all the differential theories from a general, independent, theoretical viewpoint. Such a viewpoint must remain outside the confines of one or the other differential theory. For a differential theory is only one limited approach to the psychological mode of existence as a whole. Therefore, it can never provide the ultimate basis for a total outlook on the whole psychological mode of existence.

The differential and operational theorist reflects, however, in a less proper or strict sense. Though he does not reflect on his own psychological mode of existence, he may reflect on the effectiveness of his empirical operations. He may also think about the operational translation of his hypotheses. Again, he may reflect on the possibilities of the integration of operational propositions into a logically consistent structure. Each differential theory selects its own constructs in order to develop a structure of ideas which represents the relationship of behavioral phenomena observed within its domain. These constructs, however, are determined by their usefulness for structuring the specific phenomena. They are not suitable, therefore, for an understanding of the psychological mode of existence itself.

In other words, differential and operational theories are not primordially concerned with the mode of existence of the psychologist himself. They are primarily oriented toward those behavioral phenomena which are the object of the theory in question. The so-called reflection of the differential or the operational theorist thus remains outside of himself.

The operational theorist is involved in a thoughtful consideration of the functional implications of the findings in a certain field of psychology. And the differential theorist is concerned with the systematic relationship of behavioral phenomena and operational propositions within a single area of psychology.

We should add here that some differential theories, such as the psychoanalytic and psychotherapeutic, imply a certain type of self-reflection. It differs, however, from reflection on the psychological mode of existence as a whole. First of all, self-reflection is not the primary aim of psychoanalytic and psychotherapeutic theories. Second, this limited self-reflection refers in practice to the analyst or therapist only in terms of a special purpose, such as the improvement of the therapeutic relationship. Finally, this self-reflection is not concerned with the psychological mode of existence in all its manifestations in differential theories. It refers only to the analytic or psychotherapeutic differentiation and not to the psychological mode of existence as such.

We may conclude that the differential theories never have self-reflection as a primary aim. Rather, they are an immediate outgrowth of man's spontaneous cognitive mode of existence.

Comprehensive theory, on the contrary, is a more remote development of man's cognitive mode of being. Man's spontaneous manner of knowing is not directed first toward knowing himself. He responds first of all to the phenomena which reveal themselves to his senses. Self-reflection is secondary. Another link between differential operational theories and man's spontaneous cognitive way of existence is the fruitfulness of both ways of knowing for subsequent activity. Our knowledge in daily life directs our activity. And the results of our activity supply us in turn with the knowledge of new phenomena. Differential and, more specifically, operational theories also lead to new experimental and observational activities of the psychologist. These provide him in turn with the knowledge of new phenomena. Comprehensive theory, on the contrary, cannot be translated immediately into operational terms.

The second main characteristic of differential theories is that they are limited in comprehension. They are not aimed primarily at a comprehensive knowledge of behavior. The most basic characteristic of every differential-operational theory is its commitment to a certain dimension of behavior. Such a perspective uncovers aspects of behavior while it covers up other aspects. These latter can be revealed only by a change of perspective. And changed perspectives imply other differential theories.

A differential theory aims at an integration of operational postulates and the phenomena that are discovered in the light of these postulates. The latter are determined by their capability of being translated into empirical operations. These operations are concrete, limited modes of experiment and observation. They always imply limited perspectives: only certain phenomena are revealed. Therefore, the integration of operational postulates and their corresponding phenomena is necessarily limited to that which is revealed in the light of particular perspectives. Differential theory can never seek the comprehensive integration of the perspectives of all other differential theories in the light of a total view. Logically, a differential theory *as differential* cannot possibly produce an overall view that transcends the perspective of every differential theory including its own. It may, however, seek to integrate in the light of its *own limited perspective* the findings of other differential theories.

Learning theory, for example, may consider phenomena described by psychoanalysis. But this consideration will of necessity be from the perspective of learning theory. This implies that it will not include the special aspects which reveal themselves only in the light of the psychoanalytic viewpoint. In other words, such an integration would not be a comprehensive integration but rather an absorption of the findings of one area of psychology by another. The differential theorist would merely demonstrate in such a case that he can consider from his own specific perspective the material that has been uncovered in another field of psychology. And he would imply that this material of the other field manifests not only its own particular profile but also the profile in which he is specializing.

This possibility of looking upon all phenomena of behavior from various viewpoints and of uncovering various profiles clarifies for us the very specific sense in which a differential theory can be comprehensive. That is, the differential-theoretical mode of existence in psychology is *comprehensive* in so far as it stands out toward the whole of behavior. But it is *limited-comprehensive* in so far as it views all behavior from only *one perspective,* such as the psychoanalytic, the organismic, or the psycho-physiological point of view. In the latter sense, each differential-theoretical approach will always remain limited or directed toward only one profile of behavior. Nevertheless, its contribution, incomplete as it may be, is indispensable for the understanding of behavior as a whole. The analytic approach to behavior, for example, cannot dispense with the necessity for sociological, genetic, and physiological psychology. Nor can these latter abrogate the need for the analytic method. No psychologist, whether comprehensive, differential, operational, or applied, should either underestimate or overestimate any differential approach to behavior.

The third main characteristic of differential theories is that they are mastered by the actual performance of the operations involved. The psychologist who specializes in a differential theory rooted in empirical operations conducts the necessary operations initially under competent supervision of a psychologist who is already an expert in the field. Empirical operations imply the use of experimental techniques which embody the theory concerned. When the student masters these techniques, he gains at the same time a concrete knowledge of the theory.

For example, one becomes a psychotherapist by practicing therapy under the direction of a supervisor who examines the strengths and weaknesses in the student's therapy sessions. The latter are tape-recorded or observed by means of a one-way vision screen. In this manner, it is quite possible to become an effective therapist without a profound theoretical insight into the meaning of therapeutic psychology and its relationship to the whole of psychology.

Again, a psychologist may conduct fruitful experiments regarding the learning ability of animals. He may draw valuable conclusions from these experiments. At the same time, he may have very litle theoretical insight into the relevance of these conclusions for certain aspects of human behavior. This lack of general theoretical insight does not invalidate the concrete worth of his experimentation. Sooner or later it may be evaluated by comprehensive psychologists and find its place in the whole of psychology.

Another psychologist may be trained in the administration of intelligence and aptitude tests. He is quite competent in computation. He engages in valuable research in the measurement of intelligence. It is not at all necessary, for the performance of these operations as such, that he reflect on the meaning of this measured intelligence within the whole of human behavior. To be sure, it would be rewarding for such a specialist to engage in such reflection. Indeed, most schools of psychology do stimulate insight far beyond that of mere operational technique. But a differential psychologist can perform effective, well-controlled research without being aware of its relationship to the whole of the object-pole of psychology.

Every expert in any differential-operational field of psychology becomes an expert by participating in operational research. While doing so, he develops a sensitivity for the kinds of questions raised by his specific field. He becomes keenly aware of the types of observational and experimental operations through which these questions may be answered. Differential theories, such as psychoanalytical and physio-psychological, develop their own complex of questions, methods, and operations so that every differential expert acquires a special orientation toward his own field. The psychoanalytically-oriented scientist knows by practical initiation, for example, that he cannot use the methods of cybernetics in order to understand the subjective qualities of the feelings of his patient. On the other hand, it is self-evident to the psychologist who works in the field of cybernetics that he cannot directly use constructs such as the *Oedipus complex* of Freud and the *shadow* of Jung to build a brain model.

We may conclude that the learning theorist, the client-centered therapist, the psychoanalyst, and the physiological psychologist all become experts in their differential and operational theories not by reflection but by action. They do not learn the meaning of psychology within their specific fields by means of a theoretical introduction. They learn their profession through practical experience in operational research. Practical training in a differential or operational theory develops in the student a specific interest in a particular profile of behavior and teaches him how to explore it. Reflection upon the more profound nature, meaning, and relationships of this specialized mode of psychological existence lies, as such, beyond the scope of differential and operational theory.

It should be evident by now that the theorizing of the differential psychologist is intimately bound to and limited by his concrete research. Differential theory is, therefore, essentially operational, immediately related to the concrete operations performed in research. The psychological mode of such a theorist is absorbed by one specific perspective of the object pole of psychology. He thus develops observational and experimental designs which enable him increasingly to discover new knowledge about his own area of interest. His mode of involvement with a specific profile gradually reveals its structure, variability, conditions, and functional relationships. But his concrete operations are limited in type.

Such specialization does not preclude communication and intellectual stimulation among various differential theorists. Characteristically, however, the differential-operational theorist is interested in other differential theories from his own point of view. He interacts with other theorists primarily insofar as they enlighten him in the study of the specific profile of behavior in which he is doing research.

Creativity of the Differential Theorist

Despite the limitation of his field of research, the differential-theoretical psychologist is far from a technician without creativity. A series of significant experiments or observations is an organized elaboration of an original question posed to behavior. The theorist is aware that his series of experiments as such is not his decisive contribution to science. He knows that his creative contribution is the discovery of a crucial question and the embodiment of this question in observational and experimental operations. He realizes that it is possible for him to ask an unlimited number of questions. But he also knows that an infinite number of possible questions is relatively useless in the sense that they will not lead to deeper understanding of human behavior. He no longer shares the naïve optimism of certain scientists of an earlier period who tended to forget that they were profiting from centuries of speculation which helped them to eliminate many unfruitful questions. He realizes that tentative thought, observation, speculation, and argumentation are necessary before one can pose a question to behavior which opens up really new vistas or horizons.

Let us consider the case of the psychologist who is doing admirable research in psychotherapy. It would be naïve to believe that he could be capable of effective operational questioning without the benefit of countless years of practice of therapy, of reflection on processes, of talking, arguing, hypothesizing, and publishing about psychotherapy on the part of earlier psychologists. It would be impossible to do effective contemporary research in psychotherapy if other psychologists had not practiced long ago the infant science of psychotherapy and reflected upon it. The tedious labor of discovering the most valuable perspectives and questions can require years of concentrated creative endeavor. The differential-operational theorist cannot neglect this creative, pre-operational phase of his work. If he is wise, he knows that he may lose more in the long run by such neglect than he would gain by impetuously going through the motions of skillful measurement or experiment. His observations and experiments might be well controlled and executed without contributing in the least to the understanding of the profile under study. He might conceivably produce reams of accurate reports of useless experiments about trivia.

In a sense, the pre-operational constituent of the differential-theoretical mode of existence is the crucial one which determines the significance of the research itself. This constituent is at work not only in the first beginnings of a science, for it repeats itself as long as the science lives. Over and over again, the pre-operational discovery of a possibly fruitful question is followed by the translation of this question into operations. Behavior itself gives an answer to the operational question. The answer is hidden in the so called "data" gained in observation and experimentation. The scientist must interpret this answer creatively. The period of reflection on the data may be called the post-operational constituent of the differential-theoretical mode of existence. This post-operational constituent, however, is pre-operational in relation to the *next* related experiment or observation. The differential-operational theorist reflects on the data which he has obtained in order to formulate new effective operational questions. Therefore, the pre-operational mode of existence reactualizes itself continually in scientific existence. If it did not do so, science would die out as a dynamic enterprise. It would become a monotonous repetition of what has already been done.

Reductionist Tendency in the Differential-Theoretical Mode of Existence

Having considered the chief characteristics of the differential-theoretical mode of existence, we should point out the dangers inherent in it. Every mode of existence endangers human existence as a whole insofar as it tends to identify the whole of life with itself. The same may be said of the various constituents of each individual mode of existence. Each of these limited approaches to one mode of existence sometimes attempts to absorb within itself the whole mode of which it is only one component. Differential theory, for example, is only one constituent of the whole of psychology. Yet there is often a tendency in the differential-theoretical mode to regard itself as the entire psychological mode of existence. We may carry this statement further. As we have seen, the differential-theoretical mode differentiates itself in many specific modes, such as the psychoanalytical, the behavioristic, and the physio-psychological. Observation of these specialized modes reveals that each of them sometimes tends to identify itself with the whole differential-theoretical mode or even with the entire psychological mode of existence. This phenomenon appears so frequently that it calls for explanation. We shall do this by describing some of the conditions which foster the appearance and reappearance of this phenomenon. These conditions are, first of all, the fundamental structure of our existence, which compels us to approach the object pole of psychology under certain profiles or perspectives; next, the possible seduction of successful psychological methods; and, finally, the seduction of sudden new breakthroughs in psychology.

Reductionism and the Existential Structure of Man

We must refer here to our earlier explication of implicit assumptions which have a hypothetical status in the science of psychology. According to these assumptions, man is a bodily existent, an embodied subjectivity. The fact that he exists in and through a body implies that he can attain to the universal or the totality only by many partial encounters with the multitude of phenomena. This general truth of existence must be predicated by the psychological mode of existence. Every differential-operational theory is in reality one of these many encounters with phenomena. Each one uncovers only certain phenomena insofar as diffential theory views the whole of behavior under only one perspective.

The differential theorist who is engaged in such a partial approach to reality is still driven, however, by his existential intentionality toward comprehension of the whole. The need to know the whole permeates, as it were, his quest for partial knowledge. This need may distort his awareness of the limitations of his differential perspective. It may even lead the psychologist to believe that his differential theory is a model for all behavior under all its aspects. The tremendous dynamic drive to be involved in all-that-is may even seduce him to believe that his differential theory is the model not only for all behavior but for all reality. This last distortion is called psychologism. It would seem that the existential dynamism toward comprehension is so pervasive in man that it renders the overestimation of differential theory unavoidable, at least from time to time. As we shall see later, an explicit attempt to develop a comprehensive theoretical psychology may lessen considerably this implicit attempt toward comprehension by differential theorists. For this implicit attempt to extrapolate beyond the data of differential theory can be very harmful to psychology. It could prevent a balanced understanding of behavior.

Reductionism and the Seduction of the Successful Method

We have seen that the differential-theoretical psychologist begins to master his areas of specialization by a thorough initiation into methodical research. The efficiency of his method is determined by the profile of behavior which he studies. A highly developed differential-operational theory presupposes a refined and efficient methodology which alone reveals the particular perspective desired. Such a methodology is fundamentally an experimental elaboration of one perspective which opens up a specific area of behavioral phenomena. Every other perspective, if it is well developed and embodied in an empirical methodology, should manifest a quite different methodology since it reveals a quite different field of phenomena. In other words, one criterion of the efficiency and precision of a differential-operational theory is its uniqueness. The very refinement of the psychological method of a differential field accounts for its impressive results within its own area.

The continual pressure of the existential need for universal comprehension, however, combined with the daily experience of the admirable achievements of a differential method, cannot but tempt the differential theorist to overestimate the power of this method. He may assume that the method which has been so successful in the special area of his research can also be applied, with necessary changes, in other fields of psychology. He may be seduced to believe that this method, if used in other areas, would lead to results similar to the successes in his own field. Consequently, the psychoanalyst, the learning theorist, the student of cybernetics, and the physiological psychologist may at times indulge in extrapolations beyond the confines of their respective differential theories.

This tendency may lead to the imperialism of certain theories at the expense of other possible ones. The various aspects of the object-pole of psychology can be revealed only by the development of as many methods as possible. The imperialism of only a few methods of research would imply the restriction of the whole object-pole of psychology to only those few profiles which could be explored by these methods. Such a methodical restriction of the psychological mode of existence might lead, unfortunately, to a considerable impoverishment of man's knowledge of intentional-functional behavior. It might also lead psychologists to mistake their thorough knowledge of certain aspects of behavior for a thorough understanding of behavior under all its possible perspectives.

Reductionism and the Seduction of a Crucial Breakthrough

The psychological mode of existence is a searching standing-out toward behavior by means of observation and experiment. Since the empirical or the applied psychologist cannot understand behavior from a single viewpoint, he seeks for such understanding through different viewpoints which he elaborates by means of observation and experiment. He cannot know *a priori* which specific phenomena will reveal themselves to him when he assumes a new approach and embodies it in a strict methodology. At times the results of his research are disappointing. Only through his assumption of a variety of viewpoints and their embodiment in observational and experimental methods does an unexpected realm of phenomena sometimes open up. The psychologist cannot foresee or plan this sudden disclosure of a new field of phenomena. He can only be faithful to his task of constant translation of operational hypotheses into concrete research. It is quite understandable that a sudden, unexpected breakthrough to a realm of phenomena never before revealed is an exciting event.

Frequently such a discovery changes our insights in a radical way. Then the inherent existential groping of man for universal comprehensive knowledge may unfortunately fixate itself on such a new realm of phenomena. He may be led to believe that this particular discovery is the key to the comprehensive knowledge of all behavior under all its aspects and conditions. He may be seduced into assuming, for example, that the unconscious, the libido, the stimulus-response bond, the striving for superiority, or the feedback mechanism is the ultimate explanation of all behavior. He may be inclined to forget that a discovery which is based on concrete operations can never be the last and ultimate explanation of the whole of behavior, because operations are limited in space and time. They embody a certain limited way of looking at reality, a circumscribed point of view. Therefore, they can never reveal more than a limited profile of behavior which corresponds with the limited perspective which they embody.

An explicit attempt at comprehensive theory would lessen this tendency toward over-evaluation of important but limited discoveries. Comprehensive theorists would evaluate the variety of incidental breakthroughs in the light of an open theoretical vision. Such a comprehensive theoretical psychology, on the other hand, would never attempt to obstruct the one-sided growth of differential psychologies. On the contrary, it would foster this growth as a desirable, limited specialization which enriches psychology. In the meantime, however, comprehensive theory would balance the impact of this one-sided growth by pointing out other possible profiles of behavior which have not been investigated. In other words, comprehensive psychology would foster one-sidedness *as one-sidedness.* Or, it would promote at the same time both one-sided specialization and the awareness that specialization is by definition limited, so that it can never be a basis for the understanding of behavior as a whole.

The science of psychology is of necessity dependent on the revelation of new phenomena. The order of this opening up of new profiles of behavior cannot be planned according to a hierarchy of importance of these phenomena. To be sure, psychology is in principle capable of revealing behavioral phenomena gradually and unceasingly. But the psychologist can never foresee which phenomena will reveal themselves first in the light of his research. Nor can he know *a priori* which phenomena are most important for the understanding of the whole of behavior. Therefore, the development of the science of behavior is necessarily many-sided and often unharmonious. Psychology is the result of the interplay of many one-sided differential theoretical activities carried on by numerous psychologists. It is obviously impossible for every psychologist to assume all psychological perspectives and their embodiment in empirical operations as his own. Some will inevitably devote their energy to phenomenological, experimental, or clinical research. Others will concentrate on the application of psychology to the improvement of behavior within concrete life situations. Others again will dedicate their lives as psychologists to theoretical reflection. And all of them will uncover new phenomena from their own particular, one-sided perspectives. Moreover, no authentic science of psychology is possible unless all modes of being a psychologist make their contribution to the whole.

To be really fruitful in his work, each psychologist must realize that his specialized psychological mode of existence has a relative value. He must be aware that the same is true of his psychological discoveries, no matter how exciting they are. The value of his specialized mode of existence and of the knowledge which it reveals is essential but not exclusive. It does not exclude the values of other psychological modes, of other differential-operational theories, and of the phenomena which they uncover. All differential theories and the dimensions of behavior which they uncover are of value, but we cannot determine *a priori what* their precise value is. New perspectives and new profiles of behavior will continue to open up in the future. In the light of these discoveries, the value of former discoveries may prove to be more or less than it originally seemed to be. The value of every differential-operational theory thus remains relative in so far as we cannot determine precisely what this value is.

Reductionism and the Two Main Differential-Theoretical Modes of Existence

The differential-theoretical mode of psychological existence divides itself into a variety of modes according to the diversity of aspects assumed by its theorists. While every viewpoint differs from every other, it remains possible that a whole series of perspectives may have characteristics in common. When we seek this commonality among the many perspectives studied in contemporary psychology, we discover that all these perspectives may be subsumed under two main categories. One series of approaches in differential psychology tends to reveal primarily the intentional-functional profiles of behavior; the other, the external profiles of behavior which are measurable in exact quantitative units. Examples of the intentional-functional differential theories are, among others, the psychoanalytic, the psychotherapeutic, and various clinical theories. The external behavior category of differential theories may be illustrated by the physiological, learning, sensuous-perceptual, and cybernetic theories. How are we to explain the emergence of these two main types of viewpoints which have characterized psychology from its beginning?

All science, to be sure, begins with the observation of externally perceptible phenomena. The particular phenomena with which the science of psychology originates are behavioral. The psychologist considers these phenomena from different viewpoints. He discovers that he can view behavioral phenomena under either their measurable, quantitative aspect or their qualitative, intentional-functional aspect. Both profiles of behavior, it should be noted, present themselves immediately to our perception. Even the pre-scientific observer in daily life is aware of this givenness of the two main profiles of behavior. Such awareness is commonly expressed in spontaneous questions. Somebody smiles. The observer of the smile may ask himself spontaneously: "What does it mean? Is the person who smiles pleased or is he laughing at me?" He reflects on the situation to find out which answer is true. The question reveals, however, that the observer is implicitly aware that a theoretical distinction can be made between external behavior and its intentional-functional meaning. It is to be noted that he does not make an *absolute* distinction between external behavior and its intentional-functional aspect. As long as what he observes is really behavior, it has to have some meaning, some intentionality, some function. The doubt in the questioner's mind is not a doubt regarding the meaningfulness of the behavior, but regarding *the kind* of meaning embodied in the behavior. Behavior immediately presents itself to the observer as meaningful.

When behavior is no longer intentional-functional, it ceases to be behavior. At the same time, it ceases to be the object-pole of the science of psychology. For example, the falling open of the mouth of a corpse is not behavior. It lacks the characteristic of intentional functionality. Therefore, no psychologist as psychologist devotes his time to the study of the automatic movements of dead bodies. If he observes such automatic movement at all, he does it only insofar as it is relevant to the understanding of behavior.

The spontaneous awareness of both an intentional-functional and an external measurable profile of behavior points to the two main differential-theoretical modes of existence in psychology. For science is ultimately a methodical and critical elaboration of our spontaneous awareness. Both types of psychology have produced effective scientists; both have led to discoveries which have enriched our understanding of behavior. Evidently, the comprehensive theoretical psychologist has no right to reject apodictically either one of these main types of differential psychology, since he is striving for the integration of the science of psychology as a whole. He cannot decree that either behavioristic or intentional-functional psychology is not truly psychology. He is a scientific theorist, not a philosopher. Regardless of his personal bias, he must theorize on the basis of what psychologists actually do and factually demonstrate.

On the other hand, the differential theorist, who is engaged in research that pertains to one of these two main types of psychology, may be seduced by his own need for universal knowledge. He may be inclined to perceive his own type of psychology as the only scientific one. He may expect that it alone will eventually offer a complete understanding of the whole of behavior in all its profiles. The success of the methods developed and the insights reached by his type of psychology may encourage his bias. Such unconscious extrapolation may even manifest itself in disparaging remarks about the other type. The representative of the behavioristic type of psychology may talk derisively of the "subjective nonsense" of analytical research. Such remarks spread more heat than light. No profile of behavior is totally irrelevant to the understanding of behavior. And every profile impels us to adopt a different method of investigation.

The danger of an unconscious imperialism is that one type of psychology attempts to absorb the other. Such an attempt tends to reduce the whole of behavior to one of its two main profiles. If carried out on both sides, it would inevitably lead to a dualistic conception of behavior. Such a conception can be avoided only as long as both types of psychology remain clearly aware of their limitations and maintain mutual respect. The differential-operational theorist of each type of psychology, however, is so absorbed in his concrete investigations that he has little time or energy left to immerse himself in the totally different language, methods, and problems which arise in the other type of psychology. Therefore, practically speaking, the unity of intentional-functional behavior can be safeguarded only on a higher level of theorizing which occupies itself exclusively with the respectful integration of the contributions of the two main types of psychological existence in a higher unity.

Once it is clearly understood that both main types of psychology are limited modes of standing out toward behavior, it may be confidently stated that each type extends itself in its *own* way to the *whole* of intentional-functional behavior. The approach of each type will always remain a partial approach directed primarily toward one main profile of intentional-functional behavior. Nevertheless, the contribution of each type, incomplete as it may be, is indispensable. Man is by nature bodily subjectivity or incarnated intentionality. Therefore, both the biophysiological and the intentional-functional aspects are indispensable constituents of his behavior. They are embedded in different languages, methods, and operations. They represent relative but indispensable values for our understanding of behavior as a whole.

CHAPTER FIVE

THE COMPREHENSIVE THEORETICAL MODE OF EXISTENCE IN PSYCHOLOGY

Emergence of the Comprehensive-Theoretical Mode of Existence

The psychologist studies intentional-functional behavior from a variety of aspects. Each differential mode of psychology opens up a specific area of concrete phenomena which, at first sight, seem endless in their diversity. The differential theorist, however, unites these phenomena by means of differential constructs which have an integrating function within his special field. These constructs embody the fundamental interest of his differential approach. In the last analysis, it is this theoretical perspective which unites diverse manifestations of behavior within his specific differential theory.

For example, behaviors as varied as walking, smiling, kissing, and boxing may be observed from the aspect of physiological psychology. The theorist may use a differential construct, such as muscle innervation, to indicate a physiological quality common to all these types of behavior. To be sure, a smile, a kiss, a boxing match are experienced in daily life as quite different kinds of behavior which reveal an inexhaustible richness of meanings. But in the example given, the richness of perspectives of each one of these concrete events is relegated to the background in favor of one profile—the psycho-physiological. This profile represents an aspect of behavior selected because of a specific differential approach. Other differential approaches may place the same behavior in totally different contexts, such as the psychoanalytical, client-centered, or cybernetic theories.

This differential procedure, as we have seen, is absolutely necessary because our bodily mode of existence compels us to exploration by means of perspectives. We are incapable of grasping the whole of reality at once. The need to integrate these various profiles of behavior, however, leads to the emergence of the comprehensive theoretical mode of existence.

This mode of existence aims at the unification of the differential approaches. Man's spontaneous existential interest in intentional behavior as a whole necessarily gives rise to comprehensive theory. Thus man seeks to restore the concreteness and wholeness of behavior which has been broken up into profiles by the differential modes of psychological existence. The comprehensive and differential modes are thus related to each other as synthetic and analytic studies of behavior.

Something similar to the mutual influence of differential and comprehensive theory can be observed even in the pre-scientific dimension of existence. In daily life, for instance, when we must function in a pragmatic fashion, we may consider certain objects not in their full richness but under only a few of their profiles. When we move our furniture to a new house, for example, we perceive our tables, chairs, paintings, and carpets from a point of view which differs from our usual perception of them. We may consider our paintings, for example, under two perspectives—their size and fragility. Keeping these two points in mind, we seek a safe place for our paintings among the other furniture in the moving van. At this moment we do not enjoy their subtle pastels, harmonious forms, and beautiful perspectives. Afterward, however, when the paintings adorn our new home, we no longer concentrate on size and fragility but lose ourselves in their aesthetic meaning.

Differential theory dwells much more on such abstracted profiles, however, than man does in everyday life. In daily life the painting remains primarily a painting, even if it is sometimes placed in a different context such as that of object to be moved efficiently. In differential theories such as physiological psychology or learning theory, however, a smile, a kiss, and a boxing match are nothing other than processes of a physiological nature or of conditioning and reinforcement. And both differential theories are valid because both series of constructs consider phenomena which are observable in a smile, a kiss, and a boxing match. The same may be said of a variety of other series of constructs such as experiential, social, and motivational ones.

However, it is not unthinkable that concrete behavior as a whole may evaporate, as it were, and lose its reality for a psychologist who studies behavior only insofar as it is resolved into profiles described in specific languages pertaining to widely different perspectives. This danger of loss of contact with concrete behavior as a whole increases with the development of psychology, which implies a proliferation of the psychological mode of existence into an increasing number of differential modes. Each of these necessarily develops its own conceptual frame of reference for its special profile of behavior. Moreover, each is intimately linked to empirical operations and develops its own operational language. The language, constructs, and methods of full-grown differential theories are thus very different from one another. We may even say that a differential theory demonstrates that it has attained its maximum efficiency only when it has developed an idiom of its own. This idiom of the specialist is not comprehended by the psychologist of any other differential theory so long as he—as the representative of that other theory—thinks in constructs proper to his own exclusive area of psychology.

A unified theory of behavior cannot be attained, therefore, simply by securing the sum total of the conceptual frames of reference or of the idioms characteristic of the various differential theories in psychology. They have no basic similarity to one another. Some of the differential theories, to be sure, may share a formal aspect such as a mathematical, statistical, or experimental-instrumental sophistication. But obviously this formal, external similarity is of no practical value in the scientific unification of concrete behavior as a whole.

The wholeness of behavior as it appears in psychology can be approximated only by comprehensive theoretical psychology. Such a science develops so-called foundational-integrational constructs which represent a plausible hypothesis of what behavior may be like in its wholeness. Differential theories, on the other hand, develop abstracted profiles of behavior which must be reintegrated within this hypothetical model.

A dialogue is possible between the hypothetical model of the whole and its parts, that is, between integrational constructs and differential constructs. Comprehensive theory is precisely this open on-going dialogue. In order to understand the nature, aim, and conditions of this dialogue, we must first make explicit what is implicit in the comprehensive theoretical mode of existence which, like every mode, can be analyzed in its constituents. We may distinguish five relevant constituents—the foundational, integrational, hypothetical, creative, and communicative—of this mode of existence. The following discussion of these constituents proposes to clarify the meaning and purpose of the comprehensive theoretical mode of existence and thereby of comprehensive theory as well.

The Foundational Constituent

The comprehensive-theoretical mode of existence is foundational and integrational. Comprehensive theory insofar as it is *foundational* examines the foundations, assumptions, and basic constructs of the science of psychology. It does so, first of all, by making explicit what is implicit in the subject-pole and the object-pole of the psychological mode of existence. The results of this explication, however, are kept constantly in a dialectical relationship with the findings of the differential psychologies.

Comprehensive theory insofar as it is *integrational* aims at a continuous integration of the differential psychologies in the light of the foundations, assumptions, and basic constructs developed by foundational theory. The *integrational* constituent is thus primarily concerned with the comprehensive aspect, whereas the *foundational* constituent is primarily concerned with the basic aspect of comprehensive theory.

The psychologist who studies the foundations of his science engages in a reflective mode of knowledge which is essentially different from the direct mode of knowledge which characterizes differential-operational psychology. He studies that specific mode of existence itself which is called psychology. He examines it insofar as it manifests itself in the actual and historical endeavors of scientific psychologies. He observes what psychologists do in multiverse methods within diverse areas. He attempts to uncover the basic mode of existence which is revealed through their work. Once he has delineated this phenomenon, he goes further and endeavors to make explicit what is implicit in it. He strives in this way to arrive at a better understanding of the subject-pole and the object-pole of psychology and of their mutual involvement. Thus he discovers the foundations for an integration of the differential psychologies.

The center of interest of the comprehensive theorist differs from that of the differential psychologist. The latter has refined or specialized his psychological intentionality to an interest in one of the many profiles in which behavior can appear to the human observer. His attention is totally absorbed by this specific aspect of the object-pole of psychology. He is involved in the development and practice of methods which will enable him to uncover the structure, variability, conditions, and functional relations of behavior as they appear in this one specific profile. It is not his primary aim to discover how his research is related to the psychological mode of existence as such. Neither does he consider it his task to discover and describe how his special knowledge can be integrated with the findings of other differential theories. On the contrary, his theorizing is intimately bound to and limited by his concrete research. Therefore, it is essentially operational. This does not imply that he cannot study *all* behavior. It implies only that the differential theorist *qua* differential theorist cannot study all behavior from *all* viewpoints opened up by the various differential approaches. He can study *all* behavior, however, as it appears under the one specific profile which forms the object of his research. But he cannot, at the same time and with the same method, study all behavior as it appears under all other profiles.

We should point out here that neither can the comprehensive theorist study all behavior *exhaustively* under all possible profiles. This would be impossible. First of all, the number of profiles in which behavior can appear is inexhaustible. Moreover, comprehensive theory must be constantly in readiness for the limited number of differential studies of single profiles so that it may comprehend them together. What the comprehensive theorist aims at, therefore, is the continuous integration of those profiles which have been already studied by differential psychologists. He explores these in the light of his explication of the foundations of psychology.

Consequently, a comprehensive psychology can emerge only after the development of various differential theories. The comprehensive theoretical mode of existence is essentially a reflective mode which can arise only when sufficient matter for reflection is present. In the science of behavior, this matter consists of the activities, methods, data, and theories of the differential psychologists.

One might develop a philosophical psychology, to be sure, by reflection on immediate spontaneous experience. But it would be impossible to develop on this basis a comprehensive *scientific* theory of psychology. The latter is by definition a reflection on the discoveries of scientific psychologists. Comprehensive theoretical psychology can and should be enlightened by the insights of philosophical psychology. However, its basis, source, and criterion remain the concrete phenomena uncovered by differential psychologists. For this reason, the statements of comprehensive theoretical psychology are such that postulates can be deduced from them which are open to the empirical test. Comprehensive psychology is thus organized thought about and integration of what scientific psychologists are doing, discovering, inventing, formulating, and applying.

Reflection on the foundations of the psychological mode of existence can therefore never be separated from reflection on what empirical and applied psychologists are doing. It is precisely through consideration of their activities that the comprehensive psychologist becomes aware of his own specific mode of existence, which is the *reflective* scientific mode. This mode has many constituents. It is now clear that one of these is an awareness of the generally accepted, significant results of empirical and applied psychology.

The differential psychologist is not a foundational theorist. He is engaged in actual experiments, observations, and applications. He is so much absorbed by this operational activity that he has little time to reflect on the foundations of his science. Therefore, the necessary limitation of his work necessarily leads to the emergence of comprehensive theoretical psychology as a field of specialization.

The difference between comprehensive and differential theory in psychology may be simply expressed. Both types of theory are bound to the phenomena which manifest themselves in behavioral research. Differential theory cultivates research in psychology by systematically directing the critical attention of the scientist to a certain profile of behavior. Comprehensive theory, on the other hand, fosters the understanding of behavior primarily by concentrating upon the psychological mode of existence itself insofar as it is revealed by the differential psychologists.

The development of this foundational aspect of theory is the condition for the development of the secondary or *integrational* approach of comprehensive theory. In other words, foundational theory creates a frame of reference within which the scientist can integrate the phenomena which are revealed by the differential theories. Thus an introduction to a differential theory trains a student to perceive certain isolated profiles in critical, controlled, and methodical ways. This training leads him to operational research within his specialized field of behavioral study. But reflection upon the basis, meaning, and relationships of his work and of the profile which he explores lies beyond the perspective of the differential theory itself.

Foundational theory will reveal itself as ultimately useful not only for the general understanding of behavior but also for empirical and applied psychology. All theorizing, including comprehensive, means that the psychologist perceives behavior in new ways. A new comprehensive perception develops from reflection upon differential perceptions of behavior. Every new perception, including comprehensive, will uncover new possibilities of meaning in behavior. These discoveries, in turn, will sooner or later stimulate the empirical and applied psychologist to experiment with the newly perceived possibilities. Such experimentation and application will ultimately affect the practical course of human behavior and its conditions. A similar situation may be recalled in comprehensive theoretical physics. The new comprehensive perception of Einstein uncovered new possibilities in matter. Differential-operational theorists experimented with these possibilities and as a result were able to utilize nuclear energy. Similarly, the object-pole of psychology, "behavior," may change under the impact of comprehensive theory.

Another question now arises. Does the subject-pole of comprehensive theory also change under the impact of theorizing? Does the comprehensive psychologist gain new knowledge about himself and therefore about other subjects like himself? Any theorist who explores the foundations of his science necessarily learns something about himself. The foundational theorist in psychology investigates what the psychological mode of existence is. He discovers that it is one of the modes of human intentionality rooted in existence. Therefore, he will necessarily achieve knowledge about human existence which will sooner or later affect both his self-understanding and his own behavior.

This growth in self-understanding is not the primary aim of comprehensive psychology. Nevertheless, it is a necessary consequence of the study of the psychological mode of existence. We cannot overlook the fact that growth in self-understanding satisfies a deep urge in man. This need for self-understanding is usually an explicit or implicit constituent of the total motivation which sustains the activity of the comprehensive theorist in psychology.

The Integrational Constituent

The first constituent of the comprehensive-theoretical mode of existence is, as we have seen, the foundational attitude. A secondary constituent is the integrational attitude. The purpose of the integrational task in psychology is the comprehension of the findings of differential psychologies in the light of the constructs developed in foundational theory. An examination of the origin and meaning of the word *integration* may clarify this statement. The word is derived from *integratus,* the past participle of the Latin word *integrare,* which means to make whole or to renew. Integration, then, refers to the activity of restoring an integer, an original "untouched whole". This implies that in any attempt at integration, an original whole, an image of the totality, already exists or is given. It also implies that this whole has been split up into parts which must be reintegrated. It is therefore the task of the scientist to attempt to restore this whole and not simply to fabricate. In other words, a comprehensive scientist cannot merely piece together in an arbitrary manner a number of various parts. He must follow to the best of his abilities the structure of the whole insofar as it is known to him.

The originally given whole, in the case of psychology, is intentional-functional behavior. The split-up parts of this original whole are the profiles of behavior in so far as they have been investigated and elaborated by the differential psychologists. Foundational theory attempts to make explicit what is implicit in the originally given whole of intentional-functional behavior. The function of integrational theory, on the other hand, is to reintegrate into this explicated whole the profiles of behavior which have been abstracted by the differential psychologists.

Pre-Scientific Knowledge of Behavior as a Whole

Every man has some pre-scientific notion of what intentional-functional behavior is. It would be impossible for him to respond to his fellowmen without some awareness of behavior. This is true of the psychologist as of all men. If he did not possess an implicit awareness of what behavior is before he began his scientific research, it would be impossible for him even to identify the object of his study. Without this awareness he could not, in fact, distinguish the movement of a machine from that of a child or a patient. In practice, all psychologists possess an awareness of intentional-functional behavior as a whole even though some formally deny it in theory. They demonstrate by their daily behavior in the laboratory, clinic, and classroom that they knew implicitly what behavior is even before they began to do research in it. They were aware of an originally given whole of behavior which calls for restoration. The isolated profiles which are abstracted from this whole can take on meaning only in the light of their source. In view of this fact, there is no experiential justification for the differential psychologist to maintain that he has no implicit awareness of behavior while he engages in research on one of the profiles of behavior. Psychology need not wait for innumerable phenomena revealed by single profile studies to be summed up to form the first human knowledge of what behavior is. We know implicitly what behavior is from the very beginning of our investigations. Phenomenology makes this implicit knowledge explicit.

Thus differential psychologists uncover operationally the lawful structures which become manifest when they observe behavior in certain profiles under varying conditions. Then comprehensive psychology reintegrates this newly gained knowledge within our primary awareness about the behavior of man which becomes less implicit and increasingly explicit during this scientific process.

The Pre-Scientific and the Scientific Tendency Toward Integration

The tendency toward integration or *com*prehension is inherent in man's existence. Comprehensive psychology as integration reflects what each man does spontaneously in daily life when he attempts to organize his knowledge about his own behavior and that of his fellowmen into some kind of meaningful whole. In a sense, every man is a born integrational psychologist, at least in a naïve, uncritical, pre-scientific way. For every man attempts to integrate—in a primitive manner—his experience about himself and his fellowmen. To be sure, the differential psychologist disregards this natural inclination to psychological synthesis when he concentrates on one profile of behavior during his highly specialized operations. Efficient scientific concentration in one area can only be gained at the expense of concentration on the whole. It is interesting to observe, however, that the differential psychologist, like other men, is guided in his daily life outside the laboratory by some implicit apprehension of the whole of human behavior. To be aware of behavior as a whole is unavoidable. It is an existential: it belongs to man's existence.

Science, however, is the critical and controlled elaboration of the pre-scientific modes of understanding existence. And comprehensive scientific psychology is the outgrowth of man's natural striving for a coherent comprehension of his differential perceptions of behavior. The ultimate objective of all psychology is the understanding and explanation of behavior. This is only possible on the basis of an explicit discovery and formulation of the unifying factors and universal characteristics which bind the disconnected perspectives of the science of behavior into an ordered and comprehensive system of relations. Psychology cannot stop with a disorganized enumeration of phenomena which have been discovered and accumulated in experimental and clinical observation. Neither can it be satisfied with the mere enumeration of the profiles of behavior which have been investigated by differential psychologies. Therefore, comprehensive psychology as *integrational* strives to reduce this complexity and plurality to a kind of unity.

Why Comprehensive and Not Differential Theory?

A differential theory is solely concerned with a particular aspect of behavior. Therefore it cannot integrate the perspectives of other differential theories. Freudian theory, for example, does not attempt to integrate discoveries concerning the role of conditioning in the learning process so as to change the main constructs of Freudian theory itself as a result of this open integration. Each differential theory maintains its own point of view. One of the perspectives in which Alfred Adler, for example, sees all behavior is that of striving for power. And all behavior can indeed appear in this perspective. It opens up a richness of phenomena which might have gone unnoticed if Adler had not taught us to "see" all behavior in this possible dimension. One of the differential perspectives of Freud, on the other hand, was that of man's striving for pleasure. Psychology would be the poorer if Freud had not opened our eyes to this particular profile in which all behavior can appear. Similar statements may be made about all differential theories. This situation in the science of psychology is necessary and should always be maintained. Differential-theoretical understanding of behavior is and should be the fragmentation of man's original, implicit understanding of behavior as a whole. Each differential theory should therefore concentrate on its own perspective to the exclusion of others in order to be more fruitful in its own area of psychology. The intrinsic impossibility of forming a comprehensive theory of behavior on the basis of one differential theory lies in the very nature of concentration on isolated profiles.

Foundational Constructs

How do we obtain unifying constructs which point to behavior as a whole? Foundational theory produces such constructs through a phenomenological explication of behavior, which is based on naïve, natural observation of behavior as a whole. The results of this type of observation can be reported in case studies, in literature, and sometimes in philosophy. Phenomenological explication clarifies what is essential in naïve experiences. The foundational theorist crystallizes these explicit descriptions into unifying constructs. Subjective distortions may creep in during the process of reporting on natural observation and during the phenomenological explication. Therefore, as we shall see later, intersubjective validation, experimentation, and constant checking and re-checking are necessary. Moreover, the constant dialogue between the foundational constructs and the conclusions of differential psychologies serves as a control.

Integrational Dialogue and Phenomenology

We may now ask how an integrational dialogue is possible between the constructs obtained in foundational theory and the conclusions of differential theories? This interaction is possible because foundational and differential psychology have a common ground, phenomenology. The differential psychologist, like the foundational theorist, necessarily starts from natural observation. He is necessarily engaged in some kind of explicit or implicit phenomenology, for he sees meaning and structure in natural observation. Following the process of observation, he draws conclusions concerning various phenomena. Then he investigates the lawful relationships among these phenomena. The final result of his research is never a closed system, but only a tentative one. This is necessarily so because his insight into the profile of behavior which he studies always reveals breaks in continuity. The differential psychologist fills these gaps, as it were, by means of hypotheses which bind the known facts together in his differential-theoretical model.

The comprehensive psychologist requires the help of the phenomenological psychologist in order to initiate a fruitful dialogue with the differential psychologies. The natural observation and the phenomenological explication of the differential psychologist is frequently implicit, uncontrolled, unreported, unchecked. One of the tasks of the specialist in phenomenological psychology is to perform in a critical, scientific way what has sometimes already been done in a loose, pre-scientific way by the differential psychologist. He may, for example, provide critical reports of the natural observations which have led to psychoanalytic constructs such as Oedipus complex and transference. By means of the phenomenological method, he may make explicit in a scientific way the fundamental structures of these phenomena observed by psychoanalysts. Following such a procedure, a dialogue between the phenomenological explications of behavior as a whole and those particular profiles of behavior is possible because both explications follow the same method and speak the same language. They shed light on each other. We have now arrived at a description of comprehensive and of differential phenomenological explications of behavior. A dialogue between the two provides our first insight into how they can be integrated. It gives us the necessary knowledge of the phenomena which must be integrated within a scientific system.

The Comprehensive Scientific Model

For a comprehensive scientific psychology, it is not sufficient to have a knowledge of the various relevant phenomena of behavior which are the basis of the system. An understanding of their mutual lawful relationships must be established by operational observation and experimentation. The comprehensive psychologist relates them to one another and finally to the integrational constructs which have been developed by foundational psychology. He attempts in this way to make intelligible the intentional-functional structure as a whole. He does not have at his disposal, however, all possible lawful relationships which exist among phenomena of behavior. Therefore, the only method which remains to him to make behavior as a whole intelligible, is to form an image, picture, or model of behavior which reflects the psychological knowledge which has been achieved at the present moment of the development of psychology. Such a scientific model is thus a theoretical image of behavior devised by the comprehensive psychologist. He attempts to explain and to integrate within its structure the contributions of the differential theories. The isolated profiles of behavior uncovered by these theories may now be said to delineate themselves in this model as a "Gestalt" or a well articulated structure.

The comprehensive model explains observed behavior, but it *is not* itself behavior. Therefore, this cognitive structure is not a reproduction of behavior like a photograph, a movie, or a tape recording. The scientific model of the integrational theorist is a constructed model, a tissue of ideas. It will never *mirror* intentional-functional behavior in its full concreteness, for it is the result of an intellectual process of reconstruction or *re* synthesis. As we have seen, behavior as it appears originally has been broken down into various profiles by many differential psychologists in clinics, laboratories, and consulting rooms. Therefore, the comprehensive structure of behavior which results from an intellectual *re*construction of these profiles is always one which, as such, is not given in concrete behavior. In other words, every comprehensive scientific model is projected by the theoretical psychologist on the basis of the limited knowledge produced by the differential psychologists. It is an attempt to *con*ceive and to *com*prehend the various profiles of behavior in their interconnection. It is never a direct perception of intentional-functional behavior in its own inner unity.

On the other hand, it remains true that the model of the comprehensive psychologist is existentially oriented to behavior presented to perception in the various profiles of behavior. The fact that this theoretical construction of the comprehensive psychologist points to behavior implies that the object-pole is never absent in comprehensive psychology. That is, the model is based on the givenness of the phenomena to which it points as an existential structure. It is not merely imagination; it is not a subjective configuration or synthesis in the mind of the theoretical psychologist. The integrational theory must be in conformity with the phenomena uncovered in the differential psychologies to which it refers. Therefore, the behavior to which the integrational model refers is always indirectly present in the comprehensive theory of the psychologist.

The integrational model, however, represents at the same time more than the perceptible phenomena. Its character is truly existential, for it is an intellectual, subjective grasp of phenomena which reveal themselves to the human existent. This existential character implies that it would be a meaningless structure if considered in complete isolation from the differential theories and their phenomena. The content and meaning of this structure can be better found in the differential-operational psychologies to which it refers than in itself. The more the student of psychology immerses himself in the richness of differential-operational theories, the more this comprehensive structure gains in depth and meaning for him. Therefore, the comprehensive theory of psychology can never replace the differential psychologies on which it is nourished. In a sense, it is an outline of what can be found in these psychologies. An outline is worthless if we do not know the material from which it is drawn. Comprehensive theory is for the student of psychology an instrument that enables him to comprehend the relationships between the variety of phenomena and differential theories which he encounters while immersing himself continually in the study of differential psychologies.

Integrational Constructs

Integrational theory is a scientific structure or model that increases in complexity during the dialogue between foundational constructs and differential psychologies. The growth of this complex structure implies an increase in constructs and sub-constructs which integrate differential theories and phenomena both with one another and with the foundational constructs.

We may define an integrational construct as follows:

> *A concept—expanding continually in articulation and definition—that refers hypothetically to observed behavioral phenomena, and that can be used most adequately for the integration of the greatest number and variety of phenomena and lawful relationships observed and structured by differential psychologies.*

The construct is thus not a "mental thing" isolated from the phenomena to which it points. This view of a construct is idealistic or rationalistic. Neither is it a mirror of something that exists as such outside the mind of the scientist. Such a conception would be positivistic. Existential psychology considers a scientific construct basically as a subjective structure of reference through which the scientist stands out toward a group of observed phenomena. The construct is thus a subjective-objective unity. It is a subjective structure of the scientist who explains and organizes groups of phenomena on the basis of their observed similarities. The comprehensive theorist cannot consider his constructs as absolute and final explanations of those phenomena to which they point. For new phenomena may reveal themselves in the light of new perspectives of differential psychologists. The old constructs may then prove to be inadequate to explain the new phenomena. Moreover, the continuing dialogue between foundational and differential theories may necessitate the design of new constructs. These may explain the phenomena in question no better than the former constructs did. Yet they may better facilitate the integration of these phenomena with other phenomena in the expanding integrational theory.

Therefore, the integrational construct is never an ultimate, but a provisional or hypothetical intellectual structure. The theoretical psychologist designs, defines, and redefines these conceptual structures in order to increase their accuracy as pointers to the phenomena observed; also to prevent confusion with other constructs or with identical constructs used with different meanings in other differential theories. These constructs of comprehensive psychology are called integrational constructs, although it is true that differential constructs are also to some degree integrational. Differential constructs, such as homeostasis, conditioning, reinforcement, proprium, ego, and unconditional positive regard, also point to certain groups of similar phenomena which they explain and integrate.

However, the explicit addition of the word integrational to the constructs which are developed in comprehensive psychology implies that the comprehensive psychologist seeks the highest possible degree of integrating power in his constructs. This is necessarily so, for he must use them for the integration of the variety of phenomena and lawful relationships discovered in a multitude of differential psychologies.

Examples of such integrational constructs are: existence, mode of existence, modality of existence, existential conscience, functional conscience, self, positive existential transference, negative existential transference. An example of a provisional definition of such a construct is the following existential definition of the self: "The self is an intellectual structure devised by the scientific theorist which points to the hierarchical Gestalt of the behavioral modes of existence which are observed in the subject."

Many constructs which are developed by differential theories can be related to comprehensive constructs as sub-constructs. For example, conditioning, reinforcement, ego, superego, and complex are frequently used as sub-structures in a comprehensive theory of behavior. All constructs and sub-constructs, however, tend to change their meaning to some degree in mutual dialogue. This change frequently necessitates a careful redefinition of the constructs concerned. The dialectical process tends therefore to refine the intellectual instrument through which the psychological scientist stands out toward behavior.

Sources of Integrational Constructs

There are many possible sources for integrational constructs. The primary source is the personal reflection of the comprehensive psychologist during his foundational and integrational activity. This reflection may draw on other sources in its search for intellectual structures. We have seen that comprehensive and differential psychologies yield constructs such as existence, mode of existence, profile, or perspective. We have also seen that certain integrational constructs have been developed by phenomenological philosophies and that the psychologist may borrow them. Another source is personal creative observation. Alfred Adler, as a result of his observation of his patients, created the construct of inferiority complex to account for interrelated phenomena of behavior which seemed to manifest that the patients in question felt less worthwhile, powerful, and perfect than their fellowmen and used compensations to counteract these feelings.

A main source of integrational constructs for the comprehensive theorist is the differential theories with which he must work. Differential constructs may become useful in a comprehensive theory of psychology. The comprehensive theorist enlarges, in this case, the differential or relative integrational power of these constructs into a more comprehensive power by broadening and deepening their original meaning. Examples are Rogers' construct of the self; Goldstein's and Maslow's constructs of self-actualization; Horney's construct of the idealized self; Freud's constructs of repression, defense mechanism, transference, catharsis; Gordon Allport's constructs of the proprium, of the concrete and the abstract.

The comprehensive and differential theories of other empirical sciences such as physics, biology, and physiology have developed their own constructs which may sometimes prove useful for the comprehensive theorist in psychology. However, they must be carefully redefined with an eye to the typical behavioral phenomena which the psychologist must integrate. Examples of such constructs are field, vector, and purposive behavior. Constructs may also be borrowed from many other fields such as literature, theology, history, and anthropology. Each area of human knowledge enlarges the possibility for the discovery of efficient integrational constructs and sub-constructs. The chief caution to be taken is that these borrowed constructs must be cut off from the phenomena of their original field and then critically related to the behavioral phenomena.

Quasi-Hypothetical Integrational Constructs

Foundational psychology may obtain some of its main constructs from a phenomenological-philosophical analysis of man as a whole. Concepts obtained by such analysis are descriptive and not explanatory. Ideally they are not of a hypothetical nature but are "true" descriptions of reality which, at least in principle, do not require experimental verification and in fact cannot be verified directly by experimental methods.

The psychologist *as psychologist* cannot declare that these concepts obtained from phenomenological philosophers *are* only hypothetical constructs; neither can he assert with certainty that they are not in some way "constructed" by philosophical ideas which influenced the observation and description of the philosopher. For he does not have at his disposal the training or the methods of the professional philosopher. He is compelled to abstain from any absolute judgment regarding the nature of these concepts, for he cannot support such a judgment by his own scientific methods.

On the other hand, *as a comprehensive psychologist* he must keep the structure of behavior as a whole hypothetical, always remaining ready to change it when new discoveries of differential psychologies compel him to do so. For this reason, he deals with the concepts developed by philosophical phenomenology *as if* they were hypothetical constructs. He calls them *quasi*-hypothetical constructs, which can be defined as:

Existential Foundations of Psychology

Comprehensive concepts borrowed from philosophical phenomenology which are utilized in foundational psychology "as if" they are hypothetical constructs, without making any absolute statement regarding their status as concepts or constructs.

The Hypothetical Constituent

Comprehensive psychology as an intellectual approximation of behavior is essentially provisional and hypothetical. Theoretical formulations of science are always incomplete, to be sure, as demonstrated by the revision of classical Newtonian physics. The theoretical model which seems valid today may have to be discarded tomorrow. Comprehensive psychology must therefore always remain open and dynamic. It should never succumb to the temptation to become a closed system. From this viewpoint, it may be defined as an *open progressive* integration of the historical and contemporary knowledge about intentional-functional behavior.

The hypothetical status of comprehensive psychology explains its mobility, which reveals itself in the continual emergence of new theories of behavior. Man himself is existence, radical openness to reality; he strives by nature for universal knowledge. In the psychological mode of existence, his need is for the comprehension of intentional behavior as it is in reality.

On the other hand, the comprehensive theorist knows that all psychologists are embodied subjects and are therefore placed in limited cultural periods, which call forth restricted viewpoints revealing limited aspects of behavior. The theorist also realizes that all differential psychologies combined could not possibly cover all perspectives of behavior, the number of which is inexhaustible. Consequently, he is aware that every new perspective which may be opened up by new differential psychologies may compel him to revise his comprehensive structures. Moreover, every new awareness of behavior may change behavior itself. Changes in behavior must be reflected in comprehensive theory, thus necessitating a revision of the theoretical model.

In other words, the comprehensive theorist is convinced that his theory is in principle provisional and incomplete. He realizes that comprehensive theory should never cease to develop, but should stimulate the emergence of new differential theories, which in turn will stimulate him to constantly revise his comprehensive structures. In more existential terms, the comprehensive psychologist feels dynamically driven by the existential tension between his actual limited psychological mode of existence and the comprehensive manner in which he would like to exist toward behavior. Therefore he is never satisfied with the incomplete psychological knowledge embodied even in his most advanced theoretical model. His tension reveals itself in his urgency to constantly revise his constructs and their interrelationships. Without this existential tension, both comprehensive and differential psychology would end in complacency, and there would be neither progress nor the need for progress.

It is now clear that differential theories are necessarily hypothetical with regard to the whole of behavior, for each theory is only one perspective of behavior in its entirety. It is obvious, too, that comprehensive theory under its *integrational* aspect is always open to revision, for new perspectives opened up by differential theories continually provide new material for integration. The latter may change considerably both the identity and the hierarchy of the subordinated constructs in the theoretical model. What may be less obvious is the fact that the *foundational* constituent of the comprehensive theoretical mode of existence is also hypothetical and neither absolute nor ultimate. A comprehensive theory is based on a primary foundational construct which enables the theorist to bring clarity into the complexity of differential phenomena and their relationships and to transcend their disorganized diversity. This construct helps him to reduce the plurality of differential theories to a kind of unity. To be sure, psychological integration will be successful only to the extent that this central point of reference is capable of making the multiplicity and complexity of differential theories transparent and of reducing them to unity.

What is the source of this basic construct concerning behavior? Evidently, it is not to be found in differential theories. The categories of differential psychologies refer in principle only to phenomena which are revealed under one limited perspective of a particular group of psychologists in a restricted cultural period. They are therefore essentially unable to comprehend without distortion the phenomena uncovered by other differential psychologies. Foundational categories should be sought, therefore, in the essential structure of behavior itself. Ideally, the categories obtained by the explication of the essence of behavior would be valid at all times for all people in all situations. Therefore, they would provide a lasting foundation for the organization of all phenomena of behavior revealed by all differential psychologies. Accordingly, the comprehensive psychologist attempts to establish as his primary principle of integration, an essential characteristic of behavior which is universally valid. Yet he may produce a comprehensive theory of behavior which differs from another comprehensive theory. The other psychology may claim that it too is based on an essential characteristic of all behavior. Moreover, this other may also prove that it is capable of integrating all the phenomena provided to date by differential psychologies.

The contradictions in such a case are only apparent. First of all, a comprehensive theorist may be convinced that he is explicating an essential characteristic of man, which is in fact only a characteristic of behavior in his own cultural situation but not of intentional behavior as such. It is merely quasi-essential. Or, under the pressure of his culture, the theorist may unduly emphasize one of the essential characteristics of behavior at the expense of another more basic characteristic. Yet it may still be true that the phenomena revealed by the differential theories can all be integrated without distortion in his comprehensive theory. These differential psychologies have also emerged in his same culture, which is pervaded by the same implicit view of behavior. Therefore, no differential theorist of this particular cultural period may have been impelled to adopt a perspective out of harmony with the implicit cultural view. Out of the inexhaustible number of possible perspectives, only those in tune with the cultural vision may have been selected. Thus the *Zeit Geist* may blind both the comprehensive and the differential psychologists to certain aspects of behavior.

Does this mean that a one-sided comprehensive psychology which emerges in a particular cultural period is worthless? By no means. Every successful comprehensive psychologist makes explicit a certain essential, or at least quasi-essential, characteristic of intentional behavior. He shows how the multiplicity of behavioral phenomena uncovered by differential psychologies of his culture can be integrated within this aspect. If his view is not most fundamental, then his integration can be subordinated later to a more comprehensive psychology when a more basic aspect of the essential structure is discovered. In this case, a one-sided attempt at comprehension proves to be a worthwhile stage on the road toward an increasingly comprehensive psychology. It finds a position between a differential and a truly comprehensive psychology. Moreover, such theory will provide later psychologists with an insight into the basic view of behavior which developed within a certain cultural period. Finally, when psychology discovers that a certain comprehensive theory of behavior does not work in reality, it is forced to discard it. It is able to do so only because the implicit comprehensive psychology of a cultural period has been made explicit by such a one-sided theory.

The possible and probable one-sidedness of a comprehensive theory, under its foundational aspect, makes it necessary to consider foundational constructs as provisional and hypothetical. The comprehensive psychologist should always be ready to question the foundations of his theory and to change them for more valid primary constructs which may be discovered in the evolution of human knowledge.

But how does the foundational theorist know when he should question his basic constructs? What is the criterion of the validity of the foundational constructs of a comprehensive theory? It is the primary experience of the theorist. But the theorist may easily distort his primary experience of human behavior by imagination, by anxious conformity, by ambition, by the need for the acclaim of fellow scientists, by one-sided over-apppreciation, or by other emotional attitudes imbedded in his own cultural period, which represents only a phase of the evolution of behavior. Therefore, the psychologist requires another test of the validity of his foundational constructs. This criterion is the fruitfulness of the dialogue between comprehensive theory of behavior and concrete real behavior as it appears in the development of history. A comprehensive theory tends to embody itself in concrete behavior by means of numerous explicit or implicit applications to behavior as it appears in society. The dialogue is between theory and praxis, between thought and action, speculation and reality.

If the fundamental constructs of the theory are valid, the dialogue between the theory and actual behavior will be fruitful and progressive. Theory will foster efficient and harmonious behavior. This behavior in turn will reinforce and develop the theory by its confirming answer to the tentative application of the theoretical views. Every application of theory to reality is an implicit question posed to reality. The question may be translated thus: "Are you really as we have described you? If so, manifest it by responding effectively to the application which flows from our description." Both comprehensive and differential theory are questions to reality, but the questions posed by comprehensive theory are more absolute and basic. Comprehensive theory pushes to the limit the views of behavior which underlie the differential psychologies of a cultural period. These more or less implicit concepts lead the differential theorists to pose limited questions related to the aspect of behavior which they are exploring. But comprehensive theories, because of their very comprehension, force these underlying views to reveal their limits in two ways: first, by making them explicit in foundational constructs; second, by exposing the full impact of all their implications for the whole of behavior. From this point on, a dialogue is possible between these fully explicit views of behavior and all actual behavior of people in daily reality.

The view of behavior expressed in foundational constructs may indeed be one-sided. In this case, it will be impossible at certain points to maintain the dialogue with concrete behavior. That is, at those points where other "sides" of behavior which are neglected by the "one-sided" theory of behavior reveal themselves in daily reality. Here there can be no response from reality because the theory is silent on aspects of behavior which manifest themselves in reality. Suppose, for example, that a comprehensive theory of behavior implies in its foundational constructs that human behavior is absolutely identical with animal behavior. Such a theoretical foundation is attractive, for it simplifies the process of psychology considerably and consequently promotes the "elegance" of the theory in question. But what is the result of the dialogue between this theory and the real behavior of men in daily life? As long as the psychologist poses only those questions which relate to what is animal-like and infra-personal in the behavior of man, answers will come forth readily and will reinforce the theory. When the theory is applied, for example, to the biological aspect of the behavior of hunger, a fruitful and satisfying dialogue will develop. But the comprehensive psychologist cannot restrict himself to questions related to only certain areas of behavior, for comprehensive psychology is a question to the whole of behavior under all its aspects. Therefore, as soon as the theory cited above attempts a dialogue with other human behavior such as prayer, love, faithfulness, and philosophizing, the answers of behavior will not conform to the biological categories which form the basis of this theory. The comprehensive psychologist must then admit that his basic constructs are somehow one-sided because they do not conform to reality. He experiences that a certain behavior escapes his theory, and consequently his foundational constructs can no longer be called comprehensive. In other words, the reality of behavior as it reveals itself in the history of human experience is the test of the validity of the foundational constructs of a comprehensive theory.

Ideally, differential psychologies claim only the validity of that limited aspect of behavior which they study operationally under controlled conditions. It is possible for such psychologies to test their hypotheses by experiment and controlled observation. A comprehensive theory, on the other hand, purports to explain behavior as a whole. And behavior in its totality cannot be put to experimental test, because empirical operations always presuppose the abstraction of controllable variables from the whole. How then are we to evaluate the foundational constructs of a comprehensive theory? One method is to derive from them hypothetical postulates which are then tested by differential operational psychologies. However, as we have seen, it may well be that the existing differential psychologies do not include certain profiles of behavior which have also been disregarded by the comprehensive theory. It is not unthinkable that the foundational constructs proposed in a certain culture are also implicitly present in the differential theories which emerge in the same period. In such a culture, comprehensive and differential psychologists alike may be blind to certain aspects of the reality of behavior.

The only source of evaluation possible for foundational constructs, therefore, is a close study on the part of the comprehensive psychologist of all manifestations of behavior in past and contemporary history. It is evident that concentration only on behavior reported by differential psychologies is insufficient for the validation of foundational constructs. The comprehensive psychologist should, therefore, be open to manifestations of behavior in history, literature, painting, sculpture, and other arts and sciences. These may open his eyes to aspects of behavior which are disregarded by practicing psychologists. As we shall see later, this is an area in which the comprehensive psychologist can be truly creative. By pointing out neglected aspects of intentional behavior, he can pave the way for new differential psychologies which will study these neglected profiles.

It may require a long period of time before comprehensive psychologists are able to see that their foundational constructs are one-sided in the sense that they do not respond to the full reality of behavior. The laboratory of history stretches itself over time and space. At times, entire generations of psychologists must pass by before it becomes clear that the dialogue between foundational constructs and the reality of behavior is halted, that their application is destructive rather than constructive. Then new foundational constructs must be proposed on the basis of a new explication of the primordial experience of behavior. This reconstruction of foundational theory is necessary to bring psychologists once again into contact with the reality of behavior.

It is evident that comprehensive psychology should remain hypothetical under its foundational aspect, because it is inevitable for the comprehensive psychologist to err. He is bound to be influenced in his explication of his primary experience of behavior by cultural viewpoints. No psychologist can escape his culture totally. Often the psychologists of a certain era are not even aware that their view of behavior has long ago reached an impasse. Sometimes an entire culture must die before the psychologist is able to recognize the deficiencies of his foundational constructs which have been formed under the impact of that culture. This human inclination to a one-sided way of interpreting reality teaches the comprehensive theorist to be humble in formulating his foundational constructs. He should become increasingly aware that his constructs are always subject to being proved false and that there is no substitute for the tedious test in the laboratory of history.

To understand more concretely the hypothetical character of comprehensive theory, let us look more closely at the effects of cultural influences on man's view of behavior. Man always reflects on his behavior; he communicates his thoughts to others and sometimes discovers that they share intentional behavior which he may have thought private and personal. The mutual communication of thought within a culture leads to a shared image of what behavior *is* like. Therein lies the beginning of a spontaneous psychology as a cultural concern. This psychology changes, to be sure, with the cultural situation. And this change in turn causes a change in intentional behavior itself, and likewise in the self-image which is embodied in it and which dominates the culture.

Man experiences himself and his intentional behavior differently in various periods of culture, for he is exposed to different historical situations. Each new situation implies a challenge to master its demands by the evolvement of adequate intentional behavior. Man's attempt to answer this challenge make him aware of latent potentialities which he actualizes in meeting the needs of the moment. The unfolding of particular types of intentional behavior obviously leads to the neglect of other possible types. As soon as the historical situation is mastered, man becomes aware that he has achieved a certain behavior but has disregarded other possibilities. This awareness is evoked especially in his encounter with other men who have actualized human capacities which he has disregarded. The Roman peasant, soldier, and administrator were made aware of the neglect of their potentialities for philosophy, oratory, art, and architecture by their clash with the Greeks, especially when this clash became a human encounter. On the other hand, the cultures of certain African and Indian tribes which did not encounter other cultures became frozen and petrified.

The original behavioral response of people when faced with a new situation is pre-reflective. Such intentional-functional behavior implies a new experience of self. When large numbers of people thus assume a new attitude toward themselves and their behavior, it permeates the culture by a process of pre-reflective interaction which may be compared with osmosis. This implicit, omnipresent view is not immediately expressed in an explicit psychology. Various other behavioral expressions precede a more or less clear formulation of the view because they are closer to the original experience.

The first members of a culture who are able to express a new intentional behavior and the aspect of self inherent in it are the artists of the age. They experience a refined sensitivity, a kind of radar that scans the world of meaning in which they live. Within this world of accepted meanings, they are aware of the slightest stirrings which reveal themselves in the intentional behavior of people. They are able to express these responses in poems, novels, music, and painting. Literary and artistic expression is always very close to the original intentionality expressed by a people.

Another revelation of the intentional behavior of man is the philosophical one. The philosopher of an era attempts to express the essence of all that is under the impact of the first stirrings of the new period of culture which announces itself to his alert intuition.

Although psychology is at first embodied in literature, art, and philosophy, it gradually shows distinctive characteristics which set it more and more apart. The orientation of psychological research thus depends on the implicit view of behavior which permeates a culture. Every differential and comprehensive psychologist is under its influence. He is imbued with an implicit view of behavior and of self from his earliest years, simply by living in his culture and by being immersed in its language. When a culture becomes increasingly aware of itself, the implicit view of behavior becomes explicit. Comprehensive psychology in its foundational aspect is one form of this awareness. It opens up the possibility of critical evaluation of the view of behavior inherent in the differential psychologies of the culture.

We have said that one possible evaluation for foundational constructs is the close study by the comprehensive psychologist of manifestations of behavior in past and contemporary history. Openness to all past and present revelations of behavior may lead to new insights into foundational constructs.

In fact, a pre-scientific openness to human behavior in its revelations of disturbances recorded by psychotherapists and sociologists may provide a real possibility of escape from cultural determination. Such study may lead the comprehensive psychologist to the discovery of those aspects of intentional behavior which are neglected in the contemporary foundational view of man, since their repression could well have led to disturbances in patients. Another possibility of transcending the contemporary scene may be an involvement in the foundational views of man which have dominated other periods of culture. Finally, an open study of the psychologies of man implicit in other cultures may foster the awareness of the relativity of our own foundational constructs.

We may conclude that the hypothetical nature of comprehensive psychology, even under its foundational aspect, calls for the following:

1. The study of the contemporary self-experience of man as it is embodied in his intentional behavior and implicitly present in contemporary psychologies and their orientation of research.
2. The study of the self-image expressed in cultural endeavors other than psychology, such as art, literature, social customs, language, philosophy, science, education, and patterns of worship.
3. The study of the impact of the contemporary self-experience of man on his intentional behavior, through explication of records of therapeutic, educational, and other social situations.
4. The study of behavioral indications of dissatisfaction with the dominant views of man, even though slight, and of the new self-experiences which manifest themselves in this newly emerging behavior.
5. The study of the situations which have influenced the various forms of self-experience embodied in the behavior and the behavioral products of contemporary man.

6. The comparative study of the self-image of man embodied in the behavior of the present period of our culture and those of other periods of our culture.
7. The comparative study of the foundational self-image of man which dominates the development of our whole culture in all its periods and the foundational self-images that have dominated totally different cultures in their various periods.

The type of research just proposed is demanded by the hypothetical constituent of the comprehensive-theoretical mode of existence. For this constituent compels the comprehensive theorist in psychology to respond to the whole of intentional-functional behavior in constant wonder. This sense of wonder translates itself, among other ways, as an endless questioning of his constructs and models.

The Creative Constituent

The comprehensive theoretical mode of existence, as we have emphasized, is not merely a mode of registration of data and constructs developed in differential psychologies. The integration of seemingly opposed constructs requires the continual shaping and reshaping of a theoretical model in its structure and substructures. This constant change in theoretical vision enables the psychologist to comprehend with inner consistency the ever-increasing number of phenomena and laws uncovered by the growing number of differential psychologies. A comprehensive model is not given as such in the reality of intentional behavior. It arises from systematic thought about that which is uncovered in intentional behavior by differential psychologists. It is therefore a creation of the theorist.

However, the careful and "playful" consideration of the various perspectives of psychology is necessary but not sufficient for the creation of a consistent theoretical model. First of all, the number of profiles which are uncovered by differential psychologies is limited and does not necessarily represent the most fundamental aspects of intentional behavior. Further, the constructs and data of differential psychologies may be so disparate that it is impossible to relate them in some kind of theoretical unity without resorting to views opened up by other disciplines. Therefore, the comprehensive theorist—in so far as he is able—also studies philosophies and theologies of man, anthropology, sociology, literature, and art with special reference to behavior. He may involve himself in psychotherapy, which provides an opportunity to be in direct contact with intentional-functional behavior as a whole. Nourished by all these sources of constructive thought, he ponders creatively the contributions of differential psychology. His constant creative consideration of possibilities of integration implicit in the data and constructs leads him to the creation or re-creation of his theoretical model.

Such creativity presupposes an attitude of both presence to and distance from its object. The theorist is intimately *present* to the differential psychologies and to other disciplines; he steeps himself in their thought. He is *distant* insofar as he does not allow himself to be seduced by one or the other differential psychology, so as to become himself a differential psychologist who considers the whole of intentional behavior predominantly from the viewpoint of one profile. He keeps himself similarly distant from philosophy. The ideas developed by philosophers are for him, *as an empirical scientist,* quasi-hypothetical constructs, some of which he uses as integrational constructs as long as research and observation do not refute them. This attitude of presence and distance keeps the comprehensive theorist free for a never-ending creative "play" with phenomena and constructs.

The comprehensive psychologist is creative not only in developing constantly new structures and sub-structures to embody the contributions of differential psychologies, but also in suggesting new hypotheses to be tested by them. In order to unify the variety of differential constructs and data, the theorist is forced to create integrational constructs which can be used as a sufficient explication of seemingly unrelated data. In other words, the comprehensive theorist must fill in the "gaps" left by differential research. The differential psychologists may be stimulated in turn to new investigations by his proposed theoretical solutions. They may deduce testable propositions from his theory and put them to the empirical test.

The comprehensive theorist is also creative insofar as he points out neglected aspects of research which may lead to the emergence of totally new differential fields of psychology.

Finally, comprehensive psychology is the point of departure for the clinical psychologist and psychiatrist who in their fundamental concern for the human person as a whole are disinclined to approach their clients from merely one or the other differential viewpoint. This attitude stimulates the comprehensive psychologist to formulate creative hypotheses for clinical psychology which the clinician in turn tests in his practice.

The Communicative Constituent

The comprehensive theoretical psychologist responds to the whole of behavior not only in order to express this totality in a theoretical construct, but also to communicate as an organized whole that which is seen in isolation by differential psychologists. This implicit aim of communication influences the attitude and the verbal expression of the comprehensive psychologist. He must present the contribution of psychology as a whole to his fellow psychologists, to students of psychology, to students of the arts and sciences, and to the human community at large. The growth of psychology implies an increasing differentiation in fields of specialization which develop their own language and methodology. The latter are at times difficult to understand, even for psychologists when they are not specialists in the area concerned. It is also difficult for both specialists and non-specialists to comprehend what the relevance of minute discoveries may be for the understanding of intentional behavior as a whole. Differentiation may even lead to a loss of insight into the whole if the comprehensive psychologist does not keep himself continually informed of the increasing insight into intentional behavior achieved by the painstaking labors of his colleagues in the differential psychologies. One of the functions of comprehensive psychology is thus a two-way communication of the changing structure which represents the increasing knowledge of psychologists as a community of specialized scientists.

The applied psychologist in the clinic, in education, and in industry also feels the pressing need for this type of communication. He deals with intentional behavior as a lived totality among the groups and individuals who come to him for guidance, diagnosis, and therapy. He does not have the time to acquaint himself thoroughly with the numerous reports of research submitted by the disparate differential fields in psychology, all written in their own peculiar idioms. He desires to know whether or not this research substantially affects his insight into intentional behavior, and how this changed insight may affect his treatment of his clients. When comprehensive theory has emerged into a field of psychology in its own right, pursued by many scientists all over the world, it will ideally provide the applied psychologist with this knowledge.

New students of psychology should first of all be given a general view of the science to familiarize them with the fundamental intellectual knowledge of behavior which has been achieved by comprehensive psychology at the time that they enter the field. After this, it is less difficult for them to study, in the light of this structure, the overwhelming number of differential psychologies and to assess their relevance to the whole. Comprehensive psychology communicates to them a fundamental structure.

The findings of comprehensive psychology are also relevant for other arts and sciences, for the political administration of government, for church and school, and for the public at large which obtains much of its psychological information from magazines, pamphlets, and newspapers. It is impossible for the community at large to develop a coherent insight into the significant developments in psychology by reading the inexhaustible number of published reports on isolated observations and experiments. Such a piecemeal type of knowledge may lead to confusion and to a dangerous over-estimation of certain well-publicized differential approaches at the expense of a balanced insight into the whole. In the possible future, communication specialists may be able to report with competence new discoveries in psychology within the perspective of comprehensive psychology and thus prevent harmful distortion of insight.

CHAPTER SIX

THE STUDENT AND THE STUDY OF ANTHROPOLOGICAL PSYCHOLOGY

It is one of the themes of this book that all sciences are rooted in man the scientist, and that consequently each one of them can be understood on the basis of the specific mode of existence of the scientist which led to the emergence and development of the science in question. Therefore, before developing a more concise consideration of the function of anthropological psychology in itself, we shall first reflect on the student and the study of anthropological psychology. In order to do so, we must first present an outline of the central idea of anthropological psychology which will concentrate chiefly on the scientist and his study, while in the next chapter we shall concentrate on anthropological psychology in and by itself. Because both aspects of anthropological psychology are interrelated, some overlapping will be unavoidable.

We may begin with a provisional descriptive definition of anthropological psychology which will serve our special purpose. The discussion of the various terms of this definition in relation to the student and his study will lead to an initial understanding which will find its necessary complement in the next chapter on the function of anthropological psychology. For our purposes here we may describe anthropological psychology provisionally as: *an open, personal, progressive integration of the historical and contemporary psychological knowledge about man—in the light of a phenomenological explication of the fundamental psychological structure of his personality—in order to understand his psychology.*

Open, Personal, Progressive Integration

We shall first reflect upon the expression, "an open, personal, progressive integration." As we have seen, the Latin word *integratio* is related to the verb *integrare,* to make whole. Verbs reveal a basic characteristic of the human personality, namely, his becoming, his growing towards, his reaching out, his going beyond what he is and what his world is at this moment, his humble readiness to change, his original plasticity and fluidity. This capacity for growth is one of the properties that distinguishes man from the things which surround him. The walls of his home or the stones in his path do not manifest a spontaneous inner dynamism urging them to perfect themselves. Genuine free growth, however, pervades the whole human person and embodies itself in all his activities and relations. This characteristic of becoming also imbues the persistent need of man to integrate meaningfully all that he knows about man. The developing result of his innate search for the rediscovery of the integral wholeness of man will be authentically human to the degree that it is permeated by the human characteristic of becoming, of creative, never resting openness. Unfortunately, his attempt at integration may lose its aliveness and openness when its provisional results are printed and then disregarded. The human attempt may become a fossil somewhere in a museum of books which will come to life only when another man humanizes it again by infusing new life into it. The reader or student does so by his participation in the search of the original thinker or theorist of personality, and by making it live on through his personal creative search. Sometimes, libraries are like cemeteries rather than sources of the wonder of new life. Many printed attempts at the integration of our knowledge of man remain dead because we who open the records are lacking in authentic humanness, in openness to the spontaneous search for wholeness present in our life. Under the impact of an objectivistic mechanistic education, we may perceive ourselves as objects with qualities, or as well-organized study machines. Then we are unable to infuse human life into the books which cover our desks. A printed attempt at integration of the science of man becomes for us nothing more than a finished, unchangeable "thing" that we can read, memorize, or quote, or to which we can refer as we would refer to the North Pole, the Indian Ocean, Chile, or Bagdad. We may be naïve enough to believe that this is the best way of understanding or of honoring the author.

If we ever hope to understand the author in his very act of attempting to integrate, we have to share his attempt, we have to become as it were his co-creator. We have to undergo his wrestling with thought, his moods of elation and despair, his delight when he achieves fresh observations, and above all his dynamism of becoming. Only then will we meet him; only then will we be able to recreate his work. Then we can humbly participate in the great human effort to understand the psychology of the human personality. When we experience the tentative integrations of Freud, Jung, or Adler as holy texts which can never be changed, we will never understand their creators in their act of creating, and we will never be able to participate in their work. This is why we insist that the search of anthropological psychology must be open, personal, and progressive.

Therefore we are not distressed but delighted at the appearance of so many antagonistic theories of personality. Disagreement is an encouraging sign of search, of readiness to change, of the wonderful plasticity of life, on condition, of course, that this disagreement is authentic and open and not the result of a dogmatic entrenchment in one or the other closed and final integration. Authentic disagreement is the fruit of the complexity of the problems we are faced with. Some students, comparing the unshakeable data of controlled experimentation with the ever-changing attempts to attain an integral theory of personality, may shake their heads in pity and wonder. When a new integration appears, they may ask impatiently: Is this finally "the" anthropology of man, "the" conclusive theory of person and personality? The psychologist of man will answer that there never has been and never will be such a "thing" as "the" psychology of man. If there would ever be "the" psychology of man, there would no longer be any true psychologists, for the perennial human effort to grow in the understanding of man would be buried in a closed system. This would spell the destruction of the humble awareness that we still do not know and that we never shall know perfectly all that is knowable about man's psychology. Needless to say, the extinction of this humility would be the death of science as a creative enterprise.

Indeed, the beginning student may be dumbfounded by the variety of psychological integrations and their manifold contradictions. Therefore, to commit onself unconditionally to one or the other psychological anthropology would be unwise and presumptuous. For on what basis would one decide that one phychology of man is better than the other? But even if "the" conclusive anthropology really existed, it would still be unwise to learn this integration in the same way as one would learn the structure of the nervous system or the scoring of the Stanford-Binet, for the comprehensive theory of personality expressed in this supposedly exhaustive integration would not be the truth of the student himself. The psychology of man can never become *his* psychology if he limits himself to simply learning the integration expressed by others without experiencing in his life and in the lives of others the reality of this psychology. For being a psychologist of personality is a personal enterprise, a questioning, a reply of the student himself. It is life itself which raises the question of the psychology of personality, and it is life which urges me on to rediscover and to restore the original wholeness of my own personality. My life, my existence, my being a person is mine. When I study how other men have restored the original whole of human personality, I cannot simply put my own personal existence aside as if it does not concern me, for they are talking about me, and they are integrating *my* personality. I am necessarily interested in myself because it is characteristic of man that he is in relationship to his own personality. Therefore, every man is born a true psychologist of man at least in a naïve and pre-reflective way. In the same sense every man is, by force of his very being, always attempting to restore the original whole of his being. One way in which he tries to do so is by the integration—at least in a crude and primitive way—of all his experiences about himself and his fellow man. He is always searching for the meaning of his life, and if he cannot find an integrating meaning he becomes neurotic or psychotic.

Again, one or the other specialist of certain measurable aspects of man may pretend or even believe that he is free from this human need for meaning—that he is not interested in the whole man. On closer investigation, however, we should discover in him also a psychology of man, though perhaps a very primitive one on the unconscious or half-conscious level of his existence. This natural inclination to anthropological synthesis which belongs to man's fundamental personality needs may be repressed by him in the laboratory, but it guides and directs him in his daily life even if he would be ashamed and disturbed by so unscientific a tendency.

Moreover, in spite of his protest, even his behavior in the laboratory itself and his choice of experiments is done under the impact of his unconscious anthropology. Even his disdain for the psychology of personality, or his contention that physiological-biological data obtained by experiment will sooner or later make crystal-clear the whole reality of human existence, betray his hidden view of man, for it is impossible to escape being an implicit anthropological psychologist. It belongs to man's very personality; it is greater than man is, and it is present even in the angry denial of its presence. Apparently, man must care about himself and must be a dialogue with his psychology.

This implicit psychology of man, when it becomes explicit in anthropological psychology, is authentic only when the student *himself* observes man in himself and in others; when he *himself* ponders the results of his observations; when he *himself* attempts to reply; when he *himself* clarifies his insights;

and when he *himself* searches explicitly for the restoration of the original whole of man's fundamental personality structure.

The questions and answers of the printed attempts at integration of personality knowledge, such as Freud's or Jung's, Murray's or Allport's, are not *mine*. To learn their questions and answers would no more contribute to the making of a psychologist of personality than the enumeration of the various glands or the memorizing of the rules of controlled experimentation. Only an open, personal, progressive integration will enliven and enrich the treasures of the past with one's own experience. Personal integration makes for a progressive integration which is never finished but is always open to the past, the present, and the future. This personal assimilation will make the student a "living" therapist, a "living" teacher of psychology, and a creative contributor to the science of man.

Integration of Historical and Contemporary Psychology

After this elaboration of the expression, "an open, personal, progressive integration," we must consider a further qualification of our definition of anthropological psychology which states that it is an integration "of the historical and contemporary knowledge about man." The anthropological psychologist is characterized by a *personal* search for the integral understanding of the human personality. There is no psychologist, however, who can ever begin to understand man as if there were no previous understanding of man, for many others in the course of history have tried to understand man psychologically before him, and he lives under the impact of their understanding. The psychologist is born into a community of men which communicates to him a language. Therefore, he is imbued with the historical ways of understanding man insofar as those ways are embodied in the language which he has learned to speak. It is impossible for a psychologist to try to understand man without language, and also impossible to understand man without tradition. It is interesting, for example, to realize how our language has been influenced by certain romantic, rationalistic, and religious concepts which express certain ways of seeing man in particular periods of history. More recently, certain Freudian, Adlerian, and Jungian concepts have become part of our Western languages. Such embodiments of psychological understanding have taken place throughout history in all languages. The same is true of art, monuments, and social institutions; they are all imbued with the psychological understanding of past generations.

Moreover, during all centuries great men have concentrated on the secrets of man's psychology, and they have expressed their growing understanding in classical theories and descriptions. The psychologist is under the sway of this embodied history of the understanding of man. But this does not mean that he has to abandon his quest for a personal integral understanding. On the contrary, he has to infuse new life into history. The theories of personality developed by the great psychologists of all centuries and cultures are the expression of *their personal* understanding of man. Their mission is to make us sensitive to their experience. They enable us *personally* to see something to which otherwise we would have been blind. If there had been no Freud, our conception of certain dynamics of man would have been much more naïve and superficial; or rather, we would perhaps not understand what we now do when we encounter man. Without Alfred Adler, we would not be so sensitive to the meaning of inferiority feeling and the need for compensation in man when he is placed in certain life situations. Without Hippocrates and Galen, perhaps we would not be aware of that aspect of the reality of man which has been called temperament. The psychologists of all centuries speak to us to make us capable of personal experience or observation, to make us aware of the wealth contained in the totality of man's personality. Once this is understood, there is no reason to be disturbed by the existence of many contradictory attempts at integration in the history of psychology and psychiatry. What matters is not the theory of person and personality, but *man.* In every one of the "attempts-at-integration" some aspect of man's psychology finds expression. Every truly great psychologist was struck by a certain aspect of man, such as his libido, his will to power, his religious need, the impact of his biological substructure, his observable behavior. Sometimes he was so impressed by a certain minor aspect of man's psychology that he made it the exclusive basis of his understanding of the whole of man. It became the core of his attempt at integration. In this case, the resulting integration was distorted, but nevertheless we cannot do without his special message. We cannot do without Galen, Freud, Jung, Pavlov, Watson, and all the other psychologists of man. Accordingly, the psychologist must take up the past in a creative way. He must endow the past with a new life. Evidently, he *himself* has to do this. Although anthropological psychology is an intersubjective and historical enterprise, each psychologist of man has to understand man on his own. Even those anthropological psychologists who for historical and personal reasons are inclined to favor one or the other school of psychology or psychiatry, will not *a priori* believe this or that psychological statement about man, but at most suspect its truth. The authentic psychologist of man does not accumulate knowledge of psychologists of the past, but he listens to man no matter from whom the message comes. Therefore, while studying the historical integrations of human knowledge about man, the psychologist may attempt to return to the human experience or observation which is explicated in a psychological statement. Only in his personal presence to man, or in experience or observation, is it possible for him to see and accept the meaning of this statement personally.

Intersubjective Agreement and Validation of Theory

We have stressed that the psychologist is authentic to the degree that the knowledge of the psychology of personality becomes his personal insight. Does this mean that the anthropological psychologist is forced to limit himself to a kind of monologue that expresses only his strictly personal experience or observation? The beginning student is indeed struck by the fact that the findings of experimental psychology seem much easier to agree upon than the insights of man as a whole as revealed by the various psychologies of man. This difference, however, does not mean that the latter is *only* personal, or is not open to intersubjective agreement and intersubjective validation. It is true that *in fact* there exists more agreement in the realm of physiological and biological psychology than in the realm of the psychologies of personality. There is more general agreement among physiological psychologists about the number of reinforcements needed to condition a rat than there is agreement among the psychologists of man regarding the meaning and function of man's anxiety or his sexual needs. This is so because it is easier to verify the results of an experiment with rats than the explication of the meaning of a deeply human experience, for as soon as the psychologist transcends the realm of research on the infra-human level, he cannot subject the phenomena which he studies to direct factual verification and precise control. Therefore, it is *in fact* far more difficult to come to agreement. We shall need the long and acid test of the laboratory of human history in order to come to factual agreement concerning the rightness or wrongness of our explication of man.

But the more we explicate in a scholarly way the implicit anthropology of man, the sooner we shall be able to detect our falsifications and to open the discussion which might correct these self-deceptions. The impossibility of testing these explications in the laboratory is not a reason to avoid the explication of man's psychology in as scholarly a way as possible, because mankind can never avoid harboring implicit anthropologies which guide and direct the orientation of experimentation and clinical work in psychology. These implicit anthropologies will make for a longer period of blindness to their imperfections or even falsities than a scholarly confrontation of them. By bringing them into the open, we shall be more ready for the signs in man and society which seem to indicate that our explication was not the right one because in principle the truth about man is intersubjective. Therefore, sooner or later we shall bridge our factual disagreements if they are clearly stated and thus more open to clear repudiation or confirmation by history.

Accordingly, *in principle,* the personal insight of the psychologists of personality does not mean an arbitrary insight.

We have explained that the further qualification of personal integration is an integration "of historical and contemporary knowledge about man." We have shown that this openness to all historical and contemporary knowledge about man does not exclude the personal character of our integration, and finally that our own personal integration can be taken up in the stream of the historical human enterprise of integration because personal integration does not exclude potential historical intersubjectivity.

Fundamental Structures of Personality

We have now to consider the next qualification of integration which has been formulated in the definition as "in the light of a phenomenological explication of the fundamental structures of his personality."

In elaborating the first terms of the definition, we have seen that "integration" means restoring or renewing the original, untouched, integral whole. This expression implies that anthropological psychology presupposes an originally given insight into the totality of man which has been broken up, as it were, and has to be restored. But what is breaking up this original whole? An organic whole is broken when we make one of its aspects the center of our attention in such a way that we forget about the embeddedness of this aspect in the total organic whole. Yet we are forced to break up the organic vague totality of our knowledge about man and to concentrate on certain aspects of this knowledge in order to grow to better insight into these aspects, and indirectly to a sharper view of the whole to which these aspects belong. The historical growth of the understanding of human personality is a two-way process. One pole of the process is the concentration on certain aspects of man's psychology; the other pole is the constant reintegration of the studied aspects within the whole of the original insight after their elucidation. One or the other psychologist may object and say: "We do not have an insight into the totality of man's fundamental psychology; consequently, the only way open to us is the performance of a great number of experiments. Then in the far future all the results of these experiments will be added and will reveal to us the whole of man's psychology, unknown to us up to that moment." This is an abstract theoretical conception which is at odds with the elementary phenomena of experience. Imagine for a moment that there is no awareness of man's personality structure before we start to collect data about man by means of controlled experimentation. Not having any awareness of human personality, how can we be sure that we are not studying a dream or a fantasy or a plant or a river? However, no student of human psychology has ever made such a mistake. This proves that there is some directly given notion of human psychology guiding us in our research. The psychologist is protected against mistaking the sky for man, a tree for man, the walls of his laboratory for man, by an immediately given overall knowledge of what human psychology is, what a wall is, what a tree is. In other words, there is an experiental knowledge of human psychology given to the psychologist immediately, directly, inescapably. This knowledge is not obtained by experimentation, but presupposed. The methods of experimental psychology do not determine what human psychology is, but are directed by what human psychology is. They are true to the degree that they are in accordance with this given knowledge of man's personality structure. They are worthwhile to the degree that they differentiate more clearly what we already know vaguely about man's personality structure by experience of the immediately given. This point is basic for the understanding of what anthropological psychology is.

The original integral whole for the anthropological psychologist is the fundamental personality structure of man, and it has to be restored by constantly relating all detailed studies of man to the integral whole given in his primary experience. This will not only make for a richer understanding of the whole man but also for a better understanding of various aspects of man.

The understanding of the integral components of a whole can only lead to a better understanding of this whole if our understanding of these components increases in the light of the knowledge of the whole itself. Thus a better understanding of the part gives a better understanding of the whole and vice versa. Consider a person who is interested in knowing what a house is. He already has a vague experience of a house. This given knowledge has to lead him to further understanding. Therefore, he first reflects on his original given knowledge and makes more explicit his implicit awareness of what a house is. He finds by means of this process of explication that a house is a place for people to live in. Now he can deepen his knowledge of house as a whole by the study of certain segments of the house, but always on condition that he studies them in the light of the explicated whole—a place for people to live in. He studies, for instance, what the door of a house is. He can understand this only in the light of the whole. The door of a house is a connection between the inside and the outside of the house. We need a door because people living in a house can move around and need to move around and, therefore, need an opening. Moreover, people who live in a house are also bodies that have to be protected against weather conditions. They are, moreover, personal selves that need privacy. They have property that they like to protect. These are some of the reasons why they place an object called door between the opening of the house and the outside world. This explication helps the person to understand at the same time what a door is and what a house is. We could never understand what a door in a house meant if we described it as totally independent of any idea of house whatsoever. We could then describe the door only as wooden, square, and so on. But nobody reading this information would be able to discover the meaning of "door" and at the same time obtain a more differentiated meaning of "house".

Similarly, anthropological integration is the continual restoration of the elucidated aspects of man's personality within the original whole of man's fundamental personality structure. Only a study of aspects of human personality in the light of this structure can lead to a deeper understanding of human psychology. Finally, this knowledge of fundamental personality structure is given in immediate experience in a vague, implicit way and therefore has to be explicated.

Are we not contradicting ourselves? We stress the aim to understand the personality as an integral whole and at the same time we talk about explication of our immediate experience of the human personality. Is this explication not a division of the personality which destroys the integration of the given totality? Not necessarily, because we can divide in many ways. Some of these ways respect the immediately given whole; others do not. Take, for instance, a painting by Rembrant. I see the whole of the painting in one swift glance; then, admiring the painting, I "dwell" for a moment on this, then for another moment on that detail, but all the time I am relating the particular detail of the painting to the whole and to all other details, and vice versa. When I ask myself how I select my details in such a way that they can teach me about the meaning of the whole painting, I discover that there is some kind of natural articulation present within the whole of the composition itself. In Rembrandt's painting, "Midnight Round", I dwell on the colors of the uniforms, the little drummer in the foreground, the walking attitude of the men, their rifles, the dark background from which they emerge. Continuously relating these integral parts of the composition to one another and to the whole makes me experience that this painting really means a "Midnight Round" characteristic of Amsterdam at a certain period. When I am open to the meaning of the painting, when I allow the painting in its given totality to open itself to me, then I discover a natural articulation inherent in the composition itself. I could do something else; I could refuse to allow the painting to reveal itself to me. For instance, I could divide the painting into cubic inches, and then I could handle those cubic inches statistically in terms of their equality. Or I could abstract one characteristic of the painting, for instance its colors, and make a division only according to color—so many black spots, so many grey spots, so many golden spots. In both cases, I could collect an amount of separate data. But this information could never teach me the meaning of the painting as a whole. I would know much about the measurements of the painting and about the number and the quality of the paints which were used. I would know more about other wholes, such as the "conceptual whole" of measurement or the "conceptual whole" of the color scale. But I could never directly restore those spots or measurements of painting to the meaning of the whole. The same is true of the psychology of personality. Any division by measurement alone, any division according to only one type of personality characteristic (for instance physiological ones), will make it impossible to reintegrate these units into the meaningful whole of a unique personality.

Therefore, it is not division as such that harms the understanding of personality, but the fact that a division is made independent of the fundamental structure of personality. There is a natural articulation of human personality which is given; for if human personality were not an organic unity of many natural articulations, there would be no difference between a homogeneous mass and an organism. Human personality is not like a collection of sand or a heap of stones or water in a swimming pool. The fundamental human personality is a structured whole, well articulated in the light of a unifying principle of organization. We have to find this principle of articulation and organization, and then in the light of this principle we may study certain articulations which come to the fore. For a time these articulations may gain in individuality; they may stand out in our attention; but after that they will have to be reintegrated within the whole if we wish to prevent distortion. We could compare this with the process of biological differentiation.

When we study, for instance, the genesis of the human embryo, we are faced in the first stages of its development with a rather diffuse phenomenon which does not show much differentiation. The unsophisticated observer will not recognize this embryo as a potential human child. Gradually, however, differentiation begins. Various parts emerge from the vague diffuse totality and gain dramatically in individuality and distinction. An initial trunk, arms, legs, and a head are shaping our impression of the whole of the fetus. At certain times, some parts are gaining so much individuality that they threaten to dominate our vision of the whole. The head of the fetus, at a certain phase of development, is out of proportion to the rest of the body. For a time it seems to distort the human appearance, but then it falls back into the totality of the fetus and comes into proportion with the rest of the body. This development may serve as an example of what happens in the differentiation of our initial experience of the human personality and the later study of some of these differentiated aspects of our initial experience. First we "dwell" on our initial experience of personality which is diffuse like the original human fetus. Dwelling on it reflectively, we become aware of how this initial awareness of human personality implies various organic differentiations or articulations. We try to explicate faithfully these articulations which are given in our experience without imposing on this given phenomenon our prejudices or our emotional distortions.

In the course of our explication, some aspects of human personality may temporarily gain in individuality and distinction at the cost of the view of the whole, as the head of the fetus did. Nature itself took care that the disproportionate head of the fetus acquired proportion with the organic totality from which it emerged. But the psychological knowledge of man is partly man-made. Therefore, there is no natural organic principle of organization which forces the "enlarged" aspect into proportion. This entails the possibility that our knowledge of the psychology of personality may become distorted by our losing sight of the whole; it implies also the possibility that we may start to force our distorted view of man's psychology on the reality of man himself. Then the whole process of study would be reversed. Instead of being a humble fidelity to "what is", to the psychology of man which reveals itself to us, science becomes some distortion imposed on psychology. And because of the fact that reality is more than we are, we shall necessarily lose this battle between our petty impositions and reality. Not *reality*, but we will be crushed.

Specialists of the Whole

This danger of a distortion of the whole of man's psychology is the necessary consequence of the fact that modern research is so perfected, so onesidedly directed, and therefore so time and energy consuming that it is impossible for the researcher who works in limited areas of personality to relate his findings to the explicated fundamental structure of human personality and to all the findings of all the studies of personality. Therefore, there is only one choice for humanity today: either to develop on a global scale specialists of the whole personality who counterbalance the process of individualization of certain aspects of personality, or to resign itself to an otherwise inescapable distortion of our view of man. The last course will mean our gradual destruction because we will lose contact with our own psychology. There is only one choice today: to integrate or to perish.

This necessity implies that a tremendous amount of time, energy, specified talent, skillfulness, and scholarship will be required to perform the integration of all the fields of psychological study. How can we find a solution for this problem of time, energy, talent, and special training? There are three conceivable solutions: the genius solution, the local psychology solution, and the cooperative specialist solution. The genius solution rests on the hidden assumption that it is possible to educate a sufficient number of psychologists who combine in their personality the talents and training of the phenomenological explicator of man's initial awareness, of creative theoretician and interpreter, of astute translator of differentiations into operational concepts, of skillful collector of data for detailed study, of clinical experimenter, clinical observer, perfect master of statistical measurement, and finally integrator of this detailed study within the frame of the explicated fundamental structure of personality in comparison with all the studies that have been done in the course of history in all countries and cultures. This super-psychologist would not only combine in himself these talents which usually do not go together, but also find time and energy to accomplish all these things. No psychologist can be so naïve as to believe that such genius can be produced in sufficient numbers.

Another solution, the so-called local psychology solution, suggests a division of labor in which psychologists in various countries concentrate on various phases of the knowledge of man. In an over-simplified, and therefore inaccurate example, one could imagine that the local psychology of certain countries would produce Freuds, Adlers, Jungs, Binswangers, Buytendijks, and Merleau-Pontys who would take care of the integrative phases of science, and the local psychology of certain other countries would specialize in operational translations of some of their discoveries on the infra-human level which are open to operational manipulation, measurement, and experimentation. This solution too seems inefficient—still more so when the countries concerned use different languages. When these respective psychologists do not have much direct contact with one another, the gap between the specialists of the whole personality and the specialists of certain measurable aspects of personality becomes very wide—especially when the latter had no contact with the former during their graduate study in their own national universities.

A third possibility, the cooperative specialist solution, does away with the genius psychology concept and the local psychology concept. According to this solution, no country specializes in the exclusive production of psychologists of the whole personality or of psychologists specializing in one or another measurable aspect of personality, but rather every university makes room for both talents and stimulates them without discrimination. In this case, one could obtain one's degree in any university of any country concerned by means of integrative theoretical, experimental, or clinical research. This relationship of the future specialists in the psychology of the whole man and the psychology of certain measurable aspects of man in the same countries and at the same universities would make for more efficient cooperation and would gradually contribute to the restoration of the knowledge of the whole personality. We need scholars who specialize in the integration of our knowledge of personality in the light of a phenomenological explication of man's fundamental psychological srtuctures.

Variety of Personality Theories

When the psychologists of personality attempt to integrate our knowledge of personality in the light of a phenomenological explication of man's fundamental personality structures, how can they explain the fact that there are so many integrations, such as Freud's, Jung's, Adler's, Binswanger's, or Frankl's anthropology? A first answer would be that some of these men were not trying to integrate on the basis of the fundamental structure of the human personality. If the basic categories of integrating the data and insights regarding human personality are not sought for in the explicated fundamental structure of personality, the categories will be able to contain only the phenomena of a certain group of men in a certain culture. Only the fundamental personality categories obtained by the explication of the basic structure of man's personality are valid at all times for all people in all situations, and are therefore broad enough to provide a basic organization for all psychological data, even of relative data, because their relativity has to be shown against the background of categories which are universally valid.

We must add, however, that even when anthropological psychologists are really basing their integration on the basic categories which are implicit in the primary awareness of fundamental personality structure of man—even then we may see different kinds of integration. Every integration of the psychology of man is pervaded by an original intuition, an all-illuminating light. This primary intuition enables the anthropological psychologist to bring clarity into the complexity of psychological data. This is true of the anthropologies of Freud, Jung, Adler, Horney, Binswanger, and Sullivan. There is no psychologist of personality who is satisfied with the complexity and plurality of data which are collected in experimentation and clinical observation and who is resigned to their disorderly enumeration. An anthropological psychologist is always trying to reduce the plurality to a kind of unity; he tries to discover structures; he wants to comprehend. A man such as Freud, or Jung, or Adler, or Binswanger attempting this integration does not know *beforehand* how the unity will be brought about or which structures will be discovered. The light by which he studies the psychology of man and thinks about the mutual relationships of the phenomena which he discovers is not first decided upon and then put into operation. It may perhaps be said that every new anthropological psychology begins with the vague suspicion that a certain approach will be fruitful before the psychologist of personality realizes precisely what he is doing, by what principle he is guided, by what light he is proceeding, or what fundamental intuition he is using. Usually the evident fruitlessness of a certain way of thinking about the psychology of personality in the past gives rise to and guides a new mode of thinking, but provisionally it is not at all clear in what this new mode consists. Thus, for instance, a psychologist of personality came to the conclusion that an explanation of the phenomenon of repression as involving only the need for pleasure is insufficient. Psychologists then tried to proceed along new paths; Jung pointed to the repression of the spiritual needs of the Self, Adler to the repression of the need for power. What these men are first of all interested in is a broader explanation of repression, and not reflection on the light in which they consider repression. Only much later does this light become the theme of investigation. Often such investigation is not performed by him who first made use of the light but by other anthropological psychologists. In this sense, it can be said that the psychologies of Jung, Freud, Adler, and others are much better understood by later anthropological psychologists than by these psychologists themselves.

Evidently, a psychological integration will be fruitful to the extent that its central point of reference, its basic idea of man's psychology, is capable of making the multiplicity and complexity of the psychological phenomena transparent and of reducing them to unity. For instance, we can reach no results at all in the integration of the knowledge of man's behavior with the idea "nails," while the ideas "nervous system", "libido", and "learning" offer at least some explanation.

Why is it that even when the anthropological psychologist attempts to choose as his central point of reference, as his basic principle of integration, a truly fundamental personality characteristic, he may still develop an anthropological psychology which is different from another one which was also based on a fundamental personality characteristic? First of all, an anthropological psychologist may be convinced that he is explicating a fundamental personality characteristic, while it is actually a characteristic of his own personality and of many who are in the same contemporary cultural situation, but not true of human personality as such. Or he may unduly emphasize one of the fundamental characteristics of human psychology at the cost of the others. In this case the anthropological psychologist misjudges the true character of his own fundamental personality because he has no eye for the other fundamental aspects of his personality. We may ask why this psychologist is so impressed by one aspect of his fundamental personality at the cost of the other aspects? Here only a psychological analysis could give an answer. The historical growth of his personal existence may have brought about his distorted explication of his fundamental personality, or it may have been the *Zeit Geist* which made him blind to certain aspects of his own reality.

Does this mean that such a onesided anthropological psychology is meaningless for psychology? By no means. For such a onesided psychology explains a certain fundamental aspect of the human personality and makes clear in what way the multiplicity of data about personality are integrated in this aspect. The participation of such a onesided personality theorist in the ongoing conversation of psychologists of personality helps his colleagues to transcend their own onesidedness. Secondly, when we are able to discover what type of distorted outlook made for this particular view of personality, we may learn about those people who share more or less the same emotional affliction in a certain period of culture. Their anthropological representative depicts for us their distorted world of resentment, despair, and rebellion. Finally, when we find out in reality that such a personality theory does not work, we shall be forced to question the theory concerned. This is the very moment in which we shall be born as psychologists of man. Now we are personally participating in the dialogue of mankind about the psychology of personality by means of discussions, publications, dissertations, and lectures.

Criterion of Anthropological Psychology

This brings us at once to the critical question: What is the criterion in the light of which I can see that my explication of man's basic psychological structure is true and valid? The criterion of truth is the presence of what I experience or observe. However, there is a difficulty in that I may distort my real primary experience or perception by imagination, anxiety, or by other emotional attitudes which may be ingrained in me or in my contemporary culture because of past traumatic experiences. Therefore, I need another criterion of truth for my explication of the fundamental structure of human personality. This criterion is the fruitfulness of my dialogue with the fundamental human personality in myself and in others. If this dialogue is based on a onesided explication of the fundamental psychological structure of human personality, sooner or later it will be impossible to keep the dialogue going at certain points because it will no longer touch reality, and therefore there will be no answer. Imagine, for instance, that I have explicated the fundamental structure of human personality as being absolutely identical with animal life, and that as a result of this explication I deal with the other as an animal. As long as I put only questions to him that will touch in him what is animal-like and infra-human (for instance, the biological aspect of his hunger drive), everything will be satisfactory. As soon, however, as I attempt to have a dialogue with this human person about his prayer, his love, his faithfulness, noble ideas, his philosophy, and I attempt to do it on the basis that the psychology of man is absolutely identical with that of the animal, his answers will not fit my biological categories. I will have to admit that my explication of the fundamental psychological structure of man is onesided because it does not work in reality.

In other words, the reality of the psychological life as revealing itself in collective and personal psychological history is the test of the truth of our explication. Here again, it is far easier for the psychology of the measurable aspects of man to apply the test of reality by means of experimentation. Some of these tests may indirectly prove that the implications on the infra-human level of certain explications on the formally human level are mistaken, and thereby foster a new explication. However, this proof is not usually sufficient because the reality of the psychological personality itself transcends that which can be tested by means of laboratory equipment or statistical measurement. Personality experiences such as responsibility, dread, anxiety, despair, freedom, love, wonder, or decision cannot be measured or experimented with like the infra-human aspects of personality. They are simply there and can only be explicated in their givenness. How can we find out that this explication is not a distortion? Close attention to history may be the only possible way. Entire generations of psychologists of personality may pass before it becomes clear that a certain psychological view is onesided and does not correspond to the full reality of the psychology of personality. It may become gradually clear that the prevalent view of personality contradicts reality, and a renewed explication of man's personality structure must be be attempted in order to come into contact again with his psychology. As an example, we may refer to orthodox reflexology and behaviorism. Their implicit anthropology was that man was a bundle of conditioned and unconditioned reflexes. That explication was in tune with the predominant anthropology of our most recent cultural period: man is a thing, something to be conditioned, organized, manipulated, experimented upon. At the moment, however, we see the consequences of the large scale imposition of this view of man in increasing neuroticism, self-estrangement, loneliness, despair, and boredom. Therefore, there are signs everywhere of an awakening interest in a renewed explication of man's fundamental psychological structure; other aspects of personality are emerging—man's human face is coming to the fore.

It is inevitable for man to make mistakes, to err in his psychology of personality. The psychologists of personality are always influenced in their explication by their cultural viewpoint. Often the men of a certain period of culture are not even aware that long ago they reached an impasse, and sometimes an entire life or an entire culture has to be a failure before man will recognize the deficiencies of his personality theory. This inclination to human onesidedness inspires the psychologist of personality to be modest in forming his views. To live up to the responsibility of being a psychologist of personality means a lifelong task of scholarly work.

As we have said, the explication of man's fundamental psychological structure—in the light of which explication the psychologist integrates the human knowledge about the psychology of man—is always in danger of falsification. The test of our collective history is necessary to prove the correctness or incorrectness of our explications. Humanity has no substitute for the painful test in the laboratory of history. Humanity can only prevent this test from taking longer than is necessary by making anthropological psychology the concern of sensitive scholars all over the world. These scholars must be the ears and the eyes of mankind, detecting the slightest indications that certain personality theories lead to deformation. They have to expose these indications in order that we may revise our directions when we discover that we are in blind alleys. It is not the psychologist of the measurable aspects of contemporary man in the laboratory or clinic who can assume this function. Experimentation and clinical research do not orient themselves;they are already oriented by an implicit or explicit view of personality. Therefore, it is only exceptional and accidental when they go beyond the prevalent theories of personality. Experimental research as such, and theories immediately linked to this research, cannot provide a viewpoint outside and above themselves from which to judge themselves critically. Therefore the specialist of the psychology of personality should abstain from too strong an involvement in detailed clinical or experimental research which could affect his impartiality. He has to be faithful to his unique function of being an impartial integrator of psychological knowledge in the light of man's fundamental psychological structure. The experimental or clinical psychologist is always measuring something. The comprehensive psychologist of personality is always integrating some measured aspects of the human reality and some aspects which are not measurable. Experimental and integrational research are the two poles of the axis on which turns the fascinating historical process of the discovery of the psychology of man.

Understanding Human Personality

The end of our descriptive definition, "in order to understand his psychology," announces the final aim of the anthropological endeavor: the growth in understanding of the psychology of man. The aim of any study guides the study in all of its phases. In this sense, the end is present in the very beginning and remains active as a background against which the psychologist of personality continually selects when reading, thinking, comparing, writing, or collecting data. The aim of the psychology of man is to understand man. But what is the usefulness of a psychology which makes us understand but which does not help us directly to "predict and control"? We are obsessed today by the image of the psychological laboratory, the computer, and the testing room. When we are doing things that are not directly convertible in the processes that go on in these sanctuaries of the natural sciences, we feel guilty. We tend to be disturbed when one of the highpriests of natural science in his symbolic white coat points his accusing finger in our direction and declares that we are not dedicating all of our scientific life to the service of experimentation. We feel that he may expel us from the community of scientists because we do not contribute to the increase of prediction and control.

This dogmatic attitude is due to the onesided view of personality that enslaves our society. The Gestalt of the technical prevails on the globe today.

Experimental psychology and the theories linked to it can never rise above this contemporary view of man's psychology because they are part of it. Therefore, this kind of psychology is so well accepted in our culture that it evokes guilt feelings in the psychologist of personality. In self-defense, the psychologist of personality could be tempted to demonstrate the usefulness of the comprehensive psychology of personality. He could attempt to find something in his work that equals the usefulness of motivational research, telling us which kind of package sells best; or perceptual research, informing us about the optimal conditions for vision on the road; or of human engineering, telling us how to construct an instrument panel to be used in a rocket with which we will shoot people to the moon. All these things seem far more practical, far more sound, than to talk about the psychology of personality. The effort, however, to prove an equal kind of usefulness of the psychology of personality would be in vain. A comprehensive theory of personality can never be justified by its *immediate* usefulness. Such a psychology can only justify itself by its appeal to that in man which forces him to search for an integral insight into himself and his fellow men and to grow through this understanding. The usefulness of psychology for this inner growth is frequently not understood by many psychologists of the measurable aspects of man. Many of them know only the usefulness which they experience in their laboratory or clinic or in their daily practice as industrial, educational, or motivational psychologists.

"What can you do with it?" "So what?" "How can you apply it?" "Can you translate it into an *operational* definition?" These are the questions, and the terms "do," "apply," and "operational" have a very definite meaning, limited as they are by the perspective of the world of the worker. The psychotechnics of the measuring psychologist are useful and necessary for the world of labor in which they are integrated. But the theory of personality as such seems useless to this world of labor. This psychology goes beyond the world of labor. An anthropological psychology which would be completely integrated in our contemporary world of labor would be "useless" in a higher sense. It would be useless as a means of transcending contemporary and local forms of of psychology through the integration of the psychology of men of all cultures and all centuries in order to grow in the understanding of the psychology of man as he is. An anthropological psychology which would be an integral component of the culturally and locally determined world of labor would be unable to assume a standpoint from which to view the relativity of the different kinds of psychology. The attempt to understand personality in the light of its fundamental psychological structure and of the explications of this structure during all centuries goes far beyond "usefulness" as it is strived for in the psychologies of the measurable aspects of man. The understanding of the psychology of personality as a whole is characterized by a "usefulness" which it cannot abandon under penalty of ceasing to be the unprejudiced understanding of the psychology of personality. If technical usefulness becomes our last and only guide and criterion in the understanding of personality, we will no longer be able to understand personality as personality, but we will measure personality only insofar as it can be used in the world of labor, of manipulation, prediction, and control. To know the psychology of personality from this viewpoint is important for the anthropological psychologist because it reveals an aspect of personality. But the study of the psychology of human personality as "technically useful being" can never become the exclusive basis of understanding the psychology of the whole personality, never the basis of an open comprehensive personality theory. Many introductory courses in our colleges introduce the personality not as a whole but from the viewpoint of a technocracy. The psychology of personality as personality goes beyond man's testable abilities, beyond his similarity to animals, and beyond his possibilities for adjustment to the huge glittering antiseptic buildings of our technocratic society.

We can also use the term "useful" in a sense which is totally different from its technocratic meaning. The technical usefulness of the psychology of the measurable aspects of man is that this psychology helps man to improve himself and his conditions in such a way that he becomes a better adjusted and more efficient producer and consumer in our gigantic collectives. But the usefulness of the psychology of personality is that it improves man precisely in his being man, as an independent growing self. Anthropological psychology is an aid to his self-actualization by means of participation, by making him aware that he is more than a sum of technocratic determinations by his civilization. Precisely because our society tends to treat man as a "technically useful being", this psychology of man is not only humanly useful but even necessary. This psychology of man has a really therapeutic significance in the oppressing atmosphere of a technocratic universe. The humane usefulness of the psychology of man cannot be proved outside the practice of understanding man as man. One could compare this usefulness for living with that which is proper to psychotherapy and art. Their specific kind of usefulness for man's very existence cannot be proved outside the experience of therapy itself and outside the experience of art itself. In the same way, one cannot prove the usefulness of human love. From the viewpoint of the world of labor, love is a highly impractical and time consuming affair. Its humane usefulness in a deeper sense is known only to the lovers themselves in the act of loving.

One can only understand the humane usefulness of the psychology of personality when one is "present" to the reality of the whole man. This being present to the reality of man as man is the primary experience of the psychologist of personality. Many psychologists are not present to man as man, wholly absorbed as they are in the experimentation of the laboratory, or in the psychotechnics of the testing room, or in social psychological research "about" certain aspects of man. Therefore, they are unable to understand "what this anthropological noise is all about." It cannot make sense to them. As a rule, therefore, pleas for the humane usefulness of a psychology of personality fail to convince the psychologist who is not anthropologically oriented. On the other hand, the psychologists, clinicians, or experimentalists who are already anthropologically oriented do not need such a plea because the value of this psychology clearly reveals itself in their psychological understanding of themselves and others. Only by attempting to understand oneself and one's fellowman as human can one experience what the psychology of personality really means.

Therefore, the only way in which the student can experience the value of anthropological psychology is by the actualization of his own potentialities and his own need for a continual integration of this understanding. A tremendous wealth of questions, tentative answers, anxieties, and delights are evoked in the student who confronts his own psychology and the psychology of others. Only by means of this actualization is it possible to make the student experience "true to life" what the psychology of personality really is and how incomparable is the value of the "useless" understanding of the anthropological psychologist. We are convinced that the development of our modern society and of the psychology of measurable aspects of man within society is in dire need of anthropological depth. Modern man, whether Marxist or Capitalist, is more and more in danger of becoming the victim of a technocratic mentality which pervades our society and its psychology. The more this mentality advances and extends itself in psychology, the more difficult it becomes for man to be in harmony with his psychology, with his real self, and to assent to his fundamental personality structure. The basic questions which arise in this situation are always of an anthropological nature.

CHAPTER SEVEN

ANTHROPOLOGICAL PSYCHOLOGY

Comprehensive psychology requires constructs sufficiently fundamental to integrate the contributions of various psychologies which embody isolated viewpoints in the study of intentional behavior. This variety of differential approaches can be reduced to three main categories, namely subject-oriented, object-oriented, and situation-oriented psychologies.

One series of perspectives considers human behavior in its subjective, experiential aspect. The subjective experience of man is embodied in quantifiable behavior and always refers to an object-pole in a situation. The psychologist, however, can limit his research exclusively to the subject-pole of this behavior. Many of the theories which have developed from psychiatry and psychotherapy demonstrate this perspective. The constructs and idioms of the psychologies which are predominantly subject-oriented differ from those which are oriented towards the bodily objectifiable, measurable aspects of behavior. This relative difference in method and idiom is not necessarily a difference in functional, mechanical, quantitative, process-like approach. The psychologist who specializes in the study of the subject-pole of behavior abstracts certain aspects from this behavior and isolates them for empirical study. For this differential theory he may very well use functional, mathematical, and mechanical constructs. Such an isolation of subjective variables is evident, for example, in the studies of the early introspectionists. The use of a mechanistic model is also common in psychoanalytic studies of the subject-pole of behavior. As a third category, the differential psychologies which are concerned with the situational approach to behavior have developed their own methods, constructions, and formulations. The situational aspect of behavior encompasses those social, interpersonal, environmental, cultural, and historical features which enter into behavior as a whole and without which human behavior would be unthinkable.

Comprehensive psychological theory aims at the integration of these three types of differential psychologies in an open scientific model. This model can subsequently operate as a provisional guide in the development of the field of psychology as a whole. Comprehensive theory can pursue this main purpose only when its fundamental constructs are not exclusively subject-, object-, or situation-oriented. It must transcend these three dimensions of behavior by means of constructs which represent behavior in its entirety. Comprehensive psychology thus requires a type of concept which can bridge the gaps between the three series of perspectives. Constructs are needed which are capable of reintegrating conceptually the subjective, objective, and situational aspects of intentional behavior, and which point to the original unity of behavior as it manifested itself before scientific research isolated profiles from behavior for investigation.

The transcendence of the three main types of differential constructs does not imply a devaluation of them. On the contrary, continual development of differential psychologies will remain the condition for the constant growth of comprehensive psychology. For the scientific mode of existence expands by means of an increasingly differentiated concentration on isolated aspects of its object of study.

The type of construct which transcends the three differential types is called *anthropological,* and the comprehensive theory which utilizes such constructs is named *anthropological psychology.* Anthropological constructs deal with the subjective-objective-situational Gestalt of human behavior which is rooted in the very nature of "anthropos", or man.

In this chapter we shall first discuss the meaning of the term "anthropological" and then describe the necessary and sufficient constituents of anthropological constructs in psychology.

The Term "Anthropological"

In current usage the meaning of "anthropology" is restricted to the "science of man in relation to physical character, origin and distribution of races, environmental and social relations and culture." (*Webster's New Collegiate Dictionary,* Springfield, Mass., G&C Merriam Company, 1960, p. 38.)

This restriction of the term anthropology stresses only one of the three main dimensions of "anthropos" or man, namely the cultural-social one. Etymologically, the term anthropology does not have this restricted meaning for it is derived from the Greek words, *anthropos,* which means man, and *logos,* which means word or science. Therefore, every concept, construct, word, or science which refers to man as a whole can properly be called anthropological. Man in his entirety, however, appears to us under many aspects. For example, we may refer to man insofar as he appears physically, racially, socially, and culturally. In this case, we speak of cultural anthropology. We may also perceive man in the light of other sciences or disciplines, such as medicine, history, sociology, philosophy, or theology. In these cases we can rightly speak of a medical, historical, social, philosophical, or theological anthropology. The psychologist may study man insofar as he appears to us in the entirety of his intentional-functional behavior. Such a study may be called anthropological psychology. It presupposes, however, the development of many differential psychologies through the gradual uncovering of different abstracted aspects of behavior by experiment and observation. Consequently, an anthropological psychology is possible only after this differential unveiling. The main method of such a psychology is the dialectical integration of the results of these differential approaches. In other words, anthropological psychology is a comprehensive theoretical psychology which studies *human* behavior. This concern with *human* behavior does not imply a neglect of the insights gained by the study of animal behavior. On the contrary, the contributions of animal psychology are integrated within anthropological psychology insofar as they shed light on certain aspects of human behavior which are similar to those of the behavior of animals.

Human behavior, to be sure, can be conceived and formulated in many ways. The constructs which specify the meaning of human behavior must reveal certain characteristics in order to be truly anthropological. We may call these characteristics the necessary and sufficient constituents of anthropological constructs. Briefly, anthropological constructs must transcend the predominantly subjective, objective, or situational connotations of differential constructs; they must represent fundamental human characteristics; they should be rooted in experience; they should be person-oriented, not function-oriented; and they should be appropriated by the student of human behavior in a personal way. The remainder of the present chapter will be given to a consideration of these constituents of anthropological constructs.

The First Constituent: The Transcendence of the Predominantly Subjective, Objective, or Situational Connotations of Differential Constructs

Anthropological constructs should transcend the exclusively subjective, objective, or situational connotations of the constructs of differential psychologies. These latter specialize in the study of one of these three dimensions of behavior because of scientific-methodological reasons which have already been explained. The cultural development of Western thought in the last three centuries, however, has tended to transmute these methodological distinctions into absolute ones. This absolutism leads to subjectivism, objectivism, and situationalism. Because of this unfortunate historical development, it is necessary for us, first, to discuss what we mean by an anthropological construct, abstracting from the term all possible subjectivistic, objectivistic, or situational connotations; second, to consider the development in our culture of the absolute dualism we have mentioned above;

and finally, to assess the impact of this dualism on academic and psychoanalytic psychologies.

The term "anthropological" as we shall use it excludes all subjectivistic connotations. The subjectivism which has dominated recent periods of Western culture has tended to reduce the full meaning of the term "anthropological" to only the subjective dimension of man's being. From such an impoverished viewpoint, man is explained as a subject who is initially separated from the reality in which he lives. Such a view is not rooted in our spontaneous, full experience of man as a meaningful, intentional whole who is self-evidently present to reality. It posits *a priori* that man is first of all an isolated entity. This concept implies that there must be in principle an absolute split between man and reality. This position that man is an isolated object in the world forces us to far-fetched hypotheses to account for the indisputable fact that man manifests abundantly in his daily behavior a lively intimacy and familiarity with reality. None of these hypotheses is satisfying, however, once we have started from the presupposition that man is essentially a cut-off, schizoid being who has initially no commerce whatsoever with reality as it reveals itself.

When we use the term "anthropos" or man, then we imply that man lives in an original openness for reality or, even better, that man *is* fundamentally openness for reality. This radical openness makes man different from trees, mountains, or rivers which do not have this initial understanding and freedom. We may consider man's intimacy with reality the most fundamental anthropological characteristic and the basis of all other human qualities. Man is thus a fundamental orientation or openness toward that which is not himself. Subjectivism denies or disregards this basic truth about man. A psychology which perceives the human being as fundamentally out of contact with reality can never transcend its initial subjectivism. For all later perceptions of reality will necessarily be products of this isolated subjectivity, and it will never be possible to know whether or not these products are really "out there" or merely subjective projections.

Such a fundamental subjectivism leads necessarily to just as fundamental an objectivism, which holds that man can represent in his consciousness only isolated objects from which he is absolutely separated. But man is from the beginning of life, by his very being, open for the fullness of reality, which will appear in the light of his understanding to the degree that he is faithful to his fundamental openness. Being man, therefore, does not mean being first of all an isolated self or subjectivity, whch later transcends its isolation in order to represent to itself (like a camera) isolated objects of a completely foreign reality "out there".

Psychology studies intentional behavior of man in its concrete givenness, which is always a particular realization of his original openness for reality. Therefore, psychology always studies, in the last analysis, some behavioral relationship of man to himself, to others, and to things. For man can develop only what he fundamentally is; basically he is always a behavioral relationship with reality. This relationship modifies itself according to both the inexhaustible variety of situations in which reality manifests itself and the stand which man takes toward reality. For the appearance of reality in the light of man's openness differs when man stands out toward reality as a perceiving, a thinking, a remembering, a loving, a theorizing, an imagining, a dreaming, a depressed, a paranoid, or a utilitarian subjectivity. Every mode of existence reveals a different aspect of reality. But all these modes are modifications of the fundamental "enlightening-relationship-to-the-world" which man *is*. They are special actualizations of man's existential belonging to the world, of his already-being-in-the-world.

Although man is fundamentally open for reality, at each moment of his life only certain aspects of reality enter his concrete awareness. The selection and the availability of these aspects are dependent on his attitude. The scientific attitude, for example, reveals other appearances of reality than the poetic or the philosophical one.

All-that-is can emerge and reveal itself to man in this wide-open area of reality or being. If man were not in this original open contact with reality, it would be difficult to explain how he has succeeded in coming into contact with the appearances of reality which were supposedly separated from him. This concept would necessarily lead to the idealistic explanation that man must first—in an unexplainable way—transfer the things in the world to his mind. Everything would then happen in his mind, and we could never be sure that the things outside corresponded with the "mind-things", or even that they really were "out there".

The foregoing considerations may enable us to define further our use of the term, "anthropological psychology". It is a comprehensive theoretical psychology of human behavior. Behavior is conceived as a Gestalt of observable differentiations of an original intentional-behavioral relationship of man to the world. Behavior is thus the observable differentiation of man's intentional relationships. For reasons of method, we may emphasize in this behavioral relationship: first, the intending subject-pole, man; second, the embodiment of this intentionality in measurable behavior; finally, the "situated" object-pole of this intentional behavior.

Every differential psychology should concentrate on one of these main profiles of man's existence. This concentration presupposes a temporary abstraction of the aspect concerned from the whole of man's behavior. This methodological restriction will give rise to similarly restricted constructs. Such a limitation should be distinguished from an absolute limitation. An *absolute* restriction of the object of psychology to one of these abstracted profiles would foster the conception that *only* the subjective intentionality, or *only* measurable behavior, or *only* its "situated" object-pole should be the exclusive object of psychology. Some differential psychologists, though they do not concede that they believe in an absolute limitation of the object of psychology, seem to be convinced that their own restriction is absolute. This attitude betrays itself implicitly in a "lived" refusal to consider seriously approaches to intentional behavior other than their own. Such an absolute restriction of the object of psychology, whether implicit or explicit, is not scientific but philosophical, for it is a universal and absolute statement. Any such statement on the nature of man and of his behavior is fundamentally philosophical because it can never be proved to be true or false in its absoluteness and universality by means of the scientific method itself. Psychology, to be sure, like every other science, presupposes philosophical assumptions. But the assumptions which enable an anthropological psychology to develop must be sufficiently comprehensive to allow for the integration of subjective, objective, and situational psychologies. It is evident that the assumptions which underlie the absolutism of certain differential psychologies would be useless for a comprehensive psychology, for they would defy its very integrative purpose by excluding at the start the contributions of other psychologies.

A comprehensive theoretical psychology can never use differential constructs as fundamental constructs, even if they are used in a non-absolute sense by the differential psychologist. The meaning of a differential construct is methodologically restricted to only that aspect of behavior which is studied by a particular differential approach. Anthropological psychology can utilize such constructs only when they are purified of their limited connotations. Even then, it is difficult to view them as foundational constructs because of the inherent quality of their restrictive connotations. They may be useful, however, as subconstructs or as "bridges" between foundational constructs and the discoveries of differential psychologies.

Anthropological psychology, on the other hand, requires differential psychologists who create constructs with their own *methodological* restrictions. The differential way is the only way for the psychological mode of existence to develop. Anthropological psychology resists, however, the tendency toward absolutism found in these restricted constructs. Such absolutism would hamper the development of psychology as a whole and would keep the differential psychologies in principle isolated, defensive, and mutually exclusive. It is an essential task of anthropological psychology to unmask differential constructs which are paraded as absolute symbols of the *whole* reality of human behavior.

The backgrounds of modern psychology reveal how and where the philosophical tendency to transmute certain methodologically restricted constructs into absolute ones arose.

Dualistic Philosophical Psychology

The French philosopher, scientist, physiologist, and mathematician René Descartes conceived of mind and body as two distinct substances. Both mind and matter in his thinking are complete and self-sustaining. Mind is a thinking thing and body is an extension thing. Toward the end of his life Descartes attempted a re-unification of the two. His original dualistic view, however, was in tune with the temper of his time and therefore destined to influence subsequent developments in philosophy and science, specifically in psychology and psychiatry.

The idea of the separation of mind and body turned philosophical interest toward the conscious subject. This consciousness was believed to be divorced from both body and world. Reliable knowledge was not based on an original union of the subject with the world through his body, but was merely an accurate mirroring of a world that was out there by itself, i.e., separate from the subject.

This view gave rise to two mutually exclusive starting points, namely, mind on the one hand, and body and world on the other. Each philosophical system which arose after Descartes adopted one of these starting points and denied or neglected the other. Idealistic philosophies stressed consciousness, while empiricist philosophies emphasized only body and world, which were considered to be of the same order. Idealism eliminated the world entirely as a source of knowledge and made consciousness itself—separated from the world—the absolute origin of clear and distinct ideas. Empiricism, on the contrary, held that all knowledge originates from the experience of reality which imposes itself on the perceiving consciousness. Idealism made consciousness an active, spontaneous force existing in itself in spendid isolation. Empiricism made the perceiving consciousness a passive registering apparatus determined by outside stimuli.

Anthropological Psychology

Almost every scientific psychology was rooted in either an idealistic or empiricist view of human nature, because it emerged in a cultural atmosphere satiated with Cartesian dualism and its implicit presence in both idealism and empiricism. Idealism led in psychology to introspectionism, which considered the contents of consciousness the legitimate and exclusive object of the new science. Empiricism, on the other hand, gave rise to behaviorism, which saw quantifiable bodily behavior isolated from the consciousness as the exclusive subject matter of a scientific psychology.

Originally, neither type of psychologist understood that the restriction of his attention to one aspect of behavior should be merely one of method. Each of them was inclined to posit his restriction of the subject matter of psychology as absolute and exclusive. Fortunately, this onesided dogmatic view contributed to the rich development of the two main groups of differential psychologies. The findings and theories of both idealistic and empiricist psychologies are of great value. When purified from a narrow philosophical dogmatism, they may be integrated within a comprehensive theory of behavior.

Introspectionism, which was the dominant scientific psychology until 1912, holds that psychology should develop by means of introspection or a looking-into-consciousness which reveals "contents" of consciousness. These mental contents should subsequently be described in terms of elementary sensations. Wundt and Titchener modified this development of psychology somewhat by combining the experimental method with introspection. Nevertheless, the basis of their psychology remained the method of introspection, and they shared the idealistic assumptions of the earlier members of that school. The introspective psychologist described the inner aspect of man, his consciousness, and his self-awareness. All "lower" functions or bodily-measurable, behavioral aspects were reduced to "contents of consciousness."

Behaviorism, on the other hand, excluded "consciousness" from the subject-matter of psychology and neglected the subjective aspect of behavior. This one-sided concentration on one aspect of behavior also gave rise to a large group of differential psychologies which will provide a substantial contribution to the integration of scientific knowledge of human behavior. We may cite the differential theories of such psychologists as Weiss, Lashley, Hebb, Guthrie, Hull, Spence, Skinner, and Tolman. As we have seen, the introspectionists chose to study in isolation one of the two aspects of man separated by Descartes, namely the *res cogitans*, the thinking consciousness. The behaviorists, meanwhile, concentrated their efforts on the other isolated aspect, the stimulus-response body machine, the *res extensa.* Both neglected the inherent "worldly" aspect of man's behavior. This aspect, too, became split off from the original whole as an isolated entity and gave rise to social psychologies of an environmental and cultural nature which originally tended to treat the environment as a factor in itself, insulated from intentional behavior.

Introspectionism views all bodily and measurable behavioral functions and also the world of situation of man in the light of consciousness. Like every differential psychology, it can be "differential-comprehensive" in so far as the aspect of behavior it studies is in some way present in all behavior. Consequently, introspectionism can study all behavior from its specific perspective. It errs, however, when it becomes a closed and exclusive psychology which denies the valuable knowledge gained from other differential approaches such as behaviorism and social psychology. Introspectionism alone cannot provide comprehensive psychology with the constructs required for the total integration of psychology. Comprehensive psychology cannot concentrate on consciousness to the exclusion of all other aspects of intentional-functional behavior.

The other group of differential psychologies, initiated by Watson, is based on the abstraction of the quantifiable, external aspects of behavior. Watson and some of his immediate followers adopted a radical philosophical position instead of a methodological one. Their philosophical absolutism considered behavior and consciousness as mutually exclusive. It denied the validity of any approach to behavior other than the abstracted and isolated measurable aspect. This one aspect was made absolute and was substituted for the whole. To be sure, it is worthwhile to study all behavior in the light of its measurable, external characteristics. But this "differential-comprehension" should never be confused with the "comprehensive comprehension" which integrates all differential aspects insofar as they are known at a particular point in the development of the science of behavior. Differential constructs developed by behavioristic psychologists, while valuable, are not sufficiently comprehensive to cover, for example, the contributions of introspective psychologies under their specifically "intentional" aspect.

We may conclude that a truly anthropological psychology should use fundamental constructs which are neither introspectionistic nor behavioristic, but which transcend the methodological limitations of both in order to integrate their findings into a higher unity without distortion. Only such constructs will create an open theoretical field of inquiry with stimulating interchange of ideas among all differential psychologies.

Anthropological Psychology and Non-Academic Psychology

Scientific anthropological psychology cannot overlook data or constructs presented by any school of psychology. To be truly comprehensive, it must encompass non-academic as well as academic psychologies. A crucial development outside the academic setting of the university was initiated by the psychoanalytically-oriented psychologists. The extra-academic origin of psychoanalysis is one cause among many which sometimes lead to strife between academic and psychoanalytic psychologists. The comprehensive psychologist should transcend, however, the defensive and mutually excluding attitudes maintained by certain representatives of both groups. He must seek for unity in diversity and foster the highest possible development of all psychologies. Consequently, he should give his attention to psychoanalytic as well as to behaviorist and introspectionist theories.

We have already discussed the Cartesian influence which led to the dualistic split between behaviorism and introspectionism in academic psychology. We concluded that the contructs of these psychologies are methodologically useful within the realm of differential psychology, but not to be used as fundamental anthropological constructs in a psychology which aims at synthesis and comprehension. The question now arises as to whether psychoanalytic theory is also influenced by Cartesian dualism. The answer to this question will reveal whether or not psychoanalytic constructs are sufficiently comprehensive to provide a basis for an anthropological synthesis.

An appraisal of the basic constructs of psychoanalytic theory will determine whether they encompass human behavior as a whole under all its aspects or deal with it from perhaps broad but still limited differential viewpoints. The aim of such a candid appraisal is not to discredit the contribution of psychoanalytic theory, but to assess the relative value of its findings from the viewpoint of comprehensive theory. Only the respectful integration of all contributions to psychology will lead to an understanding of the fundamental principles of the individual, social, cultural, and economic behavior of man, and to the improvement of his position in the universe. Psychologists must pool their resources. Isolationism of the differential psychologies can only render them less effective.

An evaluation of Freud's contribution from the viewpoint of comprehensive psychology leads to the conclusion that he too worked within the contemporary framework of Cartesian dualism. His view of man is obviously not based on the assumption of an original existential unity between man and world. Man in Freudian theory is biologically fixed as a pattern of innate instinctive drives prior to his having any relationship with a world which is in principle alien to his being. The world is not constitutive of his existence, but rather a collection of foreign objects to be reacted to by his fundamentally fixed biological structure. Man is not primarily an existence, a standing-out with others toward being, a participation in reality; he is fundamentally and innately a narcissistic, pleasure-seeking subjectivity. His basic libidinal and aggressive drives do not impel him to participate freely in reality, but rather to make use of objects in his world merely for instinctive gratification of his subjectivity. In other words, reality does not have an intrinsic value to be participated in respectfully, but only an utilitarian value for the subjective ego. All sense of the world "out there" is consequently determined by the isolated, subjective, instinctual forces within the organismic box. All other meanings uncovered in reality, whether personal, ethical, religious, or political, are simply imposed on reality by the absolute libidinal subject in the form of "sublimations." Man's experience of such meanings in reality is simply an illusion. He is the victim of sublimation which hides from him the fact that the only meaning of reality for him is gratification of instinctive needs. In all these viewpoints Freud mirrors, on the biological and psychological planes, the philosophical dualism introduced by Descartes.

The isolated world out there, as Freud sees it, is only "reacted to" with a pre-structured instinctive impulse which is ready to grasp it in a pre-determined way. This subjectivistic view of man led Freud to the notion that civilization was a menace to the wholesome development of the autonomous subject, and that neurosis was fundamentally a conflict between the instinctual subjectivity and any form of culture. Not only did Freud divorce the subject from his world, but he "objectivized" this isolated subjectivity as a"psychic apparatus." This apparatus comprised a host of processes and mechanisms concerned with the quantitative regulation of instinctive tensions within this now "objectified" subjective realm. Thus Freud created the constructs of release, repression, and sublimation to account for the economy within this endopsychic universe. Neurosis and criminality are expressions of the "natural and vigorous" pregiven instincts of the isolated subject, who feels painfully limited in the expression of his instinctive subjectivity by the alien cultural world in which he lives as a suppressed stranger. The basic implicit assumption of an essential split between man and his world leads necessarily to the view that social life, culture, and civilization have no real roots in the very existence of the subject.

While Freud elucidated important characteristics of the subject-pole of existence, he disregarded the possibility that man's neuroses may be due to a psychological factor which affects his existence as a whole, that is, the "situated" object-pole as well as the subject-pole. Is destructive aggression, for example, a primary instinct to hurt or destroy which is already pregiven as such in the isolated subject? Or should it be considered as a response evoked by an existential situation which is experienced as obstructive, thwarting, and interfering? The overwhelming asexual and aggressive impulses found in certain neurotic patients seem to be not merely innate forces in isolated subjects, but responses to a frustrating life situation embedded in the structure of the patient's existence during the history of his development. But Freud did not envision the development of the personality in terms of a differentiating encounter of subject and world in which both are constitutive of man's actual being. He thought of his patients much more as victims of a constant search for release of subjective tension in a strange and hostile world which they had to use for the highest possible fulfillment of their needs.

In reality, man as a whole is constituted as much by his world as by his consciousness. Man's consciousness is not separated from the world as Freud, under the impact of Cartesian dualism, believed. Consequently, Freud's viewpoint forced him to fill the isolated subjective boxes called "consciousness" and "unconsciousness" with all kinds of furniture called "internalizations" in order to explain the undeniable interaction between these subjective areas and the world. Soon the psyche was filled with a host of "internal psychic objects." The relationship of Freudian theory to the Cartesian Ego, to idealism and introspectionism, is evident in this development. To be sure, one could not have expected Freud, in spite of his genius, to emancipate himself wholly from the dualism that permeated his culture. His acute observations compelled him, in fact, to recognize the impact of significant life situations on the developing organism. But his dualism forced him to internalize these outside influences within the subject in such a way that they lived there, as it were, a dynamic life of their own. The superego was a construct which represented these totally internalized forces. Freud thus created an inner mental world of the individual divorced from the "real-world-out-there." Soon he required the constructs of projection and introversion to account for the contacts between this so-called inner world and the outer world. Impulses and emotions are not, however, isolated objects which exist in themselves within an isolated "psyche," but dynamic aspects of man's modes of existence in the world. Conflict is not an endopsychic affair, but a clash between two or more incompatible modes of existence.

Freud's theory—especially his later ego theory—was further developed by Anna Freud, William Reich, Melanie Klein, Hartmann, Kris, Alexander, Loewenstein, Winnicott, and others. These later developments reveal considerable growth toward a less dualistic view of man and his world, but they seem to be still unable to transcend completely the original split between man and world on which psychoanalytic theory is based. Nevertheless, the contribution of psychoanalytic theory to our understanding of man is monumental and should be carefully integrated within an anthropological synthesis.

Carl Jung, also, is subjectivistic in his approach to psychology. To be sure, he fills the subject box with other objects than Freud did; for example, archetypes and a racial unconsciousness. Human development becomes for him a wholly internal, somewhat mystical process within the isolated subjectivity. However, he points to significant experiences, the formulation of which is capable of being purified from the dualistic theoretical influence.

A British group of psychoanalysts, notably Melanie Klein, Fairbairn, Winnicott, and Guntrip recognized the impact of culture on behavior. At the same time, their sophisticated theory of psychic internalization of the environment fell back on the isolated subject-box-theory. The Cartesian split is revived in their theory to such a degree that man is conceived to live in two worlds at the same time, inner and outer, psychic and material. The "internal objects-psychology" of this group can also be seen as a result of the selection of the imaginative aspect of human behavior as their perspective. In their theory, imagination is not considered as world-oriented and world-revealing in principle, but as part of a relatively insulated and autonomous subjective structure. They reveal a tendency to stress the endopsychic situation and internally generated conflicts at the expense of the impact of the outer world here and now. Melanie Klein, for example, views the experience of the outer world as secondary and subordinate to the "internal" experience. Her view develops into a theory of inner psychic reality and its structuring in terms of internal objects and internal object-relations. Day and night dreams and the play of children become expressions of this relatively autonomous inner world. In the same vein, Fairbairn even concludes that the original distinction of Freud between the conscious and the unconscious now becomes less important than the distinction between the *two worlds of outer reality and inner reality.* As a result of Melanie Klein's theory, the super-ego becomes a construct which covers a whole inner world of internalized objects.

The quality and quantity of clinical material presented by this British group compels respect; so does the quality of their theorizing. They represent an original and unusual contribution to psychoanalytic and other theories. Their refreshing insights and discoveries lend themselves to integration within a comprehensive psychology of human behavior. Their constructs, while valuable and necessary from the differential viewpoint, are not sufficiently comprehensive to provide a basis for an anthropological psychology.

"Situational" Analytic Psychology

The Cartesian split, as we have seen, led to introspectionism and behaviorism in academic psychology, while an analogous development took place in non-academic psychology. In addition, the cultural interpersonal school of psychoanalytic thought represented by Alfred Adler, Harry Stack Sullivan, Karen Horney, and Erich Fromm gave rise to a series of differential theories bound together by the viewpoint of the culture, the civilization, the "others", the world. These psychologists rejected the idea that man's impulsive and emotional behavior emerges from innate instinctive drives within the organismic box. They substituted the perspective of environmental conditions, social pressures, cultural patterns, for the perspective of autonomous instinctual subjectivity. This series of differential psychoanalytic theories stresses that culture molds character and that neurosis arises from disturbances in human relationships. These theories tend, however, toward an exclusively cultural explanation of behavior which implies an underestimation of the relatively free subject who interacts with his culture. This development mirrors the situation in academic psychology in which introspectionism was one-sidedly concerned with the processes "within" the subject, while original behaviorism was geared to the perspective of the outside stimuli. Fromm, for example, sees the inclinations of man simply as the result of the social process which creates man.

Harry Stack Sullivan views the human personality as the product of the personal and social forces acting upon man from the day of his birth. The social pressure of the culture-pattern molds the personality. Sullivan recognized, however, that it is a person-integrated-in-a-situation-with-another-person-or-persons whom one studies in psychology. Such a fortunate formulation tends to transcend the Cartesian split. However, when Sullivan further outlines his theory of behavior, it becomes evident that he promotes the culture-side of the split at the expense of the subjectivity of man. His psychology is a penetrating differential study of one aspect of the human reality, namely the acculturation of the conscious and preconscious ego in relationships with the world. As a result, he evolves a theory in which the real subjectivity of man has no place, but is replaced by a social self dependent on a need for approval and acceptance. His statement which most strikingly reveals this aspect of his theory is: "The self may be said to be made up of reflected appraisals." A necessary consequence of this one-sided attention to the "situated" object-pole of human existence is a one-sided appreciation of the "real self"—just as limited as the vague entity described by Horney, Fromm, and Jung.

The series of differential psychologies initiated by the perspective of the "situated" object-pole of existence illustrates strikingly the importance of differential psychologies. They elucidate one aspect of human existence in a most remarkable manner. They are capable of viewing the whole of human reality in the light of this one perspective, because this "situational" aspect is everywhere present in man, even in the innermost reaches of his being. This one-sidedness is laudable and fruitful as a methodological principle and should be maintained as a source of insight into one aspect of human existence. It is impossible, however, to use the differential constructs of these psychologies for a comprehensive theory which is the very transcendence of these aspects. Such a theory respectfully aims to discover the appropriate place of these differential constructs in a conceptual comprehensive structure which points to human behavior as a whole.

The Second Constituent: The Representation of Fundamentally Human Characteristics

Differential psychologies deal with various isolated profiles of human behavior. Many of these profiles when taken in isolation from man as a whole are characterized by features, processes, and laws that can also be observed in animals, plants, and inanimate objects. These common aspects are abstracted, however, from the whole of man's behavior and objectivated for methodological reasons of research. The *full* meaning of these isolated features of human behavior can be grasped only when they are reintegrated within the whole by comprehensive psychology. Their meaning becomes clear when perceived again in the light of those properly human qualities of man which characterize all profiles of his behavior and their mutual interdependency.

These comprehensive, all-pervading, specifically human qualities cannot be forced into the mechanical models of certain differential psychologies such as stimulus-response, punishment-reward, tension-reduction, or homeostasis. Such frames of reference are equally applicable to nonhuman beings. Consequently, these "sets" of mechanistic constructs "catch" precisely that in man which is not specifically and exclusively true of human behavior as such. The foundational constructs of anthropological psychology should point, therefore, to precisely those unique qualities that make man distinct from every other type of being. Such unique qualities, which pervade all profiles, features, and processes of human behavior, will provide the synthesizing ideas which can inter-relate the data and theories of differential psychologies. Only such comprehensive constructs will facilitate a systematic integration, explanation, and understanding of human behavior.

This necessary concern of comprehensive psychology for man in his characteristically human qualities does not imply an underestimation of the methodological usefulness of mechanical models in certain differential psychologies. A differential mechanistic approach to certain isolated aspects of behavior remains methodologically justifiable as long as the interpretation of the results of such an approach does not go beyond the specific differential profile of behavior which is its object.

Philosophical Anthropology

Comprehensive psychology has thus to create constructs which represent the human characteristics of behavior. The discipline which is traditionally concerned with the fundamental characteristics of man is philosophical anthropology. This discipline studies the being of man, his nature, or his essence. It does so in the light of ontology, which may be defined as the study of Being as such. The anthropological psychologist, in so far as he is a foundational theorist, is necessarily interested in philosophical anthropology, and consequently in the underlying ontology on which it depends.

In every cultural period, philosophical anthropology and its underlying ontology reconsider the perennial problems of the philosophy of man in the light of contemporary knowledge and experience. The anthropological psychologist who has to deal with contemporary man in clinic, hospital, and consulting-room must integrate not only the past but also the most recent discoveries of differential psychologies. He is necessarily interested in formulations of contemporary philosophies which verbalize the contemporary predicament and self-awareness of man. However, he does not assume philosophical concepts blindly, but evaluates them in the light of both historical and contemporary contributions of differential psychologies in order to judge their applicability to these psychologies and their concomitant usefulness for the construction of comprehensive theory. Many ontological concepts are useful for comprehensive integration because of their universality, that is, their applicability to all behavior of all men. When constructs about behavior are obtained by a merely empirical study of a specific group in a particular culture, then they are useful in integrating only the data which pertain to that group. Only constructs which are obtained from an explication of man's very essence are in principle broad enough to integrate all psychological data obtained by all differential psychologies and concerning all classes of men in all periods of human history.

Certain differential psychologies, on the other hand, may develop their own implicit philosophical anthropology which is suitable only to the specific aspect of behavior which they study. The integration of the contributions of these differential psychologies presupposes, therefore, that the integrational theorist will make explicit their specific ontological assumptions. Only then is a dialogue possible between the fundamental philosophical anthropology represented in the foundational constructs of comprehensive theory and those ontological assumptions which underlie the differential psychologies. This dialogue will clarify whether or not the philosophy of man which underlies a particular differential psychology is sufficiently comprehensive to be adapted to discoveries of other differential psychologies. If it is not, the integrational theorist must purify the differential contribution of all unwarranted extrapolations arising from its implicit philosophy of man. Only such a purification will clarify precisely what the differential psychologist has established through scientific observation. Such an operation, on the basis of comprehensive anthropological constructs, is performed in comprehensive theory by means of the foundational dialectical method. This method is based on the principle that scientifically established data of differential theories can never exclude one another and are always open to integration. If the implicit philosophical anthropologies underlying the differential psychologies prove to be incompatible with one another, then the theoretical psychological interpretations may also be incompatible insofar as they are influenced by these contradictory concepts.

This dialectical activity of the comprehensive theorist does not imply that he can call himself a philosopher. First of all, he does not create philosophical concepts, but only uses them as another psychologist might use certain concepts of physiology. A differential psychologist does not become a professional physiologist because of this intellectual borrowing; neither does a comprehensive psychologist become a professional philosopher because of analogous borrowing. Furthermore, the comprehensive theorist uses only those philosophical concepts which prove relevant to the integration of the data of differential psychologies. His whole intellectual procedure is essentially different from the manner in which a professional philosopher approaches his own discipline. Finally, the comprehensive psychologist does not have the professional background in philosophy which would qualify him to construct a philosophy with authority. To continue the comparison given above, the use of philosophical concepts by a psychologist does not imply that he himself is a professional philosopher any more than the use of physiological data implies that a psychologist is a physiologist. In each case, there is only a highly selective borrowing from another discipline on the basis of discoveries in the field of psychology. This borrowing is therefore fundamentally a psychological and not a professionally philosophical or physiological activity; it presupposes, however, a previous professional activity by philosophers or physiologists. The results of this activity are assumed by the comprehensive psychologist. We may define such an assumption as a conclusion or judgment borrowed by one professional field of study from another, the intrinsic validity of which cannot be proved or disproved by the specific methods of the discipline which appropriates it. A borrowing science can prove only that the constructs borrowed are relevant to the explication and integration of its own discoveries and do not contradict the established scientific data within its own field. For example, the science of optics assumes that the laws of mathematics are valid and makes use of them to explain and integrate its own findings. However, optics makes no direct effort to prove or disprove the laws of mathematics.

The comprehensive theorist is especially interested in what psychology implicitly or explicitly borrows from ontology. For these ontological assumptions shape the basic frame of reference of psychology as a whole. The explication of ontological assumptions in foundational theory, and in the differential psychologies which are to be integrated, should not be understood as an operation which is to be performed once only. For foundational constructs should point clearly and precisely to the fundamental characteristics of man. And the insight of man concerning his basic characteristics continually grows richer, deeper, and more specific as history develops. An anthropological psychology which is open and vital profits from this growth of insight by constantly questioning its fundamental constructs and categories. Moreover, differential psychologies may be influenced in their theoretical formulations by newly emerging philosophies of man. This influence will impel the comprehensive theorist to a constant investigation of the possible presence of new philosophical elements in the formulations of differential psychologists. If such ontological changes are not clarified, they may obscure the contributions of differential observation and experimentation, and thus hinder their smooth integration within the wider frame of reference of anthropological psychology.

The Principle of Applicability

We may conclude that one necessary constituent of the comprehensive constructs of anthropological psychology is their representation of fundamental characteristics of man or those basic human qualities which characterize the meaning of human behavior as a whole. The comprehensive psychologist carefully selects and formulates his anthropological integrational constructs during the dialogue which he maintains between all differential psychologies and anthropological philosophy. This dialogue is not an arbitrary comparison between two fields of study; it is oriented by its purpose of integrating the contributions of the differential psychologies within an innerly consistent, comprehensive, anthropological frame of reference. This purpose provides the criterion of selection for the comprehensive theorist and assures a degree of inter-subjective agreement or convalidation.

In other words, for the comprehensive psychologist the criterion for the selection of foundational constructs is extrinsic to the philosophical judgment itself, but proper to his own science, by which he can determine the usefulness of these constructs for the integration of the differential contributions. When the comprehensive psychologist calls these borrowed philosophical constructs *assumptions,* he means only to indicate that they are assumptions *for him* as a scientist; he means that they are useful to him in the integrational dialogue. He cannot assert that they are *only* assumptions for he is not competent to prove such a statement by means of his own scientific methods. However, it may well be that various statements assumed by psychologists are certitudes in the disciplines from which they are borrowed.

The criterion which determines the selection of anthropological constructs is therefore the *principle of applicability.* This principle states that *the comprehensive scientific theorist of human behavior should borrow only those philosophical assumptions or constructs which can be used most adequately for the explanation and integration of the greatest number and variety of the findings of the various differential psychologies because of applicability to those findings.* This judgment concerning the usefulness of an assumption is thus psychological and not philosophical.

Not only comprehensive psychology but also differential psychologies borrow philosophical assumptions and constructs. Their criterion, however, is applicability not to the integration of *all* differential psychologies, but to the *specific* operations in which differential psychologists study certain profiles of behavior. Frequently, these constructs are limited; they are adequate tools for the explanation of behavior only insofar as it appears in the isolated perspective of a differential psychology. A stimulus-response learning theory, for example, is a differential psychology which studies the measurable stimulus-response aspects of behavior. This differential psychology may select as its philosophical concept that man is only a passive organism which is subjected to stimuli and which can be explained under all its aspects in terms of stimulus and response.

As we have seen earlier, a variety of human behaviors can indeed be perceived in the light of the perspective of a differential psychology. For this aspect may reveal itself somehow in all behavior. Such a consideration of the whole of behavior under this specific approach is not only useful but necessary for the growth of comprehensive psychology, which depends on the contributions of differential psychologies. It is clear, however, that the underlying philosophy of this one differential psychology is not necessarily applicable to many other differential psychologies which study totally different aspects of behavior. These aspects cannot appear as such in the perspective of one theory such as the stimulus-response learning theory. The ontological assumptions of the latter are useful only to the differential psychologist who attempts to perceive all behavior under only one specific aspect.

A contrast may clarify our position. Rogerian theory rests upon the assumption that man is worthy of respect and capable of assuming responsibility for his own existence. These philosophical constructs have proved useful for Carl Rogers and his students. However, a differential S-R psychologist, *as* differential S-R psychologist, cannot use Rogerian theory in his specific study because the latter does not imply aspects of behavior which reveal respect and personal responsibility.

Necessity for a Dialogue between Past and Present Psychologies

It is necessary for the comprehensive scientific theorist to keep the dialogue open not only among all contemporary differential psychologies, but also between contemporary and past psychologies. Otherwise, the pull of a successful psychology may be so strong that the comprehensive theorist succumbs to its fascination and accepts its implicit philosophy of man which is in tune with the *Zeitgeist.* The openness for all psychologies of *past* and present protects him, at least to a degree, against the seduction of the prevalent spirit of his age. Sometimes the psychology of an era will be mechanistic and deterministic; at other times, humanistic and personalistic, or environmental, or religious, or aesthetic. Every one of these psychologies may highlight one or another essential or quasi-essential aspect of human behavior. Comprehensive psychology attempts to integrate them in the light of the principle of empirical applicability to the findings of differential psychologies. This principle limits the essential task of comprehensive theoretical psychology to the creation of a useful model for the integration of scientific psychology and removes from it all pretense of creating an integral view of man as such. The latter task, which is proper to philosophy, could never be based merely on the principle of empirical applicability.

It should be clear at this point that comprehensive psychology proposes its anthropological constructs as purely provisional. On the one hand the anthropological psychologist is conscious of the limitations of the human intellect. He knows that all scientific statements are approximations at best and are always open to revision. On the other hand, he is aware of the dynamic richness of personality and the fact that the behavior of man can never be adequately encompassed by any theory.

Differences between Ontology of Man and Comprehensive Psychology

Our consideration of philosophical concepts and psychological constructs may be better clarified by a statement of the ways in which the ontology of man and comprehensive psychology differ in their fundamental purposes, criteria, and methods. As a primary object, philosophy of man studies the nature of man in the light of Being, whereas theoretical psychology investigates man's intentional- functional behavior in the light of the empirical findings of differential psychologies. Theoretical psychology borrows concepts from the philosophy of man which are used as principles of integration only insofar as they prove in some way applicable to empirical material. With respect to the reliability of their knowledge, many philosophies claim certitude, but the knowledge of comprehensive psychology is merely provisional because it is dependent on the discoveries of differential psychologies. The basic purpose of the philosophy of man is essentially non-utilitarian, but theoretical psychology is influenced by the pragmatic intention of integrating the empirical knowledge of the behavior of man so as to foster the authentic growth, development, and integration of his behavior in concrete life situations.

The criterion for the philosopher of man is whether or not a judgment provides an insight into man's nature considered in the light of Being; the criterion for the theoretical psychologist is whether or not a judgment proves capable of integrating meaningfully and consistently the *empirical* data and constructs concerning *concrete* human behavior in *concrete* life situations.

The method of the philosopher is a dialectical one in which the main voice is that of ontology. The ontologist examines empirical findings which may subsequently be used as only one minor fragment of an overall ontological view of man's nature. The method of the comprehensive psychological theorist is dialectical too, but the main voice is that of empirical data and constructs. In their light the theorist discovers the usefulness of certain philosophical concepts for the integration of the empirical data he is examining. These selected philosophical concepts become a fundamental part of a comprehensive scientific system which does not claim an overall view of man's nature, but only a provisional integration of empirical data regarding concrete ways of behavior in concrete life situations.

The Possibility of Various Comprehensive Constructs

The criterion of empirical applicability to *all* past and present differential psychologies directs the selection and choice of basic constructs by the scientific theorist. This criterion limits considerably the possible constructs which can be used without doing injustice to any differential contribution. Ideally, when a sufficient variety of differential psychologies has been developed in the course of history, all theoretical scientists would use practically the same anthropological constructs. This would necessarily be so if the theory comprehended the variety of psychologies in all their diversity without distortion or exclusion of any insight offered by them. The slightest deviation from the criterion of empirical applicability would immediately be evident in the incapacity of the theory proposed to integrate one or the other differential psychology not covered by the deficient foundational construct. Concomitantly, the theory proposed would fail to be a comprehensive theory.

However, it would seem that a sufficient variety of differential psychologies has not yet been developed. Consequently, comprehensive theorists are not yet compelled by the variety of contributions to adopt fundamental constructs which are basically the same. Actually, then, differences in fundamental constructs are still possible. Instead of new differential psychologies, there are still many cultural and sub-cultural concepts which influence the theoretical psychologist in the form of implicit philosophies. The comprehensive theorist should be aware of these implicit philosophical influences and of the danger of their conflicting with the principle of empirical applicability. In the present stage of the development of psychology, then, various comprehensive theories are still possible, all of which may apply to contributions of all the differential psychologies. However, the increase in differential psychologies will decrease the number of empirically applicable comprehensive theories.

The Third Constituent: Rootedness in Experience

An anthropological construct points to a fundamental human characteristic as it is found in real life. Consequently, it is crucial for such a construct to be based on our experience of man himself and not on wishful thinking, subjective imagination, or theoretical prejudice *about* man. In other words, anthropological constructs must be purified of all that is in disharmony with our fundamental experience of the human reality. Therefore, the first task of the foundational theorist is to study, in the light of actual experience, constructs available to him from various philosophies and differential psychologies. He will ask himself precisely what conforms with experience in these constructs and what is only hypothetical conceptualization. If the construct proves to be erroneous or distorted by prejudice, then it should be either corrected or rejected. An anthropological construct expresses at best only an approximation of fundamental human qualities. Nevertheless, experience must be the root of the construct and can never be replaced by hypotheses, models, or unverified philosophical, social, or political views. The comprehensive psychologist will build his theory on anthropological constructs, to be sure, but the constructs themselves should never be rooted in theory but in the firm ground of actual experience. It must be emphasized that the comprehensive theorist borrows from philosophy only those concepts which are rooted in experience and verifiable in experience.

The development of anthropological constructs should be an explication of that which is implicit in the human experience which they express. As we have already seen, the integration of the contributions of the differential psychologies also presupposes a basis of real experience. Only then is a dialogue possible between the experience of human behavior as a whole expressed in anthropological constructs and the experience of isolated profiles of human behavior as discovered through a purification of the formulations of differential psychologies.

In order to root both anthropological and differential constructs in real experience, natural observation and the phenomenological method are used. Natural observation enables us to describe phenomena in their immediate appearance. The phenomenological method leads us to the inner structure of these phenomena and liberates our perception of this structure from personal bias.

The requirement that anthropological constructs should be rooted in our experience of characteristically human qualities implies that one type of philosophy seems to be preferable to others in the matter of borrowing anthropological constructs. The kind of philosophy which seems to be most useful is that which is rooted in a critical phenomenology of human experience. Only such a philosophy attempts to develop, on the basis of experience, concepts which relate in principle to all that is necessarily true of all human qualities. We shall develop this subject in a later chapter on existential psychology and phenomenology.

The Fourth Constituent: Person-Orientation and Not Function-Orientation

Anthropological constructs differ distinctly from the constructs of differential psychologies in terms of personal versus functional orientation. Various differential psychologies which study certain aspects of behavior in isolation from man's behavior as-a-whole state their theories in the form of impersonal functions or equations. Such psychologies follow of necessity an analytical, objectivating procedure because of their dependency on empirical operations. Such operations can be performed only with abstracted isolated variables which are objectivated from the results of analysis of the reality under study. For the same reason, differential theories considered in terms of these isolated aspects of behavior form together a heterogeneous collection of explications of abstracted profiles of behavior without any inner relationship to one another.

Anthropological psychology, therefore, must begin with human existence in its wholeness if it is ever to reintegrate these unrelated, abstracted profiles into a meaningful, self-consistent synthesis. This specific task of comprehensive psychology requires a terminology proper to itself, for it cannot function on the same lines as the differential psychologies. The system of constructs of an anthropological psychology must refer to existence as a "living," personal, intentional whole—as it appears in real life situations. Only on such a basis of foundational constructs will comprehensive psychology be able to create a synoptic view of human behavior from a synthesis of the knowledge available in the differential psychologies. The human or personal qualities and dynamics which are characteristic of man in his natural union with the world cannot be adequately represented by a terminology which is peculiar to physiology, physics, or mathematics. Any attempt to do this would force anthropological data to fit an impersonal, infra-anthropological theory instead of developing a theory suitable to the data. Anthropological psychology transcends differential psychologies precisely at the level where the human person emerges as the unique, all-encompassing, intentional Gestalt. On this ultimate level of integration the statistical, physical, physiological, neurological, biological, biochemical, or mathematical constructs are of no avail—regardless of how well they are adapted to differential psychologies on lower levels of integration.

The use of mathematical constructs, for example, on this highest level of integration of intentional behavior would alter the identity of the subject matter. For the expression of behavior in mathematical symbols would necessarily change the conception of the personal nature of the subject. Human intentional behavior as a total dynamic structure cannot be represented by a mechanical, but only by a personal model. The anthropological constructs which compose this model must develop a new terminology capable of representing phenomena of human behavior as personal, existential, or qualitative, and not as mechanical, functional, and quantitative. These constructs are qualitative in nature and refer to the intentional presence of man in a world which has personally significant meanings for him.

Certain differential psychologies must depersonalize their abstracted profiles of behavior to determine to what degree these profiles are influenced by specific biochemical or physical laws. Such a depersonalization would be impossible, however, for a comprehensive science which studies man precisely in his very distinctness from the objects of physics, chemistry, biology, and neurology. In other words, anthropological psychology studies the intentional-functional behavior of persons who actually exist together with other people in a meaningful world. To be sure, this behavior reveals certain process-like, mechanical features which can be abstracted for close observation and study by differential psychologists. But these features are peripheral; they are not the unique core of intentional behavior. Nevertheless, they should be taken into account and reintegrated by the anthropological psychologist in his comprehensive synthesis.

Anthropological constructs, when compared with the functional thought forms in which most differential psychologies cast their facts and theories, are indisputably more personal. It would be unscientific to represent human-behavior-as-such with constructs of differential psychologies which point only to certain physiological, biological, functional, or physical attributes which human behavior has in common with other species, but which precisely for this reason are, as such, not specifically human. To do so would be to transfer a construct from an object in differential psychology to which it properly belongs to the object of anthropological psychology to which it does not properly apply.

Such an animal-morphism, bio-morphism, or machine-morphism would be highly metaphorical and would imply an artificial impersonification of the human. While such a metaphorical use of language is interesting from a literary point of view, it would be misleading in science where we expect objective statements of fact. The literary statement that man is *like* an animal or *like* a subtle machine or *like* a plant which responds to the stimulus of light is metaphorically true and based on resemblances which are really present and found by comparison. Certain differential psychologies make some of these resemblances the total isolated objects of their investigations. In such cases, these constructs are *literally* valid for these differential psychologies within their isolated areas of investigation. But the statements made by such differential psychologies about isolated impersonal aspects of behavior become metaphorical when applied to human existence in its personal wholeness.

The structural differentiations of behavioral existence which are studied in isolation by differential psychologies are perceived in anthropological psychology as *personal* differentiations. That is, they are necessarily permeated by the unique human characteristics which are represented in the fundamental anthropological constructs. In anthropological psychology, each differential aspect of human behavior is perceived in a person who is existing intentionally, not as an impersonal function going on in isolation. The impersonal aspects discovered by differential psychologies are not denied, to be sure, but respectfully integrated within the view of the whole person. All impersonal human states are pseudo-impersonal in the sense that we can always find some meaningful personal presence behind them which uses, abuses, submits to, is indifferent to, rebels against, neglects, affirms, denies, or represses them. In other words, these functions and features, which are available to man in his organism and environment, follow certain biochemical, neurological, and physical laws to which the intentional agent must adapt himself.

The total human self and its existential differentiations can thus be cast in anthropological and in differential constructs. The former represent the human reality as a whole in so far as this unique humanity is present in its existential differentiations. The differential constructs represent the reality of the many resemblances between the human reality and other physical and biological phenomena in the universe. The latter differential constructs can never represent that in which the human reality differs essentially from other realities. Both types of constructs are, in different ways, close to experience.

It would be unscientific, however, to attempt to describe the reality of the whole in terms which apply only to certain features of its dependent parts. A differential psychology of the nervous systems of body and brain can efficiently use terms such as "electric potentials" and "neuronal circuits," but it would be impossible to do justice to the total intentional presence of man to reality by means of such terms alone (except when used in a metaphorical sense). Therefore, two different languages are necessary in psychology: the anthropological language to describe man as an existing Gestalt or person, and the functional or process language to account for the functional resemblances between man and other objects. These resemblances reveal themselves most clearly when studied in isolation from man as a whole. Psychologists may well be bilingual, but they should be careful not to mix the two series of constructs by speaking metaphorically about man as a living person through the use of terms appropriate only to the differential study of certain aspects of behavior. Nor should the differential psychologist, on the other hand, apply anthropological terminology to the abstracted profile of behavior which he studies. If he did so, the anthropological terminology would become as metaphorical as the differential terminology when applied to man as a total living existence. To describe a neuron as a person is just as metaphorical as to describe a person as a neuron.

We have already stated that each differential psychology should consider the whole of behavior from its own perspective because the latter can probably be uncovered in all human behavior. This implies that every differential psychology can probably cast all behavior in its own functional constructs. At the same time, all other constructs which are used by comprehensive psychology or by other differential psychologies would become metaphorical if applied to the specific perspective of this differential psychology.

We have also pointed out the tendency toward imperialism inherent in every differential psychology which is due to the innate tendency of man toward universal comprehension. Thus highly successful differential psychologies sometimes tend to overlook the fact that their functional differential constructs cover all behavior under only one aspect, even when that aspect is related to infra-human appearances in nature. In such an attitude of perceptual blindness, a differential psychology may be tempted to identify itself with all psychology and claim that its differential constructs explain all behavior under all possible aspects.

Observation of human behavior as a whole and of functional aspects abstracted from behavior yields data which both the anthropological and the differential psychologist must ponder.

The differential psychologist who in principle deals with isolated processes may experiment with these in his laboratory and thus collect data about isolated functions *as such.* He should be careful, however, not to make unverified inferences regarding these functions when they participate in the living totality of an intentional person in a meaningful situation. It is the task of the comprehensive psychologist to study what changes these processes undergo once they are perceived as living differentiated parts of human existence.

The anthropological psychologist cannot collect data about persons as existing totalities in meaningful life situations by the method of laboratory experiment in the strict physical sense. Such experiment presupposes as a necessary condition the objectivating isolation of variables. The psychologist can collect data, however, by means of observation and experiments in personal relationships in which he can verify his anthropological constructs. Both the comprehensive psychologist and the differential psychologist must detach themselves temporarily from their data in order to examine them and to arrive at theoretical formulations of them. In both types of psychology, these data are gathered by observation. In anthropological psychology, the observation is a personal attention to an individual or individuals who move intentionally in their life situation. In certain differential psychologies, the observation is a non-personal attention to specific impersonal, isolated aspects of human and animal behavior in relation to "stimuli" in the environment.

In anthropological observation, the emerging theory should be stated in terminology appropriate to the personal nature of the phenomena studied. In differential psychologies, however, the theory should be stated in impersonal terms, the isolated aspect being impersonal because of its very objectivation.

In both cases, then, the collection of the data is by means of observation, and the constructing of theory is through intellectualizing by a temporarily detached observer; with this difference, that in differential functional psychology the observation is impersonal, while in anthropological psychology it is personal. Both theories are objective: one is the objective study of human behavior as an intentional meaningful whole; the other is an objective study of isolated behavioral aspects.

Functional or mathematical differential terminology throws no light on psychological phenomena *as psychological,* i.e., on the nature and motivated appearances of behavior *as human behavior.* Differential constructs illuminate, however, the many non-human aspects of behavior without which the whole of human behavior could not be understood or adequately explained. Therefore, comprehensive anthropological psychology requires the constant development of functional differential psychology, the discoveries of which it should respectfully integrate within itself. This work of differential psychologies cannot be done by physiologists, physicists, neurologists, or biologists because they are not concerned with the relevance of their constructs and findings to the understanding of the non-human aspects of behavior. Only the differential psychologist performs this task so necessary to the growth of the field of psychology as a whole.

The concern of differential psychologists with the mathematical, physiological, neurological, physical, or biological properties of behavior does not make them mathematicians, physiologists, neurologists, physicists, or biologists. Their primary interest is in behavior insofar as it appears under and is influenced by these different functional aspects. Other sciences develop constructs and methods which deal with these functional aspects. The differential psychologists borrow these constructs from other fields, just as the foundational theorist in psychology borrows some of his basic constructs from anthropological philosophy without becoming for this reason a professional philosopher.

Anthropological psychology deals with human intentional behavior that becomes differentiated and organized in dimensions, modes, and modalities as a result of the ever expanding development of man's "lived" personal relations to reality. Within the anthropological description of this differentiating human behavior, comprehensive psychology integrates the description of those physical and biological features which human behavior has in common with other species and which have been studied in isolation by differential psychologies. For this scientific task, anthropological psychology cannot use metaphors. It requires terminology appropriate to its subject-matter, which is the personal, motivated, intentional behavior of human beings. Anthropological constructs should not be reified as if they were things existing in themselves. They are pointers to reality. Some of the important constructs in anthropological psychology are: existence; dimensions, modes, and modalities of bodily behavioral existence; intentional behavior; human motivation; freedom; self; self-project; meaning; sense; and sign.

Various differential psychologies, on the other hand, abstract from the personal whole those characteristics which resemble features found in non-human phenomena, and must therefore express in impersonal ways the characteristics which they isolate. Comprehensive psychology proposes to be a theory of the behavior of man in terms appropriate to his personal or existential nature. However, such a theory can never be truly comprehensive if it does not have available for integration the impersonal aspects of the personal, which are rooted in the fact that human existence is also essentially a bodily, material existence in a material world. In other words, a truly comprehensive anthropological psychology would be impossible without the constant growth of functional differential psychologies.

CHAPTER EIGHT

ANTHROPOLOGICAL PHENOMENOLOGY AS MODE OF EXISTENCE

In our discussion of anthropological psychology, we have concluded that anthropological constructs must be rooted in the observation of behavior. The anthropological psychologist can fulfill this condition only through the phenomenological method. Since human experience is varied in kind and degree, there are many types of phenomenology, or the study of experience, to correspond with this variety. The subject of this and the two following chapters is mainly one type of phenomenology: anthropological phenomenology, by means of which the psychologist lays the foundation of his constructs about behavior.

Because phenomenology was first developed by philosophers, every type of phenomenology reveals this origin in its fundamental features. The non-philosophical phenomenologies study experience, however, with other purposes and under other aspects than philosophical phenomenologies do. Thus the distinct features of anthropological phenomenology emerge from its unique purpose, which is intentional behavior insofar as it is relevant to comprehensive scientific psychology and psychological praxis. Therefore, the anthropological phenomenologist does not explore the phenomena of behavior under all ontological and factual perspectives. He limits himself strictly to those aspects which are relevant to his goal: the integration of the scientific differential knowledge of behavior into a comprehensive psychology which is pertinent to psychological praxis. This purpose presupposes the use of two kinds of anthropological phenomenology.

First of all, an anthropological phenomenology is needed which examines the structure and meaning of human behavior as a whole. Such a phenomenology provides the psychologist with a matrix from which comprehensive constructs can be derived. Because these constructs are rooted in human behavior as a whole, they serve as a comprehensive model within which the differential psyychologies can be integrated. This anthropological phenomenology of the factual whole of behavior is called comprehensive or existential anthropological phenomenology.

Comprehensive psychology presupposes, however, not only a comprehensive but also a differential phenomenology. The latter is a phenomenological study of the profiles of behavior that have been formulated by differential psychologies. The anthropological psychologist must know the structure and meaning of these profiles of behavior. He should be able to establish the "reality-of-behavior" which is indicated in the abstract formulations of differential psychologists. Only then will he be able to integrate knowledge of partial behavior with knowledge of behavior as a whole.

The distinction between comprehensive and differential phenomenology, however, is not the only one to be made in anthropological phenomenology. We must also clarify anthropological phenomenology both as a fundamental mode of existence and as a method which emerges from this mode. The *mode of existence* is most relevant for the praxis of psychology. The *method* is of primary importance for the development of theoretical and experimental psychology. To be sure, the mode of existence and the method are interrelated. One cannot be understood without the other; one cannot develop fully without the other. For the sake of clarity, however, we propose first to circumscribe and discuss anthropological phenomenology as mode of existence. In the next chapter, we shall consider it as method. Both circumscriptions are provisional and open to modification.

Anthropological phenomenology is fundamentally a mode of existence of a psychologist who seeks a comprehensive or a differential knowledge of intentional behavior as it manifests itself, with the least possible imposition of psychological theory or method, personal and cultural prejudice or need, and language habit.

Discussion of the Terms of the Definition of Anthropological Phenomenology

The term "phenomenology" is derived from the two Greek words, *phainomenon* and *logos. Phainomenon,* the neuter present participle of *phainestai* (to appear), means "that which appears." *Logos* means "word," "science," or "study of words." Therefore, etymologically, phenomenology is the study of that which appears. Etymological analysis gives us some initial understanding of the meaning of phenomenology. However, the term requires further definition.

Philosophical Phenomenology and Science

Phenomenology was originally a development in philosophy. The present chapter does not deal primarily with philosophical phenomenology, for an evaluation of this subject and its prolific development into many branches falls outside the scope of a study of scientific theory in psychology. Nevertheless, it is necessary to stress from the beginning that philosophical phenomenology does not oppose science. The philosophical phenomenology of science attempts to clarify the foundations of science, its meanings, and its situation in the whole of reality. Philosophical phenomenology goes beneath science, as it were, in order to disclose its experiential roots found in the original contact between man and reality. This phenomenological quest of the philosophers of science has led us to the insight that the world of science is not the world of man's first experience. The primary world of man's original experience is not at all identical with the world of science. The latter is a secondary world, a derived construction, an abstraction. This constructed world of science is removed from the primary world of lived experience. It is, however, rooted somehow in this world of man's original experiences, for without these first experiences man could never have attained to the construction of the abstract, theoretical world of science.

Differential psychologists use mechanistic models, for example, like the stimulus-response sequence. But such a model is not experienced directly as such by man in his spontaneous life. It is a construct that is secondary, derived, abstract, fashioned by the differential psychologist himself. This useful abstraction is somehow dependent on the psychologist's experience of behavior. If he had never experienced some aspect of a situation which somehow influences behavior, as well as some aspect of behavior which is elicited by this influence, he never would have been able to devise the stimulus-response model. This dependency on experience is characteristic not only of differential-scientific but also of comprehensive-scientific models of behavior.

Philosophical phenomenology thus makes explicit the fact that science is dependent on prior experience. It denies neither the value of science nor the necessity for the constructs which science derives from experienced reality. It recognizes that the use of secondary constructs is required in science. It maintains, however, that these constructions of the scientific imagination should be rooted in the experience from which they are derived. Otherwise, science could deteriorate into a free-floating, airy enterprise, out of touch with reality.

Philosophical and Anthropological Phenomenology

The preceding discussion of the relationship between philosophical phenomenology and science helps us to clarify the relationship between philosophical and anthropological phenomenology. *Philosophical* phenomenology aids the anthropological psychologist in the discovery of the ontological foundations of both comprehensive and differential psychologies. *Anthropological* phenomenology, on the other hand, enables him to discover the ontic or factual structures of behavior. The scope of this book does not allow extensive philosophical reflection on the meaning of the terms "ontological" and "ontic." We shall indicate briefly the difference between the ontological goal of philosophical phenomenology and the ontic one of anthropological phenomenology.

The ontic analysis of anthropological phenomenology is an exploration of observable behavior in order to discover its factual structures. Such ontic clarifications are performed in order to serve the actual practice of psychology; they guide the psychologist in his conduct when he deals with behavior in clinical or private practice. Anthropological phenomenology is concerned, therefore, with only a limited set of profiles of behavior, namely those which have been or are to be investigated by differential psychologies or dealt with in psychological praxis. Even when anthropological phenomenology studies behavior as a whole, it does so on the basis of the discoveries made by differential psychologies. It seeks the underlying meaning and structure of behavior as it is revealed in this variety of profiles. It always limits itself to the study of a certain number of manifestations of behavior under the aspect of their probable mutual relationships. Consequently, anthropological phenomenology of itself can never grasp the "ontological" structure which underlies behavior as such.

This ontological structure of behavior is clearly more basic than its ontic factual structure. In fact, the ontological structure of behavior makes factual structure or actual meaning of behavior possible; it is a manifestation of Being in intentional behavior. The ultimate concern of philosophical phenomenology is thus not limited to the structure of observable behavior; it includes all manifestations of Being. Philosophical phenomenology is not concerned primarily with the actual behavior of individuals, but with the underlying ontological structure of behavior as such. It does not aim to direct people in their actual conduct, but to analyze the hidden structures and guiding concepts which are basic to all possible patterns and manifestations of any behavior whatsoever. We should add to this statement of ultimate aim the fact that some philosophical phenomenologists refer at times to ontic analysis of behavior. They do so because they realize that a grasp of the factual structure of behavior may facilitate their penetration into its ontological structure.

We may conclude that philosophical phenomenology does not restrict itself to those aspects of intentional behavior which are explored by the differential psychologists. It goes beneath this factual structure in order to find its ontological basis. We have also seen in the preceding chapter that anthropological psychology requires the explication of its own ontological assumptions and of those of the differential psychologies. This implies that the comprehensive psychologist requires the assistance of the philosophical phenomenologist who makes these assumptions explicit. The psychologist uses the conclusions derived from these assumptions if they are relevant to his ontic phenomenology of intentional behavior. The comprehensive psychologist is thus dependent on philosophical phenomenology for the explication of ontological assumptions. His main function in this realm is a selective one, namely the choice of assumptions of philosophical phenomenology in the light of their applicability to the data of the differential psychologies which he integrates. The comprehensive psychologist is thus engaged in a dialogue between the outcomes of philosophical phenomenology of behavior and those of an ontic, anthropological phenomenology of behavior.

The Aims of Anthropological Phenomenology

The distinction between philosophical and anthropological phenomenology aids in the clarification of the specific goals of anthropological phenomenology, both comprehensive and differential. One of the goals is to help the comprehensive psychologist to root his theoretical constructs in experienced behavioral phenomena. If he has obtained these constructs from philosophical phenomenology, he must still ground them explicitly in concrete behavior as revealed by differential psychologies. Ontic phenomenology also helps him to root the constructs of the differential psychologies in behavioral reality. The comprehensive psychologist must ask himself to what experiences differential psychologists really point when they use such constructs as Oedipus complex, reinforcement, feedback, repression, ego, self, and individualism.

Anthropological phenomenology thus goes beneath both the constructs of differential psychologies and the scientific and "intuitive" insights of psychoanalysts, psychotherapists, and other practising psychologists; it searches for the foundations of these constructs, statements, and intuitions in behavior itself. What the differential psychologist and the practising psychotherapist take for granted, the comprehensive psychologist studies critically. Anthropological phenomenology may therefore be called a "genuine positivism or realism," "a return to behavior itself," "a true psychoanalysis," an "authentic behaviorism." We may now return to the discussion of the terms of our original definition of anthropological phenomenology.

Anthropological Phenomenology is Fundamentally A Mode of Existence

Is Fundamentally—This phrase in the definition denotes that anthropological phenomenology is *primarily* a specific attitude or mode of existence which the psychologist assumes toward his subject matter, "intentional behavior." "Fundamentally" indicates that the phenomenological attitude is basic while methods are secondary. The specific appproach of anthropological phenomenology is, therefore, fundamentally different from other valid and necessary approaches to behavior. Among the latter are the theoretical, experimental, clinical-intuitive, and applied approaches; these presuppose attitudes in the psychologist which are fundamentally different from those of the phenomenological position. These various positions, however, presuppose and complement the phenomenological one. The distinction which we make here between existential mode or attitude and method is important for at least three reasons.

First of all, the method of phenomenology when successfully applied to a specific phenomenon lends itself to a clear codification of the steps taken to penetrate this particular phenomenon. Now, the history of science teaches us that students may memorize and blindly apply methodical rules without developing the basic attitude from which these codes have emerged. The consequence of such a development for phenomenology might be a stultification of original standards, which would then be routinely applied even in situations where a new kind of phenomenon might require modifications in the steps to be taken. Such stultification would mark the end of phenomenology as a dynamic enterprise. The development of an authentic phenomenological attitude, however, would prevent such degeneration.

A second motive for this distinction is the fact that many practicing psychologists such as diagnosticians, psychotherapists, psychoanalysts, and industrial psychologists develop a phenomenological attitude in the encounter with their clients. They attempt to understand the intentional behavior of their patients with the least possible imposition of psychological theory or method, personal and cultural prejudice or need, and language habit. In fact, certain types of training expressly instill this attitude in practicing psychologists. If such psychologists, outside the hour of encounter, engage in a controlled phenomenological explication of the intentional behavior of their clients, they are using the method of phenomenology.

A third rationale for the above distinction is found in the contemporary development of psychology and psychiatry. The pressure of cultural evolution in the Western world is stimulating in many areas a new openness for the original data beneath complex theoretical structures and superstructures. This return to phenomena has manifested itself initially in forms of psychology and psychiatry to which a controlled phenomenological method has not yet been applied. They manifest, however, a promising phenomenological attitude from which the method may emerge. In other words, the phenomenological method may be said to be present in an implicit way in these incipient phenomenological psychologies. The distinction between attitude and method will thus facilitate the appraisal of development in contemporary psychology and psychiatry.

"Fundamentally" also connotes the position of the phenomenological attitude in the hierarchy of modes of existence. It is the most fundamental scientific mode of existence. This means neither that this mode is the most valuable one in every phase of the science of behavior, nor that it is the only useful one for the investigation of every profile of behavior. On the contrary, in certain phases of scientific study and for certain profiles of behavior, other modes such as the experimental and the statistical are necessary. When we say that the anthropological phenomenological mode is most fundamental in psychology, we mean that it deals strictly with the basis of all other scientific operations, namely with lived intentional behavior itself. From this point of view, other scientific psychological modes can be said to presuppose the phenomenological mode, for the latter concerns itself with the foundation of all succeeding statements or operations in psychology.

Mode of Existence

Man is existence; it is characteristic of man to involve himseld in reality as it reveals itself to him. Existence differentiates itself in various modes-of-existence. This differentiation takes place in the course of man's encounters with concrete life situations. Each mode-of-existence integrates various modalities-of-existence such as perceiving, feeling, touching, and thinking. Thus every mode-of-existence is a multi-dimensional unity of various modalities of interest or contact. These modalities constitute the structural unity of a mode-of-existence. A common purpose, interest, or project organizes different modalities in such a way that they constitute one mode-of-existence.

In this way, the phenomenological mode-of-existence in psychology integrates various modalities of existence. The phenomenological psychotherapist, for instance, feels, perceives, understands, thinks, speaks, and behaves differently when he encounters a patient than does a psychologist whose primary aim is to implement a psychological theory. One common interest characterizes all the different modalities of behavior of the phenomenological therapist. They all manifest his purpose of reaching an initial phenomenological understanding of the intentional behavior of his patient. This means an understanding of the underlying structures of behavior with the least possible imposition of psychological theory, methodology, personal and cultural prejudice or need, and language habit. This common project organizes the various modalities which constitute phenomenological-therapeutic behavior. This example illustrates how a mode-of-existence initiates, to a great degree, "how" and "what" one sees, experiences, or encounters. For every mode-of-existence inserts man in the world in a certain manner which influences his dealing with the world. The phenomenological mode-of-existence determines to a large extent what the psychotherapist listens for and how he manages the therapeutic situation. Similar statements can be made about other forms of applied psychology.

When this open phenomenological mode-of-existence is developed in the *academic* psychologist, it stimulates him to develop strictly controlled methods in its service. These methods are directed toward the unprejudiced, non-subjectivistic discovery of behavioral phenomena themselves before they are subjected to experiment, measurement, and theory formation.

Of a Psychologist Who Aims

This phrase indicates that the phenomenological mode of existence is rooted in a personal mode of life, which is that of an individual psychologist. We are not speaking, therefore, about a phenomenological mode of existence which is rooted in other personal ways of life such as the philosophical, artistic, sociological, or theological. A personal mode of being, moreover, is influenced by personal and cultural history, and by individual interests and projects. This influence co-determines which aspect of intentional-functional-situational behavior the psychologist chooses for his own phenomenological approach. A phenomenological therapist, for example, may be interested only in emotionally disturbed college students or hospitalized patients. Similarly, other practicing psychologists have individual interests. Therefore, the personal mode-of-being-a-psychologist determines to a degree the psychologist's phenomenological mode of existence. On the other hand, the phenomenological mode itself impels him to be aware of the implications and the limitations imposed by his own choice. This same awareness leads him to observe the selected behavioral phenomena with the least possible imposition of theory or method, personal and cultural prejudice or need, and language habit. The involvement of the psychologist as an historically situated subject is, of course, unavoidable. What should be avoided is subjectivism or the unchecked influence of theoretical or methodological prejudice which would distort the behavioral phenomena.

At a Comprehensive or a Differential Understanding

The phenomenological mode of existence in the psychologist consists of two poles which interact continually. These two poles are dynamic tendencies inherent in the phenomenological quest for the structures and meanings of behavior. This quest is for the understanding of the meaning not only of different behavioral patterns but also of behavior as a whole. The psychotherapist may be interested, for example, in the structure and meaning of depressive language behavior of a patient. We call this type of phenomenological interest differential. However, he may also be interested in the patient's intentional behavior as a whole. This over-all structure colors the differentiated behavior patterns of the patient. The psychotherapist's interest in the over-all structure of behavior tends toward comprehensive phenomenology, the goal of which is the understanding of the whole of intentional behavior.

Differential phenomenology is sometimes simply called phenomenology without any limiting adjective, while comprehensive phenomenology is called existential phenomenology. Anthropological existential phenomenology is both an attitude and a controlled method. It leads to a comprehensive understanding of intentional behavior as a structured whole which is differentiated in many patterns of behavior. One should be careful, however, not to confuse this attitude and method with existentialism, which is something quite different.

Comprehensive and differential understanding of behavior influence each other. Insight into the structure and meaning of a particular behavior pattern of a patient illuminates the understanding of his intentional-behavior as a whole. Insight into the whole of his behavior, on the other hand, deepens the insight into the differentiated patterns of his behavior. Thus there exists a dialectical relationship between the comprehensive and differential components of phenomenological psychology.

Of Knowledge of Intentional Behavior As It Manifests Itself: "Phenomenological," "Objectivating," and "Naive" Knowledge of Behavior

The phenomenological mode of existence in psychology tends toward a knowledge of intentional behavior as it manifests itself. The phenomena of behavior as they reveal themselves may be contrasted with the data of behavior which are obtained by objectivation. Such data are not spontaneously experienced phenomena as they are uncovered in daily life. The process of objectivation and its resultant data are based on theorizing. Objectivation is a scientific reflection *about* behavioral phenomena instead of a penetration *into* the phenomena that are given. This reflection leads to a planned ordering of behavioral phenomena as objectivated things in a theoretical scheme instead of to an explication of the very structure and meaning of the phenomena themselves. The process of objectivation is not only useful but necessary for science. Science itself is fundamentally theory formation. As we have seen in previous chapters, comprehensive scientific theory in psychology is ultimately theory formation by means of comprehensive and differential constructs which presuppose objectivation of behavioral phenomena. But this objectivation should be preceded by phenomenological explication. The phenomenological approach is the disciplined removal of subjectivistic influences which may distort the phenomena. Such influences are usually present in the naïve experience of intentional behavior in every-day life. But subjectivistic, unrealistic distortions may also be present when behavioral phenomena are objectivated through uncritical theorizing about naïvely experienced behavior.

"Objectivating" Knowledge and the Danger of a Sophisticated Subjectivism

A special process of knowledge of intentional behavior is thus necessary between the process of naïve knowledge and that of objectivating knowledge. This intermediary function is fulfilled by phenomenological knowledge. Phenomenological insight is the result of a purification of every-day knowledge from subjectivistic influences. The psychologist who listens to naïve descriptions of every-day behavior is clearly aware that these accounts are possibly distorted by subjectivisms.

But if the psychologist is unable to approach the real structure and meaning of behavior with a phenomenological attitude, he may be caught in a sophisticated form of subjectivism. He may unwittingly substitute an artificially devised "scientific" experience of behavior for the real experience of daily life. He may "see" repressions, reinforcements, Oedipus complexes, and sublimations everywhere. This artificial "experience" of behavior is the abortive result of two sources. One is the naïve experience of every-day behavior; the other is the arbitrary interpretation of this behavior by means of an established scientific theory. Such immediate, rash interpretations cannot result from listening respectfully to the unified inner structure and meaning of behavior itself in a specific, unique situation. What really happens is that other established subjectivistic influences are substituted for or added to the subjectivistic distortions which are already present in the naïve experience itself. This impoverished, deformed, made-over subjectivistic experience is then considered to be full, real experience, equated with experience in everyday life. This "scientific" experience is called fact, and this "fact" is regarded as a first, primary, original experience of man. Through the collection of these subjectivistic "facts," one could arrive by induction at the establishment of laws of behavior which could govern the activities of practicing psychologists and their clients. This process could lead to a dogmatic psychology, autonomous and closed within itself; an empty game with empty ideas irrelevant to real intentional behavior of people in real life situations; an unchecked, uncontrolled mythology of behavior claiming to explain everything while it explains nothing. It is obvious that much harm can be done to the development of real human behavior by a practicing psychologist when his perception is distorted by a sophisticated subjectivism.

Behavior "Itself" and the Necessity of Theories "About" Behavior

When the psychologist develops the phenomenological attitude, however, he will first observe and study behavior as it manifests itself. Only afterward will he consider how scientific theory can illuminate this behavior without distorting it; or how theory should be corrected, expanded, or renewed in order to keep it in tune with behavior as it is given in reality. Both processes are necessary. The phenomenological knowledge of behavior is thus insufficient for a psychologist. He must also draw on the rich fund of insight called the science of psychology, which is an accumulation of the intellectual contributions of learned theorists of behavior. The psychologist can select wisely from this treasure-trove of theory. But this selective activity should be guided by real behavior as it reveals itself in his clients or experimental subjects. The phenomenological approach will enable him not only to select the adequate theoretical explanation but also to adapt it to the situation concerned, or even to improve on it on the basis of concrete observation. In the latter case, he will enrich the treasury of psychology so that others coming after him will have greater knowledge available than he himself had.

It should be the desire of the psychologist, however, that those following him will neither abuse his theory through the distortion of data nor substitute his theory for their own phenomenological perception. He should hope that they will listen more to behavior itself than to his expositions about behavior, that their ears will not be deafened by the noise of theories, and that their eyes will not be blinded by explications in manuscripts, journals, and books.

Intentional Behavior

The Multi-Dimensional Directedness of Behavior in Situations

The phenomenological mode of existence leads to an openness for behavior as intentional, as directed toward reality, as present in a situation which is meaningful for the behaving subject. The subject is always related in his behaving to a meaningful situation within which his behavior evolves. This is true of every dimension of behavior. By dimension of behavior we mean the expression in behavior of such experiences as perception, imagination, feeling, reminiscing, anticipation, or categorical thought. The phenomenological approach aims at the disclosure of the meaningful structures of behavior on all these levels; it proposes to unveil the "lived" behavioral structures which constitute the relationship between the behaving subject and his situation.

In other words, phenomenology is based on the observation that man and his situation are in a dialectical unity. Intentional behavior is always being-in-a-situation. For example, when I perceive a river, play a violin, show a desire for food, or reveal that I recall a humiliating incident in my past, then the river, the violin, the food, the incident, and I are in interaction with one another. They are situated objects of my intentional behavior. Such a meaningful object does not shape me as an imprint molds wax; it does not determine my behavior in an absolute and unchangeable fashion. For both my situated object and I are active participants in a living dialogue. Intentional behavior is the dialectical unity of the person who behaves and the situated object of his behavior.

In a phenomenological explication of intentional behavior, the psychologist can concentrate his attention on one of these two main aspects of intentional behavior. He can investigate either the behaving subject in his "behavioral-tending-towards" or the correlate of this tending behavior, the situated object. For example, when I explicate my intentional behavior as a therapist, I can focus my attention on my own therapeutic behavior. In this case, I make explicit the feelings, experiences, and attitudes which manifest themselves in my behavior toward my patient. On the other hand, I can explore the situated object of my therapeutic behavior. This may be an anxious patient who responds tensely to my posture, the sound of my voice, and even my choice of words. In this case, I attempt to make explicit that which is implicit in the behavior of my client in his life situation.

The behaving subject and the situated object are both necessary constituents of the same whole which is intentional behavior. One cannot exist without the other; they mutually imply each other. Object and subject of behavior are poles of the same "field," not separate but distinct. Intellectual reflection on behavior brings this distinction to light.

Openness for Intentional Behavior Is Not Introspective

Openness for the structure and meaning of intentional behavior should not be confused with the characteristic concerns of introspective psychology. Introspective psychology in its classical appearance displayed three characteristics: first, it limited itself to reflexive conscious experiences of man; second, it preferred the phenomena of sensation, perception, and categorical thought to those of feeling and emotion; third and most important, it turned exclusively to the experiencing subject as *detached from* his bodily-behaving-in-a-meaningful-situation.

The phenomenological psychologist does exactly the opposite of the introspectionist. His phenomenological mode of existence is an openness for behavior as a unitary whole, as a "field." This field does not reveal itself initially in consciousness, but in pre-reflexive, pre-conceptual, "lived" behavioral structures. Therefore, phenomenological openness leads to an interest centered more in the behavior—including language behavior—of a person than in the mere intellectual content of his words. The structures and meanings of behavior which are implicit, prelogical, and unpremeditated are more basic and valid for the phenomenological psychologist than later thoughts or theories *about* behavior, regardless of whether they are offered by unsophisticated people or by philosophers and scientists.

It is evident that man manifests more than conscious intentionality in his behavior. Man is present in his behavior not only as a rationalizing subject, but also as a living, feeling, suffering, loving, hoping, repressing, hating person who always behaves in a situation filled with meanings which he absorbs mainly in a pre-reflexive way.

The Complexity of the "Situated" Object-Pole of Intentional Behavior

The situation in which the object-pole of intentional behavior is inserted is rich and complex. We share with countless other human beings, for example, the same worlds of meaning, the worlds of our culture and subculture. Our very behavior reveals that certain situations mean the same to all of us. We were inserted very early in these shared worlds of culture which color the meanings of our individual situations. At home we learned from the behavior of our family how to eat and dress, how to use a chair, a spoon, a dish, how to act and speak properly. We were established by these communications in the cultural world-of-meaning within which our family was behaving, a world of meaning which was structured without us, long before we were born. The "lived" behavior of our family introduced us to this common cultural world, inserted us in a behavioral tradition. From that time on, we were able to behave like other people in the same culture and to encounter our fellow human beings in many customs and behavioral patterns which we all experienced as the same in our world. Our initial insertion into a world of meaning was later expanded by school, church, and society. They all helped us to be at home in our world, to share common meanings of particular situations.

The phenomenological mode of existence consequently implies an openness for structures of behavior which correlate with the historical and intersubjective cultural aspects of the meaning of a situation. However, this is not all. Certain structures of behavior correspond with interpersonal meanings developed by smaller social units, such as husband and wife, close-knit families, and other intimate associations which share certain functions, interests, or ideals.

Finally, behavior also expresses a private intentionality corresponding to purely individual meanings of the situation which arise from one's personal history. No one can communicate easily the meanings which he does not share with others either culturally or interpersonally. It is obviously important for the psychotherapist to help his clients to make explicit this private intentionality.

With the Least Possible Imposition of Psychological Theory or Method, Personal and Cultural Prejudice, and Psychological Language Habit

The anthropological psychologist must penetrate into the structure and meaning of behavior itself. But theoretical views, personal bias, and psychological jargon may dim his objective vision. He must therefore avoid these influences in order to be able to observe the phenomena of behavior itself. Consequently, the phenomenological psychologist suspends temporarily all theoretical frames of reference, all statistical, experimental, and symbolical classifications. An absolute suspension of all these influences is impossible, to be sure, but he is aware of the danger of their subtle impact on his perceptions.

We shall briefly consider these distorting influences which are pointed out in our definition. In each case, we shall discuss the temporary elimination, or at least limitation, of these subjectivistic elements by means of phenomenological suspension.

Psychological Theory or Method

Psychological theory uses constructs which, while abstracted from behavior, are definitely not behavior itself. Originally and spontaneously, we do not perceive in behavior such constructs as reinforcement, repression, compulsion, conditioning, feedback, and conditioned reflexes. No psychological construct as such is part of real behavior. Yet these constructs may unwittingly influence our view of behavior. Therefore, the anthropological psychologist attempts to prevent the impact of such constructs on his primary observation. He suspends his theoretical knowledge as far as possible, or at least attempts to be aware of its intrusion. Consequently, the phenomenological psychologist develops an attitude not only of "theoretical suspension" but also of "phenomenological vigilance." He is on guard against a permeation of his perceptions by psychological theories or scientific methods.

Differential psychologists develop their methods in view of limited projects of research. They select those profiles of behavior which are related to their particular research projects. This selective manipulation is legitimate and necessary within the framework of differential research. In phenomenological psychology, however, such manipulation and the categorical view which proceeds from it would obscure the perception of behavior as it manifests itself.

Personal and Cultural Prejudice and Needs

By personal and cultural prejudice in psychology, we mean the bias about behavior which is incorporated in the individual views of the psychologist and in the common opinions of his culture. A psychologist has his own implicit appraisal of psychology which may deeply influence his view of behavior. His personal philosophy of life colors and affects his psychological approach. Moreover, not only his personality and temperament but also his culture and subculture nourish and foster his selective perception. Most influential are those cultural trends in his environment and education which are in tune with his own personality structure and private history.

Concerning the needs of the psychologist, we may draw a conclusion similar to what we have said of his prejudices. Every psychologist develops in his personal interaction with his culture certain individual needs which may color his vision of behavior.

Language Habit

Language habit in the present context refers to the embodiment in language of psychological theories. The language concerned may be scientific or pre-scientific; likewise, psychological theories which are embedded in the language may be scientific or pre-scientific. Language is not the experience itself of behavior, but merely an expression of this experience. Words may communicate, moreover, much more than the pure experience of behavior itself. They may express, for example, the pre-scientific view of behavior assumed and fostered in a certain culture. In this case, the language habit implies not only the perception of behavior but also the pre-scientific view which guided this selective and biased perception. By the same token, the language habit conceals other aspects of behavior which fall outside the scope of the pre-scientific theory that dominates the temper of the culture.

A good example of the influence of theory on language is the term "experience." The German word for experience is "Erlebnis," the Dutch "beleving." The German "Erlebnis" is derived from "erleben," which literally means "to live an event," for "erleben" is associated with "leben" which means "to live." The Dutch "beleving" is derived from "beleven," which comes from "leven" and has the same meaning as the German word for experience, "to live." The English "experience," on the other hand, instead of indicating an awareness in the present, points to an awareness in the past. Obviously, language habit may obscure or falsify the perception of the psychologist. He may overlook or misinterpret behavior which embodies an actual "lived" presence of the subject to reality without reflection. An open perception which momentarily suspends language habit, however, may rediscover the reality of behavior which was lost in the language. Such rediscovery may impel the phenomenological psychologist to enrich the language with a new expression which clarifies the lost phenomenon. He may speak, for example, of "lived" experience, of "lived" awareness.

Language is the treasure-trove of accumulated theories, insights, and observations uncovered by a people in the course of its history; the fascinating history of a standing-out-together in certain ways toward reality. This shared involvement in reality reveals itself in ways peculiar to the cultural co-existents. The resulting insights are preserved in the constituted language of a people. This language should be a help, not a hindrance, toward further discovery of reality. Constituted language should not suppress, but support living language; should not fossilize, but foster vision; should not limit, but expand perception.

Constituted *scientific* language presents its own problems. Psychoanalytic, behavioristic, or organismic language should not paralyze, but nurture the openness of observation; should not limit, but expand perception and vision. The phenomenological psychologist may profit fully from the treasure-trove of scientific language if he is able to free himself temporarily from its influence on his perception. Perception unadulterated by theoretical tenets prepares him for a new, fresh appreciation of what other theorists have observed and formulated before him. At the same time, his open perception of behavior as it is, liberates him from the limitations inherent in the position of every theorist.

The phenomenological mode of existence with its attitudes of suspension and vigilance is fundamental for the practicing psychologist who should encounter *people* beyond all theory and classification. Only after encounter may he become aware in what sense and to what degree he may characterize their behavior by constructs *about* behavior. Theoretical psychology then becomes a light that enlightens, not a veil that dims and distorts the perception of the psychologist.

CHAPTER NINE

ANTHROPOLOGICAL PHENOMENOLOGY AS METHOD

Anthropological phenomenology comprises not only "a mode of existence" but also the method which emerges from this mode of being. Many practicing phenomenological psychologists, however, do not go beyond the phenomenological approach which influences their concrete behavior in encounter with their clients. In other words, they do not validate their phenomenological observations by means of controlling techniques. The extensive demands made on the energy and time of the general practitioner in psychology do not leave him free to carry out research projects. The phenomenological *method,* therefore, is used primarily in empirical, experimental, and theoretical psychology.

We shall first define anthropological phenomenology as method and then analyze the meanings and implications of the elements of this definition.

Anthropological phenomenology as method is a constituent of the scientific psychological mode of existence; it emerges from the phenomenological mode of existence; it is a method which translates the means and ends implicit in the phenomenological mode into well-defined procedures and objectives within concretely delineated projects of research; it develops certain checks and controls which ensure the validity and reliability of the phenomenological procedures used within such projects; its purpose is the controlled comprehensive or differential explication of behavior in order to prevent or correct subjectivistic distortions in the science of psychology.

Anthropological Phenomenology As Method Is a Constituent of the Scientific Psychological Mode of Existence

We have seen that human existence differentiates itself into various modes-of-existence. Each one of these is a *Gestalt* or structure whose constituents are unified by a specific interest of man which orients a particular aspect of his life. Scientific psychology is a mode of existence which has the specific purpose of the acquisition of scientific knowledge of behavior. The various scientific attitudes which constitute this mode are dependent on one another; together they lead to scientific discovery. The main constituents are: the implicit ontological attitude; the phenomenological attitude; and the comprehensive, differential, observational, experimental, and applied attitudes. Each one of these tends in its own specific way toward scientific knowledge of intentional behavior. All of them refer ultimately to concrete phenomena of behavior. But only phenomenology is concerned with behavior in its given concreteness. Consequently, in the hierarchy of attitudes and methods, the phenomenological is most fundamental, for it is concerned with that which all other constituents of the scientific mode presuppose and have as their basis. This unique position implies that very often a phenomenological investigation should be performed before any other scientific procedures. On the other hand, phenomenology can never replace other scientific methods which embody the other necessary constituents of the scientific psychological mode-of-being, such as experimental and statistical research.

The fact that phenomenology is a component, and not the whole, of the scientific psychological mode of existence implies that it is to some degree dependent on this mode. The unifying purpose of the science of psychology, which integrates all its subordinate structures, also regulates its fundamental phenomenological component. Thus the demands of psychology as a whole control the particular uses of phenomenological methodology. This is not to say that the phenomenology of a science is structured only by the requirements of the particular science to which it refers; its essential constitution remains dependent also on the mode of being from which it emerges. The phenomenological mode of being should therefore illuminate the methodological attitude. The basic structure of the phenomenological method is safeguarded, in fact, not by the science in which it is integrated but by the phenomenological mode from which it emerges. The concrete purpose which the phenomenological constituent serves within a science is dictated, nevertheless, by the particular science with which it is merged: the science thus determines the concrete direction, not the essential structure, of its phenomenological component.

One might draw an analogy from the position of an executive in a corporation. A company cannot mold the personalities of its directors; it expects their individual endeavors to be in tune, however, with the purpose that structures the association as a whole. The head of a steel company who centered his interest in non-steel products would soon be dismissed as a member of the board of directors. Within the framework of aims and objectives, however, every executive is stimulated to cooperate with the productive team in a creative fashion. Every director may initiate procedures which alter the company's structure in certain dimensions, but not in its essential aim: the efficient production of marketable steel. Moreover, the initiative of each executive must take into account the services of other constituents of the corporation, such as labor, management, and the sales department.

Similarly, the dependency of the phenomenological constituent on the scientific mode of existence in which it participates does not prevent its creative influence on science. Therefore, a human science which fosters the explicit, controlled development of its phenomenological component is different from one which leaves its phenomenological foundation to chance or to the bias of individual scientists. We call the relationship between psychological phenomenology and psychology a dialectical relationship. Dialogue implies a unity in opposition. Opposition means difference; unity indicates the constant mutual interaction of two dissimilar elements which cooperate closely without losing their identity.

Anthropological Phenomenology as Method Emerges from the Phenomenological Mode of Existence

This part of our definition implies that the method presupposes the phenomenological mode of existence as its matrix; every adaptation, differentiation, or refinement of the method should be influenced by the phenomenological mode of being. The psychologist should not merely repeat a phenomenological procedure which proved to be adequate in a former situation. If his approach is not constantly guided by the phenomenological attitude, he may fall into the trap of blindly applying to a new phenomenon procedures which were satisfactory in a past experiment. Only an attitude of openness will preserve his alertness to the phenomenon as it actually reveals itself. This receptivity for the peculiarity of any appearance whatever implies specific adaptations to be made in method when the psychologist examines a new phenomenon in its unique structure and meaning. In other words, the phenomenological mode and method should always coincide in theoretical, experimental, and empirical psychology, while the mode alone may be sufficient during the praxis of psychology or during the creative preparatory phase which precedes theoretical, experimental, and empirical endeavors.

Anthropological Phenomenology is a Method which Translates Means and Ends into Procedures and Objectives

"Method" is derived from the Greek words *meta* meaning "after, toward", and *hodos* signifying "way". Consequently, the etymological meaning of method is "a way to (something)".

More specifically, method denotes a systematic procedure followed in achieving an objective. Each different objective requires its own method which develops into a set of procedures and purposes that differentiate it from other methods. The basic steps and aims of the phenomenological procedure are implicitly present in the phenomenological mode of existence from which every particular phenomenological *modus operandi* originates. The systematized method makes these implicit means and ends explicit, concrete, and practical by adapting them to a specific object of research. An example of the actual development of such a phenomenological method within a specific research project will be presented in the next chapter.

The Purpose of This Phenomenological Method Is the Controlled Comprehensive or Differential Explication of Behavior

Explication

Anthropological explication is the operation of making explicit that which is implicit in behavior as it manifests itself to the psychologist. This phenomenological operation differs from both explication and explanation as such. *Explication* means a detailed description of behavior. *Explanation* means an interpretation of behavior, usually with recourse to theories, facts, and observations other than the given behavior itself. Anthropological *explication*, on the contrary, connotes an operation of the phenomenologist by which he makes explicit what is already implicitly present in behavior itself. Such explication aims at the discovery of the fundamental psychological structure of a phenomenon of behavior; it attempts to make explicit precisely what a specific behavior is and means, and consequently what distinguishes it from every other phenomenon of behavior. An authentic anthropological explication always starts from behavior itself and not from any theory *about* behavior. Some differential psychologies, such as the Freudian, the Jungian, and the Behavioristic, departing from an *a priori* view of behavior, have formulated certain universal principles concerning behavior. But an authentic phenomenological explication does not start from these theoretical principles. Such a procedure would presuppose that the specific behavior is already included, defined, and explained in the implicit theory of behavior developed by the differential psychology. The uncritical assumption of such *a priorisms* might influence the explication of the data. One might proceed from principles held by a differential psychology and, theorizing from them, arrive at a description of behavior conforming to these principles, but not necessarily to the behavior itself. Yet it is precisely the aim of the explication to determine what the behavior itself is, in order to eliminate subjectivistic influences which may have distorted the implicit philosophies and explanations of differential psychologies. To use the principles of differential psychologies in the above-mentioned deductive way would imply that a full knowledge of the fundamental structure of the behavior is already possessed.

All of us spontaneously understand the behavior of people long before we study the implicit philosophies and explanations of differential psychologies. Perhaps it is difficult for us to verbalize this naïve perception of behavior. Moreover, our natural awareness, so long as it is not subjected to a controlled explication, is influenced by subjectivistic influences. Nevertheless, this primary perception remains our only possible starting point. Every psychologist dealing with behavior starts explicitly or implicitly from his own spontaneous awareness. Otherwise, he could not talk about behavior at all. In natural, naïve perception the psychologist is present to behavior in its confusing complexity. In spontaneous presence to behavior, every detail of the fundamental structure of this behavior is not distinguished precisely as it is. The basic structure of the perceived behavior is obscured both by accidental features arising from the specific situation and by the subjectivistic prejudice of the perceiving person due to his personality, culture, and language habits.

When man speaks about behavior, he attempts to express his spontaneous perceptions, and by this formulation behavior becomes conceptual knowledge. It is simpler to perceive than to express behavior, but the attempt to do so is a necessary preparation for scientific psychology. Only when we have expressed in clear concepts, judgments, and formulations the behavior which we have perceived, can we go further in the science of behavior. For this science requires an exact concept and accurate formulation of what behavior constitutes. The precise formulation of the behavior itself is the aim of the explication which identifies and describes the necessary and sufficient constituents of the behavior concerned. The accurate distinction of the various constitutive moments of a particular type of behavior is necessary in order to prevent confusion with other types. Moreover, psychologists need a proper terminology which will enable them to communicate with other psychological scientists concerning specific behavior. Such explication of behavior provides them with a new, more explicit way of knowing. The behavior which they make explicit is already known to them, to be sure, but only in a vague way. The knowledge contained in daily spontaneous perception is imperfect, disordered, and influenced by subjectivistic bias. Science cannot stop at such knowledge; it clarifies confused knowledge by means of controlled explication. The implicit and obscure perception of a complex phenomenon of behavior changes by this process into an explicit, formulated knowledge of its foundational structure.

The point of departure for explication is therefore the undifferentiated spontaneous perception. Without this initial perception, the explication would lose its validity; the terms produced would not refer to any perceived conduct of man. What is more, perception also constitutes the final aim of the explication. For explication leads to an objective perception in which the constituent elements of behavior itself are clearly represented.

The first endeavor of the psychologist is to change naïve perception implicitly or explicitly into a more detailed conceptual knowledge. Psychologists often differ from one another in their conclusions because they formulate their original perception without first involving themselves in a scientific explication of what they have perceived. This neglect of scientific rigor in the decisive first phase of research—the phase of explication—frequently stands in appalling contrast to subsequent scientific investigations by means of statistical, experimental, and empirical procedures. In the latter, psychologists often use faultless scientific methods which nevertheless cannot correct the inexact or erroneous notions sometimes found at the basis of their investigations. Differences in explication lead to fundamental dissensions among psychologists which cannot be bridged by subsequent scientific endeavors so long as they do not return to the first and decisive operation in their science, the explication of the behavior concerned.

From what has been said, it will be clear that the ultimate norm of any explication can only be behavior itself. Explication must be restricted to the expression of what is actually given in behavior. At this stage of scientific exploration, the psychologist cannot involve himself in any implicit differential theory such as the psychoanalytic, behavioristic, stimulus-response, Jungian, or Adlerian.

Later, when the psychologist attempts to formulate his perception of behavior for fellow scientists, he must necessarily devise a series of psychological statements. This is valid so long as he faithfully follows behavior as it manifests itself and does not go beyond perception as intersubjectively validated. Such explication will be reliable only insofar as it is really an "expression" and nothing more.

Controlled Explication

The term "controlled" refers to the *validation* of the explication. This validation is of the utmost importance, for explication of behavior forms the basis for the integration of profiles of behavior by the comprehensive psychologist. If this explication is invalid, then the whole structure of comprehensive psychology supported by it will be at least temporarily distorted. Moreover, a false explication would do injustice to the differential psychology which studies the particular profile of behavior explicated by the phenomenologist. It is imperative, therefore, to ensure the validity and reliability of explications by means of adequate controls.

We may distinguish between validation in differential and validation in comprehensive phenomenological psychology.

Intra-Subjective Validation in Differential Phenomenological Psychology

The term *intra,* "within", denotes that the validation is performed by means of a critical comparison of the various phenomenological explications carried out by the same subject. This intra-subjective validation consists of procedures which verify the essential agreement among a sufficient number of explications of the same behavior in a variety of random situations when these explications are performed by the same phenomenologist.

Intra-subjective validation can be performed in a variety of ways. First of all, the psychologist himself can describe his spontaneous perceptions of an identical phenomenon in different situations, and then carry out a phenomenological explication of each one of these perceptions. He can subsequently compare the results of his various explications in order to determine whether they *essentially* agree or disagree with one another. In the case of an essential discrepancy among his explications of the same phenomenon, he must repeat the explications in order to discover the necessary and sufficient constituents of the phenomenon concerned.

Another method of intra-subjective validation is to obtain naïve descriptions of spontaneous perceptions of the phenomenon from samples of untrained subjects. The phenomenological explication begins with these naïve perceptions. Explications of the fundamental structures which appear in the descriptions, systematically compared with one another, may uncover the underlying constants. Untrained subjects usually produce a great number and variety of situations in which they engaged in the behavior under study. This fact facilitates scientific treatment, for it implies a natural variation of the independent variables. The variety of situations enables us to distinguish that which is constant from that which varies in the different situations. In this manner we may discover the foundational structure which appears in all behavior of the same kind. An added advantage is the fact that other scientists may control our procedure and repeat it, because the naïve descriptions of the original subjects can be made available to them. This validation is called *intra-subjective* because only the naïve descriptions—and not the subsequent phenomenological analyses—are provided by subjects other than the phenomenological scientist who performs the validation.

Inter-Subjective Validation of the Explication

The term *inter,* which means *between* or *among,* implies that the phenomenological explications are both performed and critically compared by different phenomenological scientists. Inter-subjective validation is the result of operations which are analogous to those performed in the intra-subjective approach; the principle difference is that they are performed by several instead of by only one phenomenologist. Like the intra-subjective, the inter-subjective validation can be achieved in various ways. A number of phenomenological scientists may independently describe their spontaneous perception of the phenomenon. After this procedure, they may make critical comparisons of their descriptions and explications.

Another possible method is to collect naïve descriptions of the phenomenon under varying conditions from random samples of unsophisticated subjects. After various phenomenologists explicate these reports independently, they may make critical comparisons.

Experimental Validation of the Explication

The phenomenological explication may also be validated indirectly by means of scientific experiments. Such validation is called indirect because it does not directly verify the phenomenological description itself; rather, it tests certain hypotheses which can be deduced from the description. These hypotheses show a typical "if . . . . then" relationship: if this phenomenological description is true, then this or that must happen when this specific experimental situation is set up. Thus the results of the subsequent experiment can affirm or deny the precision of the phenomenological explication. In the case of non-affirmation, the experiment will result in a new attempt at phenomenological explication. Phenomenology maintains, for example, that man on the proper level of his existence is always in some kind of dialogue with reality. From this phenomenological statement, we may deduce the testable hypothesis that *if* we expose man experimentally to conditions of sensory deprivation, *then* he will maintain some kind of dialogue with reality by means of imagination, emotionality, or even dreamlike, illusory, or hallucinatory activities.

Ideally, the psychological phenomenologist should make use of as many validating procedures as possible so that he can provide the theoretical comprehensive psychologist with observations which have reached the highest possible degree of validity and reliability.

Validation in Comprehensive Phenomenological Psychology

Comprehensive phenomenological psychology attempts to make implicit perception of behavior-as-a-whole explicit in order to create a comprehensive frame of reference. This structure must be capable of integrating the particular profiles of behavior which are studied in differential psychologies and which are explicated by differential phenomenological psychologists.

Comprehensive psychology, therefore, must provide the science of psychology with evidences so fundamental that they cannot be proved by more evident demonstrations. It is clear that statements which are truly self-evident cannot be proved, because every demonstration of a statement is necessarily based on other evidence. Self-evident assertions provide original and direct insight; hence their compelling impact of immediate conviction. The fact that I exist, for example, needs no demonstration; the negation of this fact would immediately lead to absurd consequences. On the other hand, the avowal that all my "higher" attitudes and activities are mere sublimations of my libido is not self-evident. I can deny this without immediately falling into absurdities. The latter claim, therefore, must be proved. The psychologist who believes it will attempt to demonstrate its validity by reducing this non-evident statement to an absolutely evident assertion.

The comprehensive psychologist must be absolutely sure that his fundamental constructs manifest this compelling character of inescapable evidence. This crucial validation is existential. Consequently, we call such existentially validated statements existential evidences. In order to understand the nature of existential validation and evidence, we must consider carefully the various types of evidence that are possible.

We shall, therefore, adapt to our specific topic of evidence in comprehensive psychology the doctrine of evidences which has been developed by the Dutch phenomenologist, Stefan Strasser. We may distinguish the types of evidence as spontaneous self-evidence, differential-scientific evidence, and comprehensive-scientific evidence. We propose that the last-named type of evidence should always be an existential evidence.

Spontaneous Self-Evidence

Certain ways of behaving appear to us in daily life as clear and obvious; their nature and meaning are so unmistakable that we feel compelled to say: "This is what it is." We do not have to reason, to explain, to theorize about it; we simply report what we spontaneously perceive. Much of the pre-scientific psychology of everyday life is based on such spontaneous evidence. In daily life it seems self-evident that a crying child is sad, pained, or angry; that the girl friend is lovely; and that the wall of the room is white. These and other naïve perceptions are the inescapable starting points not only of pre-scientific but also of scientific psychology. If psychologists themselves had not somehow perceived, for example, the behavior of crying, they could never have reflected scientifically on the conditions of this behavior. Again, psychologists would have been unable even to begin experiments on color perception if they had never experienced a naïve color perception such as that of the whiteness of the wall.

We shall see that these spontaneous self-evidences of daily life are more reliable than the differential-scientific evidences of the differential psychologies. On the other hand, spontaneous self-evidences will prove to be less reliable than existential self-evidences. For this reason, comprehensive-scientific psychology must produce only fundamental constructs which have the character of existential self-evidence.

Differential-Scientific Evidence

This type of evidence plays an important role in differential psychologies and in their empirical hypotheses. For example, the hypothesis that learning is based on a process of conditioning can be verified only by differential-scientific evidence; it cannot be validated directly by either spontaneous or comprehensive-scientific evidence. The evidences of differential psychologies are only indirect evidences. They do not make behavior itself manifest; they are deduced from spontaneous evidences by means of abstract scientific methods. The latter may consist of logical, mathematical deductions or of empirical inductions, the methods of which may differ in each differential psychology. To be sure, the conclusions of differential psychology possess their own type of evidence. Yet such scientific-differential evidences are always less reliable than naïve self-evidences.

Let us illustrate this statement with an example. When we observe the behavior of a perceiving person who looks at a white wall and reports to us what he spontaneously perceives, we may make two different statements concerning his behavior. We may simply say: "He perceives that the wall is white." As physiological psychologists, however, we may state that his behavior manifests that his sensory and nervous system is affected by light of a certain wave length which is reflected by the wall. Differential-scientific psychologists will be inclined to consider this latter statement as more scientific than the former. To the comprehensive theoretical psychologist, however, the first spontaneous report is more basic and reliable. The comparative historical study of scientific theories has made the theorist aware of the possibility that one day a second Einstein may prove the one-sidedness or incompleteness of present theory concerning the wave lengths of light. But the spontaneous report of the perceiving subject will not change fundamentally regardless of the continual change in theories.

The history of differential psychology teaches us that all differential-empirical theories are only provisional. And the comprehensive theorist also knows that, no matter what differential psychologists in the coming centuries may assert concerning color perception, they will always be obliged to start from the fact that the behavior of human subjects manifests that they spontaneously perceive color. In other words, every psychologist must start from such spontaneous pre-scientific self-evidence. The contrary is unthinkable. Moreover, differential scientists always presuppose pre-scientific knowledge when they conduct experiments in their laboratories. Therefore, pre-scientific self-evidences appear to be more basic, necessary, and reliable than indirect differential-scientific evidences.

Comprehensive-Scientific Existential Evidence

The comprehensive psychologist, while aware that the spontaneous self-evidences of daily life are more fundamental and reliable than the evidences of differential psychologies, also knows that these naïve self-evidences may be erroneous. Therefore, he cannot use them as fundamental constructs in his comprehensive frame of reference. He knows experimentally that man's perceptions and judgments and therefore his self-evidences in daily life may be influenced by such factors as optical illusion, emotion, mood,prejudice, temperament, or past experience. It is impossible, therefore, to develop a trustworthy comprehensive-scientific theory based on spontaneous self-evidences alone. This is not to deny that it is of crucial importance for a practicing psychologist, such as the psychotherapist, to develop an understanding of the spontaneous psychology of his client, which may be based on mistaken evidence which is "self-evident" only to this patient. Such a private response, while valuable in explaining the distorted universe of meaning of an individual, obviously cannot be used as a foundation for a comprehensive psychology which aims to be true for all human beings. It may be used by the comprehensive psychologist as one descriptive example of the general possibility that human behavior may develop in such or such a direction when influenced by a specific type of mistaken self-evidence. But comprehensive psychology is not merely the expression of universal possibilities of individual human development in either healthy or unhealthy directions. It is the conquest of a universal frame of reference which applies to all human behavior, and which forms the descriptive and explanatory ground for those very qualities present in every human being which make possible the development of individual deviations. An animal could never develop typically human perversions.

The comprehensive psychologist, therefore, requires a method in order to validate pre-scientific self-evidences in such a way that he may reduce them to foundational, comprehensive-scientific ones. We call these existential self-evidences. As formulated by the phenomenologist Strasser, they have the distinguishing mark that whoever would attempt to deny them would be compelled to reaffirm them, at least implicitly, in his very denial. We call these self-evidences *existential* because our very existence affirms them. Our very behavior demonstrates inescapably what we may attempt to deny intellectually. For this reason we may also call these evidences behavioral self-evidences. Even our language behavior negates the intellectual denial which may form the content of our spoken language. Let us illustrate with a few examples.

The fact that man can reflect is an existential or behavioral self-evidence. If someone were to tell us that man cannot reflect, he would contradict by his very statement the intellectual content of this communication. The very fact that he makes the statement necessarily implies that he reflects; otherwise, he could say nothing about man's ability to reflect or not to reflect. The actuality of his attempt to communicate his idea to us implies, moreover, that he believes in the possibility of our reflecting on his statement so that we may agree or disagree with him. Moreover, his concomitant behavior—his posture, his thoughtful utterance, his divorcing himself temporarily from involvement in a world of pragmatic tasks—demonstrates that he reflects. To be sure, man's ability to reflect can never be proved as such. It can only be perceived in his behavior, which communicates it in such an unmistakable way that its denial would necessarily lead to absurd consequences.

Let us take another example. The fact that we are beings who enjoy some form and some degree of freedom is an existential or behavioral self-evidence. A differential psychologist may concentrate in his particular type of research on the non-free or determined aspects of behavior. He quite rightly abstracts from the aspect of freedom as long as he stays within the limits of his differential research. He may be tempted, however, to generalize from this necessary condition for his particular type of research to all types. He may even go further and say that all human behavior, observed under all possible perspectives, reveals no evidence of freedom. He may attempt to convince us that we are never free but, on the contrary, are entirely determined by physical, physiological, and social conditions. If he does this, he denies an existential self-evidence. For the very fact that he attempts to persuade us implies a fundamental evidence. Obviously, when he speaks with us he takes into account the two possibilities that we will or will not agree with him. Otherwise he would not even try to win us over to his viewpoint. It is not a mere accident that such a differential psychologist enters into discussion with other psychologists and not with vegetables, rats, or monkeys. Only men can be converted; the differential psychologist himself is aware of this fact and *behaves* in accordance with it. This is a *behavioral* or existential way of saying that only men are free beings. This truth is thus implicitly affirmed by his behavioral attempt to deny it. Thus existential or behavioral self-evidence emerges whenever a differential psychologist attempts to deny it.

This implicit recognition of an evidence which one attempts to deny is the distinguishing mark of only existential evidences, and not of other types of evidences. For example, we can deny the fact that we perceive the wall as white without contradicting ourselves in any way. Existential evidences are more fundamental, however, than spontaneous self-evidences, for they are intimately connected with our very existence or behavior. They are characteristic features of our being. When we deny them, we contradict ourselves, not in a formal way as in logic or mathematics, but in a behavioral way. We never pretend intellectually that A is not A. But we may contradict ourselves by what we do, say, and think. Our very way of existing and behaving may reveal an implicit repudiation of our intellectual doubt. Therefore, existential or behavioral self-evidences can be critically examined and validated. They are valid for the comprehensive foundational psychologist when they are in accord with the characteristic marks of our observable behavior. If they do not conform with our characteristic modes of behavior, they are not really existential or behavioral.

It is clear that a comprehensive scientific psychology should be based essentially on existential self-evidences. Thus it will assume the character of a comprehensive phenomenological psychology. We may conclude that the method of building a comprehensive frame of reference which can integrate all the contributions of psychology consists in choosing naïve spontaneous self-evidences as a starting-point, in validating them, and in advancing from them to behavioral self-evidences.

The Different But Mutually Complementary Functions of Comprehensive and Differential Explications of Behavior

Phenomenological explication aims at disclosing structures of behavior; it reveals the "lived" structures which constitute the relationship between behaving man and the world. When explication attempts to discover the most basic, holistic structures of human behavior, we call it a comprehensive, foundational, or radical explication; for it aims at revealing those structures which comprehend in the root (*radix*) all differentiated structures peculiar to human behavior in specified situations.

We may attempt, however, to explicate a specific type of behavior not in its foundational character but merely in its "specificity" or particularity. In this case, we engage not in a comprehensive but in a differential explication. However, such situated structures of behavior, even when considered merely in their particularity, maintain their underlying universal structures. The fundamental structures of behavior appear in particular manifestations even when we abstract our attention from them temporarily in order to focus on the situational character of the behavior. We must even say that these fundamental structures of human behavior constitute the precise condition for the possibility of any personalized or situated structure of behavior whatsoever. For example, the homosexual structure of human behavior implies the fundamental sexual structure; the structure of neurotic guilt implies the universal possibility of guilt; neurotic anxiety points to the structure of human anxiety; reinforcement by rewards in specific laboratory situations reveals the general receptivity for reinforcing experiences. On the other hand, we can never observe universal structures of human behavior as such; they always appear as particularized in concrete life situations. For example, we can never observe in its pure form the basic sexuality of man; we are always faced with actual forms of sexual behavior in man's typical cultural, social, and personal situations.

Consequently, two types of controlled explication are required in psychology. One is the differential explication of situated structures of behavior insofar as they are situated. The other is the comprehensive explication of those universal structures which are implicitly present in every particular structure of behavior. Both explications start from the same data: behavior as given in concrete situations. Only the focus is different.

The differential explication is by its very nature linked to differential psychologies since they deal operationally with "situated" and "differentiated" structures of behavior. The comprehensive explication is related to comprehensive psychology since it seeks to discover those fundamental structures of behavior which comprehend all sub-structures or cultural and personal particularizations of universal structures.

Differential Explication of Behavior

The situated structures of behavior are studied empirically and experimentally by differential psychologists. One may ask, is it necessary to add to empirical research the difficult task of a controlled differential explication of the behavior under study?

The differential scientist is necessarily guided by a differential theory. In fact, operational theory is the essence of a differential science and sets it apart, on the one hand, from mere description and, on the other, from comprehensive scientific theory. However, theory is not an aim in itself; it is merely a tool—indispensable but nevertheless a tool—which helps us to understand the phenomena of behavior. Theory should be guided by phenomena, not vice versa. The phenomena themselves should be our ultimate criteria, not the implicit philosophies and abstract constructs of individual psychologists. Consequently, it is necessary that we constantly rediscover phenomena in their pure appearances, unadulterated by any theory.

Every scientific judgment of a differential psychologist ultimately refers to a phenomenon of behavior to which he is immediately present; his judgment is an abstract "mediation" of something immediate, namely the direct perception of the phenomenon. His immediate presence to an appearance of behavior may be termed his "lived" perception. Behavior as directly perceived is not the behavior the psychologist theorizes about, for his judgments *about* behavior always necessarily presuppose his perception of the behavior itself.

Perceived behavior is thus the starting point, the presupposition, the occasion of all psychological reflection and experimentation *on* behavior. For example, when a psychologist declares that a person in a certain phase of psychotherapy becomes dependent on the psychotherapist, his judgment presupposes, first of all, a perception of a structure of behavior that may be labeled "dependent"; second, the perception of a situation which may be termed therapeutic; finally, the perception of a structure of behavior that may be called therapeutic. If it were not for these perceptions, the psychologist would be unable to make his judgment concerning dependency.

The scientific views of differential psychologists about perceived behavior are always expressed in theoretical judgments. Such judgments, which are necessarily removed from perception, may contain more than what was given in the direct perception of the psychologist; they usually imply certain theoretical conceptions which may or may not be in accord with reality-perception itself. The danger of contamination of perception by prejudice necessitates the explication of the phenomena to which the constructs refer. The differential-phenomenological psychologist, therefore, will ask such questions as: In the statement of the psychologist, what is reality perception and what is merely hypothetical explanation? How far do theoretical models unconsciously influence this judgment? Is there some impact of wishful thinking, imagination, or unchecked theoretical prejudice? Has an implicit philosophical position colored the statement of fact?

Any judgment of behavior by a differential psychologist, no matter how abstract and theoretical, is ultimately a distillate from a more primary "lived" perception of the behavior. Every differential psychology is a constellation of objectivations and judgments concerning a particular aspect of behavior. This "ideal" world of judgments necessarily rests on the foundation of certain perceptions. For example, a differential psychologist may posit that learning behavior is a function of reinforcement, and he may verify this statement by experimentation. Yet his psychology of learning necessarily presupposes a perception of what he is experimenting *on* and theorizing *about,* namely a phenomenon of behavior called "learning." Without this perception, he cannot even begin to experiment. Moreover, the differential psychologist who is a learning theorist perceives learning behavior from *one* psychological viewpoint, that of the theory of conditioning. Physiological or cultural-social psychologists may take other viewpoints when observing this same type of behavior, for their psychologies are based on different positions. Other features of the behavior called learning may thus reveal themselves in the light of other perspectives which are just as real as that of conditioning. The point to note here is that none of these differential psychologists directly perceives "conditioning by reinforcement" or "neuro-physiological concomitants of the learning process" or "cultural-motivational aspects of learning behavior"; each perceives only the learning behavior of every-day life and a certain aspect of this behavior which may be labeled with one of these scientific constructs.

One might argue that the differential psychologist uses a pure theoretical knowledge which is not based on any perception when he deals with behavior statistically. However, statistics are meaningless if they do not point to something perceived which they symbolize. We must even say that statistical operations in themselves are somehow rooted in perception. For example, mathematical calculations would be meaningless to us if they did not appeal implicitly to our lived perception of reality. A percentage, for example. would mean little if we had not at some time perceived a certain quantity of concrete objects in daily life and a certain number subtracted from it and viewed in comparison to it. For this reason, the teaching of elementary mathematics to school children or primitive tribes begins with the addition and subtraction of concrete objects such as marbles or apples.

Thus, no judgment of a differential psychologist represents his "first" knowledge; it always presupposes his perception in immediate encounter with behavior. Therefore the integrational theorist must always be alert for possible non-perceptual elements in a differential judgment which might obscure or even falsify the perception of the behavior itself.

This phenomenological purification of differential judgments should be performed by specialized differential phenomenologists of each field of psychology, and not by the comprehensive phenomenologist, who performs a different function in psychology. His work is the integration of differential judgments about behavior. His final aim is to insert the differential profiles presented by phenomenologists in each field of psychology into a universal structure of systematically organized profiles of human behavior. Such profiles reveal implicitly the fundamental structures of intentional-functional behavior as a whole; in other words, they make it possible for the comprehensive psychologist to examine the elucidated phenomena further and to uncover even more fundamental structures which root these phenomena in human behavior as such.

We may conclude that differential phenomenology searches for the structure of the empirical phenomena of behavior which are discovered and named by differential psychologies. Among these are the structures of phenomena such as the Oedipal constellation, reinforcement, repression, fixation, rote-learning, the process of problem-solution, color perception, neurotic guilt, and paranoid behavior. Differential psychologists study these phenomena in so far as they appear in observable behavior under certain empirical or experimental conditions. To date, there is a deplorable scarcity of differential phenomenologists in the various fields of psychology. There is need for behaviorist, psychoanalytic, learning, perceptual, social, and psycho-physiological phenomenologists who are specialists in their fields. Because of this lack, the anthropological psychologist himself must frequently perform a phenomenological elucidation which could be done more effectively by specialized differential phenomenologists.

A concrete example of a differential phenomenological elucidation is more clarifying than an abstract discussion. Therefore, we shall present in the following chapter an outline of a specific study which illustrates a differential phenomenological procedure.

The Relationship Between Comprehensive Phenomenology and Comprehensive Theory in Psychology

The phenomenological elucidation of differential psychologies leads to the discovery of phenomena which await re-integration by the comprehensive phenomenologist into the holistic structure of man's behavior. This reconstruction will never be accomplished completely, for we shall never have at our disposal an exhaustive elucidation of all possible phenomena or perspectives of human behavior. At this point, comprehensive scientific *theory* emerges to complete the work of phenomenology. It provides the constructs that point most effectively to the holistic structure of behavior uncovered by comprehensive phenomenology. Comprehensive theory also creates the explanatory links that bind together within an understandable synthesis the phenomena discovered to date in the history of psychology. If we were to create an imaginary scale for the development of psychology from the lowest to the highest degree of integration, we might devise the following sequence: spontaneous perceptions; scientific-differential theory and data-gathering in an increasing number of differential psychologies; differential-phenomenological elucidation of the data and judgments found in different psychologies; comprehensive-phenomenological elucidation of the differentially elucidated phenomena of the differential psychologies; integration of the comprehensively elucidated phenomena into the holistic structure of human behavior already developed by comprehensive phenomenology; and finally, comprehensive theory construction on the basis of the available holistic phenomenological structure of human behavior.

The comprehensive theorist, in his attempt to provide explanatory links for human behavior-as-a-whole, will be enlightened by similar theoretical attempts in differential theories. The main difference between the two is that differential theorists attempt to explain the whole of human behavior only *insofar as* it appears in the light of their *differential* perspective. Psychoanalysts, for example, may create a differential-comprehensive theory of human behavior insofar as it appears in the perspective of dynamic motivation; learning theorists, insofar as it reveals itself under the aspect of conditioning; certain cultural-social psychologists, insofar as it is uncovered in the light of acculturation. The comprehensive theorist, however, has the task of integrating all these perspectives in an over-all explanatory construct. This synthesizing structure should not destroy valid explanations of behavior under its various differential aspects as given by differential theorists; at the same time, it should point most effectively to the elucidation of differential data by the comprehensive phenomenologist. In other words, the holistic phenomenological structure of behavior is the criterion of the comprehensive theorist in his use and evaluation of differential theories.

As we have already seen, however, even the comprehensive theorist keeps his constructs hypothetical, for he realizes that the holistic structure of behavior uncovered by the comprehensive phenomenologist may be influenced by the culture in which both the comprehensive and the differential phenomenologist are living. Therefore he continually searches in the history of both explicit and implicit psychologies of his own and of other cultures for possible evidence that his constructs are still too narrow, influenced as they may be by his own cultural frame of reference.

Comprehensive Phenomenology and Three Types of Differential Psychologies

Comprehensive phenomenology as foundational must elucidate the differential phenomena of the various fields of psychology. This elucidation clarifies the basic structure of the differential phenomenon. It manifests how and where this particular human phenomenon is rooted by its very nature in the fundamental holistic structure of human behavior as such. Comprehensive phenomenology does not elucidate the concrete situational components of the differential phenomenon, such as its cultural and individual constituents; this task has already been performed by the differential phenomenologist. Foundational phenomenology, on the contrary, places these components temporarily in the background in order to concentrate on the basic structure of behavior which transcends its situational appearances.

This foundational phenomenological elucidation is concerned with three types of differential psychology, namely differential-personal, differential-functional, and mixed personal-functional.

Differential-Personal Psychologies

Differential-personal psychologies are concerned with human behavior under one particular aspect, for example, the motivational or the perceptual profile of human behavior. Moreover, they usually limit themselves to the appearance of that behavior under certain cultural or experimental conditions. The psychology of emotionality, for instance, limits itself to the emotional aspect of human behavior; it may point to other aspects—for every perspective refers implicitly to all other perspectives—but it does not elaborate them. Nor does it attempt to point out how and where this emotionality is rooted in the holistic structure of human behavior in comparison with all other phenomena studied by all other differential psychologies. Furthermore, the psychology of emotionality usually studies emotions as they are revealed within a particular culture. The differential phenomenologist in the field of emotional psychology elucidates the concrete data of emotional behavior presented by differential psychologists, but he does not clarify the phenomenon in its fundamental rootedness in the structure of human behavior as such.

An illustration of a differential elucidation of an emotional phenomenon will be presented in the next chapter, in which we shall take as our example the experience of feeling understood by someone. The foundational phenomenologist accepts the phenomena presented by the differential field of study. The fact that, in the case cited, they are already *human* phenomena (already elucidated by the differential phenomenologist) enables the comprehensive phenomenologist to clarify their most fundamental structure, and subsequently to integrate them directly into a comprehensive phenomenology of human behavior.

Differential-Functional Psychologies

The same cannot be said of differential-functional psychologies which study isolated functions of behavior under the perspective of their similarity to measurable aspects of infra-human processes. The de-humanized function studied in artificial isolation has first to be re-humanized before it can be reintegrated in human behavior as a whole. This re-humanization implies that the psychologist must first of all investigate how this phenomenon changes when perceived as an integral part of an aspect of human behavior within a meaningful human life situation. For example, the differential phenomenologist of the psychology of conditioned learning must analyze how the laws of conditioning—discovered in animals—change in characteristically human social-cultural situations. Only when this is done will the comprehensive phenomenologist be able to seek for the most fundamental structure and meaning of the phenomenon of human learning presented to him by the differential phenomenologist. His foundation elucidation of this particular phenomenon will help him to articulate the full phenomenon of human behavior.

Mixed Personal-Funtional Psychologies

Some differential psychologies show a mixed personal-functional character. Freud's psychoanalytic psychology may serve as an example. Part of his differential theory takes the form of mechanistic descriptions of de-humanized isolated functions, while another part presents human behavior as an existential and intentional whole in living human relationships in meaningful situations; it is a mixture of process-theory and existential theory. Psychoanalytic psychology as a process-theory makes behavior an abstraction or a bundle of abstractions not directly related to the human person in his very humanity. Psychoanalysis as an existential theory studies behavior as rooted in living human existence; it is concerned with existential experience and motivation as they appear in behavior. This typical blend of functional and personal terminology in psychoanalytic theory is due to the struggle of its founder, Sigmund Freud, to make the transition from the natural science of neurophysiology to a human existential approach to the behavior of man. In his writing on the "Project", he uses the language of physics and cerebral physiology, while in his ego-psychology he uses human existential formulations. He does the latter reluctantly, forced by his spontaneous perceptions of the human predicament. In fact, he never quite decided to move in one direction or the other. The comprehensive psychologist who desires to integrate the contributions of this particular differential psychology into a comprehensive anthropological psychology is thus faced with a double task. The aspects of man's behavior which have been functionalized and dehumanized by psychoanalytic theory must first be rehumanized by differential phenomenology. Psychoanalytic theory which stresses the human quality of behavior, on the other hand, can be integrated in the same manner as the contributions of other personalized differential psychologies.

Comprehensive Phenomenology as Foundational and as Integrational

In a former chapter on the theoretical mode of existence, we distinguished between comprehensive theory as foundational and as integrational. Similar distinctions can be made concerning comprehensive phenomenology. In the preceding section we considered comprehensive phenomenology mainly in its integrational aspect, or the manner in which it deals with the phenomena presented by the differential phenomenologists. We stressed two features: first, comprehensive phenomenology has already uncovered a fundamental holistic structure of human behavior which remains open, however, to change and differentiation; second, comprehensive phenomenology elucidates differential phenomena to such a depth that it reveals how and where they insert themselves into the holistic structure of man's behavior. This continuous insertion of differential phenomena increasingly differentiates the foundational structure.

Comprehensive phenomenology *as integration* is thus the continual differentiation of the holistic structure of behavior by means of a foundational elucidation of differential phenomena.

Comprehensive phenomenology *as foundational* is the continual uncovering of the fundamental holistic features themselves. The comprehensive phenomenologist reveals this holistic structure through elucidation not only of differential psychologies, but also of phenomena not yet offered by differential psychologies but found, for example, in philosophical anthropology, in art, in literature, in the daily life of people, or even in his own experience.

In other words, while foundational and integrational endeavors are aspects of the same comprehensive phenomenological activity which mutually penetrate and sustain each other, they are not fully identical and therefore they can be distinguished intellectually.

With this conclusion in mind, we may now describe somewhat more concretely the nature of phenomenological explication in psychology. Comprehensive phenomenological explication aims at the disclosure of the "lived" structure of behavior as a whole, which constitutes the relationship between behaving man and the world. It is a fundamental method of research which leads to the discovery of that foundational structure of observable behavior which constitutes the possibility of any human behavior whatsoever. It concentrates by its very nature on behavior as a dynamic, unified interrelation with the world whose primary characteristic is intentionality. This differentiated "lived" structure of behavior is originally pre-conceptual and pre-reflexive, and it is the basis of all possible patterns of behavior. If it were not pre-reflexive, we would not need a comprehensive phenomenology to bare its structure by reflective knowledge. The pre-reflectively perceived world is the always present correlate of intentional behavior. Therefore, all phenomenology, both comprehensive and differential, implies the explication of the situation-pole, object-pole, or world-pole of behavior. Differential phenomenology explicates the particular situation, the specific world which is the counterpart of a specific pattern of behavior. Comprehensive phenomenology, on the other hand, clarifies the foundational structure of the world-pole, which is the correlate of the foundational structure of human behavior as such.

Briefly, comprehensive phenomenology in psychology is the uncovering of the primary structure of human behavior and its correlative, the primary world. Comprehensive phenomenology as *foundational* studies differential phenomena insofar as they implicitly reveal the fundamental structures of intentional-functional-situational behavior as a whole. Comprehensive phenomenology as *integrational* inserts differential phenomena into the holistic structure of human behavior. The final outcome of comprehensive phenomenology as both foundational *and* integrational is a differentiated holistic structure of human behavior. Because this outcome is never completely achieved, comprehensive theory is required to complete this unfinished structure by means of hypothetical links and explanatory constructs. The latter are developed in cooperation with the differential theories, but always in tune with the phenomenological holistic structure, which is perceived and not "thought out" as a theoretical structure is.

Comprehensive phenomenology is therefore the touchstone, the criterion for the development of comprehensive scientific theory. The dialogue between comprehensive theory and comprehensive phenomenology in psychology leads to the fusion of thought and perception, theory and reality, construct and concept. This fusion may lead to confusion if we are not aware that the fused elements retain their own origin and identity and should be so distinguished. As a result of this osmosis, foundational constructs in comprehensive theory point to the phenomenological structure of the pre-predicative, pre-conceptual, pre-logical, psychological, behavioral relationship between man and world. They thus point to the necessary condition for all the phenomena of behavior discovered and investigated in the differential psychologies. For the pre-reflexive, pre-conceptual, pre-logical structures of behavior are at the origin of human behavior, prior to any theory, construct, or experiment *about* behavior. Comprehensive phenomenology expresses human behavior as it is perceived at the present historical moment of our perceptual knowledge of behavior. Comprehensive theory completes by means of hypothetical constructs that which is not yet perceived or may never be perceived. Comprehensive phenomenology as foundational limits itself to the revelation of those structures of observable behavior which are universally necessary. Thus comprehensive theory is able to devise foundational constructs which are sufficiently comprehensive to integrate the findings of all differential psychologies.

Comprehensive psychology—both phenomenological and theoretical, foundational and integrational—is concerned with the fullness of human behavior in its total, concrete, "lived" density as it is found in real life situations. The latter are encountered in the clinic, hospital, therapy room, playground, theater, church, home, laboratory, bedroom, army barracks, school, or industrial plant. Each one of these sectors of behavior represents a different world of meaning and its correlate, a different style and structure of behavior. The ultimate aim of comprehensive scientific psychology is therefore not the foundations of human behavior, but the *practical* understanding of full human behavior in its "lived" density within concrete life situations. Practical understanding is that type of concrete insight which can lead to methodical psychological procedures conducive to concrete, observable changes in the behavior of individuals and groups. Comprehensive phenomenology alone would be insufficient for the formation of a comprehensive scientific psychology relevant to the methodical change of behavior. Only the union of comprehensive phenomenology and theory on the basis of differential phenomenology and theory, can lead to a comprehensive scientific psychology relevant to change in man's behavior.

The very nature of comprehensive scientific psychology suggests three cardinal rules for research. First of all, no new hypothetical link or explanatory construct should be devised unless phenomenological research proves to be as yet incapable of uncovering in behavior itself the integrating link which is not yet perceptible. Second, established hypothetical links and explanatory constructs should be altered when phenomenological research leads to a change or expansion of the perceptible phenomenological structure which negates these theoretical constructs. Finally, the theoretical expression of the perceived phenomenological structure should be considered as subject to change, for this theoretical "shorthand" may be an imperfect or even distorted representation of the structure.

The preceding considerations on phenomenology may lead us to a deeper understanding of the terms of the expression, "existential comprehensive scientific theory". It is called existential precisely because it attempts to keep foundational theory in tune with the results of foundational and differential phenomenology. It is called comprehensive because it attempts to integrate the contributions of differential psychologies within an increasingly differentiated holistic structure of behavior. It is called scientific because its results are checked by the differential psychologies through deduction of testable hypotheses; because its holistic-differential search is guided by the findings of differential scientific psychologies and by the needs of applied scientific psychology; and because its main integrational structure is checked directly (as far as this is possible) by means of deduction of those testable hypotheses not yet proved by differential psychologies. Existential comprehensive scientific theory, finally, is called theory insofar as its final over-all structure always has a theoretical character because, on the one hand, the outcome of phenomenological research will always be limited and requires the completion of theoretical explanatory links and, on the other hand, it requires a translation into theoretical constructs which are apt to interact with other constructs.

The Mutual Interaction Between Comprehensive and Differential Phenomenology

Differential phenomenology does not carry on its many-faceted function in complete isolation from comprehensive phenomenology. On the contrary, the differential and the comprehensive poles of psychological phenomenology complement each other in constant mutual interaction. Findings of differential phenomenology illuminate the foundations of anthropological psychology which the comprehensive phenomenologist continually attempts to elucidate. When, for example, various differential psychologists explicate different phenomena of "situated" behavior, they provide the comprehensive phenomenologist with a variety of explicated situations within which this behavior appears. Thus he is enabled to distinguish what is universal and necessary in this intentional behavior from what is due to incidental circumstances.

On the other hand, comprehensive phenomenology—in disclosing and thematizing universal structures which are at the root of human behavior—provides the differential phenomenologist with clues to the particularized presence of these structures in the situated phenomena of behavior which he explores. His perception of the universal structure facilitates that of the situated behavioral structure. Comprehensive and differential phenomenology in psychology thus maintain a dialectical relationship, stimulating each other's development. It is this dialogue which will establish the sphere for a truly existential behaviorism which will gradually integrate the divergent streams of thought in the divided world of psychology.

Without comprehensive phenomenology, psychology can never achieve synthesis and comprehensive understanding. On the other hand, comprehensive phenomenology and theory would be irrelevant and incomplete if they did not illuminate and were not illuminated by the concrete cultural, subcultural, and individual particularizations of the universal structures which they describe. This dialogue, furthermore, makes comprehensive psychology relevant for the concrete situations with which the psychologist has to cope in every-day existence.

The comprehensive scientific theorist develops a frame of constructs in accord with the structure presented by the comprehensive phenomenologist. This skeleton of constructs requires the meat of concrete data. Such data are provided by the differential psychologist and clarified in their relationship to human behavior as a whole by the differential phenomenologist. As a matter of fact, the comprehensive phenomenologist and theorist will usually illustrate the relevance of the explication of the whole structure of behavior by means of the phenomenologically elucidated data of the differential psychologies. Otherwise, their work would provide merely an abstract outline which would lose contact with the concrete ground of the differential psychologies. Hence, psychological phenomenology is a dynamic field that consists of two interdependent poles, the comprehensive and the differential.

Anthropological psychology as a differentiated whole is thus far more than an explication of the fundamental structures of behavior. We may even say that the foundational constructs would remain useless, psychologically speaking, if they could not be applied increasingly to the data of the differential psychologies. It is true that some empirical data provided by differential psychologies may prove to be incomplete or even false. This is one reason why comprehensive psychology always remains an open system, constantly in flux according to the progress of the differential psychologies. This situation implies the necessity of an unceasing dialogue, on the one hand, between comprehensive and differential phenomenology and, on the other hand, between differential phenomenology and the data of the differential psychology in which it specializes.

Such a dialogue keeps the foundational phenomenologist in constant touch with concrete profiles of situated behavior as explored by differential psychologists; it ensures the continual test of empirical applicability of his foundational constructs.

The Method of Foundational Explication

Having discussed the place and function of foundational and differential phenomenology in anthropological psychology, we may now consider the main characteristics of methodological explication as carried out respectively by foundational and differential phenomenology.

The two main phases of a phenomenological explication in psychology are that of temporary elimination of aspects of behavior and that of integration of all perspectives available after this elimination. Both procedures are necessary in foundational as well as in differential phenomenology. These two phenomenologies differ in regard to both the aspects which they temporarily eliminate from consideration and the number and type of perspectives which they must integrate. While foundational phenomenology eliminates all those particular aspects which are due to the situation in which a phenomenon appears, differential phenomenology implies at least certain selected aspects due to the cultural or developmental situation in which the phenomenon manifests itself.

We shall first consider the methodological explication which is characteristic of the foundational pole of comprehensive phenomenology. Afterwards we shall discuss the method typical of the differential pole.

The Temporary Elimination from Consideration of All Individual and Particular Aspects of Behavior

A foundational explication of behavior deals with the necessary universal structure of the behavior under study. The latter may be defined as that which remains identical in all possible variations in the subjects and situations of the behavior concerned, and which combines all necessary structural constituents discovered by differential psychologists in their varied exploration of this behavior. The fundamental structure thus admits only those constituents which remain unchanged in all possible variations of the original phenomenon of behavior. Therefore, the foundational psychologist must distance himself from all particular aspects manifested in the behavior so that he may discover only that which is universal, fundamental, and necessary for that type of behavior regardless of the situation in which it appears.

When I search for the fundamental structure of all possible dependency behavior, for example, I may explicate the behavior of a dependent child, a dependent client, a dependent student, a dependent minority group within a culture, or a dependent member of a gang of adolescents. I must eliminate, however, all reference to that in their behavior which colors their personal, developmental, cultural, or subcultural case of dependency. This act of temporary distancing from these aspects is not an act of isolating abstraction or selective attention. Such an abstraction could never provide me with an insight into the universal structure of the behavior. For this fundamental structure actually appears in those aspects which I eliminate from consideration. What I really do is to consider them insofar as they reveal the basic structure, and to distance myself from them insofar as they manifest merely situational aspects of behavior. This approach leads to a real perception of the fundamental structure of the behavior. Such perception reveals at once the necessary and sufficient constituents of, in this case, dependency-behavior. Foundational phenomenology is thus a gradual penetration into the purified primary structure of behavior which culminates in a revealing perception of this structure.

The temporary elimination of individual and particular aspects of behavior in order to perceive its universal, necessary, and sufficient constituents is not always easy. The foundational phenomenologist in psychology may therefore collect random samples of a variety of dependent behaviors among various individuals and populations. This sample enables him to observe dependent behavior from many different aspects. He may perceive what is identical in many appearances of dependent behavior and also what is different because of individual and particular aspects of the situation. He may then attempt to make explicit the underlying structure which unifies these various apearances of dependent behavior.

Integration of All Available Perspectives Following the Elimination of Individual Aspects

The foundational structure of behavior combines all necessary and sufficient structural constituents which are discovered in the light of the various perspectives assumed by differential psychologists. Therefore, foundational phenomenology in psychology is not merely a matter of eliminating all the individual and particular aspects of the behaving subject and his situation. The comprehensive phenomenologist knows that behavior presents itself in a certain perspective, which is dependent on the attitude which the psychologist assumes toward behavior. He may look at dependency behavior, for example, from the viewpoint of a psychotherapist or of a social psychologist. Each of these attitudes reveals an aspect of dependency behavior which can be explicated by the foundational phenomenologist, who may then uncover a basic and necessary constituent of all dependency behavior.

Each of these aspects, however, refers implicitly to all other aspects of behavior which may be revealed by other attitudes on the part of the perceiving psychologist. Moreover, the specific attitude adopted by the psychologist also refers to other possible attitudes which he can assume. For example, the psychologist who observes dependency behavior from the viewpoint of its emotional meaning for the subject is implicitly aware that this behavior also has physiological, social, and learning aspects. The same may be said of the phenomenologist who uncovers a basic constituent of dependency behavior by explicating any one of these other aspects. If he eliminates all individual and cultural aspects of dependency behavior as described by the social psychologist, for example, he may uncover the basic social characteristic of all dependency behavior. But he is aware, at the same time, that this characteristic is not the only constituent of dependency behavior.

Behavior as it is discovered and described by a psychologist is always a correlate of his observations, which are in turn a correlate of his specific attitude. In other words, the object of his observation is a structure of his systematically organized perspectives of the behavior, which are in accord with the various attitudes on which his observation depends.

The foundational phenomenological psychologist who searches for the universal structure of a behavior must carefully explicate the various attitudes which have been taken by psychologists toward this phenomenon of behavior. He must also analyze the different profiles of behavior which form the correlates of these observational attitudes. He therefore explores the views of all differential psychologies on this particular type of behavior and the perspectives which these views have opened up in order to assess the various profiles. He explicates each perspective in order to discover as many basic constituents as possible which together may present the total foundational structure of the behavior. This type of research will enable him to structure the behavioral phenomenon in question as a *gestalt* of systematically organized aspects discovered by the differential psychologies. Because the number of possible perspectives is virtually inexhaustible, the foundational psychologist can never claim certainty that his phenomenological explication of the universal structure of a type of behavior is exhaustive, final, and complete. Hence the description of the foundational phenomenologist always remains open to change and development in accordance with the possibility of both new findings in existing differential psychologies and the emergence of new differential psychologies, which implies the opening up of totally new perspectives and correspondingly new profiles.

Foundational phenomenology insofar as it serves comprehensive psychology never stops with the explication of only one fundamental constituent of behavior; it aims at a holistic view of man and his structures so broad that comprehensive psychology can devise constructs to integrate the findings of all differential psychologies. For this reason, foundational phenomenology in psychology should not only eliminate all individual and particular characteristics of a behavior, but also integrate the "explicated" profiles of that behavior opened up by the perspectives of all differential psychologies.

The Method of Differential Explication

Like foundational explication, differential phenomenology also entails a procedure of elimination and of integration. This activity does not aim to uncover the most fundamental structures which appear in behavior, however, but the structure of the phenomenon as it appears in certain situations and includes certain aspects of these situations. Consequently, the differential explication distinguishes itself from the foundational one by the deliberate limitation of its eliminating and integrating procedures.

The Temporary Limited Elimination from Consideration of Certain Individual and Particular Aspects of Behavior

The differential pole of comprehensive phenomenology differs from the foundational one in various ways. First of all, differential phenomenology does not abstract from all particular aspects of a behavior. The phenomenologist may, for example, be interested in the behavior of people who feel really understood in a situation. He may decide to study this behavior as it manifests itself in American teenagers who belong to a city population or in people who are in psychotherapy. He may not be interested, however, in the differences between males and females in this situation. Thus he defines the object of his phenomenology as the behavior of feeling understood as it manifests itself in urban teenagers or in therapy patients, and he temporarily eliminates from this object their being male or female.

The scope of his differential-phenomenological study obviously differs from that of a foundational phenomenologist who is interested in the universal structure of the behavior of feeling understood. Such a structure would manifest itself in all people of all times and cultures who have this experience. The foundational phenomenologist, therefore, would eliminate *all* particular cultural characteristics from his object of study. Among them would be being a teenager in a city or a client in psychotherapy.

The fact that the differential phenomenologist does not eliminate *all* individual and particular aspects from a behavior does not imply that he removes none of them. When he explores the behavior of feeling understood in teenagers, for example, he may collect samples of behavior of city teenagers in a variety of situations in which they feel understood. These samples will enable him to perceive what is identical in all situations of feeling understood in teenagers, and what is different because of those individual aspects which are not the particular developmental aspect of being a teenager. In this way, he can make explicit the structure of behavior which essentially unifies these various appearances of the behavior of teenagers who feel understood.

Integration of a Set of Perspectives Limited in Principle

A second difference between the foundational and the differential poles of anthropological phenomenology can be found in the operation of integration of perspectives.

The foundational phenomenologist aims at the integration of all perspectives opened up by all differential psychologies. The differential phenomenologist, however, is interested in the integration of only those profiles which appear in studies of psychologists who have limited themselves to a specific phenomenon. The phenomenologist who studies the behavior of feeling understood in teenagers, for example, will integrate only those perspectives which are revealed by psychologists who have studied the same behavior in the same developmental situation.

A behavior can be studied on a virtually inexhaustible number of levels, depending on what the differential phenomenologist eliminates or does not eliminate from its concretely situated structure. Thus we can imagine a continuum of degrees of elimination and a consequent continuum of differential phenomenologists in psychology, beginning with those who consider the structure of individual behavior in its peculiarities and ending with those who eliminate all particularizing factors except one. The more extensive the elimination of particulars, the greater the number of perspectives that can be integrated. Ideally, a behavior should be studied by differential phenomenologists on as many relevant levels of elimination as possible, and finally on the level of foundational elimination by comprehensive phenomenologists. The different levels of elucidation will clarify one another and lead to as perfect a grasp of the behavior in question as possible. Such a presentation of a widely and deeply elucidated phenomenon of behavior will facilitate the task of the comprehensive scientific theorist.

We have already discussed the task of the differential phenomenologist who specializes in one field, school, or area of psychology. His integration of perspectives is typically limited to those opened up by the particular psychology which is his concern. Each differential psychology is the implementation of a certain attitude toward behavior. This special viewpoint opens up a certain horizon within which behavior can appear only under certain perspectives. The differential phenomenologist who is committed to such a field of specialization is thus interested only in the integration of those perspectives which have been revealed by the attitude which defines and structures this field as a whole. For example, a differential phenomenologist in the area of dynamic-analytical psychology will integrate all *motivational* aspects of behavior which have been opened up by different psychoanalytic observers and theoreticians of this behavior, such as Freud, Jung, Adler, Horney, Fromm, Alexander, Melanie Klein, and Fairbarn. He will not integrate, for example, the perspectives of dependency behavior which have been explored by physiological and social psychologists. This task he will leave to the differential phenomenologists who specialize in these areas.

We have outlined only the two main operations of the foundational and differential poles of anthropological phenomenology. These two operations differentiate themselves in many more concrete operations, according to the rich variety of phenomena of the behavior under study. Furthermore, the phenomenologist must validate the outcomes of his research by empirical or experimental operations and create a system of checks and controls, which may differ in every specific situation.

We shall demonstrate some of these possible operations and controls in a concrete differential phenomenology of "The Experience of Really Feeling Understood by Somebody" in the following chapter.

Conclusion

Empirical observation, experimentation, measurement, and accumulation of data should be fostered in all differential psychologies. From the viewpoint of comprehensive psychology, however, much of this admirable effort is wasted if there is no phenomenological explication of *what* it is that is being observed, experimented upon, measured, correlated, and applied. In this sense, anthropological phenomenology becomes the foundation or ground of comprehensive scientific psychology, its only secure basis, and its instrument for a methodical revision of differential psychologies when necessary. Anthropological phenomenology provides comprehensive psychology with a necessary method for the solution of seemingly insolvable contradictions between statements of "fact" made by differential psychologists. It provides a return to the experienced behavioral phenomena from which these contradictory "facts" were originally derived and to which they refer. Such a return will ordinarily solve the apparent incompatibility of "facts" and enable the comprehensive psychologist to clarify what is really experienced and observed and what is theoretical, philosophical, cultural, personal, emotional, or linguistic contamination in these seemingly incompatible statements.

In our explanation of anthropological phenomenology as used in empirical psychology, we have restricted our discussion to the foundational and differential explications of intentional behavior.

As we have seen earlier, anthropological psychology also requires the explication of its ontological assumptions and of those of the differential psychologies. This task belongs primarily to philosophical anthropology. Therefore, the anthropological phenomenologist in psychology requires at this point the close collaboration of those philosophical phenomenologists who specialize in philosophical anthropology. He applies their conclusions to his own field so long as they are compatible with the evidences provided by differential psychologies. If they are incompatible, he fosters a prolonged dialogue between philosophical anthropology and the contradictory evidences of his own field until a sufficient clarification has been attained by both.

CHAPTER TEN

APPLICATION OF THE PHENOMENOLOGICAL METHOD

Existential psychology is not a special school or a specific method. It is an approach to the study of intentional - functional behavior. Therefore, a research scientist of any school or area of psychology can adopt the existential attitude without having to give up anything essential to his own differential psychology. This attitude implies continual vigilance; it guards against any form of subjectivism, which might distort research, interpretation, the formulation of conclusions, or the application of these findings to psychological practice. Subjectivism is the one-sided attempt by an investigator to impose man-made categories, methods, and schemata upon objectively-given data.

Subjectivism may take any of four forms in my work as a psychologist. In the first form, I approach my object of study, man, exclusively with the methods of physical science, even though many actual and observable aspects of man, in their objective givenness, cannot be circumscribed by such methods. Second, I may use exclusively intuitive methods in my study of man, even though the aspects of behavior under investigation lend themselves more readily to empirical and statistical methods. Third, I may consider as valid only a few of the many effective research methods developed by psychologists, even though objective aspects of my investigation require other approaches. Finally, I may fall into subjectivism by the dogmatic assertion that positive science, as a theory of man, is capable of providing all possible insights into human existence.

I call such approaches subjectivistic because they arise not from my observations of objective reality but from an *a priori* concept which I, the subject, hold about reality.

The main source of my subjectivism is my refusal to open myself first to the phenomena as they are given to me, and only then to decide which methods, categories, and statistical approaches should be developed in order to investigate these phenomena. Existential psychology demands that my potential data be observed as they exist before I attempt to interpret them.

I can open myself to the phenomena themselves in either a critical or an uncritical way. The critical method of observation implies the use of the phenomenological method. This method leads, ideally, to the type of description and classification of phenomena which can be affirmed by experts in the same field of psychology. Research performed in this way is pre-empirical, pre-experimental, and pre-statistical; it is experiential and qualitative. It sets the stage for more accurate empirical investigations by lessening the risk of a premature selection of methods and categories; it is object-centered rather than method-centered. Such preliminary exploration does not supplant but complements the traditional methods of research available to me.

I shall consider briefly the phenomenological method in relation to research in psychotherapy. Such research clearly implies scientific investigation of the *human* process of psychotherapy by means of empirical methods. The qualification "human" is crucial here. The process of human psychotherapy is not merely a bio-chemical, physiological, or gross motor process. Therefore, research in psychotherapy must take into account—at least implicitly—the specifically *human* character of the process. I wish to emphasize by the use of the term "human" that the process of therapy manifests features that are true only of human relationships. In addition, I use the term "human" to refer to man as a concrete unity, manifesting himself in concrete human behavior. This use of the word "human" implies that I reject the artificial split, introduced by Descartes, which separates man into an "internal (thinking) substance" and an "external (objective) substance." This dualism of Descartes has led to a dualism in modern psychology. There are schools of psychology which claim one-sidedly that the internal substance can be used to explain the whole man; the interior substance for them takes the form of an interior self, with drives, dynamics, needs, or complexes. Other psychologists attempt to explain the whole man in terms of the external substance; for them, man's reactive organism, artificially isolated from his intentionality and purposiveness, is his essential nature.

The anti-dualistic, or existential, viewpoint is significant for the development of research in psychotherapy. It enables me as a psychologist to perceive the behavior of man as a concrete unity of orientation and of the embodiment of this orientation in observable behavior. Thus I can use empirical methods in the study of man without fearing that I may have hidden some crucial aspect of his behavior behind a methodological screen. I can reach conclusions about him as a whole person which are susceptible to intersubjective affirmation by other observers in my field. In my research, I am no longer dependent on perceptions and insights which are accessible only to me as one single psychotherapist, or to one exclusive group of psychotherapists.

At this point I should perhaps ask myself, what is the specifically human character of my object of research? How does it differ from the object of the physical sciences? The latter study man as an organism dependent on an environment and defined biologically. Physical science can, therefore, provide me with valuable information regarding physical, physiological, and biological foundations of psychotherapy. As a human scientist, however, I study man as the originator and cultivator of his world. I do not focus my attention exclusively on biological conditions, therefore, but on all of the observable interactions between two or more persons. It would be an intrusion of subjectivism into the realm of psychotherapy were I to eliminate on principle the human interpersonal aspect of therapy from the field of scientific investigation. This aspect appears objectively and undeniably in my perception.

To be sure, my methods of study must lead to scientific propositions. However, I would hold a subjectivistic, *a priori* concept of science if I should dogmatically declare: Only those propositions are scientific which have been established by the methods of mathematics and of the natural sciences. It would be more complete to say: Only those propositions are scientific which have been proved valid according to certain rules and which can be verified by many independent observers who are experienced in this particular area of observation. Research in psychotherapy as a human science can thus be defined as the investigation of the objective aspects of therapeutic interaction by means of an objectifying approach. This approach will necessarily lead to the establishment of useful constructs, such as libido, Oedipus complex, resistance, transference, reinforcement, client-centeredness. Here again, the existential attitude will protect me from the danger of subjectivism which threatens my objectivity in every phase of my research. I must remind myself constantly of the fact that such constructs, while closely connected with my perceptions in psychotherapy, nevertheless transcend the level of perception.

The study and practice of psychotherapy, from one or another viewpoint, provide an opportunity to form these constructs. A language or framework of these constructs might even be devised on the basis of their interconnection. This frame would then permit therapists not only to organize their observations, but also to communicate with those who study psychotherapy from the same standpoint. This possibility of organization and communication by means of interconnected constructs has led to the development of various useful frames of references such as the Behaviorist, the Client-centered, and the Psychoanalytic. However, to prevent the intrusion of subjectivism, I should constantly be aware that no framework used for research and practice in psychotherapy will possess an absolutely binding character. It represents an attempt to understand, systematically and from one specific viewpoint, the potentially inexhaustible wealth of interactions which constitute the total process of psychotherapy. Such frameworks are not themselves the total possible interactions of psychotherapy, they are merely models which enable us to grasp *something* of this complete reality. The existential position in psychology implies that all such scientific frames of reference are not "true" nor "false", but only "useful" or "useless", "effective" or "ineffective". The sole criterion which the existential view demands for each frame of reference is: Does it increase our knowledge of the objective process of psychotherapy? A frame may be "effective" for the understanding of one objectified aspect of behavior while quite "ineffective" for the understanding of another. For example, the scientific model of Behaviorism is useful for the exploration of the behavior of animals in artificial surroundings, but it is inadequate for the understanding of certain specifically human aspects of the therapeutic interaction. I should become the victim of subjectivism, therefore, if I were willfully to force the objectively-given phenomena of human interaction into such a frame merely because it has been successfully used in another type of research.

I may use any methods only provisionally, always being ready to change them when they do not lead me to better understanding of the objective phenomenon under study. I should always drop methods devised by investigators, who are the *subjects* of research, if the *object* being investigated seems to expose aspects of behavior for which the methods are inadequate. Therefore it is most helpful for me to make my first approach that of a phenomenological method, which does not confine or restrict the phenomenon under study to a structure of established theoretical constructs.

To illustrate the process of such preliminary phenomenological research, I have selected one relatively simple concrete phenomenon that appears in psychotherapy. The patient at times "feels really understood" by the therapist. What is the fundamental structure and meaning of this experience of "feeling understood?" I shall answer this by outlining at least the main steps which I followed in my explication of this phenomenon.

Application of the Phenomenological Method

Preliminary Considerations*

"Feeling understood" is a human experience. When one reflects on the character of human experience, one becomes increasingly impressed by its complexity. It seems to be continually moving; it suggests an appearing and disappearing of perceptions, needs, emotions, which interact in various ways. New moments come continually to the fore, changing the total picture; a dynamic picture that would seem to forbid the rigid isolation of a perception or a feeling. These changes appear only as moments, as mutually-dependent parts of a process.

On the other hand, these mutually-dependent moments do not appear as identical with one another, nor with the process of human experience as a whole. The feeling of love for a girlfriend is quite obviously different from the feeling of being bored with a teacher. The experience of disappointment over bad weather is nothing like the feeling of delight at being understood by a sympathetic listener. In everyday life the experiences of feeling understood, feeling rejected, feeling fascinated, and feeling threatened are experienced as different from one another. Even when they are present at the same time, they are not experienced as intrinsically identical. One might feel delighted, for example, that somebody really understands him, and at the same time experience a surge of admiration for the kind person who understands. Thus people distinguish one experiential phenomenon from another. They do not seem able, however, to isolate them as rigidly as they do physical entities.

Complexity and fluidity are characteristic not only of the experiential process as a whole, but also of each specific moment of experience. "Feeling understood" is conceived of in everyday life as distinct from other moments of experience, though even a superficial observation makes it clear that this

*This part of the chapter is based on my Ph.D. dissertation submitted to the department of psychology, Western Reserve University. I wish to express my gratitude to Dwight W. Miles and George W. Albee for their encouragement and advice, and to Carl Rogers, A. H. Maslow, and Kurt Goldstein for many stimulating discussions.

specific experience also displays a complexity and fluidity of its own.

Some of the subjects whom we questioned experienced this feeling globally, as being understood in their whole person. They specified no distinct problem or specific emotion that had been grasped by the person doing the understanding. Other subjects, on the contrary, emphasized that a specific problem or a peculiar feeling had been understood by the person. Thus there was a definite distinction in emphasis. Nevertheless, in both descriptions the experience of really feeling understood was always present. And in both, mention of the emotions that seem most often to accompany this experience appears in the reports of the subjects.

Another example of the complexity and fluidity of this specific experience may be seen in the feeling of relief reported by many of the subjects. It seems to relate, in one way or another, to their experience of being understood. But we also know that relief can be found outside this specific experience, for example, after successfully passing a test. Relief, therefore, is probably not a feature that in and by itself distinguishes the experience of being understood from all other experiences.

Still another sign of complexity may be found in the differences of intensity of feeling. A subject who talks about the precious moment in a love relationship in which she felt really understood for the first time in her life, shows a deeper relief, a more overwhelming joy, than a highschool girl who tells about a teacher who understood her inferiority feeling about her lack of accomplishment in mathematics. In the former case, the elation led to gross somatic phenomena such as a pounding heart and a quivering body, while in the latter, the more moderate feelings of relief were accompanied by somatic changes so slight that the subject did not mention them.

Thus the moment of experience labeled "feeling understood" does not appear at first glance to be clearly delineated in the totality of the experience. It does not seem possible to isolate this phenomenon as one would a chemical element. Nevertheless, there must be something in the experience itself that makes us label it as "feeling understood." For feeling understood is certainly not experienced as feeling bored or feeling rejected. It must be possible to discover that which is characteristic of the feeling of being understood, that which constitutes this specific moment of experience.

Research Question Evoked by the Phenomenon

The average person is probably not pained by any problem concerning the feeling of being understood so long as his life develops smoothly. The problem poses itself only when he is in acute need of giving or receiving understanding. Then it may take such forms as: "How can I understand my wife? my girl friend? my teenage son or daughter? my employee? my boss?" Or, "How can I make myself really understood by people who do not understand me, and who misinterpret my behavior?" Many times the person works out a successful response to his question; a concrete response that helps him to find understanding in a specific situation and to respond to a certain type of person in a special way. At other times, he does not discover a satisfactory response.

For the psychologist, the phenomenon of feeling understood is thought-provoking. He becomes aware daily that this feeling may be very important in the life of an individual. He observes changes in other feelings, attitudes, and behavior that accompany or follow this emotional experience. It appears to him that the lack of this experience might hinder the full development of certain aspects of the personality. He observes this situation more dramatically when he is a clinical psychologist treating daily, in institutional or private practice, a number of clients. His considerations may make him curious about the inner structure of the phenomenon he observes. Therefore he may decide to make it an object of scientific research.

The question he will ask himself is: What is this phenomenon? What exactly is this feeling of being understood and what distinguishes it from every other subjective experience? Or, to formulate the question more exactly: *What are the necessary and sufficient constituents of this feeling?*

Another aspect of the problem of feeling understood is still to be considered—not a psychological but a philosophical-anthropological one. Approaching the feeling of being understood in a philosophical way, one would ask: "What does the existence of this feeling tell me concerning the nature of man, or how can I conceive this feeling in the light of my view of the nature of man?" To be sure, it is impossible to approach human nature directly. One can understand it only through its expression. But there are innumerably more expressions of human nature than that of feeling understood. These other expressions, at least some of them, have already provided us with philosophies of man. Therefore, conclusions concerning human nature, as they are expressed in the phenomenon of the feeling of being understood, already presuppose a more or less developed, explicit or implicit, view of man on the part of the psychologist. This presupposed specific view of man will make for different conclusions held in accordance with respectively different philosophies of man. It will vary in the light of the implicit philosophical views of man developed by various psychological scientists, for example, the Freudians, the Jungians, the Adlerians, and the Behaviorists. It would be interesting to determine what "feeling understood" would mean in the light of these various implicit philosophies.

It would also be a fascinating and challenging task to build a philosophy of man on the phenomenon being studied, as has been done by so many psychological scientists on the phenomena with which they were especially concerned. But, without denying the intellectual delight of projecting a philosophy of man from the vantage point of one or another psychological phenomenon, the existential psychologist still prefers not to transcend the limits of his empirical observation and will not do so in this study.

Method of Approach to the Phenomenon

The deductive method in science attempts to discover particular validities by beginning with universal ones. The particular validities are then assumed to be contained within the universal law. But such a method does not seem useful for the discovery of the necessary and sufficient constituents of the experience of feeling understood as introduced above.

Some psychologies, like the Freudian, the Jungian, and the Behavioristic, departing from an accepted view of man, formulated certain universal principles or laws concerning the human personality. But it does not seem desirable to start from any of these laws in order to identify the experience that is called "feeling understood." For such a procedure would presuppose that this experience is encompassed in the general implicit philosophy of man developed by the school chosen. Assuming this philosophy *a priori* might influence the explication of the data. One would proceed from certain general principles held by the school, and then, theorizing from these, might develop conclusions concerning a situation to which these principles are applicable. This situation would then be said to be the experience which people call "feeling understood."

But to determine what kind of experience is called "feeling understood" and how it is experienced is precisely the problem of our research. By using the deductive method in the way indicated, we would suppose that we already have a concept of "feeling understood," whose content and applicability are already defined. We would be assuming an answer before even exploring our problem. Therefore, in this phase of our research, the method used must necessarily be inductive. We must start from the various data of experience in order to formulate a valid description covering the various data of the sample.

We shall begin by examining man's awareness. Long before we studied psychology, even when we were children, we were aware of people, of their actions, of how they felt. We were also aware of ourselves, of our own feelings, thoughts, and desires. At that time, it was perhaps difficult for us to formulate a concept of this natural awareness. But we were sure that we experienced this way of knowing. Every human being possesses an elementary awareness of his experiences, though he may not be able to translate his awareness into clear psychological statements. This primordial human awareness encompasses an extensive field. One knows in this way all subjective experiences, such as feeling rejected, feeling thankful, feeling sorry, or feeling understood.

Every psychologist who deals with experience begins, consciously or unconsciously, with awareness. Otherwise, it would even be impossible for him to experience what people are talking about when they say that they "feel understood." He would also be unable to understand in an experiential way the external signs of the experiences of relaxation, joy, and relief in a person who feels understood. Precisely because a person himself has been aware of a particular feeling at one time or another, he is able to experience what his fellowman attempts to communicate when he says, "I feel understood."

This primary awareness of experience brings man into immediate contact with his own loving, hoping, suffering, experiencing self. Man's experience may be complex, but it is present to his awareness in its complex totality. On the other hand, although it is true that his experience is immediately present to him in all its complexity, this does not mean that every moment that is contained in a specific experience is distinguished by him exactly and distinctly as it is.

Awareness cannot be proved; no more than one can prove that red is red or that perceiving is perceiving. But everyone observes experience in himself. In others words, experience is a primary datum that in itself cannot be proved.

Explication of Awareness

When man begins to think or to speak about his experiences, he is attempting to express his awareness. It is by this formulation that awareness becomes conceptual knowledge. Only when we have expressed our experience in clear statements, concepts, and judgments can we proceed in a scientific manner. The scientific discussion of a phenomenon requires first of all an exact idea of what it contains and an accurate formulation of this idea. Such a precise formulation is our aim in attempting to identify and describe the necessary and sufficient constituents of the feeling of "being understood". The accurate distinction of the various moments in this feeling syndrome is necessary in order to prevent confusion with other subjective phenomena. We need to find appropriate terms that will enable us to communicate with other scientists concerning the phenomenon under discussion.

This formulation will provide us with a new and more explicit way of knowing the experience of feeling understood. What we wish to express is already known to us, but we know it only in a vague way. The knowledge is imperfect, confused, and disordered. Science makes clear a knowledge of experience which is vague and imprecise. In other words, science formulates explicitly what was experienced implicitly in awareness. We label this process *explication*. By explication, implicit awareness of a complex phenomenon becomes explicit, formulated knowledge of its components. The process is loosely analogous to therapy, in which the patient gradually learns to express his implicit, vague, painful self-experience in an explicitly labeled description of what is going on in his subjective life.

Explication always starts from awareness, without which it would lose its validity. One would only be expressing terms unrelated to a known reality. Moreover, awareness also constitutes the final aim of the explication. Explication produces an *enlightened* awareness in which the constituent elements of experience are precisely represented. Here again the process of psychotherapy offers an analogy. The labeling of the experience by the patient results in a sharper, enlightened awareness, for example, of his feeling of hostility.

The first endeavor of the psychologist is to change vague awareness into a more detailed conceptual knowledge. Often psychologists deviate from one another in their conclusions only because they formulate their original awareness without a scientific observation of it as it is actually present in sufficiently varied samples of subjects. This neglect of scientific rigor in the decisive first phase of research often forms a striking contrast to the following scientific build-up by means of deductive and inductive procedures. Many scientists use faultless scientific designs which are nevertheless powerless to compensate for the inexact, popular, or introspective notions which initiated their research. Thus differences in explication of awareness, the most important step in every research concerning experience, cause unnecessary but fundamental dissensions among psychologists.

The present study of the phenomenon of feeling understood will be primarily an explication of awareness. In other words, this research will deal predominantly with the first and decisive phase of the scientific objectivation of experiential phenomena.

From what has been said, it will be obvious that the norm can only be awareness itself. The psychologist must restrict himself in his explication to the expression of what is given in awareness. During the process of explication he ought not to involve himself in any implicit philosophizing, be he of a Freudian, a Behavioristic, a Stimulus-Response, a Jungian, or any other school.

When the psychologist has finally expressed awareness, he translates it necessarily into a series of psychological statements. But, in doing this, he must follow the data of awareness. He must not go beyond the content of his data in his attempt to express it. His explication is valid and reliable only insofar as it is really an "expression," uncolored by the flavor of a typical school.

Problems of Method Involved in the Explication

The possibility that the psychologist may express more than is given in the awareness, especially if he attempts to base his explication on his limited personal experience, has been indicated as a major problem. We shall deal with this problem at length.

Another factor that hinders the process of explication is the lack of descriptive concepts in psychology. This lack may be explained as follows. Phenomena of experience are different from the pure physical kind which man is aware of by means of his sensory equipment. Joy, hate, hope, guilt, love, feeling understood are never met with as such in the physical universe. The extent to which they differ from physical phenomena determines the degree of difficulty of expressing them in concepts and statements. This is so because concept-formation is very dependent on our sense-knowledge of the physical universe. This fact makes it difficult to explicate the non-physical phenomena of experience by means of concepts that find their origin in the knowledge of physical phenomena.

Many subjects, for example, describe a feeling of relief when being understood. The term "relief" seems to be an apt expression for a certain feeling. But it is by no means an original psychological label. It was first used to describe the action of someone's lifting-up of a physical object that exercised pressure on someone else's body. This lifting-up resulted in measurable changes in physical and physiological characteristics. At the same time, the subject experienced an emotion accompanying these changes. Soon the label of the physical experience, "Lifting up," "Relief," was applied to the experience itself. Gradually all experiences of becoming free of guilt, anxiety, worries, were labeled as feelings of relief. The sudden unburdening of one's bent, tired back, when somebody removes a heavy load became a striking image of what is felt when another frees us of our conflicts, anxieties, or sickly suspicions.

It is sometimes impossible to express directly certain forms of experience. The subject feels forced to use comparisons and metaphors borrowed from the world of sensible physical events and objects. By means of these indirect media he attempts to convey his inner experience. The explication of the feeling of being understood is no exception. The person who explicates has to use comparisons, metaphors and terms, as for instance, "relief," that cannot be understood in a literal way. This fact obliges us to use special safeguards because an indirect description may easily lead to inexactness.

In awareness one experiences the living, concrete, dynamic totality of feeling understood. But the explication violates this reality by breaking down its natural unity. This is so because the explication necessarily expresses itself in a series of psychological statements. Each statement expresses only a part of the concrete experience. The explication fixates that which in reality is process. The expression becomes a sum of separate formulae expressing the necessary and sufficient components of this process. It comprehends that which is concrete and individual in universal statements. It exteriorizes that which is interior. But the whole series of psychological statements, however perfect, will never express fully the living process of the experience itself.

Anyone who has never had the experience himself cannot know what it is like from its description alone. Nevertheless, the attempt to give expression to it is necessary for psychology, for the purpose of explication is not the explication itself. It aims at a new, more clear and detailed definition of an awareness, which will enable the psychologist to understand human experience more distinctly. The implications of this objectivation for personality-theory, therapy, education, test-construction, cultural and social psychology are evident.

Explication of the Self-Awareness of the Scientist

One method of explication of the experience of feeling understood is to observe one's own experience of this phenomenon and to express it as faithfully as possible. After this self-explication, one might ask a sampling of subjects whether their experiences have been similar. But this method has disadvantages and pitfalls.

The scientist who begins with his own analyzed experience may be prejudiced from the very beginning. It is far from easy to determine precisely what feeling understood is. The experience is mixed with other emotions which are dependent on a variety of conditions in the particular situation in which feeling understood is experienced. Between boy and girl, the experience of mutual understanding might be blended with the onset of love; in the therapist-patient relationship, it might be influenced by a feeling of belief in some occult power in the therapist.

Similarly, the personal experience of the scientist himself may be colored by elements that are not a part of feeling understood in its pure form. It is possible that he may not perceive that his explication is contaminated by features of the type of situation which he himself has predominantly in mind when concentrating on feeling understood. When he tries, after explicating his one-sided experience, to find out how other people feel, he may be prejudiced in his way of questioning them or of devising tests to find out whether they have had a similar experience, for he is the one who determines the classifications of his tests or questionnaires. And classifications operate as suggestive limitations for the subjects who are submitted to them.

Another disadvantage of the primary explication of one's own experience is the possibility of carrying out the process under the influence of theoretical prejudice. One might be trained, for example, in a certain personality theory. It might be that feeling understood is defined in this theory in a prescientific way, based on the impressions and feelings of the persons who represent these theories. It might even be that the psychologist is no longer aware that this vaguely defined concept of feeling understood is only an interesting "hunch" not empirically validated. In this case, the personal explication of the feeling might follow the line of the subjectivistic notion that one is trained to believe in. The result will again be slanted questionnaires, or distorted tests, always proving that the researcher is right. Other deviating experiences cannot be expressed because no provision is made in the categories for their spontaneous expression.

A further disadvantage is that the explication of one's personal experience is not open to scientific control. The expert may be prejudiced while explicating his own experience of feeling understood, but there is no way for other scientists to control the correlation between the explication and the awareness of the psychologist.

Some psychologists aim at objectivity by communicating their explication to cooperators who are expected to produce compensatory views. But the extreme complexity of the experience itself, its quality as process, its combination with many other elements in the situation render this method inadequate. The communication of what is experienced when feeling understood is easily influenced by elements of the communication-situation itself. Implicit, slight, mutual suggestions might modify in the participants, in a subtle way, the experience itself and the direction of the process of explication. Moreover, the cooperators would almost all be experts in the field of psychology. This situation could lead to a compounding of professional prejudices. For these reasons, it does not seem scientifically desirable to begin with an explication by the psychologist of his own experience of feeling understood.

Prescientific Explication by Others

Another method of explication would begin, not with one's own experience, but with the accumulation of explications obtained from samples of untrained subjects. Then the scientist would begin with his own explication of the raw observable data of the objectified experiences written down in these descriptions. In explicating these data of behavior, systematically comparing them with one another, he would attempt to find the underlying constants. Untrained subjects would probably produce a greater number and variety of situations in which they felt understood. This advantage would increase the scientific value of the method, for it would mean a natural variation of the independent variables. It would enable the psychologist to distinguish that which is constant from that which varies in the different situations. Thus he would have an increased probability of discovering the factors common to all experiences of feeling understood. Finally, the scientist would be better able to control the explication of the common human awareness objectified in the various descriptions.

The justification of this procedure rests on the following suppositions:

1. Feeling understood is a relatively common human experience.
2. Common human experience is basically identical.
3. This basically identical human experience is expressed under the same label.

Let us consider the validity of these suppositions.

The feeling of being understood is obviously a reality not only in the clinic or in the office of the therapist; it happens in daily life. People tell us that they have felt really understood at one time or another, by one person or another, in certain situations. Therefore, we may suppose that most people have at least a vague notion of what it is to feel understood.

There are people, however, who contend that they do not know what it means to feel understood. It seems to be true that a certain number of them really do not know what this feeling means because they have never had the experience. It appears, however, that most people who contend that they do not know this experience really mean that they do not know how to express it. That they do know the feeling is evident from the fact that they distinguish feeling understood from other feelings in the same way as other people do who also contend that they do know the experience. When questioned about it, they distinguish feeling understood from feelings of being hated, of being hurt, of being praised, and so on, just as the majority of people do. Therefore, they must be aware of this specific experience, at least basically and vaguely. Since a significant majority of people make this distinction regularly and in the same way, we assume that feeling understood is a relatively common human experience, in spite of the fact that not everyone is able to express it.

There are many and different circumstances in which people experience this phenomenon. Some subjects, when asked about feeling understood, will think immediately of the quiet moments of love in their lives. Others are reminded of the difficult hours in which they felt compelled to seek advice from an understanding representative of their religion. Others, again, remember a good friend who knew how to listen in a deeply interested way when a worry was confided to him. Still others cherish the moment in which they were able to communicate their elated feeling about a musical performance and were filled with joy when their companion felt the same elation, and communicated in an understanding glance and smile.

If we collect descriptions of the feeling of being understood, then we have to assume that others are focusing their attention on basically the same kind of feeling that we are when we describe our experience. This statement is founded on the supposition that experience, with all its phenomena, is basically the same in various subjects. It presupposes that other people experience basically the same sensations, perceptions, images, needs, desires, feelings, and intellectual acts that the scientist experiences.

This basic identity of experience is an axiom in psychology. The building of experimental psychology rests on this foundation. This general working hypothesis can never be proved, but it is accepted as long as, and to the extent that, it is not refuted by contrary facts. When an experimenter has the experience of seeing a rat in a maze, for example, then he presupposes that other observers have had the same experience, and that they therefore understand what he means when he expresses his experience, "rat," which follows the physical exposure of his sensory equipment to waves coming from the grey object, and impinging on the nerve ends in his sense organs. It does not seem unreasonable then to accept this axiom of the experimental psychologist, when one deals with what could be called normal individuals belonging to similar groups.

This axiom seems to be confirmed by daily experience. If there were not a basic identity of experience, then it would be impossible for us to communicate with one another. This underlying identity seems to be, in fact, the basis of the cultural uniformity represented in the labels attached to various phenomena. This is why people understand what the experimenter means when he says "rat" or "this color on the color wheel is red." Similarly, we say that other people do understand what is basically meant when somebody says, "I am happy," or "I am bored," or "I feel sad." In other words, by understanding one another regularly and continually in daily life, people feel sure that they are referring to basically the same feelings when they use the same term.

We cannot deal here with the genetic history of this uniformity. It is clear, however, that growing up in a certain culture is the common way to learn the language symbols that are used to communicate the common experiences in that culture.

The uniform cultural label helps people to understand one another in general outlines, when expressing certain experiences. The labeled experience represents, at least basically, the same feeling. It might be true that a few members of the culture deviate from the common pattern, even in general outlines. But one perceives this deviation immediately. If a person says that he feels really understood by somebody, and the other answers: "Congratulations! And when are you getting married?", then it is clear that the person responding in this manner does not understand the specific experience that is expressed. He labels with "feeling understood" an experience which, by the significant majority of people in his culture, is called "love." The deviation from the socially accepted code of labeling is evident. But it is not always so clear, especially if one is dealing with experiences that are closely related to one another, or that regularly manifest themselves at the same time.

It is improbable, for example, that the label "feeling understood" comprehends, in an absolute sense, the same elements for everyone in every situation. Our data reveals immediately that feeling relaxed, feeling "loosened up" inside, feeling relieved, feeling wanted and respected, feeling important, and feeling that one is taken seriously, approach very closely the feeling of being understood. There is also a relationship between this experience and one of insight into personal problems, or a new perception of the world.

In other words, one can only be certain that the *significant majority* of people label that experience as feeling understood which basically contains the necessary and sufficient constituents of the feeling. One cannot be certain that common people, or even scientists when dealing with this phenomenon in a philosophical or introspective way, really describe the pure feeling of being understood without blending with it other phenomena or characteristics of the specific situation in which it is experienced.

The blending of absolute and relative elements in the prescientific descriptions necessitates a second explication. The scientist now has at his disposal a number of crude, spontaneous, or prescientific explications made by untrained subjects. As we have seen, their being untrained made it probable that they would produce the data of their awareness without undue interference from implicit philosophies of schools of psychology. At the same time, the number and variety of their descriptions increase the probability that, when combined, they will touch on the underlying necessary and sufficient constituents of the experience.

These factors make it possible for the psychologist to begin the second phase of explication in a manner that is more subject to scientific control. He bases his explication on the raw data instead of on his own personal experience of feeling understood. Briefly, instead of analyzing and comparing the elements of the explicit awareness of his own experience, he analyzes and compares the written expressions of the explicit awareness of his subjects.

Scientific Phase of the Explication

The scientific explication is performed in six operations: listing and preliminary grouping, reduction, elimination, hypothetical identification, application, and final identification.

These operations do not always follow the indicated order, and tend to overlap one another. They form a set of ordered abstractions partly describing the complicated mental process that the phenomenological scientist experiences as a natural totality.

The first operation of the scientist is to classify his data into categories. These categories must be the result of what the subjects themselves are explicating. Therefore, the scientist makes his initial categories from empirical data, in this case, a sufficiently large random sample of cases taken from the total pool of descriptions. To insure the validity of this procedure, he must strive for intersubjective concurrence with other experts concerning the agreement of these initial selections with the data taken from the random sample. After this, the researcher analyzes every descriptive expression found in the samples and lists them. When necessary, the initial lists and groups are supplemented by others in order to encompass every basically different statement made by the subjects. Finally, in order to be recognized as objectively valid, the actual listing must be agreed upon by expert judges.

The final listing presents a review of the various moments of the feeling of being understood as described by various subjects. It also presents the percentages of these various elements in this particular population, a possible clue to the predominant features of the phenomenon.

Now that the elements are laid out for him in a quantitative and qualitative fashion, the researcher can proceed with the second operation of the scientific explication. He reduces the concrete, vague, intricate, and overlapping expressions of the subjects to more precisely descriptive terms. When, for example, a subject writes, "I feel a hundred pounds less heavy," or "A load is off my chest," the psychologist may reduce this statement to "a feeling of relief." To a certain extent, this operation of reduction was already active in the initial listing and preliminary grouping. It brings the necessary clearness and organization into the wealth of vivid and picturesque descriptions used by the subjects. Here also an intersubjective agreement among expert judges is necessary in order to prevent subjectivism in the selection of reduction terms. By comparing the different elements and the different descriptions in which they are used, the researcher attempts to determine those elements that might probably be said to be constituents of the experience of feeling understood.

By means of the same operation, he now attempts to eliminate those elements that probably are not inherent in the feeling of being understood as such, but rather are complexes which include being understood in a particular situation, or which represent a blending of the feeling of being understood with other phenomena that most often accompany it.

The operations of classification, reduction, and element-elimination result in the first hypothetical identification and description of the feeling of being understood. The identification is called hypothetical because it was hardly possible to take into account at once all the details of all the descriptions during the element-elimination.

Therefore, a fifth operation of the scientific explication is required, namely, the application of the hypothetical description to randomly selected cases of the sample. This tentative application may possibly result in a number of cases of feeling understood that do not correspond to the hypothetical formula. It may be that the formula contains something more than the necessary and sufficient constituents of feeling understood. In this case, the formula must be revised in order to correspond with the evidence of the cases used in the application. It may also be that some descriptions still contain elements that probably are not inherent in the experience of feeling understood as such, but rather characterize either the experience of feeling understood in a particular situation, or an experience other than the phenomenon under study. After careful analysis, the researcher again applies the operation of elimination. After such changes, the new hypothetical formula must be tested again on a new random sample of cases.

When the operations described have been carried out successfully, the formerly hypothetical identification of the phenomenon of feeling understood may be considered to be a valid identification and description. It is evidently valid only for the population represented by the samples. The validity lasts until other cases are presented which can be proved to be cases of really feeling understood, and which do not correspond to the necessary and sufficient constituents contained in the formula. The facts and only the facts remain the final criterion for the empirical scientist.

Choice of the Sample

As we have said, the subjects who write down their prescientific explications ought not to be specialists in psychology. Nevertheless, their difficult task requires certain abilities and the fulfillment of certain conditions. The chief ones are:

a. The ability to express themselves with relative ease in the English language.
b. The ability to sense and to express inner feelings and emotions without shame and inhibition.
c. The ability to sense and to express the organic experiences that accompany these feelings.
d. The experience of situations in which the subject felt really understood, preferably at a relatively recent date.
e. A spontaneous interest in his experience on the part of the subject.
f. An atmosphere in which the subject can find the necessary relaxation to enable him to put sufficient time and orderly thought into writing out carefully what was going on within him.

Which group of the population in our contemporary American culture would best fulfill these requirements? We arrived at the hypothesis that the group best suited for the prescientific explication of the experience of really feeling understood would most probably be a group of female high school seniors from an institute of learning recognized for its scholastic standards.

The high school senior, just at the end of her teen-age period, is on the threshold of adult life. Inner experience is beginning to take form more and more for her. She is in a stage of finding herself after the turbulence of the years of transition and assimilation, of meeting the new and the unexpected. This process leads her to spontaneous interest in her present and past emotional experiences that are for her as so many revelations of herself, the "self" that fascinates her in this period of synthesis. This spontaneous interest is especially true of her experience of really feeling understood. Many studies in adolescent psychology reveal that the period of her life that is now for the most part behind her was characterized by loneliness, insecurity, and bewilderment. Therefore, "really feeling understood by somebody" was a sometimes impressive experience for the lonely high school girl during this strange state of sudden self-discovery.

In order to discover the necessary and sufficient constituents of the phenomenon under study, moreover, the researcher should have at his disposal explications that cover a sufficiently wide range of situations that facilitates the isolation of that which is necessary and sufficient from that which is incidental or peculiar to specific kinds of situations.

The range of situations in which the average high school senior experiences the feeling of being understood is probably wider than it is for the average adult. The period of adolescence is replete with discoveries, emotional conflicts, new patterns of behavior, and seemingly daring adventures. These are the source of numerous anxious moments in which the teen-ager wonders whether anybody else could possibly understand her. The same situations are consequently occasions of finding understanding and enjoying this experience. In average adult life, the need for understanding is not spread over such a variety of situations as in adolescence. The average adult has found his way in life. He experiences in a culturally identical way many common life situations that are no longer new and strange to him. His need for, and his experience of, understanding seems to be more concentrated in certain areas, such as the experience of love.

Consequently, in order to obtain a sufficiently wide range of situations, a population of high school seniors seems to be preferable. A high school girl is still not absorbed, moreover, by the often hectic and disturbing influence of factory, office, or college life that might later lessen her sensitivity to experience. At the same time, since she has had a reasonably good training in English, she may now, as a senior, be skillful enough to express her inner experiences. And the school can provide the time, order, and well-organized surroundings necessary for serious concentration during the subtle enterprise of really expressing herself.

It is also recognized, at least in our culture, that the average female senses and expresses her inner feelings more easily and completely, when she really wants to, than males usually do. On the other hand, it seems probable that an increasing number of older, "adult" females in our culture, under the influence of certain vocational adjustments and social cultural variables, lose this quality to a certain degree. For all these reasons, it seemed to us that the best group of subjects available in our culture for the prescientific explication of the human experience of really feeling understood would be a group of female high school seniors who enjoy the qualities already described.

The basis of our sample is a group of 150 female high school seniors taken from five different senior classes of an all-girl Academy in Chicago, Illinois.

In accordance with our hypothesis, the average paper written by this group showed a livelier interest in self-experience and a more carefully elaborated description of it than the average papers presented by the subjects of other samples. The 150 papers represented a wide variety of situations and personalities with corresponding variety in descriptions. It was therefore relatively easy to isolate the consistent necessary and sufficient pattern. In spite of this, we made sure that a few samples, taken from a different population, presented us with the same basic picture. If analysis of these samples yielded the same necessary and sufficient constituents, it would contribute nothing to our investigation to make them as wide as our basic group, originally chosen for their supposed ease and spontaneity in sensing and expressing feelings. If the necessary and sufficient constituents had proved to be radically different, however, from those presented in the sample of the girls, we would have been obliged to expand these new samples.

In the latter samples, however, in spite of accidental differences and less spontaneous expression of feelings, we were confronted again with the same necessary and sufficient constituents. Therefore, we found no scientific necessity to increase the number of samples. They proved that the "average" self-expression of the "average" female high school senior in this specific

Academy was reliable in the essentials of its message, when given under the special conditions set up by the researcher. We combined the later samples with that of the high school seniors and formed one collection of empirical material on which to build our scientific explication.

The samples thus combined with that of the 150 female high school seniors were those of 95 male school seniors from another high school in Chicago and those of 60 female and 60 male students from a college in Pittsburgh.

Hence our total sample contained:

	150	Female High School Seniors
	95	Male High School Seniors
	60	Female College Students
	60	Male College Students
Total	365	Subjects

Formulation of the Paper Presented to the Subjects

The subjects were asked to write down their experience of really feeling understood. In every school concerned, a class hour was set apart for this task. During this hour, the subjects were free to spend as much time as they wished on this project.

Each subject received a blank paper, on top of which was the following information:

Age__________ Sex__________

1. Do *not* write your name or any other personal identification at the top of this paper.
2. Write *only* your age and sex on the top of this paper.
3. Describe how you feel when you feel that you are really being understood by somebody.
   a. Recall some situation or situations when you felt you were being understood by somebody; for instance, by mother, father, clergyman, wife, husband, girl friend, boy friend, teacher, etc.
   b. Try to describe how you felt in that situation (not the situation itself).

c. Try to describe your feelings just as they were.
d. Please do not stop until you feel that you have described your feelings as completely as possible.

This formulation was agreed upon by two other independent judges, Gene Gendlin and Anthony Barton, at that time psychologist-therapists at the Counseling Center of the University of Chicago.

Listing of the Data

A 20% random sample of 80 subjects was taken from the pool of 365 descriptions. The expressions contained in the sample were listed by three judges: Anthony Barton and Leonard Gottesman, psychologists at the Counseling Center of the University of Chicago, and the author.

A phenomenological explication bases itself on the data as presented by the subjects. This faithfulness to "the things as they appear" (phenomenon— that which appears) results in a wide range of listed expressions. Every expression revealing a moment of experience not manifested in formulations of other subjects must be written down, whether or not the researcher believes it to be worthwhile. Thus some formulations are included which are somewhat superfluous for a scientific explication aiming at the necessary and sufficient constituents of the phenomenon. Nevertheless empirical phenomenology, which is a return to the existential data, adheres to this procedure in order to exclude the influence of any implicit philosophy and to keep open for scientific control the process of explication on the basis of the prescientific data.

One advantage of this process is that disagreement among judges presents no problem. Independent listing and categorizing may reveal that one judge listed an expression of a subject that was not covered by the other judges; or it may show that one judge was not convinced that a particular expression of a subject was really covered in experience content by the formulation under which it was listed by his colleagues. The solution of the first case is to add the expression overlooked; of the second, to supplement the formulation which was doubted. In empirical phenomenology, the original expression of the subject is preferred, in principle, when an insoluble doubt arises as to whether or not a moment of experience is adequately expressed in analogous formulations.

A disadvantage is that some expressions will seem to express the same experience in overlapping ways. Nevertheless, the researcher will reduce them further only in the later process of scientific explication, so that every scientist reviewing his study may be able to control their elimination. In our case, the readjustment of the established list required the addition of a few original expressions overlooked by one or other of the judges.

With the initial list of expressions and the tentative groupings of different expressions made by the three judges as a first orientation, the author, with two other independent assistants, began the identification and classification into these broad initial classes of each expression in the 365 descriptions. Every original expression, when it represented some moment of experience not covered in the initial list, was added. The expressions were listed on the margins of graph sheets. When the analysis of a certain description yielded an expression closely similar to an expression on the margin, the index number of this description was placed in the next open square of the horizontal row corresponding to the expression listed. Hence the horizontal rows indicated both the number of subjects who used the same or analogous expressions and the index numbers of these subjects who used them. This latter information would be useful later for understanding those expressions which might be in contradiction to the formula that would be applied tentatively to the significant majority of the descriptions as a hypothetical identification of the necessary and sufficient constituents of the phenomenon described. (See "The Six Operations of the Scientific Explication.")

To insure objectivity, this further listing of the expressions in the 365 descriptions was done by three persons, two of them different from the judges who did the initial listing, namely Miss Kylikki Raitasuo, a Finnish student at the Counseling Center of the University of Chicago, Miss Sonia Eberhardt, and the author. New expressions or doubtful expressions were again brought to the attention of the other two judges of the initial listing and resolved in the manner indicated above. A similar procedure was carried out with some descriptions which on the whole did not apply to the question under study. Many subjects described not only the experience of really feeling understood, but also how they felt "when not understood," "when looking for understanding," "when trying to express themselves," and so on. The determination to categorize all data, and the awareness that in these descriptions the experience of really feeling understood might be revealed in negative or indirect ways, impelled us to list these expressions as carefully as the others.

Finally we arrived at a total of 157 different expressions listed under 16 different headings. The scope of this chapter does not make it desirable to publish the tables concerned.

Phenomenological Explication of the Data

Having listed the data quantitatively and qualitatively, we may now progress to the other operations of the phenomenological explication already described. The wealth of material could have been a source for a variety of investigations. Therefore the researcher had to be careful to remain faithful to his original objective, "the necessary and sufficient constituents of the experience of really feeling understood." Every operation of the scientific explication had to be performed in the light of this objective alone.

In the operation of further "Reduction," each one of the 157 expressions had to be tested on two dimensions:

1. Does this concrete, colorful formulation by the subject contain a moment of experience that might be a necessary and sufficient constituent of the experience of really feeling understood?
2. If so, it is possible to abstract this moment of experience and to label the abstraction briefly and precisely without violating the formulation presented by the subject?

After testing all the expressions on these two dimensions and ascertaining the moments of experience contained in them which were relevant to his objective, the researcher was able to take a second step. He now tested whether many of these seemingly different expressions really had in common the same relevant moments of experience which had just been discovered in each of them separately, by means of the former procedure.

Next, all expressions discovered in this way, as either direct or indirect representatives of a common relevant moment of experience, were brought together in a cluster. This was labeled with the more abstract formula expressing the moment common to all.

The reduction resulted in nine probably necessary and sufficient constituents, each of them heading a certain number of expressions in which they were originally contained, and each of these expressions accompanied by the percentage of descriptions in which it was present.

Next, the researcher began the final identification of each one of these moments of experience which, so far, were only "hypothetically" identified as necessary and sufficient constituents of the phenomenon of feeling understood. As indicated in the introduction, arriving at this final identification required a trying-out of the hypothetical experience-moment on random samples of cases.

The constituents which were identified in this way as being together necessary and sufficient for the experience under study had to be synthesized into one description, which then identified the total experience of really feeling understood.

Results of the Phenomenological Study

In this way, we arrived at the necessary constituents of the experience under study, with the following general operational definition: A necessary constituent of a certain experience is a moment of the experience which, while explicitly or implicitly expressed in the significant majority of explications by a random sample of subjects, is also compatible with those descriptions which do not express it. Nine constituents were finally identified as being together necessary and sufficient for the experience of "really feeling understood." These are condensed in the following table.

Table. Constituents of the Experience of "Really Feeling Understood" as Finally Identified, with Percentages of 365 Subjects Expressing Each Constituent, Explicitly or Implicitly.

Constituents of the Experience of "Really Feeling Understood"	Percentages Expressing the Constituents
Perceiving signs of understanding from a person	87
Perceiving that a person co-experiences what things mean to subject	91
Perceiving that the person accepts the subject	86
Feeling satisfaction	99
Feeling initially relief	93
Feeling initially relief from experiential loneliness	89
Feeling safe in the relationship with the person understanding	91
Feeling safe experiential communion with the person understanding	86
Feeling safe experiential communion with that which the person understanding is perceived to represent	64

The synthetic description of the experience of really feeling understood, containing these constituents, is given below, followed by a justification and explanation of each phrase of the description.

The experience of / "really / feeling understood" / is a perceptual-emotional Gestalt: / A subject, perceiving / that a person / co-experiences / what things mean to the subject / and accepts him, / feels, initially, relief from experiential loneliness, / and, gradually, safe experiential communion / with that person

/ and with that which the subject perceives this person to represent.

The experience of: The term "experience" is preferred to "feeling" because the data show that this phenomenon, commonly called feeling, contains perceptual moments too.

really: The adverb "really" added to "feeling understood" emphasizes the distinction between objective and subjective understanding. The latter includes the "what it means to me" element and the emotional involvement of the subject.

feeling understood: This popular expression is maintained because it is used by most people when they express this experience spontaneously.

is a perceptual-emotional Gestalt: The data compel us to distinguish between perceptions and feelings (emotions), the former being predominantly object-directed, the latter subject-directed. But the perceptions and emotions are interwoven in experience; the term "Gestalt" implies that the distinction we make between perceptual and emotional moments does not correspond to a separation in reality.

A subject, perceiving: The perceptual moment is mentioned first because of its priority in the explications obtained. The feeling of really being understood presupposes the perception of understanding as it is evidenced by various behavioral signs of understanding.

that a person: The subject perceives that a "person," a fellow human being, understands him in a personal way. The understanding person is not experienced only as an official, a teacher, an adult, or so on, but as being-a-person.

co-experiences: The understanding person shares at an emotional level the experiences of the subject understood. The prefix "co-" represents the awareness of the subject that the person understanding still remains another.

what things mean to the subject: The subject perceives that the person understanding experiences the events, situations, and behavior affecting the subject in the way in which they affect him, and not as they might affect others.

and accepts him: Even while sharing experiences of the subject which the person understanding does not accept personally, he manifests exclusively and consistently genuine interest, care, and basic trust toward the subject, whether or not the subject intends to change his views, feelings, or behavior.

feels, initially, relief from experiential loneliness: The initial feeling of relief is the joyous feeling that experiential loneliness, a disagreeable perceptual-emotional Gestalt, is receding to the degree that real understanding is experienced. The adjective "experiential" specifies that it is not primarily a physical loneliness, but a being-alone in certain psychological experiences.

and, gradually, safe experiential communion: This expresses that the subject gradually experiences that the self is in the relieved, joyful condition of sharing its experience with the person understanding. "Safe" emphasizes that the subject does not feel threatened by the experience of sharing himself.

with that person: The deep personal relationship between the subject and the person understanding is prevalent not only in the perceptual, but also, and still more fundamentally, in the emotional area. Therefore our synthetic description not only opens, but also closes with a reference to this person-to-person relationship.

and with that which the subject perceives this person to represent: When the person understanding typifies for the subject a certain segment of mankind, or perhaps all humans, or all beings, i.e., humanity and nature, or the all-pervading source of being, God, then the subject will experience communion with all those beings which are exemplified for him by the person understanding, and do this to the degree that this person is perceived as their representative.

Comparison with Other Approaches

As I have pointed out in an earlier article in the *Journal of Individual Psychology,* phenomenal analysis yields descriptive definitions of certain experiences which people in a given culture or subculture have in common. The experimental psychologist who works with the phenomenal method need not, however, stop here; he may deduce a number of testable hypotheses from the descriptive definition and submit these to experimental test. An example of such a study is that by Ex and Bruyn on the influence of mental set upon perception of identity and substitution. They found that paired subjects who have an intimate relationship with each other tend in their judgment to shift less toward the direction of the deviating judgment of their partner, than paired subjects who do not have such an intimate relationship. From a study such as this it becomes clear that there is no difference whatsoever in the technique of experimentation itself, with its functional-operational-statistical mechanics, as employed in phenomenological and in other psychologies.

Regarding the operations in the phenomenal analysis itself, a certain similarity to the usual analysis of an open-end question in an opinion survey will have been noted. The difference between the two methods is essentially one of objective. The phenomenal analyst restricts himself to one question, carefully aimed at obtaining spontaneous descriptions of subjective experience, and it is formulated so that the subjects are able to relate freely a wide variety of situations. The purpose is to discover the moments common to all individual experiences of the same kind. The survey analyst, on the other hand, typically uses a number of questions, which are formulated so as to obtain the specific reactions of certain populations to definite objects, persons, or events. His purpose is to understand a human experience not as such, but as an indicator of the way in which people are related to certain objects in a certain social environment. From this main difference follow certain differences in analyzing the data, which will not, however, be presented here.

In general, the differences between the phenomenological approach and other approaches lie not so much in the method as in philosophic assumptions, the nature of the hypotheses, the application of the results, and the areas of fundamental concern. While the old introspectionism was based on rationalism, and behaviorism is based on positivism, phenomenal-existential psychology is rooted in an original synthesis of certain tenets of positivism and rationalism, and of phenomenology and existential philosophy. A synthetic system of intelligible constructs, based on philosophical assumptions and tested out gradually, is still in its early phase in phenomenal-existential psychology. It is developing differently from that of other systems insofar as it is mainly concerned with the laws which govern human experience.

In forming hypotheses, phenomenal psychology tends to start from an overall analysis of the human situation in its immediate givenness; whereas introspectionism started from "objects" which were supposed to be inside the mind, isolated from the total existential situation; and behaviorism starts from the external aspects of behavior, isolated from their experiential content. The overall analysis by the phenomenologist of the concrete human situation in its givenness leads to a complex qualitative description of experiences in those situations, as we have seen above, from which further testable hypotheses may be deduced. The older psychologies tend to reduce the givenness of the situation to testable hypotheses much earlier. The result is that their hypotheses appear quite different and—at least in the opinion of the phenomenal psychologist—have less bearing on the concrete condition of human existence.

Regarding the application, the results of phenomenal psychology seem to be of greater use in reaching the deeper layers of common human existence, which is the concern of the present study. To the extent that phenomenal psychology is also and primarily interested in the explication of an experience in its individual givenness, its results are useful in problems of therapy and counseling, interpretation of personality tests, development of personality, creativity, and human relationships. The results of traditional academic psychologies seem to be of greater use in the construction of intelligence and aptitude tests, in problems of sensory perception, human engineering, mechanical learning, and industrial psychology. It is apparent, then, that the results of both kinds of psychology do not exclude but complement each other.

CHAPTER ELEVEN

ANTHROPOLOGICAL PSYCHOLOGY AND BEHAVIORISTIC ANIMAL EXPERIMENTATION

The aim of the present chapter is to make clear how the findings of animal experimentation can be integrated within a comprehensive psychology of human behavior. In other words, we shall look at the relevance of animal experimentation from the viewpoint of a comprehensive psychology of man. This does not mean that we deny that such experiments are relevant in many other important ways, even if they are not a contribution to the understanding of human psychology. Neither should the purpose of this chapter be confused with the question of the relevance of phenomenology to experimental psychology.[1]

Since the early part of the present century, experimentation in American psychology has almost exclusively used animals as subjects, and as a consequence many theories of behavior have been

---

[1]At Duquesne University one of my colleagues in experimental psychology, Dr. Amedeo Giorgi, is preparing a book on the relationship between phenomenological psychology and experimentation.

One of my students, Larry V. Pacoe, wrote a dissertation on the topic of this Chapter, which is based on my discussions with him while guiding his dissertation and on the final text of his unpublished M.A. thesis, *Anthropological Psychology and Behavioristic Animal Experimentation*, Duquesne University, June, 1963. The author graciously allowed the use in this Chapter of his final formulations on which we agreed during my guidance of his studies.

constructed on the basis of data collected from the study of subhuman organisms and the subsequent generalization of these findings and theories to human behavior. The entire process, involving experimentation, theory construction, and generalization to human behavior has been done within the behavioristic frame of reference. As we know, behaviorism approaches behavior with the methods of the physical sciences which lead to an interest in only the objectively defined and quantifiable aspects of behavior. The behaviorist aims at the construction of fully quantified theories of behavior, which implies that as he generalizes to human behavior, he is limited to dealing with only those human behaviors which can be quantified and for which he can establish some principle of similarity with the findings of animal behavior. As we have seen in earlier chapters, a comprehensive personality theory attempts to integrate all the substantiated insights of psychology insofar as they are relevant to the understanding of human behavior. Such an absorption of behaviorism's findings is only possible if the data collected by the behaviorist are clearly relevant to the understanding of human behavior.

The data collected by the behaviorist does not initially fulfill this requirement of evident relevance to the understanding of human behavior. Therefore, something further is needed. It is just this later demand with which this chapter is vitally concerned. We shall see that it is the phenomenological approach which eventually enables a comprehensive theory of personality to incorporate in a special way some of the findings of animal experimentation by means of a process of extrapolation which meets the particular needs of anthropological psychology. Our primary concern will be with a presentation and clarification of the principle of similarity as used by the behaviorists. The solution of our problem will be found in a special dimension of similarity, namely whether or not the similarity is seen at the concrete behavioral level or at the level of abstract scientific constructs. Anthropological psychology can only integrate those findings of animal experimentation which show unmistakably a correspondence between the *concrete* behavior of animal and man and not merely a correspondence on the level of abstract theoretical constructs. From our discussion it will become evident that a comprehensive theory of human behavior and the differential psychology of behaviorism require different kinds of data. Therefore, we shall at the end suggest a method of animal experimentation and a process of extrapolation which will be more directly relevant for anthropological psychology.

Most animal experimentation has been influenced by a particular differential theoretical position: behaviorism. The tenets of this differential scientific viewpoint have influenced experimental methodology, problems, selection of data, and the theoretical interpretation and extrapolation of results. To be sure, behavioristic psychology, like any other differential psychology, has differentiated itself into many divergent positions. Nevertheless, all psychologists who approach behavior from this specific differential viewpoint have certain attitudes and approaches in common that enable us to identify a psychologist as a behaviorist and not, for example, as a psychoanalyst or a self psychologist. For our aim, it is sufficient to realize that a behaviorist psychologist persistently attempts to meet the criterion of the physical sciences, that he strives after the complete quantification of all psychological variables in his experiments, and that these aims have led to a situation where the methodology dictates and necessarily limits the areas to be studied. The integrative theorist of human behavior must be aware that the data offered by the behaviorist captures only those aspects of the phenomenon which can be studied by quantitative methods, and that there may be other vitally important aspects of the phenomenon which have been ignored because they were not amenable to the available techniques.

Anthropological psychology focuses on the uniquely human aspects of man's psychological functioning and their physiological and other conditions, as well as those functions which man has in common with animals, such as conditioning. The chief concern of the behaviorist is learning, which is only one aspect of man's behavior, and touches on areas such as emotions, motivation, and anxiety only as variables associated with learning. The other possible approaches that can be taken on these phenomena are developed in other differential psychologies. Up to this point, the procedure is legitimate, but a problem emerges when the differential learning theorist wants to shift to a comprehensive psychology of human behavior and shows an inclination to explain all of human behavior in terms of learning only. Since the behaviorist has used animal experimentation as the basis for his theories, any attempt to explain human behavior must be founded on an extrapolation of animal findings. Extrapolation is defined: "To project by inference into an unexplored situation (some sequent) from observation in an explored field, on the assumption of continuity or correspondence."[2] The behaviorists are extrapolating from an area of animal behavior, which has been thoroughly explored, to the realm of human behavior in which very little experimentation has been done. The validity of this or any method of extrapolation lies on the basis of the assumption of continuity or correspondence between the two areas. In fact, the key to comprehending any method of extrapolation is to understand the principle of similarity that the scientist uses to provide a transition from one area to another.

There are different methods of extrapolation. We shall be concerned here with two main methods of extrapolation, namely, that used by the behaviorists and a method of extrapolation based on the approach of anthropological psychology. We shall compare these two methods of extrapolation on the basis of one dimension of similarity. This dimension is whether the similarity is seen at the concrete behavioral level or at the level of abstract scientific constructs. Similarity at the behavioral level demands that the scientist see correspondence between the concrete behaviors of animal and man. Similarity at the abstract, theoretical, conceptual level, however, demands only that the two behaviors meet the criteria of the scientific concepts, and there is no necessity that the observable behaviors be comparable.

---

[2]*Webster's New Collegiate Dictionary*, Springfield, Mass., G&C Merriam Company, 1960, p. 294.

The key to understanding the behavioristic approach to the study of behavior is to see clearly the behaviorist's attempt to attain objectivity, the hallmark of a natural science. Objectivity in the sense of high intrasubjective and intersubjective reliability could be attained best by using only pointer readings or physical measurements to record data.[3] The insistence on pointer readings implies another aspect of the behavioristic approach to behavior: abstraction.

Any pointer reading, any physical measurement is designed to measure only certain isolated parts of behavior such as a bar press, a change in electrical conductivity of the skin, etc. This means that only certain isolated parts of the total behavior or situation are included in the data. A Skinnerian, for example, is interested only in the bar press responses of the rat, and any other behavior is irrelevant insofar as his data is concerned. Whether the rat attempted to escape, chewed the side of the box, moved rapidly or slowly around the box is not recorded in the data, and consequently does not enter into his theory of behavior. Essentially the scientist is abstracting those aspects of the behavioral situation which fit the available methods of measurement and which are considered relevant by the theoretical system.

The behaviorist imposes the S-R paradigm on all behavior. He is interested in establishing functional relationships between the stimulating situation and the organism's response.[4] In essence, the behaviorist is assuming that all the relevant variables for understanding, predicting, and controlling behavior are implied in the S-R paradigm. Further, he assumes that by abstracting those variables from the total situation, he has the scientific essence of the organism's behavior;[5] he possesses those elemental atoms of behavior which transform the chaos, mystery, and seem-

---

[3]Leo Postman and Edward C. Tolman, "Brunswik's Probabilistic Functionalism," *Psychology: A Study of a Science,* Vol. I, Sigmund Koch, editor (New York: McGraw-Hill Book Company, Inc., 1959), p. 505.

[4]B. F. Skinner, *Science and Human Behavior* (New York: The Macmillan Company, 1953), p. 35.

[5]*Ibid.*

ing spontaneity of behavior into orderliness, clarity, and determinedness. This *a priori* S-R paradigm is partially the result of the standpoint that the behaviorist takes in relation to behavior.

In regard to the behavior he is studying, the behaviorist is an external observer who can see only the physical movements of the organism.[6] He sees the rat drink, the pigeon peck, or the human being raise his arm so many degrees. For the behaviorist, a shrug of disgust is simply an unreliable inference of the internal state of the organism, which is behind the behavior and not in it. This fixed viewpoint enables the behaviorist to group the mathematical orderliness of an organism's physically measurable behavior, but equally, it blinds him to the expressivity of behavior and to the experiential aspect of behavior.

In summary, the behaviorist's approach to the study of behavior is an adoption of the natural scientific methodology, in which the cornerstone is objectivity. This demand for objectivity is best met by physical measurement or pointer readings, which necessitate abstracting certain measurable aspects of the situation. These abstracted aspects are chosen *a priori* on the basis of the S-R paradigm, which points to the stimulating situation and the organism's response as the relevant variables which will enable the psychologist to understand, predict, and control behavior. Finally, in keeping with the traditional approach of the natural sciences, the psychologist takes the stand of an external observer who can see, scientifically speaking, only the external behavior of the organism and record his observations only in terms of physical measurement. It is from a position such as this that Skinner approaches the scientific study of behavior.

Skinner's Approach to Behavior

Skinner describes his approach in terms of a "functional analysis which specifies behavior as a dependent variable and proposes to account for it in terms of observable and manipulable physical conditions. . . ."[7] He is seeking to establish rela-

[6] *Ibid.*, pp. 35-36.
[7] *Ibid.*, p. 41.

tionships between the stimulating situation and behavior and thus to formulate scientific laws. Finally, "a synthesis of these laws expressed in quantitative terms yields a comprehensive picture of the organism as a behaving system."[8] This, in a few words, is Skinner's approach to psychology.

Skinner's method of extrapolation is based on the applicability of his abstract concepts to both animal and human behavior. From his experimentation with animals, Skinner has constructed a number of abstract concepts which he uses to explain behavior. Some of these constructs are operant conditioning, reinforcement, extinction, punishment, reinforcing schedules, etc. Each is defined in very abstract terms, such as reinforcement, which is any condition which tends to increase the probability of the response's occurring in the future.[9] On the basis of this definition, such widely divergent behaviors as a hungry rat eating a pellet and a worker getting incentive pay are considered as reinforcement. Thus, such an abstract definition can be applied to a wide variety of behaviors, regardless of the differences from one another in terms of the concrete, observable behavior. By defining his concepts abstractly in terms of probability and by not referring to the concrete behavior which is the basis of the concept, Skinner has built into his system a principle of similarity between the behaviors of all organisms. If the functional relationship as defined by his concept is the same for any two behaviors, he considers them as being subject to the same laws regardless of the difference between the concrete behaviors. This can be illustrated by returning to the previous example of the hungry rat getting a pellet for pressing a bar and the worker getting incentive pay for producing articles. It is obvious that there is no similarity in the concrete behavior of the rat and the man. However, Skinner sees a similarity in terms of his definition of reinforcement. Just as the food pellet increases the probability of the rat's pressing the bar in the future, the incentive pay increases the probability that the worker will produce

[8]*Ibid.*
[9]*Ibid.*, p. 65.

more articles. This similarity is the basis for Skinner's extrapolating the laws of behavior to man which he has created from his animal data.

In *Science and Human Behavior,* Skinner attempts to apply his concepts to such human behavior as self control, thinking, social behavior, group control, and social institutions. Skinner's discussion of self control will illustrate his method of extrapolation. Skinner begins with the assumption that man ". . . . controls himself precisely as he would control the behavior of anyone else—through the manipulation of variables of which behavior is a function."[10]

According to Skinner, an individual controls his behavior when it has both positive and negative results.[11] For example, drinking alcoholic beverages leads to confidence and sociability, which is reinforcing, and thus increases the probability of future drinking. However, a hang-over and irresponsible behavior are negatively reinforcing and have the effect of punishment—suppression of the response. The result is not a compromise between the positive reinforcing and punishment factors in which the person would drink only half as much as usual. Instead "when a similar occasion arises, the same or an increased tendency to drink will prevail, but the occasion as well as the early stages of drinking will generate conditioned adversive stimuli and emotional responses to them which we speak of as shame and guilt. The emotional response may have some deterrent effect in weakening behavior—as by 'spoiling the mood'."[12] More crucial, however, to the issue of self control, is that anything which reduces the drinking behavior is positively reinforced because it decreases the adversive stimuli such as guilt and shame. In Skinner's words, "The organism may make the punished response less probably by altering the variables of which it is a function. Any behavior which succeeds in doing this will automatically be reinforced. We call such behavior self control."[13]

---

[10]*Ibid.*, p. 228.
[11]*Ibid.*, p. 230.
[12]*Ibid.*
[13]*Ibid.*

Skinner continues the chapter with a list of the techniques of self control which point to parallels in the control of others. In his survey he enumerates physical restraint and physical aid, changing the stimulus, depriving and satisfying, manipulating emotional conditions, using adversive stimulation, drugs, operant conditioning, punishment, and doing something else.[14]

Skinner is quite aware that his survey does not explain why the individual uses these techniques. He solves this by stating that society is responsible for self control and the individual himself has little ultimate control. All self control can be accounted for by the variables in the environment and the person's history and, according to Skinner, "it is these variables which provide the ultimate control."[15]

One can see from this example of Skinner's extrapolation, that he is lifting his abstract conceptual system, which seems adequate for his animals, and placing it intact, without any modification, upon human behavior.

Skinner's first assumption that a person controls his behavior by manipulating the conditions of which the behavior is a function, is necessary for two reasons. First, in order for him to be able to apply his paradigm, both the dependent and independent variables must be observable; the observable response must be functionally related to an observable physical condition. Secondly, all of Skinner's experiments have followed a paradigm in which the experimenter manipulates the environmental situation and observes the changes in behavior. Consequently, all of his concepts are in the form: if this change is made in the stimulating situation, then the behavior will have such and such characteristics. Therefore, if he is to be able to apply his system of generalizations, he must assume that all human behavior is a function of the stimulating environment.

Also, Skinner's examination of self control illustrates the way that he uses his concept to explain both animal and human behavior. He states that the feeling of confidence which accom-

---

[14]*Ibid.*, pp. 231-240.
[15]*Ibid.*, p. 240.

panies drinking is a positive reinforcement; the confidence increases the probability that drinking will occur in the future.[16] This concept of positive reinforcement was created from such behaviors as a deprived rat's pressing a bar and receiving a pellet of food immediately afterwards. Naturally, Skinner found that the bar press response increased in frequency and that when food no longer followed the bar press, the frequency decreased. From experimental situations such as these, he created his definition of positive reinforcement, which is any stimulating condition which increases the probability of a response's occurring in the future. Skinner's extrapolation is based on the similarity between the rat and man in that they both have identifiable events which increase the probability of a given response's occurring in the future. In essence, Skinner's method of defining his concepts is in terms of the functional relationships between environmental conditions and behavior. It is important to note that there is nothing in his definition which specifies the kind of condition or behavior; he specifies only the relationship between the two variables. Thus, on this basis the bar press response of the rat and its relation to food pellets is equivalent to the drinking behavior and the feeling of confidence in man because the same concepts of behavior apply. Skinner's principle of similarity is the functional relationship between physical conditions and behavior.

One can see that Skinner's principle of similarity is abstract, in the sense that there need be no comparability between the concrete observable behaviors. It is also possible to base extrapolation on a principle of similarity in which the concrete observable behaviors of both the animal and man are comparable. Such a process, based on the phenomenological approach to psychology, may prove to be another fruitful method of seeing the similarities between animal and human behaviors.

While Skinner's method of extrapolation may prove to be productive, the anthropological psychologist is interested in a concrete phenomenological approach to studying behavior that is

---

[16]*Ibid.*, p. 230.

quite different from Skinner's abstract system. In Skinner's system, one is not able to see any comparability in the animal and human behaviors, because they are similar only in terms of the functional relationship between an unspecified stimulus and an unspecified response. Since the anthropological psychologist is interested in concrete situated behavior, another method of extrapolating animal findings to human beings must be proposed. In other words, a method of extrapolation must be found which incorporates the comparability of concrete behaviors. In order to arrive at such a proposal, this chapter initially will be concerned with the requirements of a system of extrapolation that meets the needs of anthropological psychology and phenomenology. Secondly, it will examine past and present work which points to a method of extrapolation consistent with the needs of anthropological psychology. Finally, an outline of a method of establishing similarity between the behavior of animals and man which incorporates the anthropological and phenomenological approach will be proposed.

Phenomenology and Extrapolation

One of the anthropological psychologist's main requirements for a system of extrapolation is implied in three tenets of phenomenology; namely, that all of man's knowledge is founded in the lived world of immediate experience, that man's knowledge is in the appearances of a thing or process, not behind it, and finally, that all of man's knowledge is perspective. Since these tenets are so closely related, it is practically impossible to show the implications that each has for a principle of similarity, but it is only possible to show the criterion which follows from all three as a unit.

The main requirement of relevance for anthropological psychology is that the principle of similarity in extrapolation must be built on an observable comparability between animal and human behavior. For example, if one is interested in the implications of mother-offspring relations in the monkey for the human mother-child relations, he must be able to establish comparability on the level of observable behavior. In other words, the behavioral interactions between the mother and offspring of both organisms must appear similar to a human observer. One can see that this requirement flows from the first two basic tenets of phenomenology, by the fact that it relies on the experience of a human observer to see the similarity between behaviors, and that it insists that the similarity must be in the observable behavior and not in the abstract scientific constructs.

One can immediately see that this principle of similarity differs from Skinner's in that he is interested in the concrete behavior only insofar as it can be used to establish the dependent and independent variables and the functional relation between them. In fact, the concrete behaviors and the aspects of the situation are defined as relevant on the basis of the scientist's being able to demonstrate a functional relationship between the two. So in Skinner's system there is the priority of the functional relationships between situation and behavior, and the concrete behaviors are of secondary importance. In the phenomenological system of extrapolation, the priority is quite different. The situated behaviors are the central focus and the abstract, conceptual constructs are subservient to the observable behavior. So the anthropological psychologist is seeking animal and human behaviors which appear to be observably comparable, rather than comparable in the abstract, ideal world of the scientific concept. However, this demand for concreteness does not sufficiently describe the principle of similarity, for the question remains: In what relevant dimension of behavior is the anthropological psychologist interested in finding comparable behaviors between animals and man?

Just as Skinner is interested in behavior which is a function of environmental conditions, the anthropological psychologist studies behavior from a particular standpoint. He focuses his attention on intentional behavior, which can be defined tentatively as purpose, or the orientation or directedness of the organism in its behavioral field. This definition can be concretely illustrated by placing a food-deprived rat in a variety of situations in which the food can be reached by various paths. For example, if a rat is placed in an open field situation with a variety of objects scattered throughout the box and food at one end, the rat moves through the box sniffing the different objects, and when he discovers the food, his behavior changes from sniffing to eating; if a relatively short barrier is placed between the rat and the food, he will climb over or go around it. If it is impossible for the rat to get past the barrier, he may attempt to burrow under it or chew through it, and once he is past the barrier he goes straight to the food and eats. The consistency of the rat's movements toward the food, even by long circular routes, indicates the intention or the purpose of the various behaviors.

Most psychologists deny that purpose is a legitimate area of empirical study because it violates the fundamental principle of science which rejects final causes.[17] In this view, all behaviors must be understood in terms of past events in order to fit the causal S-R paradigm. In spite of this widespread and emphatic rejection of purpose as part of behavior, there have been several psychologists who have attempted to develop a concept of purpose which is consistent with empirical psychology. The two outstanding men are E. C. Tolman and D. O. Hebb, who use purpose as an important construct in their systems.

Purpose in Tolman and Hebb

Tolman began writing about purpose as an important construct in 1925. Tolman was in the behavioristic movement from its beginning, and while he strongly believed in the basic behavioristic orientation, his writings were proposing ways of reincorporating many psychological phenomena which had been rejected by behaviorists. He wanted to reinstate purpose, cognition, ideas, and emotion as vital areas in the objective study of behavior.

In his article, *Behaviorism and Purpose,* Tolman proposes that purpose is an observable, objective, and descriptive property of

---

[17]B. F. Skinner, *Science and Human Behavior* (New York; The Macmillan Company, 1953), pp. 87-90.

behavior. Tolman defines purpose as the "persistence until character" of behavior and shows that it is present whenever, in order to adequately describe the behavior, it is necessary to give the behaviors reference objects.[18] For example, trial and error responses in a rat running a maze "are only completely describable as responses which persist until a specific 'end object,' food, is reached."[19] An error is defined as a turn in the maze that will not lead to food, and a correct response is a turn that leads to food; so that the experimenter is defining his variables in terms of purposeful behavior, whether he is aware of it or not. Tolman continues by saying, ". . . . whenever, in merely describing a behavior, it is found necessary to include a statement of something either *toward which* or *from which* the behavior is directed, there we have purpose."[20] One can see that any description of purposeful behavior cannot be a description of the organism's movement without any reference to the environmental situation, but it must communicate the relationship between the behavior and goal objects or situation. Tolman concludes:

> In short, purpose is present, descriptively, whenever a statement of the goal object is necessary to indicate (1) consistency of goal object in spite of variations in adjustment to intervening obstacles, or (2) variations in final direction corresponding to differing positions of the goal object or (3) cessation of activity when a given goal object is entirely removed.[21]

In his article, Tolman has opened a way to identify and describe purposeful behavior in organisms. One can see that Tolman's concept of purposeful behavior is similar to the anthropological psychologist's concept of intentionality. Thus with purpose or intentionality being a practical descriptive property of behav-

---

[18]Edward C. Tolman, "Behaviorism and Purpose," *Behavior and Psychological Man* (Los Angeles: University of California Press, 1961), pp. 33-35.

[19]*Ibid.*, p. 34.

[20]*Ibid.*

[21]*Ibid.*, p. 35.

ior, it opens the possibility of establishing a dimension of similarity between purposeful animal and human behavior. However, before examining the possibilities of such an approach in extrapolation, it is helpful to look briefly at a contemporary psychologist who is using the concept of purpose as an important part of his system.

D. O. Hebb is one of the few psychologists who advocate purpose as a vital aspect of the scientific study of behavior. According to Hebb:

> Behavior is classed as purposive when it shows modifiability with circumstances in such a way as to tend to produce a constant end effect; it is behavior which is free of sensory dominance, controlled jointly by the present sensory input and by the expectancy of producing the effect which is its goal. When the situation changes, the behavior changes accordingly.[22]

An example of this definition is the traditional situation in which a monkey has to get food suspended out of his reach. If boxes are available, he will pile them on top of one another to reach the food. If the boxes are absent, he may put the poles together to knock the food down. If neither the box nor pole is available, the monkey may pull the experimenter near the food and climb him to reach it. The chimp performs a wide variety of behaviors, all with the same result: obtaining the food.[23]

Both Tolman and Hebb affirm purpose as a legitimate descriptive property of behavior. The important aspect is that purpose can be determined from observation. Hebb points out one practical aspect of observation: "In principle, a number of examples of a given kind of behavior have to be observed before we can conclude that purpose is involved, since it is only in this way that we can demonstrate that the behavior adjusts itself to circumstance. In practice, however, one may know enough about the species—or about a particular animal—to be able to identify

---

[22]Donald O. Hebb, *A Textbook of Psychology* (Philadelphia: W. B. Saunders Company, 1958), p. 206.
[23]*Ibid.*

purpose in a single trial."[24] With the insights of Tolman and Hebb, it is becoming evident that a comparability of human and animal behavior along the dimension of purpose or intentionality is a possible basis for a principle of similarity.

It has been shown previously that anthropological psychology is centrally focused on intentional or purposeful behavior, and that any extrapolation based on phenomenology must have a principle of similarity which insists that the comparability of behavior must be evident on the concrete observable level and readily apparent to a human observer. Tolman's and Hebb's development of purpose as an observable, identifiable, and descriptive property of behavior has opened the possibility of establishing intentionality or purpose as a dimension of extrapolation which meets the requirements of phenomenology. Consequently, it is now possible to discuss more concretely some of the issues of such an extrapolating process.

A Phenomenological Approach to Extrapolation

In many ways a phenomenological approach to behavior is similar to naturalistic observation because both are a description of an event or process. While naturalistic observation implies reporting a unique, natural situation, the phenomenological observer is interested in repeatable events as well as unique ones. The phenomenological observer is mainly interested in discriminating the relevant and fundamental structural aspects of a situation. In order to accomplish this task, it is often necessary for him to observe a situation repeatedly and to create a formal category system which describes and records the purposeful behavior of the organism. This category system is the key to any formal scientific observation, and an examination of its properties and purpose will give insight into the concept and process of phenomenal similarity.

The category system is essentially a delineation of the observer's experience of a behavioral situation. As he begins to dif-

[24] *Ibid.*

ferentiate the relevant aspects of the situation, he can attempt to formally describe the behaviors as distinguishable behavioral units. Once he has the category system, he can then record the frequency and sequence of the behaviors in which he is interested.

In keeping with the demands of phenomenology, the category system must be constructed of descriptive language rather than inferential language. The categories must represent what appears to the observer, not what is inferred about the organism. For example, one can observe a young child being afraid of his father, but he cannot observe and describe the Oedipus complex because it is an inferential and conceptual system to explain the child's fear. Since anthropological psychology is interested in intentional behavior, the category system will focus on describing purposeful behavior of the organisms.

Tolman states that if it is necessary to refer to the objects toward which and from which an organism is moving, then the behavior is purposeful.[25] This statement points to the relevant aspect of a situation which must be referred to in order to adequately describe the purpose of an organism. One cannot describe the organism as if it were totally isolated from a situation, but the behavior must be described in reference to the goal objects in the environment. In other words, the behavior must describe the organism's movements toward or away from the significant objects in the environment. Also, the quality of the movement must be included—whether the behavior is fearful, cautious, etc.—because the quality of behavior often indicates a vital aspect of the purpose of the organism's movements.

Since the aim of this process is to establish a comparability between certain areas of human and animal behavior, the category system must be designed to reveal any existing similarity. In other words, the behavioral category systems used for both sets of behavior must have an almost point-to-point or category-to-category correspondence. For every class of animal behavior there should be a comparable class of human behavior, because

[25]Tolman, *loc. cit.*

such a system not only reflects the similarity the observer sees and incorporates into the categories, but it permits the possibility of comparing both frequency and patterning of human and animal behaviors. It is evident that a demand for a close relationship between the descriptive categories narrows the range of animals which can be used.

The animals which seem most likely to fit the demands of the category system are the primates. Not only is their anatomy most similar to man's which opens up the possibility of comparable behaviors, but also the association areas in the brain are proportionally closest to man's.[26] So while the range of possible animals is severely limited, the closeness of the primates and man increases the probability that the animal studies can make a contribution to the psychologist's understanding of human behavior.

While what has been presented is speculative, it points to the possibilities for establishing empirical dimensions of similarity between human and animal behavior. Our example has concentrated on purposeful behavior because it is of special interest to the anthropological psychologist, but it is also possible to establish emotional and cognitive dimensions of similarity as well as many other behavior patterns that are common to animals and man. Such an approach is particularly useful to anthropological psychology because it finds the similarity on the concrete behavioral level rather than the level of scientific abstraction. This is a useful approach because, as phenomenology has pointed out, the basis of all our knowledge, even our scientific knowledge, is in our experience of the way things appear to a human being. Consequently, the construction of the categories of behaviors is based on the relevant discriminations of a human observer, rather than on the basis of measurability. The categories are designed to capture the purposeful behavior of the organism by describing the relationship of the behavior

[26]Ester Milner, "Differing Observational Perspectives as a Barrier to Communication among Behavioral Scientists," *Review of Existential Psychology and Psychiatry,* Adrian van Kaam, editor (Pittsburgh: Duquesne University Press, Fall, 1962), p. 251.

to the goal objects in the situation. And finally, both the comparability of the descriptive behaviors and their patterns of occurrence point to the similarity of behaving.

The logical question is that once the similarity has been established, then how can the animal findings aid the scientist in understanding human behavior? The next section will outline the possible ways of applying the animal data to human behavior.

The Application of Animal Findings to Human Behavior

A most important consideration for the science of psychology in general is the manner in which the findings of animal experimentation are subsequently related to the study of human behavior. It is possible, for example, to attempt to use the findings to *explain* human behavior in the manner of B. F. Skinner's method of extrapolation. Or it is possible to use the animal findings to stimulate thinking in certain areas of behavior which man and animal might share as possible behaviors-in-common—to consider what may be learned from the results of animal experimentations which may have implications for broadening the scope of possible ways of understanding human behavior. It is in the latter spirit that the anthropological psychologist approaches the findings of animal experimentation.

Skinner's Approach to Application of Animal Findings to Human Behavior

Skinner's method of applying animal findings to human beings can be described briefly as an attempt to explain human behavior parsimoniously. Consistent with the methods of the natural sciences, he is attempting to explain the variety and complexity of human behavior with as small a number of concepts as possible. For example, he attempts to explain self control when drinking alcoholic beverages in terms of concepts like positive reinforcement and punishment.[27] Positive reinforcement,

---

[27]B. F. Skinner, *Science and Human Behavior* (New York: The Macmillan Company, 1953), p. 230.

in the sense of confidence, tends to increase the frequency and amount of drinking; while punishment, in terms of the possibility of irresponsible behavior, tends to suppress the drinking response. Furthermore, anything which tends to reduce the adversive stimulation of the guilt or shame associated with drinking is reinforced and, consequently, since less drinking reduces guilt and shame, it is reinforced. This reinforced decrease in drinking is what Skinner calls self control.[28] In this example, Skinner attempts to explain an already observed phenomenon in terms of positive reinforcement, punishment, and negative reinforcement. He is taking a complex event and reducing it to a limited number of concepts which he establishes on the basis of animal experimentation. Skinner is explaining behavior because he is focusing on an already observed behavior and attempting to apply his concepts to the situation in order to understand it in terms of a functional analysis. While this is what Skinner does, there is also another consideration which is important for understanding his extrapolation of animal to human behavior: his attitudes toward the validity of his applications.

Skinner's attitude toward the validity of his application of animal findings to human behavior is ambiguous because of discrepancies in his writings. In some of his statements he seems to be cautious and consistent with the empirical and tentative character of science. This attitude is epitomized in the following quotation in which he is discussing the availability of extensive animal research to be applied to human behavior:

> The use of this material often meets with the objections that there is an essential gap between man and the other animals, and that the results of one cannot be extrapolated to the other. To insist upon this discontinuity at the beginning of a scientific investigation is to beg the question. Human behavior is distinguished by its complexity, its variety, and its greater accomplishments, but the basic processes are not therefore necessarily different. Science advances from the simple to the complex; it is constantly concerned with whether the processes and laws discovered at one stage are adequate for the next. It would be rash to assert at this point

---

[28]*Ibid.*

> that there is no essential difference between human behavior and the behavior of lower species; but until an attempt has been made to deal with both in the same terms, it would be equally rash to assert that there is.[29]

The tentative quality of Skinner's attitude makes it a scientifically sound statement that most psychologists could agree with. However, Skinner makes other statements which implicitly contradict this attitude.

An example of Skinner's contradiction is contained in his discussion of self control. He explains self control in terms of a person controlling his behavior by manipulating the external stimuli of which behavior is a function. In other words, the person knows which environmental stimuli elicit a particular response; so he manipulates the situation so that the appropriate stimulus is presented which elicits the desired response. In concluding his chapter, Skinner states that his view is in conflict with the traditional concept of self control and personal responsibility. In this context he makes the following statement:

> It must be remembered that formulae expressed in terms of personal responsibility underlie many of our present techniques of control and cannot be abruptly dropped. To arrange a smooth transition is in itself a major problem. But the point has been reached where a sweeping revision of the concept of responsibility is required, not only in a theoretical analysis of behavior, but in the practical consequences as well.[30]

Skinner is implying that social institutions such as government and religion should be modified so that they can incorporate theoretical and practical attitudes which are consistent with Skinner's analysis of behavior. In the initial quote, Skinner says he is attempting to discover whether animal findings and his approach are adequate for human behavior; yet, in the latter quote he seems to assume that his approach is not only adequate, but true, to the extent that he proposes changing social institu-

---

[29]*Ibid.*, p. 38.
[30]*Ibid.*, p. 241.

tions to see behavior in terms of his analysis. Thus, it would seem that Skinner believes his extrapolation of constructs to human behavior to be valid, even though its validity has not been demonstrated. In contrast to Skinner's systems and attitudes in regard to the application of animal findings to human beings is anthropological psychology, which uses animal findings to clarify human behavior by pointing to relevant issues and implicit assumptions.

Anthropological Psychology's Application of Animal Findings to Human Behavior

In applying animal experimentation to man's psychological existence, anthropological psychology follows the lead of D. O. Hebb, who uses animal experiments to illuminate human behavior, rather than to explain human behavior.[31] Hebb's most basic principle is that animal experiments do not prove anything about human behavior. Instead, they may serve as a 'pointing to' which enables the psychologist to focus on facets of human behavior which he would not have noticed without the aid of animal experimentation. Secondly, animal experiments may point to assumptions that the psychologist has not made explicit. And finally, animal experimentations may suggest a new principle of human behavior.[32] These three ways of applying animal experimentation to the human situation summarize the possible ways that anthropological psychology hopes to use animal experimentation in constructing a theory of human behavior.

The first contribution of animal experimentation—drawing attention to important areas of human psychological functioning which previously have not been noticed—can be illustrated by Harlow's study of affection in baby monkeys.[33] He studied the

---

[31]Donald O. Hebb and W. R. Thompson, "The Social Significance of Animal Studies," *Handbook of Social Psychology*, Gardner Linzey, editor (Cambridge, Mass.: Addison-Wesley Publishing Company, Inc., 1954), p. 533.

[32]*Ibid.*

[33]Harry F. Harlow, "The Nature of Love," *The American Psychologist*, XIII (December, 1958), pp. 673-685.

variable of comfort contact or tactility in the relationship between the young monkey and mother surrogates. There were two types of mother surrogates: one made of terry cloth and the other made of wire. The mother surrogates were constructed to supply the monkeys with milk, and as soon as they were strong enough, all of the baby monkeys' food came from one of the mother surrogates. In the initial experiment, the monkeys had free access to both types of mother surrogates, but half of the population was fed solely by the wire mother and the other half was fed only by the cloth mother. However, all of the monkeys were almost exclusively with the terry cloth mothers. This was true of the monkeys who were fed by the wire mother surrogates as well.[34] Thus, it was demonstrated that physiological satisfaction may not play as important a role in the baby monkey's attachment for the mother as previously speculated. Further, the experiment has shown that comfort contact is an important variable in the baby monkey's attachment to its mother. While this experiment *proves nothing* about the role of comfort contact in the relationship between human babies and mothers, it does *suggest* this as a possible relevant variable which should be investigated on the human level. One can see from this illustration that animal experiments can bring into figure areas of human behavior which previously were ground.

Hebb has demonstrated that animal experiments can reveal implicit assumptions that the psychologist has made about man's psychological functioning.[35] A review of the literature concerning the relation of environment and heredity to the development of intelligence reveals confusion and contradiction. This, according to Hebb, stems from an implicit assumption concerning human learning. In other words, psychologists have been assuming something about human learning which they have never made explicit. They have concluded that if special experiences do not affect a child's intelligence at the age of seven or twelve, then

[34]*Ibid*, pp. 675-676.
[35]Hebb, *loc. cit.*

special experiences do not affect intelligence at any time in a child's life. Implicit in this reasoning is the assumption that the learning process and the generality of transfer learning is the same for all ages. However, this assumption is brought to light and challenged by animal experiments which indicate that in the rat early experiences have widespread and long-lasting influences on behavior. While the rat experimentation proves nothing about human behavior, it does help the psychologist to see clearly the assumptions that he has made about human behavior.[36]

Besides pointing to implicit assumptions, animal experiments can also suggest new principles for understanding human behavior.[37] Perhaps the most obvious example of a principle which has been established on a basis of animal experiments and then applied to human behavior is the principle of conditioning. While there is wide disagreement on the range of human functioning to which conditioning properly applies, it would be very difficult to construct a valid theory of human behavior which did not contain some construct comparable to conditioning. For example, Dollard and Miller[38] constructed a theory of behavior which is built entirely on the process of conditioning, while the anthropological psychologist is attempting to integrate conditioning into a theory of total human psychological functioning. Despite the disagreement concerning the range of application of conditioning as a principle of learning, it is making a valuable contribution to understanding human behavior. The three possible ways of using animal findings just illustrated demonstrate the variety of applications to human behavior. Underlying each application is the principle of similarity that the psychologist uses to make a transition from animals to man.

---

[36]*Ibid.*

[37]*Ibid.*

[38]J. Dollard and N. E. Miller, *Personality and Psychotherapy: An Analysis in Terms of Learning, Thinking, and Culture* (New York: McGraw-Hill Book Company, Inc., 1950), passim.

Conclusion

Two different methods of extrapolation have been compared according to the different principles of similarity. Skinner's method is basically an abstract conceptual similarity which focuses on the functional relationship between the stimulating situation and the organism's response. Contrary to the method most useful to the anthropological psychologist, Skinner is not interested in the similarity of concrete behavior. The needs of the anthropological psychologist are best met by a method of extrapolation which focuses on the comparability of concrete behaviors. Further, since anthropological psychology is interested in intentional behavior, the behavior of the animal and man must be comparable in their purposeful relations to goal objects. Also, it should be noted that while the method of comparing purposeful behavior was presented as a formal system, it is not always necessary to generate formal category systems with a category-to-category correspondence. Generally, a formal system is required only when one plans a long involved research project on animals to illuminate some aspect of human behavior. In many cases of extrapolation, where the psychologist is attempting to use animal experiments which already have been done, only an informal, intuitive comparability of the animal and human behaviors is required. However, to avoid confusion, the psychologist should be aware of the principle of similarity he is using.

There are more principles of similarity than the two discussed in this chapter. In fact, they represent two extreme points on a continuum, with one emphasizing the abstract conceptual similarity and the other, the concrete behavioral similarity. No one of these methods can be thought of as absolutely better than any other. Each serves a different function in a particular theoretical system. If one is seeking to explain human behavior in a minimal number of abstract scientific terms which apply to all organisms, then Skinner's method is most appropriate. However, if one is attempting to understand concrete, situated, intentional behavior, then the proposed method of anthropological psychology best meets this need. Thus, the goal of the psychologist doing the extrapolation determines the adequacy of any particular method.

And finally, the criterion for evaluating the validity of any single extrapolation must be stated in terms of the goal of psychology: the clarification and understanding of human behavior.[39] If the extrapolation clarifies some small area of human behavior, then it is relevant. However, if a psychologist is attempting to extrapolate a whole theory of behavior, then a further question must be asked: Does it adequately account for all relevant behavior? Since animal behavior lacks the range and amplitude of man's functioning in such areas as language and association, the answer is usually negative. This limitation does not negate extrapolation, because it has been demonstrated that animal studies can contribute to the psychologist's understanding of human psychological existence.

---

[39]Hebb, *loc. cit.*

CHAPTER TWELVE

EXISTENTIAL AND HUMANISTIC PSYCHOLOGY

A clarification of the relationships of existential and humanistic psychology demands first of all a discussion of the function of implicit views of life in the development of science, art, and culture. We shall then consider more specifically the existential image of man in its relation to existential and humanistic psychology. Finally, the introduction of the concept of anthropological psychology is relevant to the understanding of our discussion.

An at least implicit view of human nature continually directs man's social and personal endeavors. Initially, such a view influences cultural development pre-reflectively; we "live" the anthropological orientation that is ours without thinking about its structure and its subtle, continual influence. Nevertheless, this submerged evidence of life is a decisive power in the dynamic evolvement of our culture, of religion, science, art, and education. The intimate structure of this guiding image of man alters in the course of human history, which is a story of humanization despite prolonged periods of regression and decline. All progress in humanization presupposes the enlightenment of man, first in certain areas of life, then in the global view of reality. We realize, therefore, that new insights in the arts and sciences gradually lead to striking transformations in the outlook of man and concomitantly in the pattern of his culture. The partial light of each one of these areas of insight does not alter our view of man significantly, for each of them is too specialized to effect a metamorphosis of the fundamental light that orients the unfolding of man's civilization. Many innovations in the limited areas of cultural specialization, however, carry implications for the wisdom of living; these implications—far transcending their limited fields of origin—filter down into the pre-reflective realm of consciousness where they collide and fuse, erode former convictions, and insert a new awareness that leads to a rebirth of central vision. We live such a new image in attitude and action before we know it rationally. Sooner or later, however, we feel compelled to reflect on it, to make it explicit so that we may know what propels us so powerfully, to scrutinize it critically, and to utilize it as a principle of renewal within various reflective fields of thought and performance. In this attempt we are not alone, for a similar transformation of vision emerges simultaneously all over the globe in sensitive men who participate in the evolution that marks the historic period in which we live.

When a pre-reflective view of man's nature has been raised to the level of reflective thought and action, it tends to give rise to a corresponding humanism or a project of improvement of the human condition in the light of the newly explicated vision. This innate humanistic tendency explains the appearance of successive humanisms such as positivistic, atheistic, Christian, Marxist, romantic, technical, rationalistic, and behavioristic humanisms. Each newly emerging humanism may find a reverberation in a corresponding humanistic psychology which studies certain psychological aspects of man as relevant in the light of the parallel humanistic movement and of the specific view of man from which the latter emerged.

If the history of humanization is nourished by an implict vision of man, we may ask ourselves which view orients contemporary humanization? It is not simple to answer this question, since various visions are simultaneously present in a society which is fluid and pluralistic. The purpose of the present chapter limits us to the consideration of one contemporary view of man emerging in this century: the existential vision. We are concerned here not with a philosophical or psychological view of man, but with a "lived" pre-philosophical and pre-psychological image which can be explicated in a psychological, philosophical, theological, sociological, or any other reflective direction. As a corollary of contemporary development, an existential image of man seems to be present in sensitive people of almost all Western nations, cultures, and religions, and in the representatives of the most diverse professions and disciplines. We are already moving beyond this stage of the unknown "lived" image that emerged almost unnoticed as a result of the forces of evolution. We can already find reflective expressions and elaborations of this implicit view in many arts and sciences, one of which is the science of psychology. When we study these various expressions, we realize at once that each specific mode of knowledge makes explicit only that aspect of the implicit contemporary image of man that is relevant to the specificity of the mode of knowledge concerned. For example, philosophy may make explicit the ontological, whereas psychology would stress the psychological aspect of such an implicit view. Moreover, each art or science re-evaluates in a unique way its own structure, methodology, content, applications, and problems in the light of this explicated aspect of the contemporary image of man. In the elaboration of the explicated aspect, the art or science concerned increasingly transcends and expands this initial explication by means of its own traditions and methods of exploration, experimentation, and theory construction. An existential psychology, for example, should be fundamentally different in these respects from existential physics, philosophy, sociology, or physiology.

We may ask why it is that the various explications of aspects of the existential image are fundamentally distinct. These elaborations are different because of the uniqueness of the aspect on which each one of them concentrates, and because of the basic difference of methodology by means of which each of them explores its unique perspective and incorporates it within the traditional dialogue of its own field of competence. In spite of these differences, some restricted dialogue and mutual enrichment is possible among, for example, existential physiology, philosophy, psychology, and physics. The different aspects which each one of these disciplines develops in its own way are rooted in the same image of man. Moreover, a variety of developments of the same original vision is possible even within one discipline concerned with one specific aspect of the pre-reflective image. This diversity of development is especially observable in philosophy, where the explication and elaboration of the same philosophical aspect can lead to diverse developments in accordance with the personal or cultural orientation of the philosopher concerned. No existential philosophy, therefore, can set itself up as "the" authoritative explication of the contemporary existential image of man. Each existential philosophy is a different *philosophical* explication of this pre-philosophical image. Each one of these philosophical explications is influenced by the cultural or personal orientation of the philosopher concerned.

Consequently, existential psychology should never be a simplistic application of any specific existential philosophy. Existential psychology is a unique explication and elaboration of the psychologically relevant aspects of the implicit existential image of man, just as theoretical physics is a unique assimilation of the dimensions that are relevant to physics.

As soon as psychology has discovered and totally assimilated this relevant aspect—partly by means of existential psychology—the prefix *existential* should be dropped, for psychology as such will then be existential, which simply means that psychology will have assimilated this relevant perspective and will be in tune with the latest phase of the evolution of human insight. After this assimilation, psychology will again await its further fundamental enrichment by its assimilation of the next development of our view of man, which will emerge as a result of the next phase of the human evolution. Physics, being an earlier established science, has already gone through the phase of assimilation of contemporary insight. Theoretical physics has already assimilated the insights implied in the existential view, for example, that of perspectivity. Gradually, the field of physics adopted this view under the influence of theoretical physics.

Therefore, the prefix *existential* would now be superfluous in this field. We may add that assimilation is a two-way process in which both the assimilating field and the assimilated aspect are progressively transformed.

Existential psychology is thus a temporary attempt to assimilate into the science of psychology those aspects of the contemporary existential image of man which are directly relevant for the evolvement of empirical, clinical, and theoretical psychology. This movement of reconstruction by assimilation will tend to become superfluous as soon as psychology has fundamentally restructured, deepened, and expanded itself by the integration of insights which have recently emerged in Western humanity as an inescapable result of its cultural and historical evolution.

Evidently, such a new impetus in psychology may give rise to a new type of humanistic psychology, namely an existential humanistic psychology which is fundamentally different from a rationalistic or a behavioristic humanistic psychology, related respectively to the humanism of the eighteenth century enlightenment and nineteenth century scientism. This fundamental difference does not imply that an existential humanistic psychology discards the contributions made by a rationalistic and a behavioristic humanism. On the contrary, existential psychology fosters respect for these contributions insofar as they remain relevant within the light of contemporary insight. Existential psychology is a leaven of positive reconstruction which gives rise to re-evaluation, not elimination of positions of prevalence among the theories, methods, and data with which the field of psychology was enriched in the past as a result of implicit or explicit former views of man and reality. A humanistic psychology which is existential will share in this respectful attitude of the movement of reconstruction from which it sprang.

A discussion of the meaning of anthropological psychology is relevant here. In current usage, the meaning of "anthropology" is restricted to "the science of man in relation to physical character, origin, and distribution—or races, environmental and social relations, and culture." (*Webster's New Collegiate Dictionary,* Springfield, Mass., G and C Merriam Company, 1960, p. 38.) This restriction of the term "anthropology" stresses only one of the three main dimenions of "anthropos" or man, namely the cultural-social one. Etymologically, the term "anthropology" does not have this restricted meaning, for it is derived from the Greek words *anthropos,* which means man, and *logos,* which means word or science. Therefore, every concept, construct, word, or science which refers to man as a whole may be properly called anthropological. Man in his entirety, however, appears to us under many aspects. For example, we may perceive man insofar as he appears physically, racially, socially, or culturally. In the latter case, we speak of cultural anthropology. We also perceive man in the light of other sciences or disciplines, such as medicine, history, sociology, philosophy, or theology. In these cases, we may rightly speak of a medical, historical, social, philosophical, or theological anthropology. The psychologist too may study man insofar as he appears in the entirety of his behavior. Such a study may be called anthropological psychology.

It presupposes, however, the development of many differential psychologies through the gradual uncovering of different abstracted aspects of behavior by observation and experimentation. Consequently, an anthropological psychology is possible only after this differential revelation. The main method of such a psychology is the dialectical integration of the results of these differential approaches. In other words, anthropological psychology is a comprehensive theoretical psychology which studies *human* behavior. This concern with human behavior does not mean that it neglects the insights gained by the study of animal behavior. On the contrary, the contributions of animal psychology are integrated within anthropological psychology insofar as they shed light on certain aspects of human behavior which are similar to those of the behavior of animals. Anthropological psychology thus integrates the insights and data of the various empirical, clinical, and theoretical psychologies within a theory of man that is linked to one or the other implicit image of man such as the positivistic, rationalistic, behavioristic, or existential image. We find the counterpart of anthropological psychology in other fields of learning related to man, such as the anthropological physiology developed by Frederick Buytendijk, and the anthropological medicine developed by V. von Weisacker.

Humanistic and anthropological psychology are both interested in man. The interest of anthropological psychology is primarily academic, scientific-theoretical, while that of a humanistic psychology—in the tradition of the great humanisms—is primarily the improvement of the human condition by means of concrete psychological research. Anthropological psychology can be relevant to humanistic psychology insofar as its integrative comprehensive knowledge of the psychology of man can be used by the humanistic psychologist for the promotion of his humanistic aims; it may even suggest to him certain types of research to be done in order to close the gaps in our theoretical knowledge which prevent us from fostering the humanization of man in certain areas of his psychological development.

We are now ready to formulate a few tentative definitions which may elucidate our discussion.

Psychology: The science of behavior. (The meaning of the term "behavior" in this definition will differ according to the implicit view of man that at a certain moment of the history of humanization dominates culture and science. From an existential viewpoint, for example, behavior that is the object of psychology is always intentional and purposive.)

Existential Psychology: A temporary movement towards fundamental reconstruction of scientific psychology by means of the assimilation of the psychologically relevant insights implicit in the pre-philosophical contemporary view of man that is called existential.

Humanistic Psychology: A lasting movement concerned with the improvement of conditions of the humanization of man by means of psychological research in the light of one or the other view of man.

Existential Humanistic Psychology: A humanistic psychology that operates in the light of the existential image of man.

Anthropological Psychology: A scientific-theoretical movement within psychology that integrates empirical, clinical, and theoretical psychologies within an open theory of personality that serves as a comprehensive frame of reference for all the significant theories and data in the field.

Existential Anthropological Psychology: An anthropological psychology that roots its comprehensive frame of reference in the existential image of man.

BIBLIOGRAPHY

Allport, Gordon W. "The Psychology of Participation," *Psychological Review,* 53, 1945, 117-132.

Becoming. New Haven: Yale University, 1955.

Personality and Social Encounter. Boston: Beacon Press, 1960.

Pattern and Growth in Personality. New York: Holt, Rinehart and Winston, 1961.

Angyall, A. *Foundations for a Science of Personality.* New York: Commonwealth Fund, 1941.

"A Theoretical Model for Personality Studies," *J. Pers.,* 20, 1951, 131-142.

Argyle, Michael. *The Scientific Study of Social Behavior.* London: Methuen and Company, Ltd., 1957.

Arnold, Magda. *Emotion and Personality.* 2 vols. New York: Basic Books, Inc., 1961.

Arnold, Magda and Gasson, J. *The Human Person.* New York: Ronald Press, 1954.

Barnett, H. G. *Innovation: The Basis of Cultural Change.* New York: McGraw-Hill Book Co., Inc., 1965.

Barral, Mary Rose. *Merleau-Ponty: The Role of the Body Subject in Interpersonal Relations.* Pittsburgh: Duquesne University Press, 1965.

Bergmann, Gustav and Spence, Kenneth W. "Operationism and Theory Construction," *Psychological Theory.* Melvin H. Marx, ed. New York: The Macmillan Company, 1951.

Bergson, Henri. *The Creative Mind,* trans. Mabelle L. Anderson. New York: The Philosophical Library, Inc., 1946.

Bertalanffy, Ludwig von. *Problems of Life.* New York: Harper and Brothers, 1952.

Bevan, William. *Scientific Woozle Hunters? An Opinion in Outline.* Kopenhagen: Einar Munksgaards Forlag, 1953.

Binswanger, L. *Grundformen und Erkenntnis menschlichen Daseins.* Zurich: Max Niehans, 1942.

Trans. Jacob Needleman, *Being-in-the-World.* New York: Basic Books Inc., 1963.

Boas, George. *Dominant Themes of Modern Philosophy.* New York: The Ronald Press Company, 1957.

Boelen, Bernard J. "Philosophical Orientation," (pamphlet). Pittsburgh: Duquesne University, 1958.

Boring, Edwin G. "A History of Introspection," *Psychological Bulletin,* 50, 1953, 169-189.

A History of Experimental Psychology. Second Edition. New York: Charles Scribner's Sons, 1958.

Brentano, F. *Psychologie vom empirischen Standpunkte.* Leipzig: Duncker and Humblot, 1847.

Brown, Clarence W. and Ghiselli, Edwin E. *Scientific Method in Psychology.* New York: McGraw-Hill Book Co., Inc., 1955.

Buber, Martin. *I and Thou,* trans. Ronald Gregor Smith. New York: Charles Schribner's and Sons, 1958.

Buytendijk, F.J.J. "The Phenomenological Approach to the Problem of Feelings and Emotions," *Feeling and Emotions.* The Mooseheart Symposium in cooperation with the University of Chicago. New York, Toronto, London: McGraw-Hill Book Co., Inc., 1950.

De Vrouw. Haar Verschijning, Natuur en Bestaan. Utrecht, Holland: Spectrum, 1951.

Phénoménologie de la rencontre. Paris: Desclée de Brouwer, 1952.

La Femme. Bruges: Editions Desclee de Brouwer, 1954.

Cohen, Morris R. and Nagel, Ernest. *An Introduction to Logic and Scientific Method.* New York: Harcourt, Brace and Co., 1934.

David, Henry P., and von Bracken, Helmut. *Perspectives in Personality Theory.* New York: Basic Books, Inc., 1957.

Descartes, R. *Discourse on Method,* trans. Laurence J. Lafleur. New York: The Liberal Arts Press, 1956.

Meditations, trans. Laurence J. Lafleur. New York: The Liberal Arts Press, 1951.

Oeuvres de Descartes. Leopold Cert (ed.). Paris: Charles Adam & Paul Tanner, 1897.

De Waelhens, A. *Une philosophie de l'ambiguité. L'Existentialisme de Maurice Merleau-Ponty.* Louvain: Publs. Universitaires de Louvain, 1957.

Dollard, J. and Miller, N.E. *Personality and Psychotherapy: An Analysis in Terms of Learning, and Culture.* New York: The McGraw-Hill Book Co., Inc., 1950.

Dondeyne, Albert. *Contemporary European Thought and Christian Faith,* trans. Ernan McMullin and John Burnheim. Pittsburgh: Duquesne University Press, 1958.

Farber, Leslie H. "Despair and the Life of Suicide," *Review of Existential Psych. & Psychiatry,* Vol. II, (Feb., 1962), 125.

Farber, M. *The Foundations of Phenomenology.* Cambridge, Massachusetts: Harvard University Press, 1943.

"The Function of Phenomenological Analysis." *Phil. and Phenom.* Res. I (1941), 431-441.

Phenomenology as a Method and as a Philosophical Discipline. Buffalo, New York: University of Buffalo Press, 1928.

Feigl, Herbert. "Philosophical Embarrassments of Psychology," *The American Psychologist,* XIV (March, 1959), 115-128.

Fingarette, H. *The Self in Transformation,* Harper Torchbooks (New York, 1965).

Frankl, Viktor E. *The Doctor and the Soul: An Introduction to Logotherapy,* trans. Richard and Clara Winston. New York: Alfred A. Knopf, 1955.

From Death-Camp to Existentialism: A Psychiatrist's Path to a New Therapy, trans. Ilse Lasch. Boston: Beacon Press, 1959.

Frings, M. S. *Max Scheler.* Pittsburgh: Duquesne University Press, 1965.

Gatch, Vera Mildred and Maurice Kahn Temerlin, "The Belief in Psychic Determinism and Behavior of Psychotherapist," *Review of Existential Psychology and Psychiatry,* V (Winter, 1965).

Gendlin, E. T. "Need for a New Type of Concept," *Review of Existential Psychology and Psychiatry,* II, 37.

Goldstein, Kurt. *Human Nature in the Light of Psychopathology.* Cambridge: Harvard University Press, 1947.

The Organism. Boston: Beacon Press, 1963.

Gruhle, Hans W. *Verstehende Psychologie. Erlebnislehre.* Stuttgart: Georg Thieme Verlag, 1956.

Guillaume, P. *Psychologie.* Paris: Presses Universitaires de France, 1943.

Gurwitsch, Aron. *Field of Consciousness.* Pittsburgh: Duquesne University Press, 1964.

Gusdorf, E. G. *Speaking.* Chicago: Northwestern University Press, 1965.

Hall, Calvin S. and Gardner Lindzey. *Theories of Personality.* New York; John Wiley & Sons, Inc., 1957.

Harlow, Harry F. "The Nature of Love," *The American Psychologist,* XIII (Dec., 1958), 673-685.

Hebb, Donald O. *The Organization Of Behavior.* New York: John Wiley & Sons, Inc., 1949.

Hebb, Donald O. and Thompson, W.R. "The Social Significance of Animal Studies," *Handbook of Social Psychology.* Vol. I. Gardner Linzey, ed. Cambridge, Mass.: Addison-Wesley Publishing Co., Inc., 1954.

Hebb, Donald O. *A Textbook of Psychology.* Philadelphia: W.B. Saunders Co., 1958.

Heidegger, Martin. *Essays in Metaphysics,* trans. Kurt F. Leidecker. New York: Wisdom Library, a Division of Philosophical Library, Inc., 1960.

Existence and Being. Introduction by Werner Brock. Chicago: Henry Regnery Company, 1949.

An Introduction to Metaphysics, trans. Ralph Manheim. New Haven: Yale University Press, 1959.

The Question of Being, trans. William Kluback and Jean Wilde. New York: Twayne Publishers, Inc., 1958.

Being and Time. New York: Harper Bros., 1962.

Hengstenberg, Hans-Eduard, *Philosophische Anthropologie*. W. Kohl-Hammer Verlag (Stuttgart, 1957.).

Hilgard, Ernest P. *Theories of Learning*. New York: Appleton-Century-Crofts, Inc., 1956.

Holland, James G. and B.F. Skinner, *The Analysis of Behavior*. New York: McGraw-Hill Book Company, Inc., 1961.

Halton, Gerald and Roller, Duane. *Foundations of Modern Physical Science*. Reading, Mass.: Addison-Wesley Publishing Co., Inc., 1958.

Husserl, Edmund. *Cartesian Meditations,* trans. Dorion Cairns. The Hague. Netherlands: Martinus Nijhof, 1960.

Logische Untersuchungen: Zur Phänomenologie und Theorie der Erkenntniss. Halle: Niemeyer, 1901.

James, William. *The Principles of Psychology*. New York: Holt, 1890.

Jaspers, Karl. *Existenzerhellung*. Berlin: J. Springer, 1932.

Man in the Modern Age, trans. by Eden and Cedar Paul. New York: Doubleday Anchor Books, Doubleday & Company, Inc., 1957.

Jessor, Richard. "Phenomenological Personality Theories and the Data Language of Psychology," *Psychological Review,* 63 (1956), 173-180.

"The Problem of Reductionism in Psychology," *Psychological Review,* LXV (June, 1958), 170-178.

Kaplan, Bernard "Radical Metaphor, Aesthetic and the Origin of Language," *Review of Existential Psychology and Psychiatry,* II, No. 1.

Kelly, George A. *The Psychology of Personal Constructs.* New York: W.W. Norton & Co., 1955.

Kemeny, John G. *A Philosopher Looks at Science.* Princeton: Van Nostrand, 1959.

Kimble, Gregory A. "Psychology as a Science," *The Scientific Monthly,* LXXVII (September, 1953), 156-160.

Principles of General Psychology. New York: The Ronald Press Co., 1956.

Koch, Sigmund. "Clark L. Hull," *Modern Learning Theory.* William K. Estes and others, eds. New York: Appleton-Century-Crofts, Inc., 1954.

Psychology :A Study of a Science. 3 vols. New York: McGraw-Hill Book Co., Inc., 1959.

Kockelmans J. *Phenomenology and Physical Science.* Pittsburgh: Duquesne University Press, 1966.

Köhler, Wolfgang. *Gestalt Psychology.* New York: Liveright, 1929.

Gestalt Psychology. New York: The New American Library (Mentor Books), 1959.

Kuenzli, Alfred E. (ed.). *The Phenomenological Problem.* New York: Harper & Bros., 1959.

Kwant, Remy C. "De ambiguïteit van het feit," *Gawein* Nijmegen (Holland), III, 1, 1954, 9 - 23.

Encounter, trans. Robert C. Adolfs. Pittsburgh: Duquesne University Press, 1960.

The Phenomenological Philosophy of Merleau-Ponty. Pittsburgh: Duquesne University Press, 1964.

Phenomenology of Language. Pittsburgh: Duquesne University Press, 1965.

Phenomenology of Social Existence. Pittsburgh: Duquesne University Press, 1965.

Laing, R. D. *The Divided Self.* Chicago: Quadrangle Books, Inc., 1960.

Landsman, T. "Four Phenomenologies," *Journal of Individual Psychology,* 14 (No. 1, 1958), 29-37.

Lanteri-Laura, Georges. *La Psychiatrie Phénoménologique.* Paris: Presses Universitaires de France, 1963.

Lauer, Quentin J. *The Triumph of Subjectivity.* New York: Fordham University Press, 1958.

Luijpen, William A. *De psychologie van de verveling.* Amsterdam: H.J. Paris, 1951.

Existential Phenomenology, trans. Henry J. Koren. Pittsburgh: Duquesne University Press, 1960.

Phenomenology and Metaphysics. Pittsburgh: Duquesne University Press, 1965.

MacDougall, William and John B. Watson. *The Battle of Behaviorism - An Exposition and an Exposure.* New York: W.W. Norton & Company, Inc., 1929.

MacLeod, R. B. "The Place of Phenomenological Analysis in Social Psychological Theory." In J. H. Rohre and Sherif (eds.), *Social Psychology at the Crossroads.* New York: Harper, 1951, 215-241.

"The Phenomenological Approach to Social Psychology," *Psychological Review,* 54 (1947), 193-210.

Mahony, M. J. *Cartesianism.* New York: Fordham University Press, 1925.

Mandler, George and William Kessen. *The Language of Psychology.* New York: John Wiley & Sons, Inc., 1959.

Marcel, Gabriel. *Being and Having.* London: Dacre Press, 1949.

The Mystery of Being. 2 vols. Trans. René Hague. Chicago: Henry Regnery Company, 1950.

Man Against Mass Society, trans. G. S. Fraser. Chicago: Henry Regnery Company, 1950.

The Philosophy of Existence. London: Harvill Press, 1954.

Marx, M. H. (ed.). *Psychology Theory.* New York: The MacMillan Company, 1951.

Maslow, A. H. "A Theory of Motivation," *Psychological Review,* 50, (1943), 370-396.

Motivation and Personality. New York: Harper & Brothers, 1954.

May, Rollo and others (eds.). *Existence: A New Dimension In Psychiatry and Psychology.* New York: Basic Books Inc., 1958.

May, Rollo. *Existential Psychology.* New York: Random House, 1961.

"Toward the Ontological Basis of Psychotherapy," *Existential Inquiries,* I (September, 1959), 5-7.

Mendel, W. M. "Expansion of a Shrunken World," *Review of Existential Psychology and Psychiatry,* I (Winter, 1961), 27-32.

Merleau-Ponty, M. *Phenomenology of Perception.* New York: Humanities Press, 1962. Gallimard, 1945.

The Structure of Behavior. Boston: Beacon Press, 1963.

"What is Phenomenology," *Cross Currents,* 6 (Winter, 1955), 59-70.

Milner, Ester. "Differing Observational Perspectives as a Barrier to Communications Among Behavioral Scientists," *Review of Existential Psychology and Psychiatry,* II (Fall, 1962), 249-258.

Morgan, Clifford L. *Introduction to Psychology.* New York: McGraw-Hill Book Company, Inc., 1961.

Mounier, Emmanuel. *Traité du Caractère.* Paris: Éditions du Seuil, 1947.

Moustakas, Clark E. (ed.) *The Self. Explorations in Personal Growth.* New York: Harper and Brothers, 1956.

Murphy, Gardner. *Historical Introduction to Modern Psychology.* New York: Harcourt, Brace & Company, 1949.

Nédoncelle, Maurice. *La réciprocité des consciences. Essai sur la nature de la personne.* Aubiers: Éditions Montaigne, 1942.

Nuttin, J. *Psychoanalysis and Personality.* New York: Sheed and Ward, 1953.

Osgood, Charles E. *Method and Theory in Experimental Psychology.* New York: Oxford University Press, 1956.

Perls, Frederick, Ralph Hefferline and Paul Goodman. *Gestalt Therapy.* New York: Julian Press, 1958.

Pieper, Josef. *Leisure, The Basis of Culture,* trans. Alexander Dru. New York: Pantheon Books, Inc., 1952.

Postman, Leo and Edward C. Tolman. "Brunswik's Probabilistic Functionalism," *Psychology: A Study of Science.* Vol. I, Sigmund Koch, ed. New York: McGraw-Hill Book Company, Inc., 1959.

Pratt, Carroll C. *The Meaning of Music.* New York: McGraw-Hill, 1931.

Rather, L. J. "Existential Experience in Whitehead and Heidegger," *Review of Existential Psychology and Psychiatry,* I (Spring, 1961).

Reymert, Martin L., (ed.) *Feeling and Emotions.* The Mooseheart Symposium in cooperation with the University of Chicago. New York, Toronto, London: McGraw-Hill Book Company, Inc., 1950.

Rogers, Carl. *Counseling and Psychotherapy.* New York: Houghton-Mifflin Co., 1942.

Psychotherapy and Personality Change. Chicago: University of Chicago Press, 1954.

"Some Observations on the Organization of Personality," *American Psychologist,* 2 (1947), 358-368.

"The Loneliness of Contemporary Man," *Review of Existential Psychology and Psychiatry.* I (Spring, 1961), 94-101.

Rogers, Carl R. and B. F. Skinner. "Some Issues Concerning the Control of Human Behavior," *Science,* 124 (1956), 1057-1066.

Sartre, Jean P. *The Emotions: Outline of a Theory,* trans. by Bernard Frechtman. New York: Philosophical Library, 1948.

Schachtel, Ernest. *Metamorphosis.* New York: Basic Books, Inc., 1959.

Scheler, M. *Man's Place in Nature.* Boston: Beacon Press, 1961.

Wesen und Formen der Sympathie Phänomenologie und Theorie der Sympathiegefühle. Frankfurt-Main: G. Schulte-Bulmke, 1948.

Severin, Frank T. *Humanistic Viewpoints in Psychology.* McGraw-Hill Book Co., (New York, 1965).

Skinner, Burrkus F. "Are Theories of Learning Necessary," *Psychological Review,* LVII (March, 1950), 193-216.

Science and Human Behavior. New York: The Macmillan Co., 1953.

Smith, Brewster. "The Phenomenological Approach in Personality: Some Critical Remarks," *The Journal of Abnormal and Social Psychology,* 45 (1950), 516-522.

Snygg, D. and A. W. Combs. *Individual Behavior.* New York: Harper, 1949.

"The Need for a Phenomenological System of Psychology," *Psychological Review,* 48 (1941), 404-424.

"The Phenomenological Approach in the Problem of 'Unconscious' Behavior: A Reply to Doctor Smith," *The Journal of Abnormal and Social Psychology,* 45 (1950), 523-528.

Sonneman, Ulrich. *Existence and Therapy.* New York: Grune & Straton, 1954.

Spranger, E. *Lebensformen Geisteswissenschaftliche Psychologie und Ethik der Persönlichkeit.* Halle, (Saale): Max Niemeyer Verlag, 1930.

Spiegelberg, H. *The Phenomenological Movement.* 2 vols. The Hague, Netherlands: Martinus Nijhoff, 1960.

Stevens, S. S. "Psychology and the Science of Science," *Psychological Theory.* Melvin H. Marx, ed. New York: The Macmillan Co., 1957.

Strasser, S. *Das Gemüt. Grundgedanken zu einer Phanomenologischen Philosophie und Theorie des Menslichen Gefühlslebens.* Utrecht: Het Spectrum, Freiburg: Verlag Herder, 1956.

The Soul in Metaphysical and Empirical Psychology, trans. Henry J. Koren. Pittsburgh: Duquesne University Press, 1957.

"Phenomenological Trends in European Psychology," *Phil. and Phenom. Research,* XVIII, (September, 1957).

Phenomenology and the Human Sciences, Pittsburgh: Duquesne University Press, 1964.

"Phenomenologies and Psychologies," *Review of Existential Psychology and Psychiatry*, V, No. 1, (Winter, 1965).

Straus, Erwin W., ed. *Phenomenology: Pure and Applied.* Pittsburgh: Duquesne University Press, 1964.

Sullivan, J. W. N. *The Limitations of Science.* New York: The New American Library, (Mentor Books), 1933.

Tolman, Edward C. "Behaviorism and Purpose," *Behavior and Psychological Man.* Los Angeles: University of California Press, 1961.

"Operationalism, Behaviorism and Current Trends in Psychology," *Behavior and Psychological Man.* Los Angeles: University of California Press, 1961.

Tauber, Edward S. and Maurice R. Green. *Prelogical Experience.* New York: Basic Books, Inc., 1959.

van der Berg, J. H. and Linschoten, J. *Persoon en Wereld.* Utrecht: Erven J. Bijleveld, 1953.

The Phenomenological Approach to Psychiatry. An Introduction to Recent Phenomenological Psychopathology. Springfield, Illinois: Charles C. Thomas, 1955.

van der Berg, J. H. and Buytendijk, F. J. J. (ed.) *Scientific Contributions to Phenomenological Psychology and Psychopathology.* Springfield, Illinois: Charles C. Thomas, 1955.

Van Breemen, P. "De mens en de Moderne natuurwetenschap," *Streven* (Brussels) 3, 1956, 212-220.

"De Natuurwetenschap zelfgenoegzaam?", *Streven* (Brussels), 3, 1957, 635-644.

van Croonenburg, E. J. *Gateway to Reality* (An Introduction to Philosophy), Pittsburgh, Duquesne University Press, 1964.

van de Hulst, H. C., and van Peursen, C. A. *Phaenomenologie en natuurwetenschap.* Utrecht: Erven J. Byleveld, 1953.

van Laer, Henry, *Philosophico-Scientific Problems.* Pittsburgh: Duquesne University Press, 1964.

The Philosophy of Science. (Part I, Science in General). Pittsburgh: Duquesne University Press, 1964.

The Philosophy of Science. (Part II, A Study of the Division and Nature of Various Groups of Sciences). Pittsburgh: Duquesne University Press, 1964.

van Kaam, Adrian. "The Addictive Personality," *Humanitas,* Vol. 1, No. 2 (Fall, 1965).

van Kaam, Adrian and L. V. Pacoe. "Anthropological Psychology and Behavioristic Experimentation," in *Festschrift Dr. Straus,* eds. Griffith, R.M., and von Baeyer, W., Berlin, Heidelberg, New York: Springer-Verlag, 1966.

van Kaam, Adrian. "Assumptions in Psychology," *Journal of Individual Psychology,* Vol. 14 (1958), 22-28.

"Clinical Implications of Heidegger's Concepts of Will, Decision, and Responsibility," *Review of Existential Psychology and Psychiatry.*

"Commentary on 'Freedom and Responsibility Examined'," *Behavioral Science and Guidance, Proposals, and Perspectives,* eds. Lloyd-Jones and E. M. Westervelt. New York: Teachers College, Columbia University Press, 1963.

"Counseling and Existential Psychology," *Harvard Educational Review* (Fall, 1962). This article was later published in *Guidance—An Examination,* New York: Harcourt, Brace & World, 1965.

"Differential Psychology," *The New Catholic Encyclopedia,* Washington, D.C.: The Catholic University of America, 1966.

"The Existential Approach to Human Potentialities," *Explorations in Human Potentialities,* ed. Herbert A. Otto. Springfield, Illinois: Charles C. Thomas, 1966.

"Existential Psychology," *The New Catholic Encyclopedia,* Washington, D.C.: The Catholic University of America, 1966.

"Existential and Humanistic Psychology," *Review of Existential Psychology and Psychiatry,* (Fall, 1965).

"Existential Psychology as a Theory of Personality," *Review of Existential Psychology and Psychiatry,* (Winter, 1963).

"Die existentielle Psychologie als eine Theorie der Gesamtpersönlichkeit," *Jahrbuch für Psychologie und medizinische Anthropologie,* 12. Jahrgang Heft 4.

"The Fantasy of Romantic Love," *Modern Myths and Popular Fancies,* Pittsburgh: Duquesne University Press, 1961.

"The Field of Religion and Personality or Theoretical Religious Anthropology," *Insight,* Vol. 4, No. 1. (Summer, 1965).

"Freud and Anthropological Psychology," *The Justice,* (Brandeis University), (May, 1959).

"The Goals of Psychotherapy from the Existential Point of View," *The Goals of Psychotherapy,* ed. Alvin R. Mahrer. New York: Appelton-Century-Crofts, 1966.

"Humanistic Psychology and Culture," *Journal of Humanistic Psychology,* Vol. 1 (Spring, 1961), 94-100.

"The Impact of Existential Phenomenology on the Psychological Literature of Western Europe," *Review of Existential Psychology and Psychiatry,* Vol. I (1961), 63-92.

"Francis Libermann," *The New Catholic Encyclopedia,* Washington, D.C.: The Catholic University of America, 1966.

A Light to the Gentiles. Milwaukee: Bruce Publishing Co., 1962.

"Motivation and Contemporary Anxiety," *Humanitas,* Vol I, No. 1 (Spring, 1965).

"The Nurse in the Patient's World," *The American Journal of Nursing,* Vol. 59, (1959), 1708-1710.

Personality Fulfillment in Spiritual Life. Denville, New Jersey: Dimension Books, Inc., 1966.

"Phenomenal Analysis: Exemplified by a Study of the Experience of 'Really Feeling Understood'," *Journal of Individual Psychology,* Vol. 15 (1959), 66-72.

"A Psychology of the Catholic Intellectual," in *The Christian Intellectual,* (Samuel Hazo, ed.). Pittsburgh, Pennsylvania: Duquesne University Press, 1963.

"A Psychology of Falling-Away-From-The-Faith," *Insight,* Vol. 2, No. 2 (Fall, 1963), 3-17.

"Religion and Existential Will," *Insight,* Vol. 1, No. 1 (Summer, 1962).

"Religious Counseling of Seminarians," *Seminary Education in a Time of Change,* eds. James Michael Lee and Louis J. Putz. Notre Dame, Indiana: Fides Publishers, Inc., 1965.

"Review of *The Divided Self* by R. D. Laing." *Review of Existential Psychology and Psychiatry* (Winter, 1962), 85-88.

Religion and Personality. New Jersey: Prentice-Hall, Inc., 1965.

"Sex and Existence," *Review of Existential Psychology and Psychiatry,* (Spring, 1963.)

"Sex and Personality," *The Lamp,* Vol. 63, No. 7 (July, 1965.)

"Structures and Systems of Personality," *The New Catholic Encyclopedia,* Washington, D.C.: The Catholic University of America, 1966.

The Third Force in European Psychology. Greenville, Delaware: Psychosynthesis Research Foundation, 1960. (Greek translation, Athens, Greece, 1962.)

The Vocational Director and Counseling. Derby, New York: St. Paul Publications, 1962.

van Melsen, A. G. *The Philosophy of Nature.* Pittsburgh: Duquesne University Press, 1952.

Science and Technology. Pittsburgh: Duquesne University Press, 1961.

From Atomos to Atom (The History of the Concept "Atom.") Pittsburgh: Duquesne University Press, 1952.

Verplanck, William S. "Burrhus F. Skinner," *Modern Learning Theory.* William K. Estes and others, eds. New York: Appleton-Century-Crofts, Inc., 1954.

Waelhens, Alphonse de. *Existence et Signification.* Paris: Beatrice-Nauwelaerts, 1958.

Watson, John B. *Behaviorism.* New York: W. W. Norton & Company, Inc., 1924.

Wertheimer, Max. *Productive Thinking.* Enlarged edition. New York: Harper & Bros., 1959.

Wolman, Benjamin. *Contemporary Theories and Systems in Psychology.* New York: Harper & Bros., 1960.

Woodworth, Robert S. *Contemporary Schools of Psychology.* Revised edition. New York: The Ronald Press Company, 1948.

Woodworth, Robert and Harold Schlosberg. *Experimental Psychology.* Revised edition. New York: Henry Holt and Company, 1954.

Wright, William Kelley. *A History of Modern Philosophy.* New York: The Macmillan Company, 1941.

UNPUBLISHED MATERIALS

Barton, Anthony. "The Experience of Estrangement." Unpublished Master's Thesis. University of Chicago, 1960.

Greiner, Dorothy. "Anthropological Psychology and Physics." Unpublished Master's Thesis. Duquesne University. Pittsburgh, Pennsylvania, 1962.

"A Foundational-Theoretical Approach Toward a Comprehensive Psychology of Human Emotion." Unpublished Doctoral Dissertation. Duquesne University. Pittsburgh, Pennsylvania, 1964.

Kraft, W.F. "Anthropological Psychology and Phenomenology." Unpublished Master's Thesis. Duquesne University. Pittsburgh, Pennsylvania, 1962.

"An Existential Anthropological Psychology of the Self." Unpublished Doctoral Dissertation. Duquesne University. Pittsburgh, Pennsylvania, 1965.

Linschoten, J. "Das Experiment in der phaenomenologischen Psychologie." (Paper read in Bonn, Germany, 1955.)

Pacoe, Larry V. "Anthropological Psychology and Behavioristic Animal Experimentation." Unpublished Master's Thesis. Duquesne University. Pittsburgh, Pennsylvania, 1963.

Reeves, Jeanne C. "An Introduction to the Methodology of Anthropological Psychology." Unpublished Master's Thesis. Duquesne University. Pittsburgh, Pennsylvania, 1962.

Rogers, Carl. "A Theory of Therapy, Personality and Interpersonal Relationships, as Developed in the Client-Centered Framework." Unpublished Paper. Chicago: University of Chicago, 1956.

Smith, David. "Anthropological Psychology and Ontology." Unpublished Master's Thesis. Duquesne University. Pittsburgh, Pennsylvania, 1960.

van Kaam, Adrian, "The Experience of Really Feeling Understood by a Person." Unpublished Doctoral Dissertation. Western Reserve University. Cleveland, Ohio, 1958.

van Kaam, Adrian. "Counseling and Psychotherapy from the Existential Viewpoint." (To be published in 1967).

van Kaam, Adrian and Healy, Kathleen. *The Demon and the Dove: Personality Development Through Literature* (To be published in 1967).

van Kaam, Adrian. *Personality Fulfillment in Religious Life.* (To be published in 1967 by Dimension Books, Denville, New Jersey).

INDEX

Index

Index

Index

Index